Brothers Chapman

Portrait and Biographical Album of Sumner County

Brothers Chapman

Portrait and Biographical Album of Sumner County

ISBN/EAN: 9783337098452

Printed in Europe, USA, Canada, Australia, Japan

Cover: Foto ©Raphael Reischuk / pixelio.de

More available books at **www.hansebooks.com**

Portrait and Biographical Album

Sumner County, Kansas.

Containing Full Page Portraits and BIOGRAPHICAL SKETCHES

OF PROMINENT AND REPRESENTATIVE CITIZENS OF THE COUNTY AND OF THE PRESIDENTS OF THE UNITED STATES

TOGETHER WITH PORTRAITS & BIOGRAPHIES OF ALL THE GOVERNORS OF THE STATE

CHICAGO. CHAPMAN BROS. 1890.

PREFACE.

THE greatest of English historians, MACAULAY, and one of the most brilliant writers of the present century, has said: "The history of a country is best told in a record of the lives of its people." In conformity with this idea the PORTRAIT AND BIOGRAPHICAL ALBUM of this county has been prepared. Instead of going to musty records, and taking therefrom dry statistical matter that can be appreciated by but few, our corps of writers have gone to the people, the men and women who have, by their enterprise and industry, brought the county to a rank second to none among those comprising this great and noble State, and from their lips have the story of their life struggles. No more interesting or instructive matter could be presented to an intelligent public. In this volume will be found a record of many whose lives are worthy the imitation of coming generations. It tells how some, commencing life in poverty, by industry and economy have accumulated wealth. It tells how others, with limited advantages for securing an education, have become learned men and women, with an influence extending throughout the length and breadth of the land. It tells of men who have risen from the lower walks of life to eminence as statesmen, and whose names have become famous. It tells of those in every walk in life who have striven to succeed, and records how that success has usually crowned their efforts. It tells also of many, very many, who, not seeking the applause of the world, have pursued "the even tenor of their way," content to have it said of them as Christ said of the woman performing a deed of mercy—"they have done what they could." It tells how that many in the pride and strength of young manhood left the plow and the anvil, the lawyer's office and the counting-room, left every trade and profession, and at their country's call went forth valiantly "to do or die," and how through their efforts the Union was restored and peace once more reigned in the land. In the life of every man and of every woman is a lesson that should not be lost upon those who follow after.

Coming generations will appreciate this volume and preserve it as a sacred treasure, from the fact that it contains so much that would never find its way into public records, and which would otherwise be inaccessible. Great care has been taken in the compilation of the work and every opportunity possible given to those represented to insure correctness in what has been written, and the publishers flatter themselves that they give to their readers a work with few errors of consequence. In addition to the biographical sketches, portraits of a number of representative citizens are given.

The faces of some, and biographical sketches of many, will be missed in this volume. For this the publishers are not to blame. Not having a proper conception of the work, some refused to give the information necessary to compile a sketch, while others were indifferent. Occasionally some member of the family would oppose the enterprise, and on account of such opposition the support of the interested one would be withheld. In a few instances men could never be found, though repeated calls were made at their residence or place of business.

CHAPMAN BROS.

CHICAGO, April, 1889.

PORTRAITS AND BIOGRAPHIES

OF THE

GOVERNORS OF KANSAS,

AND THE

PRESIDENTS

OF THE

UNITED STATES

PRESIDENTS.

GEORGE WASHINGTON.

THE Father of our Country was born in Westmorland Co., Va., Feb. 22, 1732. His parents were Augustine and Mary (Ball) Washington. The family to which he belonged has not been satisfactorily traced in England. His great-grandfather, John Washington, emigrated to Virginia about 1657, and became a prosperous planter. He had two sons, Lawrence and John. The former married Mildred Warner and had three children, John, Augustine and Mildred. Augustine, the father of George, first married Jane Butler, who bore him four children, two of whom, Lawrence and Augustine, reached maturity. Of six children by his second marriage, George was the eldest, the others being Betty, Samuel, John Augustine, Charles and Mildred.

Augustine Washington, the father of George, died in 1743, leaving a large landed property. To his eldest son, Lawrence, he bequeathed an estate on the Patomac, afterwards known as Mount Vernon, and to George he left the parental residence. George received only such education as the neighborhood schools afforded, save for a short time after he left school, when he received private instruction in mathematics. His spelling was rather defective.

Remarkable stories are told of his great physical strength and development at an early age. He was an acknowledged leader among his companions, and was early noted for that nobleness of character, fairness and veracity which characterized his whole life.

When George was 14 years old he had a desire to go to sea, and a midshipman's warrant was secured for him, but through the opposition of his mother the idea was abandoned. Two years later he was appointed surveyor to the immense estate of Lord Fairfax. In this business he spent three years in a rough frontier life, gaining experience which afterwards proved very essential to him. In 1751, though only 19 years of age, he was appointed adjutant with the rank of major in the Virginia militia, then being trained for active service against the French and Indians. Soon after this he sailed to the West Indies with his brother Lawrence, who went there to restore his health. They soon returned, and in the summer of 1752 Lawrence died, leaving a large fortune to an infant daughter who did not long survive him. On her demise the estate of Mount Vernon was given to George.

Upon the arrival of Robert Dinwiddie, as Lieutenant-Governor of Virginia, in 1752, the militia was reorganized, and the province divided into four military districts, of which the northern was assigned to Washington as adjutant general. Shortly after this a very perilous mission was assigned him and accepted, which others had refused. This was to proceed to the French post near Lake Erie in Northwestern Pennsylvania. The distance to be traversed was between 500 and 600 miles. Winter was at hand, and the journey was to be made without military escort, through a territory occupied by Indians. The trip was a perilous one, and several times he came near losing his life, yet he returned in safety and furnished a full and useful report of his expedition. A regiment of 300 men was raised in Virginia and put in command of Col. Joshua Fry, and Major Washington was commissioned lieutenant-colonel. Active war was then begun against the French and Indians, in which Washington took a most important part. In the memorable event of July 9, 1755, known as Braddock's defeat, Washington was almost the only officer of distinction who escaped from the calamities of the day with life and honor. The other aids of Braddock were disabled early in the action, and Washington alone was left in that capacity on the field. In a letter to his brother he says: "I had four bullets through my coat, and two horses shot under me, yet I escaped unhurt, though death was levelin' my companions on every side." An Indian sharpshooter said he was not born to be killed by a bullet, for he had taken direct aim at him seventeen times, and failed to hit him.

After having been five years in the military service, and vainly sought promotion in the royal army, he took advantage of the fall of Fort Duquesne and the expulsion of the French from the valley of the Ohio, to resign his commission. Soon after he entered the Legislature, where, although not a leader, he took an active and important part. January 17, 1759, he married Mrs. Martha (Dandridge) Custis, the wealthy widow of John Parke Custis.

When the British Parliament had closed the port of Boston, the cry went up throughout the provinces that "The cause of Boston is the cause of us all." It was then, at the suggestion of Virginia, that a Congress of all the colonies was called to meet at Philadelphia, Sept. 5, 1774, to secure their common liberties, peaceably if possible. To this Congress Col. Washington was sent as a delegate. On May 10, 1775, the Congress re-assembled, when the hostile intentions of England were plainly apparent. The battles of Concord and Lexington had been fought. Among the first acts of this Congress was the election of a commander-in-chief of the colonial forces. This high and responsible office was conferred upon Washington, who was still a member of the Congress. He accepted it on June 19, but upon the express condition that he receive no salary. He would keep an exact account of expenses and expect Congress to pay them and nothing more. It is not the object of this sketch to trace the military acts of Washington, to whom the fortunes and liberties of the people of this country were so long confided. The war was conducted by him under every possible disadvantage, and while his forces often met with reverses, yet he overcame every obstacle, and after seven years of heroic devotion and matchless skill he gained liberty for the greatest nation of earth. On Dec. 23, 1783, Washington, in a parting address of surpassing beauty, resigned his

commission as commander-in-chief of the army to to the Continental Congress sitting at Annapolis. He retired immediately to Mount Vernon and resumed his occupation as a farmer and planter, shunning all connection with public life.

In February, 1789, Washington was unanimously elected President. In his presidential career he was subject to the peculiar trials incidental to a new government; trials from lack of confidence on the part of other governments; trials from want of harmony between the different sections of our own country; trials from the impoverished condition of the country, owing to the war and want of credit; trials from the beginnings of party strife. He was no partisan. His clear judgment could discern the golden mean; and while perhaps this alone kept our government from sinking at the very outset, it left him exposed to attacks from both sides, which were often bitter and very annoying.

At the expiration of his first term he was unanimously re-elected. At the end of this term many were anxious that he be re-elected, but he absolutely refused a third nomination. On the fourth of March, 1797, at the expiration of his second term as President, he returned to his home, hoping to pass there his few remaining years free from the annoyances of public life. Later in the year, however, his repose seemed likely to be interrupted by war with France At the prospect of such a war he was again urged to take command of the armies. He chose his subordinate officers and left to them the charge of matters in the field, which he superintended from his home. In accepting the command he made the reservation that he was not to be in the field until it was necessary. In the midst of these preparations his life was suddenly cut off. December 12, he took a severe cold from a ride in the rain, which, settling in his throat, produced inflammation, and terminated fatally on the night of the fourteenth. On the eighteenth his body was borne with military honors to its final resting place, and interred in the family vault at Mount Vernon.

Of the character of Washington it is impossible to speak but in terms of the highest respect and admiration. The more we see of the operations of our government, and the more deeply we feel the difficulty of uniting all opinions in a common interest, the more highly we must estimate the force of his talent and character, which have been able to challenge the reverence of all parties, and principles, and nations, and to win a fame as extended as the limits of the globe, and which we cannot but believe will be as lasting as the existence of man.

The person of Washington was unusally tall, erect and well proportioned. His muscular strength was great. His features were of a beautiful symmetry. He commanded respect without any appearance of haughtiness, and ever serious without being dull.

John Adams

JOHN ADAMS,

JOHN ADAMS, the second President and the first Vice-President of the United States, was born in Braintree (now Quincy), Mass., and about ten miles from Boston, Oct. 19, 1735. His great-grandfather, Henry Adams, emigrated from England about 1640, with a family of eight sons, and settled at Braintree. The parents of John were John and Susannah (Boylston) Adams. His father was a farmer of limited means, to which he added the business of shoemaking. He gave his eldest son, John, a classical education at Harvard College. John graduated in 1755, and at once took charge of the school in Worcester, Mass. This he found but a "school of affliction," from which he endeavored to gain relief by devoting himself, in addition, to the study of law. For this purpose he placed himself under the tuition of the only lawyer in the town. He had thought seriously of the clerical profession but seems to have been turned from this by what he termed "the frightful engines of ecclesiastical councils of diabolical malice, and Calvanistic good nature," of the operations of which he had been a witness in his native town. He was well fitted for the legal profession, possessing a clear, sonorous voice, being ready and fluent of speech, and having quick perceptive powers. He gradually gained practice, and in 1764 married Abigail Smith, a daughter of a minister, and a lady of superior intelligence. Shortly after his marriage, (1765), the attempt of Parliamentary taxation turned him from law to politics. He took initial steps toward holding a town meeting, and the resolutions he offered on the subject became very popular throughout the Province, and were adopted word for word by over forty different towns. He moved to Boston in 1768, and became one of the most courageous and prominent advocates of the popular cause, and was chosen a member of the General Court (the Legislature) in 1770.

Mr. Adams was chosen one of the first delegates from Massachusetts to the first Continental Congress, which met in 1774. Here he distinguished himself by his capacity for business and for debate, and advocated the movement for independence against the majority of the members. In May, 1776, he moved and carried a resolution in Congress that the Colonies should assume the duties of self-government. He was a prominent member of the committee of five appointed June 11, to prepare a declaration of independence. This article was drawn by Jefferson, but on Adams devolved the task of battling it through Congress in a three days' debate.

On the day after the Declaration of Independence was passed, while his soul was yet warm with the glow of excited feeling, he wrote a letter to his wife which, as we read it now, seems to have been dictated by the spirit of prophecy. "Yesterday," he says, "the greatest question was decided that ever was debated in America; and greater, perhaps, never was or will be decided among men. A resolution was passed without one dissenting colony, 'that these United States are, and of right ought to be, free and independent states.' The day is passed. The fourth of July, 1776, will be a memorable epoch in the history of America. I am apt to believe it will be celebrated by succeeding generations, as the great anniversary festival. It ought to be commemorated as the day of deliverance by solemn acts of devotion to Almighty God. It ought to be solemnized with pomp, shows, games, sports, guns, bells, bonfires, and illuminations from one end of the continent to the other, from this time forward for ever. You will think me transported with enthusiasm, but I am not. I am well aware of the toil, and blood and treasure, that it will cost to maintain this declaration, and support and defend these States; yet, through all the gloom, I can see the rays of light and glory. I can see that the end is worth more than all the means; and that posterity will triumph, although you and I may rue, which I hope we shall not."

In November, 1777, Mr. Adams was appointed a delegate to France, and to co-operate with Benjamin Franklin and Arthur Lee, who were then in Paris, in the endeavor to obtain assistance in arms and money from the French Government. This was a severe trial to his patriotism, as it separated him from his home, compelled him to cross the ocean in winter, and exposed him to great peril of capture by the British cruisers, who were seeking him. He left France June 17, 1779. In September of the same year he was again chosen to go to Paris, and there hold himself in readiness to negotiate a treaty of peace and of commerce with Great Britian, as soon as the British Cabinet might be found willing to listen to such proposals. He sailed for France in November, from there he went to Holland, where he negotiated important loans and formed important commercial treaties

Finally a treaty of peace with England was signed Jan. 21, 1783. The re-action from the excitement, toil and anxiety through which Mr. Adams had passed threw him into a fever. After suffering from a continued fever and becoming feeble and emaciated he was advised to go to England to drink the waters of Bath. While in England, still drooping and desponding, he received dispatches from his own government urging the necessity of his going to Amsterdam to negotiate another loan. It was winter, his health was delicate, yet he immediately set out, and through storm, on sea, on horseback and foot, he made the trip.

February 24, 1785, Congress appointed Mr. Adams envoy to the Court of St. James. Here he met face to face the King of England, who had so long regarded him as a traitor. As England did not condescend to appoint a minister to the United States, and as Mr. Adams felt that he was accomplishing but little, he sought permission to return to his own country, where he arrived in June, 1788.

When Washington was first chosen President, John Adams, rendered illustrious by his signal services at home and abroad, was chosen Vice President. Again at the second election of Washington as President, Adams was chosen Vice President. In 1796, Washington retired from public life, and Mr. Adams was elected President, though not without much opposition. Serving in this office four years, he was succeeded by Mr. Jefferson, his opponent in politics.

While Mr Adams was Vice President the great French Revolution shook the continent of Europe, and it was upon this point which he was at issue with the majority of his countrymen led by Mr. Jefferson. Mr. Adams felt no sympathy with the French people in their struggle, for he had no confidence in their power of self-government, and he utterly abhored the class of atheist philosophers who he claimed caused it. On the other hand Jefferson's sympathies were strongly enlisted in behalf of the French people. Hence originated the alienation between these distinguished men, and two powerful parties were thus soon organized, Adams at the head of the one whose sympathies were with England and Jefferson led the other in sympathy with France.

The world has seldom seen a spectacle of more moral beauty and grandeur, than was presented by the old age of Mr. Adams. The violence of party feeling had died away, and he had begun to receive that just appreciation which, to most men, is not accorded till after death. No one could look upon his venerable form, and think of what he had done and suffered, and how he had given up all the prime and strength of his life to the public good, without the deepest emotion of gratitude and respect. It was his peculiar good fortune to witness the complete success of the institution which he had been so active in creating and supporting. In 1824, his cup of happiness was filled to the brim, by seeing his son elevated to the highest station in the gift of the people.

The fourth of July, 1826, which completed the half century since the signing of the Declaration of Independence, arrived, and there were but three of the signers of that immortal instrument left upon the earth to hail its morning light. And, as it is well known, on that day two of these finished their earthly pilgrimage, a coincidence so remarkable as to seem miraculous. For a few days before Mr. Adams had been rapidly failing, and on the morning of the fourth he found himself too weak to rise from his bed. On being requested to name a toast for the customary celebration of the day, he exclaimed " INDEPENDENCE FOREVER." When the day was ushered in, by the ringing of bells and the firing of cannons, he was asked by one of his attendants if he knew what day it was? He replied, "O yes; it is the glorious fourth of July—God bless it—God bless you all." In the course of the day he said, "It is a great and glorious day." The last words he uttered were, "Jefferson survives." But he had, at one o'clock, resigned his spirit into the hands of his God.

The personal appearance and manners of Mr. Adams were not particularly prepossessing. His face, as his portrait manifests, was intellectual and expressive, but his figure was low and ungraceful, and his manners were frequently abrupt and uncourteous. He had neither the lofty dignity of Washington, nor the engaging elegance and gracefulness which marked the manners and address of Jefferson

THOMAS JEFFERSON,

THOMAS JEFFERSON was born April 2, 1743, at Shadwell, Albemarle county, Va. His parents were Peter and Jane (Randolph) Jefferson, the former a native of Wales, and the latter born in London. To them were born six daughters and two sons, of whom Thomas was the elder. When 14 years of age his father died. He received a most liberal education, having been kept diligently at school from the time he was five years of age. In 1760 he entered William and Mary College. Williamsburg was then the seat of the Colonial Court, and it was the abode of fashion and splendor. Young Jefferson, who was then 17 years old, lived somewhat expensively, keeping fine horses, and much caressed by gay society, yet he was earnestly devoted to his studies, and irreproachable in his morals. It is strange, however, under such influences, that he was not ruined. In the second year of his college course, moved by some unexplained inward impulse, he discarded his horses, society, and even his favorite violin, to which he had previously given much time. He often devoted fifteen hours a day to hard study, allowing himself for exercise only a run in the evening twilight of a mile out of the city and back again. He thus attained very high intellectual culture, alike excellence in philosophy and the languages. The most difficult Latin and Greek authors he read with facility. A more finished scholar has seldom gone forth from college halls; and

there was not to be found, perhaps, in all Virginia, a more pureminded, upright, gentlemanly young man.

Immediately upon leaving college he began the study of law. For the short time he continued in the practice of his profession he rose rapidly and distinguished himself by his energy and acuteness as a lawyer. But the times called for greater action. The policy of England had awakened the spirit of resistance of the American Colonies, and the enlarged views which Jefferson had ever entertained, soon led him into active political life. In 1769 he was chosen a member of the Virginia House of Burgesses. In 1772 he married Mrs. Martha Skelton, a very beautiful, wealthy and highly accomplished young widow.

Upon Mr. Jefferson's large estate at Shadwell, there was a majestic swell of land, called Monticello, which commanded a prospect of wonderful extent and beauty. This spot Mr. Jefferson selected for his new home; and here he reared a mansion of modest yet elegant architecture, which, next to Mount Vernon, became the most distinguished resort in our land.

In 1775 he was sent to the Colonial Congress, where, though a silent member, his abilities as a writer and a reasoner soon become known, and he was placed upon a number of important committees, and was chairman of the one appointed for the drawing up of a declaration of independence. This committee consisted of Thomas Jefferson, John Adams, Benjamin Franklin, Roger Sherman and Robert R. Livingston. Jefferson, as chairman, was appointed to draw up the paper. Franklin and Adams suggested a few verbal changes before it was submitted to Congress. On June 28, a few slight changes were made in it by Congress, and it was passed and signed July 4, 1776. What must have been the feelings of that man—what the emotions that swelled his breast—who was charged with the preparation of that Declaration, which, while it made known the wrongs of America, was also to publish her to the world, free, sovereign and independent. It is one of the most remarkable papers ever written ; and did no other effort of the mind of its author exist, that alone would be sufficient to stamp his name with immortality.

In 1779 Mr. Jefferson was elected successor to Patrick Henry, as Governor of Virginia. At one time the British officer, Tarleton, sent a secret expedition to Monticello, to capture the Governor. Scarcely five minutes elapsed after the hurried escape of Mr. Jefferson and his family, ere his mansion was in possession of the British troops. His wife's health, never very good, was much injured by this excitement, and in the summer of 1782 she died.

Mr. Jefferson was elected to Congress in 1783. Two years later he was appointed Minister Plenipotentiary to France. Returning to the United States in September, 1789, he became Secretary of State in Washington's cabinet. This position he resigned Jan. 1, 1794. In 1797, he was chosen Vice President, and four years later was elected President over Mr. Adams, with Aaron Burr as Vice President. In 1804 he was re-elected with wonderful unanimity, and George Clinton, Vice President.

The early part of Mr. Jefferson's second administration was disturbed by an event which threatened the tranquility and peace of the Union; this was the conspiracy of Aaron Burr. Defeated in the late election to the Vice Presidency, and led on by an unprincipled ambition, this extraordinary man formed the plan of a military expedition into the Spanish territories on our southwestern frontier, for the purpose of forming there a new republic. This has been generally supposed was a mere pretext ; and although it has not been generally known what his real plans were, there is no doubt that they were of a far more dangerous character.

In 1809, at the expiration of the second term for which Mr. Jefferson had been elected, he determined to retire from political life. For a period of nearly forty years, he had been continually before the public, and all that time had been employed in offices of the greatest trust and responsibility. Having thus devoted the best part of his life to the service of his country, he now felt desirous of that rest which his declining years required, and upon the organization of the new administration, in March, 1809, he bid farewell forever to public life, and retired to Monticello.

Mr. Jefferson was profuse in his hospitality. Whole families came in their coaches with their horses,—fathers and mothers, boys and girls, babies and nurses,—and remained three and even six months. Life at Monticello, for years, resembled that at a fashionable watering-place.

The fourth of July, 1826, being the fiftieth anniver-

sary of the Declaration of American Independence, great preparations were made in every part of the Union for its celebration, as the nation's jubilee, and the citizens of Washington, to add to the solemnity of the occasion, invited Mr. Jefferson, as the framer, and one of the few surviving signers of the Declaration, to participate in their festivities. But an illness, which had been of several weeks duration, and had been continually increasing, compelled him to decline the invitation.

On the second of July, the disease under which he was laboring left him, but in such a reduced state that his medical attendants, entertained no hope of his recovery. From this time he was perfectly sensible that his last hour was at hand. On the next day, which was Monday, he asked of those around him, the day of the month, and on being told it was the third of July, he expressed the earnest wish that he might be permitted to breathe the air of the fiftieth anniversary. His prayer was heard—that day, whose dawn was hailed with such rapture through our land, burst upon his eyes, and then they were closed forever. And what a noble consummation of a noble life! To die on that day,—the birthday of a nation,—the day which his own name and his own act had rendered glorious; to die amidst the rejoicings and festivities of a whole nation, who looked up to him, as the author, under God, of their greatest blessings, was all that was wanting to fill up the record his life.

Almost at the same hour of his death, the kindred spirit of the venerable Adams, as if to bear him company, left the scene of his earthly honors. Hand in hand they had stood forth, the champions of freedom; hand in hand, during the dark and desperate struggle of the Revolution, they had cheered and animated their desponding countrymen; for half a century they had labored together for the good of the country; and now hand in hand they depart. In their lives they had been united in the same great cause of liberty, and in their deaths they were not divided.

In person Mr. Jefferson was tall and thin, rather above six feet in height, but well formed; his eyes were light, his hair originally red, in after life became white and silvery ; his complexion was fair, his forehead broad, and his whole countenance intelligent and thoughtful. He possessed great fortitude of mind as well as personal courage ; and his command of temper was such that his oldest and most intimate friends never recollected to have seen him in a passion. His manners, though dignified, were simple and unaffected, and his hospitality was so unbounded that all found at his house a ready welcome. In conversation he was fluent, eloquent and enthusiastic ; and his language was remarkably pure and correct. He was a finished classical scholar, and in his writings is discernable the care with which he formed his style upon the best models of antiquity.

James Madison

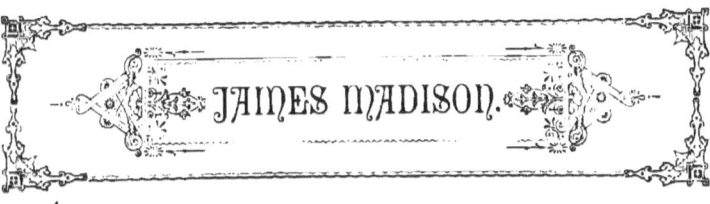

JAMES MADISON.

AMES MADISON, "Father of the Constitution," and fourth President of the United States, was born March 16, 1757, and died at his home in Virginia, June 28, 1836. The name of James Madison is inseparably connected with most of the important events in that heroic period of our country during which the foundations of this great republic were laid. He was the last of the founders of the Constitution of the United States to be called to his eternal reward.

The Madison family were among the early emigrants to the New World, landing upon the shores of the Chesapeake but 15 years after the settlement of Jamestown. The father of James Madison was an opulent planter, residing upon a very fine estate called "Montpelier," Orange Co., Va. The mansion was situated in the midst of scenery highly picturesque and romantic, on the west side of South-west Mountain, at the foot of Blue Ridge. It was but 25 miles from the home of Jefferson at Monticello. The closest personal and political attachment existed between these illustrious men, from their early youth until death.

The early education of Mr. Madison was conducted mostly at home under a private tutor. At the age of 18 he was sent to Princeton College, in New Jersey. Here he applied himself to study with the most im-

prudent zeal; allowing himself, for months, but three hours' sleep out of the 24. His health thus became so seriously impaired that he never recovered any vigor of constitution. He graduated in 1771, with a feeble body, with a character of utmost purity, and with a mind highly disciplined and richly stored with learning, which embellished and gave proficiency to his subsequent career.

Returning to Virginia, he commenced the study of law and a course of extensive and systematic reading. This educational course, the spirit of the times in which he lived, and the society with which he associated, all combined to inspire him with a strong love of liberty, and to train him for his life-work of a statesman. Being naturally of a religious turn of mind, and his frail health leading him to think that his life was not to be long, he directed especial attention to theological studies. Endowed with a mind singularly free from passion and prejudice, and with almost unequalled powers of reasoning, he weighed all the arguments for and against revealed religion, until his faith became so established as never to be shaken.

In the spring of 1776, when 26 years of age, he was elected a member of the Virginia Convention, to frame the constitution of the State. The next year (1777), he was a candidate for the General Assembly. He refused to treat the whisky-loving voters, and consequently lost his election; but those who had witnessed the talent, energy and public spirit of the modest young man, enlisted themselves in his behalf, and he was appointed to the Executive Council.

Both Patrick Henry and Thomas Jefferson were Governors of Virginia while Mr. Madison remained member of the Council; and their appreciation of his intellectual, social and moral worth, contributed not a little to his subsequent eminence. In the year 1780, he was elected a member of the Continental Congress. Here he met the most illustrious men in our land, and he was immediately assigned to one of the most conspicuous positions among them.

For three years Mr. Madison continued in Congress, one of its most active and influential members. In the year 1784, his term having expired, he was elected a member of the Virginia Legislature.

No man felt more deeply than Mr. Madison the utter inefficiency of the old confederacy, with no national government, with no power to form treaties which would be binding, or to enforce law. There was not any State more prominent than Virginia in the declaration, that an efficient national government must be formed. In January, 1786, Mr. Madison carried a resolution through the General Assembly of Virginia, inviting the other States to appoint commissioners to meet in convention at Annapolis to discuss this subject. Five States only were represented. The convention, however, issued another call, drawn up by Mr. Madison, urging all the States to send their delegates to Philadelphia, in May, 1787, to draft a Constitution for the United States, to take the place of that Confederate League. The delegates met at the time appointed. Every State but Rhode Island was represented. George Washington was chosen president of the convention; and the present Constitution of the United States was then and there formed. There was, perhaps, no mind and no pen more active in framing this immortal document than the mind and the pen of James Madison.

The Constitution, adopted by a vote 81 to 79, was to be presented to the several States for acceptance. But grave solicitude was felt. Should it be rejected we should be left but a conglomeration of independent States, with but little power at home and little respect abroad. Mr. Madison was selected by the convention to draw up an address to the people of the United States, expounding the principles of the Constitution, and urging its adoption. There was great opposition to it at first, but it at length triumphed over all, and went into effect in 1789.

Mr. Madison was elected to the House of Representatives in the first Congress, and soon became the avowed leader of the Republican party. While in New York attending Congress, he met Mrs Todd, a young widow of remarkable power of fascination, whom he married. She was in person and character queenly, and probably no lady has thus far occupied so prominent a position in the very peculiar society which has constituted our republican court as Mrs. Madison.

Mr. Madison served as Secretary of State under Jefferson, and at the close of his administration was chosen President. At this time the encroachments of England had brought us to the verge of war.

British orders in council destroyed our commerce, and our flag was exposed to constant insult. Mr. Madison was a man of peace. Scholarly in his taste, retiring in his disposition, war had no charms for him. But the meekest spirit can be roused. It makes one's blood boil, even now, to think of an American ship brought to, upon the ocean, by the guns of an English cruiser. A young lieutenant steps on board and orders the crew to be paraded before him. With great nonchalance he selects any number whom he may please to designate as British subjects; orders them down the ship's side into his boat; and places them on the gundeck of his man-of-war, to fight, by compulsion, the battles of England. This right of search and impressment, no efforts of our Government could induce the British cabinet to relinquish.

On the 18th of June, 1812, President Madison gave his approval to an act of Congress declaring war against Great Britain. Notwithstanding the bitter hostility of the Federal party to the war, the country in general approved; and Mr. Madison, on the 4th of March, 1813, was re-elected by a large majority, and entered upon his second term of office. This is not the place to describe the various adventures of this war on the land and on the water. Our infant navy then laid the foundations of its renown in grappling with the most formidable power which ever swept the seas. The contest commenced in earnest by the appearance of a British fleet, early in February, 1813, in Chesapeake Bay, declaring nearly the whole coast of the United States under blockade.

The Emperor of Russia offered his services as mediator. America accepted; England refused. A British force of five thousand men landed on the banks of the Patuxet River, near its entrance into Chesapeake Bay, and marched rapidly, by way of Bladensburg, upon Washington.

The straggling little city of Washington was thrown into consternation. The cannon of the brief conflict at Bladensburg echoed through the streets of the metropolis. The whole population fled from the city. The President, leaving Mrs. Madison in the White House, with her carriage drawn up at the door to await his speedy return, hurried to meet the officers in a council of war. He met our troops utterly routed, and he could not go back without danger of being captured. But few hours elapsed ere the Presidential Mansion, the Capitol, and all the public buildings in Washington were in flames.

The war closed after two years of fighting, and on Feb. 13, 1815, the treaty of peace was signed at Ghent.

On the 4th of March, 1817, his second term of office expired, and he resigned the Presidential chair to his friend, James Monroe. He retired to his beautiful home at Montpelier, and there passed the remainder of his days. On June 28, 1836, then at the age of 85 years, he fell asleep in death. Mrs. Madison died July 12, 1849.

James Monroe

JAMES MONROE.

AMES MONROE, the fifth President of The United States, was born in Westmoreland Co., Va., April 28, 1758. His early life was passed at the place of nativity. His ancestors had for many years resided in the province in which he was born. When, at 17 years of age, in the process of completing his education at William and Mary College, the Colonial Congress assembled at Philadelphia to deliberate upon the unjust and manifold oppressions of Great Britian, declared the separation of the Colonies, and promulgated the Declaration of Independence. Had he been born ten years before it is highly probable that he would have been one of the signers of that celebrated instrument. At this time he left school and enlisted among the patriots.

He joined the army when everything looked hopeless and gloomy. The number of deserters increased from day to day. The invading armies came pouring in; and the tories not only favored the cause of the mother country, but disheartened the new recruits, who were sufficiently terrified at the prospect of contending with an enemy whom they had been taught to deem invincible. To such brave spirits as James Monroe, who went right onward, undismayed through difficulty and danger, the United States owe their political emancipation. The young cadet joined the ranks, and espoused the cause of his injured country, with a firm determination to live or die with her strife for liberty. Firmly yet sadly he shared in the melancholy retreat from Harleam Heights and White Plains, and accompanied the dispirited army as it fled before its foes through New Jersey. In four months after the Declaration of Independence, the patriots had been beaten in seven battles. At the battle of Trenton he led the vanguard, and, in the act of charging upon the enemy he received a wound in the left shoulder.

As a reward for his bravery, Mr. Monroe was promoted a captain of infantry; and, having recovered from his wound, he rejoined the army. He, however, receded from the line of promotion, by becoming an officer in the staff of Lord Sterling. During the campaigns of 1777 and 1778, in the actions of Brandywine, Germantown and Monmouth, he continued aid-de-camp; but becoming desirous to regain his position in the army, he exerted himself to collect a regiment for the Virginia line. This scheme failed owing to the exhausted condition of the State. Upon this failure he entered the office of Mr. Jefferson, at that period Governor, and pursued, with considerable ardor, the study of common law. He did not, however, entirely lay aside the knapsack for the green bag; but on the invasions of the enemy, served as a volunteer, during the two years of his legal pursuits.

In 1782, he was elected from King George county, a member of the Legislature of Virginia, and by that body he was elevated to a seat in the Executive Council. He was thus honored with the confidence of his fellow citizens at 23 years of age; and having at this early period displayed some of that ability and aptitude for legislation, which were afterwards employed with unremitting energy for the public good,

he was in the succeeding year chosen a member of
the Congress of the United States.

Deeply as Mr. Monroe felt the imperfections of the old
Confederacy, he was opposed to the new Constitution,
thinking, with many others of the Republican party,
that it gave too much power to the Central Government,
and not enough to the individual States. Still he retained the esteem of his friends who were its warm
supporters, and who, notwithstanding his opposition
secured its adoption. In 1789, he became a member
of the United States Senate; which office he held for
four years. Every month the line of distinction between the two great parties which divided the nation,
the Federal and the Republican, was growing more
distinct. The two prominent ideas which now separated them were, that the Republican party was in
sympathy with France, and also in favor of such a
strict construction of the Constitution as to give the
Central Government as little power, and the State
Governments as much power, as the Constitution would
warrant. The Federalists sympathized with England,
and were in favor of a liberal construction of the Constitution, which would give as much power to the
Central Government as that document could possibly
authorize.

The leading Federalists and Republicans were
alike noble men, consecrating all their energies to the
good of the nation. Two more honest men or more
pure patriots than John Adams the Federalist, and
James Monroe the Republican, never breathed. In
building up this majestic nation, which is destined
to eclipse all Grecian and Assyrian greatness, the combination of their antagonism was needed to create the
right equilibrium. And yet each in his day was denounced as almost a demon.

Washington was then President. England had espoused the cause of the Bourbons against the principles of the French Revolution. All Europe was drawn
into the conflict. We were feeble and far away.
Washington issued a proclamation of neutrality between these contending powers. France had helped
us in the struggle for our liberties. All the despotisms
of Europe were now combined to prevent the French
from escaping from a tyranny a thousand-fold worse
than that which we had endured. Col. Monroe, more
magnanimous than prudent, was anxious that, at
whatever hazard, we should help our old allies in
their extremity. It was the impulse of a generous
and noble nature. He violently opposed the President's proclamation as ungrateful and wanting in
magnanimity.

Washington, who could appreciate such a character,
developed his calm, serene, almost divine greatness,
by appointing that very James Monroe, who was de-
nouncing the policy of the Government, as the minister
of that Government to the Republic of France. Mr.
Monroe was welcomed by the National Convention
in France with the most enthusiastic demonstrations.

Shortly after his return to this country, Mr. Monroe was elected Governor of Virginia, and held the
office for three years. He was again sent to France to
co-operate with Chancellor Livingston in obtaining
the vast territory then known as the Province of
Louisiana, which France had but shortly before obtained from Spain. Their united efforts were successful. For the comparatively small sum of fifteen
millions of dollars, the entire territory of Orleans and
district of Louisiana were added to the United States.
This was probably the largest transfer of real estate
which was ever made in all the history of the world.

From France Mr. Monroe went to England to obtain from that country some recognition of our
rights as neutrals, and to remonstrate against those
odious impressments of our seamen, but England was unrelenting. He again returned to England on the same mission, but could receive no
redress. He returned to his home and was again
chosen Governor of Virginia. This he soon resigned
to accept the position of Secretary of State under
Madison. While in this office war with England was
declared, the Secretary of War resigned, and during
these trying times, the duties of the War Department
were also put upon him. He was truly the armor-
bearer of President Madison, and the most efficient
business man in his cabinet. Upon the return of
peace he resigned the Department of War, but continued in the office of Secretary of State until the expiration of Mr. Madison's administration. At the election held the previous autumn Mr. Monroe himself had
been chosen President with but little opposition, and
upon March 4, 1817, was inaugurated. Four years
later he was elected for a second term.

Among the important measures of his Presidency
were the cession of Florida to the United States; the
Missouri Compromise, and the " Monroe doctrine,"

This famous doctrine, since known as the " Monroe
doctrine," was enunciated by him in 1823. At that
time the United States had recognized the independence of the South American states, and did not wish
to have European powers longer attempting to sub-
due portions of the American Continent. The doctrine
is as follows : "That we should consider any attempt
on the part of European powers to extend their system to any portion of this hemisphere as dangerous
to our peace and safety," and "that we could not
view any interposition for the purpose of oppressing
or controlling American governments or provinces in
any other light than as a manifestation by European
powers of an unfriendly disposition toward the United
States." This doctrine immediately affected the course
of foreign governments, and has become the approved
sentiment of the United States.

At the end of his second term Mr Monroe retired
to his home in Virginia, where he lived until 1830,
when he went to New York to live with his son-in-
law. In that city he died, on the 4th of July, 1831

J. Q. Adams

JOHN QUINCY ADAMS.

JOHN QUINCY ADAMS, the sixth President of the United States, was born in the rural home of his honored father, John Adams, in Quincy, Mass., on the 11th of July, 1767. His mother, a woman of exalted worth, watched over his childhood during the almost constant absence of his father. When but eight years of age, he stood with his mother on an eminence, listening to the booming of the great battle on Bunker's Hill, and gazing on upon the smoke and flames billowing up from the conflagration of Charlestown.

When but eleven years old he took a tearful adieu of his mother, to sail with his father for Europe, through a fleet of hostile British cruisers. The bright, animated boy spent a year and a half in Paris, where his father was associated with Franklin and Lee as minister plenipotentiary. His intelligence attracted the notice of these distinguished men, and he received from them flattering marks of attention.

Mr. John Adams had scarcely returned to this country, in 1779, ere he was again sent abroad. Again John Quincy accompanied his father. At Paris he applied himself with great diligence, for six months, to study; then accompained his father to Holland, where he entered, first a school in Amsterdam, then the University at Leyden. About a year from this time, in 1781, when the manly boy was but fourteen years of age, he was selected by Mr. Dana, our minister to the Russian court, as his private secretary.

In this school of incessant labor and of enobling culture he spent fourteen months, and then returned to Holland through Sweden, Denmark, Hamburg and Bremen. This long journey he took alone, in the winter, when in his sixteenth year. Again he resumed his studies, under a private tutor, at Hague. Thence

in the spring of 1782, he accompanied his father to Paris, traveling leisurely, and forming acquaintance with the most distinguished men on the Continent; examining architectural remains, galleries of paintings, and all renowned works of art. At Paris he again became associated with the most illustrious men of all lands in the contemplations of the loftiest temporal themes which can engross the human mind. After a short visit to England he returned to Paris, and consecrated all his energies to study until May, 1785, when he returned to America. To a brilliant young man of eighteen, who had seen much of the world, and who was familiar with the etiquette of courts, a residence with his father in London, under such circumstances, must have been extremely attractive but with judgment very rare in one of his age, he preferred to return to America to complete his education in an American college. He wished then to study law, that with an honorable profession, he might be able to obtain an independent support.

Upon leaving Harvard College, at the age of twenty, he studied law for three years. In June, 1794, being then but twenty-seven years of age, he was appointed by Washington, resident minister at the Netherlands. Sailing from Boston in July, he reached London in October, where he was immediately admitted to the deliberations of Messrs. Jay and Pinckney, assisting them in negotiating a commercial treaty with Great Britian. After thus spending a fortnight in London, he proceeded to the Hague.

In July, 1797, he left the Hague to go to Portugal as minister plenipotentiary. On his way to Portugal, upon arriving in London, he met with despatches directing him to the court of Berlin, but requesting him to remain in London until he should receive his instructions. While writing he was married to an American lady to whom he had been previously engaged,—Miss Louisa Catherine Johnson, daughter of Mr. Joshua Johnson, American consul in London; a lady endowed with that beauty and those accomplishment which eminently fitted her to move in the elevated sphere for which she was destined

He reached Berlin with his wife in November, 1797; where he remained until July, 1799, when, having fulfilled all the purposes of his mission, he solicited his recall.

Soon after his return, in 1802, he was chosen to the Senate of Massachusetts, from Boston, and then was elected Senator of the United States for six years, from the 4th of March, 1804. His reputation, his ability and his experience, placed him immediately among the most prominent and influential members of that body. Especially did he sustain the Government in its measures of resistance to the encroachments of England, destroying our commerce and insulting our flag. There was no man in America more familiar with the arrogance of the British court upon these points, and no one more resolved to present a firm resistance.

In 1809, Madison succeeded Jefferson in the Presidential chair, and he immediately nominated John Quincy Adams minister to St. Petersburg. Resigning his professorship in Harvard College, he embarked at Boston, in August, 1809.

While in Russia, Mr. Adams was an intense student. He devoted his attention to the language and history of Russia; to the Chinese trade; to the European system of weights, measures, and coins; to the climate and astronomical observations; while he kept up a familiar acquaintance with the Greek and Latin classics. In all the universities of Europe, a more accomplished scholar could scarcely be found. All through life the Bible constituted an important part of his studies. It was his rule to read five chapters every day.

On the 4th of March, 1817, Mr. Monroe took the Presidential chair, and immediately appointed Mr. Adams Secretary of State. Taking leave of his numerous friends in public and private life in Europe, he sailed in June, 1819, for the United States. On the 18th of August, he again crossed the threshold of his home in Quincy. During the eight years of Mr. Monroe's administration, Mr. Adams continued Secretary of State.

Some time before the close of Mr. Monroe's second term of office, new candidates began to be presented for the Presidency. The friends of Mr. Adams brought forward his name. It was an exciting campaign. Party spirit was never more bitter. Two hundred and sixty electoral votes were cast. Andrew Jackson received ninety-nine; John Quincy Adams, eighty-four; William H. Crawford, forty-one; Henry Clay, thirty-seven. As there was no choice by the people, the question went to the House of Representatives. Mr. Clay gave the vote of Kentucky to Mr. Adams, and he was elected.

The friends of all the disappointed candidates now combined in a venomous and persistent assault upon Mr. Adams. There is nothing more disgraceful in the past history of our country than the abuse which

was poured in one uninterrupted stream, upon this high-minded, upright, patriotic man. There never was an administration more pure in principles, more conscientiously devoted to the best interests of the country, than that of John Quincy Adams; and never, perhaps, was there an administration more unscrupulously and outrageously assailed.

Mr. Adams was, to a very remarkable degree, abstemious and temperate in his habits; always rising early, and taking much exercise. When at his home in Quincy, he has been known to walk, before breakfast, seven miles to Boston. In Washington, it was said that he was the first man up in the city, lighting his own fire and applying himself to work in his library often long before dawn.

On the 4th of March, 1829, Mr. Adams retired from the Presidency, and was succeeded by Andrew Jackson. John C. Calhoun was elected Vice President. The slavery question now began to assume portentous magnitude. Mr. Adams returned to Quincy and to his studies, which he pursued with unabated zeal. But he was not long permitted to remain in retirement. In November, 1830, he was elected representative to Congress. For seventeen years, until his death, he occupied the post as representative, towering above all his peers, ever ready to do brave battle for freedom, and winning the title of "the old man eloquent." Upon taking his seat in the House, he announced that he should hold himself bound to no party. Probably there never was a member more devoted to his duties. He was usually the first in his place in the morning, and the last to leave his seat in the evening. Not a measure could be brought forward and escape his scrutiny. The battle which Mr. Adams fought, almost singly, against the proslavery party in the Government, was sublime in its moral daring and heroism. For persisting in presenting petitions for the abolition of slavery, he was threatened with indictment by the grand jury, with expulsion from the House, with assassination; but no threats could intimidate him, and his final triumph was complete.

It has been said of President Adams, that when his body was bent and his hair silvered by the lapse of fourscore years, yielding to the simple faith of a little child, he was accustomed to repeat every night, before he slept, the prayer which his mother taught him in his infant years.

On the 21st of February, 1848, he rose on the floor of Congress, with a paper in his hand, to address the speaker. Suddenly he fell, again stricken by paralysis, and was caught in the arms of those around him. For a time he was senseless, as he was conveyed to the sofa in the rotunda. With reviving consciousness, he opened his eyes, looked calmly around and said "*This is the end of earth;*" then after a moment's pause he added, "*I am content.*" These were the last words of the grand "Old Man Eloquent."

Andrew Jackson

NDREW JACKSON, the seventh President of the United States, was born in Waxhaw settlement, N. C., March 15, 1767, a few days after his father's death. His parents were poor emigrants from Ireland, and took up their abode in Waxhaw settlement, where they lived in deepest poverty.

Andrew, or Andy, as he was universally called, grew up a very rough, rude, turbulent boy. His features were coarse, his form ungainly; and there was but very little in his character, made visible, which was attractive.

When only thirteen years old he joined the volunteers of Carolina against the British invasion. In 1781, he and his brother Robert were captured and imprisoned for a time at Camden. A British officer ordered him to brush his mud-spattered boots. "I am a prisoner of war, not your servant," was the reply of the dauntless boy.

The brute drew his sword, and aimed a desperate blow at the head of the helpless young prisoner. Andrew raised his hand, and thus received two fearful gashes,—one on the hand and the other upon the head. The officer then turned to his brother Robert with the same demand. He also refused, and received a blow from the keen-edged sabre, which quite disabled him, and which probably soon after caused his death. They suffered much other ill-treatment, and were finally stricken with the small-pox. Their mother was successful in obtaining their exchange, and took her sick boys home. After a long illness Andrew recovered, and the death of his mother soon left him entirely friendless.

Andrew supported himself in various ways, such as working at the saddler's trade, teaching school and clerking in a general store, until 1784, when he entered a law office at Salisbury, N. C. He, however, gave more attention to the wild amusements of the times than to his studies. In 1788, he was appointed solicitor for the western district of North Carolina, of which Tennessee was then a part. This involved many long and tedious journeys amid dangers of every kind, but Andrew Jackson never knew fear, and the Indians had no desire to repeat a skirmish with the Sharp Knife.

In 1791, Mr. Jackson was married to a woman who supposed herself divorced from her former husband. Great was the surprise of both parties, two years later, to find that the conditions of the divorce had just been definitely settled by the first husband. The marriage ceremony was performed a second time, but the occurrence was often used by his enemies to bring Mr. Jackson into disfavor.

During these years he worked hard at his profession, and frequently had one or more duels on hand, one of which, when he killed Dickenson, was especially disgraceful.

In January, 1796, the Territory of Tennessee then containing nearly eighty thousand inhabitants, the people met in convention at Knoxville to frame a constitution. Five were sent from each of the eleven counties. Andrew Jackson was one of the delegates. The new State was entitled to but one member in the National House of Representatives. Andrew Jackson was chosen that member. Mounting his horse he rode to Philadelphia, where Congress then held its

s. sions, —a distance of about eight hundred miles. Jackson was an earnest advocate of the Democratic party. Jefferson was his idol. He admired Bonaparte, loved France and hated England. As Mr. Jackson took his seat, Gen. Washington, whose second term of office was then expiring, delivered his last speech to Congress. A committee drew up a complimentary address in reply. Andrew Jackson did not approve of the address, and was one of the twelve who voted against it. He was not willing to say that Gen. Washington's administration had been " wise, firm and patriotic."

Mr. Jackson was elected to the United States Senate in 1797, but soon resigned and returned home. Soon after he was chosen Judge of the Supreme Court of his State, which position he held for six years.

When the war of 1812 with Great Britain commenced, Madison occupied the Presidential chair Aaron Burr sent word to the President that there was an unknown man in the West, Andrew Jackson, who would do credit to a commission if one were conferred upon him. Just at that time Gen. Jackson offered his services and those of twenty-five hundred volunteers. His offer was accepted, and the troops were assembled at Nashville.

As the British were hourly expected to make an attack upon New Orleans, where Gen Wilkinson was in command, he was ordered to descend the river with fifteen hundred troops to aid Wilkinson. The expedition reached Natchez; and after a delay of several weeks there, without accomplishing anything, the men were ordered back to their homes. But the energy Gen. Jackson had displayed, and his entire devotion to the comfort of his soldiers, won him golden opinions; and he became the most popular man in the State. It was in this expedition that his toughness gave him the nickname of "Old Hickory."

Soon after this, while attempting to horsewhip Col. Thomas H. Benton, for a remark that gentleman made about his taking a part as second in a duel, in which a younger brother of Benton's was engaged, he received two severe pistol wounds. While he was lingering upon a bed of suffering news came that the Indians, who had combined under Tecumseh from Florida to the Lakes, to exterminate the white settlers, were committing the most awful ravages. Decisive action became necessary. Gen. Jackson, with his fractured bone just beginning to heal, his arm in a sling, and unable to mount his horse without assistance, gave his amazing energies to the raising of an army to rendezvous at Fayetteville, Alabama.

The Creek Indians had established a strong force on one of the bends of the Tallapoosa River, near the center of Alabama, about fifty miles below Fort Strother. With an army of two thousand men, Gen. Jackson traversed the pathless wilderness in a march of eleven days. He reached their fort, called Tohopeka or Horse-shoe, on the 27th of March, 1814. The bend

of the river enclosed nearly one hundred acres of tangled forest and wild ravine. Across the narrow neck the Indians had constructed a formidable breastwork of logs and brush. Here nine hundred warriors, with an ample suply of arms were assembled.

The fort was stormed. The fight was utterly desperate. Not an Indian would accept of quarter. When bleeding and dying, they would fight those who endeavored to spare their lives. From ten in the morning until dark, the battle raged. The carnage was awful and revolting. Some threw themselves into the river; but the unerring bullet struck their heads as they swam. Nearly every one of the nine hundred warrios were killed A few probably, in the night, swam the river and escaped. This ended the war. The power of the Creeks was broken forever. This I old plunge into the wilderness, with its terrific slaughter, so appalled the savages, that the haggard remnants of the bands came to the camp, begging for peace.

This closing of the Creek war enabled us to concentrate all our militia upon the British, who were the allies of the Indians No man of less resolute will than Gen. Jackson could have conducted this Indian campaign to so successful an issue Immediately he was appointed major-general.

Late in August, with an army of two thousand men, on a rushing march, Gen. Jackson came to Mobile. A British fleet came from Pensacola, landed a force upon the beach, anchored near the little fort, and from both ship and shore commenced a furious assault The battle was long and doubtful. At length one of the ships was blown up and the rest retired.

Garrisoning Mobile, where he had taken his little army, he moved his troops to New Orleans. And the battle of New Orleans which soon ensued. was in reality a very arduous campaign. This won for Gen. Jackson an imperishable name. Here his troops, which numbered about four thousand men, won a signal victory over the British army of about nine thousand. His loss was but thirteen, while the loss of the British was two thousand six hundred.

The name of Gen. Jackson soon began to be mentioned in connection with the Presidency, but, in 1824, he was defeated by Mr. Adams. He was, however, successful in the election of 1828, and was re-elected for a second term in 1832. In 1829, just before he assumed the reins of the government, he met with the most terrible affliction of his life in the death of his wife, whom he had loved with a devotion which has perhaps never been surpassed. From the shock of her death he never recovered.

His administration was one of the most memorable in the annals of our country; applauded by one party, condemned by the other. No man had more bitter enemies or warmer friends. At the expiration of his two terms of office he retired to the Hermitage, where he died June 8, 1845. The last years of Mr. Jackson's life were that of a devoted Christian man.

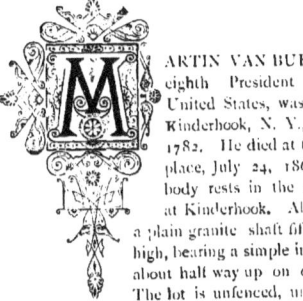

ARTIN VAN BUREN, the eighth President of the United States, was born at Kinderhook, N. Y., Dec. 5, 1782. He died at the same place, July 24, 1862. His body rests in the cemetery at Kinderhook. Above it is a plain granite shaft fifteen feet high, bearing a simple inscription about half way up on one face. The lot is unfenced, unbordered or unbounded by shrub or flower.

There is but little in the life of Martin Van Buren of romantic interest. He fought no battles, engaged in no wild adventures. Though his life was stormy in political and intellectual conflicts, and he gained many signal victories, his days passed uneventful in those incidents which give zest to biography. His ancestors, as his name indicates, were of Dutch origin, and were among the earliest emigrants from Holland to the banks of the Hudson. His father was a farmer, residing in the old town of Kinderhook. His mother, also of Dutch lineage, was a woman of superior intelligence and exemplary piety.

He was decidedly a precocious boy, developing unusual activity, vigor and strength of mind. At the age of fourteen, he had finished his academic studies in his native village, and commenced the study of law. As he had not a collegiate education, seven years of study in a law-office were required of him before he could be admitted to the bar. Inspired with a lofty ambition, and conscious of his powers, he pursued his studies with indefatigable industry. After spending six years in an office in his native village, he went to the city of New York, and prosecuted his studies for the seventh year.

In 1803, Mr. Van Buren, then twenty-one years of age, commenced the practice of law in his native village. The great conflict between the Federal and Republican party was then at its height. Mr. Van Buren was from the beginning a politician. He had, perhaps, imbibed that spirit while listening to the many discussions which had been carried on in his father's hotel. He was in cordial sympathy with Jefferson, and earnestly and eloquently espoused the cause of State Rights; though at that time the Federal party held the supremacy both in his town and State.

His success and increasing reputation led him after six years of practice, to remove to Hudson, th. county seat of his county. Here he spent seven years constantly gaining strength by contending in the courts with some of the ablest men who have adorned the bar of his State.

Just before leaving Kinderhook for Hudson, Mr. Van Buren married a lady alike distinguished for beauty and accomplishments. After twelve short years she sank into the grave, the victim of consumption, leaving her husband and four sons to weep over her loss. For twenty-five years, Mr. Van Buren was an earnest, successful, assiduous lawyer. The record of those years is barren in items of public interest. In 1812, when thirty years of age, he was chosen to the State Senate, and gave his strenuous support to Mr. Madison's administration. In 1815, he was appointed Attorney-General, and the next year moved to Albany, the capital of the State.

While he was acknowledged as one of the most prominent leaders of the Democratic party, he had the moral courage to avow that true democracy did not require that "universal suffrage" which admits the vile, the degraded, the ignorant, to the right of governing the State. In true consistency with his democratic principles, he contended that, while the path leading to the privilege of voting should be open to every man without distinction, no one should be invested with that sacred prerogative, unless he were in some degree qualified for it by intelligence, virtue and some property interests in the welfare of the State.

In 1821 he was elected a member of the United States Senate; and in the same year, he took a seat in the convention to revise the constitution of his native State. His course in this convention secured the approval of men of all parties. No one could doubt the singleness of his endeavors to promote the interests of all classes in the community. In the Senate of the United States, he rose at once to a conspicuous position as an active and useful legislator.

In 1827, John Quincy Adams being then in the Presidential chair, Mr. Van Buren was re-elected to the Senate. He had been from the beginning a determined opposer of the Administration, adopting the "State Rights" view in opposition to what was deemed the Federal proclivities of Mr. Adams.

Soon after this, in 1828, he was chosen Governor of the State of New York, and accordingly resigned his seat in the Senate. Probably no one in the United States contributed so much towards ejecting John Q. Adams from the Presidential chair, and placing in it Andrew Jackson, as did Martin Van Buren. Whether entitled to the reputation or not, he certainly was regarded throughout the United States as one of the most skillful, sagacious and cunning of politicians. It was supposed that no one knew so well as he how to touch the secret springs of action; how to pull all the wires to put his machinery in motion; and how to organize a political army which would, secretly and stealthily accomplish the most gigantic results. By these powers it is said that he outwitted Mr. Adams, Mr. Clay, Mr. Webster, and secured results which few thought then could be accomplished.

When Andrew Jackson was elected President he appointed Mr. Van Buren Secretary of State. This position he resigned in 1831, and was immediately appointed Minister to England, where he went the same autumn. The Senate, however, when it met, refused to ratify the nomination, and he returned home, apparently untroubled; was nominated Vice President in the place of Calhoun, at the re-election of President Jackson; and with smiles for all and frowns for none, he took his place at the head of that Senate which had refused to confirm his nomination as ambassador.

His rejection by the Senate roused all the zeal of President Jackson in behalf of his repudiated favorite; and this, probably more than any other cause, secured his elevation to the chair of the Chief Executive. On the 20th of May, 1836, Mr. Van Buren received the Democratic nomination to succeed Gen. Jackson as President of the United States. He was elected by a handsome majority, to the delight of the retiring President. "Leaving New York out of the canvass," says Mr. Parton, "the election of Mr. Van Buren to the Presidency was as much the act of Gen. Jackson as though the Constitution had conferred upon him the power to appoint a successor."

His administration was filled with exciting events. The insurrection in Canada, which threatened to involve this country in war with England, the agitation of the slavery question, and finally the great commercial panic which spread over the country, all were trials to his wisdom. The financial distress was attributed to the management of the Democratic party, and brought the President into such disfavor that he failed of re-election.

With the exception of being nominated for the Presidency by the "Free Soil" Democrats, in 1848, Mr. Van Buren lived quietly upon his estate until his death.

He had ever been a prudent man, of frugal habits, and living within his income, had now fortunately a competence for his declining years. His unblemished character, his commanding abilities, his unquestioned patriotism, and the distinguished positions which he had occupied in the government of our country, secured to him not only the homage of his party, but the respect of the whole community. It was on the 4th of March, 1841, that Mr. Van Buren retired from the presidency. From his fine estate at Lindenwald, he still exerted a powerful influence upon the politics of the country. From this time until his death, on the 24th of July, 1862, at the age of eighty years, he resided at Lindenwald, a gentleman of leisure, of culture and of wealth; enjoying in a healthy old age, probably far more happiness than he had before experienced amid the stormy scenes of his active life.

W. H. Harrison

WILLIAM HENRY HARRISON.

ILLIAM HENRY HARRI-
SON, the ninth President of
the United States, was born
at Berkeley, Va., Feb. 9, 1773.
His father, Benjamin Harrison, was in comparatively opulent circumstances, and was
one of the most distinguished
men of his day. He was an
intimate friend of George
Washington, was early elected
a member of the Continental
Congress, and was conspicuous
among the patriots of Virginia in
resisting the encroachments of the
British crown. In the celebrated
Congress of 1775, Benjamin Harrison and John Hancock were
both candidates for the office of
speaker.

Mr Harrison was subsequently
chosen Governor of Virginia, and
was twice re-elected. His son,
William Henry, of course enjoyed
in childhood all the advantages which wealth and
intellectual and cultivated society could give. Having received a thorough common-school education, he
entered Hampden Sidney College, where he graduated
with honor soon after the death of his father. He
then repaired to Philadelphia to study medicine under
the instructions of Dr. Rush and the guardianship of
Robert Morris, both of whom were, with his father,
signers of the Declaration of Independence.

Upon the outbreak of the Indian troubles, and notwithstanding the remonstrances of his friends, he
abandoned his medical studies and entered the army,
having obtained a commission of Ensign from Presi-

dent Washington. He was then but 19 years old.
From that time he passed gradually upward in rank
until he became aid to General Wayne, after whose
death he resigned his commission. He was then appointed Secretary of the North-western Territory. This
Territory was then entitled to but one member in
Congress and Capt. Harrison was chosen to fill that
position.

In the spring of 1800 the North-western Territory
was divided by Congress into two portions. The
eastern portion, comprising the region now embraced
in the State of Ohio, was called "The Territory
north-west of the Ohio." The western portion, which
included what is now called Indiana, Illinois and
Wisconsin, was called the "Indiana Territory." William Henry Harrison, then 27 years of age, was appointed by John Adams, Governor of the Indiana
Territory, and immediately after, also Governor of
Upper Louisiana. He was thus ruler over almost as
extensive a realm as any sovereign upon the globe. He
was Superintendent of Indian Affairs, and was invested with powers nearly dictatorial over the now
rapidly increasing white population. The ability and
fidelity with which he discharged these responsible
duties may be inferred from the fact that he was four
times appointed to this office—first by John Adams,
twice by Thomas Jefferson and afterwards by President Madison.

When he began his administration there were but
three white settlements in that almost boundless region,
now crowded with cities and resounding with all the
tumult of wealth and traffic. One of these settlements
was on the Ohio, nearly opposite Louisville; one at
Vincennes, on the Wabash, and the third a French
settlement.

The vast wilderness over which Gov. Harrison
reigned was filled with many tribes of Indians. About

the year 1806, two extraordinary men, twin brothers, of the Shawnese tribe, rose among them. One of these was called Tecumseh, or "The Crouching Panther;" the other, Olliwacheca, or "The Prophet." Tecumseh was not only an Indian warrior, but a man of great sagacity, far-reaching foresight and indomitable perseverance in any enterprise in which he might engage. He was inspired with the highest enthusiasm, and had long regarded with dread and with hatred the encroachment of the whites upon the hunting-grounds of his fathers. His brother, the Prophet, was an orator, who could sway the feelings of the untutored Indian as the gale tossed the tree-tops beneath which they dwelt.

But the Prophet was not merely an orator: he was, in the superstitious minds of the Indians, invested with the superhuman dignity of a medicine-man or a magician. With an enthusiasm unsurpassed by Peter the Hermit rousing Europe to the crusades, he went from tribe to tribe, assuming that he was specially sent by the Great Spirit.

Gov. Harrison made many attempts to conciliate the Indians, but at last the war came, and at Tippecanoe the Indians were routed with great slaughter. October 28, 1812, his army began its march. When near the Prophet's town three Indians of rank made their appearance and inquired why Gov. Harrison was approaching them in so hostile an attitude. After a short conference, arrangements were made for a meeting the next day, to agree upon terms of peace.

But Gov. Harrison was too well acquainted with the Indian character to be deceived by such protestations. Selecting a favorable spot for his night's encampment, he took every precaution against surprise. His troops were posted in a hollow square, and slept upon their arms.

The troops threw themselves upon the ground for rest; but every man had his accoutrements on, his loaded musket by his side, and his bayonet fixed. The wakeful Governor, between three and four o'clock in the morning, had risen, and was sitting in conversation with his aids by the embers of a waning fire. It was a chill, cloudy morning with a drizzling rain. In the darkness, the Indians had crept as near as possible, and just then, with a savage yell, rushed, with all the desperation which superstition and passion most highly inflamed could give, upon the left flank of the little army. The savages had been amply provided with guns and ammunition by the English. Their war-whoop was accompanied by a shower of bullets.

The camp-fires were instantly extinguished, as the light aided the Indians in their aim. With hideous yells, the Indian bands rushed on, not doubting a speedy and an entire victory. But Gen. Harrison's troops stood as immovable as the rocks around them until day dawned: they then made a simultaneous charge with the bayonet, and swept every thing before them, and completely routing the foe.

Gov. Harrison now had all his energies tasked to the utmost. The British descending from the Canadas, were of themselves a very formidable force; but with their savage allies, rushing like wolves from the forest, searching out every remote farm-house, burning, plundering, scalping, torturing, the wide frontier was plunged into a state of consternation which even the most vivid imagination can but faintly conceive. The war-whoop was resounding everywhere in the forest. The horizon was illuminated with the conflagration of the cabins of the settlers. Gen Hull had made the ignominious surrender of his forces at Detroit. Under these despairing circumstances, Gov. Harrison was appointed by President Madison commander-in-chief of the North-western army, with orders to retake Detroit, and to protect the frontiers.

It would be difficult to place a man in a situation demanding more energy, sagacity and courage; but General Harrison was found equal to the position, and nobly and triumphantly did he meet all the responsibilities.

He won the love of his soldiers by always sharing with them their fatigue. His whole baggage, while pursuing the foe up the Thames, was carried in a valise; and his bedding consisted of a single blanket lashed over his saddle. Thirty-five British officers, his prisoners of war, supped with him after the battle. The only fare he could give them was beef roasted before the fire, without bread or salt.

In 1816, Gen. Harrison was chosen a member of the National House of Representatives, to represent the District of Ohio. In Congress he proved an active member; and whenever he spoke, it was with force of reason and power of eloquence, which arrested the attention of all the members.

In 1819, Harrison was elected to the Senate of Ohio; and in 1824, as one of the presidential electors of that State, he gave his vote for Henry Clay. The same year he was chosen to the United States Senate.

In 1836, the friends of Gen. Harrison brought him forward as a candidate for the Presidency against Van Buren, but he was defeated. At the close of Mr. Van Buren's term, he was re-nominated by his party, and Mr. Harrison was unanimously nominated by the Whigs, with John Tyler for the Vice Presidency. The contest was very animated. Gen Jackson gave all his influence to prevent Harrison's election; but his triumph was signal.

The cabinet which he formed, with Daniel Webster at its head as Secretary of State, was one of the most brilliant with which any President had ever been surrounded. Never were the prospects of an administration more flattering, or the hopes of the country more sanguine. In the midst of these bright and joyous prospects, Gen. Harrison was seized by a pleurisy-fever and after a few days of violent sickness, died on the 4th of April; just one month after his inauguration as President of the United States.

John Tyler

OHN TYLER, the tenth President of the United States. He was born in Charles-city Co., Va., March 29, 1790. He was the favored child of affluence and high social position. At the early age of twelve, John entered William and Mary College and graduated with much honor when but seventeen years old. After graduating, he devoted himself with great assiduity to the study of law, partly with his father and partly with Edmund Randolph, one of the most distinguished lawyers of Virginia.

At nineteen years of age, he commenced the practice of law. His success was rapid and astonishing. It is said that three months had not elapsed ere there was scarcely a case on the docket of the court in which he was not retained. When but twenty-one years of age, he was almost unanimously elected to a seat in the State Legislature. He connected himself with the Democratic party, and warmly advocated the measures of Jefferson and Madison. For five successive years he was elected to the Legislature, receiving nearly the unanimous vote or his county.

When but twenty-six years of age, he was elected a member of Congress. Here he acted earnestly and ably with the Democratic party, opposing a national bank, internal improvements by the General Government, a protective tariff, and advocating a strict construction of the Constitution, and the most careful vigilance over State rights. His labors in Congress were so arduous that before the close of his second term he found it necessary to resign and retire to his estate in Charles-city Co., to recruit his health. He, however, soon after consented to take his seat in the State Legislature, where his influence was powerful in promoting public works of great utility. With a reputation thus constantly increasing, he was chosen by a very large majority of votes, Governor of his native State. His administration was signally a successful one. His popularity secured his re-election.

John Randolph, a brilliant, erratic, half-crazed man, then represented Virginia in the Senate of the United States. A portion of the Democratic party was displeased with Mr. Randolph's wayward course, and brought forward Mr. John Tyler as his opponent, considering him the only man in Virginia of sufficient popularity to succeed against the renowned orator of Roanoke. Mr. Tyler was the victor.

In accordance with his professions, upon taking his seat in the Senate, he joined the ranks of the opposition. He opposed the tariff; he spoke against and voted against the bank as unconstitutional; he strenuously opposed all restrictions upon slavery, resisting all projects of internal improvements by the General Government, and avowed his sympathy with Mr. Calhoun's view of nullification; he declared that Gen. Jackson, by his opposition to the nullifiers, had abandoned the principles of the Democratic party. Such was Mr. Tyler's record in Congress,—a record in perfect accordance with the principles which he had always avowed.

Returning to Virginia, he resumed the practice of his profession. There was a split in the Democratic party. His friends still regarded him as a true Jeffersonian, gave him a dinner, and showered compliments upon him. He had now attained the age of forty-six. His career had been very brilliant. In consequence of his devotion to public business, his private affairs had fallen into some disorder; and it was not without satisfaction that he resumed the practice of law, and devoted himself to the culture of his plantation. Soon after this he removed to Williamsburg, for the better education of his children; and he again took his seat in the Legislature of Virginia.

By the Southern Whigs, he was sent to the national convention at Harrisburg to nominate a President in 1839. The majority of votes were given to Gen. Harrison, a genuine Whig, much to the disappointment of the South, who wished for Henry Clay. To conciliate the Southern Whigs and to secure their vote, the convention then nominated John Tyler for Vice President. It was well known that he was not in sympathy with the Whig party in the North; but the Vice President has but very little power in the Government, his main and almost only duty being to preside over the meetings of the Senate. Thus it happened that a Whig President, and, in reality, a Democratic Vice President were chosen.

In 1841, Mr. Tyler was inaugurated Vice President of the United States. In one short month from that time, President Harrison died, and Mr. Tyler thus found himself, to his own surprise and that of the whole Nation, an occupant of the Presidential chair. This was a new test of the stability of our institutions, as it was the first time in the history of our country that such an event had occured. Mr. Tyler was at home in Williamsburg when he received the unexpected tidings of the death of President Harrison. He hastened to Washington, and on the 6th of April was inaugurated to the high and responsible office. He was placed in a position of exceeding delicacy and difficulty. All his long life he had been opposed to the main principles of the party which had brought him into power. He had ever been a consistent, honest man, with an unblemished record. Gen. Harrison had selected a Whig cabinet. Should he retain them, and thus surround himself with counsellors whose views were antagonistic to his own? or, on the other hand, should he turn against the party which had elected him and select a cabinet in harmony with himself, and which would oppose all those views which the Whigs deemed essential to the public welfare? This was his fearful dilemna. He invited the cabinet which President Harrison had selected to retain their seats. He reccommended a day of fasting and prayer, that God would guide and bless us.

The Whigs carried through Congress a bill for the incorporation of a fiscal bank of the United States. The President, after ten days' delay, returned it with his veto. He suggested, however, that he would approve of a bill drawn up upon such a plan as he proposed. Such a bill was accordingly prepared, and privately submitted to him. He gave it his approval. It was passed without alteration, and he sent it back with his veto. Here commenced the open rupture. It is said that Mr. Tyler was provoked to this measure by a published letter from the Hon. John M. Botts, a distinguished Virginia Whig, who severely touched the pride of the President.

The opposition now exultingly received the President into their arms. The party which elected him denounced him bitterly. All the members of his cabinet, excepting Mr. Webster, resigned. The Whigs of Congress, both the Senate and the House, held a meeting and issued an address to the people of the United States, proclaiming that all political alliance between the Whigs and President Tyler were at an end.

Still the President attempted to conciliate. He appointed a new cabinet of distinguished Whigs and Conservatives, carefully leaving out all strong party men. Mr. Webster soon found it necessary to resign, forced out by the pressure of his Whig friends. Thus the four years of Mr. Tyler's unfortunate administration passed sadly away. No one was satisfied. The land was filled with murmurs and vituperation. Whigs and Democrats alike assailed him. More and more, however, he brought himself into sympathy with his old friends, the Democrats, until at the close of his term, he gave his whole influence to the support of Mr. Polk, the Democratic candidate for his successor.

On the 4th of March, 1845, he retired from the harassments of office, to the regret of neither party, and probably to his own unspeakable relief. His first wife, Miss Letitia Christian, died in Washington, in 1842; and in June, 1844, President Tyler was again married, at New York, to Miss Julia Gardiner, a young lady of many personal and intellectual accomplishments.

The remainder of his days Mr. Tyler passed mainly in retirement at his beautiful home,—Sherwood Forest, Charles-city Co., Va. A polished gentleman in his manners, richly furnished with information from books and experience in the world, and possessing brilliant powers of conversation, his family circle was the scene of unusual attractions. With sufficient means for the exercise of a generous hospitality, he might have enjoyed a serene old age with the few friends who gathered around him, were it not for the storms of civil war which his own principles and policy had helped to introduce.

When the great Rebellion rose, which the Staterights and nullifying doctrines of Mr. John C. Calhoun had inaugurated, President Tyler renounced his allegiance to the United States, and joined the Confederates. He was chosen a member of their Congress; and while engaged in active measures to destroy, by force of arms, the Government over which he had once presided, he was taken sick and soon died.

JAMES K. POLK.

AMES K. POLK, the eleventh President of the United States, was born in Mecklenburg Co., N. C., Nov. 2, 1795. His parents were Samuel and Jane (Knox) Polk, the former a son of Col. Thomas Polk, who located at the above place, as one of the first pioneers, in 1735.

In the year 1806, with his wife and children, and soon after followed by most of the members of the Polk family, Samuel Polk emigrated some two or three hundred miles farther west, to the rich valley of the Duck River. Here in the midst of the wilderness, in a region which was subsequently called Maury Co., they reared their log huts, and established their homes. In the hard toil of a new farm in the wilderness, James K. Polk spent the early years of his childhood and youth. His father, adding the pursuit of a surveyor to that of a farmer, gradually increased in wealth until he became one of the leading men of the region. His mother was a superior woman, of strong common sense and earnest piety.

Very early in life, James developed a taste for reading and expressed the strongest desire to obtain a liberal education. His mother's training had made him methodical in his habits, had taught him punctuality and industry, and had inspired him with lofty principles of morality. His health was frail; and his father, fearing that he might not be able to endure a sedentary life, got a situation for him behind the counter, hoping to fit him for commercial pursuits.

This was to James a bitter disappointment. He had no taste for these duties, and his daily tasks were irksome in the extreme. He remained in this uncongenial occupation but a few weeks, when at his earnest solicitation his father removed him, and made arrangements for him to prosecute his studies. Soon after he sent him to Murfreesboro Academy. With ardor which could scarcely be surpassed, he pressed forward in his studies, and in less than two and a half years, in the autumn of 1815, entered the sophomore class in the University of North Carolina, at Chapel Hill. Here he was one of the most exemplary of scholars, punctual in every exercise, never allowing himself to be absent from a recitation or a religious service.

He graduated in 1818, with the highest honors, being deemed the best scholar of his class, both in mathematics and the classics. He was then twenty-three years of age. Mr. Polk's health was at this time much impaired by the assiduity with which he had prosecuted his studies. After a short season of relaxation he went to Nashville, and entered the office of Felix Grundy, to study law. Here Mr. Polk renewed his acquaintance with Andrew Jackson, who resided on his plantation, the Hermitage, but a few miles from Nashville. They had probably been slightly acquainted before.

Mr. Polk's father was a Jeffersonian Republican, and James K. Polk ever adhered to the same political faith. He was a popular public speaker, and was constantly called upon to address the meetings of his party friends. His skill as a speaker was such that he was popularly called the Napoleon of the stump. He was a man of unblemished morals, genial and courteous in his bearing, and with that sympathetic nature in the joys and griefs of others which ever gave him troops of friends. In 1823, Mr. Polk was elected to the Legislature of Tennessee. Here he gave his strong influence towards the election of his friend, Mr. Jackson, to the Presidency of the United States.

In January, 1824, Mr. Polk married Miss Sarah Childress, of Rutherford Co., Tenn. His bride was altogether worthy of him,—a lady of beauty and culture. In the fall of 1825, Mr. Polk was chosen a member of Congress. The satisfaction which he gave to his constituents may be inferred from the fact, that for fourteen successive years, until 1839, he was continued in that office. He then voluntarily withdrew, only that he might accept the Gubernatorial chair of Tennessee. In Congress he was a laborious member, a frequent and a popular speaker. He was always in his seat, always courteous; and whenever he spoke it was always to the point, and without any ambitious rhetorical display.

During five sessions of Congress, Mr. Polk was Speaker of the House Strong passions were roused, and stormy scenes were witnessed; but Mr Polk performed his arduous duties to a very general satisfaction, and a unanimous vote of thanks to him was passed by the House as he withdrew on the 4th of March, 1839.

In accordance with Southern usage, Mr. Polk, as a candidate for Governor, canvassed the State. He was elected by a large majority, and on the 14th of October, 1839, took the oath of office at Nashville. In 1841, his term of office expired, and he was again the candidate of the Democratic party, but was defeated.

On the 4th of March, 1845, Mr. Polk was inaugurated President of the United States. The verdict of the country in favor of the annexation of Texas, exerted its influence upon Congress; and the last act of the administration of President Tyler was to affix his signature to a joint resolution of Congress, passed on the 3d of March, approving of the annexation of Texas to the American Union. As Mexico still claimed Texas as one of her provinces, the Mexican minister, Almonte, immediately demanded his passports and left the country, declaring the act of the annexation to be an act hostile to Mexico.

In his first message, President Polk urged that Texas should immediately, by act of Congress, be received into the Union on the same footing with the other States. In the meantime, Gen. Taylor was sent with an army into Texas to hold the country. He was sent first to Nueces, which the Mexicans said was the western boundary of Texas. Then he was sent nearly two hundred miles further west, to the Rio Grande, where he erected batteries which commanded the Mexican city of Matamoras, which was situated on the western banks.

The anticipated collision soon took place, and war was declared against Mexico by President Polk. The war was pushed forward by Mr. Polk's administration with great vigor. Gen. Taylor, whose army was first called one of "observation," then of "occupation," then of "invasion," was sent forward to Monterey. The feeble Mexicans, in every encounter, were hopelessly and awfully slaughtered. The day of judgement alone can reveal the misery which this war caused. It was by the ingenuity of Mr. Polk's administration that the war was brought on.

"To the victors belong the spoils." Mexico was prostrate before us. Her capital was in our hands We now consented to peace upon the condition that Mexico should surrender to us, in addition to Texas, all of New Mexico, and all of Upper and Lower California. This new demand embraced, exclusive of Texas, eight hundred thousand square miles. This was an extent of territory equal to nine States of the size of New York. Thus slavery was securing eighteen majestic States to be added to the Union. There were some Americans who thought it all right: there were others who thought it all wrong. In the prosecution of this war, we expended twenty thousand lives and more than a hundred million of dollars. Of this money fifteen millions were paid to Mexico.

On the 3d of March, 1849, Mr. Polk retired from office, having served one term. The next day was Sunday. On the 5th, Gen. Taylor was inaugurated as his successor. Mr Polk rode to the Capitol in the same carriage with Gen. Taylor; and the same evening, with Mrs. Polk, he commenced his return to Tennessee. He was then but fifty-four years of age. He had ever been strictly temperate in all his habits, and his health was good With an ample fortune, a choice library, a cultivated mind, and domestic ties of the dearest nature, it seemed as though long years of tranquility and happiness were before him. But the cholera—that fearful scourge—was then sweeping up the Valley of the Mississippi. This he contracted, and died on the 15th of June, 1849, in the fifty-fourth year of his age, greatly mourned by his countrymen.

Zachary Taylor

ZACHARY TAYLOR.

ACHARY TAYLOR, twelfth President of the United States, was born on the 24th of Nov., 1784, in Orange Co., Va. His father, Colonel Taylor, was a Virginian of note, and a distinguished patriot and soldier of the Revolution. When Zachary was an infant, his father with his wife and two children, emigrated to Kentucky, where he settled in the pathless wilderness, a few miles from Louisville. In this frontier home, away from civilization and all its refinements, young Zachary could enjoy but few social and educational advantages. When six years of age he attended a common school, and was then regarded as a bright, active boy, rather remarkable for bluntness and decision of character. He was strong, fearless and self-reliant, and manifested a strong desire to enter the army to fight the Indians who were ravaging the frontiers. There is little to be recorded of the uneventful years of his childhood on his father's large but lonely plantation.

In 1808, his father succeeded in obtaining for him the commission of lieutenant in the United States army; and he joined the troops which were stationed at New Orleans under Gen. Wilkinson. Soon after this he married Miss Margaret Smith, a young lady from one of the first families of Maryland.

Immediately after the declaration of war with England, in 1812, Capt. Taylor (for he had then been promoted to that rank) was put in command of Fort Harrison, on the Wabash, about fifty miles above Vincennes. This fort had been built in the wilderness by Gen. Harrison on his march to Tippecanoe. It was one of the first points of attack by the Indians, led by Tecumseh. Its garrison consisted of a broken company of infantry numbering fifty men, many of whom were sick. Early in the autumn of 1812, the Indians, stealthily, and in large numbers, moved upon the fort. Their approach was first indicated by the murder of two soldiers just outside of the stockade. Capt. Taylor made every possible preparation to meet the anticipated assault. On the 4th of September, a band of forty painted and plumed savages came to the fort, waving a white flag, and informed Capt. Taylor that in the morning their chief would come to have a talk with him. It was evident that their object was merely to ascertain the state of things at the fort, and Capt. Taylor, well versed in the wiles of the savages, kept them at a distance.

The sun went down; the savages disappeared, the garrison slept upon their arms. One hour before midnight the war whoop burst from a thousand lips in the forest around, followed by the discharge of musketry, and the rush of the foe. Every man, sick and well, sprang to his post. Every man knew that defeat was not merely death, but in the case of capture, death by the most agonizing and prolonged torture. No pen can describe, no immagination can conceive the scenes which ensued. The savages succeeded in setting fire to one of the block houses. Until six o'clock in the morning, this awful conflict continued. The savages then, baffled at every point, and gnashing their teeth with rage, retired. Capt. Taylor, for this galiant defence, was promoted to the rank of major by brevet.

Until the close of the war, Major Taylor was placed in such situations that he saw but little more of active service. He was sent far away into the depths of the wilderness, to Fort Crawford, on Fox River, which empties into Green Bay. Here there was but little to be done but to wear away the tedious hours as one best could. There were no books, no society, no intellectual stimulus. Thus with him the uneventful years rolled on Gradually he rose to the rank of colonel. In the Black-Hawk war, which resulted in the capture of that renowned chieftain, Col Taylor took a subordinate but a brave and efficient part.

For twenty-four years Col. Taylor was engaged in the defence of the frontiers, in scenes so remote, and in employments so obscure, that his name was unknown beyond the limits of his own immediate acquaintance. In the year 1836, he was sent to Florida to compel the Seminole Indians to vacate that region and retire beyond the Mississippi, as their chiefs by treaty, had promised they should do. The services rendered he.e secured for Col. Taylor the high appreciation of the Government; and as a reward, he was elevated to he rank of brigadier-general by brevet; and soon after, in May, 1838, was appointed to the chief command of the United States troops in Florida.

After two years of such wearisome employment amidst the everglades of the peninsula, Gen. Taylor obtained, at his own request, a change of command, and was stationed over the Department of the Southwest. This field embraced Louisiana, Mississippi, Alabama and Georgia. Establishing his headquarters at Fort Jessup, in Louisiana, he removed his family to a plantation which he purchased, near Baton Rogue. Here he remained for five years, buried, as it were, from the world, but faithfully discharging every duty imposed upon him.

In 1846, Gen. Taylor was sent to guard the land between the Nueces and Rio Grande, the latter river being the boundary of Texas, which was then claimed by the United States. Soon the war with Mexico was brought on, and at Palo Alto and Resaca de la Palma, Gen. Taylor won brilliant victories over the Mexicans. The rank of major-general by brevet was then conferred upon Gen. Taylor, and his name was received with enthusiasm almost everywhere in the Nation. Then came the battles of Monterey and Buena Vista in which he won signal victories over forces much larger than he commanded.

His careless habits of dress and his unaffected simplicity, secured for Gen. Taylor among his troops, the *sobriquet* of "Old Rough and Ready.'

The tidings of the brilliant victory of Buena Vista spread the wildest enthusiasm over the country. The name of Gen. Taylor was on every one's lips. The Whig party decided to take advantage of this wonderful popularity in bringing forward the unpolished, unlettered, honest soldier as their candidate for the Presidency. Gen. Taylor was astonished at the announcement, and for a time would not listen to it; declaring that he was not at all qualified for such an office. So little interest had he taken in politics that, for forty years, he had not cast a vote. It was not without chagrin that several distinguished statesmen who had been long years in the public service found their claims set aside in behalf of one whose name

had never been heard of, save in connection with Palo Alto, Resaca de la Palma, Monterey and Buena Vista. It is said that Daniel Webster, in his haste remarked, " It is a nomination not fit to be made."

Gen. Taylor was not an eloquent speaker nor a fine writer His friends took possession of him, and prepared such few communications as it was needful should be presented to the public. The popularity of the successful warrior swept the land. He was triumphantly elected over two opposing candidates,— Gen. Cass and Ex-President Martin Van Buren. Though he selected an excellent cabinet, the good old man found himself in a very uncongenial position, and was, at times, sorely perplexed and harassed. His mental sufferings were very severe, and probably tended to hasten his death. The pro-slavery party was pushing its claims with tireless energy, expeditions were fitting out to capture Cuba ; California was pleading for admission to the Union, while slavery stood at the door to bar her out. Gen. Taylor found the political conflicts in Washington to be far more trying to the nerves than battles with Mexicans or Indians

In the midst of all these troubles, Gen. Taylor, after he had occupied the Presidential chair but little over a year, took cold, and after a brief sickness of but little over five days, died on the 9th of July, 1850. His last words were, " I am not afraid to die. I am ready. I have endeavored to do my duty." He died universally respected and beloved. An honest, unpretending man, he had been steadily growing in the affections of the people; and the Nation bitterly lamented his death.

Gen. Scott, who was thoroughly acquainted with Gen. Taylor, gave the following graphic and truthful description of his character:—" With a good store of common sense, Gen. Taylor's mind had not been enlarged and refreshed by reading, or much converse with the world. Rigidity of ideas was the consequence. The frontiers and small military posts had been his home. Hence he was quite ignorant for his rank, and quite bigoted in his ignorance. His simplicity was child-like, and with innumerable prejudices, amusing and incorrigible, well suited to the tender age. Thus, if a man, however respectable, chanced to wear a coat of an unusual color, or his hat a little on one side of his head; or an officer to leave a corner of his handkerchief dangling from an outside pocket,—in any such case, this critic held the offender to be a coxcomb (perhaps something worse), whom he would not, to use his oft repeated phrase, ' touch with a pair of tongs.'

"Any allusion to literature beyond good old Dilworth's spelling-book, on the part of one wearing a sword, was evidence, with the same judge, of utter unfitness for heavy marchings and combats. In short, few men have ever had a more comfortable, laborsaving contempt for learning of every kind."

Millard Fillmore

MILLARD FILLMORE.

ILLARD FILLMORE, thirteenth President of the United States, was born at Summer Hill, Cayuga Co., N. Y., on the 7th of January, 1800. His father was a farmer, and owing to misfortune, in humble circumstances. Of his mother, the daughter of Dr. Abiathar Millard, of Pittsfield, Mass., it has been said that she possessed an intellect of very high order, united with much personal loveliness, sweetness of disposition, graceful manners and exquisite sensibilities. She died in 1831; having lived to see her son a young man of distinguished promise, though she was not permitted to witness the high dignity which he finally attained.

In consequence of the secluded home and limited means of his father, Millard enjoyed but slender advantages for education in his early years. The common schools, which he occasionally attended, were very imperfect institutions; and books were scarce and expensive. There was nothing then in his character to indicate the brilliant career upon which he was about to enter. He was a plain farmer's boy; intelligent, good-looking, kind-hearted. The sacred influences of home had taught him to revere the Bible, and had laid the foundations of an upright character. When fourteen years of age, his father sent him some hundred miles from home, to the then wilds of Livingston County, to learn the trade of a clothier. Near the mill there was a small villiage, where some

enterprising man had commenced the collection of a village library. This proved an inestimable blessing to young Fillmore. His evenings were spent in reading. Soon every leisure moment was occupied with books. His thirst for knowledge became insatiate and the selections which he made were continually more elevating and instructive. He read history biography, oratory, and thus gradually there was enkindled in his heart a desire to be something more than a mere worker with his hands; and he was becoming, almost unknown to himself, a well-informed, educated man.

The young clothier had now attained the age of nineteen years, and was of fine personal appearance and of gentlemanly demeanor. It so happened that there was a gentleman in the neighborhood of ample pecuniary means and of benevolence,—Judge Walter Wood,—who was struck with the prepossessing appearance of young Fillmore. He made his acquaintance, and was so much impressed with his ability and attainments that he advised him to abandon his trade and devote himself to the study of the law. The young man replied, that he had no means of his own, no friends to help him and that his previous education had been very imperfect. But Judge Wood had so much confidence in him that he kindly offered to take him into his own office, and to loan him such money as he needed. Most gratefully the generous offer was accepted.

There is in many minds a strange delusion about a collegiate education. A young man is supposed to be liberally educated if he has graduated at some college. But many a boy loiters through university hall and then enters a law office, who is by no means a.

well prepared to prosecute his legal studies as was
Millard Fillmore when he graduated at the clothing-
mill at the end of four years of manual labor, during
which every leisure moment had been devoted to intense mental culture.

In 1823, when twenty-three years of age, he was
admitted to the Court of Common Pleas. He then
went to the village of Aurora, and commenced the
practice of law. In this secluded, peaceful region,
his practice of course was limited, and there was no
opportunity for a sudden rise in fortune or in fame.
Here, in the year 1826, he married a lady of great
moral worth, and one capable of adorning any station
she might be called to fill,—Miss Abigail Powers.

His elevation of character, his untiring industry,
his legal acquirements, and his skill as an advocate,
gradually attracted attention; and he was invited to
enter into partnership under highly advantageous
circumstances, with an elder member of the bar in
Buffalo. Just before removing to Buffalo, in 1829,
he took his seat in the House of Assembly, of the
State of New York, as a representative from Erie
County. Though he had never taken a very active
part in politics, his vote and his sympathies were with
the Whig party. The State was then Democratic,
and he found himself in a helpless minority in the
Legislature, still the testimony comes from all parties,
that his courtesy, ability and integrity, won, to a very
unusual degree the respect of his associates.

In the autumn of 1832, he was elected to a seat in
the United States Congress. He entered that troubled
arena in some of the most tumultuous hours of our
national history. The great conflict respecting the
national bank and the removal of the deposits, was
then raging.

His term of two years closed; and he returned to
his profession, which he pursued with increasing reputation and success. After a lapse of two years
he again became a candidate for Congress; was re-
elected, and took his seat in 1837. His past experience as a representative gave him strength and
confidence. The first term of service in Congress to
any man can be but little more than an introduction.
He was now prepared for active duty. All his energies were brought to bear upon the public good. Every
measure received his impress.

Mr. Fillmore was now a man of wide repute, and
his popularity filled the State, and in the year 1847,
he was elected Comptroller of the State.

Mr. Fillmore had attained the age of forty-seven
years. His labors at the bar, in the Legislature, in
Congress and as Comptroller, had given him very considerable fame. The Whigs were casting about to
find suitable candidates for President and Vice-President at the approaching election. Far away, on the
waters of the Rio Grande, there was a rough old
soldier, who had fought one or two successful battles
with the Mexicans, which had caused his name to be
proclaimed in trumpet-tones all over the land. But
it was necessary to associate with him on the same
ticket some man of reputation as a statesman.

Under the influence of these considerations, the
names of Zachary Taylor and Millard Fillmore became
the rallying-cry of the Whigs, as their candidates for
President and Vice-President. The Whig ticket was
signally triumphant. On the 4th of March, 1849,
Gen. Taylor was inaugurated President, and Millard
Fillmore Vice-President, of the United States.

On the 9th of July, 1850, President Taylor, but
about one year and four months after his inauguration, was suddenly taken sick and died. By the Constitution, Vice-President Fillmore thus became President. He appointed a very able cabinet, of which
the illustrious Daniel Webster was Secretary of State.

Mr. Fillmore had very serious difficulties to contend
with, since the opposition had a majority in both
Houses. He did everything in his power to conciliate
the South; but the pro-slavery party in the South felt
the inadequacy of all measures of transient conciliation.
The population of the free States was so rapidly increasing over that of the slave States that it was in-
evitable that the power of the Government should
soon pass into the hands of the free States. The
famous compromise measures were adopted under Mr.
Fillmore's administration, and the Japan Expedition
was sent out. On the 4th of March, 1853, Mr. Fillmore, having served one term, retired.

In 1856, Mr. Fillmore was nominated for the Presidency by the "Know Nothing" party, but was beaten
by Mr. Buchanan. After that Mr. Fillmore lived in
retirement. During the terrible conflict of civil war,
he was mostly silent. It was generally supposed that
his sympathies were rather with those who were endeavoring to overthrow our institutions. President
Fillmore kept aloof from the conflict, without any
cordial words of cheer to the one party or the other.
He was thus forgotten by both. He lived to a ripe
old age, and died in Buffalo. N. Y., March 8, 1874.

FRANKLIN PIERCE.

RANKLIN PIERCE, the fourteenth President of the United States, was born in Hillsborough, N. H., Nov. 23, 1804. His father was a Revolutionary soldier, who, with his own strong arm, hewed out a home in the wilderness. He was a man of inflexible integrity; of strong, though uncultivated mind, and an uncompromising Democrat. The mother of Franklin Pierce was all that a son could desire,—an intelligent, prudent, affectionate, Christian woman. Franklin was the sixth of eight children.

Franklin was a very bright and handsome boy, generous, warm-hearted and brave. He won alike the love of old and young. The boys on the play ground loved him. His teachers loved him. The neighbors looked upon him with pride and affection. He was by instinct a gentleman; always speaking kind words, doing kind deeds, with a peculiar unstudied tact which taught him what was agreeable. Without developing any precocity of genius, or any unnatural devotion to books, he was a good scholar; in body, in mind, in affections, a finely-developed boy.

When sixteen years of age, in the year 1820, he entered Bowdoin College, at Brunswick, Me. He was one of the most popular young men in the college. The purity of his moral character, the unvarying courtesy of his demeanor, his rank as a scholar, and genial nature, rendered him a universal favorite. There was something very peculiarly winning in his address, and it was evidently not in the slightest degree studied: it was the simple outgushing of his own magnanimous and loving nature.

Upon graduating, in the year 1824, Franklin Pierce commenced the study of law in the office of Judge Woodbury, one of the most distinguished lawyers of the State, and a man of great private worth. The eminent social qualities of the young lawyer, his father's prominence as a public man, and the brilliant political career into which Judge Woodbury was entering, all tended to entice Mr. Pierce into the fascinating yet perilous path of political life. With all the ardor of his nature he espoused the cause of Gen. Jackson for the Presidency. He commenced the practice of law in Hillsborough, and was soon elected to represent the town in the State Legislature. Here he served for four years. The last two years he was chosen speaker of the house by a very large vote.

In 1833, at the age of twenty-nine, he was elected a member of Congress. Without taking an active part in debates, he was faithful and laborious in duty, and ever rising in the estimation of those with whom he was associated.

In 1837, being then but thirty-three years of age, he was elected to the Senate of the United States; taking his seat just as Mr. Van Buren commenced his administration. He was the youngest member in the Senate. In the year 1834, he married Miss Jane Means Appleton, a lady of rare beauty and accomplishments, and one admirably fitted to adorn every station with which her husband was honored. Of the three sons who were born to them, all now sleep with their parents in the grave.

In the year 1838, Mr. Pierce, with growing fame and increasing business as a lawyer, took up his residence in Concord, the capital of New Hampshire. President Polk, upon his accession to office, appointed Mr. Pierce attorney-general of the United States; but the offer was declined, in consequence of numerous professional engagements at home, and the precarious state of Mrs. Pierce's health. He also, about the same time declined the nomination for governor by the Democratic party. The war with Mexico called Mr. Pierce in the army. Receiving the appointment of brigadier-general, he embarked, with a portion of his troops, at Newport, R. I., on the 27th of May, 1847. He took an important part in this war, proving himself a brave and true soldier.

When Gen. Pierce reached his home in his native State, he was received enthusiastically by the advocates of the Mexican war, and coldly by his opponents. He resumed the practice of his profession, very frequently taking an active part in political questions, giving his cordial support to the pro-slavery wing of the Democratic party. The compromise measures met cordially with his approval; and he strenuously advocated the enforcement of the infamous fugitive-slave law, which so shocked the religious sensibilities of the North. He thus became distinguished as a "Northern man with Southern principles." The strong partisans of slavery in the South consequently regarded him as a man whom they could safely trust in office to carry out their plans.

On the 12th of June, 1852, the Democratic convention met in Baltimore to nominate a candidate for the Presidency. For four days they continued in session, and in thirty-five ballotings no one had obtained a two-thirds vote. Not a vote thus far had been thrown for Gen. Pierce. Then the Virginia delegation brought forward his name. There were fourteen more ballotings, during which Gen. Pierce constantly gained strength, until, at the forty-ninth ballot, he received two hundred and eighty-two votes, and all other candidates eleven. Gen. Winfield Scott was the Whig candidate. Gen. Pierce was chosen with great unanimity. Only four States—Vermont, Massachusetts, Kentucky and Tennessee—cast their electoral votes against him. Gen. Franklin Pierce was therefore inaugurated President of the United States on the 4th of March, 1853.

His administration proved one of the most stormy our country had ever experienced. The controversy between slavery and freedom was then approaching its culminating point. It became evident that there was an "irrepressible conflict" between them, and that this Nation could not long exist "half slave and half free." President Pierce, during the whole of his administration, did every thing he could to conciliate the South; but it was all in vain. The conflict every year grew more violent, and threats of the dissolution of the Union were borne to the North on every Southern breeze.

Such was the condition of affairs when President Pierce approached the close of his four-years' term of office. The North had become thoroughly alienated from him. The anti-slavery sentiment, goaded by great outrages, had been rapidly increasing; all the intellectual ability and social worth of President Pierce were forgotten in deep reprehension of his administrative acts. The slaveholders of the South, also, unmindful of the fidelity with which he had advocated those measures of Government which they approved, and perhaps, also, feeling that he had rendered himself so unpopular as no longer to be able acceptably to serve them, ungratefully dropped him, and nominated James Buchanan to succeed him.

On the 4th of March, 1857, President Pierce retired to his home in Concord. Of three children, two had died, and his only surviving child had been killed before his eyes by a railroad accident; and his wife, one of the most estimable and accomplished of ladies, was rapidly sinking in consumption. The hour of dreadful gloom soon came, and he was left alone in the world, without wife or child.

When the terrible Rebellion burst forth, which divided our country into two parties, and two only, Mr. Pierce remained steadfast in the principles which he had always cherished, and gave his sympathies to that pro-slavery party with which he had ever been allied. He declined to do anything, either by voice or pen, to strengthen the hand of the National Government. He continued to reside in Concord until the time of his death, which occurred in October, 1869. He was one of the most genial and social of men, an honored communicant of the Episcopal Church, and one of the kindest of neighbors. Generous to a fault, he contributed liberally for the alleviation of suffering and want, and many of his townspeople were often gladened by his material bounty.

James Buchanan

JAMES BUCHANAN.

JAMES BUCHANAN, the fifteenth President of the United States, was born in a small frontier town, at the foot of the eastern ridge of the Alleghanies, in Franklin Co., Penn., on the 23d of April, 1791. The place where the humble cabin of his father stood was called Stony Batter. It was a wild and romantic spot in a gorge of the mountains, with towering summits rising grandly all around. His father was a native of the north of Ireland; a poor man, who had emigrated in 1783, with little property save his own strong arms. Five years afterwards he married Elizabeth Spear, the daughter of a respectable farmer, and, with his young bride, plunged into the wilderness, staked his claim, reared his log-hut, opened a clearing with his axe, and settled down there to perform his obscure part in the drama of life. In this secluded home, where James was born, he remained for eight years, enjoying but few social or intellectual advantages. When James was eight years of age, his father removed to the village of Mercersburg, where his son was placed at school, and commenced a course of study in English, Latin and Greek. His progress was rapid, and at the age of fourteen, he entered Dickinson College, at Carlisle. Here he developed remarkable talent, and took his stand among the first scholars in the institution. His application to study was intense, and yet his native powers enabled him to master the most abstruse subjects with facility.

In the year 1809, he graduated with the highest honors of his class. He was then eighteen years of age; tall and graceful, vigorous in health, fond of athletic sport, an unerring shot, and enlivened with an exuberant flow of animal spirits. He immediately commenced the study of law in the city of Lancaster, and was admitted to the bar in 1812, when he was but twenty-one years of age. Very rapidly he rose in his profession, and at once took undisputed stand with the ablest lawyers of the State. When but twenty-six years of age, unaided by counsel, he successfully defended before the State Senate one of the judges of the State, who was tried upon articles of impeachment. At the age of thirty it was generally admitted that he stood at the head of the bar; and there was no lawyer in the State who had a more lucrative practice.

In 1820, he reluctantly consented to run as a candidate for Congress. He was elected, and for ten years he remained a member of the Lower House. During the vacations of Congress, he occasionally tried some important case. In 1831, he retired altogether from the toils of his profession, having acquired an ample fortune.

Gen. Jackson, upon his elevation to the Presidency, appointed Mr. Buchanan minister to Russia. The duties of his mission he performed with ability, which gave satisfaction to all parties. Upon his return, in 1833, he was elected to a seat in the United States Senate. He there met, as his associates, Webster, Clay, Wright and Calhoun. He advocated the measures proposed by President Jackson, of making reprisals against France, to enforce the payment of our claims against that country; and defended the course of the President in his unprecedented and wholesale removal from office of those who were not the supporters of his administration. Upon this question he was brought into direct collision with Henry Clay. He also, with voice and vote, advocated expunging from the journal of the Senate the vote of censure against Gen. Jackson for removing the deposits. Earnestly he opposed the abolition of slavery in the District of Columbia, and urged the prohibition of the circulation of anti-slavery documents by the United States mails.

As to petitions on the subject of slavery, he advocated that they should be respectfully received; and that the reply should be returned, that Congress had no power to legislate upon the subject. "Congress," said he, "might as well undertake to interfere with slavery under a foreign government as in any of the States where it now exists."

Upon Mr. Polk's accession to the Presidency, Mr. Buchanan became Secretary of State, and as such, took his share of the responsibility in the conduct of the Mexican War. Mr. Polk assumed that crossing the Nueces by the American troops into the disputed territory was not wrong, but for the Mexicans to cross the Rio Grande into that territory was a declaration of war. No candid man can read with pleasure the account of the course our Government pursued in that movement.

Mr. Buchanan identified himself thoroughly with the party devoted to the perpetuation and extension of slavery, and brought all the energies of his mind to bear against the Wilmot Proviso. He gave his cordial approval to the compromise measures of 1850, which included the fugitive-slave law. Mr. Pierce, upon his election to the Presidency, honored Mr. Buchanan with the mission to England.

In the year 1856, a national Democratic convention nominated Mr. Buchanan for the Presidency. The political conflict was one of the most severe in which our country has ever engaged. All the friends of slavery were on one side; all the advocates of its restriction and final abolition, on the other. Mr. Fremont, the candidate of the enemies of slavery, received 114 electoral votes. Mr. Buchanan received 174, and was elected. The popular vote stood 1,340,618, for Fremont, 1,224,750 for Buchanan. On March 4th, 1857, Mr. Buchanan was inaugurated.

Mr. Buchanan was far advanced in life. Only four years were wanting to fill up his threescore years and ten. His own friends, those with whom he had been allied in political principles and action for years, were seeking the destruction of the Government, that they might rear upon the ruins of our free institutions a nation whose corner-stone should be human slavery. In this emergency, Mr. Buchanan was hopelessly bewildered. He could not, with his long-avowed prin-

ciples, consistently oppose the State-rights party in their assumptions. As President of the United States, bound by his oath faithfully to administer the laws he could not, without perjury of the grossest kind, unite with those endeavoring to overthrow the republic. He therefore did nothing.

The opponents of Mr. Buchanan's administration nominated Abraham Lincoln as their standard bearer in the next Presidential canvass. The pro-slavery party declared, that if he were elected, and the control of the Government were thus taken from their hands, they would secede from the Union, taking with them, as they retired, the National Capitol at Washington, and the lion's share of the territory of the United States.

Mr. Buchanan's sympathy with the pro-slavery party was such, that he had been willing to offer them far more than they had ventured to claim. All the South had professed to ask of the North was non-intervention upon the subject of slavery. Mr. Buchanan had been ready to offer them the active co-operation of the Government to defend and extend the institution.

As the storm increased in violence, the slaveholders claiming the right to secede, and Mr. Buchanan avowing that Congress had no power to prevent it, one of the most pitiable exhibitions of governmental imbecility was exhibited the world has ever seen. He declared that Congress had no power to enforce its laws in any State which had withdrawn, or which was attempting to withdraw from the Union. This was not the doctrine of Andrew Jackson, when, with his hand upon his sword-hilt, he exclaimed. "The Union must and shall be preserved!"

South Carolina seceded in December, 1860; nearly three months before the inauguration of President Lincoln. Mr. Buchanan looked on in listless despair. The rebel flag was raised in Charleston; Fort Sumpter was besieged; our forts, navy-yards and arsenals were seized; our depots of military stores were plundered; and our custom-houses and post-offices were appropriated by the rebels.

The energy of the rebels, and the imbecility of our Executive, were alike marvelous. The Nation looked on in agony, waiting for the slow weeks to glide away, and close the administration, so terrible in its weakness At length the long-looked-for hour of deliverance came, when Abraham Lincoln was to receive the scepter.

The administration of President Buchanan was certainly the most calamitous our country has experienced. His best friends cannot recall it with pleasure. And still more deplorable it is for his fame, that in that dreadful conflict which rolled its billows of flame and blood over our whole land, no word came from his lips to indicate his wish that our country's banner should triumph over the flag of the rebellion. He died at his Wheatland retreat, June 1, 1868.

ABRAHAM LINCOLN.

BRAHAM LINCOLN, the sixteenth President of the United States, was born in Hardin Co., Ky., Feb. 12, 1809. About the year 1780, a man by the name of Abraham Lincoln left Virginia with his family and moved into the then wilds of Kentucky. Only two years after this emigration, still a young man, while working one day in a field, was stealthily approached by an Indian and shot dead. His widow was left in extreme poverty with five little children, three boys and two girls. Thomas, the youngest of the boys, was four years of age at his father's death. This Thomas was the father of Abraham Lincoln, the President of the United States whose name must henceforth forever be enrolled with the most prominent in the annals of our world.

Of course no record has been kept of the life of one so lowly as Thomas Lincoln. He was among the poorest of the poor. His home was a wretched log-cabin; his food the coarsest and the meanest. Education he had none; he could never either read or write. As soon as he was able to do anything for himself, he was compelled to leave the cabin of his starving mother, and push out into the world, a friendless, wandering boy, seeking work. He hired himself out, and thus spent the whole of his youth as a laborer in the fields of others.

When twenty-eight years of age he built a log-cabin of his own, and married Nancy Hanks, the daughter of another family of poor Kentucky emigrants, who had also come from Virginia. Their second child was Abraham Lincoln, the subject of this sketch. The mother of Abraham was a noble woman, gentle, loving, pensive, created to adorn a palace, doomed to toil and pine, and die in a hovel. "All that I am, or hope to be," exclaims the grateful son "I owe to my angel-mother."

When he was eight years of age, his father sold his cabin and small farm, and moved to Indiana Where two years later his mother died.

Abraham soon became the scribe of the uneducated community around him. He could not have had a better school than this to teach him to put thoughts into words. He also became an eager reader. The books he could obtain were few; but these he read and re-read until they were almost committed to memory.

As the years rolled on, the lot of this lowly family was the usual lot of humanity. There were joys and griefs, weddings and funerals. Abraham's sister Sarah, to whom he was tenderly attached, was married when a child of but fourteen years of age, and soon died. The family was gradually scattered. Mr. Thomas Lincoln sold out his squatter's claim in 1830, and emigrated to Macon Co., Ill.

Abraham Lincoln was then twenty-one years of age. With vigorous hands he aided his father in rearing another log-cabin. Abraham worked diligently at this until he saw the family comfortably settled, and their small lot of enclosed prairie planted with corn, when he announced to his father his intention to leave home, and to go out into the world and seek his fortune. Little did he or his friends imagine how brilliant that fortune was to be. He saw the value of education and was intensely earnest to improve his mind to the utmost of his power. He saw the ruin which ardent spirits were causing, and became strictly temperate; refusing to allow a drop of intoxicating liquor to pass his lips. And he had read in God's word, "Thou shalt not take the name of the Lord thy God in vain;" and a profane expression he was never heard to utter. Religion he revered. His morals were pure, and he was uncontaminated by a single vice.

Young Abraham worked for a time as a hired laborer among the farmers. Then he went to Springfield, where he was employed in building a large flat-boat. In this he took a herd of swine, floated them down the Sangamon to the Illinois, and thence by the Mississippi to New Orleans. Whatever Abraham Lincoln undertook, he performed so faithfully as to give great satisfaction to his employers. In this adventure his employers were so well pleased, that upon his return they placed a store and mill under his care.

In 1832, at the outbreak of the Black Hawk war, he enlisted and was chosen captain of a company. He returned to Sangamon County, and although only 23 years of age, was a candidate for the Legislature, but was defeated. He soon after received from Andrew Jackson the appointment of Postmaster of New Salem. His only post-office was his hat. All the letters he received he carried there ready to deliver to those he chanced to meet. He studied surveying, and soon made this his business. In 1834 he again became a candidate for the Legislature, and was elected Mr. Stuart, of Springfield, advised him to study law. He walked from New Salem to Springfield, borrowed of Mr. Stuart a load of books, carried them back and began his legal studies. When the Legislature assembled he trudged on foot with his pack on his back one hundred miles to Vandalia, then the capital. In 1836 he was re-elected to the Legislature. Here it was he first met Stephen A. Douglas. In 1839 he removed to Springfield and began the practice of law. His success with the jury was so great that he was soon engaged in almost every noted case in the circuit.

In 1854 the great discussion began between Mr. Lincoln and Mr. Douglas, on the slavery question. In the organization of the Republican party in Illinois, in 1856, he took an active part, and at once became one of the leaders in that party. Mr. Lincoln's speeches in opposition to Senator Douglas in the contest in 1858 for a seat in the Senate, form a most notable part of his history. The issue was on the slavery question, and he took the broad ground of the Declaration of Independence, that all men are created equal. Mr. Lincoln was defeated in this contest, but won a far higher prize.

The great Republican Convention met at Chicago on the 16th of June, 1860. The delegates and strangers who crowded the city amounted to twenty-five thousand. An immense building called "The Wigwam," was reared to accommodate the Convention. There were eleven candidates for whom votes were thrown. William H Seward, a man whose fame as a statesman had long filled the land, was the most prominent. It was generally supposed he would be the nominee Abraham Lincoln, however, received the nomination on the third ballot. Little did he then dream of the weary years of toil and care, and the bloody death, to which that nomination doomed him: and as little did he dream that he was to render services to his country, which would fix upon him the eyes of the whole civilized world, and which would give him a place in the affections of his countrymen, second only, if second, to that of Washington.

Election day came and Mr. Lincoln received 180 electoral votes out of 203 cast, and was, therefore, constitutionally elected President of the United States. The tirade of abuse that was poured upon this good

and merciful man, especially by the slaveholders, was greater than upon any other man ever elected to this high position. In February, 1861, Mr. Lincoln started for Washington, stopping in all the large cities on his way making speeches. The whole journey was frought with much danger. Many of the Southern States had already seceded, and several attempts at assassination were afterwards brought to light. A gang in Baltimore had arranged, upon his arrival to "get up a row," and in the confusion to make sure of his death with revolvers and hand-grenades. A detective unravelled the plot. A secret and special train was provided to take him from Harrisburg, through Baltimore, at an unexpected hour of the night. The train started at half-past ten; and to prevent any possible communication on the part of the Secessionists with their Confederate gang in Baltimore, as soon as the train had started the telegraph-wires were cut. Mr. Lincoln reached Washington in safety and was inaugurated, although great anxiety was felt by all loyal people.

In the selection of his cabinet Mr. Lincoln gave to Mr Seward the Department of State, and to other prominent opponents before the convention he gave important positions.

During no other administration have the duties devolving upon the President been so manifold, and the responsibilities so great, as those which fell to the lot of President Lincoln. Knowing this, and feeling his own weakness and inability to meet, and in his own strength to cope with, the difficulties, he learned early to seek Divine wisdom and guidance in determining his plans, and Divine comfort in all his trials, both personal and national Contrary to his own estimate of himself, Mr. Lincoln was one of the most courageous of men. He went directly into the rebel capital just as the retreating foe was leaving, with no guard but a few sailors. From the time he had left Springfield, in 1861, however, plans had been made for his assassination, and he at last fell a victim to one of them. April 14, 1865, he, with Gen. Grant, was urgently invited to attend Fords' Theater. It was announced that they would be present. Gen. Grant, however, left the city. President Lincoln, feeling, with his characteristic kindliness of heart, that it would be a disappointment if he should fail them, very reluctantly consented to go. While listening to the play an actor by the name of John Wilkes Booth entered the box where the President and family were seated, and fired a bullet into his brains. He died the next morning at seven o'clock.

Never before, in the history of the world was a nation plunged into such deep grief by the death of its ruler. Strong men met in the streets and wept in speechless anguish. It is not too much to say that a nation was in tears. His was a life which will fitly become a model. His name as the savior of his country will live with that of Washington's, its father; his countrymen being unable to decide which is the greater.

Andrew Johnson

ANDREW JOHNSON.

ANDREW JOHNSON, seventeenth President of the United States. The early life of Andrew Johnson contains but the record of poverty, destitution and friendlessness. He was born December 29, 1808, in Raleigh, N. C. His parents, belonging to the class of the "poor whites" of the South, were in such circumstances, that they could not confer even the slightest advantages of education upon their child. When Andrew was five years of age, his father accidentally lost his life while heroically endeavoring to save a friend from drowning. Until ten years of age, Andrew was a ragged boy about the streets, supported by the labor of his mother, who obtained her living with her own hands.

He then, having never attended a school one day, and being unable either to read or write, was apprenticed to a tailor in his native town. A gentleman was in the habit of going to the tailor's shop occasionally, and reading to the boys at work there. He often read from the speeches of distinguished British statesmen. Andrew, who was endowed with a mind of more than ordinary native ability, became much interested in these speeches; his ambition was roused, and he was inspired with a strong desire to learn to read.

He accordingly applied himself to the alphabet, and with the assistance of some of his fellow-workmen, learned his letters. He then called upon the gentleman to borrow the book of speeches. The owner, pleased with his zeal, not only gave him the book but assisted him in learning to combine the letters into words. Under such difficulties he pressed onward laboriously, spending usually ten or twelve hours at work in the shop, and then robbing himself of rest and recreation to devote such time as he could to reading.

He went to Tennessee in 1826, and located at Greenville, where he married a young lady who possessed some education. Under her instructions he learned to write and cipher. He became prominent in the village debating society, and a favorite with the students of Greenville College. In 1828, he organized a working man's party, which elected him alderman, and in 1830 elected him mayor, which position he held three years.

He now began to take a lively interest in political affairs; identifying himself with the working-classes, to which he belonged. In 1835, he was elected a member of the House of Representatives of Tennessee. He was then just twenty-seven years of age. He became a very active member of the legislature, gave his adhesion to the Democratic party, and in 1840 "stumped the State," advocating Martin Van Buren's claims to the Presidency, in opposition to those of Gen. Harrison. In this campaign he acquired much readiness as a speaker, and extended and increased his reputation.

In 1841, he was elected State Senator; in 1843, he was elected a member of Congress, and by successive elections, held that important post for ten years. In 1853, he was elected Governor of Tennessee, and was re-elected in 1855. In all these responsible positions, he discharged his duties with distinguished ability, and proved himself the warm friend of the working classes. In 1857, Mr. Johnson was elected United States Senator.

Years before, in 1845, he had warmly advocated the annexation of Texas, stating however, as his reason, that he thought this annexation would probably prove "to be the gateway out of which the sable sons of Africa are to pass from bondage to freedom, and become merged in a population congenial to themselves." In 1850, he also supported the compromise measures, the two essential features of which were, that the white people of the Territories should be permitted to decide for themselves whether they would enslave the colored people or not, and that the free States of the North should return to the South persons who attempted to escape from slavery.

Mr. Johnson was never ashamed of his lowly origin; on the contrary, he often took pride in avowing that he owed his distinction to his own exertions. "Sir," said he on the floor of the Senate, "I do not forget that I am a mechanic; neither do I forget that Adam was a tailor and sewed fig-leaves, and that our Savior was the son of a carpenter."

In the Charleston-Baltimore convention of 1860, he was the choice of the Tennessee Democrats for the Presidency. In 1861, when the purpose of the Southern Democracy became apparent, he took a decided stand in favor of the Union, and held that "slavery must be held subordinate to the Union at whatever cost." He returned to Tennessee, and repeatedly imperiled his own life to protect the Unionists of Tennesee. Tennessee having seceded from the Union, President Lincoln, on March 4th, 1862, appointed him Military Governor of the State, and he established the most stringent military rule. His numerous proclamations attracted wide attention. In 1864, he was elected Vice-President of the United States, and upon the death of Mr. Lincoln, April 15, 1865, became President. In a speech two days later he said, "The American people must be taught, if they do not already feel, that treason is a crime and must be punished; that the Government will not always bear with its enemies; that it is strong not only to protect, but to punish. * * The people must understand that it (treason) is the blackest of crimes, and will surely be punished." Yet his whole administration, the history of which is so well known, was in utter inconsistency with, and the most violent

opposition to, the principles laid down in that speech.

In his loose policy of reconstruction and general amnesty, he was opposed by Congress; and he characterized Congress as a new rebellion, and lawlessly defied it, in everything possible, to the utmost. In the beginning of 1868, on account of "high crimes and misdemeanors," the principal of which was the removal of Secretary Stanton, in violation of the Tenure of Office Act, articles of impeachment were preferred against him, and the trial began March 23.

It was very tedious, continuing for nearly three months. A test article of the impeachment was at length submitted to the court for its action. It was certain that as the court voted upon that article so would it vote upon all. Thirty-four voices pronounced the President guilty. As a two-thirds vote was necessary to his condemnation, he was pronounced acquitted, notwithstanding the great majority against him. The change of one vote from the *not guilty* side would have sustained the impeachment.

The President, for the remainder of his term, was but little regarded. He continued, though impotently, his conflict with Congress. His own party did not think it expedient to renominate him for the Presidency. The Nation rallied, with enthusiasm unparalleled since the days of Washington, around the name of Gen. Grant. Andrew Johnson was forgotten. The bullet of the assassin introduced him to the President's chair. Notwithstanding this, never was there presented to a man a better opportunity to immortalize his name, and to win the gratitude of a nation. He failed utterly. He retired to his home in Greenville, Tenn., taking no very active part in politics until 1875. On Jan. 26, after an exciting struggle, he was chosen by the Legislature of Tennessee, United States Senator in the forty-fourth Congress, and took his seat in that body, at the special session convened by President Grant, on the 5th of March. On the 27th of July, 1875, the ex-President made a visit to his daughter's home, near Carter Station, Tenn. When he started on his journey, he was apparently in his usual vigorous health, but on reaching the residence of his child the following day, was stricken with paralysis, rendering him unconscious. He rallied occasionally, but finally passed away at 2 A. M., July 31, aged sixty-seven years. His funeral was attended at Greenville, on the 3d of August, with every demonstration of respect.

ULYSSES S. GRANT.

ULYSSES S. GRANT, the eighteenth President of the United States, was born on the 29th of April, 1822, of Christian parents, in a humble home, at Point Pleasant, on the banks of the Ohio. Shortly after his father moved to George-town, Brown Co., O. In this re-mote frontier hamlet, Ulysses received a common-school edu-cation. At the age of seven-teen, in the year 1839, he entered the Military Academy at West Point. Here he was regarded as a sound, sensible young man of fair abilities, and of sturdy, honest character. He took respectable rank as a scholar. In June, 1843, he graduated, about the middle in his class, and was sent as lieutenant of in-fantry to one of the distant military posts in the Mis-souri Territory. Two years he past in these dreary solitudes, watching the vagabond and exasperating Indians.

The war with Mexico came. Lieut. Grant was sent with his regiment to Corpus Christi. His first battle was at Palo Alto. There was no chance here for the exhibition of either skill or heroism, nor at Resaca de la Palma, his second battle. At the battle of Monterey, his third engagement, it is said that he performed a signal service of daring and skillful horsemanship. His brigade had exhausted its am-munition. A messenger must be sent for more, along a route exposed to the bullets of the foe. Lieut. Grant, adopting an expedient learned of the Indians, grasped the mane of his horse, and hanging upon one side of the animal, ran the gauntlet in entire safety.

From Monterey he was sent, with the fourth infantry, to aid Gen. Scott, at the siege of Vera Cruz. In preparation for the march to the city of Mexico, he was appointed quartermaster of his regiment. At the battle of Molino del Rey, he was promoted to a first lieutenancy, and was brevetted captain at Cha-pultepec.

At the close of the Mexican War, Capt. Grant re-turned with his regiment to New York, and was again sent to one of the military posts on the frontier. The discovery of gold in California causing an immense tide of emigration to flow to the Pacific shores, Capt. Grant was sent with a battalion to Fort Dallas, in Oregon, for the protection of the interests of the im-migrants. Life was wearisome in those wilds. Capt. Grant resigned his commission and returned to the States; and having married, entered upon the cultiva-tion of a small farm near St. Louis, Mo. He had but little skill as a farmer. Finding his toil not re-munerative, he turned to mercantile life, entering into the leather business, with a younger brother, at Ga-lena, Ill. This was in the year 1860. As the tidings of the rebels firing on Fort Sumpter reached the ears of Capt. Grant in his counting-room, he said,— "Uncle Sam has educated me for the army; though I have served him through one war, I do not feel that I have yet repaid the debt. I am still ready to discharge my obligations. I shall therefore buckle on my sword and see Uncle Sam through this war too."

He went into the streets, raised a company of vol-unteers, and led them as their captain to Springfield, the capital of the State, where their services were offered to Gov. Yates. The Governor, impressed by the zeal and straightforward executive ability of Capt. Grant, gave him a desk in his office, to assist in the volunteer organization that was being formed in the State in behalf of the Government. On the 15th of

June, 1861, Capt. Grant received a commission as Colonel of the Twenty-first Regiment of Illinois Volunteers. His merits as a West Point graduate, who had served for 15 years in the regular army, were such that he was soon promoted to the rank of Brigadier-General and was placed in command at Cairo. The rebels raised their banner at Paducah, near the mouth of the Tennessee River. Scarcely had its folds appeared in the breeze ere Gen. Grant was there. The rebels fled. Their banner fell, and the star and stripes were unfurled in its stead.

He entered the service with great determination and immediately began active duty. This was the beginning, and until the surrender of Lee at Richmond he was ever pushing the enemy with great vigor and effectiveness. At Belmont, a few days later, he surprised and routed the rebels, then at Fort Henry won another victory. Then came the brilliant fight at Fort Donelson. The nation was electrified by the victory, and the brave leader of the boys in blue was immediately made a Major-General, and the military district of Tennessee was assigned to him.

Like all great captains, Gen. Grant knew well how to secure the results of victory. He immediately pushed on to the enemies' lines. Then came the terrible battles of Pittsburg Landing, Corinth, and the siege of Vicksburg, where Gen. Pemberton made an unconditional surrender of the city with over thirty thousand men and one-hundred and seventy-two cannon. The fall of Vicksburg was by far the most severe blow which the rebels had thus far encountered, and opened up the Mississippi from Cairo to the Gulf.

Gen. Grant was next ordered to co-operate with Gen. Banks in a movement upon Texas, and proceeded to New Orleans, where he was thrown from his horse, and received severe injuries, from which he was laid up for months. He then rushed to the aid of Gens. Rosecrans and Thomas at Chattanooga, and by a wonderful series of strategic and technical measures put the Union Army in fighting condition. Then followed the bloody battles at Chattanooga, Lookout Mountain and Missionary Ridge, in which the rebels were routed with great loss. This won for him unbounded praise in the North. On the 4th of February, 1864, Congress revived the grade of lieutenant-general, and the rank was conferred on Gen. Grant. He repaired to Washington to receive his credentials and enter upon the duties of his new office.

Gen. Grant decided as soon as he took charge of the army to concentrate the widely-dispersed National troops for an attack upon Richmond, the nominal capital of the Rebellion, and endeavor there to destroy the rebel armies which would be promptly assembled from all quarters for its defence. The whole continent seemed to tremble under the tramp of these majestic armies, rushing to the decisive battle field. Steamers were crowded with troops. Railway trains were burdened with closely packed thousands. His plans were comprehensive and involved a series of campaigns, which were executed with remarkable energy and ability, and were consummated at the surrender of Lee, April 9, 1865.

The war was ended. The Union was saved. The almost unanimous voice of the Nation declared Gen. Grant to be the most prominent instrument in its salvation. The eminent services he had thus rendered the country brought him conspicuously forward as the Republican candidate for the Presidential chair.

At the Republican Convention held at Chicago, May 21, 1868, he was unanimously nominated for the Presidency, and at the autumn election received a majority of the popular vote, and 214 out of 294 electoral votes.

The National Convention of the Republican party which met at Philadelphia on the 5th of June, 1872, placed Gen. Grant in nomination for a second term by a unanimous vote. The selection was emphatically indorsed by the people five months later, 292 electoral votes being cast for him.

Soon after the close of his second term, Gen. Grant started upon his famous trip around the world. He visited almost every country of the civilized world, and was everywhere received with such ovations and demonstrations of respect and honor, private as well as public and official, as were never before bestowed upon any citizen of the United States.

He was the most prominent candidate before the Republican National Convention in 1880 for a re-nomination for President. He went to New York and embarked in the brokerage business under the firm name of Grant & Ward. The latter proved a villain, wrecked Grant's fortune, and for larceny was sent to the penitentiary. The General was attacked with cancer in the throat, but suffered in his stoic-like manner, never complaining. He was re-instated as General of the Army and retired by Congress. The cancer soon finished its deadly work, and July 23, 1885, the nation went in mourning over the death of the illustrious General.

Sincerely
R.B.Hayes

RUTHERFORD B. HAYES.

UTHERFORD B. HAYES, the nineteenth President of the United States, was born in Delaware, O., Oct. 4, 1822, almost three months after the death of his father, Rutherford Hayes. His ancestry on both the paternal and maternal sides, was of the most honorable character. It can be traced, it is said, as far back as 1280, when Hayes and Rutherford were two Scottish chieftains, fighting side by side with Baliol, William Wallace and Robert Bruce. Both families belonged to the nobility, owned extensive estates, and had a large following. Misfortune overtaking the family, George Hayes left Scotland in 1680, and settled in Windsor, Conn. His son George was born in Windsor, and remained there during his life. Daniel Hayes, son of the latter, married Sarah Lee, and lived from the time of his marriage until his death in Simsbury, Conn. Ezekiel, son of Daniel, was born in 1724, and was a manufacturer of scythes at Bradford, Conn. Rutherford Hayes, son of Ezekiel and grandfather of President Hayes, was born in New Haven, in August, 1756. He was a farmer, blacksmith and tavern-keeper. He emigrated to Vermont at an unknown date, settling in Brattleboro, where he established a hotel. Here his son Rutherford Hayes the father of President Hayes, was

born. He was married, in September, 1813, to Sophia Birchard, of Wilmington, Vt., whose ancestors emigrated thither from Connecticut, they having been among the wealthiest and best families of Norwich. Her ancestry on the male side are traced back to 1635, to John Birchard, one of the principal founders of Norwich. Both of her grandfathers were soldiers in the Revolutionary War.

The father of President Hayes was an industrious frugal and opened-hearted man. He was of a mechanical turn, and could mend a plow, knit a stocking, or do almost anything else that he choose to undertake. He was a member of the Church, active in all the benevolent enterprises of the town, and conducted his business on Christian principles. After the close of the war of 1812, for reasons inexplicable to his neighbors, he resolved to emigrate to Ohio.

The journey from Vermont to Ohio in that day when there were no canals, steamers, nor railways was a very serious affair. A tour of inspection was first made, occupying four months. Mr. Hayes determined to move to Delaware, where the family arrived in 1817. He died July 22, 1822, a victim of malarial fever, less than three months before the birth of the son, of whom we now write. Mrs. Hayes, in her sore bereavement, found the support she so much needed in her brother Sardis, who had been a member of the household from the day of its departure from Vermont, and in an orphan girl whom she had adopted some time before as an act of charity.

Mrs. Hayes at this period was very weak, and the

subject of this sketch was so feeble at birth that he was not expected to live beyond a month or two at most. As the months went by he grew weaker and weaker, so that the neighbors were in the habit of inquiring from time to time " if Mrs. Hayes' baby died last night." On one occasion a neighbor, who was on familiar terms with the family, after alluding to the boy's big head, and the mother's assiduous care of him, said in a bantering way, " That's right! Stick to him. You have got him along so far, and I shouldn't wonder if he would really come to something yet."

" You need not laugh," said Mrs. Hayes. " You wait and see. You can't tell but I shall make him President of the United States yet." The boy lived, in spite of the universal predictions of his speedy death; and when, in 1825, his older brother was drowned, he became, if possible, still dearer to his mother.

The boy was seven years old before he went to school. His education, however, was not neglected. He probably learned as much from his mother and sister as he would have done at school. His sports were almost wholly within doors, his playmates being his sister and her associates. These circumstances tended, no doubt, to foster that gentleness of disposition, and that delicate consideration for the feelings of others, which are marked traits of his character.

His uncle Sardis Birchard took the deepest interest in his education; and as the boy's health had improved, and he was making good progress in his studies, he proposed to send him to college. His preparation commenced with a tutor at home; but he was afterwards sent for one year to a professor in the Wesleyan University, in Middletown, Conn. He entered Kenyon College in 1838, at the age of sixteen, and was graduated at the head of his class in 1842.

Immediately after his graduation he began the study of law in the office of Thomas Sparrow, Esq., in Columbus. Finding his opportunities for study in Columbus somewhat limited, he determined to enter the Law School at Cambridge, Mass., where he remained two years.

In 1845, after graduating at the Law School, he was admitted to the bar at Marietta, Ohio, and shortly afterward went into practice as an attorney-at-law with Ralph P. Buckland, of Fremont. Here he remained three years, acquiring but a limited practice, and apparently unambitious of distinction in his profession.

In 1849 he moved to Cincinnati, where his ambition found a new stimulus. For several years, however, his progress was slow. Two events, occurring at this period, had a powerful influence upon his subsequent life. One of these was his marriage with Miss Lucy Ware Webb, daughter of Dr. James Webb, of Chilicothe; the other was his introduction to the Cincinnati Literary Club, a body embracing among its members such men as Chief Justice Salmon P. Chase,

Gen. John Pope, Gov. Edward F. Noyes, and many others hardly less distinguished in after life. The marriage was a fortunate one in every respect, as everybody knows. Not one of all the wives of our Presidents was more universally admired, reverenced and beloved than was Mrs. Hayes, and no one did more than she to reflect honor upon American womanhood. The Literary Club brought Mr. Hayes into constant association with young men of high character and noble aims, and lured him to display the qualities so long hidden by his bashfulness and modesty.

In 1856 he was nominated to the office of Judge of the Court of Common Pleas; but he declined to accept the nomination. Two years later, the office of city solicitor becoming vacant, the City Council elected him for the unexpired term.

In 1861, when the Rebellion broke out, he was at the zenith of his professional life. His rank at the bar was among the the first. But the news of the attack on Fort Sumpter found him eager to take up arms for the defense of his country.

His military record was bright and illustrious. In October, 1861, he was made Lieutenant-Colonel, and in August, 1862, promoted Colonel of the 79th Ohio regiment, but he refused to leave his old comrades and go among strangers. Subsequently, however, he was made Colonel of his old regiment. At the battle of South Mountain he received a wound, and while faint and bleeding displayed courage and fortitude that won admiration from all.

Col. Hayes was detached from his regiment, after his recovery, to act as Brigadier-General, and placed in command of the celebrated Kanawha division, and for gallant and meritorious services in the battles of Winchester, Fisher's Hill and Cedar Creek, he was promoted Brigadier-General. He was also brevetted Major-General, "for gallant and distinguished services during the campaigns of 1864, in West Virginia." In the course of his arduous services, four horses were shot from under him, and he was wounded four times.

In 1864, Gen. Hayes was elected to Congress, from the Second Ohio District, which had long been Democratic. He was not present during the campaign, and after his election was importuned to resign his commission in the army; but he finally declared, " I shall never come to Washington until I can come by the way of Richmond." He was re-elected in 1866.

In 1867, Gen. Hayes was elected Governor of Ohio, over Hon. Allen G. Thurman, a popular Democrat. In 1869 was re-elected over George H. Pendleton. He was elected Governor for the third term in 1875.

In 1876 he was the standard bearer of the Republican Party in the Presidential contest, and after a hard long contest was chosen President, and was inaugurated Monday, March 5, 1875. He served his full term, not, however, with satisfaction to his party, but his administration was an average on...

J. A. Garfield

JAMES A. GARFIELD.

JAMES A. GARFIELD, twentieth President of the United States, was born Nov. 19, 1831, in the woods of Orange, Cuyahoga Co., O His parents were Abram and Eliza (Ballou) Garfield, both of New England ancestry and from families well known in the early history of that section of our country, but had moved to the Western Reserve, in Ohio, early in its settlement.

The house in which James A. was born was not unlike the houses of poor Ohio farmers of that day. It was about 20 x 30 feet, built of logs, with the spaces between the logs filled with clay. His father was a hard working farmer, and he soon had his fields cleared, an orchard planted, and a log barn built. The household comprised the father and mother and their four children—Mehetabel, Thomas, Mary and James. In May, 1823, the father, from a cold contracted in helping to put out a forest fire, died. At this time James was about eighteen months old, and Thomas about ten years old. No one, perhaps, can tell how much James was indebted to his brother's toil and self-sacrifice during the twenty years succeeding his father's death, but undoubtedly very much. He now lives in Michigan, and the two sisters live in Solon, O., near their birthplace.

The early educational advantages young Garfield enjoyed were very limited, yet he made the most of them. He labored at farm work for others, did carpenter work, chopped wood, or did anything that would bring in a few dollars to aid his widowed mother in her struggles to keep the little family together. Nor was Gen. Garfield ever ashamed of his origin, and he never forgot the friends of his struggling childhood, youth and manhood, neither did they ever forget him. When in the highest seats of honor the humblest friend of his boyhood was as kindly greeted as ever. The poorest laborer was sure of the sympathy of one who had known all the bitterness of want and the sweetness of bread earned by the sweat of the brow. He was ever the simple plain, modest gentleman.

The highest ambition of young Garfield until he was about sixteen years old was to be a captain of a vessel on Lake Erie. He was anxious to go aboard a vessel, which his mother strongly opposed. She finally consented to his going to Cleveland, with the understanding, however, that he should try to obtain some other kind of employment. He walked all the way to Cleveland. This was his first visit to the city After making many applications for work, and trying to get aboard a lake vessel, and not meeting with success, he engaged as a driver for his cousin, Amos Letcher, on the Ohio & Pennsylvania Canal. He remained at this work but a short time when he went home, and attended the seminary at Chester for about three years, when he entered Hiram and the Eclectic Institute, teaching a few terms of school in the meantime, and doing other work. This school was started by the Disciples of Christ in 1850, of which church he was then a member. He became janitor and bell-ringer in order to help pay his way. He then became both teacher and pupil. He soon "exhausted Hiram" and needed more; hence, in the fall of 1854, he entered Williams College, from which he graduated in 1856, taking one of the highest honors of his class. He afterwards returned to Hiram College as its President. As above stated, he early united with the Christian or Disciples Church at Hiram, and was ever after a devoted, zealous member, often preaching in its pulpit and places where he happened to be. Dr. Noah Porter, President of Yale College, says of him in reference to his religion:

" President Garfield was more than a man of strong moral and religious convictions. His whole history, from boyhood to the last, shows that duty to man and to God, and devotion to Christ and life and faith and spiritual commission were controlling springs of his being, and to a more than usual degree. In my judgment there is no more interesting feature of his character than his loyal allegiance to the body of Christians in which he was trained, and the fervent sympathy which he ever showed in their Christian communion. Not many of the few 'wise and mighty and noble who are called' show a similar loyalty to the less stately and cultured Christian communions in which they have been reared. Too often it is true that as they step upward in social and political significance they step upward from one degree to another in some of the many types of fashionable Christianity. President Garfield adhered to the church of his mother, the church in which he was trained, and in which he served as a pillar and an evangelist, and yet with the largest and most unsectarian charity for all 'who love our Lord in sincerity.'"

Mr. Garfield was united in marriage with Miss Lucretia Rudolph, Nov. 11, 1858, who proved herself worthy as the wife of one whom all the world loved and mourned. To them were born seven children, five of whom are still living, four boys and one girl.

Mr. Garfield made his first political speeches in 1856, in Hiram and the neighboring villages, and three years later he began to speak at county mass-meetings, and became the favorite speaker wherever he was. During this year he was elected to the Ohio Senate. He also began to study law at Cleveland, and in 1861 was admitted to the bar. The great Rebellion broke out in the early part of this year, and Mr. Garfield at once resolved to fight as he had talked, and enlisted to defend the old flag. He received his commission as Lieut.-Colonel of the Forty-second Regiment of Ohio Volunteer Infantry, Aug. 14, 1861. He was immediately put into active service, and before he had ever seen a gun fired in action, was placed in command of four regiments of infantry and eight companies of cavalry, charged with the work of driving out of his native State the officer (Humphrey Marshall) reputed to be the ablest of those, not educated in war whom Kentucky had given to the Rebellion. This work was bravely and speedily accomplished, although against great odds. President Lincoln, on his success commissioned him Brigadier-General, Jan. 10, 1862; and as "he had been the youngest man in the Ohio Senate two years before, so now he was the youngest General in the army." He was with Gen. Buell's army at Shiloh, in its operations around Corinth and its march through Alabama. He was then detailed as a member of the General Court-Martial for the trial of Gen. Fitz-John Porter. He was then ordered to report to Gen. Rosecrans, and was assigned to the "Chief of Staff."

The military history of Gen. Garfield closed with his brilliant services at Chickamauga, where he wor the stars of the Major-General.

Without an effort on his part Gev Garfield was elected to Congress in the fall of 1862 from the Nineteenth District of Ohio. This section of Ohio had been represented in Congress for sixty years mainly by two men—Elisha Whittlesey and Joshua R. Giddings. It was not without a struggle that he resigned his place in the army. At the time he entered Congress he was the youngest member in that body. There he remained by successive re-elections until he was elected President in 1880. Of his labors in Congress Senator Hoar says : "Since the year 1864 you cannot think of a question which has been debated in Congress, or discussed before a tribunal of the American people, in regard to which you will not find, if you wish instruction, the argument on one side stated, in almost every instance better than by anybody else, in some speech made in the House of Representatives or on the hustings by Mr. Garfield."

Upon Jan. 14, 1880, Gen. Garfield was elected to the U. S. Senate, and on the eighth of June, of the same year, was nominated as the candidate of his party for President at the great Chicago Convention. He was elected in the following November, and on March 4, 1881, was inaugurated. Probably no administration ever opened its existence under brighter auspices than that of President Garfield, and every day it grew in favor with the people, and by the first of July he had completed all the initiatory and preliminary work of his administration and was preparing to leave the city to meet his friends at Williams College. While on his way and at the depot, in company with Secretary Blaine, a man stepped behind him, drew a revolver, and fired directly at his back. The President tottered and fell, and as he did so the assassin fired a second shot, the bullet cutting the left coat sleeve of his victim, but inflicting no further injury. It has been very truthfully said that this was "the shot that was heard round the world." Never before in the history of the Nation had anything occurred which so nearly froze the blood of the people : for the moment, as this awful deed. He was smit ten on the brightest, gladdest day of all his life, and was at the summit of his power and hope. For eighty days, all during the hot months of July and August, he lingered and suffered. He, however, remained master of himself till the last, and by his magnificent bearing was teaching the country and the world the noblest of human lessons—how to live grandly in the very clutch of death. Great in life, he was surpassingly great in death. He passed serenely away Sept. 19, 1883, at Elberon, N. J., on the very bank of the ocean, where he had been taken shortly previous. The world wept at his death, as it never had done on the death of any other man who had ever lived upon it. The murderer was duly tried, found guilty and executed, in one year after he committed the foul deed.

CHESTER A. ARTHUR,

CHESTER A. ARTHUR, twenty-first President of the United States was born in Franklin County, Vermont, on the fifth of October, 1830, and is the oldest of a family of two sons and five daughters. His father was the Rev. Dr. William Arthur, a Baptist clergyman, who emigrated to this country from the county Antrim, Ireland, in his 18th year, and died in 1875, in Newtonville, near Albany, after a long and successful ministry.

Young Arthur was educated at Union College, Schenectady, where he excelled in all his studies. After his graduation he taught school in Vermont for two years, and at the expiration of that time came to New York, with $500 in his pocket, and entered the office of ex-Judge E. D. Culver as student. After being admitted to the bar he formed a partnership with his intimate friend and room-mate, Henry D. Gardiner, with the intention of practicing in the West, and for three months they roamed about in the Western States in search of an eligible site, but in the end returned to New York. where they hung out their shingle, and entered upon a successful career almost from the start. General Arthur soon afterward married the daughter of Lieutenant Herndon, of the United States Navy, who was lost at sea. Congress voted a gold medal to his widow in recognition of the bravery he displayed on that occasion. Mrs. Arthur died shortly before Mr. Arthur's nomination to the Vice Presidency, leaving two children.

Gen. Arthur obtained considerable legal celebrity in his first great case, the famous Lemmon suit, brought to recover possession of eight slaves who had been declared free by Judge Paine, of the Superior Court of New York City. It was in 1852 that Jonathan Lemmon, of Virginia, went to New York with his slaves, intending to ship them to Texas, when they were discovered and freed. The Judge decided that they could not be held by the owner under the Fugitive Slave Law. A howl of rage went up from the South, and the Virginia Legislature authorized the Attorney General of that State to assist in an appeal. Wm. M. Evarts and Chester A. Arthur were employed to represent the People, and they won their case, which then went to the Supreme Court of the United States. Charles O'Conor here espoused the cause of the slave-holders, but he too was beaten by Messrs Evarts and Arthur, and a long step was taken toward the emancipation of the black race.

Another great service was rendered by General Arthur in the same cause in 1856. Lizzie Jennings, a respectable colored woman, was put off a Fourth Avenue car with violence after she had paid her fare. General Arthur sued on her behalf, and secured a verdict of $500 damages. The next day the company issued an order to admit colored persons to ride on their cars, and the other car companies quickly followed their example. Before that the Sixth Avenue Company ran a few special cars for colored persons and the other lines refused to let them ride at all.

General Arthur was a delegate to the Convention at Saratoga that founded the Republican party. Previous to the war he was Judge-Advocate of the Second Brigade of the State of New York, and Governor Morgan, of that State, appointed him Engineer-in-Chief of his staff. In 1861, he was made Inspector General, and soon afterward became Quartermaster-General. In each of these offices he rendered great service to the Government during the war. At the end of Governor Morgan's term he resumed the practice of the law, forming a partnership with Mr. Ransom, and then Mr. Phelps, the District Attorney of New York, was added to the firm. The legal practice of this well-known firm was very large and lucrative, each of the gentlemen composing it were able lawyers, and possessed a splendid local reputation, if not indeed one of national extent.

He always took a leading part in State and city politics. He was appointed Collector of the Port of New York by President Grant, Nov. 21 1872, to succeed Thomas Murphy, and held the office until July, 10, 1878, when he was succeeded by Collector Merritt.

Mr. Arthur was nominated on the Presidential ticket, with Gen. James A. Garfield, at the famous National Republican Convention held at Chicago in June, 1880. This was perhaps the greatest political convention that ever assembled on the continent. It was composed of the leading politicians of the Republican party, all able men, and each stood firm and fought vigorously and with signal tenacity for their respective candidates that were before the convention for the nomination. Finally Gen. Garfield received the nomination for President and Gen. Arthur for Vice-President. The campaign which followed was one of the most animated known in the history of our country. Gen. Hancock, the standard-bearer of the Democratic party, was a popular man, and his party made a valiant fight for his election.

Finally the election came and the country's choice was Garfield and Arthur. They were inaugurated March 4, 1881, as President and Vice-President. A few months only had passed ere the newly chosen President was the victim of the assassin's bullet. Then came terrible weeks of suffering, —those moments of anxious suspense, when the hearts of all civilized nations were throbbing in unison, longing for the recovery of the noble, the good President. The remarkable patience that he manifested during those hours and weeks, and even months, of the most terrible suffering man has often been called upon to endure, was seemingly more than human. It was certainly God-like. During all this period of deepest anxiety Mr. Arthur's every move was watched, and be it said to his credit that his every action displayed only an earnest desire that the suffering Garfield might recover, to serve the remainder of the term he had so auspiciously begun. Not a selfish feeling was manifested in deed or look of this man, even though the most honored position in the world was at any moment likely to fall to him.

At last God in his mercy relieved President Garfield from further suffering, and the world, as never before in its history over the death of any other man, wept at his bier. Then it became the duty of the Vice President to assume the responsibilities of the high office, and he took the oath in New York, Sept. 20, 1881. The position was an embarrassing one to him, made doubly so from the facts that all eyes were on him, anxious to know what he would do, what policy he would pursue, and who he would select as advisers. The duties of the office had been greatly neglected during the President's long illness, and many important measures were to be immediately decided by him; and still farther to embarrass him he did not fail to realize under what circumstances he became President, and knew the feelings of many on this point. Under these trying circumstances President Arthur took the reins of the Government in his own hands; and, as embarrassing as were the condition of affairs, he happily surprised the nation, acting so wisely that but few criticised his administration. He served the nation well and faithfully, until the close of his administration, March 4, 1885, and was a popular candidate before his party for a second term. His name was ably presented before the convention at Chicago, and was received with great favor, and doubtless but for the personal popularity of one of the opposing candidates, he would have been selected as the standard-bearer of his party for another campaign. He retired to private life carrying with him the best wishes of the American people, whom he had served in a manner satisfactory to them and with credit to himself

Grover Cleveland

S. Grover Cleveland.

TEPHEN GROVER CLEVE-
LAND, the twenty-second President of the United States, was
born in 1837, in the obscure
town of Caldwell, Essex Co.,
N. J., and in a little two-and-a-
half-story white house which is still
standing, characteristically to mark
the humble birth-place of one of
America's great men in striking con-
trast with the Old World, where all
men high in office must be high in
origin and born in the cradle of
wealth. When the subject of this
sketch was three years of age, his
father, who was a Presbyterian min-
ister, with a large family and a small salary, moved,
by way of the Hudson River and Erie Canal, to
Fayetteville, in search of an increased income and a
larger field of work. Fayetteville was then the most
straggling of country villages, about five miles from
Pompey Hill, where Governor Seymour was born.

At the last mentioned place young Grover commenced going to school in the "good, old-fashioned
way," and presumably distinguished himself after the
manner of all village boys, in doing the things he
ought not to do. Such is the distinguishing trait of
all geniuses and independent thinkers. When he
arrived at the age of 14 years, he had outgrown the
capacity of the village school and expressed a most

emphatic desire to be sent to an academy. To this
his father decidedly objected. Academies in those
days cost money; besides, his father wanted him to
become self-supporting by the quickest possible
means, and this at that time in Fayetteville seemed
to be a position in a country store, where his father
and the large family on his hands had considerable
influence. Grover was to be paid $50 for his services
the first year, and if he proved trustworthy he was to
receive $100 the second year. Here the lad com-
menced his career as salesman, and in two years he
had earned so good a reputation for trustworthiness
that his employers desired to retain him for an in-
definite length of time. Otherwise he did not ex-
hibit as yet any particular "flashes of genius" or
eccentricities of talent. He was simply a good boy.

But instead of remaining with this firm in Fayetteville, he went with the family in their removal to
Clinton, where he had an opportunity of attending a
high school. Here he industriously pursued his
studies until the family removed with him to a point
on Black River known as the "Holland Patent," a
village of 500 or 600 people, 15 miles north of Utica,
N. Y. At this place his father died, after preaching
but three Sundays. This event broke up the family,
and Grover set out for New York City to accept, at a
small salary, the position of "under-teacher" in an
asylum for the blind. He taught faithfully for two
years, and although he obtained a good reputation in
this capacity, he concluded that teaching was not his

calling for life, and, reversing the traditional order, he left the city to seek his fortune, instead of going to a city. He first thought of Cleveland, Ohio, as there was some charm in that name for him; but before proceeding to that place he went to Buffalo to ask the advice of his uncle, Lewis F. Allan, a noted stock breeder of that place. The latter did not speak enthusiastically. "What is it you want to do, my boy?" he asked. "Well, sir, I want to study law," was the reply. "Good gracious!" remarked the old gentleman; "do you, indeed? What ever put that into your head? How much money have you got?" · Well, sir, to tell the truth, I haven't got any."

After a long consultation, his uncle offered him a place temporarily as assistant herd-keeper, at $50 a year, while he could "look around." One day soon afterward he boldly walked into the office of Rogers, Bowen & Rogers, of Buffalo, and told them what he wanted. A number of young men were already engaged in the office, but Grover's persistency won, and he was finally permitted to come as an office boy and have the use of the law library, for the nominal sum of $3 or $4 a week. Out of this he had to pay for his board and washing. The walk to and from his uncle's was a long and rugged one; and, although the first winter was a memorably severe one, his shoes were out of repair and his overcoat—he had one—yet he was nevertheless prompt and regular. On the first day of his service here, his senior employer threw down a copy of Blackstone before him with a bang that made the dust fly, saying "'That's where they all begin." A titter ran around the little circle of clerks and students, as they thought that was enough to scare young Grover out of his plans; but in due time he mastered that cumbersome volume. Then, as ever afterward, however, Mr. Cleveland exhibited a talent for executiveness rather than for chasing principles through all their metaphysical possibilities. "Let us quit talking and go and do it," was practically his motto.

The first public office to which Mr. Cleveland was elected was that of Sheriff of Erie Co., N. Y., in which Buffalo is situated; and in such capacity it fell to his duty to inflict capital punishment upon two criminals. In 1881 he was elected Mayor of the City of Buffalo, on the Democratic ticket, with especial reference to the bringing about certain reforms

in the administration of the municipal affairs of that city. In this office, as well as that of Sheriff, his performance of duty has generally been considered fair, with possibly a few exceptions which were ferreted out and magnified during the last Presidential campaign. As a specimen of his plain language in a veto message, we quote from one vetoing an iniquitous street-cleaning contract: "This is a time for plain speech, and my objection to your action shall be plainly stated. I regard it as the culmination of a most bare-faced, impudent and shameless scheme to betray the interests of the people, and to worse than squander the people's money." The *New York Sun* afterward very highly commended Mr. Cleveland's administration as Mayor of Buffalo, and thereupon recommended him for Governor of the Empire State. To the latter office he was elected in 1882 and his administration of the affairs of State was generally satisfactory. The mistakes he made, if any, were made very public throughout the nation after he was nominated for President of the United States. For this high office he was nominated July 11, 1884, by the National Democratic Convention at Chicago, when other competitors were Thomas F. Bayard, Roswell P. Flower, Thomas A. Hendricks, Benjamin F. Butler, Allen G. Thurman, etc.; and he was elected by the people, by a majority of about a thousand, over the brilliant and long-tried Republican statesman, James G. Blaine. President Cleveland resigned his office as Governor of New York in January, 1885, in order to prepare for his duties as the Chief Executive of the United States, in which capacity his term commenced at noon on the 4th of March, 1885. For his Cabinet officers he selected the following gentlemen: For Secretary of State, Thomas F. Bayard, of Delaware; Secretary of the Treasury, Daniel Manning, of New York; Secretary of War, William C. Endicott, of Massachusetts; Secretary of the Navy, William C. Whitney, of New York; Secretary of the Interior, L. Q. C. Lamar, of Mississippi; Postmaster-General, William F. Viles, of Wisconsin; Attorney-General, A. H. Garland, of Arkansas.

The silver question precipitated a controversy between those who were in favor of the continuance of silver coinage and those who were opposed, Mr. Cleveland answering for the latter, even before his inauguration.

Benj. Harrison

Benjamin Harrison.

ENJAMIN HARRISON, the twenty-third President, is the descendant of one of the historical families of this country. The head of the family was a Major General Harrison, one of Oliver Cromwell's trusted followers and fighters. In the zenith of Cromwell's power it became the duty of this Harrison to participate in the trial of Charles I, and afterward to sign the death warrant of the king. He subsequently paid for this with his life, being hung Oct. 13, 1660. His descendants came to America, and the next of the family that appears in history is Benjamin Harrison, of Virginia, great-grandfather of the subject of this sketch, and after whom he was named. Benjamin Harrison was a member of the Continental Congress during the years 1774–5–6, and was one of the original signers of the Declaration of Independence. He was three times elected Governor of Virginia.

Gen. William Henry Harrison, the son of the distinguished patriot of the Revolution, after a successful career as a soldier during the War of 1812, and with a clean record as Governor of the Northwestern Territory, was elected President of the United States in 1840. His career was cut short by death within one month after his inauguration.

President Harrison was born at North Bend, Hamilton Co., Ohio, Aug. 20, 1833. His life up to the time of his graduation by the Miami University at Oxford, Ohio, was the uneventful one of a country lad of a family of small means. His father was able to give him a good education, and nothing more. He became engaged while at college to the daughter of Dr. Scott, Principal of a female school at Oxford. After graduating he determined to enter upon the study of the law. He went to Cincinnati and then read law for two years. At the expiration of that time young Harrison received the only inheritance of his life; his aunt dying left him a lot valued at $800. He regarded this legacy as a fortune, and decided to get married at once. Taking this money and go to some Eastern town and begin the practice of law. He sold his lot, and with the money in his pocket, he started out with his young wife to fight for a place in the world. He decided to go to Indianapolis, which was even at that time a town of promise. He met with slight encouragement at first, making scarcely anything the first year. He worked diligently, applying himself closely to his calling, built up an extensive practice and took a leading rank in the legal profession. He is the father of two children.

In 1860 Mr. Harrison was nominated for the position of Supreme Court Reporter, and then began his experience as a stump speaker. He canvassed the State thoroughly, and was elected by a handsome majority. In 1862 he raised the 17th Indiana Infantry, and was chosen its Colonel. His regiment was composed of the rawest of material, but Col. Harrison employed all his time at first mastering military tactics and drilling his men, when he therefore came to move toward the East with Sherman his regiment was one of the best drilled and organized in the army. At Resaca he especially distinguished himself, and for his bravery at Peachtree Creek he was made a Brigadier General, Gen. Hooker speaking of him in the most complimentary terms.

During the absence of Gen. Harrison in the field the Supreme Court declared the office of the Supreme Court Reporter vacant, and another person was elected to the position. From the time of leaving Indiana with his regiment until the fall of 1864 he had taken no leave of absence, but having been nominated that year for the same office, he got a thirty-day leave of absence, and during that time made a brilliant canvass of the State, and was elected for another term. He then started to rejoin Sherman, but on the way was stricken down with scarlet fever, and after a most trying siege made his way to the front in time to participate in the closing incidents of the war.

In 1868 Gen. Harrison declined re-election as reporter, and resumed the practice of law. In 1876 he was a candidate for Governor. Although defeated, the brilliant campaign he made won for him a National reputation, and he was much sought, especially in the East, to make speeches. In 1880, as usual, he took an active part in the campaign, and was elected to the United States Senate. Here he served six years, and was known as one of the ablest men, best lawyers and strongest debaters in

that body. With the expiration of his Senatorial term he returned to the practice of his profession, becoming the head of one of the strongest firms in the State.

The political campaign of 1888 was one of the most memorable in the history of our country. The convention which assembled in Chicago in June and named Mr. Harrison as the chief standard bearer of the Republican party, was great in every particular, and on this account, and the attitude it assumed upon the vital questions of the day, chief among which was the tariff, awoke a deep interest in the campaign throughout the Nation. Shortly after the nomination delegations began to visit Mr. Harrison at Indianapolis, his home. This movement became popular, and from all sections of the country societies, clubs and delegations journeyed thither to pay their respects to the distinguished statesman. The popularity of these was greatly increased on account of the remarkable speeches made by Mr. Harrison. He spoke daily all through the summer and autumn to these visiting delegations, and so varied, masterly and eloquent were his speeches that they at once placed him in the foremost rank of American orators and statesmen.

On account of his eloquence as a speaker and his power as a debater, he was called upon at an uncommonly early age to take part in the discussion of the great questions that then began to agitate the country. He was an uncompromising anti-slavery man, and was matched against some of the most eminent Democratic speakers of his State. No man who felt the touch of his blade desired to be pitted with him again. With all his eloquence as an orator he never spoke for oratorical effect, but his words always went like bullets to the mark. He is purely American in his ideas and is a splendid type of the American statesman. Gifted with quick perception, a logical mind and a ready tongue, he is one of the most distinguished impromptu speakers in the Nation. Many of these speeches sparkled with the rarest of eloquence and contained arguments of greatest weight. Many of his terse statements have already become aphorisms. Original in thought, precise in logic, terse in statement, yet withal faultless in eloquence, he is recognized as the sound statesman and brilliant orator of the day

Governors.

Yours, very truly,
C. Robinson

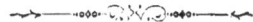

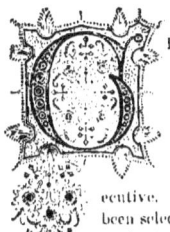HARLES ROBINSON, the first Governor of Kansas, was elected under the Wyandotte Constitution, and upon the admission of the State, Jan. 29, 1861, was inaugurated as Chief Executive. No better man could have been selected to lay the foundations of the State, for his mind was creative, original and vigorous. Rarely working by copy, he belongs to the class who think and originate, and with whom precedence and text-books have little authority. At this time a great State was to be formed from most incongruous elements. It required men of genius and originality to formulate laws and a constitution, and to this work the vigor and ingenuity of Robinson were peculiarly adapted. Men of all classes, sorts and conditions, had rushed to this section upon different objects bent—some to assist in building up a State, some to make money, to secure notoriety and political preferment, but more, perhaps, as cosmopolitans, having little interest in its reputation or its future.

That the work before Gov. Robinson was accomplished in a praiseworthy manner, a grateful people readily acknowledge. In his course, which necessarily was opposed to the rough and irresponsible element, he made many enemies and was impeached by the House, but on his trial by the Senate no evidence was adduced to connect him with any illegal transaction, and a case of malicious prosecution was clearly established, which left his good name untarnished.

In reviewing the career of a prominent public man, it cannot be called complete without the story of his early life. Gov. Robinson was born at Hardwick, Mass., July 21, 1818, and received a good common-school and academic education, besides two years' drill at Amherst College. His father, Charles Robinson, was a pious and conscientious man, who cherished an inherent hatred of slavery, and the latter quality of his father's character Charles inherited in a marked degree. Upon religious subjects, however, he was always independent and liberal, and is considered heterodox, although for the great principles of Christianity, which serve to improve society and make better men and women, he has the highest regard.

There is but little which is ideal or sentimental in the nature of Gov. Robinson, as his life has been spent principally dealing with men upon practical principles. Before completing his studies he was obliged to leave college on account of ill-health, and his eyes failing him from hard study, he walked forty miles to consult a celebrated physician, Dr. Twichel, of Keene, N. H., and there became so sensibly impressed with both the quackeries of medicine as so often practiced, and the real utility of the healing art as a science, that he determined to study medicine, and after a preparatory course entered for a series of lectures at Woodstock, Vt., and Pittsfield, Mass., and from the school of the latter he was graduated, receiving his diploma with the high honors of the class. Subsequently he became connected with the celebrated

Dr. J. G. Holland in the management of a hospital. In 1849 he started out as a physician to a colony bound overland to California. They arrived in Kansas City April 10, and on the 10th of May following, left with ox and mule teams for the Pacific Slope.

On the 11th of May, thirty-nine years ago, riding his horse at the head of a colony of gold-seekers, Gov. Robinson ascended Mt. Oread, where now stands the State University of Kansas, whose Regent he has been for thirteen consecutive years, as well as its faithful, intelligent and generous friend. In his note book at that time he wrote that if the land was opened to settlement and entry, he would go no further, as there seemed to be gold enough for all human wants in the rich soil of the Kaw Valley, and beauty enough in the rolling prairies beyond to meet all the aspirations of ordinary men. He pushed on, however, to California, and there followed a variety of occupations, being miner, restauranteur, editor and member of the Legislature. Then he returned to Massachusetts, and in 1852 commenced the publication of the Fitchburg News, which he conducted two years.

At the time of the repeal of the Missouri Compromise, and the intense excitement coincident with the organization of the Territories of Kansas and Nebraska, Gov. Robinson was sent out by the New England Aid Society to Kansas, charged with saving it to freedom. In the darkest hours of that long struggle, as well as in its hour of victory, he seemed to be the one safe counselor and leader of the Free-State forces. His California experience had rounded and ripened a robust nature, and the perils that the hero of the squatter troubles had passed through in that strange combination of craft and cunning, fitted and schooled him for his Kansas work. In the "Wakarusa War," when the city of Lawrence, only 600 strong, was besieged by an opposing force of 1,200, Dr. Robinson, as he was called in those days, was chosen Major General of the Free-State party. He constructed forts and rifle-pits which did their service, but as a negotiator and diplomat he excelled. He wanted Kansas to be lawfully free, and felt justified in availing himself of any agency which would assist him in accomplishing this. Although the recognized leader of the Free-State forces, it was not Robinson, but Lane, that the Quantrell ruffians sought when they massacred in cold blood 180 of the inoffensive citizens of Lawrence.

In 1855 the Free-State men had been driven from the polls. Robinson was among the first to repudiate the authority of the bogus laws, and was unanimously chosen a delegate to the convention which met at Topeka to formulate a State government. From May, 1856, until September, he was a prisoner at Lecompton, charged with treason. After serving his term as the first Governor of the State, he was, in 1872, chosen a member of the Lower House of the Legislature, and in 1874 elected State Senator and re-elected in 1876. At the last election he came within forty-three votes of beating his opponent for the State Senate, and where the party majority of the latter was about 1,500.

Gov. Robinson has been twice married. By his first wife, Miss Sarah Adams, daughter of a highly respected Massachusetts farmer, two children were born and both died in infancy. The mother died in 1846. On the 30th of October, 1851, he was married to Miss Sarah D. T. Lawrence, daughter of a distinguished Massachusetts lawyer, and connected with the celebrated Lawrence family of that State. Of this union there are no children. Mrs. Robinson is a lady of high literary culture, and has written one of the best of the many books which have been published on Kansas. Though highly accomplished, she is not much of a society woman, being content to dwell quietly at home on their farm, which lies five miles out from Lawrence, and is the resort of many friends, who meet a refined and elegant hospitality.

In 1856 Gov. Robinson pre-empted a portion of the land which, upon his journey to California, he had viewed with so much admiration. He now has one of the finest homes in his section of country, where he resides in affluent circumstances, busying himself in looking after his farm, esteemed by his neighbors, and amply honored by the great State, in laying the firm foundations of which he rendered such efficient service over a quarter of a century ago.

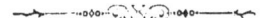

THOMAS CARNEY, the second Governor of Kansas, was born in Delaware County, Ohio. Aug. 20, 1824. His ancestry was a mixed one, composed of Irish and German. His father, James Carney, was of Irish descent, being the grandson of one of the same name, who came to this country and assisted the Colonies in the war with Great Britain. His mother was remotely of German descent, and like his father was born in Pennsylvania. They removed to Ohio the year before the birth of Gov. Carney. They were Presbyterians, in which faith Mr. C. was reared.

The portion of Ohio in which Mr. Carney was born was then a wilderness, and the family engaged in farming, the land having to be cleared first. The father died when the lad was but four years old, leaving the mother with four children, the eldest being only six years of age, the early life of young Carney therefore was spent in work of the hardest kind, from the moment he was old enough to be of any assistance. From the age of seven to eighteen he worked on the farm belonging to the family, and then started for himself as a farm hand for six months, at $10 a month. From the time he was eleven years of age until he left home, he was the teamster of the family, and carried the products of the farm to Newark, thirty-six miles, his motive power being a yoke of oxen for most of the time.

He attended school some during the winter months, and after he was eighteen went to school in Berkshire, Ohio, for six months. After this he commenced a long, persistent and weary search for employment in a store, and was finally successful in Columbus, where he remained in the employ of a retail dry-goods house for two years, and then took service with a wholesale dry-goods establishment in Cincinnati. He obtained, while in the retail house, $50 a year and his board for the first year's service, and for the second year $100. At the end of this period he was given a quarter interest in the firm, with his name at the head of it. A rise of so great rapidity is unprecedented. He resided in Cincinnati twelve years.

Mr. Carney's health became impaired by his devotion to business, and in 1857 he visited the West, and commenced business in Leavenworth in the spring of 1858. In 1861 he was elected to the State Legislature, and in 1862 was elected Governor. He entered on his duties the 1st of January, 1863, at a time when Kansas affairs were in a most critical condition.

In 1864 he was elected to the United States Senate, but as there was some doubt as to whether or not the time at which the election was held was the proper one, he declined the position. He was soon after elected Mayor of Leavenworth, and was re-elected. Since that period, 1866, he has occupied himself wholly with his private business.

The earlier struggles of the future Governor were arduous and severe, but probably had their effect in strengthening him for the career for which he was destined. When he took possession of the gubernatorial office, in January, 1863, he found the State of Kansas but little better than a political and financial wreck. A local writer referring to that period says, that the "State was in peril at almost every point, and its settled portions were one extended camp. A rebel force hovered on its eastern and southern borders, while Indians were murdering and scalping in the west. Nothing short of a constant vigilance could prevent the rebel enemy invading the State and butchering the people."

An appeal was made to the military authorities for assistance and to Gov. Carney for protection. It was at a time when the General Government was too busy with the Rebellion to give close attention to matters in a new and remote State, and hence the Governor was obliged to depend on his own resources. He was equal to the emergency. The State had no money, no men, no arms, no ammunition, with which to protect itself, but even this did not discourage him. He visited the menaced regions, and soon satisfied himself that something had to be done, or the State would be overwhelmed by the perils which threatened it. In the counties which were more particularly threatened, the population became uneasy, and removals were being made to places of safety by so many of the residents that there loomed up a probability that the entire region would become a desert.

After looking over the ground, Gov. Carney determined to raise a force of 150 men from citizens of the menaced region, and to employ them as a patrol along the border, so that no hostile movement could be made without detection, and the people could be warned of danger in time to rally at the necessary points for defense, all being armed and organized into military organizations. This patrol was hired by the Governor for the public defense out of his private means. He agreed to pay $1 a day each, for man and horse, the United States Government furnishing the rations. He put this force in the field, and kept it in active operation, at a cost to himself of over $10,000. At the same time he was a Captain in the home guards, and many a night was on guard like the private soldier.

The little patrol put in the field by the Governor preserved the borders from invasion so long as it lasted, which was some three months. At a later period the Governor was notified by the commander of the Federal forces that he was able to care for the safety of the State, and thereupon the patrol was abolished. Almost immediately after it was disbanded Quantrell made his raid into Kansas, and Lawrence was attacked, burned, and its residents massacred. Concerning this feature of the transaction the Governor says: "While this patrol was on the border the arrangements were such that the different members could speak with each other

every hour, and thus be in a position to almost instantly communicate with the residents in case of invasion. When the Government notified me that it could take care of the border I disbanded the patrol, and within three days Lawrence was in ashes and 180 people were foully murdered. The military was scattered in squads over a distance of twenty-five miles along the border, and when Quantrell moved into Kansas he had no difficulty in marching between the Federal divisions. The march of Quantrell was entirely unknown and wholly unexpected. Not a living soul knew that he was in the State when he arrived before Lawrence. A man living on the route taken by the guerrillas saw them, and mounted a horse and undertook to carry the information to Lawrence. His horse fell and the rider's neck was broken, and thus the sole witness of the invasion was silenced."

It will show the benevolent disposition of the Governor to state that from his own pocket he gave $500 to the widow of the man who undertook to carry the warning of danger to Lawrence.

The entire official career of Gov. Carney was of the stormiest and most perplexing character, and it is certain that, with an official head less clear and efficient, the embarrassments and perplexities of Kansas would have proved insoluble. Cool, self-possessed, firm, intelligent, he guided the State through the storms, breakers, whirlpools and rocks, which were encountered, and finally reached the harbor, with the vessel much battered but sound in frame and in all essential particulars.

The following is a copy of a resolution passed by the Kansas Legislature after his term of office had expired:

"Resolved by the House of Representatives of the State of Kansas, that the thanks of this House and the people of the State of Kansas are justly due to Hon. Thomas Carney, late Governor of the State of Kansas, for the honest, faithful and impartial manner in which he discharged his executive duties."

Gov. Carney is possessed of ample wealth, which he uses to the best advantage. His wife was Rebecca Canady, of Kenton, Ohio, who has devoted much of her time for a number of years in caring for the orphaned children of the State. His children are four in number, all boys.

No man in Kansas is more honored and respected than he, and no man has done more, either in a public or private way, for the advancement of the State and its institutions. Its railroads, bridges, churches, school-houses, and its citizens needing assistance, all bear witness to his liberality and bounty.

Samuel J. Crawford

AMUEL J. CRAWFORD, the third Governor of the State of Kansas, was born in Lawrence County, Ind., April 10, 1835. His ancestors were Scotch-Irish, who emigrated to America at an early period in Colonial days. His paternal grandfather served in the war of the Revolution as a soldier from the State of North Carolina, and his maternal grandfather was a planter in the same State. His father, William Crawford, emigrated, in 1815, to the then Territory of Indiana, and located in Lawrence County, where he became a successful farmer. Although born, reared and educated in a slave State, the elder Crawford had imbibed unconquerable prejudice to the institution of slavery, and as a consequence turned his back upon friends and kindred and sought a home in the Northwest Territory, in which slavery and involuntary servitude had been forever inhibited.

The subject of this sketch was reared upon his father's farm, and received a common-school and academic education. At the age of twenty-one he became a student at law in the office of the Hon. S. W. Short, of Bedford, Ind., pursuing his studies until the fall of 1857, when he entered the Law College at Cincinnati, from which institution he was graduated in 1858.

In March, 1859, he bade adieu to home and friends, proceeded to the Territory of Kansas, and located in Garnett, the county seat of Anderson County. Here he practiced his profession of the law, and was elected a member of the first State Legislature, which convened at Topeka, March 27, 1861.

The attack upon Ft. Sumter, following swiftly after the Montgomery Secession Convention, the failure of the Peace Conference, the Proclamation of Jefferson Davis calling for 100,000 men, and the seizure of Government property by Floyd and Twiggs, without protest from the Executive, thrilled loyal Kansas to the very core. President Lincoln made his first call for 75,000 volunteers in April, 1861. Responding to this call, Mr. Crawford resigned his seat in the Legislature, returned home, recruited a company, was chosen its Captain, assigned to the 2d Kansas Infantry, and mustered into the United States service. He served with the regiment, participating under the gallant Gen. Lyon in the battle of Wilson's Creek and various other battles of the Missouri Campaign fought during the summer and fall of 1861. In the winter of 1861-62, the regiment was re-organized, and became the 2d Kansas Cavalry. Capt. Crawford was assigned to the command of Company A, and soon thereafter promoted to the command of a battalion. He participated with his regiment in the battles of Newtonia, Old Ft. Wayne, Cane Hill, Prairie Grove, Van Buren, and various other engagements fought by Gen. Blunt during the Trans-Mississippi campaign of 1862.

It was in these engagements that Capt. Crawford developed extraordinary ability as a cavalry leader. At the battle of Old Ft. Wayne he charged the enemy's lines and captured a battery under circumstances which almost forbade the venture, and for which achievement he was complimented in General Orders. At the battles of Cane Hill and Prairie Grove he acquitted himself with great credit, and was again complimented by the commanding General. In March, 1863, although holding the rank of Captain, he was assigned to the command of the 2d Kansas Cavalry, and led the regiment in the campaign of that year through the Indian Territory and Western Arkansas, which resulted in the battles of Perryville, McAllister and the Backbone Mountain, and the capture of Ft. Smith by the Federal arms. The 2d Kansas Cavalry covered itself with glory in these memorable campaigns.

In October, 1863, Capt. Crawford was promoted to be Colonel of the 83d United States Infantry, and with his regiment accompanied Gen. Steele on the Shreveport, La., expedition, which moved southward, in March, 1864, from Ft. Smith and

Little Rock to co-operate with Gen. Banks in his Red River campaign, participating in the battles of Prairie De Hand and Saline River. At the latter affair Col. Crawford charged and captured a battery, which his men brought off the field by hand, all the artillery horses having been killed or disabled. This battle resulted in a complete victory for the Union forces, to which consummation Col. Crawford's regiment largely contributed. After this battle he returned with the 7th Corps to Little Rock, and thence, with the Kansas Division, under the command of Gen. Thayer, to Ft. Smith, Ark. In July, 1864, Col. Crawford commanded an expedition into the Choctaw Nation in pursuit of the rebel General, Standweighty, whom he routed.

September 8, 1864, while still in the field, Col. Crawford was nominated as the Republican candidate for Governor of Kansas. Obtaining leave of absence, he bade adieu to the gallant army with which he had served so long, and on the 9th of October returned to Kansas. Upon arriving at Ft. Scott he learned that a heavy body of the enemy, under Gen. Price, was moving westward through Central Missouri, with the design of laying Kansas in waste. He hastened to Kansas City, arriving October 17, reported to Gen. Curtis, commanding the Federal forces there concentrating to resist Gen. Price, and was assigned to duty as a volunteer aid on his staff. A few days subsequently the battles of the Blue, Westport and Mine Creek were fought, and at the latter engagement Col. Crawford ordered and participated in a charge with two brigades of cavalry, which resulted in the capture of the Confederate Generals, Marmaduke and Cabell, 500 prisoners and eight pieces of artillery. This battle closed his military career in the war for the suppression of the Rebellion, and on April 13, 1865, he was promoted by the President of the United States to the rank of Brigadier General by brevet, for meritorious services in the field.

On the 7th of November, 1864, Col. Crawford was elected Governor of the State of Kansas, and in 1866 was re-chosen for a second term. During his holding of the gubernatorial office, he re-organized and consolidated the Kansas Volunteer Regiments, and secured the enactment of new laws, under which the State Militia was placed on war footing for the protection of the people against rebel invasions and Indian incursions. He devoted much of his time to the establishment and maintenance of the various State institutions, and on retiring from office he left the Deaf Mute, Blind and Insane Asylums, the State University, the Agricultural College and State Normal School, in successful operation. He also gave considerable attention to the preparation and dissemination of pamphlet literature respecting the advantages of his State, with the view of encouraging emigration thereto.

During the memorable years of 1867 and 1868, hostile bands of Indians hovered on the borders of Kansas, driving back the settlers, checking the construction of the railroads and threatening to cut off communication between Kansas and the Western States and Territories. For two years an Indian war of savage barbarity was carried on. Many settlers were killed, scalped, and their bodies mutilated. Large amounts of property were captured and destroyed. Women and even children were outraged, and others carried into captivity to suffer a fate worse than a thousand deaths.

The Federal forces stationed on the border and the State troops furnished by Gov. Crawford were inadequate for the protection of the people. The Indians followed their custom of making war during the summer months, and then retreating to their homes in the Indian Territory to be fed, clothed and nurtured by the Government in winter. Finally, in August, 1868, the settlements of Northwest Kansas were raided by these Indians, who killed and wounded some forty persons, carried women into captivity, and also committed other atrocities. As soon as the terrible details of this last massacre reached the ears of Gov. Crawford, he proceeded at once to the scene of disaster, saw that the dead were properly buried and the wounded cared for, returned to Topeka, organized a regiment of cavalry, resigned the office of Governor, and with his regiment accompanied Gen. Sheridan on his historic campaign into the interior of the wild country bordering on Texas, where the hostile tribes had always felt secure from punishment during the winter season. These Indians were attacked and captured in the Washita Valley, in December, 1868, and several of their chiefs held as hostages until the captive white women were delivered up.

Gov. Crawford returned home after the close of this campaign and has since been successfully engaged in the practice of his profession. Nov. 27, 1866, he was married to Miss Isabel M. Chase, an estimable and accomplished lady, of Topeka, where they now reside, and the union has been blessed by two children, daughter and son. Gov. Crawford is possessed of an imposing presence, his height being six feet two inches, with the accompaniment of a Herculean frame, symmetrically proportioned, and a pair of shoulders Atlas might fairly envy. His manners are the very essence of courtesy and gentleness, and altogether he presents a marked type of the energetic, patriotic and sturdy sons of the great West—*suaviter in modo, fortiter in re*—with whom the high sense of duty stands first and foremost in every relation of life.

Respectfully
N. Green

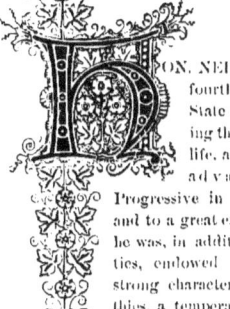

HON. NEHEMIAH GREEN, fourth Governor of the State of Kansas was, during the years of his active life, a man essentially in advance of his time. Progressive in thought, cultured, and to a great extent self-educated, he was, in addition to these qualities, endowed by nature with a strong character and deep sympathies, a temperament sanguine yet sedate, and with a steady inspiration to good deeds. He is now a confirmed invalid, having been confined to his room for the last three years, an uncomplaining sufferer. Comparatively few are aware of the fact that this affliction, overtaking him in the prime of life, is due to his exertions while an officer in the army, relieving his exhausted soldiers by himself carrying their guns and haversacks, during which a blood vessel was ruptured, and since Mr. Green has never seen a well day.

Mr. Green was born March 8, 1837, in Grassy Point Township, Hardin Co., Ohio. His father, Shepard Green, was a native of Washington County, Pa., where he was born August 2, 1808, and the son of Nehemiah Green, Sr., who was born in England, and came to America during revolutionary times. He espoused the cause of the Colonists, and while doing his duty as a soldier, was taken prisoner and conveyed to England, where he was confined until after the surrender of Cornwallis, when he was exchanged. He then located in Washington County, Pa.

Shepard Green, when a boy in his teens, went to Ohio and was one of the early settlers of Champaign County. There he learned the tinner's trade, which he followed a few years, but after marriage he purchased a tract of timber land in Grassy Point Township, Hardin County, and put up a log house. In that humble dwelling the subject of this sketch was born. The country was wild and new, and there were no railroads for many years afterward. The State road, known as the Sandusky & Dayton road, passed by the farm, and after a few years Shepard Green put up a hotel which he conducted for several years, and which was made a stage station. Many distinguished guests sought entertainment under its roof; among them were Henry Clay, Tom Corwin, and Richard M. Johnson. About 1850 Mr. Green removed to Logan County, where his death occurred July 26, 1880.

For his wife Shepard Green chose in early manhood Miss Mary A. Fisher. This lady was born at Fairfax Court House, Va., and was the daughter of William Fisher, a Virginian by birth, and one of the earliest pioneers of Ohio, he locating first on the Scioto river above Columbus. Later he removed to Logan County, where he purchased timber land, improved a farm and died. The mother of our subject made her home with her parents until her marriage, learning to card, spin and weave, and when her children were small she made the greater part of the cloth in use in the family. Having no stove, her cooking was performed many years by a fire-place. She died at the home farm in Logan County, Ohio, in 1859.

Both Shepard Green and his excellent wife were conscientious members of the Methodist Episcopal Church, and the father for many years was one of its chief pillars. His house was the headquarters of the pioneer preachers, and services were frequently held there. Politically, he was an Old Line Whig. The parental family included nine children, all of whom lived to mature years, viz: William F., Louis F., Nehemiah, Nancy, Fanny, Shepard, George S., Mary and Emma. The sons all served in the Union army during the Civil War.

When the Green family changed their residence to Logan County, Ohio, Nehemiah was a lad of thirteen years. He continued attending the subscription school until sixteen years old during the winter season, and in the meantime improved his opportunities for useful knowledge. His desire was for a finished education, and now to his great satisfaction he was permitted to enter Wesleyan University at Delaware, Ohio, where he studied two years. In 1855 he left school to visit the Territory of Kansas. The journey was made by steamer on the Ohio, Mississippi and Missouri rivers to Kansas City; thence by team to Douglas County, this State, Mr. Green made a claim twelve miles south of Lawrence, and during that spring the troubles began between the Free State and Pro-Slavery men.

Mr. Green was an ardent Free State man, and was prominently identified with John Brown, Jim Lane, Montgomery Bain, Gov. Robinson and Marcus Parrott, with whom he participated in the trials, struggles and triumphs which followed. He remained in Kansas until late in 1857, then returned to Ohio and entered the ministry, becoming a member of the Cincinnati Methodist Episcopal Conference. He was stationed at Aberdeen and Williamsburg until the first call by President Lincoln for troops to quell the Rebellion.

It was not long before Mr. Green proffered his services as a soldier of the Union, enlisting as a private in Company B 89th Ohio Infantry. Two weeks later he was commissioned by Gov. Todd, as First Lieutenant and served with his regiment in Kentucky and West Virginia. He was in the campaign which drove Kirby Smith out of the Blue Grass State and Loring out of the Kanawa Valley. While on the Kirby Smith campaign he ruptured a blood vessel and suffered hemorrhages and has not seen a well day since. In 1863 he was obliged to resign. He recuperated in a measure and in 1864 enlisted in the Ohio National Guards and was Sergeant Major of the 153d Regiment, serving in the Army of the Potomac. He received his discharge in September, 1864, and, returning to Kansas, resumed his ministerial labors, being placed in charge of the Methodist Episcopal Church at Manhattan.

In the meantime Mr. Green had kept himself well posted upon State and national events and was looked upon as a fit representative of the people's interest in legislative halls. In 1866 he was nominated for Lieutenant-Governor and elected. In 1868 the Cimaron War broke out and Kansas was asked to raise a regiment of cavalry for the United States service. Gov. Crawford resigned and was appointed Colonel of the regiment and Mr. Green was then sworn in as his successor, administering the duties of his office until the close of the term. Executive business had in the meantime accumu-

lated while Gov. Crawford was raising the regiment, and the military and contingent fund had been exhausted while the whole frontier was threatened by hostile Indians. The soldiers and their horses had to be fed and the former clothed, Gov. Green was equal to the emergency and borrowed money, while at the same time letting contracts subject to the approval of the Legislature to carry on all business, both military and civil. He visited the various military posts, traveling in an ambulance, and personally inspecting the militia. The war ended with the capture and destruction of the bands of Indians commanded by Black Kettle and Little Raven, by Gen. Custer.

After the expiration of his term of office Gov. Green delivered the great seal of the State to his successor and resumed preaching. In due time he was chosen Presiding Elder of Manhattan District, which included the western half of the north half of the State. He followed up the frontier and laid the foundation for many prosperous churches. He thus labored actively in the church until 1873, when failing health compelled him to retire. That year he settled on his farm in Grant Township, Riley County. This farm comprises 810 acres of land. Gov. Green lived a few years in comparative quiet but in 1880 was brought forward again by his old constituents, elected to the State Legislature and took an important part in the proceedings being finally elected Speaker pro tem. During this term the principal subjects acted upon were education, transportation, agriculture and temperance. Mr. Green took an important part in the proceedings to compel the Union Pacific Railroad to acknowledge its obligation to the State. A measure was passed which forced the matter to the Supreme Court when the Company surrendered every point and although its offices were moved from the State, agreed to accept service on any local agent.

The marriage of Nehemiah Green and Miss Ida K. Lettingwell, of Williamsburg, Ohio, was celebrated in 1860. This lady was born at that place and was the daughter of Sidney and Melissa (Bryant) Lettingwell. She became the mother of three children and died in 1871. The eldest child, Glenzen S., is a resident of Oregon. Effie married Dr. William B. Sweatman, and they live in Parkersville, Morris Co., this State. Alice is the wife of Prof. John E. Edgerton, Principal of the schools of White City. In 1873 Mr. Green contracted a second marriage with Miss Mary Sturdevant. This lady was born in Rushville, N. Y. and is the daughter of Josiah and Hannah (Peabody) Sturdevant, who were natives respectively of New England and New York State; they spent their last years in Rushville, N. Y. Of this union there have been born two children—Burtis W. and Ned M.

James A. Harvey

James M. Harvey

AMES M. HARVEY, fifth Governor of the State of Kansas, and a Virginian by birth, is a native of Monroe County, and was born Sept. 21, 1833. His parents, Thomas and Margaret (Walker) Harvey, were also natives of the Old Dominion, but removed from that State when their son James M. was quite young. He acquired his education in the public and select schools of Indiana, Illinois and Iowa, and following his tastes and talents, became a finished practical surveyor and civil engineer. Mr. Harvey, in the year 1859, just before Kansas was freed from Territorial enthrallment, and when she was struggling to become one of the sisterhood of States, removed hither, settling in Riley County. He at once became warmly interested in the affairs of this section of country, and distinguished himself for his ability, intelligence and enthusiastic support of the measure which was to make the Territory a full member of the American Union. The pursuit of agriculture at that time offered a more ample income than his profession, and in this he at once engaged, but the seclusion of the farm did not conceal his eminent ability and his talents from the public, and he was a prominent factor in the affairs of Kansas for a period of nearly thirty years.

It was not long after his arrival here until the Civil War was precipitated upon the country, and James M. Harvey enlisted as a soldier of the Union army, and was soon given a Captain's commission in the 4th and 10th Regiments, which were consolidated. He served with honor in the campaign in which his command took part, and was mustered out in 1864. The following year, and also in 1866, he was elected to represent his county in the Kansas Legislature, where he displayed such power as to attract the leading men of the commonwealth, and in which he gave unmistakable indications of the distinction he would achieve in the future. After serving his terms creditably as a member of the House, he was, in 1867–71, a member of the Senate, and in the latter year was elected Governor.

The duties of these various offices Mr. Harvey discharged with that fidelity and ability which entitled him to still higher distinction, and accordingly on the assembling of the State Legislature, in 1874, he was elected to fill the vacancy occasioned by the resignation of Alexander Caldwell, United States Senator. This vacancy had been temporarily filled by the appointment of Robert Crozier, but the Legislature promptly recognized the claims of Mr. Harvey, and gave him the merited compliment of his regular election to that position. He took his seat on the 12th of February, and in this, as in all other places which he was called upon to fill, discharged his duties with great credit to himself and honor to his State until the 4th of March, 1877, at which time his term expired.

During Mr. Harvey's incumbency of the Governor's office much important work was done by the Legislature, including the issuance of bonds for the military expenses of the Indian War, and providing a military contingent fund for the protection of the frontier of the State against Indian depredations—these two objects calling for $275,000; and also the further issuance of bonds to aid in completing the west wing of the State Capitol, $70,000; to defray the expenses of raising the 19th Regiment, $14,000; and $1,500 was appropriated to buy seed wheat for destitute farmers on the frontier. During that term also the east wing of the new capitol at Topeka was so far completed that on December 25 they were occupied by the State officers. At that date there had been expended on the wing completed and on the west wing, on which work was still progressing, the sum of $117,588.29. At the annual election, which occurred Nov. 8, 1870, Gov. Harvey received over 19,000 majority over his Democratic opponent. For United States Senator, to serve the unexpired term of Caldwell, the balloting commenced January 27, and was continued four days, no candidate receiving the required seventy votes necessary to a choice. On the 2d of February, Mr. Harvey was elected on a joint vote of seventy-six as against fifty-eight thrown for all other candidates.

During the twelfth session of the Kansas Legislature, James M. Harvey, Governor, thirty-eight laws were passed. Among them were bills authorizing or legalizing the issuance of municipal bonds; the State Board of Agriculture was created; $3,000 was appropriated for the relief of Western settlers, and $2,500 for the Freedman's University of Quindaro; the boundaries of Kingman and Harvey Counties were defined, the latter named in honor of James M.; two new judicial districts were created, the Thirteenth and Fourteenth; the salaries of State officers and Judges of the Supreme Courts and Districts Courts were increased; and an act passed providing for the sale of Normal School lands; Commissioners were also appointed to provide for the settlement of losses by Indian depredations between 1860 and 1871.

Gov. Harvey upon retiring from public life returned to his farm at Vinton, Riley County, where he resided for a time, and then returned to the vicinity of his old home in Virginia, and is now living in Richmond. On the 4th of October, 1854, he was united in marriage with Miss Charlotte Cutter, of Adams County, Ill., and of this union there were born six children, four daughters and two sons, namely: Clara, Emma, Lillian, Martha, James N. and John A.

The assuring smile of peace fell upon Kansas for the first time in her existence when the war of the Rebellion ended, and about the time Mr. Harvey, after serving valiantly in the ranks of the Union army, returned to Riley County, and was called upon to assist in the further great work which lay before both legislators and people. It was a time demanding the best efforts of its wisest men, and Mr. Harvey in his sphere was equal to the emergency, and to the perplexing duties devolving upon him as Legislator, Senator and Governor. Twelve years of turmoil and strife had trained the inhabitants to know no rest save in motion, and no safety except in incessant vigilance. Under this discipline their character had become as peculiar as the experiences through which they had passed. A restless energy was the controlling element, and the life of ease and peace was one so foreign to their experience as to strike them as almost unnatural. They, however, under the fortunate rule of a wise executive, turned to the pursuit of the peaceful arts and conquered the right to the free soil they now tread. Mines were opened, railroads built, husbandry and manufactures brought wealth and plenty, and peace and prosperity reigned.

Along with the happy state of affairs just above mentioned, there were also built up the indispensable adjuncts of churches, schools and charitable institutions, together with happy homes, villages and cities, and all else which marks the development of a civilized and free people. Every man who at that critical period performed his duty deserves to be perpetuated in history. Among these James M. Harvey was likewise equal to the emergency, and is amply entitled to have his name enrolled among the patriots of that period, who labored efficiently in bringing about the future prosperity of the commonwealth which now occupies a proud position among the States west of the Mississippi.

Thomas A. Osborn

Thomas A. Osborn.

THOMAS A. OSBORN, one of the most popular and distinguished gentlemen who ever served the State of Kansas as her Executive, is to-day an honored citizen of that great commonwealth and a resident of her capital city. He was chosen to this high position at a critical time in the history of the State. While it is true that no commonwealth in our glorious galaxy of States has been so sorely tried or passed through so many and such severe ordeals, there have been some periods of greater trials than others. One crisis after another has come upon this people, but there was always a firm and wise hand ready and able to guide the ship of State through the storm and over the shoals. Kansas found in the person of Mr. Osborn a safe leader, a patriot and a statesman. From the year 1872 to 1877 was an important period in the history of Kansas, and during this time Thomas A. Osborn stood at the head of its affairs. Many vital questions were forced upon the Executive during these eventful years, and the record he made then will ever endear him to the hearts of the people of the State he so efficiently served. When tried he was not found wanting, but demonstrated that he possessed a sound judgment, a keen foresight, and an unfaltering devotion to the well-being and prosperity of the State. Though a staunch Republican as a citizen, as a Governor he was non partisan, and worked impartially to the betterment and welfare of the whole people. Not only

has he been a valued citizen of the State because he so ably filled the Gubernatorial Chair for two terms, but because for over a quarter of a century he has stood in the front rank of her most progressive and patriotic citizens, aiding in every laudable enterprise having for its object the public good.

Thomas A. Osborn was born nearly fifty-two years ago, at Meadville, Pa., Oct. 26, 1836. He attended the common schools of his neighborhood during his boyhood, and at the age of fifteen commenced life as a printer by carrying the newspapers of the office. Here he served a full apprenticeship, and in the meantime pursued the course of study which had been interrupted by the necessity of making his own living. By his labors at the case he was enabled in due time to earn enough money to pay his way through Allegheny College, and in 1856 he commenced the study of law in the office of Judge Derrickson, of his native town. The year following he came to Michigan, and was soon afterward admitted to the bar. In November, 1857, he migrated to Kansas, and began his career in the Territory at Lawrence, as a compositor in the office of the *Herald of Freedom*. Such was his fidelity to duty, and his industry and efficiency, that he was soon promoted to the position of foreman, and in March, 1858, the editor of the paper, after a two-weeks absence, expressed his thanks "to his worthy foreman, T. A. Osborn, Esq., for the very satisfactory manner in which he has conducted its columns."

Before Mr. Osborn was twenty-two years old he commenced the practice of law at Elwood, Doniphan County, and soon acquired a fine reputation in his chosen profession. Politically, he was a strong

Republican and Free-State man, and in 1859 was elected Senator from Doniphan County to the first State Legislature, taking his seat in 1861, when twenty-five years old. The year following he was chosen President *pro tem* of the Senate during the absence of the Lieutenant Governor, and during the impeachment trial of Gov. Robinson and others. His next promotion was his election to the office of Lieutenant Governor over his competitor, Hon. J. J. Ingalls.

In 1864 Mr. Osborn received the appointment of United States Marshal in Kansas, by President Lincoln, and occupied the position until 1867, residing during and after his term of office at Leavenworth. In the fall of 1872 he accepted from the hands of his party the nomination for Governor of Kansas. The convention assembled at Topeka, and their candidate was elected by a majority of 34,000. He was duly inaugurated in January, 1873, and served with so great ability and rendered such satisfaction that he was again chosen at the State Convention of his party for a second term. The following November he was duly elected, and served another two years.

It is proper in this connection to give a *resume* of some of the occurrences in Kansas at the time Gov. Osborn occupied the position of State Executive. In May, 1874, during his second year as Governor, the Indians on the southwestern frontier commenced depredations upon the settlers in Barbour County, which were confined for a time to the stealing of their cattle and horses. In an attempt to recover some of the plunder, a detachment of United States Cavalry fatally wounded a son of Little Robe, a chief of the Cheyennes. This incited the Indians to open outrages, and in June five murders were committed. These outrages alarmed the entire southwestern border, and action was at once taken to place the more exposed points in as good a condition of defense as was possible. Companies were organized and armed in readiness for an emergency, and stockades were constructed by the settlers at Medicine Lodge, Kiowa, Sun City, and at points midway between the two latter places. Notwithstanding these precautions, hundreds of people deserted their homes and sought protection in the larger towns. In July other murders were committed, and suspicion pointed strongly to the Osage Indians. Early in August a party of these, twenty-five in number, appeared near the town of Kiowa, claiming to be out on a buffalo hunt, and upon being ordered to return to their reservation they refused to do so. This was communicated to Capt. Ricker, who was in command of a company of mounted militia, and who in setting out to find them, overtook them about fifteen miles northeast

of Medicine Lodge. In the skirmish which ensued four Indians were killed. The savages now grew more bold and decided in their onslaught upon the white settlers, and by the 1st of September they had slain sixteen citizens, six of whom were residents of Lawrence and peaceably engaged in surveying public lands forty miles south and twenty miles west of Dodge City. Gov. Osborn was compelled to keep the volunteer militia companies on the border in active service until nearly the close of 1874, and between those who urged extreme measures and those who, more timid, advised a policy of extreme forbearance, he was in a position requiring great ingenuity and temperance of action. Few men in his position could have done better, and more would probably have failed in assisting to bring all these troubles to a peaceable conclusion.

After leaving the Gubernatorial Chair in 1877, Mr. Osborn was appointed by President Hayes, United States Minister to Chili. In this position he remained for four years, when he was tendered by President Garfield the position of Minister to the Empire of Brazil. This he accepted, and remained near the court of Don Pedro until the administration of President Cleveland came into power.

Mr. Osborn's record as a foreign Minister was not only highly creditable to our own Nation, but doubly so to him as an official and a citizen of the great peace-loving Republic of America. While in Chili he was quite active in trying to bring to an end the bloody war in which that country was engaged with Peru and Bolivia, and in 1880 presided over a conference of representatives of the belligerent power on board the American man-of-war "Lackawanna" in the bay of Arica, which had in view that object. He also interested himself in bringing to a peaceful conclusion the long-pending boundary dispute between Chili and the Argentine Republic. For his valued and able services in this connection he received the thanks of both nations.

Since Gov. Osborn's return to the United States he has occupied himself in various enterprises, and while not entirely eschewing politics, has made known his desire to be excused from filling further official positions. He stood at the head of the Kansas delegation to the National Republican Convention in 1888, and in that august assembly was a prominent figure. He is a man whose opinions are universally held in respect, and one who has no unimportant influence in the councils of his party. His early life and training served to build up within him that patience and self-reliance, and that perseverance in behalf of a worthy principle, which has been the secret of his standing among his fellowmen, and distinguished him as a man of more than ordinary ability, and one eminently to be trusted.

George T. Anthony

George T. Anthony.

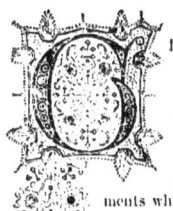

EORGE T. ANTHONY, the seventh Governor of the State of Kansas, came of an excellent family of the Empire State, who were orthodox Quakers religiously, and who in point of the elements which go to make up the bone and sinew of the social fabric, possessed all the characteristics of that peculiar people. He was born in Mayfield, Fulton Co., N. Y., June 9, 1824, and spent his boyhood and youth on a farm, acquiring his education mostly in the winter season, and making himself useful at agricultural pursuits in summer. About the age of nineteen he commenced learning the tin and copper smith's trade at Union Springs, Cayuga County, which he followed as a journeyman five years, then repaired to Ballston Spa, and clerked in a hardware store until his removal to Medina, in 1850.

In the town above mentioned Mr. Anthony found his future wife, Miss Rose A. Lyons, to whom he was married Dec. 14, 1852, and thereafter for a period of nine years was engaged in trade in hardware, tin and stoves, and also carried on the manufacture of stoves and agricultural implements. Later he engaged in the commission business, and in due time was made Loan Commissioner for Orleans County, being thus occupied three years.

During the late Rebellion and under the call of July 2, 1862, for additional troops, Mr. Anthony was selected by request of Gov. Morton as one of a committee of seven to raise and organize troops in the Twenty-eighth District of New York, embracing the counties of Orleans, Niagara and Genesee. In August following he was authorized to recruit an independent battery of light artillery of six guns, and which was subsequently known as the 17th New York Independent Battery. Such was the industry with which he set about this commission, that in four days the maximum number was secured and mustered into service, with Mr. Anthony as Captain, and they proceeded at once to Washington.

Capt. Anthony served with his battery until the close of the war, operating between Washington and Richmond, and in front of the latter city and Petersburg, being with the 18th Army Corps during the last year of the war. He was breveted Major for services in the last campaign ending at Appomattox Court House, and after the surrender of the Confederate forces, was mustered out of service at Richmond, Va., June 12, 1865.

In November, 1865, Mr. Anthony changed his residence from Rochester, N. Y., to Leavenworth, this State, and became editor of the Leavenworth *Daily Bulletin*, also of the Leavenworth *Daily Conservative*, filling the position two years and one-half. He subsequently assumed proprietorship of the *Kansas Farmer*, which he conducted six years. In the meantime such had been the zeal with which he interested himself in the affairs of a State struggling for recognition, and only needing good men for leaders, that he was recognized as a man eminently fitted for promotion, and in December, 1867, was appointed United States Internal Revenue Assistant Assessor, and the following year Collector of Internal Revenue. For three years he was President of the Kansas State Board of Agriculture, and for two years held the same position on the Board of Centennial Managers for the State, and was discharging the duties of the three offices at the time of his election as Governor, on the 7th of November, 876.

Gov. Anthony, while State Executive, presided wisely as counselor over the many difficult questions arising at that time, and retired from the office with the best wishes of those who had realized how faithfully he had endeavored to perform his duty. He continued his residence in Leavenworth after the expiration of his term of office, and thereafter was employed much of the time in a responsible position, in connection with the extension of the great Santa Fe Railroad through New Mexico and into Old Mexico.

That Gov. Anthony was popular during his incumbency of the Executive office, is indicated by the fact that the county seat of Harper County was named in his honor. Over the establishment of this town there was much earnest debate in regard to its location and many other important details in connection therewith. It is now a city of importance, and was honored with a post-office in the summer of 1878. At first the service was only weekly, but in due time became daily, and it was made a money-order office in 1880. Previous to this, however, a bank had been established in a small frame structure standing on the street, and its business was soon conducted in a store building, with a capital of $20,000. The Globe Mills were put up in 1880-81, at a cost of over $25,000, and in due time commanded a large trade from points in the Indian Territory, as well as the surrounding towns.

Churches and newspapers sprang up in due time in the town of Anthony, and various lodges of the different societies were named in honor of the Governor. The town itself lies on the edge of a beautiful valley, a trifle over two miles from the geographical center of Harper County, and the site was selected after much deliberation by the Town Company, which had been formed at Wichita for the purpose, as it was found desirable to establish a town not far from the center of Harper County, which embraced large tracts of beautiful rolling land. The projected town was considered a matter of serious importance, and not the least among the matters connected with its establishment was the name by which it should be called. The descendants of Gov. Anthony may be pardoned if in preserving their family history they keep properly in view this fact in connection therewith. The town site was made to cover 320 acres, and the first work of the company was to build a barracks for the accommodation of emigrants, and to dig three public wells.

About as soon as the announcement went forth that the "city of Anthony" was ready for settlement, about a dozen box houses sprang up as if by magic, and were soon followed by a store of general merchandise, a hardware and a drug-store, and closely upon the heels of these came a physician and an attorney. The new town grew rapidly, and now occupies a proud position among the other cities adjacent, going in some respects ahead of those which are older. As may be supposed, the patriot, the ex-soldier, and one of the most conscientious men who ever occupied the Gubernatorial Chair of Kansas, has watched its growth with lively interest.

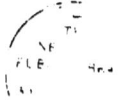

John P. St. John.

JOHN P. ST. JOHN, eighth Governor of the State of Kansas, was born in Brookfield, Franklin Co., Ind., Feb. 25, 1833. The family is of Huguenot descent. Daniel St. John, the paternal grandfather, was a native of Luzerne County, Pa., and for sixty years was one of the foremost ministers of the Universalist denomination, preaching with unswerving faith the doctrines he had espoused, and illustrating their purity by a guileless and untarnished reputation. He was the friend and contemporary of Murray, Ballou, Streeter and Thomas, and was numbered with them as one of the American fathers of this religious faith. He was also a Freemason, and at the time of his death, which occurred in Broad Ripple, Ind., was the oldest member of the fraternity in the State.

The subject of this sketch was the son of Samuel St. John, who was born in Orange County, N. Y., and was a man of more than ordinary ability. The mother, Sophia (Snell) St. John, was of English extraction, a lady of rare intelligence, with a character adorned by all the Christian virtues. The children of farmers in the rural districts of Indiana forty years ago were taught by such instructors as the limited means of the inhabitants could command, and who dispensed knowledge usually only two short terms each year. Under these circum-stances the early education of John P. St. John was acquired. He soon mastered the elementary branches taught in the district school, but determined to carry on his education as soon as he could secure the means, and for this purpose, while yet a youth, entered a store, but devoted his leisure hours to his books.

In 1852 Mr. St. John made his way to the Pacific Slope, and employed himself at whatever he could find to do—wood-chopping, steamboating, mining, merchandising, etc. During the period of eight years, which were pregnant with adventure, hardship, danger and toil, if not of profit, he made voyages to Central America, South America, Mexico, Oregon and the Sandwich Islands. He was engaged in the Indian Wars of Northern California and Southern Oregon in 1852–53, in which he suffered all the perils and hardships incident to the struggles of that time, and was several times wounded in the service.

During his mining life in California the long-cherished predilection of Mr. St. John for the legal profession ripened into a definite purpose. He accordingly procured a few elementary law books, and under circumstances calculated to try the courage of one less determined, he commenced his law studies in his mining camp, reading each evening after the close of the day's labor by the light of a burning pine knot or the camp fire. He thus pursued his studies laboriously for two years. In 1860 he returned eastward with but little more of this world's goods than when he set out eight years before, but equipped with a rich experience, a

knowledge of the world and a fair idea of common
law. With the view of perfecting himself still
further in his studies, he entered the office of
Messrs. Starkweather & McLain, at Charleston, Ill.,
and at the expiration of a year's time was admitted
to practice at the bar, and became a member of the
firm above mentioned.

The anticipated professional career of Mr. St.
John, however, was rudely broken in upon by the
mutterings of Civil War, and laying aside his personal interests, he enlisted as a private in Company
C, 68th Illinois Infantry. The regiment was soon
sent to Alexandria, Va., and St. John was assigned
to detached duty as Assistant Adjutant General.
He continued in this capacity until his term of
enlistment had expired, but subsequently at Camp
Mattoon, Ill., he was placed in command of the
troops there, given the commission of Captain, and
upon the organization of the 143d Illinois, was
elected Lieutenant Colonel of this regiment. They
operated subsequently in the Mississippi Valley, and
Col. St. John continued in the service until 1864,
when he retired to private life, and resumed the
practice of law in connection with Judge McLain
the surviving partner of the old firm.

In February, 1865, Mr. St. John with his family
removed to Independence, Mo., where he first
became prominent as a politician, and as a most
effective and popular orator. During his four-
years residence at that point he took an active part
in the political campaign of 1868, making an effective and vigorous canvass of Western Missouri in
behalf of the nominees of the Republican party. In
May, 1869, he changed his residence to Olathe,
Kan., and associated himself with M. V. B. Parker
for the practice of law. This continued until 1875,
and Mr. St. John then formed a partnership with
Hon. I. O. Pickering, of Olathe, and continued the
practice of his profession until pressing public
duties forced him to abandon it.

The prominence of Gov. St. John in public life
seems to have become his unsought, and as the result of circumstances entirely outside his individual purposes or designs. Up to 1872 he had given
only such attention to political affairs as was
vouchsafed by all intelligent and patriotic voters.
He had held unsought the various local offices

which fall to the lot of responsible citizens in the
administration of town affairs, and as an ardent Republican had done acceptable work on the stump
during the canvass of 1868. Four years later he
was elected State Senator from Johnson County,
and at once took a leading position, both on the
floor as a debator, and in the committee rooms as
an efficient business member.

The temperance movement found a sturdy and
fearless advocate of prohibition in Mr. St. John.
Consequently when the question came to be an
issue in the politics of Kansas, he was at once recognized as the fit exponent and defender of the
then unpopular doctrine. The Kansas State Temperance Convention accordingly nominated him as
its candidate for Governor, in 1876. He declined
the nomination, although in full accord with the
convention on the issue it presented. That same
fall he was on the first ballot in the Republican
convention, the leading gubernatorial candidate.
On the seventh ballot he withdrew his name, which
action resulted in the nomination and subsequent
election of Hon. George T. Anthony.

At the Republican State Convention held two
years later at Topeka, in August, 1878, Mr. St.
John received the Republican nomination for
Governor. Considering the distracting element of
a third party, the campaign was brilliant and effective, and the result one of the most decisive political victories ever achieved in the State. In 1880,
in a total vote of 198,238, Mr. St. John was re-
elected by a majority over the next highest candidate of 51,647 and a majority over all of 32,170, a
fact which shows how satisfactory to the people
had been the manner in which he had discharged
the duties of his office during his first term.

The great exodus of the colored people from the
Southern States to Kansas began in 1879, and Gov.
St. John at once took an active interest in their
behalf. Through his influence, personal and official,
the necessities of thousands of these destitute and
suffering people were relieved and themselves
placed in a position to become self-sustaining. In
1882 his friends nominated him as Governor for a
third term, but he failed of a re-election. In 1884
he was the nominee of the Prohibition party for
President, and received 150,000 votes.

G. W. Glick

George W. Glick.

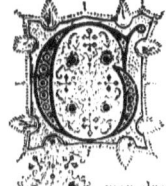EORGE W. GLICK, ninth Governor of Kansas, was its first Democratic State Executive. He was born at Greencastle, Fairfield Co., Ohio, July 4, 1827, and on the paternal side is of German descent. His great-grandfather, Henry Glick, was one of five brothers who left the beautiful Rhine country prior to the Revolutionary War. In this immortal struggle they all participated and subsequently settled in Pennsylvania. George Glick, grandfather of the Governor, served as a soldier in the War of 1812, and was severely wounded at the battle of Ft. Meigs.

Isaac Glick, the father of George W., and who was prominent as a farmer and stock-raiser of Sandusky County, Ohio, held for three consecutive terms the office of Treasurer of that county, and was a man accounted above reproach, both in his business and private character. He married Miss Mary Sanders, daughter of George Sanders, who was a soldier patriot in the War of 1812, in which he ranked as a Captain and bore the marks of his bravery in bodily wounds of a serious nature. Mrs. Mary (Sanders) Glick is a lady of high culture and great piety, active in the work of Christian charity, and of that retiring disposition which fully carried out the command of the great teacher, "Let not thy right hand know what thy left hand doeth." As a boy, George W. Glick was more than usually studious, and acquired a good English education, embracing the higher mathematics and the languages, which lent a polish to his practical sense and business qualifications, and enabled him to succeed almost uniformly in his undertakings. When he was a little lad of five years the family removed to Lower Sandusky, now Fremont, where, after completing his education, he entered the law office of Buckland & Hayes, the junior member of the firm being afterward President of the United States. In due time he passed a thorough examination in connection with the Cincinnati Law School students, and was admitted to the bar by the Supreme Court.

Mr. Glick commenced the practice of his profession at Fremont, Ohio, where his careful attention to the interests of his clients secured him a large patronage. Later he removed to Sandusky City, and in 1858 was made the Congressional nominee of the Democratic party in his district, but declined the honor in the presence of the convention, but accepted later the nomination for State Senator. Although defeated, he ran nearly 2,000 votes ahead of his party ticket. Later he was elected Judge Advocate General of the 2d Regiment of the Seventeenth Division of the Ohio Militia, with the rank of Colonel, receiving his commission from Gov. Salmon P. Chase.

Late in 1858 Mr. Glick came to Kansas, locating in Atchison, and associated himself in the practice of law with Hon. Alfred G. Otis. This gentleman was well versed in jurisprudence, and as Judge of the Second Judicial District from January, 1877, to January, 1881, won golden opinions as an administrator of justice. The firm of Otis & Glick continued fifteen years, and was finally dissolved in consequence of a throat affection from which Mr. Glick had suffered for some time. The firm settled up its affairs annually, never a dispute occurring, its last settlement having been effected within an hour.

At the first election held under the Wyandotte

Constitution, Dec. 6, 1859, Mr. Glick was made the Democratic nominee for Judge of the Second Judicial District, and received a vote larger than that of any candidate on his ticket. He was elected a member of the House of Representatives from the city of Atchison, in 1862, and each consecutive year thereafter until 1867. He was re-elected in 1875 and again in 1880. During these years he was Chairman of the Judiciary Committee, and was chosen to fill this position by the Republican Speakers of the House, who manifested the utmost confidence in his wisdom and integrity. Thereafter he served on the most important committees existing, and during the session of 1876 was Speaker *pro tem* of the House. In May, 1874, he served as State Senator, having been elected to fill the vacancy caused by the resignation of the Hon. Joseph C. Wilson. From this time on Mr. Glick was constantly called into requisition by his party, being in 1866 a delegate to the Union Convention at Philadelphia, and in 1870 a member of the Democratic State Central Committee. Subsequently he was a member of the State Central Relief Committee, and was commissioned a Centennial Manager by Gov. Thomas A. Osborn in 1876. Subsequently he was elected Treasurer of the Board of Managers, and was present at the first meeting in Philadelphia, when the arranging of the display was completed. In July, 1882, he was nominated by acclamation as the Democratic candidate for Governor, and at the election received considerable support outside of his party.

Mr. Glick was County Commissioner of Atchison County upon his accession to the office of Governor, and was also holding the position of Auditor. In his election to this office he received about forty-six per cent of the votes cast, and was outdone by only one man in this respect, namely, John P. St. John, who, in 1880, received about fifty-eight per cent. Although a man of temperate habits, he does not consider prohibition a sovereign remedy for the evils arising from the use of, and traffic in, intoxicating drinks. In February, 1876, while a member of one House and during the tendency of the proposed amendment to the Dram Shop Act, he entered a protest, which was spread upon the House Journal, in which he maintained that the Prohibitory Liquor Law had, wherever tried, failed to accomplish its purpose, and that this proposition was conceded by all who were not controlled by fanaticism; that no one would attempt to enforce such a law, and that regulation and control of the traffic was an absolute necessity for the preservation of the peace and good order of society, and that this control was made of no effect by the proposed amendment.

Mr. Glick furthermore contended that the revenue derived from the sale of intoxicating liquors aided in paying the burdensome expenses following the wake of such sales, and that by the proposed law the burdens upon the public were increased while its ability to prevent them was decreased. He believed that if the bill became a law it would increase the number of places where liquor would be sold, thereby resulting in the increase of the evils of the traffic, and also the expenses of protecting life and property and preserving the public peace.

The early Kansas railroads found in Gov. Glick a staunch and efficient assistant, and he was one of the first Directors of the Central Branch of the Union Pacific, running west from Atchison. He was also a Director of the Atchison, Topeka & Santa Fe—the important transportation line of the State and of the country west of the Mississippi. From the time of the organization of the Atchison & Nebraska, he was its President to its completion, and spent four years of incessant labor in order to effect its construction from Atchison to the capital city of Omaha. He organized the Atchison Gas Company and secured the building of the works. Many of the buildings in the city of Atchison, both business and dwelling-houses, were erected by him, and he has generously disbursed his capital to encourage those enterprises best calculated to increase the importance of the city.

Mr. Glick was married at Massillon, Ohio, Sept. 17, 1857, to Miss Elizabeth, daughter of Dr. A. Ryder, of Fremont, that State. While he was State Executive his son Frederick was his private secretary. This son and a daughter Jennie are his only children. Mr. Glick was the first Master of the Shannon Hills Grange of the Patrons of Husbandry. He has been a member of the Masonic fraternity nearly forty years, and aided in organizing the Royal Arch Chapter and Commandery, of Atchison.

John A. Martin.

HE tenth Governor of Kansas was born March 10, 1839, at Brownsville, Pa., and in his early days, after an ordinary education, learned the printer's trade. In 1857 he went to Pittsburgh, and was employed in the office of the *Commercial Journal*, and early in October of that year he emigrated to Kansas and located in Atchison. He purchased the office of the *Squatter Sovereign* in February, 1858, and changed its name to the *Freeman's Champion*, and on the 20th of the month commenced his editorial career in this State, by the issue of the first number of the paper which he has since been identified with. He was always a staunch free-State man, and an earnest and ardent Republican, being among the organizers of that grand old party in his native State. He was Secretary of the Wyandotte Constitutional Convention, and was elected State Senator before he was of age.

During the summer of 1861 Mr. Martin assisted in organizing the 8th Kansas Infantry, of which he was appointed Lieutenant Colonel. The regiment served on the Missouri border during the fall and winter of 1861. Early in 1862 he was appointed Provost Marshal of Leavenworth, and in March of the same year his regiment was ordered to Corinth, Miss., Lieut. Col. Martin in command. A few weeks after, when at Corinth, the regiment with the division to which it was attached, was ordered to join Gen. Buell in Tennessee, and thereafter during the whole war it served in the Army of the Cumberland. Lieut. Col. Martin was promoted to be Colonel on the 1st of November, 1862, and was Provost Marshal of Nashville, Tenn., from December, 1862, to June, 1863. The regiment, under his command, took part in the battles of Perryville and Lancaster, Ky., the campaign against Tullahoma and Chattanooga, the battle of Chickamauga, the siege of Chattanooga, the storming of Mission Ridge, the campaign of East Tennessee, in the winter of 1863–64, the campaign from Chattanooga to Atlanta, and the subsequent pursuit of Hood northward. Col. Martin commanded the 3d Brigade, 1st Division, 20th Army Corps, on the second day of the battle of Chickamauga, and during the siege of Chattanooga, and commanded the 1st Brigade, 3d Division, 4th Army Corps, from August, 1864, until his muster out at Pulaski, Tenn., Nov. 17, 1864.

In a lengthy description of the battle of Mission Ridge, published in the New York *Times* of July

18, 1876, Maj. Gen. Thomas J. Wood, who commanded the 3d Division, 4th Corps, Army of the Cumberland, says:

"Willich's brigade, in the center, had with it the heroic, accomplished Martin, Colonel of the 8th Kansas. What that regiment could not take it was not worth while to send any other regiment to look for. Martin was among the foremost to set the example of the upward movement, and among the first to reach the crest."

In a letter published in the Cincinnati *Commercial* of Jan. 24, 1876, the late Brig. Gen. August Willich, commander of the 1st Brigade, 3d Division, 4th Army Corps, after stating that the orders he received at Orchard Knob, concerning the advance to Mission Ridge, were to "take the rifle pit at the foot of Mission Ridge, and to keep that position," and describing the advance to the base of the ridge and the capture of the rifle pits there, says:

"Herein the work assigned by Gen. Grant was accomplished. But now the fire of the enemy became very severe; the shells rent the ground in every direction; our lines were infiladed from the different spurs of the ridge, where the enemy was protected against our fire by his works and his dominant position. There appeared at first thought to Gen. Willich, holding position about 100 yards behind the rifle pits, to be only three chances, viz: To obey orders and to be shot without effective resistance; to fall back, or to charge. The second chance being out of the question, I galloped with Lieut. Green, of my staff, up to the 8th Kansas, lying in line behind the rifle pits. Col. Martin, commanding the regiment, seeing me, jumped on the breastworks and shouted: 'Here we are, General, what more?' 'Forward, storm! We have to take the works on the ridge,' was the answer. The Colonel: 'Altogether, boys, forward! Hip, hip, hurrah!' Like one man, the whole line, with one leap, cleared the breastworks; forward they moved and the air was soon filled with the sound, 'Forward! Forward!' extending more and more, right and left."

Returning home, Col. Martin resumed control of the Atchison *Champion* early in January, 1865, and on the 22d of March issued the first number of the *Daily Champion*. He has been commander of the department, a delegate to the National Republican Conventions of 1860, 1868, 1872 and 1880; was a United States Centennial Commissioner, and one of the Vice Presidents of that body; was one of the incorporators of the State Historical Society, of which he was President for one term; was elected by the two Houses of Congress one of the Board of Managers of the National Soldiers' Home, in 1878, and re-elected in 1882, being now Second Vice President of that body. He was married, June 1, 1871, to Miss Ida Challiss, eldest daughter of Dr. William L. Challiss, of Atchison, and has seven children.

At the Republican State Convention, held in Topeka July 17, 1884, the rules were suspended and John A. Martin was nominated for Governor by acclamation. At the November election following he was elected Governor by a plurality of 38,495 votes. At the Republican State Convention, held in Topeka July 7, 1886, he was again unanimously nominated for a second term, and at the November election following was elected Governor by a plurality vote of 33,918. He was the first and only Governor of Kansas who was twice unanimously nominated by his party for that office, and has served with distinction, filling the honored position occupied by his able predecessors with equal ability, and giving to the people as the Chief Executive of the populous and growing State, satisfaction. He is a man of honest, upright character, and abhors trickery and deceit, and in looking over his long and useful life he may well feel a just pride at the position he has won in the esteem and confidence of honest men, and the respect of all good citizens. There are but few men of the stirring State of Kansas who have been more closely identified with all public movements for the general welfare and prosperity of the State than John A. Martin. His name may be found on almost every page of the memorable history of Kansas, from the holding of the first Republican Convention, held at Osawatomie in 1859, until to-day, when he is the leading spirit among the enterprising men of the most progressive State of the Nation. A man of excellent judgment, moved by honest purpose and love for the general welfare of the whole State, he is always found identified with the right, and, as might be expected, popular with the people.

HON. L. U. HUMPHREY. This distinguished gentleman was chosen Governor of Kansas, at the election held in November, 1888. He had made for himself an honorable record on the deadly battle-field, as well as in the more monotonous, though not less courage-requiring hours of political life, in the fields of journalism, in the forensic arena, and in the various capacities in which he has labored for the public weal. It is not our purpose in this brief sketch, to dwell at great length upon his private life, his public record sufficing to indicate that his character is noble, and his example a worthy one.

Gov. Humphrey was born in Stark County, Ohio, July 25, 1844. His father, Col. Lyman Humphrey, who was a native of Connecticut, of English descent, and a lawyer of distinction, died when the subject of this sketch was but eight years of age. At the outbreak of the Civil War, in 1861, Gov. Humphrey was attending the High School at Massillon, and his fervid, patriotic heart was thrilled to the utmost, with an enthusiastic desire to serve his country, and uphold the flag which he had been taught to revere. Though only a boy of seventeen, he enlisted in Company I, 76th Ohio Infantry, a regiment famous for its bravery, and for the eminent men who belonged to it. Such was the gallantry, and the proper conception of a soldier's duties exhibited by him, that he had been promoted to the office of 1st Lieutenant, had acted as Adjutant of his regiment, and had commanded a company for a year, before he was out of his minority.

Much active service was experienced by Capt. Humphrey, and among the battles in which he participated, were those of Donelson, Pittsburg Landing, Corinth, the siege of Vicksburg, Chattanooga, Atlanta, and the fighting around that city, he being under fire five or six weeks in that single campaign. He was with Sherman in his march to the sea, was present at the capture of Savannah, and was engaged in many other trying scenes. He was with his regiment in the campaign through the Carolinas, and took part in the battle of Bentonville, as well as in the capture of Gen. Joe Johnston's army. He was twice wounded, once at Pittsburg Landing, and once at Chattanooga, but refused to retire from the field. During the four years of his military service, he never was absent from duty for a day. The regiment of which he was a member, belonged to the 1st Brigade, 1st Division, 15th Corps, Army of the Tennessee.

At the termination of the war Capt. Humphrey resumed the studies which had been interrupted by the "irrepressible conflict," feeling the need of a more thorough education to fit him to act well his part in the battle of life. He entered Mt. Union College, and soon after matriculated in the law department of the Michigan University, from which he was graduated after having completed his studies in the legal profession. Returning to his native State he was admitted to practice in the several courts of Ohio, in 1868, but feeling that the West would afford a broader field for his labors, he removed to Shelby County, Mo., where for a time he assisted in editing the *Shelby County Herald.*

The newer State of Kansas, which had already become the home of many men eminent in various walks of life, seemed to beckon Capt. Humphrey still further West, and in February, 1871, he crossed the Missouri and located at Independence. He formed a law partnership with the Hon. Alexander M. York, the attempt at whose bribery by Senator Pomeroy in 1873, during the contest for United States Senatorial honors, brought his name prominently before the people of Kansas as an opponent to fraud and corruption. The legal relation between the two gentlemen lasted until 1876, after which time Gov. Humphrey continued the practice of his chosen profession alone. The Independence *Tribune* was founded by Messrs. A .M. York, W. T. Yoe and L. U. Humphrey, the latter withdrawing from the firm at the expiration of a year.

Gov. Humphrey had not long been a resident of Kansas before his talents were known and his fitness for public office appreciated. In 1871, the year of his arrival in the State, he was honored by the Republican nomination as candidate for a seat in the State Legislature, but because of his vigorous opposition to the issue of questionable bonds to the L. L. & G. Railroad Company, he was defeated by a small vote. In 1876 he was vindicated by an election to the House from a district formerly Democratic, and served two years as a member of the Republican State Central Committee. In 1877 Melville J. Salter having accepted a position in the land office at Independence, resigned his position as Lieutenant Governor, and our subject was chosen to fill the vacancy. His principal opponent was the Democratic candidate, Thomas W. Waterson, who received 24,740 votes, while Mr.

Humphrey received 62,750, his majority over all other candidates being 27,381. The following year he was re-elected; the convention which nominated him having, after a protracted and exciting struggle, placed John P. St. John at the head of the ticket.

In 1884 Mr. Humphrey was elected to the State Senate for the term of four years, and upon the organization of that Legislative body was chosen President, pro tem, by a unanimous vote. On July 25, 1888, that being the forty-fourth anniversary of his birth, he was nominated for Governor of the State of Kansas, and was elected by the splendid majority of 73,361. Gov. Humphrey carried 101 out of the 106 counties in the State, his opponent in the contest being no less prominent a person than Judge John Martin.

Gov. Humphrey has been frequently called upon to preside as a Judge, pro tem, of the District Court, an honor which indicates the degree of confidence reposed in him by the public. He has been an active Republican, and has an enviable record both as a speaker and writer in behalf of the principles to which he is a devotee. He is deeply interested in the promulgation of the fundamental doctrines of true government, and the loyal principles for which our forefathers in earlier years and our nearer kinsmen in recent times, gave their strength and even their lives. He belongs to the Loyal Legion, a body made up of those who, like himself, are intensely patriotic. Also is a member of the G. A. R., and a prominent Mason. His affability, his frankness, and his justice in dealing with men, has won for him a high place in the esteem of all with whom he comes in contact, either personally or through the medium of his published addresses. His keen perception as to the wants of the growing State, his desire that she shall be built up in all the elements that constitute the true greatness and glory of a government or of a people, and the powers of discrimination, which lead him to discern right from wrong, justice from injustice, especially qualify him for the high office to which the people called him.

Gov. Humphrey was married at Independence on Christmas Day, 1872, to Miss Leonard, daughter of James C. Leonard. They have two children, Lyman L. and A. Lincoln.

ONE of the most important factors in the business development and prosperity of a city, county or State, is its railroad communications. A retrospection of the history of the South Platte Country since the advent of railroad facilities, will convince the careful observer of the immense benefit resulting from the introduction of this essential adjunct of commercial enterprise. The following brief sketches of the leading railroads of this section of the great commonwealth will form an interesting feature of this ALBUM. It may be remarked in this connection that the roads referred to are not only the important corporations of Kansas, but stand among the first in the Nation.

The Missouri Pacific Railway System.

THIS great system, which now threads its way through several States west of the Mississippi River, has been a potential factor in the development of Missouri and Kansas, and with its accustomed enterprise, a short time ago penetrated with its lines into the rich agricultural districts of Nebraska, to compete in this growing State with its rapidly accumulating business. It was also among the pioneer roads in Kansas, and its many branches now traverse in different directions the most thickly settled portions of the State. It has contributed in a large measure, by its liberal and aggressive policy toward the rapid development of the great resources of Kansas. It is interesting to note briefly its history, as it was the first road built West from St. Louis, as early as 1850–51. The preliminary steps to build the road were taken, and it has since gradually extended its lines, like the arteries and veins of the human system, until it has encompassed in its range the best portions of Missouri, Kansas and Nebraska, and has even reached out and tapped the large commercial centers of Texas and Colorado. In Missouri its several lines and connections pierce the great coal and mineral fields of the State, enabling it to lay down in Kansas City, Topeka, Leavenworth, Atchison, Wichita, Omaha and Lincoln, cheaper than any other roads, these essential adjuncts so necessary in the development of commercial centers, and even the settlers in the outlying districts of Kansas and Nebraska have fuel laid down to them more cheaply on account of this road.

Its splendid and far-reaching management extends to its patrons, both in freight and passenger traffic, the best facilities for reaching the sea-board and the great Eastern marts of trade. The growth and development of the Missouri Pacific system have been rapid and fully abreast of the times. Its local business is enormous and rapidly increasing. In respect to its through business no other road or system in the West is better equipped than this. Its steel rail tracks, well ballasted road-beds and superior passenger coaches constitute it one of the greatest railroad systems of the West. Its superb fast train between St. Louis and Denver via Kansas City and Pueblo, is unquestionably the most elegant and best equipped train of any road which enters the Peerless City of the Plains. It runs more passenger trains and finer coaches between St. Louis and Kansas City than any other road, and the volume of its freight traffic between the above-mentioned emporiums of the State of Missouri, is vastly greater than any other line. It has contributed in a marked and wonderful degree toward the building up of the various cities along its numerous lines. Kansas City has felt its influence more than that of any other road centering there, largely on account of its lines that lead into the heart of the coal, iron and granite fields of Missouri, and the extensive timber districts of Arkansas, and by its connecting lines with the extensive and growing cattle interests of Texas and the Southwest.

It gives to its numerous and rapidly increasing patronage in Nebraska and Kansas, unsurpassed facilities for reaching the great health resorts of Arkansas and Texas over its line from Omaha to St. Louis, about five hundred miles in extent. It runs the finest trains between these two cities, passing through Weeping Water, where connection is made with the line from Lincoln, the State capital, thence to Nebraska City and Falls City, in Nebraska, and St. Joseph, Atchison, Leavenworth, before reaching Kansas City. The length of its main line and branches is over 322 miles, its northern terminus being Omaha, where connections are made with all the roads centering in that metropolis. The line from Omaha to Falls is 115 miles, the Crete branch 58 miles, Lincoln to Auburn 76 miles, Warwick to Prosser and Hastings 73 miles. Various extensions and divisions are constantly being made in Nebraska. Thus it will be seen that this road already taps the two leading cities in the State,

Omaha and Lincoln, besides Nebraska City, rapidly growing into importance, and likewise Hastings.

Kansas is literally covered by the lines and branches of the Missouri Pacific Railway, which amount in mileage in the State to over three thousand. The Central Branch Division extends from St. Joseph and Atchison, through the northern portion of the State out toward the western line, giving the rich counties in these tiers and the flourishing cities and towns, direct outlet to Omaha, Kansas City and St. Louis.

Another main stem extends through the central portion of the State, from Kansas City to Pueblo, over which through trains are run from St. Louis and Kansas City to Pueblo and Denver. Still farther to the south is the Ft. Scott, Wichita & Western Railway, extending from the eastern to the southwestern portion of the State, and giving a direct outlet from Hutchinson, Wichita, and the growing country in this part of this State, Kansas City and St. Louis. In the extreme south of the State, the Denver, Memphis and Atlantic Division, extends from Chetopa through Larned and the western part of the State, opening up the rich country tributary to Larned, Conway Springs, Winfield, Arkansas City and Coffeyville, and giving it a direct outlet also to St. Louis. A new division has already been surveyed, and work commenced from Ft. Scott through to Tipton in Missouri, on the Main Line which will bring Central and Southern Kansas nearer than they have ever been before to St. Louis and the great centers of the East. Perhaps the most momentous event in the history of the road for the past year, has been the completion of the small portion amounting to about eighty-two miles, of the Kansas & Arkansas Valley Railway, extending from Ft. Smith up through the Indian Territory to Coffeyville. It is hardly realized as yet, what this means for the great country west and south of the Missouri River. This, it will readily be seen by a glance at the map, gives a direct line between the great cotton and iron producing country of the Southeast, and the corn, wheat, pork and beef producing region of the West, formed by the divisions of the Missouri Pacific Railway, south from Omaha, St. Joseph and Kansas City—also from Denver, Pueblo and Wichita to

Coffeyville, the Kansas & Arkansas Valley Railway, extending from Coffeyville via Wagoner to Ft. Smith, a division of the great Iron Mountain Route, which, as is well known, forms a part of the Missouri Pacific System. From Ft. Smith, the Little Rock & Ft. Smith Railroad—another division of the Iron Mountain Route extends to Little Rock, connecting with other divisions there for Texarkana, Arkansas City, Hot Springs and Memphis. The Iron Mountain Route which has been before mentioned as a part of this system, extends from St. Louis to the South and West, to Memphis, Little Rock, Hot Springs and Texarkana, and runs through Pullman Buffet Sleeping Cars in connection with the various Texas Lines to Galveston on the Gulf of Mexico, and to Laredo and El Paso, on the Rio Grande River, connecting at those points for California and the City of Mexico, and the interior States of the Republic of Mexico. This constitutes largely the Railway System of the State of Arkansas, passing through it from northeast to southwest, from Poplar Bluff to Texarkana, and from east to west, connecting Memphis and Arkansas City with Ft. Smith. The total mileage of the Missouri Pacific System is five thousand and ninety-four miles. Hence the reader will readily observe that this great System is one of the most important which traverses the growing States west of the Mississippi River; on account of its extensive mileage and ramifications the System is destined to promote in a large degree, the development of the material interests of the country through which it passes.

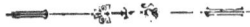

Chicago, Rock Island & Pacific

IS among the oldest and most important trunk lines, having Chicago for its eastern terminus—the completion of this road in Illinois marked an important era in the development of the northern and western portion of the State, as well as contributing to the upbuilding of many thriving manufacturing cities on its line—notably Joliet, Moline, Rock Island and Davenport; also with its two branches extending to Peoria, has opened up good markets for the extensive coal and agricultural resources of that locality, likewise giving a rapid impetus to the commercial and manufacturing resources of Peoria. Moline (except Chicago), is probably the most important and extensive manufacturing city on the line, and through the enterprise of the great Rock Island Route it has been enabled to lay down its manufactured wares to the farmers of Southern Iowa, Northern Missouri and Kansas, cheaper than by any other road, and the vast lumber interests of the cities of Rock Island and Davenport have by means of this line been enabled to reach the most important, as well as the most remote, places in Kansas. The Rock Island has always been in the very van of railroad progress; while always solid and substantial, yet it has ever been steadily and constantly building new lines and extending its system until it now ramifies into the best regions of the Mississippi and Missouri Valleys. Its lines extending to Denver, Colorado Springs, and other points in Colorado, offer unsurpassed facilities, to the tourist or man of business for elegant and comfortable traveling; its superb dining cars have among travelers made it renowned as among the best roads of the West. In brief the Rock Island Company has by a judicious system of permanent improvements, and by the introduction of all modern appliances which tend to the preservation of life and property, placed itself in such a condition, materially and physically, that its financial future cannot be affected by the contingencies which seriously affect other roads. Its success as one of the great highways of the West is an assured reality. It might be appropriately noted here that while much of this road's past success may be attributed to its admirable geographical location, embracing a very rich section of the country for local traffic, and with a termini on Lake Michigan, the Mississippi and Missouri Rivers and Denver, the heart of the Rocky Mountain regions, equally as much is due to the stability of the management, and to the fact that the property has never yet become the foot-ball of speculators. It is not surprising that the Chicago, Rock Island & Pacific has maintained a firm position as an investment in the moneyed centers of the world, and it has acquired a well-merited popularity with the traveling and shipping public. Its steel rails and well ballasted road-bed have long since made it the favorite with shippers, and its freight traffic is immense and growing. At Council Bluffs and Omaha, connections are made with all roads centering there. It is the most direct and shortest route between Omaha and Chicago—and hence the favorite of shippers. At Davenport a branch diverges to the Southwest, and extends to Kansas City, Leavenworth, Atchison and St, Joseph.

At St. Joseph the road crosses the Missouri and enters Kansas; at Horton the line diverges and extends up into Nebraska as far as Nelson; from Fairbury, Neb., the line extends through Northern Kansas to Denver, and Colorado Springs. From Horton the line leads in a southwesterly direction through Topeka, the capital of the State; thence to Herington, Hutchinson and to Liberal, the latter place on the line of the Indian Territory. At McFarland a spur extends in a northwestern direction through Manhattan and Clay Center to Belleville, where a junction is made with the main line to Denver, Col.; at Herington a short branch goes to Abilene and Salina. From Herington the line passes south through Wichita and Wellington to Caldwell, on the line of the Indian Territory.

With its accustomed energy this road was the first to complete its line into the Oklahoma country, passing through Kingfisher, and having El Reno for its Southern terminus.

CHARACTERISTICS OF THE ROAD.

The whole number of miles operated by the Chicago, Rock Island & Pacific Railway at the present time, including second tracks and sidings, is about four thousand and ninety-three miles. The main track mileage in the following States is: Illinois, 236 miles; Iowa, 1,066.10; Missouri, 286.70; Kansas, 1,117.37; Nebraska, 140.97; Colorado, 376.06; and Indian Territory, 106.75—186.70 second track, and about 565.15 side track.

This company has a contract for joint use of track with the Hannibal & St. Joseph between Kansas City and Cameron Junction; with the Union Pacific Railway from Kansas City to North Topeka, also from Union to Denver; and with the Denver & Rio Grande between Denver and Pueblo.

The principal shops of this company are located at Chicago, Ill.; Rock Island, Ill.; Stewart, Iowa; Trenton, Mo.; Horton and Goodland, Kan.; and Roswell, Colo. Solid trains, carrying all classes of passengers, are run through between Chicago, Kansas City and Topeka; through trains to Wichita, El Reno (Ft. Reno), Hutchinson, Dodge City, Salina and Abilene. The line is equipped with first-class baggage, mail, smoking cars and coaches; chair cars of the latest improved pattern of chairs, and Pullman Palace Sleeping Cars. Dining cars are now running on all through passenger trains between Colorado points and Chicago, and also between Council Bluffs and Chicago, and eating-houses are located at convenient points on all divisions for the accommodation of local trains. It is contemplated to establish dining-car service on the whole line, in the near future. In regard to freight traffic, the management has a comprehensive system of through cars and way-billing to all prominent points in the West, Northwest and Southwest. Having their own rails between Chicago, Peoria and Kansas City, St. Joseph, Omaha and Denver, no delays or transfers between Chicago and any of these points. Also run through cars to the Pacific Coast via all lines having terminals on the coast. Less than car-load shipments to all prominent points in through cars, thus avoiding transfers and delay. Special attention is paid to live stock from all points on the line. At present there is one hundred and eighty-seven miles of double track being operated, one hundred and eighty-one miles of which is located in Illinois, between Chicago and Rock Island; the balance in Iowa, from Davenport to what is known as Double Track Junction, about six miles west of Davenport on the Council Bluff line.

The experience of the past has clearly demonstrated that whatever is undertaken by the managers of the Rock Island is not merely done, but done well, that they possess to an almost unlimited extent the confidence of Eastern and European capitalists, and that they are remarkably shrewd and far-seeing in anything which affects the present or the future interests of their property.

It will be observed that all the great leading

marts of trade in Kansas are tapped by this road, thereby giving to that portion of the West a strong and substantial competitive market with the great Eastern commercial centers.

Atchison, Topeka & Santa Fe Railway,

OPULARLY known as the Santa Fe Route. The initial lines of this great system were first built from Atchison to Topeka, in 1869, and for many years the former city was the Eastern terminus of the road. The management of the Santa Fe, with wonderful energy, pushed out its lines in every direction, into the young and growing State of Kansas, and in the majority of instances preceding settlement and civilization. This road was the first to penetrate across the southern part of Colorado, via Pueblo and Trinidad into New Mexico, until its lines penetrated the old adobe town of Santa Fe, whose citizens were half Spanish and half Mexican. As its course penetrated the wilderness it sometimes followed the old Santa Fe Trail, and generally not far distant at any time from the "trail" which had been made famous years before by trappers and also by the Government freighters. The marvelous growth and development of the State of of Kansas is in a great measure due to the enterprise and public spirit of the managers of the Santa Fe System. Not only did they devote their energy to the upbuilding of the road, but at great expense they maintained emigration and Colonial agents in the various countries of Europe, as well as in the Eastern, Middle and Southern States, thereby advertising the State of Kansas as no other State has heretofore been done. Its climate, its soil and great advantages to the home seeker were at times fully portrayed by the enterprise of this road—every fostering care was given to the stock and ranch men, to the merchant, the mechanic and the manufacturer to settle in Kansas—as a result we have here a State in the center of the Union, of boundless agricultural resources, settled by a wide-awake, enterprising and prosperous people. The Santa Fe owns and operates more miles of road in

Kansas than any other line, with its vast system of East and West, North and South lines reaching every important town in the State, and penetrating sixty-three counties in Kansas. The magnitude of its business is immense. Its lines beginning at the Missouri River towns in Kansas are St. Joseph, Atchison, Leavenworth and Kansas City; extends south to Coffeyville, Arkansas City, Hunnewell, Caldwell, New Kiowa (thence to the Pan Handle of Texas), and north to Superior, in Nebraska; Concordia, Clay Center Minneapolis, and other Northern Kansas cities. Its main lines and branches reach nearly every important city in the State. St. Joseph, on the Missouri side of the river, has a population of nearly one hundred thousand, and its wholesale trade is heavy throughout the West. Atchison is a growing city of about twenty thousand people; the Soldiers' Orphans Home of the State is located here. Leavenworth, with her thirty thousand people, is an important manufacturing center. Leavenworth was the earliest famous city of Kansas, as it was the original outfitting point for travel and traffic across the plains. The Kansas system may be described as a main east and west line, over four hundred miles in length, with branch lines extending in every direction where an area of particularly rich country, or some other special advantages invited a line of rails.

The road from Topeka, after 1869, was extended west and south, and then east to Kansas City by purchase of a line built by another company. From Kansas City, in 1887–88 the line was extended to Chicago, under the name of the Chicago, Santa Fe & California Road; in 1887, also the purchase of the Gulf, Colorado & Santa Fe Road, and the extension of the Kansas lines through the Indian Territory to Texas, gave the company a line to the Gulf of Mexico. So that at the present time the Santa Fe System proper begins at Chicago, passes through Illinois, Iowa, Missouri, Kansas, Colorado, Indian Territory, Texas, New Mexico, Arizona and California, and has for its Southern terminals Galveston, on the Gulf of Mexico, and El Paso, on the Mexican frontier; and for its Western terminals San Diego and Los Angeles, on the Pacific Coast, (San Francisco being practically a Pacific-Coast terminal, as it is reached via Mojave, over the tracks of the Southern Pacific Railway); and for its Northern terminals Chicago. St. Joseph, Mo., Superior, Neb., and Denver, the capital of Colorado.

Chicago to Kansas City is practically an air line, being the most straight and direct of any road between the two cities. It passes through a large number of important towns in Illinois, including Joliet, with its great steel works, and other manufacturing interests. The next important place is Streator, a few miles south of the latter place; a branch extends to the thriving city of Pekin, on the Illinois River. From Streator the main line crosses the Illinois at Chillicothe, and extends through Peoria and Knox Counties to the beautiful and enterprising city of Galesburg, here it comes in competition with several lines of the Burlington System; thence running in a southwesterly direction through a rich and populous section, crossing the Mississippi at Ft. Madison, on a magnificent steel bridge. Here the company have established shops, that being the terminus of the two operating divisions of the road. From Ft. Madison by a spur Keokuk is reached. The line through Missouri shows very heavy construction work, made to secure what was desired in the way of distance and grades. Along the Santa Fe new towns are springing up, and new industries are being developed. Twenty miles east of Kansas City the Missouri River is crossed by a steel bridge, so that the line enters Kansas City on the south side of the river. From Kansas City to Topeka the line runs on the South bank of the Kansas River; at Wilder and Holliday are points for the departure of branch lines—one northwest to Atchison, and the other southwest through Ottawa and Southern Kansas, being known as the Southern Kansas division of the Santa Fe System. From Lawrence to Topeka the road is still in the Kansas Valley, through a veritable garden. Native trees of great height overhang the railway here and there, and in the spring and summer the crops look green and luxuriant. The approach to Topeka is through the long yards, and by the vast machine shops of the Santa Fe Company, across various broad streets to a commodious brick station.

The general offices of the road are in Topeka.

and occupy a handsome and commodious building near the State capitol. From Topeka to Denver the Santa Fe Route runs for about seventy-five miles in a southwesterly direction to the upper waters of Neosho River, at Emporia, passing through Osage County, where are found some of the richest coal fields of the West. At Newton the line diverges south through Southern Kansas, the Indian Territory and Texas to Galveston; continuing west from Newton the first city of importance reached is Hutchinson; here are some of the heaviest salt works in the United States, besides other extensive manufacturing interests. West of Hutchinson the line extends through a fertile, prosperous and rapidly growing district. The line is beautified here and there by many thriving cities and villages. At La Junta, in Colorado, the line for New Mexico, Arizona and beyond, turns south. Pueblo, sixty-five miles due west of La Junta, for years the terminus of the Santa Fe System, is a growing manufacturing city. It is admirably located with reference to the great ore-producing cañons of Colorado. All roads leading to it, coal, iron, silver, gold, lead, copper, building stone, everything in fact which is produced in the greatest mining State in the Union, roll naturally down hill to Pueblo. Beyond Pueblo to the west are many thriving cities founded on mining and agriculture, notably; Leadville, the greatest mining camp in Colorado; while forty miles north, on the line of the Santa Fe, are the lovely villages of Colorado Springs, and Manitou, nestling at the foot of Pike's Peak. Manitou is at the mouth of a deep cañon, and is one of the most lovely summer resorts in America. Near here is the famous "Garden of the Gods," whose wondrous beauty and grandeur is unsurpassed. From Colorado Springs westward, through Manitou and up the cañon beyond Pike's Peak, the Colorado Midland Railway is pushing its way far toward the the western borders of the State. Eighty miles north of Colorado Springs the Santa Fe line terminates at Denver, a magnificently built city of nearly two hundred thousand people. It is probable that no American city has so many features of unique beauty as Denver. Its splendid public buildings, and its broad avenues lined with beautiful residences, cozily located at the foot of the snow-capped mountains of the Rocky range, render it unlike any other city of its size in the world. The ride from Pueblo to Denver along the foot of the mountains is one never to be missed. The snow-covered peaks, the many combinations of sun and cloud, and rain and snow; the marvelous atmosphere, all combine to surprise and charm the beholder.

From Newton to Galveston, the line leaving the main east and west line in Kansas at Newton, runs directly south to Galveston. The first place of importance reached is the phenomenal city of Wichita, located on the Big and Little Arkansas Rivers, a city of thirty-five thousand people, where only a few years ago was an Indian trading-post. Wichita is one of the most remarkable cities in the West. It has a heavy and growing wholesale trade, and a large amount of manufacturing business, including the Burton Stock Car Works, the Dold & Whitaker Meat-Packing establishments. The city is handsomely laid out, and has many handsome public buildings, commodious business houses and spacious residences, situated on broad avenues, lined with beautiful shade trees. South of Wichita is a cluster of growing cities, comprising Winfield, Wellington, Arkansas City and Caldwell. Wichita and Arkansas City have profited much by the opening up of Oklahoma to settlement. Entering the Indian Territory the line passes through a magnificent agricultural country, as yet almost wholly undeveloped. In Texas the principal cities on the line between the Indian Territory and Galveston, are Gainesville, Paris, Ft. Worth, Cleburne, Dallas, Morgan, Temple, Brenham, Houston and Richmond. Galveston, the terminus, is a rapidly growing city of fifty thousand inhabitants. It is charmingly situated on the Gulf Coast, and has an unsurpassed climate in both summer and winter.

From La Junta to El Paso, the line leaving La Junta climbs to the summit of the Raton Range, seventy-six hundred and twenty-two feet above the sea. On the way up it passes through the important Colorado towns of El Moro and Trinidad. The village of Raton is an important division point for the railway, and then comes Las Vegas and its famous hot springs, six miles distant from the main line, but connected with it by a short line with good equipments. At the Hot Springs is the Phenix Hotel. The springs are unsurpassed anywhere in the world, and the hotel is conducted by the company in the most generous manner imaginable. The springs are forty-two in number, and are hot and cold, and have a variety of mineral properties which render them remarkably strong in their curative power. South of Las Vegas the line passes through fertile valleys, heavy forests, and black and rugged canons, until the valley of the Rio Grande is reached. A branch line from Lamy extends up the mountain to Santa Fe, the capital of New Mexico, next to St. Augustine, the oldest city in America. Santa Fe has a new State House, and its quaint old churches and dwellings are interspersed with modern structures. It should be seen before the peculiar charm of its antiquity has been entirely destroyed. Albuquerque, Socorro and San Marcial are the chief points between Santa Fe and El Paso. All are important points for the business of mining, cattle raising and general commerce. From Rincon a branch line leads to Deming, where junction is made with the Southern Pacific Railway, and to Silver City, and to the other mining towns of Southern New Mexico. It is the fortunate destiny of New Mexico generally, and the Rio Grande Valley particularly, to soon take front rank in the line of fruit production. The grapes produced in the Lower Rio Grande Valley are not surpassed in either quality or quantity by the product of any part of the Continent.

From Albuquerque to the Pacific Coast, in the heart of New Mexico, due west, the Atlantic & Pacific Railroad forms the main Santa Fe Route to California. The line passes through a great mining and stock-raising country, where the climate is perfect. Prescott, the capital of Arizona, is reached by a branch from Prescott Junction. Constant changes of scenery characterize the line, and the crossing of the Colorado Canon is one of the most remarkable accomplishments known in the railroad world. In Southern California the lines of the California Central & Southern reach every important city. Barstow, San Bernardino, Colton, San Diego, National City, Los Angeles, and a hundred other beautiful towns offer unequaled inducements to the seeker after health, wealth and pleasure.

San Francisco and other cities of Central and Northern California are reached by the lines of the Southern Pacific by virtue of a special arrangement for traffic. Between Chicago and Kansas City meals are served on the finest dining cars; on the other lines and branches are superb eating-houses and hotels. No expense is spared in securing elegant accommodations; the supplies are secured from the best markets East and West.

From the resume thus given of the facilities possessed by the Santa Fe Railway, for interchanging traffic at its termini and various junctions, it must be apparent to the reader that the line is admirably situated, and that in many respects it occupies a strategic position, superior to that of other trans-Missouri and Mississippi railroads. These advantages have been utilized in the past, as they will be in the future, in developing the localities through which the various branches extend, and to build up the permanent prosperity of the property whose history is so closely interwoven with the settlement, development and prosperity of the West beyond the Missouri River. Its local traffic compares favorably with that of other competing lines. To this purely local traffic must be added the contributions of its several termini, all large cities and prominent trade centers in the Missouri and Mississippi Valleys. With the growth and steady development of the manufacturing and other industries of Chicago, Kansas City, St. Joseph, Atchison, Leavenworth, Topeka, Wichita, Galveston, El Paso, Pueblo and Denver, the Santa Fe Railway must materially make corresponding strides toward attaining that proud financial position which has been the life dream of its originators and present owners. Under the present progressive and conservative management, all advantages of geographical position, and all the resources of the through line will be constantly utilized in building up the future prosperity of the road itself, and in developing the extended area of Chicago's commercial supremacy. The Land Grant from the Government amounted substantially to three million acres. In brief its commanding geographical position, coupled with its direct Eastern alliance for through business, must render the Santa Fe eventually one of the most remunerative of our Western railroads.

SUMNER COUNTY,

KANSAS.

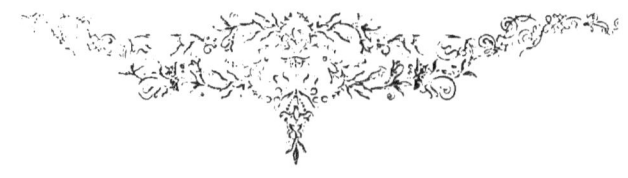

INTRODUCTORY.

THE time has arrived when it becomes the duty of the people of this county to perpetuate the names of their pioneers, to furnish a record of their early settlement, and relate the story of their progress. The civilization of our day, the enlightenment of the age and the duty that men of the present time owe to their ancestors, to themselves and to their posterity, demand that a record of their lives and deeds should be made. In biographical history is found a power to instruct man by precedent, to enliven the mental faculties, and to waft down the river of time a safe vessel in which the names and actions of the people who contributed to raise this country from its primitive state may be preserved. Surely and rapidly the great and aged men, who in their prime entered the wilderness and claimed the virgin soil as their heritage, are passing to their graves. The number remaining who can relate the incidents of the first days of settlement is becoming small indeed, so that an actual necessity exists for the collection and preservation of events without delay, before all the early settlers are cut down by the scythe of Time.

To be forgotten has been the great dread of mankind from remotest ages. All will be forgotten soon enough, in spite of their best works and the most earnest efforts of their friends to perserve the memory of their lives. The means employed to prevent oblivion and to perpetuate their memory has been in proportion to the amount of intelligence they possessed. The pyramids of Egypt were built to perpetuate the names and deeds of their great rulers. The exhumations made by the archeologists of Egypt from buried Memphis indicate a desire of those people

to perpetuate the memory of their achievements. The erection of the great obelisks were for the same purpose. Coming down to a later period, we find the Greeks and Romans erecting mausoleums and monuments, and carving out statues to chronicle their great achievements and carry them down the ages. It is also evident that the Mound-builders, in piling up their great mounds of earth, had but this idea—to leave something to show that they had lived. All these works, though many of them costly in the extreme, give but a faint idea of the lives and characters of those whose memory they were intended to perpetuate, and scarcely anything of the masses of the people that then lived. The great pyramids and some of the obelisks remain objects only of curiosity; the mausoleums, monuments and statues are crumbling into dust.

It was left to modern ages to establish an intelligent, undecaying, immutable method of perpetuating a full history—immutable in that it is almost unlimited in extent and perpetual in its action; and this is through the art of printing.

To the present generation, however, we are indebted for the introduction of the admirable system of local biography. By this system every man, though he has not achieved what the world calls greatness, has the means to perpetuate his life, his history, through the coming ages.

The scythe of Time cuts down all; nothing of the physical man is left. The monument which his children or friends may erect to his memory in the cemetery will crumble into dust and pass away; but his life, his achievements, the work he has accomplished, which otherwise would be forgotten, is perpetuated by a record of this kind.

To preserve the lineaments of our companions we engrave their portraits, for the same reason we collect the attainable facts of their history. Nor do we think it necessary, as we speak only truth of them, to wait until they are dead, or until those who know them are gone; to do this we are ashamed only to publish to the world the history of those whose lives are unworthy of public record.

Whitfield Townsend

BIOGRAPHICAL.

HITFIELD TOWNSEND, whose portrait is presented on the opposite page of this volume, was one of Sumner County's well-known men. He was the owner of a fine estate in Wellington Township, which during his residence upon it of about seven years he developed from an unbroken tract of prairie land to a fine condition, erecting upon it a large frame dwelling, adequate barns and other necessary buildings; he further added to its value by planting an orchard, and in various ways embellishing it. Mr. Townsend was born in St. Clair County, Ill., October 24, 1823, and was a son of George Whitfield Townsend, who is supposed to have been born in Tennessee, from which State he removed to Illinois, becoming a pioneer of St. Clair County. There he bought a large tract of land and carried on the pursuit of agriculture quite extensively, continuing to abide in that county until his death. He of whom we write was reared and educated there, the school which he attended being held in a log house, with a fire-place and home-made furniture, the seats made by splitting logs, hewing them to a tolerably smooth surface on one side, and inserting wooden pins in the other side for legs. In this temple of learning, under the instruction of teachers whose curriculum comprised little else than the "three R's," he acquired all the education possible to be obtained, and developed the sturdy nature befitting the son of a pioneer.

Mr. Townsend assisted his father on the farm and resided with his parents until their death, and for a time thereafter continued to live on the old homestead. He then located on land adjoining it, added a kitchen to the small house that was already on the place, and made other improvements as rapidly as possible. In 1880, renting the farm, which is still owned by his family, he came to this county, where he had previously purchased three hundred and twenty acres of prairie land, comprising the west half of section 19, in Wellington Township. When he took possession the only improvements consisted of a small house and straw stable, but these were soon replaced by more substantial structures. On this now beautiful estate, which he brought to a high state of cultivation, Mr. Townsend breathed his last January 20, 1887, deeply mourned by a large circle of friends and acquaintances, to whom his high moral and Christian character had endeared him. In the family circle he had been a loving companion and parent, and here his loss was still more deeply felt.

Mr. Townsend was twice married. His first wife, Jane Bradsby, so far as known, was a native of Illinois. She died on the home farm in St. Clair County, fifteen months after her marriage, leaving no children. The second matrimonial alliance of Mr. Townsend was contracted March 18, 1866, the bride being Mrs. Annie (Huseman) Cook. She was born in Bielefeld, in the Westphalen district of Minden, Prussia. Her father, Henry Huseman, was a native of the same place, and there followed the occupation of farming until his death, in 1845. The wife of Henry Huseman bore the maiden name of Wilhelmina Westerbeck, and was a native of the same locality, where she was reared by strangers, having been left an orphan at an early age. On the death of her husband she was left with four children to care for, and a few years later started with three of her brothers to America. While on board a Mississippi River steamer she was attacked with cholera and died, her remains, together with those of one of her brothers, being taken ashore and buried on the banks of the river. The surviving brothers—Phillip and Albert—settled in Burlington, Iowa. This was in 1853. Mrs. Townsend found a home with a family named Damke, in St. Louis, for a year and a half, and then spent six years with the family of Maj. Walker in the same city.

In that city, in 1861, Annie Huseman was united in marriage with Herman Cook, a teamster by occupation and a native of Germany. After their marriage they removed to St. Clair County, Ill., where Mr. Cook rented a farm, and where he departed this life in 1865. His widow later became the wife of our subject. To Mr. and Mrs. Townsend came five children—Thadis S., the first born, was with them only from December 17, 1869, to July 19, 1872; Virginia, James, Whitfield and Annie are still spared to their widowed mother. Mrs. Townsend possesses many womanly qualities and virtues of character, and is displaying good judgment in the management of her worldly affairs and the rearing of the fatherless ones who are left to her care. She is a member of the Christian Church, with which she united at the age of twenty-one years, and in which her late husband was an Elder for many years.

GEORGE G. HUMPHREYS. The life of this gentleman affords an excellent representation of the success that attends on energy and perseverance, and of the reputation which may be gained by an upright life and a steadfast character, without becoming famous, or having

one's name spread broadcast over the world. The influence of these quiet lives is that to which our country owes its greatest debt of gratitude, in the example set before the young, as well as in the personal deeds.

Born in Champaign County, Ohio, February 16, 1825, Mr. Humphreys has spent many years in agricultural work, has participated in the pioneer work of development, and with but limited educational advantages in his boyhood, has kept himself well informed regarding general topics and current events. He has also won an honorable record in the ranks of his country's defenders during the attempt to destroy the Union. His parents, Thomas and Nancy Humphreys, took up their abode in Champaign County, Ohio, when that section of the country was very new and sparsely settled. There the early years of our subject were passed, and while acquiring a limited education in the subscription schools, which he attended only during the winter seasons and which he abandoned entirely when about fourteen years old, he assisted the other members of the family in the development of his father's farm.

The first marriage of Mr. Humphreys was celebrated in March, 1846, his chosen companion being Miss Mary Howver, a native of the Buckeye State, who shared his fortunes until December, 1855, when she was called from time to eternity. She bore two children: Cornwell, deceased, and Nancy J., the wife of Joseph Piatt of Wellington. Mr. Humphreys contracted a second matrimonial alliance, taking as his companion Mrs. Mary Howver, nee Gleason. She was the widow of Peter Howver, a native of Champaign County, Ohio, who was born in 1828, reared in his native State, and married in 1847. To him she bore two children—Lydia, the wife of Thomas Berkley of Vermilion County, Ill., and William, who resides with our subject.

Mrs. Humphreys is the daughter of Arah Gleason, a native of New York. He married Lydia Safford, a native of the same State. She bore her husband twelve children, named as follows: Amanda M., is deceased; Mary M.; Martha is deceased; Phebe lives in Champaign, Ill.; James, Lydia, Nathaniel R., an infant son who died unnamed, and Minnie, all deceased; Lorinda lives in Filer City, Mich.; Charles is a minister of the Congregational Church, now located in Angola Ind.; and George is a farmer in Holt County, Neb. Arah Gleason died at the home of our subject the 2d of June, 1870, aged seventy years, having been born June 5, 1800. Mrs. Lydia Gleason departed this life June 11, 1886, aged nearly eighty-one years, she was born August 2, 1805.

Mr. Humphreys enlisted in the Federal army August 12, 1862, placing his name upon the muster-roll of Company B, Ninety-fourth Illinois Infantry, and becoming an integral part of the Western army. He took part in the battles at Springfield, Prairie Grove, Van Buren, the siege of Vicksburg, Red River, Algiers, Brownsville, (Texas), Fts. Morgan, Gaines, Spanish and Blakeley, the siege of Mobile, and others of minor importance. He was honorably discharged August 29, 1865, and returned to DeWitt County, Ill., in which he had resided prior to his gallant service in the army. Some time subsequently to the war he lived in Vermilion County, Ill., three years. In 1878 he turned his footsteps westward with the determination to become a citizen of Kansas, and selecting this county as his place of abode, settled on the farm where he still resides. It is located in Belle Plaine Township and comprises a quarter of section 23; has been brought to a high state of cultivation and affords its owner a comfortable subsistance. When he took possession of it, it was in an almost primitive condition, the only improvement having been the breaking of thirteen acres of the sod. Its present fine condition and the improvements of various kinds which it bears, are a standing monument to the efforts of Mr. Humphreys.

Both Mr. and Mrs. Humphreys belong to the Methodist Episcopal Church at Belle Plaine, and the former has served as Steward of the organization. It is a matter of course that he belongs to the G. A. R. Post.

The father of our subject was a native of Ireland, who, upon emigrating to America in 1792, settled in Erie County, Pa., whence he afterward removed to Ohio. He belonged to a long-lived race and himself lived to be one hundred and twelve

years and six months old, dying in 1850. He was a soldier in the War of 1812. The mother of our subject was a native of Kentucky. She bore her husband six children, as follows: William, a resident of DeWitt County, Ill.; Elizabeth, wife of Patrick Gorman, of the same county; James, who lives in Ohio; our subject; Joseph H., of Baxter Springs, Kan., and an infant who died unnamed.

ON. T. A. HUBBARD. The Rome Park Stock Farm, located in Jackson Township, which has attained a reputation throughout Sumner County, is one of the most fitting monuments to the industry and perseverance of its proprietor with whose name we introduce this sketch. Mr. Hubbard makes a specialty of fine cattle, horses and hogs, in which he has met with unqualified success and he has done much to raise the standard of this industry in Southern Kansas. He may be properly called a self-made man—one who has been endowed by nature with fine abilities and who has been fortunate in choosing that wise course which has enabled him to increase his talent ten-fold.

The first eleven years of the life of Mr. Hubbard were spent in McKean County, Pa., near the town of Tarpert,and Centerville, Allegany County, N. Y., where his birth took place December 22, 1843. His father, Jeremiah Hubbard, was a native of Vermont as was also his paternal grandfather, Abner Hubbard. The first mentioned was reared among his native hills and when approaching manhood employed himself as a boatman on Lake Champlain. Later he followed the trade of a shoemaker. He finally left Vermont and settled in Cattaraugus County, N. Y., whence, later, he removed to Allegany County, purchasing a tract of land where he prosecuted farming until 1851. That year he emigrated to Michigan, settling in Barry County and securing land from the United States. He at once put up a frame house and proceeded to clear the farm, constructing a comfortable homestead upon which he spent the remainder of his days; he departed hence about

1863. The wife and mother, Mrs. Eliza (Sherman) Hubbard, was born in Connecticut and died in Barry County, Mich., about 1874. Of this union there were born three children. By a previous marriage Jeremiah Hubbard had become the father of seven children.

The subject of this sketch attained to manhood on a farm in the Wolverine State, obtaining a practical education in the common schools. Upon the outbreak of the Civil War he was only seventeen years old, but after watching the conflict for a time he resolved to assist in the preservation of the Union. On October 1, 1861, he enlisted in Company B., Thirteenth Michigan Infantry, first seeing the smoke of battle at Stevenson, Ala., in 1862. He was afterward a participant in all the battles fought by Gens. Rosecrans and Sherman until the close of the war. At Chickamauga, September 19, 1863, his company suffered almost annihilation, being reduced to four members. Young Hubbard was three times wounded and was conveyed to the hospital at Nashville, where he remained until his wounds permitted him to travel, when he was sent home on a furlough, remaining sixty days. He rejoined his regiment at Chattanooga, Tenn., and in January following veteranized and was granted a furlough. He returned home and assisted in recruiting a full regiment and afterward returning to Chattanooga performed engineer duty until the fall of 1864.

Mr. Hubbard's regiment was now sent to Nashville to assist in driving Gen. Forrest from Tennessee, and he later joined Sherman's army at Rome, Ga., going from there on the famous march to the sea. His regiment was in the rear and burned the bridges over the Chattahoochie River, thus severing the connection and cutting off all communication of Gen. Sherman's army with the outside work. After this long tedious march was ended by the capture of Ft. McAllister and Savannah, the army went into camp for a brief rest. They then started on the march through the Carolinas, the most remarkable winter campaign on record. Young Hubbard said the general order was reveille at 4:30 A. M., march at 6, one day's rations for five days and live off the country, and forty rounds of cartridges in the cartridge box. Railroads were destroyed and the country stripped of nearly everything on which an army could subsist, consequently the boys in blue found their lines cast in anything but pleasant places, yet manfully, and on the whole cheerily, they marched along "shouting the battle cry of freedom."

At Bentonville, N. C., the Fourteenth Corps met the gallant Joe Johnston and were threshed unmercifully, but the Union army soon got into position and after three days hard fighting, Sherman was victorious in the last great battle of the war. Mr. Hubbard says that he escaped without a scratch but did some tall running. The army then marched to Goldsboro, where the boys got their first mail for sixty days. There also they heard the general order of Gen. Sherman which was for rest and a supply of stores from the rich granaries of the North. After a short rest they marched to Raleigh, soon after which Johnston surrendered. Then followed the famous march to Richmond, Va., then to Washington, D. C., and participation in the Grand Review, after which the corps was transported back to Louisville, Ky., where it went into camp. Young Hubbard was promoted to be First, or Orderly Sergeant, and after a season of rest, camp duty and drill he was mustered out, July 25, 1865, and returned to his old haunts in Michigan, receiving his honorable discharge at Jackson, August 10.

Mr. Hubbard purchased his father's old farm in Yankee Spring Township, Barry County, Mich., during the War and lived upon it until 1872. That year he came to Kansas to visit friends in Marion County and while here explored the surrounding country. Emigrating finally into Sumner County he resolved to purchase land and selected the northwest quarter of section 26, in what is now Jackson Township. On the 4th of July, that year, he filed his claim in the general land office at Wichita and the following year July 5, 1873, secured his title to the land. He settled upon it a few months later and lived there for a number of years. Wichita, for some years was his nearest market and to that point he hauled his grain residing upon that farm until 1880. In the meantime Mr. Hubbard had become quite prominent in local affairs and after filling other positions of trust and responsibility was selected Register of Deeds, which necessitated his removal to Wellington, January 1880. He resided there until the March of 1889, then returned to his farm of eight hundred acres. In the meantime he had retained the management of this and in 1882 commenced the breeding of Poland-China swine, becoming interested the following year in Berkshires. He now (1889) has a herd of probably four hundred head of full blooded animals of both kinds and is said to be the second largest breeder of swine in the United States. He has been in the habit of carrying off the blue ribbons at the State and County Fairs in which he has competed with the best herds west of the Mississippi. He secured the general sweepstake prize for the best herd of swine of any age or breed at two of the Kansas State Fairs and the same at the Bismarck Fair. He likewise received the first prize at the State Fairs at Lincoln, Neb., and at the Fairs in Kansas City and St. Louis, Mo., in several classes. He also gives much attention to the breeding of Shorthorn cattle, of which he has two hundred and fifty head of high-grade Kentucky Short-horns and he has twenty-four head of graded Percheron horses. It cannot be denied that the live stock interests of the Sunflower State have been greatly augmented by the labors and efforts of Mr. Hubbard.

The subject of this sketch was married November 3, 1869, at the bride's home in Michigan to Miss Almira I. Barto. Mrs. Hubbard was born in Kalamazoo County, Mich., February 1, 1849, and is the daughter of Orin Barto, a native of Hinesburg, Vt. Her paternal grandfather, David Barto, was a native of France and upon coming to America settled in Vermont. In that State David Barto was reared to manhood and prosecuted farming there until 1854. That year he emigrated to Michigan, locating in Kalamazoo County, where he spent the remainder of his life. He married Miss Polly Stevens, whom it is supposed was likewise a native of the Green Mountain State. After the death of her husband, Grandmother Barto went to Montana to visit her children and died there. The father of Mrs. Hubbard was reared and married in the Green Mountain State where he lived until about 1831 and then emigrated to

Michigan during the earliest settlement of Kalamazoo County. He journeyed by Lake Champlain and the Champlain Canal, then by the Erie Canal and the lakes to Detroit, whence he proceeded the balance of the journey by team. He purchased a tract of timber land when bear, deer and wolves were plentiful, and constructed a good farm which he occupied until 1865. That year, selling out, he removed to Barry County where he purchased a farm upon which he resided until the death of the wife and mother, about 1881. Afterward he made his home with his children until his death, which took place at the home of his daughter in Mecosta County, in January, 1882.

The mother of Mrs. Hubbard bore the maiden name of Esther Averill. She was born in Vermont and was the daughter of Truman Averill, likewise a native of the Green Mountain State and who emigrated to Kalamazoo County, Mich., as early as 1829. He was thus among the first settlers of that region. He possessed all the hardy elements of the pioneer and improved a farm from the wilderness, where he spent the remainder of his days. Mrs. Esther (Averill) Barto departed this life October 17, 1884.

The Republican party has received the cordial endorsement of Mr. Hubbard since he became a voting citizen. He has kept himself well informed upon current events and while a resident of Michigan was Clerk of Yankee Springs Township for a period of six years. Upon coming to Kansas he served the people of Jackson Township as Road Overseer one year and Trustee of said township two terms, and in 1875 was elected to the State Legislature, serving to such good purpose that he was returned in 1876. While a member of the General Assembly he was on various important committees, including Ways and Means, and Railroads, and was Chairman of the committee on Roads and Highways. He voted every time for nine days for Mr. Plumb for United States Senator. He was elected Register of Deeds in 1879 and re-elected in 1881. He served as a delegate to numerous State and county conventions and in 1889 was a delegate to the third Deep Harbor Convention which met at Topeka. Socially he belongs to Wellington Lodge, No. 150, F. & A. M., Sumner

Chapter No. 37, R. A. M., St. John Commandery, No. 24, K. T., Wellington Lodge, No. 24, A. O. U. W., and James Shield Post, January, 1890, the President appointed Mr. Hubbard Supervisor of Census for the Fourth District in Kansas, about one-fourth part of the State. Mr. Hubbard has about eight hundred or one thousand appointments to make in his district.

AMES R. GIDEON. The home of this gentleman and his family is pleasantly located on section 22, Belle Plaine Township, of which he is quite an early settler. He now owns three hundred and twenty acres of valuable land, in the accumulation of which he has been ably assisted by his devoted wife, who shared in all the hardships of their early years in the West, and who with him is now enjoying the fruit of useful and industrious lives, the respect of all who know them, and the devotion of their children.

Mr. Gideon was born in Loudoun County, Va., December 28, 1828, to Henry and Nancy (Miller) Gideon, who were natives of the same county, and of German ancestry. His grandfather, Peter Gideon, was a soldier in the Revolutionary War, and his uncle, George Gideon, took part in the war of 1812. To his parents eleven children were born, of whom all survive save David, the ninth on the family roll. Jacob lives in Hall County. Neb.; Alfred, in Macon County, Ill.; Joseph, in Muscatine County, Iowa; Ann, the wife of Samuel Garvey, in Sangamon County, Ill.; Peter, in Hall County, Neb.; Valentine and Sanford, in Omaha, Neb.; Mary E., the wife of Andrew Bennett, in Madison County. Iowa; and Oliver, in Hall County, Neb.

While still a small infant James R. Gideon accompanied his parents in their removal to Champaign County, Ohio, where they were among the early settlers, taking up their abode there while wild hogs and bears and Miami Indians were still numerous in the region. The parents endured such hardships as fell to the lot of Ohio pioneers, and the boyhood of our subject was passed amid frontier scenes. When he was fourteen years old the family emigrated to Sangamon County, Ill., where he was reared to manhood. His entire boyhood and youth having been spent where there were no free schools, and where all educational work was kept up by subscriptions, he had not the advantages afforded the youth of this day and age, but acquired what knowledge he could under the circumstances which surrounded him, and added to his information by reading in later years.

In the spring of 1873, Mr. Gideon with his family, which at that time comprised his wife and four children, removed to Sumner County, Kan., and settled on the farm which they still occupy. Fourteen acres of the quarter section on which he located was broken ground, and a 12x14 foot house, made of planks, was the only other improvement. He has not only well improved the acreage of which he first took possession, but has added to his landed estate, and successfully carried on his agricultural work.

A quarter of a century ago, on September 20, 1864, the rites of wedlock were celebrated between Mr. Gideon and Miss Catherine Blue. She is of Irish descent in both her paternal and maternal lineage, and a daughter of Robert and Martha (Blue) Blue, both of whom were natives of Kentucky. Her paternal grandfather is supposed to have been a Revolutionary soldier. Her parents were early settlers in Menard County, Ill., where her birth occurred September 1, 1846. The family circle of which she made one comprised seven children, five of whom still live. One died in infancy, and Elizabeth in mature years; Eliza is the wife of Edward Vaughn, of Christian County, Ill.; John lives in Springfield, Ill.; Emily is the wife of Anthony Kinnamon, of Macon County, Ill.; and Nancy, the wife of Hiram Hendrix, of Nebraska.

Eleven children have come to bless the union of Mr. and Mrs. Gideon, and nine still live: Anne is the wife of Robert Nugent, of Belle Plaine Township, this county; and Martha, the wife of Julius Bender, also of this county; Peter, Minnie, Oliver, Mabel, Edward, Ettie and Katie still linger under the parental roof-tree. Mr. Gideon is a believer in the principles of the Democratic party, and therefore casts his vote in its favor. For several years he has served on the School Board of his district, and evinces an interest in educational matters, and in all other movements which tend to elevate and improve society and forward the interests of the community.

GEORGE RINEHART, a prosperous farmer of Jackson Township, owns two hundred and forty acres of good land on sections 22 and 23; one hundred and sixty acres on the former, and eighty on the latter section. His entire farm is under high cultivation, is well improved and stocked, and fully supplied with all necessary buildings. His family residence, barns and other buildings are all frame structures, erected in a tasty and substantial manner, and are a credit to his enterprise. His success in his chosen vocation is owing to his unremitting energy and intelligent adaptation of necessary means to secure the desired results. He holds a high place in the neighborhood as a man and friend, and is entirely worthy of the esteem which he receives from all who have the pleasure of his acquaintance.

David Rinehart, father of our subject, was born in Pennsylvania, it is thought in Northumberland County. His father, Valentine Rinehart, was a native of Pennsylvania, and thence removed to Ohio while the latter State was in the first stage of its settlement. They crossed the mountains in wagons drawn by horses, and wound slowly along through the almost trackless forests till they reached their destination in the county of Stark, where they were among the very first settlers. Upon his arrival in the county he took up a tract of Government land, a portion of which was heavily timbered and the rest oak openings. It was hard work clearing the land, but he persevered until he had a nice farm, upon which he lived till he fell asleep to awake in that land where the inhabitants never grow weary or faint with the toil which is the common lot of man on this sphere.

The father of our subject was eighteen years of age when he accompanied his parents to Ohio. He remained under the parental roof till he married and set up in housekeeping for himself. Following his marriage he removed to Carroll County, Ohio, where he bought a tract of heavily timbered land, which he proceeded to clear and fit for agricultural purposes. His first care, however, was to build a house, which he constructed out of logs. It was only a humble cabin, but it sheltered a noble heart, fired with the resistless spirit of progression, which has made the American name famous over the whole world. Mr. Rinehart split puncheon for the floor of his little cot, and constructed a chimney out of earth and sticks. This lowly abode was the birthplace of the subject of this sketch, and in that vicinity he grew to manhood.

Timber was of no appreciable value in that part of the country during the youth of George Rinehart, consequently they rolled large logs together and burned them to get them out of the way. Diligent labor on the part of the father of our subject was rewarded with a fair measure of success, and he was soon enabled to abandon the "little old log cabin" for a substantially built two-story house of hewn logs in which he passed the greater part of his life. There were no railroads in that neighborhood during the youth of our subject, and they were obliged to carry all their produce to the town of Bolivar, on the Ohio Canal. In 1883 David Rinehart sold his farm, but purchased another in the same township, where he removed and resided till his death, April 7, 1886. The maiden name of the mother of our subject was Elizabeth Snyder. She was born in Pennsylvania, and is a daughter of John Snyder. She is an estimable woman, and still lives on the homestead in Rose Township, Carroll County, Ohio. The union of Mr. and Mrs. David Rinehart resulted in the birth of six children, of whom four survive, and are named as follows: George, Sarah A., Valentine and James H.

The subject of this sketch was born in Rose Township, Carroll County, Ohio, March 6, 1835. He was reared in his native township, and received such education as was afforded by the schools of his district. There were no free schools in his neighborhood in those days, and the people were obliged to maintain such centers of education as they desired at their own expense. The first school that George attended was taught in a log building, heated by an open fireplace. He was an industrious youth, and early began assisting his father in clearing and cultivating his land. Upon reaching his majority he took to himself a wife in the person of Miss Harriet Walls. Their nuptials were celebrated March 18, 1856, and they went to housekeeping on eighty acres of land in Rose Township, which was given to Mr. Rinehart by his father, and which had a log house already built upon it. Mrs. Rinehart was a native of the same township as her husband. Her birth occurred October 17, 1835, and her active life was spent in her native place.

In 1863 Mr. Rinehart removed from Ohio to Kansas, locating in Sumner County, where he now resides. In the year following, on the 3d of September, his wife departed this life for a better, leaving four children to the care of their bereaved father. They were named respectively: Sarah E., David O., John E. and Hugh M. The second marriage of our subject took place October 19, 1865, to Miss Martha Emily Walters, a native of Coshocton County, Ohio, and daughter of George and Martha (Thompson) Walters. This union resulted in the birth of three children, whose names are Edward E., Walter O. and Emma A.

Mr. Rinehart was reared in the Lutheran Church, and Mrs. Rinehart was reared in the Presbyterian faith, but since taking up their residence in Sumner County they have both united with the Presbyterian denomination which worships at Rome. They are highly respected in the community for their many good qualities, and have a large circle of friends. Mr. Rinehart is a staunch Republican in politics, but does not usually take a very deep interest in purely political affairs.

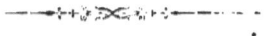

ALEXANDER CARNAHAN, Register of Deeds, Sumner County, although he has not resided in this county many years, has gained a high standing among her citizens, being known as a man of strict probity, varied knowledge, and more than ordinary culture. He was elected to the office which he now holds in 1889, at which time he removed to Wellington,

where he now makes his home. In politics he is a Republican, and is proud of the fact that he cast his first Presidential ballot for James A. Garfield.

The subject of this sketch was born upon land in Pennsylvania which his great-grandfather had entered from the Government, and where his father and grandfather were born and spent their lives. His grandfather was well known throughout Western Pennsylvania, and occupied many prominent and useful positions in his day. He served in the War of 1812 under Gen. Harrison. He was County Commissioner for a long term of years, being a member of the board when the location of the court house was decided; the ballot was a tie, and it fell to his lot to cast the deciding vote, which he did in favor of the present site. He also served as a member of the State Legislature with credit to himself and satisfaction to his constituents. He died in 1879 at the advanced age of ninety years. He was a member of the United Presbyterian Church. The maiden name of his wife was Nancy Smith. Unto them were born seven children, of whom but two are now living—George R., who resides on the old homestead, and David T., a prominent minister in the Presbyterian Church.

William Carnahan, the father of our subject, died in March, 1865, at the age of forty-three years. He was the father of eight children, one of whom was born after his own death. His widow was spared to see her family grow to womanhood and manhood, her death occurring March 16, 1887. She had fulfilled all her duties as a good Christian and devoted wife and mother, in a manner to call forth the highest praise.

The gentleman whose name introduces this biographical compendium opened his eyes to the light in Union Township, Allegheny County, Pa., February 28, 1852. He is the second son of his parents, and was left fatherless at the age of thirteen years. After taking a special course in the University of Pittsburg he concluded to try his fortunes in the West, and having journeyed as far as Illinois, spent a year in that State. He then came to Belle Plaine, Kan., during the winter and purchased a tract of wild land in Sedgwick County, which he improved, and upon which he resided until the spring of 1883. He then sold and removed to Sumner County, where he bought two hundred and forty acres, nearly all raw land. This he improved and made his home until his election to the office of register of deeds, being engaged in general farming and stock-raising, proving his ability as an agriculturist, and placing himself in a front rank among the farmers.

An important step in the life of Mr. Carnahan was taken in 1879, when he became the husband of Miss Emma Kimble. She is a native of Pickaway County, Ohio, the daughter of Solomon and Sarah Kimble, and is a woman of intelligence, refinement and fine character. She is a devoted member of the Presbyterian Church, as is her husband, and like him she holds a high position in the esteem of the community. Mr. and Mrs. Carnahan are the parents of three children who are living, and of one —Maggie A.,—who died when a year old.

LOUIS N. PHILLIPPI. Few men within the limits of Morris Township have attained to a better position through a course of industry and good management than the subject of this biographical outline, who is the owner of one of its finest farms, embracing three hundred and twenty acres on section 6. Mr. Phillippi is in possession of the true secret of comfort and profit, paying others to do his hard work and keeping out a close eye to the general management, noting the receipts and disbursements and knowing at all times where he stands financially. He is a man liberal and progressive in his ideas and one evidently who was born to make his mark in his community

The native place of our subject was in Westmoreland County, Pa., and the date of his birth July 16, 1834. He was the fourth in a family of six children born to John and Eve (Brant) Phillippi, both of whom were natives of the Keystone State, where they were reared and married and where they spent their entire lives. John Phillippi was a farmer by occupation and he likewise officiated as an exhorter in the United Brethren Church. He died at the old homestead in Westmoreland County in 1851. The mother survived her husband for a period of thirty-two years, remaining a widow and

departed this life at the age of eighty. The farm which the father secured in his early manhood is still in the family and considered one of the finest estates in Westmoreland County.

Young Phillippi acquired such education as was furnished by the common school and at the age of eighteen years started out for himself, engaging for about one year with a partner in the mercantile business. He was then broken up by the rascality of his partner, losing nearly all he had and assuming the debts of the concern, all of which he liquidated to the full extent. He continued in business for eleven years and was then burned out, with no insurance. He then moved to Stahlstown, continuing there also in the mercantile business for eleven years in all, and in the meantime traded a farm which he had purchased for a three story house, two lots and a stable. This also was destroyed by fire, and no insurance. In 1870 he removed to Wayne County, Ohio, and was in business there two years. Then pushing on further Westward he settled on a farm in Effingham County, Ill., where he sojourned four years.

Selling out then again, we next find Mr. Phillippi at Altamont, where he again associated himself with a partner and at the end of three years found himself again a loser, and forced to commence once more at the foot of the ladder. This brings Mr. Phillippi up to 1879, in which year he came to this State and settled in Ness County, where he sojourned five years, living in a sod house and was never able to raise a crop during the whole time. Finally, securing a small stock of notions and jewelry he packed them into trunks and traveled on the railroad from one town to another, disposing of his merchandise, and thus managed to clear $100 above expenses every month. After thus securing a sufficient sum of money he, in 1885, came to this county and purchased three hundred and twenty acres of partially improved land, embracing his present homestead. This last venture proved highly successful. He has now a well-developed farm which yields in abundance the rich crops of the Sunflower State and is also largely devoted to the breeding of cattle and swine.

While a resident of Pennsylvania Mr. Phillippi, in 1855, took unto himself a wife and helpmate,

Miss Mary, daughter of William and Jane (Grove) Weaver. Parents and daughter were natives of the same township in Pennsylvania as our subject. Mrs. Phillippi was born September 10, 1837, and was the eldest in a family of five children. The mother died April 16, 1887. Mr. Weaver is still living in Pennsylvania, being now past eighty years old. There have also been born five children to Mr. and Mrs. Phillippi, four of whom are living. John is a resident of Halstead, this State; Imelda, Edgar and Bertram are at home with their parents. The latter are members of the Methodist Episcopal Church in which Mr. Phillippi has been for many years a Class-Leader and Steward. He identified himself with the Masonic fraternity while a resident of his native State and at the present time belongs to the lodge at Argonia. For over fifteen years he has been a member in good standing of the A. O. U. W., holding various offices, and he also belongs to the Farmers' Alliance. He cast his first Presidential vote for John C. Fremont, at the organization of the Republican party and has since been an active supporter of its principles. After the outbreak of the Civil War he endeavored to enter the ranks as a Union soldier in the Two Hundred and Eleventh Pennsylvania Infantry, but was rejected on account of physical disability. He, however, was elected sutler and sent a man in his place. The latter robbed him of $4,000 worth of goods which had been purchased on thirty days' time.

ANTHONY WINDELL. Considering the limited amount of capital with which this subject of this notice commenced life in Kansas a few years since, his success has been almost phenomenal. This has only been brought about by the most unflagging industry and the exercise of good judgment, in addition to the practice of a close economy. He has now a well-improved farm in Morris Township, free from encumbrance, with convenient modern buildings and a very fine apple orchard, besides trees of the smaller fruits. The homestead is beautifully located, and is invariably an object of admiration to

all who pass by it. The proprietor is a man held in high respect in his community—a respect which he has earned by his straightforward dealings with his fellow-men.

The early tramping ground of Mr. Windell was in Harrison County, Ind., where he first opened his eyes to the light November 27, 1842. He was the tenth in a family of eleven children born to Anthony and Elizabeth (Cunningham) Windell, the father a native of the Shenandoah Valley, Va., and the mother born in Hardin County, Ky. Both went to Indiana with their respective parents early in life, and were there married. The father carried on farming in Harrison County, eliminating a good homestead from the wilderness, and departed this life in 1855. The mother survived her husband for a period of twenty-one years, remaining a widow and passing away in September, 1876. Anthony Windell, Sr., served in the Black Hawk War as Captain of the celebrated Yellow Jacket camp of Indians. Eleven of the children of the parental family are living.

Young Windell attended the common school during the winter seasons in his boyhood, and assisted his father on the farm until a lad of fourteen years. Then, starting out on his own account, he was employed on a farm until after the outbreak of the Civil War. In January, 1862, when a little over nineteen years of age, he enlisted as a Union soldier in Company B, Fifty-third Indiana Infantry, under the command of Col. W. Q. Gresham. They remained on duty at Indianapolis for a time, guarding prisoners, then repaired to Savannah and Corinth, and subsequently took part with Gen. Hurlbut's Division—the Seventeenth Army Corps—in the engagements which followed. Mr. Windell met the enemy at Hatchie's Run and the siege of Vicksburg, about which time his term of enlistment expired. He then veteranized, while on the Black River, near Vicksburg. Subsequently, while on a foraging expedition, he fell over a cliff and was seriously injured, so that he was obliged to accept his honorable discharge, in December, 1864, for disability.

Upon leaving the army, Mr. Windell returned to Indiana and resumed farming, sojourning there until 1875. He then removed to Texas and settled in Dallas County, but soon became dissatisfied with his surroundings, and we next find him in Cowley County, this State. He sojourned there also only a brief season, then coming to this county, located upon the land which he now owns and occupies. The outlook at that time was anything but encouraging, the land being as the Indians had left it. Mr. Windell first secured one hundred and sixty acres, to which he has since added, and has now three hundred and twenty acres, one hundred and ninety of which are under the plow. He has expended no small amount of time and hard cash in erecting his buildings, gathering together the necessary machinery and putting the farm in good running order. His orchard comprises fifty apple trees in good bearing condition, this alone being the source of a handsome income. Otherwise, he raises the usual crops of this region and also considerable live stock.

Mr. Windell was married in Harrison County, Ind., April 29, 1865, to Miss Emily C., daughter of Henry and Annie (Pennington) Sieg. Mrs. Windell was the third in a family of thirteen children, and was born in Indiana November 19, 1841. Her parents were natives respectively of Virginia and Indiana, to which latter State the father removed when a young man, and was there married. They were residents thereafter of Harrison County, where the father died in 1865. The mother is still living at the old homestead, and is now sixty-five years old.

Mrs. Windell acquired her education in the common school, and remained under the parental roof until her marriage. Twelve children have been born to this couple, ten of whom are living. Mary Madeline is the wife of John T. Johnson, a resident of Morris Township, this county, and they have one child; Anna Florence married Charles Holland, and they live on a farm in Morris Township; Elizabeth remains with her parents; Sarah is the wife of Samuel H. Brooks, of Harper County; Charles, Alice, Minnie, Ida, Amanda and Atta are at home with their parents. Mr. and Mrs. Windell are members in good standing of the Christian Advent Church. Mr. Windell belongs to the Farmer's Alliance, in which he officiates as Assistant Lecturer. He takes an interest in political af-

fairs and gives his support to the Republican party.

The maternal grandfather of Mrs. Windell was Dennis Pennington, a native of Tennessee, who emigrated to Indiana in time to assist in organizing the Territorial Government. He was a man of fine talents and executive ability, and was a member of the Indiana Legislature many years after it was admitted into the Union as a State. He married Miss Elizabeth English, a native of Kentucky, whose father was one of the earliest settlers of the Blue Grass State. Mr. English was murdered by Indians, who captured his wife and three children. The wife soon escaped with her youngest child, but Elizabeth and her brother were kept in captivity for a period of twelve years. Peace was then declared, and a treaty was made with the Indians by which they released all their white prisoners, and the two were thus returned to their friends. Mr. Windell, our subject, was one of six sons, three of whom entered the Union service during the Civil War, and John died, in 1862, at home; Washington was the Captain of Company F, Thirty-eighth Indiana Infantry.

When Mr. Windell came to Kansas he reached Wichita with a wife and six children and $5.50 in money. He hired an ox-team to break his prairie farm land, then returned to Cowley County and broke an equal number of acres for the owner of the oxen.

NTON WENGLER. The farmers of Oxford Township have a worthy representative in this gentleman, who in less than a decade has made of his estate one of the finest and most productive in the vicinity. That farm was purchased by him in 1880, and was but slightly improved at that time, and the one hundred and sixty acres which comprise it now bear a fine orchard, grove and hedges, a comfortable and substantial dwelling, and other adequate farm buildings.

Mr. Wengler was born in Madison County, Mo., March 16, 1850, and is the son of Anton and Catherine (Shumer) Wengler, natives of Germany, who settled in Missouri on coming to the United States, and there remained until the death of the father in 1872. Our subject was reared and educated at his native place, and his boyish eyes witnessed some of the ravages of the late Civil War. He was married January 27, 1876, to Miss Lizzie Emde, of Burlingham County, and continued to reside in Missouri until he came to this place.

The wife of Mr. Wengler was born August 22, 1855, and is a daughter of Henry and Mary Emde, who were natives of Germany, and identified themselves with the farming communities of Missouri upon coming to the United States. To Mr. and Mrs. Wengler five children have been born, all of whom are still spared to them. They bear the names of Catherine, John, Bertha, Lizzie and Mary, and it is the intention of the parents to give them the best advantages in the way of schooling, and such moral and practical training as shall fit them for useful lives.

An enterprising and energetic farmer, an intelligent and honorable man, and a reliable citizen, Mr. Wengler is respected by his neighbors, and his worthy wife shares in their esteem.

ASPER C. MANEE. There are few farms in Sumner County upon which the proprietors have labored to better advantage than that which is owned and occupied by the subject of this sketch. His well-tilled fields produce in abundance the rich crops of the Sunflower State, but Mr. Manee has made a specialty of fruit-growing, in which industry he excels. Upon coming to this county, in 1872, he purchased one hundred and sixty acres of land on section 7, Falls Township, and subsequently pre-empted one hundred and ten acres on section 6. In 1877 he re moved to his present quarters, where he has a neat and substantial residence, good outbuildings, an abundance of fruit and shade trees and all the other appliances of modern farm life.

Mr. Manee was born on Staten Island, N. Y., January 16, 1821, and is the son of Isaac and Maria (Cropsey) Manee, who were natives respectively of Staten Island and Long Island. The father

was a ship carpenter by trade and during his early manhood served as a soldier in the War of 1812, afterward receiving a pension. He spent his entire life on his native island. The paternal grandfather, Abraham Manee, was also born on Staten Island. His ancestors were of old Huguenot stock and were prominent people in their day among the early Colonists. Grandfather Cropsey was likewise a soldier in the Revolutionary War.

Mrs. Maria (Cropsey) Manee was the daughter of Harmonis Cropsey, whose ancestors came from Holland. Of her union with Isaac Manee there were born ten children, viz.: Harmon, Anna E., Abraham, Jasper C., Isaac, Harmon, 2d; Susan, Nicholas, Ellen J., and one who died unnamed in infancy. Jasper C., of this sketch, was the fourth child and was reared on his native island, attending school until a lad of fourteen years. He was unusually bright and ambitious and at an early age became anxious to start out in the world for himself. When leaving school he repaired to New York City and commenced serving an apprenticeship to the silversmith's trade with which he occupied himself until 1849. At that time the California gold excitement was attracting many young men to the Pacific Slope and Mr. Manee joined the caravan journeying thither, entering the mines, and engaged in searching for the yellow ore with fair success until 1855.

Six years of life in the extreme wild West sufficed to satisfy Mr. Manee and he gladly returned to his native place, but only to sojourn one year or less. He now found he could no longer content himself in the place of his birth or any where else in the East, and in 1856 he again set his face toward the Mississippi, which he crossed a second time, coming then to Jefferson County, this State, and taking up a homestead claim in Jefferson Township. About this time the border troubles commenced and Mr. Manee was one of the very few men who had the courage to maintain their position among the Indians and highway assassins who infested the country. In addition to the danger of an encounter with these, there were also many hardships to endure in endeavoring to develop a homestead and make a living.

Mr. Manee, however, stood his ground, remaining

RESIDENCE OF I. R. WINTERS, SEC. 9. CALDWELL TP, SUMNER CO. KAN.

a resident of Jefferson County until 1872 and becoming a prominent man in his community. He served as a County Commissioner several years and held the minor offices. Such was his course as a citizen, that he enjoyed the confidence and esteem of all who knew him and no man was more warmly interested in the welfare and advancement of his adopted county. However, in 1872, desiring a change of location and believing he could better himself in Sumner County, he removed hither.

During the progress of the Civil War Mr. Mance joined the Jefferson County militia and assisted in driving the rebel General Price from Independence. He is a Republican, politically, and during the times which tried men's souls he steadfastly maintained his loyalty to the Union. While a resident of New York City, Mr. Mance, on the 2d of August, 1846, was united in the bonds of wedlock with Miss Eliza J. Denton. Mrs. Mance was born in Connecticut in 1831, and when about eighteen years old removed with her parents to West Milton, N. J. Her union with our subject resulted in the birth of six children, and the mother died at the homestead in Jefferson County, Kan., in 1864. With the exception of an infant who died unnamed, the children were christened respectively: Harmon, Jasperena, Jessie, Avery, and Lucy. Three of these are living and making their homes in Caldwell.

Mr. Mance has a pleasant and commodious residence, which is represented by a fine view on another page of this work.

ISAAC R. WINTERS. A front rank among the farmers of Sumner County is occupied by the above named gentleman, and his assured position in financial circles has been accomplished by his own efforts and his wise use of the strength and ability bestowed upon him by nature. He has not only a high standing among farmers and fruit-growers, but enjoys a meritorious war record and a reputation for uprightness and Christian character which make it a special pleasure to represent him in this volume.

Before entering upon the sketch of the life of our subject, it may be well to devote a few lines to his progenitors. His father, John S. Winters, was born in the Green Mountain State, December 12, 1812, and in his boyhood was taken by his parents, Mr. and Mrs. Thomas Winters, to Preble County, Ohio. He entered the ministry of the United Brethren Church when twenty-one years of age, preaching his first sermon in Preble County, Ohio. In Darke County, Ohio, March 29, 1832, he was united in marriage with Miss Prudence, daughter of Nathaniel Harris. She was born in that county in 1813, and her death took place in 1886. About the year 1850 Elder Winters moved to Logansport, Ind., and preached in that vicinity until his death, in May, 1883. The parental family comprised nine children: Eli, Isaac R., Maria, John B., Marvin, Sophia, San Francisco, Theophilus R. and Elvira.

Isaac R. Winters was born in Preble County, Ohio, February 21, 1838, and passed the first twelve years of his life in his native county. From that time until 1871 his home was in Cass County, Ind., whence he removed to Kansas, and the following spring pre-empted one hundred and sixty acres on section 9, Caldwell Township; he immediately identified himself with the agriculturists and the better class of citizens of Sumner County. He has given all his time to general farming and fruit growing, improving his land and bringing it to a state of cultivation second to none in the vicinity. He is a member of the Farmers' Alliance and of the Christian Church.

In 1861 Mr. Winters determined to devote his energy to the preservation of the Union, and joining the army as a private in Company B, Forty-sixth Indiana Infantry, became an integral part of the Army of the Cumberland, having for his commanding officers three of the most noted generals in contemporaneous history—Logan, Sherman and Grant. Although he participated in struggles on many a hard-fought field, he fortunately escaped wounds and retained such excellent health that he was never an inmate of the hospital. At New Madrid, Ruddles Point, St. Charles (Ark.), Ft. Pemberton, Ft. Gibson, Champion Hills, Siege of Vicksburg, Jackson (Miss.), Grand Coteau (La.) and Mansfield he bore the part of a brave soldier, as well as in the minor engagements and weary marches. Under all circumstances he manifested the same loyal and uncomplaining spirit, and the same determination that his share in the great conflict should be bravely borne. In November, 1865, he received his honorable discharge at Louisville, Ky., and once more resumed the peaceful occupations which had been interrupted by the call to arms.

In Cass County, Ind., October 14, 1868, the rites of wedlock were celebrated between Mr. Winters and Miss Mary E. McCoy. The bride was born in Pulaski County, Ind., July 19, 1816, and departed this life March 29, 1873. She had borne her husband three children: Amy, Frank P. and Harry P., the latter of whom died March 4, 1873, at the age of three months. On May 30, 1874, Mr. Winters was again married, taking as his companion Mrs. Sarah M. Malone, of Sumner County, widow of Ezekiel S. Malone. She is a daughter of Ezekiel V. and Icyphena (Marrs) Lisenby; her father was born in Washington County, Tenn., on February 14, 1808, and her mother in Monroe County, Ky., February 25, 1816. Mrs. Lisenby departed this life September 14, 1884; her husband still survives, and is making his home with our subject.

On another page of the ALBUM will be found a lithographic view of the residence of Mr. and Mrs. Winters.

JOSEPHUS W. FORNEY, State Senator for Sumner County, Twenty-eighth District, is a pioneer of Belle Plaine Township, and has for a number of years enjoyed a good legal practice in Belle Plaine. He is the possessor of an excellent education, his collegiate course having been due to his own efforts, and has thoroughly learned the principles of justice and equity.

Mr. Forney is of German and English ancestry, and needs to go back but three generations on the genealogical tree ere reaching Germany. His grandfather Forney was born in Maryland, but spent the greater part of his life in Guernsey County, Ohio, where he settled in 1814, and where John Forney, father of our subject, was born. The latter is still living there and is now well advanced in years. He married Miss Eliza Wilson, and to this union on September 26, 1841, a son was born, of whose history this sketch will give an outline.

Reared to manhood on a farm in his native county and State, he of whom we write received an elementary education in the district schools, and took up the profession of a teacher at the age of sixteen years. For nine winters he was occupied in the instruction of others and during this time he took the scientific course in Madison College at Antrim, Ohio, attending during the summer months and paying his tuition and other expenses with the money he earned in teaching. In 1858, he began the study of the law alone, continuing his reading in this way until 1861, when he entered the office of Col. J. D. Taylor, at Cambridge, Ohio, with whom he read between two and three years.

Mr. Forney was admitted to the Ohio State bar in 1863. In the winter of 1864 he re-enlisted, becoming a member of Company B, One Hundred and Eighty-fifth Ohio Infantry and receiving the commission of Lieutenant, which office he filled during the remainder of his service. The greater part of his second term of service was spent in post duty in various States, and he was honorably discharged in July, 1865, although not virtually released until the spring of 1866.

Returning to the Buckeye State, Mr. Forney engaged in the practice of his profession in Cambridge, until some time during the year 1867, when he opened an office in St. Charles, Iowa. After sojourning in that town until the spring of 1871, he came to Belle Plaine, since which time he has given this section the benefit of his legal knowledge and professional skill. The fall after his arrival here he pre-empted one hundred and sixty acres of land in Belle Plaine Township, comprising the northwest quarter of section 18, upon which he settled, being practically its first occupant as it was virtually bare of improvement. For ten years he made his home upon his farm but still attended to his legal duties—keeping an office in town.

In the fall of 1888 our subject was elected State

Senator for a term of four years, his practical knowledge of the life and needs of the agriculturist, and his forensic skill, alike fitting him for the position, and his constituents confidently expect their varied interests to be advanced through his instrumentality. Mr. Forney is a member of the A. F. & A. M. and has served as Secretary of the lodge. He also belongs to the G. A. R. Post at Belle Plaine and for two years was its Commander.

His political adherence is given to the Republican party. He and his wife are members of the Methodist Episcopal Church and endeavor to carry the principles of their faith into the details of their daily life.

His marriage took place July 3, 1870, and the lady in whom he found the traits of mind and character which he thought most desirable in a life companion, was Miss Sarah E. Ergenbright. She is a native of Clay County, Ind., and a daughter of William Ergenbright. The happy union has been blessed by the birth of six children—May, Nora, John, Lyda, James G., and Minnie, and the loving parents have been bereaved of the last named.

COL. GEORGE BURTON, Postmaster of Argonia, is what may be termed "a gentleman to the manor born," possessed of more than ordinary intelligence and that courteous bearing which wins for him friends wherever he goes. He comes of substantial Irish ancestry, and was born March 7, 1819, in the city of Dublin, where he spent the first thirteen years of his life. Then, equipped with only a limited education, he started out in the world for himself, embarking as cabin boy on an ocean vessel and from that time until 1842 his life was spent on the water—the sea and lakes. The next four years were occupied at various businesses and in 1846 he entered the volunteer service of the United States during the war with Mexico, being a member of Company G, Fourth Illinois Infantry, under Col. Ed. Baker. He served for one year and returned a Third Sergeant. He and ex-Gov. Richard Oglesby, who was then a Sergeant in Company K, frequently reported together.

He served under Gen. Taylor until a part of the army was ordered to join Gen. Scott, and he participated in the battles of Vera Cruz, Natural Bridge, Cerro Gordo and other minor engagements. Later he was under the command of Gen. Shields and under Division Commander, Gen. Twiggs.

Upon retiring from the service Mr. Burton repaired to Tazewell County, Ill., where he operated a sawmill until 1849. Being seized then with an attack of the California gold fever, he set out overland across the plains and worked in the mines until the fall of 1850. In returning home he went down the coast as far as Cape St. Lucas, where the vessel "Louisa Boston" was sunk in the harbor of Mazatlan, and he rode a mule from there to Durango, and finally succeeded in reaching home safely after being chased in Mexico by the Apache Indians. He now resumed sawmilling and was engaged in the mercantile business for probably two years. He in 1852, crossing the Mississippi, took up his abode in Decatur County, Iowa, where he operated as a general merchant three years and also engaged in farming. He became prominent in local affairs and was County Auditor for three years until the outbreak of the Civil War.

Watching the conflict which ensued with more than ordinary interest, Col. Burton in June, 1861, organized a military company in Leon, Iowa, of which he was elected Captain and which was assigned to the Fourth Iowa Infantry, under command of Col. Dodge. He fought at the battle of Pea Ridge, skirmishing all through Arkansas, was in the fight at Chickasaw Bayou, and then at Arkansas Post, Lookout Mountain, Mission Ridge, Ringgold, Ga., and Woodville, Ala. On the 2d of May, 1862, he was commissioned Lieutenant-Colonel of the Fourth Iowa Infantry. At the battle of Pea Ridge he was wounded by a canister shot through the left arm, and at Cherokee Station received a sabre cut in the left hand. He resigned his commission April 10, 1864, and returning to Iowa resumed the duties of a private citizen.

Col. Burton became well-known in the Hawkeye State and in 1869 was elected Auditor of Decatur County, which office he held three years. Later, for the same length of time he engaged in the livestock business, purchasing cattle in Indian Territory, and selling them in Iowa. In 1875 he settled on a farm near Mayfield, this county, where he sojourned until 1883, coming that year to Argonia and engaging in the mercantile business. He also began speculating considerably. On the 2d of April, 1888, he was appointed to the office of Postmaster, the duties of which have since occupied his time and attention until February 1, 1890.

In 1848, Col. Burton was united in marriage with Miss Jane Waring, who died in 1863, leaving no children. In 1865, the Colonel contracted a second marriage with Miss Martha S. Walton. This lady was born in Ohio and is the daughter of George and Martha Walton who spent their last days in Iowa. Of this union there were no children. Mrs. Burton was a very excellent lady and a member in good standing of the Methodist Episcopal Church. The Colonel takes an interest in politics, voting the straight Democratic ticket. He is Past Grand in the I. O. O. F., belongs to the Encampment, is a Knight of Pythias and a member of the Chapter in Masonry.

The father of our subject was John Burton, a native of Dublin, Ireland, and a manufacturer of cotton cloth. The mother bore the maiden name of Martha Whitehead and she also was born in Dublin. They came to America in 1833, settling in Cleveland, Ohio, and about 1842, removed to Bloomington, Ill. There the mother died in 1835 and the father in 1848. Only two of the five children born to them are living—G. B. and Eliza, now Mrs. Burnes, the latter being a resident of Leroy, McLean County, Ill.

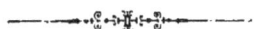

JOSEPH T. McCLUER is the owner and occupant of an excellent farm in Ryan Township, and is one of the best farmers in all the section roundabout. His industry has been unremitting, his energy unfailing, and all who know him rejoice in the success which is crowning his efforts to secure a competence. He came to this locality in the spring of 1878, preempted a tract of raw land, and with but seventy-

five cents in his pocket, began a struggle which only his love for his family, his self-respect, and his conscientious determination to do his best in the battle of life, made endurable. He was not able to bring his family here until late in the fall, after his own arrival, but he is now comfortably situated, with stock and all necessary farm tools and appliances, and freed from all but a slight incumbrance upon his property.

The father of our subject was born in Rockbridge County, Va., near the Natural Bridge. He was christened Samuel, and adopted the occupation of a farmer. He was married in Ohio in 1832, to Miss Hannah Sharp, who died in 1849, after having borne eleven children, five of whom are living. After the death of his wife Samuel McCluer removed to Illinois, settling in Peoria County, where he died August 16, 1859.

The subject of this sketch was the eighth in order of birth in the parental family, and first opened his eyes to the light in Adams County. Ohio, January 29, 1841. He received a common-school education, partly in his native State and partly in Illinois, and at the early age of thirteen began life for himself. He worked in the coal mines in Peoria and Fulton Counties, Ill., until his twenty-first year, when the breaking out of the Civil War aroused all the patriotic fervor and loyal devotion of his young heart, and he determined to devote the opening years of his manhood to his country's cause.

Enlisting in Company C, Forty-seventh Illinois Infantry, August 18, 1861, young McCluer was sent with his comrades to St. Louis to acquire his first instruction in army discipline and tactics in the barracks there. Thence they went to Otterville, Mo., thence to Island No. 10, to Pittsburg Landing, Corinth. Iuka, thence back to Corinth. on to Vicksburg, next entering the Red River expedition under Gen. Banks, and subsequently going to Mobile, Ala. Mr. McCluer participated in all these battles except that of Pittsburg Landing, where his command arrived the day after the contest. He also took part in the battle of Nashville under Gen. Thomas. At Corinth he was struck on the left arm by a minie ball, but was not disabled, and at Pleasant Hill, on the Red River, he had a very narrow escape from death, being knocked down by a ball which grazed the back of his neck. He enlisted as a private, and was promoted to the rank of Sergeant. At the expiration of his term of enlistment, when at Black River Bridge, Miss., he re-enlisted and served until February 22, 1865.

The short list of heavy engagements in which Mr. McCluer took part makes up a very small portion indeed of his army record, but all who are familiar with the history of the "irrepressible conflict," can readily fill in the details of experience spreading over a period of nearly four years. Especially can those who have witnessed the life in camp, who know the drill which is necessary in preparing for active campaigns, and the watchfulness and care that are ever required, appreciate the service rendered by those gallant men who, like our subject, were conscientious, brave and painstaking in every detail of a soldier's life.

When mustered out of the service Mr. McCluer returned to Peoria County, Ill., spending the summers in farming and the winters in working in the mines for a few years. The farm which he preempted in this county comprises one hundred and sixty acres of land, all improved and one hundred and ten acres under the plow. He has put on all the improvements, raises all the stock the farm will support, and now has thirty head of cattle, thirty of hogs and six horses. During the season of 1889 he raised thirty-five hundred bushels of corn on eighty-four acres, eleven hundred bushels of wheat on eighty acres, and eleven hundred bushels of oats on forty acres. With the grain he has raised and the sale of his soldier's claim in Garfield Township, he has paid off $1,200 indebtedness, and is now feeling quite comfortable in regard to the claims upon him. The dwelling in which the family resides was built in 1885. The next year he went to Garfield County, where he remained two years, securing his soldier's homestead.

In Illinois, August 16, 1866, Mr. McCluer was united in marriage with Mrs. Margaret Obarr, nee Bradley. She is a daughter of Thomas D. and Mary A. (Jordan) Bradley, natives of Mississippi, who removed to Tennessee, where the father died in 1861. Mrs. Bradley removed to Illinois two years later and settled in Fulton County, whence she came to Kansas in 1881. She is now living with our subject, and has reached the advanced age of seventy-five years. She is the mother of six children, the wife of our subject being the second in order of birth, and her natal day April 2, 1842. Mrs. McCluer was the recipient of a common-school education, is a lady of estimable character, and of many domestic virtues. She has borne her husband six children, five of whom are now living, named respectively: Lucy A., George W., Samuel D., and Oscar and Ernest (twins). The eldest daughter is a member of the Christian Church and Sunday-school, the parents also being active in the Sunday-school work, and members of the Church of Christ at Milan.

Mr. McCluer is a member of the Southern branch of the Farmers' Alliance. He is Treasurer of School District No. 23, and has been a member of the board since the district was organized. He has served as Road Overseer. He keeps himself posted in political matters, and now votes the Union Labor ticket; he was previously a Greenbacker. It is needless to state that he is highly esteemed by his fellow-citizens, among whom his character is above reproach.

———————

WILLIAM B. MALABY. This gentleman is prominent among the leading men of Springdale Township as an advanced advocate of the Union Labor movement, and one who keeps himself thoroughly posted upon the leading topics of the day, advocating progressive measures in all things as far as is wise and prudent. He has the honor of being one of the pioneer settlers of this county, becoming first a resident of Palestine Township. His native place was in Fayette County, Pa., and the date of his birth July 23, 1818. He was the eldest of the twelve children of his parents, ten of whom are living, making their homes mostly in Kansas.

George A. Malaby, the father of our subject, was a native likewise of the Keystone State, and occupied himself as a farmer and bricklayer. He was married in early manhood to Miss Esther A.

Johnson, a maiden of his own county, and they resided there until 1851. Then emigrating to LaSalle County, Ill., they lived there sixteen years, and next removed to Marshall County. After a three years' residence in the latter, they, in 1870, disposed of their property and transported themselves and their household goods across the Mississippi to Kansas, settling in this county. The father departed this life at his home in Palestine Township, August 1, 1878; the mother is still living at the old homestead, and is aged fifty-nine years.

The Malaby family removed to Illinois when William B. was a little lad six years of age. He attended school for a few winters thereafter, and at the age of twenty years commenced farming on his own account. He came to Kansas in 1870, settling in this county on the 7th of August, when there was not a woman within its limits, and when the Osage Indians mostly owned and occupied the land. Herds of buffalo roamed over the prairie, and Mr. Malaby spent days at a time without seeing the face of a human being. Settlers soon began coming in, however, and there was soon a growing community. But few are living in this county who came to this region at that time. Mr. Malaby located first on what was known as the McCamon farm, and labored as best he could without capital, and with few conveniences or farm implements. Later he removed to the John Widick farm in Palestine Township. About 1872, he with the Deaver Bros., put up the first livery stable in Belle Plaine, which he operated one year.

Mr. Malaby was married in February, 1873, to Martha S., step-daughter of Joseph Daniels, of Palestine Township. Mrs. Malaby was born May 2, 1855, in Illinois, and by her union with our subject, became the mother of three children: William L. F. was born March 20, 1875; Joseph E. A., February 22, 1877; and Ross E., July 13, 1879. Mrs. Martha Malaby died at her home in Palestine, July 22, 1881. Our subject was married again July 17, 1882, to Miss Margaret, daughter of Alfred and Susan Rice, who were natives of Gallatin County, Ill. Mrs. Rice died in 1880. Mr. Rice is still living in Illinois. Mrs. Margaret Malaby was born December 15, 1860, in Gallatin County, Ill., where she was reared and attended the common school.

This union resulted in the birth of four children: Clarence L., born May 13, 1880; Myra Helena, March 31, 1886; Norah Esther, January 4, 1888, and Howard Raymond, August 5, 1889. The present wife of our subject is a member in good standing of the Presbyterian Church.

Mr. Malaby is President of the Farmers' Alliance, Springdale Lodge, No. 656, and has been a member of the school board of his district for the past five years. He has just completed his second term as Township Trustee. He takes an active interest in politics, and until about three years ago, was a stanch supporter of the Republican party. His sympathies are now with the Union Labor movement, of which he is a leader in this locality. His farm embraces three hundred and twenty acres of good land, the greater part of which is under a good state of cultivation. Upon taking possession of this in 1877, pre-empting it from the Government, it presented an appearance widely different from that of the present, having upon it no improvements whatever, lying as the Indians had left it. Mr. Malaby put up his present residence in 1882. He is quite extensively interested in the breeding of live-stock, cattle, horses, sheep, and swine. He has planted large numbers of fruit trees, having two orchards, including four hundred apple trees, one hundred cherry trees, and fifty of peach. As a pioneer settler of this region, he is regarded with more than ordinary interest, and as one who has made for himself a good record, he is eminently worthy of representation in a work designed to perpetuate the names and deeds of the early settlers of Sumner County.

WILLIAM A. McLAIN, one of the progressive farmers of Jackson Township, was born in Hillsboro Township, Montgomery County, Ill., October 20, 1845. His father, Addison McLain, was a native of Greensborough, N. C., where he was reared and married. In 1835 he left his native State to find his home in the then far Northwest. He journeyed with teams across the mountains, traversed the States of Tennessee and

Kentucky and entered the State of Indiana, where he remained one year. At the expiration of that time he again started Westward, and reached Illinois, where, being pleased with the country, he located in Montgomery County of which he was one of the first settlers. He bought a tract of land which was covered with timber and had a log house upon it, the one in which our subject was born. The region in which he fixed his abiding place was sparsely settled at that time and deer and other wild game abounded. St. Louis, sixty-five miles distant, was their nearest market and they were obliged to draw their grain and pork there and back with teams.

Addison McLain improved his place and made it into a fine productive farm which yielded him a good income in the latter years of his life, and which was his residence until his death, which occurred in 1873. The maiden name of the mother of our subject was Catherine Lowy. She is a native of North Carolina and now resides in the homestead in Hillsboro, Ill. Mr. and Mrs. A. McLain were the parents of eight children of whom two are deceased.

The subject of this notice was reared and educated in his native county and made that his home until 1883. In 1876 he visited Texas and bought land in Hunt and Kaufman Counties but did not settle there. He returned to Illinois and in 1878 made a trip to Sumner County, Kan., traveling by rail as far as Hutchison, then finishing the journey in a wagon. The nearest railroad point at that time was at Wichita and the country was but sparingly settled in that portion of the State. When Mr. McLain examined Sumner County's advantages, present and prospective, he was so pleased with the outlook that he bought the southwest quarter of section 10, Jackson Township. Following his purchase of land in Sumner County, our subject returned to Illinois where he continued to reside until 1883. In that year he removed to Kansas and located on the land which he had previously purchased.

As soon as possible after the arrival of Mr. McLain in his new home he erected good, substantial frame buildings, enclosed his farm with a strong fence, planted fruit and shade trees and in every respect brought it up to a high standard of excellence. June 30, 1887, our subject and Miss Olive Finefrock were united in the holy bonds of matrimony and began housekeeping on the farm which was then in a high state of development and productiveness. Mrs. McLain is a native of Ohio. She is a member of the Presbyterian Church at Rome, and a refined, cultivated, Christian lady, whom it is a pleasure to know. Mr. McLain is a Republican in politics and takes a moderate share in the active work of his party. They are the parents of one child, named—Charles Sumner.

JOSHUA WRIGHT is a well-known dweller in Belle Plaine, and was, for about thirteen years, a member of the agricultural class of Belle Plaine Township. He spent some time in serving his country during the trying days of the War of the Rebellion, was elected Captain on the organization of the company, and has since that time been known by that title. He has acquired a sufficient amount of this world's goods to allow him to give up active work and to enjoy the repose that seems so fitting after a life of industry and well-doing. He and his estimable wife are regarded with confidence and esteem by all who know them.

The paternal grandfather of our subject was born in England, but having become a citizen of the Colonies prior to the Revolutionary War, entered the Colonial army and met his death at the hands of the British. His son, Jonathan, was born in Virginia, was bound out when a child, taken to Kentucky, and there grew to manhood. He married Miss Sarah Read, and became the father of twelve children, of whom three only beside our subject are now living. Mrs. Parmelia Turley lives in Orange County, Ind., and Aaron and Emmett in Lawrence County, of the same State. The parents had removed to that State in 1802, taking their place among the pioneers of Orange County, where they endured the privations and hardships incident to such life, rearing their family among the frontier surroundings and bestowing upon them such ad-

vantages as the circumstances would admit. The
father died November 17, 1838, and the mother did
not long survive, her death taking place August 4,
1840.

In the State and county in which his parents so
long resided, Capt. Wright was born, December
20, 1822, spending his boyhood amid the scenes
of the frontier, where a sturdiness of character is
developed and habits of observation learned that
take the place of extended schooling. Even before the death of his parents, he was obliged to
begin labor for his own support, at the age of
sixteen going out to work by the month or day.
On April 8, 1842, he was united in marriage with
Miss Parmelia Hall also a native of Orange County,
Ind., who has borne her share in the burdens of
life by her husband's side since the day of their
union, and has faithfully endeavored to fill her
place as a wife and mother. She is becoming advanced in years, having been born September 27,
1823.

The parents of Mrs. Wright were William and
Sophia (Dabney) Hall, who, like her husband's
parents, were early settlers in the county in which
she was born. Her father was a native of Kentucky and of English descent. The household
band comprised twelve children, of whom the following now survive: Mrs. Nancy Stewart, of Iowa;
Mrs. Polly Fender, of Kansas; Mrs. Wright; and
Mariutha, wife of George Moore, of Lawrence
County, Ind.

In the spring of 1849 Capt. Wright, with his
wife and two children, removed to Jefferson
County, Iowa, where he resided for over a quarter
of a century, and whence, in 1876, he came to
Kansas. He located on a farm near Belle Plaine,
in this county, and remained there until February, 1889, when he became a citizen of the village.
His farm comprised 160 acres of well-improved
land, which he sold some time since. The enlistment of Capt. Wright took place in July, 1862,
as a member of the Nineteenth Iowa Infantry, and
he was elected Captain of Company D. The command became a part of the Army of the Southwest, and participated in numerous skirmishes and
various engagements. During the battle of Prairie Grove the Captain received a wound in the
right arm, and still carries a musket ball embedded
in that member as a trophy from the battle-field.
He now receives a pension of $20 per month on
account of his injury. During the same engagement he received two other slighter wounds. In
July, 1863, he was discharged and returned to his
home to again take up the life of a civilian. He
was connected with the home militia in Iowa after
his return from the seat of war.

To Capt. and Mrs. Wright eight children have
been born, of whom Sarah J., Eliza M. and Mary
E. have been removed from them by death. Matilda is the wife of Henry Kline, of this county;
Rhoda E., the widow of David Snider, also lives
in this county; George W. makes his home in Iowa;
Millard is mining in Colorado; and William operates a farm in Belle Plaine Township, this county.
The parents of this family have been identified
with the Christian Church and are active members
of society. Capt. Wright belongs to the Grand
Army of the Republic, and gives his political adherence to the Republican party. He has served
as Justice of the Peace here for nearly six years.

GEORGE W. HENDERSON. This gentleman represents a large amount of wealth
and influence, and is considered one of the
most stirring and useful citizens of Morris Township. He has built up one of its most valuable
farms and has been no unimportant factor in the
growth and development of this region, having
by his very example promoted, to a large extent,
its material interests. He occupies a substantial
modern dwelling, and has all the other necessary
farm buildings, together with modern machinery
and the appliances requisite for the successful
prosecution of agriculture. Among the other good
things which have fallen to his lot in life is the
possession of an intelligent and helpful wife, who
not only manages her household affairs in a most
praiseworthy manner, but is at the same time the
efficient helpmate of her husband in many of his
business enterprises, being a safe counselor at all
times. Thus, in addition to being in the enjoy-

ment of a model home, they are most happily situated in their domestic relations. There have been born to them two children only—Marshall E., April 1, 1875, and Rose Myrtle, July 23, 1877. The son and daughter are being given a good education, including instruction in music, in which art they are quite proficient.

Mr. Henderson has made his permanent location many miles from his birthplace, which was in Sussex County, N. J., and the date thereof July 12, 1829. He was the eldest in a family of seven children, four of whom are living, the other three being located in Kansas and Iowa. The father, Eleazer, was an iron manufacturer, and like his wife, who in her girlhood was Mary Castimore, was a native of New Jersey. This branch of the Henderson family is of Irish and French descent, while the mother traced her forefathers to England and Germany.

The parents of our subject were reared and married in New Jersey, residing there until 1839. That year they removed to Pennsylvania, where they lived until 1857. Still looking Westward, they next removed across the Mississippi to Fayette County, Iowa, where the iron manufacturer changed his occupation to that of a farmer. The wife and mother departed this life at the homestead, in Fayette County, in 1876, at the age of seventy-four years. The father subsequently took up his abode with his son, George W., and died at his house, April 5, 1882, aged seventy-five years, four months and fifteen days.

After emerging from the common school, Mr. Henderson, in 1877, took a thorough course in the business college at St. Joseph, Mo. He left the parental roof when a youth of seventeen years, commencing an apprenticeship at wagon-making and wheelwrighting, at which he was employed continuously thereafter for a period of twenty years. He completed his apprenticeship in Pennsylvania, and during the years mentioned resided in that State and Illinois. In the spring of 1856 he preceded his family to Iowa, settling in Fayette County, where he followed his trade and purchased a farm, upon which he resided until 1859. He then recrossed the Father of Waters, and took up his abode in Centralia, Ill., where he sojourned until

the fall of 1856. In the meantime he spent one year in the Quartermaster's Department at Nashville and Chattanooga, Tenn., employed in putting up hospitals and warehouses.

In the fall of 1865 Mr. Henderson came to Kansas, and settling in Doniphan County, engaged in farming. He lived there until 1881, and his next removal was to this county, where he secured possession of the land which he now owns and occupies. When a little over twenty-one years old he was married, January 28, 1851, in Pennsylvania, to Miss Hannah M. Venrick. The two children born of this union are sons—William, a resident of Trinidad, Col.; and Alexander, employed in the freight depot of the Missouri Pacific Railroad at Leavenworth. Mrs. Hannah M. Henderson departed this life at her home in Iowa, May 2, 1857. The second marriage of Mr. Henderson occurred August 1, 1861, with Miss Mary Beaver, and she also became the mother of two children—George L., a resident of this county; and Ella, the wife of Edward Brooks, of New Mexico. Mrs. Mary Henderson died October 23, 1873.

The present wife of our subject, to whom he was married, at Pana, April 22, 1874, was in her girlhood Miss Hattie L. Yeager. Her parents were Moses and Margaret (Campbell) Yeager, natives of Pennsylvania, and the father engaged in farming pursuits. They removed with their respective parents to Ohio, where they were married, and whence they emigrated to Indiana, probably fifty years ago. After a sojourn there of twenty years, they went over into Illinois, and then, in 1884, came to this State, settling in Argonia. Mr. Yeager died February 6, 1888, at the age of seventy-four years. His widow is still living, and is aged seventy-six. Four of their six children are living. Mrs. Henderson was the second, and was born March 11, 1841, in Rush County, Ind. As a child, she was a bright beyond her years, made good use of her time in school, fitting herself for a teacher, and followed this profession for a period of seventeen years in Indiana and Illinois.

Mr. and Mrs. Henderson are devoted members of the Methodist Episcopal Church, in which they have been active workers, especially in the Sunday-school. Mr. Henderson officiating as Superin-

tendent and teacher of the Bible Class, and in the
church proper he has held the offices of Class-
Leader and Steward. He is rather conservative in
politics and strongly in favor of prohibition. He
voted for Abraham Lincoln in 1860, but is now
rather independent, aiming to support the men
whom he considers will best serve the interests of
the people. For seven years he has been Treasurer of his school district. He was elected a Trustee of Morris Township, but resigned. He served
at one time as Justice of the Peace in Morris Township. He belongs to the Grange, the Farmers' Alliance and the A. H. T. A.

Mr. Henderson's farm embraces three hundred
and twenty acres of choice land, which is devoted
to the raising of grain and stock, he making a
specialty of cattle, horses and swine. The present
residence was put up in 1881. It is handsomely
finished and furnished, and is considered one of the
best structures of its kind in Morris Township.
Mr. Henderson is one of those men whose name
will be held in remembrance long after he has been
gathered to his fathers.

WYATT B. GOAD, Postmaster at Mayfield,
is of English extraction, and a native of
Tennessee, born in Smith County, May 3,
1845. His early boyhood was passed in his native
State, and in 1857 he accompanied his parents to
Kentucky, continuing his education in the common schools there, and growing to early manhood
on the farm which his father owned and operated.
He had been taught to love his country, and the
spirit of loyalty which was implanted within his
breast led him to desire to assist in the preservation of the Union, and he therefore, in the spring
of 1862, although but seventeen years of age, enlisted at Glasgow, Ky., was enrolled in Company
C. Thirty-seventh Kentucky Infantry, and served
twenty two months; he then re-enlisted in the
Fifty-fifth Regiment, Company E. Infantry, until
May 24, 1865, when he was honorably discharged
at Covington. Although he was not called upon
to take part in any of the most famous battles of

the war, he bore his part bravely in the battles of
Mt. Sterling, Cynthiana, and King Salt Works in
Virginia, a few minor engagements, in the routine
duties of camp life, and in various marches.

When mustered out of the service, young Goad
returned to Kentucky, and remained in that State
until 1882, when he came to Wellington, Kan., and
for two years followed his trade as a carpenter in
this vicinity. He then moved on to a farm, and
for about three years carried on the pursuit of
agriculture. Having received the appointment of
Postmaster, he took possession of the office, September 20, 1887. Mr. Goad is a Republican, never
failing to exercise his right to the elective franchise in behalf of what he considers most conducive
to the welfare of the country. He is an honorable
and upright man, and throughout his entire life has
exhibited a spirit of prudence and industry, and a
cordial, friendly nature in his dealings with mankind.

In November, 1866, Mr. Goad was united in
marriage with Miss Harriet R. Bullock, who was
born October 2, 1834, and who died May 23, 1880.
Mr. Goad subsequently became the husband of
Mrs. Nannie Owens, widow of James T. Owens, the
rites of wedlock being celebrated between them
September 28, 1880. Mrs. Goad is a daughter of
Thomas and Emily (William) Franklin, natives of
Virginia, and was born March 28, 1852. Her
mother died in Warren County, Ky., at the age of
fifty-five years, and her father is still living there.
She has borne her husband one child, Thomas H.,
whose natal day was February 1, 1883.

The paternal grandfather of our subject was
Joshua A. Goad, who was born in Virginia about
the year 1770, and who died at Carthage, Tenn., at
the advanced age of eighty-five years. His son,
Henry, was born in Colfax County, Va., October 9,
1800, and was six years old when the family removed to Tennessee. In 1857 he became a resident of Kentucky, where his death occurred April
20, 1885. He was a Republican in politics, and a
member in good standing of the Methodist Episcopal Church.

The wife of Henry Goad, and the mother of our
subject, bore the maiden name of Martha Duke,
and was born in Jackson County, Tenn., January

28, 1806, and is still living in Monroe County, Ky. Her parents, McKange and Annie (Brooks), Duke, were natives of Virginia. and her father was a planter and slave trader. Mr. and Mrs. Duke died in Jackson County, Tenn. The family of Mr. and Mrs. Henry Good comprised eight children— Martha, Harvey, Sallie A., Henry, C. Mathew, Mary, Wyatt and Katherine. Three of this family are deceased, Martha having died at the age of three years. Mathew in infancy, and Henry at the age of thirty-five. The latter was a Union soldier during the Civil War.

JOHN L. MEARS. If a man's character may be determined by his surroundings, that of Mr. Mears and his no less capable and worthy wife, possesses all the elements of thrift, industry and good citizenship. We find them in the midst of pleasant surroundings, the occupants of a well-developed farm on section 14. Dixon Township, having a substantial dwelling with convenient outbuildings, fruit and shade trees and the land under a good state of cultivation. The family occupies a good position in the community, and the fact that they are well spoken of by their neighbors is sufficient indication of the sterling worth of character which has had its influence upon those with whom they have become associated.

A native of Muskingum County, Ohio, Mr. Mears was born May 29, 1837, being the eleventh child of the Rev. William and Elizabeth (Latham) Mears, who were natives of the city of London, England. The father for a period of forty years officiated as a minister of the Baptist Church. Upon coming to America, in 1830, he located in Zanesville, Ohio, being among its earliest settlers and teaching the first school established there. He purchased one hundred and sixty acres of land north of the town site and after a residence of three years in the town removed to his farm, where he built up a permanent homestead and where his death took place in 1869. The mother survived her husband for a period of fifteen years, dying in Ohio in 1884.

They were the parents of thirteen children, eight of whom grew to mature years. Six are now living, making their homes in Ohio, Kansas and Nebraska.

Young Mears lived at the farm with his parents until a youth of nineteen years, learning the arts of sowing and reaping and choosing agriculture for his life vocation. In the fall of 1856, starting out for himself he sought the Great West and settled on a tract of new land in Tama County, Iowa. He was one of the earliest pioneers of that region and not realizing his hopes of making a fortune, returned, after about two years, to his old home in Ohio. Sojourning there until 1877 he again turned his steps Westward, coming to this State and settling on a tract of raw land, from which he has since constructed his present farm. He commenced at first principles in its development and has himself effected all the improvements upon it. He put up a new residence in 1888, and has one hundred and thirty acres under the plow. He makes a specialty of swine.

Miss Mary, daughter of Abraham C. and Mary (Wallwork) Romine, was wedded to John L. Mears, October 10, 1860, in Ohio. Mrs. Mears was born September 3, 1838, near Zanesville, Ohio. Her father was a native of Columbus, Ohio, and a plasterer by trade, which he followed the greater part of his life and died in Ohio in 1889. The mother was born in the city of London, England, and came with her parents to America when quite young. She passed away prior to the decease of her husband, her death occurring in 1884 in Ohio. Of the three children born to them only two are living, the one besides Mrs. Mears being Mrs. Black, a resident of Ohio.

Six children have been born to Mr. Mears and his estimable wife, the eldest of whom, Mary Louisa, is the wife of James Mack, and the mother of two children; James Baxter married Miss Vesta Thurlow, and is a resident of Milan, Kan.; Alice is the wife of Thomas Looper, a resident of Belle Plaine, this State; Laura married J. M. Bunker, is the mother of one child, and lives in Ryan Township; J. Welcome and Ellen Blanche remain at home with their parents,

Mr. and Mrs. Mears are connected with the

Church of God. Mr. Mears was formerly a Class-Leader in the Methodist Episcopal Church and is identified with the Masonic fraternity, in which he has held the office of Junior Deacon. For a period of eight years he has served on the school board of his district and he has also officiated as Road Overseer. His political sympathies are with the Union Labor party.

In 1863, during the progress of the Civil War, Mr. Mears enlisted in Company E, One Hundred and Fifty-ninth Ohio Infantry, and was promoted to Corporal in the one-hundred days' service. His duties lay around Camp Bradford in Maryland. After serving his first term he re-enlisted in Company B, One Hundred and Eighty-ninth Battalion, Ohio Infantry, and was stationed at Camp Chase, being held as a reserve, and as it was near the close of the war was not required in the active service.

ALFRED LASHLEY is the owner and occupant of a valuable farm on section 33, Oxford Township, where he is engaged in general farming. He came to this county in January, 1886, and the following August purchased one hundred and sixty acres, which he soon afterward began improving, putting upon it such outbuildings as are usually erected by an enterprising farmer, and substantial fences, and cultivating it thoroughly. He has also set out shade trees, a wind-break, and an orchard which is considered as fine as any to be seen in this vicinity. The estate is ably conducted, and the fortunate owner is a fine representative of the class to which he belongs.

John Lashley, the grandfather of our subject, was a native of New Jersey, his wife's maiden name was Grace Bortons, and moved to Ohio, when it was a new country, and in Warren County, June 8, 1829, a son was born to him. That son, David Lashley, grew to maturity in his native State, married, settled on a farm, and is still living in his native county. His wife bore the maiden name of Sarah Slack, and she was born in the same county as himself, her natal day being July 2, 1826. Her parents, Job and Rebecca (Searle) Slack, were early

settlers in the Buckeye State, to which they came from Pennsylvania, and the father was a mechanic. To David and Sarah Lashley, seven children were born: Rebecca A., our subject, Sylvester S., William H., Florence E., and Robert B., still survive; Marshall E. is deceased.

The subject of this biography is a native of Warren County, Ohio, where his eyes first opened to the light November 26, 1857. He received a good education in the common schools of his native county, and completed his studies at Waynesville, and at the age of twenty-two years, left his home to become a resident of Kansas. He is not only succeeding in his agricultural work, but is winning the respect of all with whom he comes in contact, by his honorable dealing, his intelligence, friendliness, and excellent moral principles. He has already a good financial standing, and bids fair to become one of the wealthy men of the township ere middle age. He is a member of the Farmers' Alliance, and casts his vote with the Republican party. He belongs to the United Brethren Church.

Sylvester Lashley, brother of our subject, was also born in Warren County, Ohio, and there grew to maturity. His natal day was November 23, 1859, and after finishing his education, and remaining with his parents until twenty-two years old, he came to this county in February, 1882, and has since spent the most of his time here. He, however, took up a claim in Grant County, on which he resided, and which he proved up on.

GEORGE S. HILL, manager of the business of the Rock Island Lumber Company, at Caldwell, is comparatively a young man starting out with the promise of making for himself an excellent record. He was born in East Sullivan, Me., June 15, 1859, and is the son of Thomas B. and Pruda (Simpson) Hill, who were likewise natives of the Pine Tree State, and born in the same place as their son. Thomas B. Hill followed the seas the greater part of his life, but is now located at East Sullivan, Me., where they are peacefully spending their declining days. There were born to them five children, namely: Elwood W., George S., H. Ernest, Arthur T., and Helen C., all of whom are living, making their homes principally in Maine, Kansas and Nova Scotia.

The subject of this notice, the second child of his parents, removed with them when quite young, to East Sullivan, in his native State, where he attended the common school. After becoming sufficiently advanced in his studies, he entered East Maine Conference Seminary, at Bucksport, where he completed his studies. He commenced his business career as clerk in a store of general merchandise at Bucksport, Me., in 1883. That year he sought the Far West, and in September took up his abode in Caldwell, and engaged in the lumber business, in which he has since been interested. He has improved his opportunities for information in this line of trade, and is thoroughly posted as to its details. Although meddling very little with politics, he gives his support to the Republican party, and occupies a good position among the Knights of Pythias.

After becoming a resident of Caldwell, Mr. Hill formed the acquaintance of Miss Emma G. Cragin, to whom he was wedded March 11, 1886. Mrs. Hill was born in Groton, Mass., July 31, 1864, and is the daughter of Rodney and Jennie (Gill) Cragin, who were natives of Groton, Mass., and are now in Caldwell, Kan. Mr. and Mrs. Hill occupy a neat home in the central part of the city, also a good position, socially, among its people.

ALVIN B. McALLISTER. Although by no means an old man, this gentleman is one of the old settlers of the county, to which he came in the spring of 1870, opening a bachelor's hall in Belle Plaine Township, assisting in the development of the agricultural resources of this section, and seeing the country around him grow to a well-cultivated, well-settled and prosperous region. The characteristics which make of the "canny Scot" so reliable a citizen, so staunch a friend, and so brave a soldier when called to battle, have been manifested in the career of the gen-

tleman above-named, who from both lines of descent derives these traits, and that pride in the family name which is also a leading trait in the Scotch character.

James and Nancy (Andrew) McAllister were natives of Franklin County, Pa., and the parents of eleven children, of whom our subject is the tenth in order of birth. Of this family all the survivors except our subject are living in Pennsylvania—Margaret and John make their home in Adams County; Alexander is deceased; Mary, Agnes and Samuel live in Adams County; Sarah is the wife of John Young, of York County; Martha and Theodore live in Adams County, and Robert is deceased. The father of this family died about the year 1870, and the mother survived him about four years. The parental home was within one and a half miles of the town of Gettysburg, and the McAllister estate formed a part of the historic and memorable battlefield.

The subject of this biography was born September 15, 1844, was reared to manhood on a farm in Adams County, Pa., and received his education in the common schools. He was still in his teens at the outbreak of the Civil War, but with the patriotism and enthusiasm manifested by so many of the youth of the land, he entered the Union army in December, 1863, as a member of Company B, Twenty-first Pennsylvania Cavalry. The band to which he belonged became a part of the Second Brigade, Second Division of the Army of the Potomac, under the command of Gen. Crook, since so widely known as a successful Indian fighter. Mr. McAllister participated in the fight at Dinwiddie Court-House, at Farmerville, Sailor's Creek, in the engagement prior to the surrender of Lee at Appomattox Court-House, and in numerous affrays of minor importance, his conduct in every position doing honor to the family name.

After receiving an honorable discharge, in June, 1865, Mr. McAllister returned to his native county and State, whence in the spring of 1868 he emigrated to Kansas. For some two years he remained near Junction City, and then coming to this county, pre-empted one hundred and sixty acres of land on Cow Skin Creek, Belle Plaine Township. There he lived about two years, at the expiration of which time he bought the quarter-section, upon which he now lives, paying $2,200 for it. About sixty acres of breaking had been done upon it, and a shanty of cottonwood boards, ten by twelve feet, had been constructed. This "shack," to use the Western term, was the bachelor home of Mr. McAllister until a better structure could be put up and take its place.

For a number of years Mr. McAllister practiced the self-denials and endured the discomforts of life in a bachelor's hall, which, although sufficiently jolly at times, is scarcely the ideal of home life, and he then, on January 1st, 1884, took to himself a wife in the person of Miss Emma North. His bride was born in Ohio, and is a daughter of Wesley and Amelia (Moore) North, who settled in this county about the year 1872, and a sketch of whom appears on another page of this work. By dint of energy and hard work Mr. McAllister had brought his land to a fine state prior to his marriage, and is able to provide his loved companion and bright family with all the comforts of life, and he receives an ample return in the neatness, order and added cheerfulness to be found under his roof. Three children have come to bless the home—Ray, born October 10, 1884; and Nellie and Norna (twin girls) November 16, 1886.

Mr. McAllister has served as Clerk of Belle Plaine Township three terms. He belongs to the Grand Army of the Republic Post, at Belle Plaine, is a Republican in his political opinions and ballots, and both he and his wife are members in good standing in the Presbyterian Church.

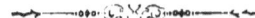

JONATHAN H. DAVIS, a Sumner County pioneer of 1873 and one of the Trustees of Jackson Township, is a citizen deserving of more than a passing notice. He was born near Greenville, Bond County, Ill., October 19, 1840, and is the son of Matthew Davis, a native of Trigg County, Ky. The paternal grandfather, the Rev. Jonathan Davis, a preacher of the Ironclad Baptist persuasion, was born and reared in Virginia. Jonathan Davis when a young man left his na-

tive soil and removing to Kentucky, established himself among the earliest pioneers of Trigg County. He remained there until about 1815, then emigrated to what was then the Territory of Illinois, locating in what is now Bond County. There, likewise, he was one of the first settlers. The removal from the Blue Grass State was made with teams, and a portion of the way had to be cut through the wilderness in order for the travelers to reach their destintaion. The earthly plans and expectations of Grandfather Davis and his family were cut short in one brief year by his death. The widow and her seven children soon afterward returned to Kentucky and resided in Trigg and Christian Counties. Matthew, the father of our subject, sojourned in that region until 1838, then returned to Illinois accompanied by his mother and two brothers. This time they located about the center of Bond County, where Matthew purchased a tract of wild land, part prairie and part timber, and built a log house. In the meantime he was married and in that humble dwelling the subject of this sketch was born.

Matthew Davis was a resident of Bond County, Ill., until October, 1843, when he sold out and removed to Montgomery County. There he purchased a partially-improved farm near the town of Donelson. Of this twenty acres had been cleared and a set of log buildings had been erected. Deer and other wild animals were plentiful. It was before the days of railroads and St. Louis, sixty miles distant, was the nearest market. Stoves were unknown and the mother performed her cooking by the fireplace. She also spun and wove wool and flax and clad her children in cloth made by her own hands. The father was in ill health for some years and the children were trained to habits of industry at an early age. Matthew Davis departed this life at the old homestead in Montgomery County, Ill., in 1858. He was married in Illinois to Miss Sarah Bentley, a native of Giles County, Tenn. Grandfather Richard Bentley was a native of Virginia, whence he removed to Tennessee and from there to Bond County, Ill., during its earliest settlement. He there spent the closing years of his life, dying in 1873, in the eighty-ninth year of his age. The maiden name of his wife was Elizabeth Hayes.

The mother of Mr. Davis came to this county in 1873 and died at his home in Jackson Township in August, 1886. Of her children, seven in number, the eldest, Margaret C. A., became the wife of David D. Moss, now deceased. Jonathan H. was the second born; Nancy, Clarissa E., Richard B. and James B. are residents of Jackson Township; Sarah E. married E. M. Desart and lives in South Haven Township. Jonathan H. was reared to man's estate in Montgomery County, Ill., where he attended the pioneer schools conducted on the subscription plan. The temple of learning was a log house with slab benches and a fireplace extending nearly across one end. The chimney was made outside of earth and sticks and the system of instruction corresponded very well with the surroundings of the pupils. Young Davis being the eldest son he, after the death of his father necessarily assumed much of the care of the family and he remained with his mother, superintending the farm until a man of twenty-seven years. He made his home there until coming to Kansas in 1873, and after retiring from the management of the farm occupied himself as a carpenter.

The journey to the Sunflower State was made by Mr. Davis overland with a team of horses and a wagon, he being accompanied by his wife and his brother, Richard B. They arrived in this county on the 6th of April, 1873, when the country was thinly settled and Wichita, forty miles away, was the nearest market and railroad station. Mr. Davis entered a claim to a tract of Government land on section 27, in what is now Jackson Township, filing the same in the land office at Wichita. He put up a box house, 12x14 feet in dimensions and commenced at first principles in the development of a farm. He resided there five years, effecting good improvements, then sold out and removed to that whereon he now resides. Deer, buffalo and other wild game was plentiful a few miles west of his present homestead at the time of his settlement here. He has watched the march of events in his adopted State with that interest only felt by the intelligent and public-spirited citizen, and in adding to the value of the taxable property of Sumner County has thus contributed his full quota to its prosperity.

The wife of Mr. Davis, to whom he was married in Montgomery County February 23, 1873, was in her girlhood Miss Elizabeth Desart. Mrs. Davis was born in Edgar County, Ill., and is the daughter of George and Emily (Martin) Desart, who were natives of Ohio and New York and are now deceased. This union resulted in the birth of three children, all daughters—Olive, Emily and Augusta. They are a bright and promising trio and, it is hardly necessary to state, the pride of their parents' hearts.

Mr. Davis cast his first Presidential vote for Gen. McClellan and has since remained a steadfast supporter of the principles of the Democratic party. He is serving his sixth term as the Trustee of Jackson Township, and has been the candidate of his party for the State Legislature. He belongs to Lodge No. 255, A. F. & A. M., and is prominently connected with the Methodist Episcopal Church.

CORNELIUS I. CUSHMAN. The farming community of South Haven Township recognizes in Mr. Cushman one of its most faithful representatives, although he has only been a resident of Kansas since 1883. That year he came to this county supplied with a reasonable amount of hard cash, and purchased three hundred and thirty-three acres of wild land on section 9. By a course of unflagging industry, he has now one hundred acres under the plow, has erected a substantial frame residence with a barn, corn crib, granary and other necessary structures, and has set out an apple orchard, together with trees of the small fruits. He makes a specialty of live stock, mostly cattle and swine of good grades.

A native of Windsor County, Vt., Mr. Cushman was born June 21, 1839, and was there reared to manhood on a farm. His father, John Cushman, Jr., was also of New England birth, and the son of John, Sr., who was born, and reared his family chiefly in Vermont, where he spent his last days. John, Jr., remained a resident of his native county until reaching manhood, and was then married to Miss Fanny, daughter of Raszell Spaulding. There were born to them seven children, of whom Cornelius I. was next to the youngest. He and his brother, Edmund E., are the only surviving members of the family.

Mr. Cushman remained a resident of his native State until November, 1868, then, leaving New England, emigrated to Illinois, and was a resident of Jacksonville until the winter of 1873. Next, crossing the Mississippi, he established himself as a resident of Fairmount, Neb., where he was employed as a clerk in a store three years. In the meantime, in 1876, he was married to Miss Isabel Perry. There were born to them one child, a son, Aubert J., and Mrs. Cushman died April 28, 1879, aged twenty-nine years. In 1876, Mr. Cushman removed to Clay County, Neb., where he prosecuted farming until coming to this county.

Our subject contracted a second marriage April 1, 1889, with Miss Hannah M., daughter of Carson and Christina E. (Meyer) Ehlers. Mrs. Hannah Cushman was born in Adams County, Ill., of parents who were natives of Germany. Her mother came to America with her mother and sister in 1856, and located in Illinois. Mr. Ehlers came to the same state in 1851, and was there married. In 1886 they came to Kansas and purchased a farm in Falls Township, upon which they still live. In the fatherland they were members in good standing of the German Lutheran Church.

During the progress of the late Civil War, Mr. Cushman enlisted as a Union soldier in Company A, Twelfth Vermont Infantry, and served as a private nine months. Politically, he votes independently. He became a member of the Independent Order of Odd Fellows, in Illinois, and joined the Farmers' Alliance after coming to this county.

The Cushman family, it is supposed, originated in England, and the first representative in America was one Robert Cushman, who was born about 1585, and was one of the band who left his native land for the sake of religious freedom. To him had been given the responsible task of going to London and hiring a vessel larger than the Mayflower, of "burden about nine score," and to see that she was sent around to Southampton, there to meet their companions from Holland. These facts are selected from a work compiled as the "Cushman Genealogy." The Cushmans later flourished in

both Massachusetts and Vermont, and were people generally well-to-do, noted for their industry, honesty and moral worth generally. They experienced all the inconveniences and discomforts incidental to the early settlement of New England, and in all the relations of life conducted themselves in a manner which, as the records show, should be a matter of pride to their descendants.

~~─ 0 ─ ─ ─ ~~

JOHN EIKLOR. The number of comparatively young men who occupy positions of public responsibility, carry on extensive business operations, and own large and valuable estates in the great expanse west of the Mississippi River, is a continual source of surprise and comment to Eastern visitors, who are accustomed to see such places occupied either by men of middle age or as an inheritance from those who have lived long in the East. The above-named gentleman, though still young, is in a position of financial prosperity highly creditable to his own energy and ability, and is justly considered one of the most substantial and progressive agriculturists of Greene Township.

Mr. Eiklor came to this county in January, 1878, and pre-empted one hundred and sixty acres of land on section 29, and to that acreage he has added until his landed estate now comprises eight hundred acres, principally located in Greene Township, and bearing improvements which are more than usually adequate, substantial, and attractive in appearance. He is one of the largest dealers in stock in this county, his herd of cattle numbering some five hundred head. Since youth he has been engaged in farming, and endeavors in every department of agriculture to keep up with the times in the use of modern and labor saving machinery; he takes the advantage of every opportunity to increase the quantity and quality of his farm products, and keeps fine grades of stock, exhibiting good judgment in the qualities most desirable in them. That he has met with success in his under-

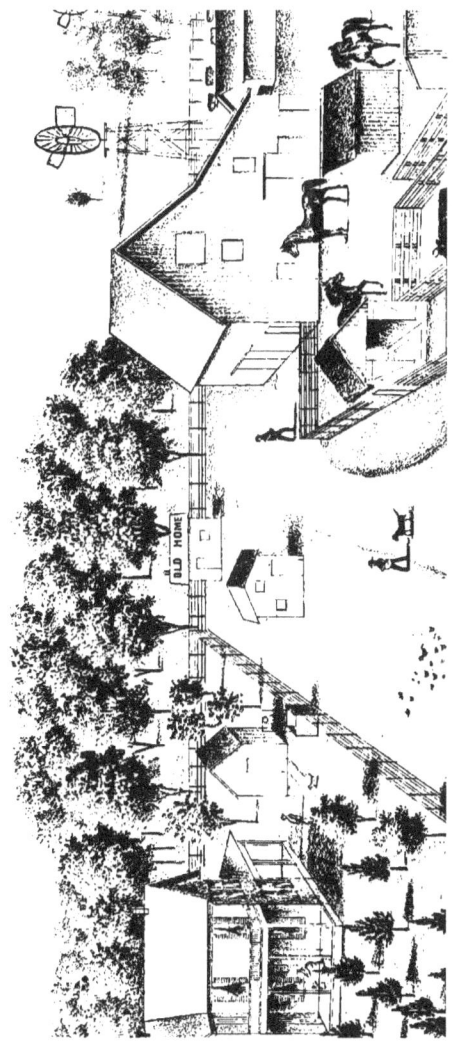

takings is evidenced by a lithographic engraving of his homestead, presented elsewhere in this volume.

The birth of Mr. Eiklor took place February 2, 1852, in DeKalb County, Ill., which was his home until he reached the age of twelve years. Then, accompanying his parents to McLean County, he there grew to manhood, making it his home until he came West. There also his father died, about two years after settling in the county. Mr. Eiklor was united in marriage with Miss Emeline Olmsted, also a native of DeKalb County, December 17, 1872. Four bright children—Daisy, Andrew, Herman and Lawrence—have come to bless their union. Mrs. Eiklor is a woman of intelligent and cultured mind, practical domestic acquirements, and consistent Christian character.

Mr. Eiklor belongs to the Republican party, and while neither an aspirant for political honors nor what is commonly known as a politician, is deeply interested in the success of the principles in which he believes, and in the election of the candidates in whose hands he believes the reins of Government will be most wisely held. Both he and his wife are members of the Methodist Church, and it is needless to say that they have many warm friends in the community and are held in high esteem by all who know them.

HARLES F. HORNER, in whose death this county lost one of her earliest pioneers and most highly esteemed citizens, was a native of Gettysburg, Adams County, Pa., his natal day having been April 29, 1818. He was a son of John and Jane Horner, of the same county, was reared on a farm, and received his early education in the district schools. He lost his mother by death when he was about seventeen years old. He remained in his native State until eighteen years of age, when he came to Kansas, following various occupations here during the first years of his sojourn. He and his brother, D. W. Horner, herded cattle here before Sumner County was organized, and they built one of the first houses within its limits.

Among the employments in which Mr. Horner was engaged, was that of milling, but his principal occupation was buying and selling cattle. In 1870 he pre-empted land in Belle Plaine Township, his location being on the Arkansas bottoms, where he resided a short time, and then moved to within a half mile of the village of Belle Plaine, where he was a resident until his death. That sad event occurred on the 9th of January, 1889, and was made doubly sad by the suddenness with which the dreadful blow fell. Mr. Horner seemed as well as usual during that day except for a slight pain in his back, of which nothing serious was thought. During the evening, however, it was thought best to call a physician, and his devoted wife sent word to his brother, that "Charley" did not seem well. The brother and a friend went to the house about eleven o'clock, found Mr. Horner in good spirits, and inclined to joke about the matter. Shortly after their arrival the Doctor gave him a soothing potion, and requested him to lie down and try to sleep. He was attended up stairs to his room by his wife, who, after seeing him comfortably disposed for rest, returned below, thinking he would fall asleep in a few minutes, but on going back to the room a short time afterward, she found that life had departed. Although no noise had been perceptible to those below, it was evident from the position of the lifeless body, that Mr. Horner had risen and fallen across the bed. So suddenly did apoplexy remove an honored citizen from the midst of his fellowmen.

The family from which a kind and loving husband and father was thus removed, comprised a wife and three children. Mrs. Horner, who has the sympathy of many devoted friends in her sad bereavement, is a native of Gettysburg, Pa., a daughter of John and Margaret A. Knox, of that place, and was united in marriage with him whose loss she now mourns, November 7, 1883. The first child born of this happy union, is Edith, whose natal day was August 24, 1884; John B. added his presence to the family circle May 23, 1886; and Margaret C., October 16, 1888. Mrs. Kate M. Horner is a member of the Presbyterian Church, in which her deceased husband held high standing. She still lives near Belle Plaine, owning her residence with ten acres of land surrounding it, and one hundred and sixty acres near Conway Springs.

Mr. Horner belonged to the Masonic fraternity, and gave his political affiliation to the Republican party. Like other pioneers he had endured some of the hardships attending the early settlers, and as he had no one to start him in life, his success was due to his personal efforts and capability. The prosperity at which he had arrived was a source of rejoicing to all who knew him, as he had ever manifested the generous and whole-souled spirit which viewed with favor every movement that would advance the interests of the community, would elevate the standard of morality and good citizenship, and lead to a higher and nobler civilization.

⋖⊰⊹⊱⊰❖⊱⊹⊰⊱⋗

HARLES RUMBLE. If great credit is due to the men and women who do the pioneer work in any section of country and open the way for the advance of civilization, how much greater credit should be accorded those who take their places upon the frontier in one section after another, doing a double share of the labor and undergoing a double share of the privations and dangers which surround the lives of the early settlers. The gentleman above named, who is now the owner of a fine tract of land in Wellington Township, is not only a pioneer of this county but in another section of this State was also an early settler and developed a tract of land, reclaiming it from the primitive condition and making of it a valuable estate.

Mr. Rumble is a native of "Merrie England," in which country his parents, Mr. and Mrs. John Rumble, were also born and where they were reared and married. In 1834 they left their native land and, with their children, crossed the Atlantic and settled near Toronto, Canada, in a section which was then sparsely inhabited. There the father of our subject was employed at various occupations for a few years when he purchased twenty acres of land twenty miles from Toronto, in Vaughn Township, where he built a set of log buildings and lived

until after the death of his wife. He then sold his property and lived with his children in the Dominion, all of whom except our subject remained there. The family comprised eight sons and daughters— Thomas, William, Robert, John, George, Charles, Mary and Lucy.

The subject of this sketch was about six years old when the family came to the New World, and he was reared in Canada, whence about the year 1855 he removed to the United States. He located in LaSalle County, Ill., which was then a new country in which Ottawa, twenty miles distant from his home, was the nearest railroad station and depot for supplies. He purchased a tract of prairie land in Otter Creek Township, which was unbroken and unimproved and upon which he at once erected a frame house 16x14 feet, and began other necessary improvements and which he cultivated and made his home until 1871. He then sold and turning his face Westward, arrived in this county on the 9th of May.

Mr. Rumble thought best to rent a farm and raise a crop that year while looking about for a place that would suit him as a permanent location. The people who were living here in the year 1874 will always remember that as the "grasshopper year" and our subject, with other residents, suffered the loss of his entire crop, as the grasshoppers came in clouds and devoured every green thing, leaving corn-stalks as bare as bean poles. In the fall of that year Mr. Rumble purchased the southeast quarter of section 8, in Wellington Township, which was an unbroken tract of prairie land. He continued his work as a renter for two years and then located upon his own estate where he has since resided and where he began making improvements immediately after taking possession. It is a fine body of land lying on the Slate Creek bottoms and capable of producing excellent crops. During the first few years of Mr. Rumble's residence here antelope were to be seen from his door, and deer and bison were plentiful a few miles farther west; Wichita was the nearest railroad station and market for farm produce, and all the travel throughout this vicinity was accomplished with teams or on foot.

The lady who for over thirty years presided over

the household economy of Mr. Rumble's home, faithfully discharging the duties which devolved upon her sphere in life and encouraging him in his labors, was a native of Clearfield County, Pa., and the rites of wedlock were celebrated between them in 1854. Her maiden name was Elizabeth Corle, and she was a daughter of Isaac and Jane Corle, natives, respectively, of New Jersey and Pennsylvania. The union of Mr. and Mrs. Rumble resulted in the birth of seven children— Isaac, Miriam J., Lucy May, Mary A., Rella Belle, Phœbe A., and Elizabeth R. The wife and mother was torn from her family by the hand of death May 18, 1885, deeply regretted by many friends and especially by the home circle wherein her virtues were best known and understood.

⁕───⟨✲⟩───⁕

EORGE M. D. HINCKLE, a representative farmer and stock-raiser residing on section 9, Belle Plaine Township, is the subject of this brief biography. He was born March 28, 1846, in Frederick County, Va., to Daniel and Mary J. (Duckwall) Hinckle. The parents were born natives of Virginia, the father of Daniel Hinckle having settled in Frederick County, upon his arrival as an emigrant from Germany many years before. The parental family consisted of five children, named respectively: Mary C., wife of John Shade, resides in Sedgwick County, Kan.; Rebecca, deceased; George M. D., the subject of this notice; Sarah E. is the wife of Dr. W. B. Hollis, and resides in Virginia; and William A. P., who resides in Belle Plaine Township, Kan.

Mr. Hinckle was reared in his native State to the occupation of a farmer. His educational advantages were limited, being confined to the early subscription schools of the State, which were far from being efficient in either method or scope of instruction. Realizing the benefits to be conferred by knowledge, our subject was not discouraged at the little opportunities which were within his reach, but applied himself diligently to reading and study of such subjects as were presented to him from time

to time. By this means he became well acquainted with all the leading topics of the day, and has always kept abreast of the general trend of modern thought.

When Mr. Hinckle was in his twentieth year, he left home and went to Portland Ky., where he clerked in a store for about ten months, then went north as far as Macoupin County, Ill., where he hired out as a farm-hand. He followed the latter occupation for about two years, receiving $25 per month, and his board. Subsequently he rented land in the same county, and farmed it one season then moved to Montgomery County, Ill., where he operated a farm two years for another man, receiving one-half of the products as his share. He left Illinois in the spring of 1872, and located on section 34, Salem Township, Sedgwick County, Kan., where he resided a number of years. He then went to Mulvane, Kan., where he handled stock for a time, then removed to his present place in the spring of 1886, where he has since lived.

Upon first coming to Kansas, Mr. Hinckle preempted one hundred and sixty acres in Sedgwick County, when it was in a perfectly raw condition, with no improvements, and but few neighbors. The usual hardships of a pioneer fell to his lot, but he was made of sterner stuff than to mind a little trouble when the object in view was a home of his own. He persevered in his work, and, after keeping bachelor's hall for some time, in 1874, on the 10th of November, was united in marriage to Miss Lillie Wilson, a daughter of David O., and Cornelia D. Wilson. They are now residents of Stevens County, Kan., but were at the time of the marriage of their daughter, residents of Sedgwick County. Mrs. Hinckle was born January 14, 1858, in Randolph County, W. Va., is a lady of domestic habits, and is a model wife and mother. There have been born to Mr. and Mrs. Hinckle, three children, who are named respectively: Pearl; Earl, deceased; and Mabel. Mr. Hinckle and his wife are both active and efficient members of the church known as the United Brethren in Christ. They are not only regular in their attendance upon its services, and liberal contributors to its financial prosperity, but in many other ways are zealous in their labors of love for the Lord. Their duties to their home and church, do not, however, interfere with their participation in the pleasures and refinements of society, nor in their obligations to the community in general. They are ever ready to assist the right whether in political affairs of the State or Nation, or in the more immediate concerns of their own county.

Mr. Hinckle owns three hundred and twenty acres of land in Sumner County in addition to that already mentioned as belonging to him in Sedgwick County. He is a self-made man, having accumulated all his present property since he began life as an humble hired farm hand. Industry and good management have been the principal factors in the success which he has achieved. He is not a politician, and has no desire for office, preferring home life to the agitation of public affairs, but, nevertheless, he keeps posted in all issues of national or local importance. He affiliates with the Prohibition party, but is not a strict party man, aiming to vote for the best man irrespective of party. He was a member of the Patrons of Husbandry when that organization had an existence. His experience in this county dates back to its beginning. He has witnessed its gradual improvement and development from a wild prairie where the Indian and buffalo held full sway, to the present, when the forces emanating from the brain of man have changed it to a fit residence for refined people, and made it the dwelling place of cheerful prosperity.

The parents of Mr. Hinckle were both members of the denomination known as the United Brethren in Christ, and were worthy and devout people. The father of Mr. Hinckle was a local preacher in that church. Mr. and Mrs. Hinckle are natives of Virginia and West Virginia, respectively, where they have many friends.

RICHARD B. DAVIS. For the past sixteen years Mr. Davis has been a continuous resident of this county, and during this time has lived at his present homestead on section 27, Jackson Township. He shared in the labors and struggles of the early pioneers, and has made for himself a good record, having been a peaceful and law-abiding citizen, attending closely to his own concerns, and in assisting in the development of a good farm, has thus contributed his quota to the growth and prosperity of his adopted county.

Mr. Davis is a native of Illinois, having been born in Bear Creek Precinct, Montgomery County, November 20, 1846. He is the second son of Matthew and Sarah (Bentley) Davis, further mention of whom is made in the sketch of the brother of our subject, J. H. Davis, on another page in this volume.

As soon as large enough, young Davis was sent to the pioneer school of his neighborhood, and at an early age, he also was required to assist in the labors of the farm as far as his strength would permit. His father died when he was a lad of twelve, and he continued at the homestead during the years which followed, assisting his mother in the support of the family, and remaining under the old roof-tree until 1873. Then, in company with his brother, Jonathan H., he started out for the country west of the Mississippi, overland with a team, making his way to this county. Much of the land in this region was at that time owned by the Government, and was thinly settled, presenting a wild picture of frontier life.

The land selected by Mr. Davis, comprised the southeast quarter of section 28, in what is now Jackson Township, and after he had filed his claim, he returned to Illinois to settle up his affairs. In the fall of that same year, he started on the return journey to Kansas, accompanied by his mother, his sisters, and a younger brother, journeying as before, overland with a team. The mother, upon her arrival here, selected the southwest quarter of section 27, as her property, entering the same at the Land Office at Wichita. Upon this land a house was at once put up, and other buildings added as time and means allowed. Mr. Davis and his brothers proceeded with the improvement of the joint farm, and the mother resided with them until her death, in August, 1886.

The two sisters, Nancy and Clarissa, continue their residence at the homestead. The latter now presents the picture of a thoroughly improved farm, which has been enlarged from its original proportions, comprising now two hundred and forty acres, and embellished with substantial buildings.

Mr. Davis for the past few years has given considerable attention to stock-raising, in which industry he has been fairly successful. He still pursues his life of single blessedness, his sisters presiding over his domestic affairs, and he has accumulated a sufficiency of this world's goods to defend him against want in his declining years. In summing up the list of the early pioneers of this county, it must be acknowledged that Mr. Davis, one of the most worthy, has performed well his part, and is amply worthy of representation in a work designed to perpetuate their names and deeds.

JOHN T. McMILLAN, one of the earliest settlers of Sumner County, resides on the southwest quarter of section 34, Belle Plaine Township. He was born December 6, 1833, in Jefferson County, Ind., to John and Mary (Shannon) McMillan. The father was a native of Ayr, Scotland, and emigrated to America in October, 1803, locating first in New York and afterward removing to Lexington, Ky., September 12, 1805. He was a fine architect and followed that profession in both of the above-named places for a number of years. The mother of our subject was born in Fayette County, Ky., and was a daughter of George Shannon, who settled in Jefferson County, Ind., in the early days of its history when everything was new and the future gave little promise of the wonderful development that was to come.

The father and mother of our subject were united in marriage April 26, 1815. They had a family of eight children, of whom John T. is the youngest in order of birth. Their eldest son, George, was a minister of the United Presbyterian Church until death relieved him. The rest of the family were all members of the Presbyterian faith. The Shannon family was of considerable note in that new country, as they invested in quite a body of choice land, and the uncle of this subject, George Shannon, was the first Surveyor in this part of the State, and did much valuable work for the community in which he lived.

The subject of this notice was reared in his native county, and after a thorough course in the common school, he attended the Hanover College awhile. This institution is located in Hanover, Ind., and is the oldest Presbyterian college in the State. The father of our subject was a hardware merchant for a number of years and besides this, he was the owner of two fine farms, one of which he had farmed himself, and after the death of his father, John T. being then not quite twelve years of age, he and his mother lived on the farm and followed agricultural pursuits until the year 1856. His mother died September 21, 1855, and a portion of 1857 he spent in Illinois and other places. He then leased out the homestead which he had fallen heir to, and in the fall of 1858, concluded to go to Texas, and leaving the Hoosier State at Madison, on board a new steamer, the "Diana," which had just been built for the Galveston and Houston trade, he thus proceeded down the Ohio and Mississippi Rivers to New Orleans, where he crossed on the Gulf to Galveston, Tex. The passage across the Gulf came very near being of a serious nature, had the "Diana" not reached a harbor at Vermillion Bay, just in time to escape a fearful storm, in which two Gulf steamers were badly disabled. The passage across the Gulf occupied several days before reaching Galveston, but our subject enjoyed the novel experience of a taste of sea life on a common river steamboat. In a few more days he reached his destination, Houston, Tex., where his friends met him, rejoicing, as the report had been there for several days, that the "Diana" was lost. Mr. McMillan remained at that place for some time engaged in mercantile pursuits. He was a resident of the Lone Star State for six or seven years, residing in different counties and following different occupations, but principally engaged in an agency, after leaving Texas. He finally drifted Northward again and in July, 1865, found himself once more in his native State, where he remained some two or three years. He concluded to settle again on the old homestead, and was married the first time to Miss Sarah A. Leap. The marriage was celebrated at the home of the bride, near Hanover, Ind., January 4, 1866. She was a refined and gentle woman, but unfitted, physically, to cope with the rigors of their changeable climate. So in the spring of 1868 they removed to Kansas, hoping it might benefit his wife's health, and first located in Lawrence, Douglas County, where he remained but a short time, then went to Labette County, where he engaged in the milling business. His first venture was with a sawmill which he operated with good success in that county, until he had the sad misfortune of losing his wife, who had previous to this time borne her husband two children: Cora A., and Ada E., who are at rest beneath the green sod with their loving mother. So not long after Mr. McMillan's sad bereavement he removed his sawmill west to Cowley County, on the Walnut River, three miles below Winfield, where it was operated one season with good success, during which time he located for pre-emption a quarter section of land in Sumner County on section 31, the same on which he now lives, which was done in the fall of 1870. He afterward decided to remove his mill to Oxford, Sumner County, and in addition to the sawmill he also put up a gristmill at the same place, which was the first to be erected in that part of the State. He operated the mill in that place for about three years, in the meantime controlling territory from thirty to fifty miles around, as he was the only gristmill owner within a radius of that distance. He is proud of the distinction of being the first to grind (grain) wheat, corn, and buckwheat in his section of the country where it was so much needed. After this Mr. McMillan went East onto the Mississippi River and engaged again in the sawmill business for two or three years, after which time he had the misfortune to have his mill burned up. He then went to the mountains in Colorado to look for his fortune but was not very successful. He was in the milling business altogether about twelve years. After Mr. McMillan returned from the mountains he then went onto his land where he now resides, and commenced improving with a determination of making a home of it. Mr. McMillan was again married on the 29th of December,

1879, to Miss Hattie M. Dickinson, a young lady of great decision and force of character, and the daughter of George W. Dickinson, of Madison, Ind. They are the parents of one daughter, Pearl B.

Mr. McMillan owns three hundred and sixty acres of land under a high state of cultivation. He turned the first furrow on his place at a time when there was no wagon road near, nothing but the hunter's trail. There was no town laid off in the county when he settled in it and he has lived to see it develop from that primitive state of wildness to its present condition of wealth, culture and refinement. In common with most pioneers he endured some privations and hardships but he feels amply repaid for his sacrifices by the present prosperous condition in which everything is progressing in his adopted State and county. He is a friend and helper of everything tending to the upbuilding of the community either from a material or intellectual point of view.

Mr. and Mrs. McMillan are members of the Presbyterian Church and take a deep interest in the religious education of the rising generation and are highly esteemed in church and society circles. Mr. McMillan is a Democrat and is distinguished as the first Democrat to locate in the county. He takes only a moderate share in purely party affairs, but keeps himself well posted in regard to those questions of the time that concern all good American citizens and is ever ready to lend a helping hand to whatever promises good to the nation or his own community.

ALBERT D. SPARR, Postmaster of Millerton and its pioneer merchant, is widely and favorably known to the people of this part of Sumner County as a man who has been for many years identified with her closest interests. Notwithstanding a varied experience and many years spent in business channels, he is a comparatively young man, having been born February 11, 1850. His native place was in Blair County, Pa., and his parents were John and Susannah (Shultz) Sparr, who were likewise natives of the Keystone State, within whose limits they reared their family of ten children, of whom Albert D. was the eldest. The father occupied himself at farming until his death, which took place in his native State in 1865. He was a man of many excellent qualities and a member in good standing of the Lutheran Church. He had been twice married, becoming by his first union the father of two children.

The subject of this sketch, in 1869, leaving his native State, made his way to Peoria County, Ill., and sojourned there until April, 1873. Then crossing the Father of Waters, he came to this county and pre-empted one hundred and sixty acres in London Township, where he lived until 1876. In the meantime he had been joined by his widowed mother. That year he sold out and purchased an improved farm of one hundred and sixty acres in Conway Township. He occupied that four years, effecting many improvements, then retiring from the active labors of farm life removed to the village of Millerton, which had just been laid out. Soon afterward he added to the importance of the embryo town by putting up a substantial residence and purchasing a stock of goods of his brothers, Edmund and Martin L., who had opened the first store in the town. He entered upon his career as business merchant, which he has since followed successfully, building up a good business.

Mr. Sparr was appointed Postmaster in the fall of 1886, a position which he still holds and in which he has given general satisfaction. In the fall of 1887 he was elected Township Assessor, and has since been annually re-elected. In the meantime he has served as Clerk of the School Board and is the only Notary Public in Millerton, having held this office since November, 1885. He has also served as Township Clerk. Every movement calculated to advance the welfare of the place has been warmly seconded by Mr. Sparr, who may be looked upon as decidedly one of the city fathers.

Mr. Sparr remained a bachelor until twenty-eight years old and then took unto himself a wife and helpmate, Miss Mary F. Martin, to whom he was wedded April 25, 1888. This lady was born in Jasper County, Mo., and was the daughter of Joshua and Sarah (Vance) Martin. Mr. Martin was a stanch Union man during the war and was a man who was highly respected in his community. He was shot and instantly killed by bushwhackers July 29, 1863, at his home in Joplin, Mo. These bushwhackers claimed to be Union men and accused Mr. Martin of secretly working in behalf of the rebel army. It was confidently believed, however, that they were rebels and accomplished his death to effect their purpose. Prior to this they had burned his house with the most of its contents, together with his barn, granary, corn cribs and all the buildings on the farm with the outstanding grain. Mrs. Martin was compelled to flee for her life on foot, as her teams and stock were also driven off, she being thus left without means or resources of any kind. Upon one occasion her thirteen-year-old son, who had gone to mill with an ox-team, was waylaid by the outlaws and the wagon and team taken from him, he being compelled to walk home. The Martin family were not by any means the only sufferers from marauders in that region, as Unionists generally were treated in the same manner by the rebel element.

Mrs. Martin spent the winter of 1863-64 in Carthage, Mo., and the following spring came with her family of eight children to Kansas, traveling from Ft. Scott with a freighting train. (Her two younger children, twins, were born in September, 1863, a short time after the death of their father). She was destitute of money, but having extended much kindness to a sick soldier in Missouri, the United States supply train men on this account assisted her in getting to Kansas, providing all the necessities for her and her children on the journey to Ft. Scott, and at that point hired a team by which she was conveyed to Lawrence, in the vicinity of which she had a brother living. The latter was unable to go down to Carthage after her because it was dangerous for a Northern man to visit that region.

Mrs. Martin lived for a time in Douglas County, this State, until one of her sons, Joseph, came to Illinois Township, this county, and took up a claim, after which she joined him. Four of her children are now residents of this county, and she makes her home among them. Joshua Martin was a prominent

member of the Baptist Church, in which he officiated as Deacon. He was born in Kentucky and
went to Missouri with his parents when a mere boy.
He was first married to Miss Elizabeth Edwards,
who bore him eight children and died in Joplin.

The mother of Mrs. Sparr was a widow when
she married Mr. Martin, her first husband having
been Isaac N. Thompson, who died in 1860, while
on his way to California, leaving two children.

There have been born to Mr. and Mrs. Sparr five
children, viz: Luther L., Ernest E., Albert D., Mil-
son V. and Zora Q. They are all living at home.
Mr. and Mrs. Sparr, as may be supposed, enjoy the
esteem and confidence of a host of friends. Beside
his village and farm property Mr. Sparr has a business house at Conway Springs, a part of which is
occupied as the post-office. For four years he conducted a store on his farm, abandoning it when the
railroad was built and the station located at Millerton.

⟶ ⟶ ⟶ ⟶⟪╬╪⟫⟶ ⟶ ⟶ ⟵

AMUEL F. CLINARD. This gentleman
is numbered among the old settlers of
Sumner County, and is well known as an
enterprising and progressive farmer, a
reliable citizen, and a man of upright life and
character. His attractive farm consists of three
hundred and twenty acres on sections 17 and 8,
Greene Township, and is a productive and valuable
estate.

Mr. Clinard was born in Clermont County, Ohio,
March 22, 1844, and is a son of Henry and Sarah
(Ferguson) Clinard. The parents removed to
Pettis County, Mo., when our subject was about
five years old, and in that and Saline Counties he
grew to manhood. The father was a blacksmith
and gave his son every advantage possible in the
way of acquiring an education. The young man
attended Jones Commercial Academy at St. Louis
about six months, and also attended the Missouri
State Normal School at Kirksville, for more than
half a year. He adopted the profession of a
teacher, and for seven or eight years was engaged
in pedagogical labors in Pettis and Saline Counties,
proving his efficiency in the school room, and sow-

ing seed which would develop and bring forth
fruits of usefulness in the lives of his pupils long
after he had left their midst.

In the summer of 1876, Mr. Clinard came to this
county and pre-empted one hundred and sixty
acres on section 17, immediately beginning work
upon the same, which is now in a fine state of productiveness and improvement. Since settling here
Mr. Clinard has given his attention almost wholly
to farming and stock-raising, and is demonstrating
the fact that book lore is not incompatible with
success in the more mechanical employments, when
practical common sense and good judgment are
brought to bear with one's theoretical knowledge.
He has added to his landed estate since his first
settlement, now holding the amount mentioned at
the beginning of this article, the whole comprising
a home with which any man might well be pleased.

In Saline County, Mo., February 27, 1879, Mr.
Clinard was united in marriage with Mrs. Magda-
line (Carmean) Stanley, who was born in Ross
County, Ohio, December 26, 1845, and who is an
educated woman, of noble Christian character, and
one who in every department of life is faithful and
efficient in the discharge of her duties, so letting
her light shine in the midst of her associates. Mrs.
Clinard is a daughter of John and Susannah
(DeHaven) Carmean, and at the date of her marriage
with our subject was the widow of Winfield S.
Stanley, who died in Saline County, Mo., February
11, 1876. By her first marriage she became the
mother of two children, Frank M. and Mattie E.
To herself and Mr. Clinard three children have
come: Pearlie M., now brightening their fireside,
while John H. and Rhoda were taken from them in
their infancy.

In the spring of 1880, Mr. Clinard was elected
Trustee of Greene Township, being the first incumbent of that office, a position which he held for
five consecutive years. He has also held some of
the school offices, and in every position manifests
an intelligent understanding of the duties accruing
to it and an earnest determination to fulfill them to
the best of his ability. In politics he favors the
principles of the Democracy and therefore supports
them with his vote. He belongs to the Farmers'
Alliance. Both himself and wife are professing

Christians, the one being a member of the Baptist and the other of the Methodist Church, and both having high standing in their respective denominations.

ROSTIEN L. WRIGHT. No citizen of South Haven is held in higher respect than the subject of this notice, who was one of the first men upon the ground after the laying out of the town and had the honor of serving as the first City Treasurer. He is at present engaged in the grocery business, including cigars, tobacco and confectionery, and by his straightforward method of dealing with his fellow-citizens, has earned their confidence and esteem as well as a substantial patronage.

Mr. Wright was born in Montgomery County, Ohio, February 9, 1850, and spent his early years in Springfield, Yellow Springs and Dayton, that State. His father, Isaac K. Wright, a native of Philadelphia, Pa., was engaged during his later years as a merchant tailor, and died at Philadelphia in 1868. His mother bore the maiden name of Mitchell and is now living in Cowley County, Kan.

Mr. Wright after reaching his majority, came, in October, 1871, across the Mississippi, joining a corps of men who had been appointed to survey the Indian Territory. He operated with them two years and at the expiration of this time, located on a pre-emption claim at a time when few white settlers had come to this section and when buffalo and other wild animals roamed at will over the country. Erecting a frame house, young Wright thereafter lived by himself for about ten years, carrying on farming and keeping bachelor's hall. He had a dairy of from ten to twenty cows, from which he manufactured quantities of butter. He hired men to assist him in his farm operations, doing the cooking for the whole crowd, and afterward occupied for some time an old log building that had formerly been utilized as a trading post.

Finally, however, realizing the fact that it was not good for man to be alone, Mr. Wright, in September, 1881, was wedded in Cowley County,

this State, to Miss Lydia A., daughter of N. C. and Margaret (Raszell) Heizer. This lady was born in Fayette County, Ind., in 1852, of parents who were natives of Indiana and who are now living in Sumner County. Mr. and Mrs. Wright remained on the farm in Cowley County until the spring of 1885, then Mr. Wright purchasing a farm in Guelph Township, this county, removed to it, living there until February, 1887. His next removal was to the embryo town of South Haven. Here he associated himself with a partner, J. M. Johnson, and they engaged in the dry-goods and grocery business. In April following Mr. Wright established a new grocery store by himself, which he has since successfully conducted. There have been born to him and his estimable wife two children: Maggie E. and Carrie C. Mr. and Mrs. Wright are actively connected with the Methodist Episcopal Church.

The parents of Mrs. Wright came to Kansas in 1877, settling first in Cowley County and later removed to South Haven Township, this county. Mr. Heizer was born in Fayette County, Ind., and his wife was a native of Decatur County, that State. The latter with her parents, Nehemiah and Nancy A. (Wherrett) Raszell removed to Fayette County where she was reared, and where her parents spent the remainder of their lives.

ALBERT M. COLSON, President of the Citizen's Bank of Caldwell, is also extensively engaged as a dealer in live stock and is one of the leading men of Southern Kansas. By a course of industry and prudence, he has become independent, financially, while his genial and companionable temperament draws around him friends wherever he goes. He is a gentleman of fine business abilities, and enjoys the distinction of being one of the first settlers of Sumner County. A native of Eaton, Madison County, N. Y., he was born March 13, 1843, and is the son of Brackley and Susan (Salter) Colson.

Brackley Colson was a native of Connecticut

and a hatter by trade, at which he worked the greater part of his life. He accumulated considerable means and lived to a ripe old age, dying in 1885, after having passed his ninety-second year. The wife and mother was born in Massachusetts and outlived her husband one month only, dying in 1885 at the age of eighty-seven years. Their married life had embraced the long period of sixty-seven years. There were born unto them nine children of whom Albert M. was the youngest.

Mr. Colson was reared in his native town, receiving such advantages as were afforded by the common school. He was variously employed until the outbreak of the Civil War, then enlisted as a private in Company C, Ninety-first New York Infantry, which was first assigned to the Department of the Gulf and later went with the Fifth Army Corps under the command of Gen. Warren. After a faithful service of four years, during which he shared with his comrades the various dangers and hardships in the army, Mr. Colson received his honorable discharge in July, 1865. Soon afterward he emigrated to the Pacific Coast, following various pursuits for a number of years. We find him first in Kansas in 1870, locating in this county, of which he has since been a continuous resident. He arrived here prior to its organization and upon this important occasion was elected Superintendent of Public Instruction. He soon took up his residence in Caldwell and in due time became a member of the City Council and finally the Mayor. He has watched the growth and development of the town with unabated interest, and has contributed his full quota toward bringing it to its present condition.

In 1887 in company with other leading residents of Caldwell, Mr. Colson assisted in organizing the Citizens Bank, of which he was elected President, a position which he has since held with credit to himself and satisfaction to all concerned. He came to the Sunflower State poor in purse, and has had no assistance from any one, financially. By industry and good management, he has accumulated a comfortable property, including considerable real estate in this county, besides the Caldwell zern Hotel at Caldwell. He has for some years dealt considerably in live stock, realizing ample returns therefrom. He cast his first Presidential vote for Lincoln and remains a loyal adherent of the Republican party. He is a Mason in good standing and Commander of Upton Post, No. 27, G. A. R. at Caldwell. He is also a K. of P., Uniform Rank. Mr. Colson was first wedded in 1871, to Miss Mary Goldey of Milan, this State. This lady was born in Iowa and after becoming the mother of one child, a daughter, Fawnie, died at their home in Caldwell in 1879. The following year Mr. Colson contracted a second marriage with Mrs. Mary J. Garetson. Mrs. Mary Colson was born in Litchfield, Ill., April 11, 1853. Of her first marriage there was born two children, a daughter, Katie and son Charlie who died July 11, 1877. The Colson residence is pleasantly located in the north part of the city and is the frequent resort of its most intelligent and cultured people.

~~~~~~~~~~~~

MRS. MARGARET E. CAPPS. One of the finest farms in Belle Plaine Township belongs to the lady with whose name we introduce this sketch and embraces two hundred and forty acres of well-developed land on sections 1 and 12. It is embellished with good buildings with fruit and shade trees and is supplied with the most approved machinery for the successful prosecution of agriculture. Mrs. Capps is a lady of more than ordinary intelligence and fine business capacities and manages her property with rare good judgment. Socially, she occupies a leading position in her community.

Mrs. Capps was born in Sangamon County, Ill., September 2, 1818, and is the daughter of James P. and America (Morris) Hilyard, who were natives of Virginia. Mr. Hilyard removed from the Old Dominion with his parents when a small boy to Sangamon County, Ill., they locating among its earliest pioneers. His wife, America, also came to that region with her parents when a young girl. They lived there for some time after their marriage, Mr. Hilyard engaging in agricultural pursuits. In the meantime he served as a soldier during the war with Mexico and afterward removed from Sangamon to Macon County, where he made his home four years.

Mr. Hilyard came to Kansas in 1870, taking up his abode in Greenwood County. The parental household consisted of fourteen children of whom Margaret E. was the fourth in order of birth. She was a maiden of seventeen years when the family removed to Macon County and she was there married November 24, 1867, to Ephraim James. Mr. James was born near Columbus, Ohio, March 19, 1837, and became a resident of Macon County, Ill. After their marriage Mr. and Mrs. James continued to live there until their removal to Kansas in 1874. They settled in Belle Plaine Township, Mr. James purchasing six hundred and fifty acres of land upon which he engaged quite extensively in farming until the illness which resulted in his death, April 14, 1884.

To Mr. and Mrs. James there was born a family of eight children, the eldest of whom, a daughter, Laura J., is the wife of O. C. Watson of Belle Plaine; William lives in Belle Plaine Township; Powell died when one year old; Emma, Elmer, Albert, George and Sybil, remain at home with their mother. Mrs. Margaret E. James was a second time married April 19, 1888, to E. S. Capps, a native of Illinois and of English parentage.

In religious belief Mrs. Capps is a Universalist, as was also her first husband. Mr. James was an intelligent man and took a warm interest in educational affairs.

HOMAS R. MORDY. Among the residents of Sumner County, who claim English birth and parentage, this gentleman is numbered. As a successful agriculturalist, an early settler and a prominent citizen, he well deserves notice in a volume of this character. He now resides on a farm in Belle Plaine Township, which from an eighty-acre tract, he has increased two-fold, besides redeeming the soil from its primitive condition and erecting substantial buildings on the homestead. He is identified with all important movements in the history of the township,

and is a member of the Subordinate Lodge of I. O. O. F. at Belle Plaine, also of the Encampment at Mulvane, being a charter member of both organizations. Politically, he supports the principles of the Republican party, and is at present serving his third term as Treasurer of the Twenty-fourth School District.

Durham County, England, was the native place of our subject, and the date of his birth February 13, 1845. He was the youngest son born to John and Dorothy (Robson) Mordy, who were born in England, and after passing their entire lives on its soil, also passed to rest there. Our subject's education has been principally self-obtained, as in his youth he had very limited advantages. He was reared in his native county, and until the age of seventeen years, remained under the parental roof. Then, commencing for himself, he worked in the Durham County coal mines until he resolved to come to America.

Taking passage in the steamer "Louisiana," which sailed from the port of Liverpool April 26, 1864. Mr. Mordy arrived in New York City on the 11th of May. Thence he went to Pennsylvania and worked in coal mines, principally in Schuylkill County. He was there during the Mollie McGuire period, but in the spring of 1866 removed to Tuscarawas County, Ohio, whence, after spending a short time engaged in digging coal and farming, he returned to Pennsylvania. He once again sought the Buckeye State, where he was united in marriage August 22, 1867, with Emma Beberly, who was born in Germany July 10, 1844 and was the daughter of Charles and Theresa Beberly. When about two years of age she came with her mother to the United States.

Mr. and Mrs. Mordy have a family of bright and intelligent children, five in number. The eldest, James, is deceased. Cora, Thomas, Simon, John and Vivian are at home and are receiving good educational advantages. In January, 1878, Mr. Mordy, with his wife and children, came from their home in the Buckeye State to Sumner County, Kan., having in the former place traded a horse and buggy and seventy bushels of corn, for the eighty-acre farm where they now live. This land was practically unimproved, when he settled on it, being in about the same condition left by the Indians. It required many years to bring the farm up to its present high state of cultivation, while prudent economy enabled him to purchase another eighty acres. Upon coming to the Sunflower State he had $6 ahead. His present prosperity is due in no small measure to the assistance he has received from his wife, who has been his helpmate and counselor for years. He has witnessed the gradual development of the county and has contributed his share to the same. His farm is a monument to his industry, and is being subjected to constant improvements.

APT. GEORGE D. ARMSTRONG. This gentleman first set foot upon the soil of Kansas during the early settlement of this county, when the land now lying within its limits was the property of Uncle Sam and when few settlers had ventured into this region. He landed here in June, 1871, and at once entered a claim to the northeast quarter of section 33, in what is now Avon Township, filing his claim in the Land Office at Wichita. He was not then married and did not build upon his land until the following year, when he put up a solid oak frame house which thereafter remained his residence until 1879. Then selling out, he purchased his present farm, which occupies the southeast quarter of section 3, Jackson Township. Here he has erected a set of frame buildings, has gotten together the requisite farm machinery, planted a large variety of fruit trees and surrounded his dwelling with shade and ornamental trees. His property is now numbered among the attractive rural homes of the county where is indicated in a marked manner the enterprise of the proprietor, his industry as an agriculturist and his worth as a member of the community.

Mr. Armstrong was born a little over fifty years ago, December 3, 1839, in Shelby County, Ohio, where he spent the first ten years of his life and then removed with his parents to Illinois. He was a young man approaching the twenty-second year

of his age at the outbreak of the Civil War and that same year, in October, 1861, proffered his services to assist in the preservation of the Union, enlisting in Company F, Fifty-ninth Illinois Infantry. A few months later, however, in April, 1862, he was obliged to accept his discharge on account of disability. Upon recovering from his ailment, however, he in July following, re-enlisted in Company B, Ninety-seventh Illinois Infantry and had the satisfaction of serving until the enemies of the Government had been subjugated. He participated in many of the important battles of the war, meeting the enemy at Pea Ridge, Chickasaw Bluffs, the siege of Vicksburg, Port Gibson, Raymond, Champion Hills, Black River Bridge, Ft. Blakely and other minor engagements. After the close of the war he received his honorable discharge and was mustered out at Galveston, Tex.

At the second enlistment of Mr. Armstrong in the army, he was mustered in as private and later for gallant and meritorious conduct on the field, was promoted through the different grades and finally was given a Captain's commission. He justly looks upon that period of his life as something to be proud of. In August, 1865, Mr. Armstrong returned to Illinois and in connection with farming, worked at the trade of a plasterer, which he had learned prior to entering the army. He sojourned in Coles County until 1870 and spent the following year in California. In 1871 he came to Kansas.

Mr. Armstrong found a wife and helpmate in this county, having been married October 13, 1872, to Miss Sarah A. Gregson. Mrs. Armstrong is a native of Indiana and the daughter of Joseph and Elizabeth (Montgomery) Gregson, who came to this county at an early day, settling in Avon Township; they are now residing in Avon. Of the seven children born to the Captain and his excellent lady, three died in infancy. The survivors are Irving, Albert, Minnie and Edwin. Since coming to this county Mr. Armstrong has identified himself with its most important interests, especially in the rural districts and among the fruit growers. He is a leading member of the State and Sumner County Horticultural Societies and belongs to the Southern Kansas Farmers' Alliance. James Shields

Post, No. 57, G. A. R. recognizes Capt. Armstrong as one of its most worthy members. He and his estimable wife are prominently connected with the Methodist Episcopal Church.

The immediate progenitor of Capt. Armstrong was John S. Armstrong, who was born September 30, 1806, in Gallia County, Ohio. The paternal grandfather, Andrew Armstrong, a native of Mifflin County, Pa., was born March 15, 1777, and was reared in his native county. He emigrated to Ohio during the early settlement of the State and was married in Gallia County, October 4, 1803, to Miss Susan Snider. Grandmother Armstrong was born in North Carolina June 18, 1779. Her father, John Snider, was born in September, 1751, in North Carolina and removed to Ohio during the pioneer days of Gallia County, where he constructed a home in the wilderness and spent his last years.

Andrew Armstrong after his removal to Ohio sojourned a few years in Gallia County, then removed to Clark County and finally to Shelby County. In the latter he entered a tract of heavily timbered land from which he cleared a farm and there resided until his death on the 25th of March, 1840. His wife had died in Clark County, August 24, 1817. Their son, John S., the father of our subject, when becoming his own man, took up his abode in Miami County where he sojourned a few years, but about 1815, settled in Logan County. There he proceeded as had his father and grandfather before him, purchasing a tract of timber land and constructing a farm. Upon this, however, a few acres had been cleared and there had been erected a double log house. This was long before the days of railroads in that region and for some years thereafter the town of Sidney, twenty-five miles away, was the nearest market and trading point. Upon the building of the first railroad, John Armstrong secured the contract to supply the timber for one mile of the road. Much more lumber was then employed in the construction of a track than is now used, heavy timbers then being laid lengthwise the road bed, the cross ties being laid upon them and upon these another layer of lengthwise timbers upon which were spiked the iron rails. Father Armstrong cleared considerable of his land, residing there until about 1851.

In the above-mentioned year the father of our subject, selling out his interest in the Buckeye State, started overland for Illinois with teams. He was accompanied by his wife and seven children, and upon arriving in Cumberland County purchased a tract of land in Long Point Precinct, comprising one hundred and sixty acres of timber and the same of prairie. The latter embraced a part of what was known as Parker's Prairie. A hewed log house was put up, the first ever built in that region. No railroads were made in Illinois for several years thereafter and Terre Haute, forty miles distant, was the nearest market, milling place and depot for supplies. Deer were plentiful and the Armstrongs could often see droves of them passing not very far from their own doorway. They lived there until 1863, then the father, selling out once more, changed his abode to Coles County, purchasing a farm six miles southeast of Mattoon. In 1871 he made another removal, selling out again and settling in Bond County, purchasing an improved farm near Greenville. There John Armstrong spent his last years, dying on the 20th of June, 1880.

The mother of Mr. Armstrong of this sketch bore the maiden name of Priscilla Dye. She was born in Miami County, Ohio, July 12, 1818, and was the daughter of John Minor Dye who was born August 24, 1773, and was one of the earliest pioneers of Miami County. He was a man of great industry and perseverance and improved a large farm from the wilderness near which the city of Troy afterward grew up. There he spent his remaining days, passing away April 1, 1842, at the age of sixty-nine years. He was married to Elizabeth Clyne who was born in June, 1775, and died January 5, 1852.

Mrs. Priscilla (Dye) Armstrong departed this life at her home in Bond County, Ill., March 31, 1879. To her and her husband was born a family of twelve children, two of whom, James and Samuel died young. They were named respectively: Andrew M., James, George D., Elizabeth A., John C., Henry C., Charles M., Priscilla, T. Alexander, Mary E., Samuel S., and Walter Grant.

Joseph Gregson, Mrs. Armstrong's father, was born in Indiana in 1828, and was married June 1,

1854, to Miss Elizabeth Montgomery, who was born in Ohio in 1836. Of this union there were born eight children, as follows: Sarah A., Mary C., William C., Joseph F., Carrie E., Alvin W., Commodore P., Lee W. All of these are living.

JOSEPH THEW, one of the early settlers of Oxford, came to this county before the railroad was built through, and purchased a farm of one hundred and sixty acres, adjoining the village of Oxford on the west. With the exception of the soil having been broken, no improvements whatever had been made on the place, but going at once to work, our subject planted out an orchard, erected a good residence, setting out a grove and in other ways improved the farm.

Upon coming to Kansas, Joseph Thew was accompanied by his wife, whose maiden name was Mary Hayward, and who was born in England May 20, 1821. When four years of age she accompanied her parents to the United States, and settled with them in Pennsylvania. Her father, Isaac Hayward, was a farmer by occupation. Her mother, Ann Shepard, was also a native of England. Later the family removed to Ohio, where Mary met and married Joseph Thew, the wedding being celebrated December 20, 1843. The father afterward located near Ft. Wayne, Ind., and lived there until his death in 1884, and after a residence in the Hoosier State of about twenty years.

Mrs. Thew first began housekeeping in Marion County, Ohio, where her husband was engaged in the shoe business and where their children were born. They were six in number and are all living, and named respectively: Olive Ann, J. Wesley, Francis, Ella, A. Lizzie and William. Mr. and Mrs. Thew removed to Indiana when their youngest son William was eighteen months old. After a short sojourn there they located in Noble County, the same State, where Mr. Thew continued in the same business as before. In that county they resided for eighteen years, coming thence to Kansas in 1877.

Having purchased his farm before coming to this State, Mr. Thew came directly here via the railroad to Wichita. He conveyed his lumber from the latter city and put up at the first good house in the country, and it is still in a good condition. He was not a politician, but was a member for many years of the Methodist Episcopal Church. He was born in England in 1819 and when six years of age with his father removed to Ohio, settling in Morrow County. His father, Richard Thew, there engaged as a farmer. Here our subject grew to manhood and lived until his marriage, which occurred as above stated, in 1843. He was one of the leading men of the township in which he resided, and highly spoken of by all who knew him. He died in Oxford after a long illness, January 8, 1883. Of his children, Olive married Albert Rice of this township, and has one child, Frank. J. W. married Miss Quintilla Flowers, by whom he has two children —Grace and Lenna. He lives in Oxford. F. H. married Emma Frink, and they have three children- Iva, Bessie and Bernie. Ella married D. F. Owens, of Dodge City, Kan. They have two children, Mabel and William. A. Lizzie married D. A. Griffith, now of Chicago. Their two children are Ethel and Mansure. William married Ann A. Gibbons, and has one child, Joseph. Mr. and Mrs. Thew lost two children, Ellen M. and Charles Wesley.

Mrs. Thew was again married in this township to William G. Lewis, who came to Kansas in the summer of 1877, settling at Belle Plaine, and there lived until coming to Oxford. He was born in 1837 in Pittsburg, Pa., where he lived until coming West and taking up a claim.

BENJAMIN F. HAMILTON, M. D., Coroner of Sumner County, and a leading physician and surgeon of Wellington, was first elected to his present office in November, 1887. He was re-elected in 1889, having filled the office most acceptably to the people. He located in Wellington, in the fall of 1884.

Dr. Hamilton was born near Meadon, Mercer County, Ohio, August 31, 1857, and there grew to mature years. He completed his education at Valparaiso, Ind., and subsequently taught school five years in Ohio, a part of which time he was Superintendent of the Mendon schools. In the meantime for three years he occupied his leisure hours in the reading of medicine and later placed himself under the instruction of Dr. J. B. Haines, of Mendon. When sufficiently prepared he took a course of lectures in the Ohio Medical College at Cincinnati, from which he was graduated in the class of 1883. He commenced the practice of his profession in his native place and in the fall of 1884, coming to Kansas, settled first at Millerton, Sumner County, whence in the spring of 1886 he removed to Wellington. He is now in the enjoyment of a lucrative business and is looked upon as a valuable member of the community. He has never sought office but keeps himself well posted in political affairs and gives his support to the Republican party.

Dr. Hamilton was married August 23, 1885 in Wellington, Kan., to Miss Luella Mann. Mrs. Hamilton was born in Shelby County, Ill., September 5, 1866, and is the daughter of John and Maggie Mann, who were natives of Illinois. Mr. Mann is at present engaged in the hardware business at Wellington. He came to Sumner County in 1884. To the Doctor and his estimable wife there have been born two children, only one of whom is living, a babe unnamed. Barrus F. died at the age of one year, three months and seventeen days. The father of our subject was Justin D. Hamilton, a native of Mercer County, Ohio, who married Eliza J. Snavely. He was bred to farming pursuits and with his estimable wife occupies the old homestead where he was born.

ARMOUR C. LAMBE. In making notice of the men who came to this county during the period of its early settlement, the name of Mr. Lambe could by no means be properly omitted from the category. His career has been signalized by unflagging industry and a perseverance that was bound to overcome all obstacles. He met with the usual difficulties and drawbacks of life in a new country at a time when a long journey was involved in going to market and mill, and when the country was poorly supplied with the facilities for either agriculture or any other industry. He not only watched the march of events with a warm interest and faith in the future of the Sunflower State, but in building up one of its most creditable homesteads has contributed his full quota to bring about the welfare and prosperity of his adopted county. He is now in possession of a well-tilled farm of one hundred and sixty acres, whereon he has effected good improvements and is in a condition to rest upon his oars.

Mr. Lambe, besides the property above mentioned, owns another body of land on section 23, the homestead proper lying on section 28, and both are largely devoted to stock-raising. His native place was County Tyrone, Ireland, and the date of his birth September 25, 1830. He lived there until a youth of sixteen years, attending the common schools and learning the art of agriculture as conducted in the Emerald Isle. When a youth of sixteen years, desirous of bettering his condition, and seeing little prospect of this upon his native soil, he set out with his father for America, settling in Clinton County, Ill. He lived there until a young man of twenty years, then emigrated to St. Louis, Mo., and for ten years thereafter had charge of an omnibus line. At the expiration of this time, tired of city life, he returned to Clinton County, Ill., and engaged in farming. He sojourned there until coming to Kansas in 1870. In this State he first took up his abode in Montgomery County, but only lived there about one year, removing the following spring to Sumner County. He pre-empted one hundred and sixty acres of land on section 28, where he established his abiding place and has since remained.

Mr. Lambe after coming to this State was married in Coffeyville, Montgomery County, April 21, 1871, to Miss Mary Sproul. The lady was born in Pike County, Ill., June 10, 1854. The result of this union was five children, who bear the names respectively of Charles B., William J., Nettie, Maggie and Armour C., Jr. Mr. Lambe was in St. Louis, Mo., during the progress of the Civil War, and was identified with the Home Guards,

Upon becoming a voting citizen, Mr. Lambe identified himself with the Democratic party, of which he has since been a uniform supporter. Recognizing his ability and sound sense, the Democrats of this county nominated him in 1881 to represent them in the State Legislature, and tendered him the same compliment in 1889. The party being in the minority, he was defeated with the balance of his ticket. He has officiated as Township Trustee and Justice of the Peace for a period of six years, Mr. and Mrs. Lambe are prominently identified with the Christian Church, in whose welfare and advancement they take an active interest.

The father of our subject was John Lambe, also a native of County Tyrone, Ireland, and a farmer by occupation. After coming to this country he prosecuted farming in Clinton County, Ill., where he died.

———◦◦◦———

LEWIS A. SALTER. The legal profession of this county embraces many able men, and among them may be properly numbered Mr. Salter, who is a prominent citizen of Argonia, and in the enjoyment of a thriving business. He is a young man still, just having passed the thirty-second year of his age, having been born January 7, 1858. His native place was in the vicinity of Marshall, Calhoun County, Mich. His parents were Melville J. and Sarah Elizabeth (Hinkle) Salter, natives respectively of New York and Pennsylvania. The paternal grandfather, David N. Salter, was a native of Vermont, a farmer by occupation, and spent the closing years of his life in Michigan.

Melville J. Salter sought the State of Michigan in early manhood and was there married. He continued a resident of the State until February, 1871, coming then to Kansas and locating in Neosha County. Later he removed to Bourbon County, settling at Pawnee Station, where he now lives, engaged in the mercantile business with two of his sons. The latter and Lewis A. comprise the household circle. The elder Salter was Register of the United States Land Office at Independence for

about eight years, during which time the family lived at Independence. The father of our subject was elected Lieutenant-Governor in 1874, and again in 1876 of Kansas.

The subject of this sketch was the eldest born of his parents, and pursued his early studies in the common schools of his native township. After the removal of the family to Kansas, he entered the State Agricultural College at Manhattan, from which after a three years' course, he was graduated in 1879. Subsequently for two years he employed himself on his father's farm.

Our subject, Lewis A., subsequently removed to Cherry Vale and engaged in the hardware trade with Messrs. Carson & Baldwin. In 1882, he removed to Argonia and opened a hardware establishment with the same gentlemen, they operating under the firm name of Carson, Baldwin & Salter. A year later Messrs. Carson & Baldwin sold out their interest to Mr. O. Kinsey, and under the firm name of Salter & Kinsey the business was conducted until the fall of 1885. Mr. Salter then sold out and embarked in the real estate and insurance business, in the meantime improving his leisure hours in the reading of law, and was admitted to the bar in 1887. He has been successful in both in his practice and his other interests, and is the owner of two hundred acres of valuable land, one and one half miles southwest of Argonia, where his residence now is.

The marriage of Lewis A. Salter and Miss Susannah M., daughter of Oliver and Terrissa A. Kinsey, occurred at Silver Lake, Shawnee County, this State, in September, 1880. Mrs. Salter was born in 1860, in Ohio, and was given a good education, developing at an early age uncommon brightness and intelligence. She is a lady who has read extensively and keeps herself well informed upon all the leading topics of the day. She sympathizes entirely with her husband in his political views, being with him a stanch Republican with prohibition tendencies. She became so thoroughly interested in the well-being of the city of Argonia that she was considered fully competent to stand at the head of the municipal affairs, and in the spring of 1887 was elected Mayor, serving her term of one year acceptably and with great credit. She was

Samuel Butterworth

the first lady holding this position in the State of Kansas, and it was considered a great triumph for her sex, she receiving letters of congratulation from all over the world. Mr. Salter has always been an active politician, prominent in his party, and is frequently sent as a delegate to the county and State conventions. In Neosha County he was a member of the school board, and in (Sumner County) City Clerk and Notary Public. He was the Master Workman in the A. O. U. W., Argonia Lodge, No. 171, in which he has held many other offices. He and his estimable wife are members in good standing of the Baptist Church, in which Mr. Salter has officiated as clerk and trustee.

There have been born to Mr. and Mrs. Salter five interesting children, viz.: Clarence E., Francis Argonia, who was the first child born in the city; Winfred A., Melva Olive and Bertha Elizabeth.

AMUEL BUTTERWORTH is one of the leading farmers of Oxford Township, where he owns a valuable farm of four hundred acres, his residence being on section 31. He was born in England, April 14, 1833, and when nine years of age was brought to the United States by his father, Gonther Butterworth, who settled in Pequanick, near Bridgeport, Conn., where he remained about four years. They then removed to Fall River, Mass., where our subject remained seven years, his next place of residence being Shirley, whence he came West to Illinois, settling on a farm in DeWitt County. The father left Massachusetts in 1849, and went to California, where he died.

Samuel Butterworth, of whom we write, made his home in DeWitt County, Ill., until 1874, though he had spent some time in Canada. In that country, on March 16, 1874, he was united in marriage with Mrs. Mary E. Alyea, and came at once to this county, where he had purchased a farm a few months before. When Mr. Butterworth purchased the place it was in almost its primitive condition, and he has put upon it the fences and other

improvements that are expected of an enterprising farmer, and has so cultivated and conducted it that he now has one of the finest farms in the southwestern part of the township.

Mrs. Butterworth was born in County Prince Edward, Canada, December 31, 1851, and is a daughter of James and Sarah (Abrams) Cummings. Her father was born in Ireland, and her mother in Rome, N. Y., their home after marriage being in Canada, where their daughter also resided until her marriage to her present husband. Mr. and Mrs. Butterworth have one son, James S. Sarah Alyea, the daughter of Mrs. Butterworth and her first husband, is now the wife of Charles Brant, of this township.

Until recently Mr. Butterworth belonged to the Republican party, but he is now in sympathy with free trade. He has been Trustee of the School District for four years, and his continuance in office is proof of his fitness for the position. He is a member of the Methodist Episcopal Church, while his wife belongs to the Friends' Church. Both receive their due measure of respect from their associates therein, as well as from the community in general.

A lithographic portrait of Mr. Butterworth may be found on another page of this volume.

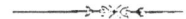

EWIS J. MATSON, the popular liveryman of Argonia, established himself at his present headquarters in August, 1889, with a fair outlook for the future. He is well-to-do, financially, owning a good farm in Morris Township, and may be properly classed among the leading citizens of his town. He was born March 26, 1844, in Ohio, and was the seventh in a family of nine children, the offspring of James and Mary (Kels) Matson, the former of whom departed this life at his home in Pennsylvania, in 1851, and the latter died in Nebraska, in 1881. Seven of their children are still living, located in Nebraska, Pennsylvania, and Kansas.

James Matson was one of the early pioneers of

the Buckeye State, whence he removed to New York State, sojourning there one year, and from there went to Bradford County, Pa. The parents were married in New York State. The mother was a native of Vermont, and descended from a substantial Dutch family, who settled in New Jersey.

Young Matson commenced "paddling his own canoe" at the age of fifteen years. He worked on a farm and chopped cord wood until the outbreak of the Civil War, then made two separate attempts to enter the army, both of which were failures, because of his youth in one instance, and the negligence of a mustering officer in the other. In 1863, however, he succeeded in getting into the Pennsylvania State Militia, for a term of three months, and finally in September, 1864, he enlisted in Company K, Second New York Cavalry, as a recruit. This regiment operated in the Shenandoah Valley, and assisted in fighting the famous battle of Winchester the day before Mr. Matson joined it. He served under Gen. Phil Sheridan in the lamented Gen. Custer's Division, going on several scouting expeditions. He served under Custer until April, 1865, and in all the engagements under that dashing commander. At the battle of Five Forks he was wounded through the left knee by a minie ball. At the field hospital near Dinwiddie court house, he submitted to amputation of the left leg above the knee. He was then conveyed to City Point, thence to Harwood hospital near Washington, from there to Lincoln hospital at Washington, and thence back to Harwood, where he received his honorable discharge, September 2, 1865.

Returning now to Bradford County, Pa., Mr. Matson sojourned there one year, then selling his farm, removed to Muscatine, Iowa. He lived there on a farm one year, then changed his residence to Mercer County, Mo., where he remained ten years. During this time he took charge of a stock of tinware for another party, adding a stock of groceries himself, and carried on this business for some time, returning then to his farm.

In March, 1877, Mr. Matson first struck the soil of Kansas, and secured a tract of land on section 8, Morris Township, this county. He occupied this until August, 1889, then renting his farm, established himself in his present business in Argonia.

He was married on the 8th of January, 1864, to Miss Julia Ann, daughter of George and Eliza (Fox) Locke. Mr. Locke was a carpenter by trade, which he followed in Bradford County, Pa., until his death September 11, 1851. There were born to him and his excellent wife, three children, only one of whom is living, Mrs. Matson. She was born April 26, 1846, in Bradford County, Pa., and was left fatherless five years later. Mr. Locke dying in 1851. The mother subsequently married Isaiah Carr, and is now a resident of Kansas. Miss Julia Ann remained with her mother until her marriage, which took place in Bradford County, Pa. Seven children have been born of her union with our subject, five of whom are living. The eldest, George L., is operating his father's farm; Willis A. lives with his parents; Marian E. is the wife of Simon Dobson, and lives in Argonia; Elnora is the wife of Joseph Varner, and they also live on the home farm; Cora is with her parents. Mr. and Mrs. Matson belong to the Christian Advent Church, in which Mr. Matson is a Class Leader. He is also a Master Workman in the Ancient Order of United Workmen, a member of the Grange, and the Grand Army of the Republic, at Argonia, in the latter of which he has been surgeon and Senior Vice Commander. He votes the straight Republican ticket, although conservative in his ideas. He has officiated as Road Overseer in his district, and as a member of the school board.

The deceased children of Mr. and Mrs. Matson are: Harry, who died in Missouri when one year old, and Cecil Clay, who died at the home farm in this county in 1886, in his fourth year.

GALE S. DOWIS, general merchant, of Perth, established himself in business here in 1883, and by his good management and strict attention to business details, has built up a lucrative and steadily increasing patronage. He is a gentleman just past the fifty-fourth year of his age, having been born December 12, 1835, and his native place was the town of Barboursville, Ky. His ancestry from away back were Southerners. His father, Robert Dowis, was born in South Carolina, whence he emigrated to the Blue Grass State with his parents when a child. The family were among the earliest settlers of Knox County, where the father followed farming and died at the early age of forty-one years.

The paternal grandfather of our subject was also a native of South Carolina and lived to the advanced age of ninety years, spending his last days in Knox County, Ky. Robert Dowis was married in early manhood to Miss Nancy Steele, who was born in Virginia and who is now living in Knox County, Ky., at the age of eighty-eight years. She is a daughter of William and Annie Steele, who were likewise natives of the Old Dominion. To her and her husband were born a family of nine children, viz.: Martha, Helen, Jackson, Gale S., Jasper, Franklin, Elizabeth, Robert and Dallas.

The subject of this notice was the fourth child of his parents and was reared in his native county, although he attended school for a time in Tennessee. Upon approaching manhood he was occupied in various pursuits until the outbreak of the Civil War when, on the 20th of August, 1861, he enlisted as a soldier in the Union army, being then twenty-six years old. He was assigned to Company I, Seventh Kentucky Infantry, served as Sergeant until January, 1862, was then promoted to be Second Lieutenant and at the end of two months was again promoted to the rank of First Lieutenant, in which position he served until May, 1864, when he was promoted to the rank of Captain. He was discharged from the service on the 5th of October, 1864, by reason of the expiration of term of service. He participated in the seige of Vicksburg and various other engagements. After leaving the army he returned to his native county, sojourning there until 1865.

In the year above mentioned Mr. Dowis turned his face toward the country west of the Mississippi, removed to Jackson County, Mo., where he sojourned until 1883. In the meantime he was married, March 17, 1867, in Jackson County, to Miss Betty H. Dupuy. This lady was born in Shelby County, Ky., in 1845, and by her union with our subject became the mother of four children, viz:

Nellie, Cora, Robert and Albert. Robert died in infancy; Nellie is married and living in Guthrie, Oklahoma; Cora and Albert are at home. Mr. Dowis was not quite twenty-one years old upon the organization of the Republican party, but he endorsed its principles and has remained its loyal adherent.

JESSE A. BURNETTE, attorney-at-law in the city of Caldwell, and who is making for himself a good record among his brethren of the legal profession, is a gentleman still young in years, having been born May 26, 1859. His native place was Cocke County, Tenn., to which his father, James B. S. Burnette, removed in boyhood, living there until December, 1869. That year he set out for the Far West and located in Fremont County, Iowa, where he sojourned until 1874. He then removed to Atchison County, Mo., where he now resides. He was born in Buncomb County, N. C., in 1821, and has followed farming all his life. He served in the Confederate army during the late Civil War in an East Tennessee Regiment. Without making any great stir in the world, he has pursued the even tenor of his way as a peaceable and law-abiding citizen and is a member in good standing of the Baptist Church. The paternal grandfather of Mr. Burnette, William by name, was also a native of North Carolina and the son of a hero of the Revolution.

Mrs. Rebecca (Young) Burnette, the mother of our subject, was born in Cocke County, Tenn., of parents who were North Carolinians by birth. One of her grandfathers served in the Continental army and met his death on the battle-field at King's Mountain. Mrs. Burnette is sixty-three years old.

The parental family consisted of twelve children, of whom Jesse A. was the seventh in the order of birth. His boyhood days were spent in his native county until he was eleven years of age, when he accompanied his parents, first in their removal to Iowa and then to Missouri. He worked on a farm and attended the common schools until approaching manhood, then completed his education at

Amity College, College Springs, Iowa. He utilized the knowledge which he had acquired in teaching school and employed his spare moments in reading law. In the latter he made such good progress that in the spring of 1885 he was admitted to the bar in Atchison County, Mo.

Soon after entering the ranks of the legal profession young Burnette repaired to Mobeetie, the county-seat of Wheeler County. Tex., where he commenced the practice of his profession and taught school one year. At the expiration of this time, leaving the Lone Star State, he came to this county and located in Caldwell, opening an office, and has since given his attention to the duties of his profession. He has served as City Attorney three terms and is evidently on the highway to prosperity, being in the enjoyment of a lucrative practice and able from time to time to lay up something for a rainy day. He is a working member of the Republican party, and is identified with the Ancient Order of United Workmen and Modern Woodmen of America.

The marriage of Mr. Burnette with Miss Kate Pursel was celebrated at the bride's home in Atchison County, Mo., May 20, 1886. Mrs. Burnette was born in that county October 20, 1863, and is a daughter of Alex and Annie Pursel, who are now residents of Atchison County, Mo. Two daughters have been born of this union, named, respectively, Imogen and Emma.

ELSON SMITH. One of the finest stock farms in Jackson Township has been developed and improved by Mr. Smith and is eligibly located where it is amply watered by two branches of Shoo Fly Creek—this creek being fed by springs and during the coldest weather has never been known to have its current interrupted by the formation of ice. In the industry to which Mr. Smith devotes the most of his time and attention, he has been very successful and ships annually numbers of cattle and hogs.

A native of the Buckeye State, Mr. Smith was born in Chillicothe, Ross County, March 7, 1833, and is the son of Jacob and Eliza (Hanes) Smith, the former a native of New York State and the latter of Ross County, Ohio. Jacob Smith, when a young man emigrated to Ohio and was there married. He purchased a tract of land near Delphi, Ross County, where he prosecuted farming until his death, in 1838. The mother had also died several years prior to the decease of her husband and the latter married a second time. Five children were subsequently cared for by the stepmother, who kept the family together about three years and then Nelson went to live with his guardian, David Holderman, a farmer of Ross County, Ohio. Grandfather Frederick Hanes was a native of Germany and emigrated to America when a young man, settling among the pioneers of Ross County, Ohio. He took up a tract of timber land from which he cleared a farm and there spent the remainder of his days.

Young Smith attended school a part of each year during his boyhood and the balance of the time worked on the farm with his guardian until fourteen years old. He then entered the employ of his brother-in-law, David Whetsel, with whom he remained for a period of seven years during which he was absent from his duties but three days. Mr. Whetsel was a stock dealer and there being no railroads young Smith assisted him in driving his cattle across the mountains to the Eastern markets. Upon one occasion he went to New York City with a drove of cattle. He had saved his earnings and when twenty-two years old had a snug little sum of money with which he went to Illinois and purchased land in Macon County, two and one-half miles from Decatur, the county seat. Mr. Smith resided in Illinois until 1877, then, selling out, came to Kansas locating in this county, when the nearest railroad station was at Wichita. He had visited this region previously and purchased one hundred and sixty acres of land on the southeast quarter of section 22, Jackson Township. There were fifteen acres broken, but no buildings. Mr. Smith rented a house near by in which he resided with his family one and one-half years, then put up a dwelling on his own land, which he has since occupied. As his capital increased, being prospered in his labors, he added to his landed possessions and is now the owner of three hundred and twenty acres, all fenced and improved with modern buildings. He is now enjoying the fruits of his industry and feels well repaid for the toils and sacrifices which he endured when settling upon what was very nearly approaching the frontier.

The marriage of Nelson Smith and Miss Susanna May was celebrated at the bride's home in Ross County, Ohio, September 6, 1855. Their union has been blest by the birth of five children: Frank, Beman, Chancey, Maggie and Clara. Mrs. Smith was born in Green Township, Ross County, Ohio, and is the daughter of Francis and Barbara (Betzer) May, who were likewise natives of Ross County, Ohio. It is believed that the paternal grandfather, George May, was born in Germany and if so, he emigrated to America at a very early day and was reared in Pennsylvania. He was among the earliest pioneers of Ross County, where he cleared a farm and spent the remainder of his life. Francis May was reared in his native county where, upon reaching man's estate he purchased an improved farm, which he lived upon until 1858. Then removing to Macon County, Ill., he settled in Decatur where he resided until his death, about 1887. The mother of Mrs. Smith was the daughter of William Betzer, a native of Pennsylvania and of German ancestry. He likewise was a pioneer of Ross County, Ohio, and died there. His daughter, Barbara, was taught in her girlhood to card wool and flax, also to spin and weave and made her home with her parents until her marriage. She spent her last days in Decatur, Ill., passing away prior to the decease of her husband. Mrs. Smith remained with her parents until her marriage.

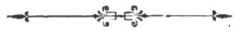

IRA M. VICKERY. In noting the leading farmers and stock-raisers of Walton Township, Mr. Vickery is deserving of special mention. He has by a course of plodding industry and good management become one of the leading land-owners of this section, holding the warranty deeds to

eight hundred acres lying in the counties of Cowley and Sumner, his residence being on the Indian Territory line. He came to this county in 1883 and commenced operations upon his present estate, which has yielded bountiful returns, rendering the owner practically independent.

The subject of this sketch was born in Oswego County, N. Y., November 2, 1838, and is the son of William and Hannah L. (Manwarren) Vickery, both also natives of the Empire State and the latter born in Oswego County. William Vickery lived in that county from a child of four years, until 1857, when he set out for the far West, settling in Doniphan County in 1858, before Kansas was admitted into the Union as a State. Taking up land, he prosecuted farming successfully, becoming well-to-do and leaving an estate valued at $10,000. His death took place in 1865 when he was sixty-two years old. He was for many years a member of the Christian Church.

The mother of our subject was born in 1816 and is still living, making her home with our subject. Her father, John Manwarren, likewise a native of New York State, served as a soldier in the War of 1812, and his father, carried a musket on behalf of the Colonists in the Revolutionary War. To William and Hannah Vickery there was born a family of eight children, namely: Fanny L., Ira M., William M., Lucy A., Hannah A., William E., Lillie H. and Frank. Four of these are living and located in Colorado and Kansas.

The subject of this sketch was the second child of his parents and was reared on the farm in Oswego County, N. Y. He attended the common schools and later Falley Seminary, and at an early age was trained to those habits of industry and frugality which have probably been the secret of his success in life. He came to Kansas Territory with the family in 1857, working still with his father until after the outbreak of the Civil War. That same year he joined the army, enlisting as a private in Company A, Seventh Kansas Cavalry, and served with the Sixteenth Army Corps in Missouri, Arkansas, Tennessee, Kentucky, Alabama and Mississippi. He maintained his position in the ranks until the close of the conflict, escaping wounds and imprisonment and received his honorable discharge at Ironton, Mo., July 20, 1865, on account of disabilities from a horse falling on him.

After retiring from the service Mr. Vickery returned to Doniphan County, this State, remaining there until removing to his present homestead. He gives his entire attention to farming and stock-raising. Aside from his membership with the Church of God, he is not identified with any organization, social, religious or political, not even casting his vote for President. On the 30th of January, 1866, Mr. Vickery was united in marriage with Miss Georgia A. Smith. This lady was born in Randolph County, Ala., in 1847, and is the daughter of David D. and Sarah H. (Thrasher) Smith of that State. Mr. Vickery formed the acquaintance of his wife in Alabama during the war. There have been born to them six children, viz.: Clara J., Minnie L., Ivan W., Willie M., Jesse A. and Nannie E. Clara J. and Jesse A. died at the ages of three years and fourteen months respectively.

IRA T. GABBERT, M. D., one of the ablest physicians and surgeons of Caldwell, aside from occupying a high position in the medical profession, is also numbered among the business men of this place. He is intelligent and progressive in his ideas, a man who keeps himself thoroughly posted upon leading events and for whom is predicted a career of more than ordinary success. He was born December 3, 1852, in the town of Weston, Platte County, Mo., and is the son of William and Frances (Hamner) Gabbert. William Gabbert was born in Warren County, Ky., about 1816.

The father of our subject when a young man removed to Southern Indiana, sojourning there until about 1840. Thence he emigrated across the Mississippi to Platte County, Mo., where he still resides. He has followed agricultural pursuits the most of his life, accumulating a large property, and is now retired from active labor, with the exception of occupying himself as a money-loaner. He is an active member of the Christian Church, contributing liberally of his means to further the cause of

the Master. Politically, he is a sound Republican and socially, belongs to the Free and Accepted Masons and Modern Woodmen of America, of which he is Examining Physician.

Mrs. Frances (Hamner) Gabbert, the mother of our subject was born in Virginia about 1818, and is still living. The parental family included eight children, Ira T. being the fifth in order of birth. He was reared in his native town, receiving a collegiate education. In 1878 he began reading medicine under the instruction of Dr. J. W. Martin, of Weston and subsequently attended three courses of lectures in Jefferson Medical College, Philadelphia, from which in 1882, he was graduated with high honors. He began the practice of his profession in Kansas City, Mo., but a year later came to this county, establishing himself in Caldwell of which he has since been a resident. His close attention to business gained him the esteem and confidence of his fellow-citizens and he soon found himself in the midst of a lucrative business. In addition to this he conducts a thriving drug store, of which he became part owner in 1886 and sole proprietor in the spring of 1889. He has also dealt largely in real estate. As a member of the Knights of Pythias he has taken the Uniformed Rank degree, and in politics is a straight Republican.

Dr. Gabbert was married in Gap, Lancaster County, Pa., October 2, 1889, to Miss Elizabeth Slaymaker. This lady was born in Lancaster County, Pa., in 1860 and is the daughter of John and Elizabeth Slaymaker, who were likewise natives of the Keystone State and the mother is still living at Gap, Pa. The father died at Williamstown about 1875.

JOSEPH M. JOHNSON, a prominent citizen of Creek Township, is the proprietor of one of the finest homes within its limits, and is apparently surrounded with all the good things of life. He has been more than ordinarily successful as an agriculturist, and is considerably interested in sheep-raising, an industry which he believes is far too much neglected among the fertile districts of the Sunflower State. The career of Mr. Johnson has been eminently creditable to him as a man and a citizen, but that perhaps upon which he prides himself most is the fact that during the late Civil War he was a brave and gallant soldier of the Union Army. In viewing the wealth and prosperity of this great country, he justly feels that he was one of the humble instruments in preserving to her her continued prosperity and standing among the nations.

Coming of substantial Pennsylvania stock, Mr. Johnson was himself a native of the Keystone State, and born in Fayette County, December 21, 1832. He acquired a practical education in the common-schools, and at an early age developed the independence of character which has made him a successful man in life. He left home before reaching his majority, emigrating to Delaware County, Iowa, and was there employed on a farm the greater part of the year. He then returned to his native State, sojourning there and engaging in in farming mostly until 1858. He had, however, learned the tanner's trade, at which he worked a part of the time. During the year last mentioned, he went to LaSalle County, Ill., but in 1859, returned to Pennsylvania, remaining there until after the outbreak of the Civil War.

On the 27th of August, 1861, Mr. Johnson signalized his patriotism by enlisting as a Union soldier in Company I, Eighty-fifth Pennsylvania Infantry. When the organization of the regiment was completed, the "boys in blue" were sent to Washington City and attached to the Army of the Potomac, which was then under the command of Gen. McClellan. Mr. Johnson took part in the battle of Williamsburg, the siege of Yorktown and the fights at Savage Station, Seven Pines, Jones' Ford and Black Water. Later, in North Carolina, he met the enemy at Southwest Creek, Kniston, Whitehall, Goldsboro, the sieges of Morris Island and Fts. Wagner and Gregg, and was at White Marsh Island in Ga., Gloucester Point, Va., Bermuda Hundred and in the skirmish near the Richmond & Petersburg Railroad.

At Richmond, Mr. Johnson was wounded in the thigh by a minie ball, and sent to the general hospital at Fortress Monroe. On the 30th of August, 1863, he was wounded in the face and breast by a shell, one piece of which he still carries in his breast. He entered the service as a private, and was first promoted to Orderly Sergeant. On the 4th of March, 1863, he was tendered the commission of Second Lieutenant. After his wounds were healed, he returned to his regiment and served the balance of his time in the army as Regimental Quartermaster. He was given an honorable discharge November 22, 1864.

Returning now to Pennsylvania, Mr. Johnson sojourned there until 1869. That year he came to this State, settling first on a farm in Waubansee Township. In 1871 he came to this county, locating first in Palestine Township, where he lived eight years. His next removal, in 1879, was to Creek Township, of which he has since remained a resident. His farm embraces two hundred acres of thoroughly-cultivated land with all the modern improvements. The residence, a well-built and convenient structure, was erected in 1885. Mr. Johnson has given considerable attention to fruit growing, having an orchard of 80 apple trees, 50 cherry trees, 30 pears, and 1,000 peach trees, besides the smaller fruits, and he gives considerable attention to stock-raising.

Mr. Johnson was first married November 10, 1853, to Miss Margaret Diamond, and there were born to them three children, only two of whom are living. The daughter, Catherine Jane, is the wife of Frederick Rinehart, of Springdale Township, and they are the parents of eight children; William A. B. married Miss Myra Brown, is the father of two children, and lives in Riley County, this State. Mrs. Margaret Johnson departed this life at her home in Illinois many years ago. Mr. Johnson was again married September 27, 1860, to Miss Hannah, daughter of John and Sarah (Clovis) Ganoe. This lady was born March 19, 1838, in Fayette County, Pa. Her father was a native of that State, and her mother was born in Maryland; the father is deceased, and the mother resides in Pennsylvania.

To Mr. Johnson and his present wife have been born twelve children, ten of whom are living. Martha E. is the wife of George W. Lewis, of Ewell, and they have one child; Jesse E. is unmarried, and remains at home with his parents; Dessie

May is the wife of William Dempsey, and they live five miles northeast of Conway Springs; Benjamin A., Phebe A., Sarah E., Quindora L., Mary E., Kate S. and Joseph E. sojourn under the parental roof. Mr. Johnson belongs to the Cumberland Presbyterian Church, while his estimable wife is a Baptist in her religious views. Politically, Mr. Johnson supports the principles of the Republican party. He is Trustee of Creek Township, serving his third term. He was Justice of the Peace for three terms, and is a member of the School Board, taking a warm interest in educational matters, and having been a school official in Pennsylvania and other places where he has resided. Socially, he belongs to the Independent Order of Odd Fellows at Milan, in which he has passed through all the Chairs, and is now Past Grand. He is also identified with the Grand Army of the Republic at Milan, in which he has been Senior Vice Commander.

The parents of our subject were Simon and Jane (Jefferys) Johnson, natives of Pennsylvania, and the father a farmer by occupation. The parents were reared and married in their native State, where they spent their entire lives. The father died in 1853, at the age of fifty-five years, having been born in 1798. The mother was born April 2, 1805, and died in Pennsylvania about 1880. Of the twelve children born to them, eight are now living located mostly in Pennsylvania. Simon Johnson was a prominent man in his community, and served as a Justice of the Peace for many years.

JOSEPH T. BRENEMAN, M.D. Among the old landmarks of Wellington may be numbered Dr. Breneman, who, as the result of a long and successful practice, has become fully established, both as a physician and a citizen. He does business at a well-equipped office on the corner of Washington and Harvey Avenues, and occupies a pleasant residence at No. 1028 South Washington. His professional career has been signalized by close study and extensive reading, resulting in a thorough understanding of the most modern and approved methods adopted by the medical fraternity of the present day.

Dr. Breneman was born twelve miles east of Findlay, Hancock County, Ohio, January 23, 1849, but when a boy of seven years, was taken by his parents to New Middletown, Mahoning County. He there developed into manhood, and completed his literary education. When a young man of twenty years, he removed with the family to Iowa County, Iowa, where the father took up new land and improved a homestead. Joseph T., after following the profession of a teacher for a time, began reading medicine under the instruction of Dr. W. W. Orris of Victor, Iowa, and later entered Bennett Medical College of Chicago, where he remained from 1872 until 1874. He commenced the practice of his profession at Morris, Iowa, remaining there until 1877. That year he entered the Iowa State university, and took two full courses, being graduated on the 5th of March, 1879. He then resumed practice at Morris until the fall of that year, when he changed the field of his operations to Audubon, Iowa, where he sojourned four years, and conducted a drug store for three years, doing a good business.

Dr. Breneman became a resident of Wellington in 1883, and for two years conducted a drug store here in connection with his practice. He now gives his entire attention to the latter, and has met with unqualified success. He was for a time a member of the Board of United States Pension Examiners under the administration of President Cleveland. Although a warm supporter of the Democratic party since becoming a citizen, he has never aspired to office. He is identified with the Independent Order of Odd Fellows and the Knights of Pythias.

Dr. Breneman was first married in Iowa City, Iowa, to Miss Allace Ewing. She was the daughter of Frank Ewing. Of this union there was no issue. She departed this life at Salom, Iowa, May 16th, 1877.

On the 13th of May, 1883, Dr. Breneman was wedded to Miss Fanny Humptry, of West Union, Iowa. This lady was born in West Union, and is the daughter of William H. Humptry, a farmer by occupation, and now deceased. This union resulted in the birth of three children—Fay Alice, Hazel and a babe, George H. The father of our subject was Christian B. Breneman, who was born in Mahoning County, Ohio, in 1814. He married Miss Mary A. Robison and engaged in farming. In 1869, leaving the Buckeye State, he removed to Iowa, and thence to Kansas in the spring of 1884 His death took place at his residence in Wellington, November 10, 1884; the mother is still living, and makes her home with the Doctor.

ICHAEL TROUTMAN. The State of Illinois parted with a most excellent citizen in October, 1872, when Mr. Troutman left the fertile lands of Macon County, hoping for still better things in Kansas. He first settled in Avon Township, near Wellington, where he lived about two years, then removed to South Haven Township, where he had secured possession of a claim of one hundred and sixty acres, upon which he removed, and where he continued to live until 1879. Then, selling out, he came to Harmon Township, and selected his present homestead on section 13. Here he has erected good buildings, and operates largely as a stock dealer and feeder, reaping therefrom a comfortable income.

Mr. Troutman was born in Fulton County, Ind., April 17, 1852, and lived there until a youth of seventeen years. He then went to Macon County, where he sojourned until coming to this State. He has had a lifelong experience as an agriculturist, and enjoys nothing better than watching the growing grain and gathering in the harvest. His farm, two hundred and sixty-two acres in extent, has all been brought to a good state of cultivation, and yields abundantly the rich crops of Southern Kansas.

One of the most interesting and important events in the life of our subject was his marriage in Oxford Township, April 20, 1876, to Miss Delilah Elder. This lady was born in Kosciusco County, Ind., April 1, 1857, and is the daughter of Lewis

and Elizabeth (Firestone) Elder, who were natives of Pennsylvania and Ohio. Mr. Elder died in Kosciusco County, Ind., about 1860. The mother is still at the old home in Indiana. The parental household consisted of eight children, seven of whom are living. There have been born to Mr. and Mrs. Troutman five children, only one of whom is living, a son, George H., who was born April 26, 1882, in Kansas. The deceased are Fayette, Joseph M., Veda and James E. Mrs. Troutman is a lady highly esteemed in her community, one who has been a devoted wife and mother, looking carefully after the ways of her household, and by her wise management, prudence and economy, has assisted her husband materially in his struggles for a home and a competence. Mr. Troutman, politically, supports the principles of the Democratic party, and has held the office of Township Trustee.

The parents of our subject were Joseph and Phebe (Clark) Troutman, natives of Kentucky and Indiana, and who are now residents of South Haven Township, this county.

ARNER A. TILTON is one of the prominent business men of Oxford, where he is engaged in the sale of clothing and gentlemen's furnishing goods. His business establishment is furnished with a complete and well-assorted stock, and is conducted in a manner creditable to the business tact and energy of its owner, and on the principles of honorable dealing with all. Mr. Tilton owns a fine farm of three hundred and twenty acres in Greene Township, which he still supervises, in addition to the management of his excellent business in this city.

The birth of our subject took place in Goshen, Hampshire County, Mass., October 21, 1820, and he lived in his native place until sixteen years old, attending the public schools and in intervals working with his father, who was a tanner and farmer. In 1836 the family removed to Hawley, and two years later to South Deerfield, Franklin County. Young Tilton finished his education at North

Hampton, and when about of age left the parental roof and started in life for himself, occupying his time in teaching and tanning. He finally went into the business of manufacturing buttons and doing all kinds of turning and sawing at South Deerfield, continuing in this business until 1852. He then went to California, via Cape Horn, and engaged in ranching and mining. At Grass Valley, Nevada County, he carried on his mining work, and at Iowa City, Placer County, conducted his search for the precious metal. After four years spent in these employments he went to Sacramento, where for about eighteen months he dealt in wood and coal. He then returned to the occupation of mining, working in various parts of the State until 1860, when he returned home via the Isthmus of Panama.

After some time spent in farming at his former place of abode, Mr. Tilton removed to Toledo, Ohio, and engaged in the milk business and tobacco growing. In 1877 he left the Buckeye State to become a resident of Kansas, and having purchased a farm which was almost entirely in its primitive condition, he set about its improvement and cultivation. He erected good buildings, brought the soil to a fine state of productiveness, and now has as fine a farm as one could desire. After living upon the rural estate for six years, Mr. Tilton came to this place, and with his son, C. G., opened a dry-goods and grocery establishment, but not long after changed to the line of trade which he has conducted during the past five years.

Mr. Tilton is descended from one of three brothers who emigrated from Devonshire, England, in 1660, and who settled in Martha's Vineyard, N. H., and New Jersey respectively. From the New Jersey settler descended Theodore Tilton. From the Martha's Vineyard branch descended Salathiel Tilton, the grandfather of our subject, who was born on the Island. His son, Benjamin B., father of our subject, was born in Goshen, Mass., October 20, 1796. He learned the trade of a tanner, and always made his home in the old Bay State, being gathered to his fathers in October, 1876, when he lacked but a few days of being eighty years old. His wife bore the maiden name of Clymena Warner, and she was born in 1802,

and died in 1847 of consumption. She was a daughter of Capt. Warner, who took part in the first fighting done by Vermont during the Revolution, and in after years settled in Williamsburg, Hampshire County, Mass., his occupation being that of a farmer. The parents of our subject reared three children.

The marriage of our subject took place in June, 1843, in South Deerfield, Mass., his bride being Miss Harriet N., daughter of Col. Zebediah Graves, whose character and acquirements well fitted her for the duties of wife and mother. Their union has resulted in the birth of four children— Theressa M. is now the wife of Mr. Cole, of Glen St. Mary, Fla.; C. G. is engaged in general merchandising in this city; Mrs. Flora A. Dewey lives in Avondale, Ala.; Edward W. resides in Tacoma, Wash.

Mr. Tilton is not an aspirant for political honors, and takes no interest in political affairs, except in so far as to exercise the elective franchise, and his vote is given to the Union Labor party. He is a man highly spoken of by all who know him, for his business integrity and ability, his good principles and his kindly nature.

------◆◆◆◆------

G EORGE W. CLARK, proprietor of the Wellington Carriage Works, is an old resident of Sumner County, to which he came in January, 1871, the first settlement in this county having been made the preceding fall. Although identified with the history of this county at so early a date, Mr. Clark has not been a continuous resident. He is one of those gallant soldiers who entered the Union army soon after the breaking out of the Rebellion, and spent several of his best years in the service of his country, receiving various injuries, but ever faithful to the cause he loved.

Mr. Clark was born at Coshocton, Ohio, September 18, 1840, and while quite young accompanied his parents to New Philadelphia, where he remained till seventeen years old. He then went to Fairfield, Iowa, and entered a blacksmith-shop with the purpose of learning the trade. After sojourning there two years he went to Burlington, and the war having broken out, enlisted in Company I, Sixth Iowa Infantry, his enrollment taking place June 17, 1861.

The command to which Mr. Clark belonged was sent to Missouri, with Gen. Fremont as their leader under Sherman. They then went to Shiloh, where Mr. Clark participated in the first engagement, and subsequently took part in the battles of Corinth, Holly Springs, Memphis, Vicksburg, Jackson (Miss), Missionary Ridge, Knoxville, and the various combats preceding the taking of Atlanta, thence accompanying Sherman on his march to the sea, and being mustered out after having served a little more than three and a half years. The first wound which he received was at Jones' Ford, Miss., on the Black River, in July, 1863, from the effects of which he was sent from the field hospital to Paducah, Ky. While forming the part of the right wing at Atlanta, on the 27th of July, 1864, he was again wounded, the injury being sufficiently serious to detain him in the hospital for some time. The explosion of a shell at Dallas caused partial deafness of each ear, and an injury received at Griswoldville, Ga., caused his discharge.

After being mustered out of the service Mr. Clark went to Pittsburg, Pa., and being desirous of enlarging his fund of information and knowledge, attended school there for a year. In 1867 he came to this State, and engaged in blacksmithing at Salina, where he remained until 1869. He then removed to Hays City, and took a contract to furnish wood for the railroad. The following January he came to Sumner Township, this county, and put up the first blacksmith-shop therein, and a store being subsequently started by C. Gifford, both situated on the old cattle trail, the place received the name of Austin, and our subject was its Postmaster for some time. In 1875 he went to the Wichita Agency, where he was employed by the Government for about five years. He then went to Texas, and purchased seven hundred head of cattle, and moving them to the territory occupied himself in the cattle business until 1886. He then sold out, came to this place, and with O. G. Brown engaged in carriage manufacturing. He now has a

fine two-story and basement edifice, 50x100 feet, built of stone, in which all kinds of work pertaining to carriage-making are carried on.

The marriage license of Mr. Clark and Miss Catherine Wright was the first issued. The bride was born at Bladensburg, Iowa, and in 1871 accompanied her parents to this county, of which they were early settlers. She died in December, 1873, leaving no children. On April 10, 1878, Mr. Clark contracted a second matrimonial alliance, the lady with whom he was united being Mrs. Anna M. Egner. She was born in Batesville, Ark., and is a daughter of Reuben Harpham, who is well-known in this county.

Mr. Clark belongs to the Grand Army of the Republic and to the Masonic fraternity. He is highly spoken of by all who know him, as a man of strict integrity in all business transactions, and honorable in his social life.

The father of our subject was an Englishman, who came to the United States when a young man, and spent some time in New York State, there marrying Miss Anna Syron, and afterward settling in Coshocton, Ohio. While in this place he worked in a sawmill, although his trade was that of a baker and confectioner. He changed his location to New Philadelphia, where his death took place about the year 1846, when he was forty years old. The mother of our subject was born near Trenton, N. J., about the year 1824, and after the death of Mr. Clark remained a widow for a number of years, eventually marrying again, and surviving until 1881.

L UCIUS S. CAMPBELL, M. D. During his ten years' residence in the city of Wellington, Dr. Campbell has fully established himself in the confidence and esteem of his fellow-citizens. The story of his life is in its main points as follows: He was born in the town of Ferrisburg, Addison County, Vt., October 26, 1826, and is the son of Capt. George Campbell, a native of Mansfield, Conn. His paternal grandfather is supposed to have been likewise a native of Connecticut and tradition says that the family in America was perpetuated by four brothers who emigrated from Scotland. Grandfather Campbell followed farming all his life which it is supposed he spent in Connecticut. Capt. George Campbell was reared in his native State whence he went to Vermont and after his marriage located in Vergennes, where he established a tannery and in addition to the manufacture of leather, also made boots and shoes. This was before the days of railroads and transportation was effected via Lake Champlain and the Champlain Canal.

The father of our subject remained a resident of Vergennes a number of years, then purchasing property in Ferrisburg, put up a sawmill and bought a tannery. He was occupied with these until his death, which occurred in October, 1845. He earned his title of Captain by commanding a company of State Militia a number of years. Politically, he was an old line Whig and he was for many years identified with the Masonic fraternity. He was twice married.

The maiden name of the mother of our subject, who was the second wife of Capt. George Campbell, was Harriet E. Powers. She was born in Ferrisburg, Vt., and was the daughter of Capt. Joseph Powers, a native of Massachusetts. Capt. Powers received only limited educational advantages in his youth, being a good-sized boy when first attending school. That very first day the British invaded Lexington and young Powers left the schoolhouse and joining the citizens assisted in driving the British back to Boston. He also participated in the battle of Bunker Hill and continued in the Federal service until the close of the war. Then removing from Massachusetts to Vermont he settled in Ferrisburg where he spent his last days.

Mrs. Campbell accompanied her son, Lucius S. to Wisconsin and thence to Michigan, spending her last days at his home in Glen Arbor. Her death took place in 1858. She was the mother of four children, only two of whom lived to mature years. Six children were born to Capt. George Campbell by his first wife. Lucius S. was reared in his native county, receiving a good education. After leaving school he taught one term in Shoreham, Vt. In 1848 he went to Tolland, Conn., and com-

menced the study of medicine with Dr. J. C. Eaton. Thence in 1850 he emigrated to Wisconsin and practiced for a short time in Fond du Lac County. There being then a good opening for a builder and contractor, he embarked in this business and resided there eight years. His next removal was to Glen Arbor, Mich., where he erected a sawmill and engaged in the lumber business two years. Then returning to Wisconsin he superintended the erection of seven buildings at Lapeer.

During the Civil War Mr. Campbell, at St. Louis, Mo., entered the Quartermaster's Department of the Second Missouri Light Artillery as regimental wheelwright. He remained with the army in Missouri a few months and was then sent to the frontier, being in the service about one year. When the war closed he received his honorable discharge with his regiment at St. Louis. Next visiting the Southwest, he sojourned briefly at Springfield and from there traced his steps to Douglas County, Mo., where he put up a steam sawmill. Later in Dallas County, he erected the first steam saw and grist mills within its borders. Later he operated similarly in Marshfield, Webster County, taking a contract also for building the court house and several other important structures. He spent a few months following in New Orleans and then coming to this county established himself in a drug store at Marshfield which he operated until 1879. Then selling out he came to Wellington which was at that time a town of about twelve hundred inhabitants. He purchased lot No. 20, block 59, Washington Avenue, and erected a frame building which was destroyed by fire in 1883. He at once put up an iron clad building and resumed business within a short time.

In 1884 Dr. Campbell erected one of the best buildings in Wellington, 25x100 feet in dimensions two stories in height and with a fire-proof metal roof. In October, that year he sold his stock of drugs and rented the building. In the meantime he was studying medicine and in 1883 attended the Cincinnati Medical College to which he returned in 1885, and in 1886 was regularly graduated. He is now following his profession with flattering success.

Dr. Campbell was married in 1871 to Miss Josephine E. Straw. This lady was born in New Hampshire, in 1850, and is the daughter of Jacob and Lucy Straw. Her mother is living at Springfield Mo., and her father is deceased. The two sons born of this union bear the names of Robert G. and Lucius S. During his early manhood Dr. Campbell, politically, affiliated with the old Whig party and upon its abandonment cordially endorsed Republican principles. He was a charter member of the I. O. O. F. Encampment at Marshfield, Mo., and at the same place identified himself with the Masonic fraternity. He has been a charter member of three lodges of the Knights of Pythias. He and his little family occupy a neat home in the northeast part of the city, and a good position in its social circles.

JACOB H. ALLEN. This gentleman is a veritable pioneer of Sumner County, having entered what are now its limits before it was yet surveyed or organized, and when every foot of the land was held by the Government, which has since been sold for $1.25 per acre. Mr. Allen is a large land-owner, his acreage in Wellington Township amounting to six hundred and forty acres, while he has a half-interest in sixteen hundred and sixty-three acres in Falls Township. He farms a portion of the land and rents the remainder, his home being on section 23, Wellington Township, where he has a commodious and tasteful dwelling, accompanied by all necessary outbuildings, substantially erected and conveniently disposed.

The grandfather of our subject was one of the first settlers of Montgomery County, Ohio, where he cleared and operated a large farm, upon which his son, Scott Allen, father of our subject, was born and reared. On reaching mature years the latter married Rebecca, daughter of Jacob Hosier, an early settler of the same county.

After his marriage Scott Allen leased a farm in Fayette County, and lived upon it until 1847, when he bought land in Shelby County and removed there. In the latter county he remained

until his death, October 10, 1869, although during that period he changed farms two or three times. His wife had been taught to card, spin and weave, and when her children were small she used to weave the cloth and fashion their garments therefrom with her own hands. She also departed this life in Shelby County, the date of her decease being in the fall of 1888. To Mr. and Mrs. Scott Allen, twelve children were born, nine of them attaining to years of maturity.

Jacob H. Allen was born in Fayette County, Ohio, April 6, 1842, and was but five years old when his parents changed their residence to Shelby County, where he attended school as opportunity offered, and in early boyhood began to assist his father upon the farm, continuing his labors as strength would admit. The breaking out of the Civil War roused in our subject a desire to do a man's work in the armies of his country, and in July, 1861, though still lacking some months of being of age, he entered the Union army as a member of Company B, Twentieth Ohio Infantry.

The army life of Mr. Allen carried him into various parts of Kentucky, Tennessee, Mississippi, Louisiana, Alabama and Georgia, and he participated in a number of the most noted and bloody conflicts of the Rebellion. Among the engagements in which he took part were those at Ft. Donelson, Shiloh, La Grange, Bolivia, Grant Junction, Corinth, Vicksburg, Jackson, Black River, Snake Creek and Ft. Gibson. He joined Sherman's command in Georgia, and took part in the battle of Jonesburg and the engagements around Atlanta. Like all faithful soldiers he had a weary round of camp duties to perform at times, and much arduous marching to undergo, but they were all cheerfully fulfilled until the expiration of his term of service, in October, 1864, when he was honorably discharged.

On being mustered out of the service Mr. Allen went to Louisville, where he spent six months driving a Government Post team. He then went to Washington, Iowa, and rented some land on which he began farming for himself, and where he remained until November 2, 1869, on which day he started on horseback for this State. He stopped in Miami County and rented a farm, upon which he resided until late in the fall of 1870, when he started on horseback for the Western frontier, and reaching this county, located a claim, built a dug-out, and began his labors as a pioneer farmer. He occupied the dug-out a twelve month, and then erected a frame house, and as time rolled on added to his original quarter-section and made various marked improvements, some of which have been noted above.

On April 10, 1874, Mr. Allen was united in marriage with Mary E. Sullivan, an estimable lady, who was born in Wisconsin and was a daughter of Hiram and Mary Sullivan. She died on the 13th of October, 1878, after having borne two children—Ralph J. and Minnie E. After having remained a widower several years, Mr. Allen contracted a second matrimonial alliance, the ceremony taking place November 15, 1883, and the bride being Miss Mary E. Gregson, a native of Rochester, Fulton County, Ind. Mrs. Allen has borne her husband two children—Fred and Glenn. She is a member of the Christian Church, and an intelligent and noble-hearted woman.

The grandparents of the present Mrs. Allen were William and Mary (Myers) Gregson, the former born in North Carolina in 1803, and the latter a native of Lexington, Ky., while their marriage took place in the Hoosier State, to which Mr. Gregson had gone when a young man. He was an early settler in Morgan County, where on April 23, 1834, a son was born to him, who was christened James R., and who became the father of Mrs. Allen. William Gregson carried on a farm in Morgan County, whence he subsequently removed to Fulton County, which he made his home until 1873, when he came West and lived with his children in this county until his death, November 1, 1876. His companion survived him until March 24, 1887, when she also fell asleep, and was buried beside her husband in Prairie Lawn Cemetery.

James R. Gregson was but an infant when his parents removed to Fulton County, where he was reared and attended the pioneer schools. He remained with his parents until his marriage to Christina, daughter of Michael and Sarah (Mc-Mahon) Morris, who was born in Fayette County, Ohio, October 15, 1837. He then purchased a tract of timber land, comprising eighty acres, and located five and a half miles from Rochester, built a frame house and log stable thereon, cleared half of the land and resided there until 1873. He then sold his Indiana property and came to this county, traveling by rail to Wichita, which was then the western terminus of the road, and thence continuing his journey with a team. He bought the southeast quarter of section 24, where the sod had been turned on a half acre, and a small board shanty had been erected. Wellington then contained but a few houses, Wichita was the nearest railroad station, and for some years continued to be the market for this locality. Herds of buffaloes roamed over the prairies a few miles west, and deer and smaller game were abundant. Mr. Gregson immediately began to improve his farm, and at the time of his death, July 20, 1884, was in possession of a productive and valuable estate. While Wichita was yet the market for produce, he drew eight hundred bushels of grain there one year.

ILLIAM R. WALLACE. Few, if any, of the dwellers of this county have a more realizing sense of pioneer life than the above-named gentleman, who, as boy and man, has labored in frontier development. He is one of those to whom Belle Plaine Township owes its improvement, and that he has many friends is attested by the fact that he has been elected Mayor of Belle Plaine, in which town he has lived for a few years past. He was born in DeWitt County, Ill., January 13, 1844, to Charles C. and Rebecca R. Wallace, natives of Kentucky, whence his father had gone to the Prairie State at an early day, laboring among the pioneers there. His paternal ancestors were Scotch-Irish, and his grandfather Wallace is said to have been a soldier in the War of 1812. Our subject is the oldest son in a family of four children, of whom the other survivors are: Elizabeth A., wife of C. A. Stewart, of Kansas City; and James D., of Girard, Kan.

Mr. Wallace was reared to manhood among the

scenes of pioneer life, and having lost his father when he was but eight years old, and living on a farm, he was early obliged to assume control of the farm, and the support of the family depended to a considerable extent on his efforts. His education was therefore somewhat limited, although he attended the district schools of the county in which he lived, and for about two years was a student in the schools of Atlanta, Ill. On the 2d of August, 1862, having but a short time before attained to eighteen years of age, he became a member of Company C, One Hundred and Sixth Illinois Infantry, which was a part of the army of the Mississippi, under the command of Gen. Grant. The duties of Mr. Wallace for some time, were to form one of the body which was watching Johnston to prevent him from breaking through Grant's lines while the latter was besieging Vicksburg. He subsequently did duty in Arkansas, and was shifted around to various places doing guard duty. On March 19, 1865, after an army life of over thirty-two months, he was honorably discharged, leaving the service with a worthy record as a member of the rank and file who so faithfully carried out the orders of their commanders.

Returning to Illinois Mr. Wallace remained there until the summer of 1874, at which time he was numbered among the inhabitants of this county. In the meantime, December 28, 1871, he was united in marriage with Miss Elizabeth A., daughter of James and Sarah Temple, of Pike County, Ill., a lady to whose housewifely skill and Christian character he owes the physical comforts of his home, and the sympathy and good counsel which every true man finds agreeable. The happy union has been blessed by the birth of the following children: Helen, born December 22, 1872; Nora, April 1, 1875; Edna, September 7, 1882; and Charles, deceased.

Upon becoming a citizen of Kansas Mr. Wallace first located on a farm in the northern part of Belle Plaine Township, and after operating the same some five years, removed to the town where he now lives, and where, with the exception of two years which was spent in Wellington, he has since been a continuous resident. He still owns one hundred and fifty acres of outlying land in the town-

ship. He was Township Trustee there three different terms, and for two years he served as Register of Deeds for Sumner County. In April, 1889, he was elected Mayor of Belle Plaine, the term of office being one year. He is a member of the G. A. R. Post, and he and his wife are members of the Christian Church, in which he has officiated as an Elder for a number of years. In politics he is a true-blue Republican.

ANIEL E. HOLLIDAY, now following the peaceful pursuits of agriculture on a one hundred and sixty-acre farm, comprising a portion of section 24, Harmon Township, looks upon that period of his life which was spent in the Union army as the one most creditable in his whole career. He enlisted as a private soldier, October 1, 1863, at the organization of Company C, which was assigned to the Ninety-first Ohio Infantry, and served until the close of the war. Prior to this, however, he had been in the army in the employ of Capt. John Cook, of the Fifty-sixth Ohio Infantry, one year. Upon entering the ranks, he went with his comrades to the front and participated in the battles of Cloyd Mountain, Lynchburg, Stevenson Depot, Winchester, Opequan, Cedar Creek and others, thirteen general engagements in all. With the exception of receiving a slight flesh wound, which did not incapacitate him from service, he escaped unharmed, and was mustered out at Cumberland, Md., after which he received an honorable discharge at Camp Denison, Ohio.

At the expiration of his first term of service, Mr. Holliday enlisted in Company D, Eighteenth Regular United States Infantry, in which he served three years, going to the Far West among the Indians. Upon returning to the pursuits of civil life, he took up his abode in Warren County, Ill., where he was engaged in agricultural pursuits for about four years. At the expiration of this time he came to Kansas, locating in Miami County, where he engaged in farming until the spring of 1878. That year, coming to this county, he purchased his present farm in Harmon Township, of which he has since been a resident. His land is all in a productive condition, enclosed and divided with good fences and embellished with substantial modern buildings. Both as a farmer and a citizen he may be accounted a success.

Mr. Holliday was married in Paulding County, Ohio, June 10, 1869, to Miss Sarah Drake. This lady was born in Licking County, that State, April 11, 1851, and is the daughter of the Rev. James H. and Caroline Drake, who were natives of Ohio, [and are now living in Wayne County, Iowa. Eight children have been born of this union, viz: Arthur O., Oliver M., Clara, Frank, Milton Garfield, Lulu B., Robert L. and George A. Mr. Holliday gives his support to the Republican party, and has taken quite an active part in political affairs. He has held the office of Township Clerk and served at different times on the School Board of his district. He is a member in good standing of Belle Plaine Post, No. 337, G. A. R., with headquarters at Belle Plaine. Both he and his wife are prominently connected with the Methodist Episcopal Church.

When entering the regular army, Mr. Holliday was at once promoted to Second Sergeant, and served in that capacity for eighteen months. He was then made a First Orderly Sergeant, with which rank he was mustered out. While in the volunteer army he was detached, and served about six months as Orderly of his regiment at department headquarters, and at the headquarters of Gen. George Crook.

JOHN E. HUTSON, one of the leading farmers and stockmen of Caldwell Township, has been a resident of Kansas for about twenty years, and during the extended period of his sojourn here has made many warm friends. He inherits the thrift and sturdy integrity of his Scotch ancestry, and has succeeded in amassing a comfortable property. He was equally for-

tunate in the selection of a helpmate, his wife being a lady of culture and refinement. She was Miss Rettie, daughter of James and Eliza (Black) Stevens, and was born June 12, 1850, in Jefferson County, Ohio, though at the time of her marriage she was living in Miami County, Kan. Mr. and Mrs. Hutson are the parents of six children, as follows: Ella, Della, Eddie, Jessie, Nellie K. and Asa.

In Greene County, Mo., our subject was born December 1, 1842, his parents being William and Elizabeth (Ryan) Hutson. The former was born in Ray County, Tenn., and removed to Greene County, Mo., in 1842. After the late war he removed to Douglas County, Kan., and subsequently to Miami County, where he died in 1872, having attained to the age of sixty-four years. His entire life from boyhood had been spent in tilling the soil, with the exception of three years, which he devoted to the service of his country. In 1861 he joined the Union army in Company E, Thirty-seventh Missouri Infantry, but was afterward transferred to Company B, Seventh Missouri Cavalry, and held the rank of Lieutenant. He served three years, and during the term of his enlistment participated in many of the hard-fought battles of the war. He was a Republican, and a member of the Methodist Episcopal Church. His father, David Hutson, was a native of Tennessee, and a soldier of the War of 1812.

The mother of our subject was born in Ray County, Tenn., and has now reached the ripe age of seventy-six years. She is a daughter of Abner Ryan, who was also a native of Tennessee. She is the mother of eleven children, of whom our subject is the fourth in order of birth.

The gentleman whose name initiates this sketch was reared on the farm in Johnson County, and received a common-school education. He was not yet of age when the Civil War broke out, but during the first year of that struggle he joined the Union forces as a private in Company L, First Missouri Battery, and served with that command in Missouri, Arkansas, Tennessee, Mississippi and Pennsylvania, until the winter of 1862, when his term of service expired. He then returned to Sedalia, Mo., and re-enlisted, becoming a member

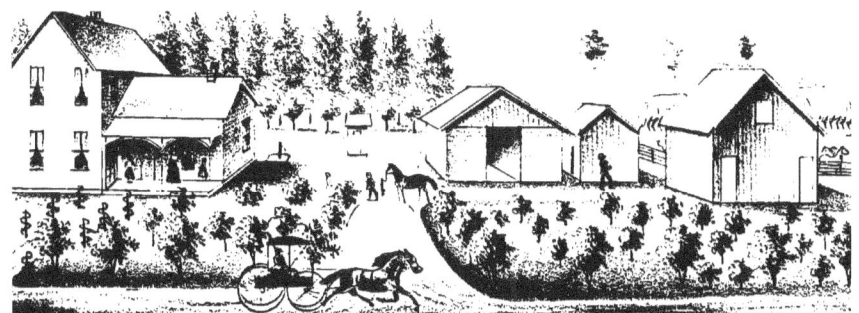

FARM RESIDENCE OF GEORGE LINN, SEC. 4., DIXON TP, SUMNER CO. KANS.

RESIDENCE OF J.E.HUTSON, SEC.4 CALDWELL TP, SUMNER CO. KAN.

of Company L, Second Missouri Battery, in which he served until the close of the war, most of the time in the Sixteenth Army Corps. There are few men who took part in as many hard engagements as did Mr. Hutson, and he had a share in many minor conflicts, in much heavy marching, and in the usual camp duties which pertain to a soldier's life. The list of hotly-contested fields upon which he bore a gallant part, includes Vicksburg, Gettysburg, Shiloh, Stone River, Nashville, Franklin (Tenn.) and Chickamauga. At the latter place his commanding officers fell, and he assumed their duties during the battle. He took part in the famous Georgia campaign with Sherman's army, and with the 60,000 marched through to the sea. During his term of service he received seven bullet wounds, although none were of a serious nature. Just before his term of service expired he was, with three companions, out scouting on Powder River, Wyo. Ter., when they were encountered by the Indians, and all were killed with the exception of our subject. Being able to run barefooted, he escaped, though being compelled to run for a long distance on prickly pears, the thorns penetrated his feet, and it required three days for the physician to extract them. Even after that, for many months the small particles would work through his feet. The last battle our subject was engaged in was with Price at Pleasanton, Kan.

The limits of a sketch like this will not allow of any detailed account of Mr. Hutson's experiences during the Rebellion, and we can only say that he was ever found ready at the word of command, and that his conduct on the field of battle, and in many positions where even greater moral courage was needed than in those exciting scenes, was such as became a brave and loyal young man. He was honorably discharged at St. Louis, Mo., in November, 1865, and took up his residence in Miami County, Kan., (having first become a resident of this State in 1861). In 1870 he removed to Labette County, and three years later to Sumner County, purchasing two hundred and two acres of land on section 4, Caldwell Township, where he has since resided. He has given his entire attention to farming and the stock business, and has one of the best improved farms in

the township. All that he has, has been made by his own unremitting industry, his prudent economy, and the exercise of a discriminating judgment regarding the agricultural needs of the community, the best methods of cultivation, and the number and kind of stock of which he could readily dispose.

Mr. Hutson belongs to the Grand Army of the Republic and to the Independent Order of Odd Fellows. A firm believer in the principles of the Republican party, he exercises the right of suffrage in its behalf and upholds it with his personal influence. He is a member of the Methodist Episcopal Church, and endeavors to live in a manner consonant with his belief; consequently he gains the respect of all who know him, and among his associates has many warm friends.

By careful labor and systematic business management, Mr. Hutson has become the possessor of a commodious residence, which, with its convenient accessories, is represented by a view elsewhere in this work.

EORGE LINN. The Linn homestead, which is pleasantly situated on section 4, Dixon Township, invariably attracts the attention of the passing traveler as one which has evidently been built up by a man possessing more than ordinary industry and enterprise. A handsome residence still further embellishes it, and is represented on another page of this volume by a lithographic engraving. The proprietor is a self-made man in the broadest sense of the term, having begun at the foot of the ladder in life, and made his way unaided, bending his energies to the accomplishment of a certain purpose, and he has reason to be proud of the result of his efforts. He has been a hard worker, and a good manager, and has surrounded himself and his family with all the comforts and many of the luxuries of life.

In noting the career of the successful citizen, the mind naturally reverts to those from whom he drew his origin. The subject of this sketch is the son of

Jacob Linn, and was born February 12, 1849, in Stark County, Ohio, being the thirteenth in a family of fourteen children, ten of whom are still living. The mother, who in her girlhood was Miss Elizabeth Allen, was a native of the Keystone State, where both she and her husband developed into mature years, and where they lived nearly twenty years after their marriage. Then removing to Ohio, they settled on a farm in Stark County, where they spent the remainder of their days. The elder Linn was a blacksmith by trade, which he followed more or less until the close of his life. He departed hence in 1848, after having made the record of an honest man and a good citizen. The mother survived her husband nine years, dying in Ohio in 1857.

Mr. Linn spent his early years in his native township, and acquired his education by a somewhat limited attendance at the common school. He was only nine years old at the time of his father's death, after which he went out to work among strangers, giving his earnings to his widowed mother. He continued this course until his marriage, giving even the proceeds of his summer's work before that event, to his mother. He was united in wedlock with Miss Helen E., a daughter of the Rev. Jonathan M. and Mary (Brown) West, the former a minister of the Church of God, preaching for many years in Ohio, Missouri and Kansas. Both he and his wife were natives of Pennsylvania. He departed this life at his home in Missouri in 1881. The mother died in Ohio in 1887. They were the parents of nine children, three of whom are still living. Mrs. Linn was born January 22, 1840, in Stark County, Ohio, and there obtained her education in the common school.

Our subject and his wife became the parents of five children, namely: Mary J., born September 5, 1861; Dora B., June 19, 1863; Emma L., March 21, 1868, died June 23, 1871; Helen A., born October 3, 1870; and George N., April 11, 1874. The latter is at home with his parents. Mary J. is the wife of William Keplinger, and they live in Navarre, Stark County, Ohio; Dora B. is at home with her parents; Helen A. is the wife of Corwin Bryant, of Meade County, this State, and they have one child, Floyd, an infant. Mr. Linn's children

have been given a good education, and are, like their parents, intelligent and bright, reflecting credit upon the home training.

Until the early part of 1885, Mr. Linn remained a resident of his native State, then decided upon seeking the farther West. Setting out for Kansas, he arrived in this county on the 28th of February, settling at once upon his present farm. This embraces one hundred and fifty-six acres of fertile land, and Mr. Linn owns besides a quarter-section, two and one-half miles southeast of Argonia on the Chikaskia River bottoms. The latter is operated by a tenant. The homestead proper is embellished with good buildings, including a neat residence, put up in 1885, at a cost of $1,200. Eighty acres of the land are devoted to the raising of grain, and the ordinary crops, and the balance is utilized principally for live-stock, Mr. Linn being considerably interested in cattle, horses and swine.

In politics, Mr. Linn votes the Democratic ticket. He has been somewhat prominent in local affairs, serving as Treasurer of Dixon Township two terms. In Ohio he was for many years a member of the school board of his district, and served as Township Trustee two terms. Socially, he belongs to Argonia Lodge, I. O. O. F., and is foreman in the Ancient Order of United Workmen. Mrs. Linn, a lady greatly respected in her community, is connected with the Presbyterian Church.

RUDOLPH J. TRACY. Among the solid men of Dixon Township may be most properly mentioned Mr. Tracy, whom we find in independent circumstances, financially, the result of his own industry and good management. He is one of the many who may be termed "self-made," having sprung from an humble position in life, and without any other aid than his native good sense and steady application has attained to a worthy position and is deserving of more than a passing mention. It is to perpetuate the record of such men that the present work has been instituted, in the hope that the story of their lives, perused by a generation to come, will become an incentive to those who may be similarly situated.

Mr. Tracy first opened his eyes to the light on the other side of the Atlantic, in the Kingdom of Prussia, December 13, 1849. He is thus a little past the age of forty years, still a young man, and having already acquired a competence, may reasonably hope for many years in the enjoyment of this world's goods. He comes of substantial German stock, being the son of George and Catherine (Yerka) Tracy, who were likewise natives of that country and born under the reign of the good old Emperor, Wilhelm. They were reared and married in their native Province, whence they emigrated to America in 1860, settling first in the city of Baltimore, Md. In 1867 they emigrated to the West, settling in Lisbon, Iowa. From there in 1870, they came to Kansas, locating in Sedgwick County, where the mother still lives. The parental household comprised seven children, only two of whom are living—Rudolph J. and Augusta, the latter a resident of Wichita.

Mr. Tracy was a lad of only eleven years when coming to America, and immediately upon his arrival began to work in a factory at Baltimore, turning over his earnings to his mother. After coming West, he was employed on a railroad, and spent one season in Nebraska, part of the time chopping wood near old Ft. Cottonwood, past which wild Indians frequently roamed and displayed feelings which were anything but friendly. After removing to Sedgwick County, this State, the Tracy family, who were among the earliest pioneers, occupied a dug-out for some time, and Rudolph J. subsequently was employed in freighting between Wichita and Emporia.

At the age of twenty-two years, Mr. Tracy was united in marriage, on the 9th of January, 1872, at Wichita, with Miss Euphemia L. Lane, the ceremony being performed by the first probate judge at Wichita. Mrs. Tracy was a daughter of Reuben C. and Susannah (Mood) Lane, who were natives of Ohio, where they were reared and married. The father was a farmer by occupation, and, leaving the Buckeye State in 1851, settled in Illinois. Two years later, with his family, he pushed on further

Westward into Iowa, locating on a farm in Madison County, where they sojourned until 1870. That year they moved to Sedgwick County, this State, of which they were residents until 1877. Their next removal was to this county, where they remained until 1881. They then removed to Edwards County, where the father now lives, the mother having died, in 1871, near Wichita. Mr. Lane is living with his third wife. During the Civil War he enlisted in Company H, Twenty-third Iowa Infantry and served gallantly until the close. By his first wife he became the father of thirteen children, six of whom are living, and of whom Mrs. Tracy was the eldest. She was born January 9, 1852, in Ohio.

The seven children born to Mr. and Mrs. Tracy were named respectively: Harmon F., Emma L., George C., Henry M., Vernon R., Luella A. and Benjamin Levi. They form a bright and intelligent group, acquiring their education in the district school, and all living at home with their parents. Mr. and Mrs. Tracy were in former years members of the Cumberland Presbyterian Church. They now perform the office of guardian to Elmer R. Tracy, a nephew, who is the only surviving member of his family. Mr. Tracy takes an active interest in politics, and uniformly votes the Republican ticket. He is liberal and progressive in his ideas, a member of the Grange and also of the Farmers' Alliance. He has little ambition for office, and aside from serving as Road Overseer, has held himself aloof from responsibility in this line.

The estate of Mr. Tracy embraces three hundred and twenty acres of prime land, all improved, and upon which he has built four and one-half miles of fencing. The greater part of his land is under the plow, and twenty-five acres are devoted to an apple orchard and nearly all other kinds of fruit. Several thousand evergreens add beauty to the premises, including five red cedars, which Mr. Tracy brought with him from the battlefield of Pea Ridge. These also are in a flourishing condition. The present residence was completed in 1888.

When Mr. Tracy came to Sedgwick County, this State, he brought with him a capital of thirty cents and seven bushels of feed for his team. After completing his house in this county, he had nothing left and was $50 in debt. In 1878, his dwelling, with all its contents, was destroyed by fire. He has thus met with reverses, but he never allowed himself to give way to discouragements, simply following the rule of always doing the best he could under all circumstances.

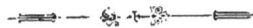

AWSON W. COOLEY. The Oxford Bank is one of the flourishing institutions of Sumner County, and is now operating under a State charter obtained May 15, 1885. It was organized by J. H. Allen and D. W. Cooley as a private enterprise, opening its doors for business in November, 1883. These two gentlemen were President and Cashier respectively, and the capital was $10,000, which has been increased to a stock of $25,000, while a few wealthy farmers are added to the stockholders, and the same officers retain the positions which they assumed at the opening of the institution.

Our subject is a son of John B. Cooley, who was born in the Empire State, February 7, 1817, and reared on a farm, but who became a steamboat captain. On October 18, 1838, John Cooley was united in marriage with Miss Wealthy A. Winchester, who was born in Wyoming County, September 30, 1820. The home of the family was in New York State until the fall of 1866, when they removed to Brookfield, Mo., and thence to Rogers, Ark., in the spring of 1883. In the latter place the father departed this life, May 21, 1888, and the widow is still living. John Cooley was quite prominent in local politics, though not an aspirant for office. He belonged to the Democratic party. The parental family comprised five children, of whom our subject was the first born—George W. is now living in New York City; Marion L. lives in Las Vegas, N. M.; Frank P. died in 1878; Donna died March 27, 1862.

The subject of this sketch opened his eyes to the light in Wyoming County, N. Y., August 11, 1839, and remained in his native place until sixteen years of age. He then went to Wisconsin, where he sojourned until the fall of 1860, when he returned to his native State, and the following spring offered his services to uphold the Union, being one of the first volunteers in the State or country. Three days after Ft. Sumter was fired upon he enlisted in Company C, Hawkins' Zouaves, which was mustered into service on the 3d of May, and is said to have been the first organized regiment of volunteers in the war. It was attached to the Ninth Army Corps, and for some time formed a part of the Army of the Potomac. The command was first sent to Fortress Monroe, and took part in the capture of Hatteras, Roanoke Island and Elizabethtown; in engagements at Winton and Camden Court-House; and in the terrible conflicts at Antietam and Fredericksburg. The regiment was one of those that suffered the greatest loss in battle, Hawkins' Zouaves being ever in the thick of the fight or in the most exposed position, and the gallantry of the members of that band is unquestioned. Mr. Cooley was discharged at Suffolk, and returned to New York, and until the close of the war was in the employ of the Government in the Quartermaster's Department.

After peace was declared Mr. Cooley went to Brookfield, Mo., and there remained until 1869, when he changed his place of abode to Baxter Springs, Kan. In the spring of 1871 he came to this county, and took up a claim which now forms a part of the town of Wellington, being one of the few settlers in the vicinity, and building the first frame house on the prairie where Wellington now stands. The dwelling is still standing in what is now the Rose Hill Addition, and our subject continued to occupy it until the population of the town was about twelve hundred, and in place of the buffaloes which covered the plains when he came here, herds of cattle were to be seen over its broad expanse.

Mr. Cooley removed from Wellington to Missouri, and spent two years as a traveling salesman, afterward going into the mercantile and banking business at Golden City, Mo., where he remained about two years. He then came to Oxford, and organized the bank of which he has since had sole charge and which is in a very prosperous condition.

owing to his business tact and good management. He was married in Oneida County, N. Y., October 26, 1870, to Miss Estella M. Temple, who was removed from him by death October 17, 1885. Mr. Cooley contracted a second matrimonial alliance October 26, 1886, the bride being Miss Anna Milner, who was born in Ohio, January 10, 1855.

Mr. Cooley is a member of the Masonic fraternity, and his good character, as well as his ability and uprightness in business life, command the respect of his fellow-citizens, and insure his popularity among them.

Mr. Cooley takes great pleasure in the preservation of some family relics which have been handed down to him. Among them is a deed given to his grandfather, Grove Cooley, by the Holland Land Company in November, 1733. There is also a demit from the Dryden (N. Y.) Lodge of Master Masons to Grove Cooley, dated February 6, 1820. The commission of John B. Cooley as Captain in the Ninety-ninth Infantry (New York State Militia) dated October 3, 1839, and signed by W. H. Seward, is a valued relic of the Black Hawk War, to which our subject's father had started, although he did not get to the front until the Indian troubles were settled.

JOHN S. EPPERSON. In the person of the subject of this notice we have one of the most liberal-minded and public-spirited men of Sumner County. This fact is duly recognized by his fellow-citizens, who, in November, 1888, elected him County Commissioner, the duties of which office he is discharging in a manner creditable to himself and satisfactory to his constituents. He is a lifelong agriculturist by occupation, although he is now retired from active labor and is living at his ease, having accumulated a competence. A Republican of the first water, he takes a warm interest in political affairs, and has been the Treasurer of Avon Township in the past, and a member of the School Board. He and his estimable wife are members in good standing of the Chris-

tian Church, and have taken a prominent part in its prosperity and welfare. Mr. Epperson holding its various offices, and in fact being one of the chief pillars. For forty years both Mr. and Mrs. Epperson have labored conscientiously to further the Master's cause.

Madison County, Ky., was the native place of Mr. Epperson, and the date of his birth June 27, 1827. His father, Charles Epperson, likewise a native of the Blue Grass State, emigrated to Indiana where he sojourned a few years, then pushed on further Westward into Benton County, Iowa, where he spent his last years. The maiden name of the mother was Martha Woolery, and she is now with our subject. Mr. Epperson was a young man of twenty years when he accompanied his father's family from Indiana to Iowa, in which State he continued to reside until 1870. In the meantime he was married, in Benton County, November 27, 1848, to Miss Nancy E. Forsyth. In August, 1870, he removed with his family to Independence, this State, and November 7, 1872, came to this county. Soon afterward he entered one hundred and sixty acres of land on section 3, Avon Township, and in November following removed to it, and there has since continued to reside. His sound sense and the spirit of enterprise which has signalized his operations have had the effect, not only to place him in a good position, financially, but also to establish him in the esteem and confidence of his fellow-citizens. He has built up one of the best homesteads in this part of Sumner County, his well-tilled fields yielding him a handsome income.

In his labors and struggles Mr. Epperson has found a most efficient assistant in his amiable and estimable wife. Mrs. Nancy E. (Forsyth) Epperson was born in Decatur County, Ind., July 5, 1831, and is the daughter of Judge J. S. Forsyth, who was formerly the County Judge of Benton County, Iowa, for a period of four years, and for the same length of time was the Sheriff of Boone County, Ind. He came with his family to Kansas in 1872, and made his home with our subject, in Avon Township, where his decease occurred in 1877. His wife died in 1850.

Prior to their removal to this State Mr. and Mrs. Epperson had charge of the Benton County

(Iowa) Poor Farm for three years, and the institution under the management of Mr. Epperson underwent many improvements and reforms. There have been born to Mr. and Mrs. Epperson six children, the eldest of whom, a daughter, Martha J., became the wife of W. G. Hollingsworth, and died in Harmon Township, this county, April 28, 1887; Harry married Miss Susie Nottingham, and is farming in Scott County; Julius married Miss Ella Seeger, and is farming in Harmon Township; Alma is the wife of W. H. C. Bowers, of Wellington; Mary and Florence remain at home with their parents.

JACOB SMITH, one of the leading farmers in Walton Township, was born in Prussia, September 8, 1841, to Anthony and Elizabeth (Keiser) Smith. They emigrated to America in 1857, and settled in St. Clair County, Ill., where the father lives, and where the mother died on the 24th of August, 1889. The father had been a manufacturer of woolen goods in Germany, but adopted a farmer's life after becoming a resident of the United States, and was in easy financial circumstances, and was a devout member of the Catholic Church. He was the father of five children—Mary, Catherine, Jacob, John and Christina, all living but the first born.

The gentleman whose name initiates this sketch, was but a boy when his parents came to America, and he was brought up on the farm in St. Clair County, Ill. In 1869 he took up his residence in Montgomery County, Kan., lived there until 1872, and then removed to Cowley County, and preempted one hundred and twenty acres of land. He subsequently bought six hundred acres in Cedar Township, of that county, and lived on the same until 1885, when he removed into Arkansas City, continuing to reside in that town until the spring of 1888, when he moved to his present home. His home farm comprises one hundred and sixty acres on sections 12 and 13, Walton Township, which bears marked improvements, the whole estate evinc-

ing careful management and skillful oversight. He is now devoting his entire attention to farming and stock-raising, and is adding to his prosperity, and placing his affairs on a still more substantial financial basis. In addition to his farm in this county, he owns one hundred and sixty acres in Cedar Township, Cowley County, and some valuable real estate in Arkansas City. All his property has been acquired since he became a resident of this State, and is a proof of his unflagging industry and business ability. He is a devout member of the Catholic Church, a reliable citizen, and his social, kindly nature are manifested in his associations with his neighbors and in his domestic relations.

An important step in the life of Mr. Smith was taken in 1871, when he became the husband of Miss Katie Gallagher, of Cowley County, whose capable and tasteful conduct of the household economy makes his home pleasant, and his heart happy. Mrs. Smith was born in Canada. She has borne her husband two children, Mary and Anthony, who are yet under the parental roof.

MAKE HACKNEY, a pioneer of 1871, came to this county in the fall of that year from Adams County, Ill., and purchased one hundred and sixty acres of land on section 27, Harmon Township. Of this township he has since been a resident, making good improvements on his farm, eighty acres of which, however, he has disposed of, having the remaining eighty in a fine state of cultivation.

The subject of this notice was born in Chatham County, N. C., November 7, 1846, and when a small boy removed with his parents to Adams County, Ill., where he grew to manhood. He spent his time after the manner of most farmer's sons, attending the district school in winter and making himself useful about the homestead in summer until after the outbreak of the Civil War. On the 24th of February, 1864, when a young man of eighteen years, he enlisted in Company B, Fiftieth Illinois Infantry and served eighteen months, operating with his regiment mostly with Gen. Sherman. He saw active fighting, and after being mustered out at Springfield returned to Adams County, Ill., and occupied himself at farming until his removal to Kansas.

On the 14th of March, 1867, Mr. Hackney was married, at the bride's home in Schuyler County, Ill., to Miss Maggie Baxter. This lady was born in Carroll County, Ohio, December 9, 1847, and is the daughter of John and Ellen Baxter, who are natives of Ohio and spending their last years in Brown County, Kan. There have been born to Mr. and Mrs. Hackney six children, two of whom, John and Etta, died in infancy. The survivors are Ella, Emma, Myrtle and Jessie. Mr. Hackney votes the straight Republican ticket, and has held some of the school offices of this district. He belongs to the Ancient Order of United Workmen and Belle Plaine Post, G. A. R.

The parents of our subject were John and Milly (Dorsett) Hackney, natives of North Carolina and now residents of Schuyler County, Ill. The parental household included six children.

RALPH A. BROWN, M. D. This promising young physician of South Haven established himself here in the spring of 1886, and bids fair in the near future to take a leading position among the practitioners of this county. His native place was Ashtabula County, Ohio, his birth occurring April 6, 1858, and in 1861 his parents, George P. and Mary (Seymour) Brown, removed to Richmond, Ind., where the early school days of the boy were spent. Ten years later they changed their residence to Indianapolis, and in that city Ralph A. developed into manhood. The family consisted of four sons —Charles C., Ralph, George A. and Walter S.

In 1877 the Brown family removed to Ann Arbor, Mich., in order that the boys might receive the advantages of a thorough education. The four were all graduated from the Michigan

State University. During this time the mother kept house for her sons, while the father was engaged as a traveling salesman. Later, the parents removed to Bloomington, Ill., where they now reside, the father being publisher of the Illinois *School Journal*. He is a well-educated man, and in former years served as Superintendent of the Richmond Public Schools. Later, he was Principal and Superintendent of the High Schools of Indianapolis. The elder Brown identified himself some years ago with the Ancient Free & Accepted Masons, of which he still remains an honored member.

The paternal grandfather of our subject was William Brown, a native of England, who crossed the Atlantic when a young man, locating in the Dominion of Canada. Later, he emigrated to New York State, where he was married to Miss Mary Piper, a lady of Irish ancestry. Finally leaving New York State, they removed to Ohio, where they reared a large family and died. Ralph A., our subject, was graduated from the schools of Indianapolis in 1875, and in due time entered the medical department of the University of Michigan, from which he emerged in 1880, well equipped for the duties of his chosen profession. He, however, spent one year in the hospital at Ann Arbor, and then established himself in Boone County, Ind., where he remained until the fall of 1885. Then, on account of failing health, he spent several months traveling.

Returning to Indianapolis, in January, 1886, Dr. Brown was married to Miss Cora J., daughter of James M. and Mary (Connell) Smith. This lady was born December 28, 1864, in Boone County, Ind., and was the daughter of an early pioneer of that region. Her mother died when she was a small child. Her father, an attorney-at-law, is still a resident of Tipton. Mrs. Brown received a careful home training and a good education, and at an early age developed a rare taste for music, in which she became quite proficient and is now an experienced and skillful pianist.

Dr. Brown, by his strict attention to the duties of his profession, is rapidly gaining a foothold in his community, no less as a physician and surgeon than as a business man and a member of the community. He is a regular attendant at the Christian Church, of which Mrs. Brown is a devoted member, and he served one year as Superintendent of the Sunday-school. While a resident of Boone County, Ind., he became a member of the Independent Order of Odd Fellows. He votes the Independent ticket, and was the first City Clerk of South Haven. There has been born to the Doctor and his estimable lady one child, a son, Ralph S., August 25, 1889.

FREDERICK W. BAUM. The farming community of Falls Township recognizes in Mr. Baum one of its most enterprising and successful men. He was born in the Kingdom of Prussia, December 10, 1848, and is the son of Frederick C. and Johanna F. Augusta (Finke) Baum, who were likewise natives of that kingdom, and who emigrated to America in 1853. They settled in Calhoun County, Ill., and there spent the remainder of their lives, the father engaged in farming pursuits. In former years, in his native land, he had been a weaver. He was a highly-educated man, and possessed of more than ordinary intelligence. There were born to him and his excellent partner two children only—Johanna F. Augusta and Frederick W. The former died in Illinois, Frederick W. is consequently the only surviving member of his family.

Mr. Baum was a lad of fifteen years when leaving his native land, and he sojourned with his parents in Calhoun County, Ill., until the outbreak of the Civil War. In 1861, at an early stage in the conflict, he joined the Union army as a private in Company C. Tenth Missouri Infantry, and served with that command until November, 25, 1863. He participated in many of the important battles which followed, and at Missionary Ridge received a wound which necessitated the amputation of his left leg, between the ankle and the knee. Consequently he received his honorable discharge, in the spring of 1864, at St. Louis, Mo.

Upon leaving the army, Mr. Baum returned to Illinois where he spent one year, then repaired to St. Louis, Mo., and for a time officiated as City Weigher. He followed various pursuits until May, 1868, when he came to Kansas, locating in Johnson County, and sojourning there until 1871. In December, that year, he came to this county, and the following January purchased a claim on sections 7 and 18, Falls Township, upon which he located and where he has since resided. His industry and perseverance brought him ample returns, and he added to his possessions in due time by the purchase of additional land, until he is now the owner of two hundred acres, which have become the source of a fine income. At the time of his settlement here, the country was wild and new, infested with Indians and highwaymen, who frequently made life a burden to settlers on the frontier. His first dwelling, constructed very imperfectly with the aid of limited tools and material, offered very little protection against the elements, and for awhile the only door was a blanket. Mr. Baum had no property worthy of mention when coming to this county, and naturally feels warmly attached to the Sunflower State, which has made of him a comparatively wealthy man. He is a strong defender of the principles of the Republican party, and belongs to Upton Post, No. 27, G. A. R., of Caldwell.

On the 25th of September, 1864, Mr. Baum was married to Miss Fredericka D. Wernecke. Mrs. Baum is a native of the same country as her husband, and was born November 13, 1841. Her parents were Andrew and Dorothy (Franke) Wernecke, who were likewise natives of Prussia. The mother died there when Mrs. Baum was a child of eight years. Mr. Wernecke came to this country in 1857, and settled in Warren County, Mo., where he was severely dealt with during the war on account of his Union sentiments. He became well-to-do, and died there in 1880, aged sixty-seven years. To Mr. and Mrs. Wernecke were born five children, named Fredericka D., Theresa, Wilhelmina F., Gustaf and F. Herman. Mr. Wernecke was married a second time, his wife being Louisa Sontag, and unto them were born two children—Louisa B. and Anna.

To Mr. and Mrs. Baum there has been born a family of six children, namely: Edward, Benjamin,

FARM RESIDENCE OF F.W.BAUM SECS. 7 & 8 (200 ACRES) SOUTH HALF FALLS TP. SUMNER CO. KAN.

Walter, Lydia, Ada and Arthur. Edward, Benjamin and Arthur are deceased; the other three are at home with their parents. We direct the attention of the reader to a lithographic view of the residence of our subject, found elsewhere in this volume.

APT. LEWIS K. MYERS is one of the original Town Site Company of Wellington, which place has been his home since the spring of 1871, although he has been absent temporarily at various times. During his early years he learned considerable of the privations, toils and needs of the pioneer, and was well qualified to take a position among the frontiersmen in this State. During the Civil War he was a gallant soldier, and his title is an honorable testimony to his faithfulness and courage.

The paternal grandfather of our subject was George Myers, who was probably born in Pennsylvania, and was the son of German parents. He moved from the Keystone State to Jefferson County, Ohio, where the latter part of his life was spent. He reared eight sons and four daughters, all of whom married and also reared families. One of his sons, Abraham Myers, was born in Washington County, Pa., and was nearly grown when his parents moved to Ohio. In Jefferson County he married Miss Margaret Spiller, a native of Washington County, Pa. Her parents are presumed to have been natives also of the Keystone State, and her maternal grandfather, Jackson, was made a captive by a small band of Indians. Two brothers, John and Andrew Poe, attacked the savages and enabled Mr. Jackson to make his escape.

Abraham Myers purchased a tract of one hundred and sixty acres in Knox Township, Jefferson County, on which there was an improved water power and grist mill. There he resided, carrying on the occupations of a miller and a farmer, until 1843, when he sold and purchased land in Carroll County, on which he resided over a decade. Selling that he went to Iowa, and settled in Union County, where he took Government land and built

a log house. The removal from Ohio was made by teams and they camped by the way. There were no railroads west of the Mississippi until two years after his settlement in the Hawkeye State, in which he had lived but a few months when his demise took place, the date of the event being October, 1854. His widow survived until January, 1860, when she too passed away.

The subject of this biography was born in Jefferson County, Ohio, May 15, 1832, and was reared in his native State, his youth being spent in study and in assisting his father upon the farm. Before the family moved to Iowa, whither he accompanied them, he had taught one term of winter school. The family was among the earliest settlers of Union County, Iowa, where Indians still lingered and where deer and other kinds of wild game were abundant. Soon after their arrival there young Myers began surveying and he also entered several tracts of land under the Government land laws. After his father's death he and his older brother improved the land which his father had taken. He had not long been a resident of the State ere he received the appointment of Deputy County Surveyor, and in 1859 he was elected County Surveyor and two years later was elected to the office of Sheriff.

The breaking out of the Civil War found Mr. Myers filling the two positions last named which he resigned to take his place among the defenders of the Union. In August, 1862, he enlisted in Company H., Twenty-ninth Iowa Infantry, and was mustered into the service as First Lieutenant and not long after promoted to the Captaincy, retaining the command of the company until his discharge. The most important battles in which he participated were at Helena, Ark., Little Rock, Saline River, and Spanish Fort. At the latter place he was severely wounded and was transferred to the hospital at New Orleans, and as soon as he was able to travel was granted a furlough and returned home. He rejoined his command at Mobile, whence they went to the mouth of the Rio Grande, where the order for his discharge reached him.

Returning to his former home in Iowa, Capt. Myers remained there until 1871, and in February of that year came to Kansas, traveling by rail to

Emporia, which was then the western terminus of the railroad, and thence by stage to Wichita. Thence he started with a team and accompanied by others for a point two and a half miles southeast of the present site of Wellington, which was designated as Meridian and had been named by the Governor as the temporary county seat of the newly organized county of Sumner. A village had been staked out there but no buildings had been erected, a tent in the timber near by being the residence of one of the proprietors of the town site. The Government survey of the county was not yet completed and there was not a building where Wellington now stands, the land, like that in other parts of the county, being still held by the Government.

Capt. Myers made no claim here, but returned to Wichita, bought a pony and set out to explore the country northwest of that town. Late in March, however, he returned to Sumner County, and with seven other gentlemen formed a Town Site Company and made claim to the land now occupied by the city of Wellington. On the 4th of April, 1871, he made the first survey and at once platted the town. On the same day he got a man to remove his log cabin to this place and at once erected it here. Other buildings went up about the same time and soon quite a little village was started. In September an election was held to determine the location of the county seat, and Wellington was one of the five towns which competed for that honor. None of them had a majority of the votes cast and W. P. Hackney, the representative, secured the passage of the present law that governs county seat elections in Kansas, and at the fifth election Wellington was victorious. The township built a stone court house that was leased to the county, rent free, for ten years, and which was occupied as the Seat of Justice until 1881, when the present handsome and commodious structure was erected.

The wife of Capt. Myers bore the maiden name of Mary Guthridge and their marriage was celebrated October 30, 1860. The bride was born in Champaign County, Ohio, April 24, 1840, and her father, Darius J. Guthridge, was a native of the same county. In 1851 he removed to Iowa, his first settlement in that State being on the line of Union and Clarke Counties, where he was one of the pioneers. He opened a general store there and when the town of Afton was started the following year, he moved his stock of goods and opened the first store in the new town. There he continued to reside until 1880, when he was gathered to his fathers. He was a successful business man, a natural orator, and possessed an eminently social nature. His wife, whose maiden name was Mary J. Owens, died in Ohio while quite young. Mrs. Myers received the best training and education which her father's means could compass in the circumstances which surrounded them during her youth, and grew to a worthy womanhood. She has borne her husband three children—William A., Edith and May; the elder of the girls is now a teacher in the schools in the county.

Capt. Myers is the only member of the original Town Site Company who now resides in Wellington. His social and benevolent nature has led him to take a decided interest in the social orders and he belongs to several lodges. He is a member of James Shield Post No. 57, G. A. R., Wellington Lodge No. 150, A. F. & A. M.; Sumner Chapter No. 37, R. A. M., and St. John Commandery No. 24, K. T. It is needless to state that he is well respected, not only in the city in whose welfare he has ever been interested, but wherever his character and works are known.

FRANKLIN E. KNOWLES is the owner and occupant of an improved and cultivated farm in Osborn Township, which was taken by him as a pre-emption claim in 1876, since which time he has become well-known as a business man of Wellington, where he was for some years engaged in carrying on a meat market. He is a son of Henry and Sarah (Waters) Knowles, who became residents of this county in 1877. His father was born in New York State, and after living there many years, became a resident of McHenry County, Ill. After coming to this State, he engaged in the cattle business, and is still so occupied. Mrs. Henry Knowles is a native of Michigan, and is the mother of seven children—Ellen, Wesley, Frank E., Eva, Alice, Flora, and Charles.

The gentleman whose name initiates this sketch, first opened his eyes to the light in McHenry County, Ill., April 5, 1853, and was reared in Marengo, receiving a common-school education, and supplementing it by a commercial course of study. When, in the Centennial year, he determined to become a citizen of Kansas, he took up one hundred and sixty acres on section 8, Osborn Township, and made such improvements as were necessary, coupled with his residence thereon, to enable him to prove up. He then engaged in business in Wellington, continuing it until 1886, when he sold out, and in February, 1889, owing to ill health, he abandoned it and returned to his farm.

The lady whose housewifely skill and amiable disposition makes a happy home for Mr. Knowles, was in her maidenhood Miss Maggie E. Culley, and the rites of wedlock were celebrated between them May 30, 1883, Mrs. Knowles was born in Logan County, Ill., February 28, 1861, and is the daughter of James and Margaret (Jackson) Culley, who are also natives of the Prairie State. She has borne two children, Harley and Edna, both of whom have been removed from their loving parents by the hand of death.

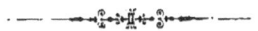

RANK K. ROBBINS, President of the First National Bank of Wellington, came to Sumner County, in May, 1887, and succeeding Reuben H. Harpham in the position which he now holds, has since retained that place, to which he was elected in January, 1888-89-90, and re-elected the following year. He was also incumbent of the office of cashier for two years, but in January, 1890, Mr. R. L. Beattie was elected cashier. Though so short a time a resident of this city, Mr. Robbins is a prominent and popular citizen, his excellent moral character and business tact winning respect, and his affable and social nature gaining warm friends.

His father, Daniel Robbins, was born in Kentucky about the year 1795, and went to Illinois at an early day, becoming one of the first settlers of Dewitt County, and laying out the town of Dewitt, then called Marion. About the year 1837, Daniel Robbins married Miss Rebecca Day, and being elected County Judge in 1850, removed to Clinton, the county seat, where he continued to reside until his death in 1869. He was Postmaster of that city for a number of years, and was a prominent politician, being a life-long Whig and Republican. His widow married R. Rollins, and is now living in McLean County.

The subject of our sketch was born in Dewitt County, Ill., November 17, 1847, and grew to maturity in Clinton, where he learned the profession of a druggist, and engaged in that business, following it for some eight years in that place, under the firm name of Day & Robbins. He then carried on the same business in Kenney for nine years, and until the date of his removal to this State. While in Kenney, he was united in marriage with Miss Lura Randolph, the ceremony taking place on December 28, 1876, at the home of the bride's father, J. H. Randolph, a prominent farmer of that county. Mrs. Robbins was born there May 22, 1859, was well-educated, and possessed many fine traits of character. While en route to San Antonio, Tex., for her health, in December, 1881, she was called from earth, her decease taking place in New Orleans. She had borne two children, of whom one, a daughter, Edna, is still living.

Though only a boy in his teens, Mr. Robbins enlisted October 5, 1864, in Company K, of Gov. Oglesby's old Regiment, the Eighth Illinois Infantry. They were sent to Memphis, Tenn., and on to the Mississippi River, taking part in the charge at Spanish Fort, and also charging Ft. Blakeley, and going into Mobile at the head of the troops, the colors of that regiment being the first planted on the fort by the Union soldiers. Mr. Robbins served until October 5, 1865, when he was honorably discharged, and returned from Texas to his home, having fortunately escaped wounds or capture.

During his residence at Kenney, Ill., Mr. Robbins was appointed Postmaster by President Hayes, and served eight years, until the change of administration. He was an active Republican worker in that county, but not an aspirant for office, being content to serve his party in the ranks. He belongs to the Masonic fraternity, the Knights of Pythias, and the Independent Order of Odd Fellows, and for two years represented the Odd Fellows Lodge in the Grand Lodge of the State, at Springfield, Ill.

LBERT R. QUICK, Assistant Cashier of the Stock Exchange Bank at Caldwell, may be classed as a self-made man, as he began life for himself with only what nature had bestowed upon him in the way of capital, if we except a common-school education. He began a business career early in his teens, and young as he is has an enviable reputation in Sumner County for his business ability and good character.

The paternal ancestors of our subject were from Holland, and the Keystone State was the family abiding place for many years. In that State Emanuel B., the father of our subject, was born about 1814, and he breathed his last in Milford, in 1881. He was a shoemaker and worked at his trade all his life, securing a comfortable support and being in easy financial circumstance at the time of his death. He served as one of the Commissioners of Pike County several years, and had good standing in the Methodist Episcopal Church. His wife, whose maiden name was Catherine Ennis, was also born in the Keystone State, still survives and is in good health although she is now about seventy-three years old. The parental family was made up of two sons and a daughter, who were christened Edgar, Bella and Albert R.

In Milford, Pike County, Pa., October 1, 1852, the eyes of our subject first opened to the light, and his early years were passed amid the usual surroundings of boyhood in the family of a tradesman. Having acquired a good understanding of the common-school branches, at the age of fifteen years he began clerking in a general store, subsequently engaging in general merchandising for himself and enjoying a very successful business career in that line until 1881, when he sold out and moved West. He located in Emporia, Kan., and for a time was engaged in the stock business, after which he entered the employ of the Atchison, Topeka & Santa Fe Railroad as agent. In 1885 he was located at Caldwell and served in the capacity of agent at that place until the following year, when he was tendered the position which he is now filling in the Stock Exchange Bank. He is well qualified for the post which he occupies and is regarded by business men as a very careful and accurate cashier. He is a stockholder in the bank and also owns valuable real estate in Caldwell. In politics he is a Democrat and is a Master Mason in one of the social orders.

In 1873 Mr. Quick was united in marriage with Miss Mae E. Chapman, of Readfield, Me., a daughter of Ira S. and Elizabeth (Taylor) Chapman. Two sons and one daughter have been born to Mr. and Mrs. Quick, and they bear the names of Harry C., J. Wallace and Bell H.

HOMAS V. OGDEN. This gentleman is one of the oldest settlers of Sumner County, and one of the most substantial and highly respected citizens of Wellington, where he is engaged in the livery business and horse dealing. His establishment is situated on Lincoln Avenue, and is well patronized, and is well supplied with vehicles and steeds, thirty to forty head of equines being usually kept. Mr. Ogden was born in Fulton County, Ill., August 11, 1834, and in the spring prior to his eighteenth birthday accompanied his parents to this county. They settled six miles east of Wellington, which was then but a small village, the father taking up a raw quarter section in Avon Township, erecting a frame house upon it and beginning its further improvement. Our subject can well remember when buffaloes roamed over these prairies, and when deer and smaller game abounded.

Mr. Ogden remained with his parents until about nineteen years of age, when he took a quarter section of land in the same township, three miles east of this place, and began reclaiming the raw prairie and putting upon it such improvements as are usually made by enterprising agriculturalists. He broke one hundred and twenty acres of the sod, and put the balance under good fences for use as pasture, set out an orchard and grove, erected good buildings, and made one of the fine farms of the county. For the past five years he has rented his estate, and has been carrying on the livery business here, proving his business ability in its management, and winning esteem by his honorable conduct and good character. He votes with the Democratic party, but has no political aspirations, and has little to do with party affairs except in exercising the right of suffrage.

The father of our subject, T. V. Ogden, Sr., was born in Ohio, and married Miss Sarah Boardwine, of Fulton County, Ill., where he settled as a farmer. His wife is a native of Virginia, but lived in Illinois some time previous to her marriage. Their family comprises eight children, all still living. The senior Mr. Ogden is well-known as one of the early settlers of this county, and as a successful farmer, now owning three hundred acres in Falls Township, twenty miles southwest of this place. He and his wife are worthy parents of the son who is taking a high stand among the young men of the county, and who bids fair to become still more prominent and influential in the years to come.

EDMUND ROCKHOLD. This gentleman, in the spring of 1889, established himself as a farmer in Downs Township, purchasing eighty acres of land on section 13, where he still lives and carries on general farming. He has attained to considerable prominence in the community, being a stanch supporter of the Republican party, and is an Elder of the Cumberland Presbyterian Church. He is now approaching the sixty-fifth year of his age, having been born March 19, 1825, and is a native of Baltimore County, Md., where for many years his father, the Rev. Edmund

Rockhold, a native of the same county, officiated as a minister of the Methodist Protestant Church. The latter was born in 1770, and departed this life in Baltimore County, Md., at the age of seventy-six years.

The paternal grandfather of the subject of this notice was Jacob Rockhold, a native of England, who emigrated to America in 1760, locating in Baltimore County, Md., where he carried on farming and died at the age of seventy-six years, six months and twenty days. The mother of our subject was in her girlhood Miss Susan Miller, she was a native of the same county as her husband and son, and spent her last days in Butler County, Ohio, passing away at the age of sixty-three years. Her parents were Jacob and Elizabeth (Marshall) Miller. Grandfather Miller was born in Germany, whence he emigrated to the United States at an early day, settling in Pennsylvania, where he married his wife, who was a native of that State. Subsequently they removed to Maryland, where Grandfather Miller died when eighty-seven years old. He was a miller by occupation, a steady-going, prudent and industrious man who enjoyed the esteem and confidence of his fellow-citizens. Grandmother Miller died at the age of seventy-eight years in Stark County, Ohio.

To Edmund Jr., and Susan (Miller) Rockhold there was born a family of five children, namely: Edmund, Susan, Hannah, William and John. The subject of this notice was the first-born and is the only living member of the family. He was reared on a farm in his native county, and received the educational advantages afforded by the common schools. When a man of twenty-seven years, he, in 1852, removed to Butler County, Ohio, and after the outbreak of the Civil War, enlisted as a Union soldier in September, 1863, in Company B, One Hundred and Thirty-fourth Ohio Infantry. He only served until the following year, being mustered out and returning to his old haunts in Butler County. He remained there until the spring of 1889, then turned his face to the country west of the Mississippi.

Mr. Rockhold was married in his native State October 20, 1846, to Miss Eliza Elderdice. Mrs. Rockhold was born in Frederick County, Md.,

June 20, 1820, and is the daughter of Hugh and Catherine (Meyers) Elderdice, who were natives of Ireland and Pennsylvania, respectively. The grandmother on the mother's side was a Barbara Martin, and on the father's side, was Mary Stewart, who was Scotch-Irish, and was of royal blood. Mr. Elderdice was a farmer by occupation, and removed from his native State to Maryland, where he and his excellent wife spent their last days. To Mr. and Mrs. Rockhold there have been born seven children, viz.: Kate, James, Abbie, Mary, Tillie, Ella and John C. Mary was taken from the home circle when a young woman of twenty-seven years; James died when a promising youth of sixteen; Abbie died at the age of three years. John C. married Miss Rose DeFreese and lives in Spivey, and is Roadmaster of the Mulvane extension of the Santa Fe Railroad; Mary married J. W. Hoover, who is County Superintendent of Schools; Kate is married to B. F. Grove, of York, Pa.

JOHN R. SIMONS is the owner and occupant of a pleasant home in Wellington Township, where he has been living since 1884. Early in life he began agricultural labors and the management of a farm, proving very successful in his occupation and ever manifesting an industry and good judgment highly creditable to his natural qualities and his training. He is a man of probity and intelligence, a reliable citizen, and stands well in the regard of his associates and fellow-citizens.

Wales claims the honor of being the birthplace of our subject and of the ancestral line for generations. His grandfather, Edward Simons, spent his entire life in that land. Edward Simons, Jr., the father of our subject, was born in Denbigh shire, was there reared and educated and lived until 1843, when accompanied by his wife and four children he came to America. His first settlement was made in Kendall County, Ill., and among the frontiersmen of Oswego Township he began the development of a tract of wild land which he had

purchased. At that date and for some years after, there were no railroads in the Prairie State, and Chicago, then a city of about seven thousand inhabitants, was the nearest market and a drive of forty miles was necessary to reach it. The parents of our subject resided in Illinois until 1886 when they came to Kansas to spend their last days with our subject. Both are still living at an advanced age, the father will be ninety in June and the mother eighty-eight years of age. The maiden name of the mother was Margaret Roberts and she also is a native of Wales. She has borne nine children, two of whom, Hannah, and our subject, still survive.

He whose name initiates this sketch was born in Hope, Wales, about two and a half years before the family moved to America and he therefore has no recollection of the land of his nativity. He, however, well remembers the pioneer life in Illinois, where as soon as he was large enough he began to assist his father on the farm and being the only son, while yet in his teens had its management placed upon his shoulders. After his marriage he purchased two hundred and forty acres in the same township, and in addition to his farming operated a threshing machine twenty seasons. He sold his Illinois property in 1884 and coming to Wellington bought one hundred and sixty acres of land adjoining the town and at once began farming here. Two years later he took advantage of the boom and sold the greater part of his land at a good advance on its original price, but still occupies the house into which he first moved on becoming a resident of this State.

In 1864 Mr. Simons was united in marriage with Miss Susannah R. Minkler, an estimable lady possessed of many womanly qualities. She had borne live children: Burton R., Louisa E., Minkler E., Ivah A., and Kansas. The oldest daughter is the wife of Samuel J. Lumbard, attorney-at-law, of Chicago, Ill.

The father of Mrs. Simons is Smith G. Minkler, who was born in Albany County, N. Y., and whose father, Peter Minkler, is presumably a native of the same State. In 1835, Peter Minkler and his family joined a colony and journeyed to Illinois, traveling with teams. A graphic description of their journey, as told by Smith Minkler, appears in the history of Kendall County. Ill., which was published a few years since. In that county the elder Mr. Minkler located, being one of the first settlers in what is now Kendall Township, where he secured a tract of Government land upon which he resided until his death.

Smith G. Minkler was a young man when the family moved from New York and he reached man's estate in Kendall County. where he was married and where he also secured a tract of Government land, building upon it a log house in which Mrs. Simons was born. At the time of his settlement, deer, wolves and other kinds of game were plentiful in the vicinity. Indians still lingered there, and the surrounding country was very sparsely settled. The greater part of the land was prairie and was the last to be settled, as the first comers thought it would not produce crops and therefore cleared the groves. When the land Smith Minkler took came into market he was short $16 of the requisite amount of money to pay for it and he started out to hire the money. He traveled a long distance on horseback before he could find any one possessing that amount, but he finally obtained the loan, giving a mortgage on the farm to secure it. He has been a continuous resident of that place since he first located upon it. He very early developed an interest in fruit culture and started a nursery, and for many years past has been an influential member of the Northern Illinois Horticultural Society, and has served both as its President and its Treasurer. He has served as Steward and Trustee of the Methodist Episcopal Church and has been a Class-Leader for many years, his wife also being a member of that denomination. To him and his wife five children were born, of whom four reached years of maturity. They are: Betsey, Mrs. Simons, Ellis T., and Florence.

The mother of Mrs. Simons, and wife of Smith Minkler, was in her maidenhood Miss Sarah A. Burton. She was born near Yarmouth, England, and is a daughter of Nathaniel and Susannah (Ransom) Burton, both of whom were natives of the Mother Country, whence they came to America about 1836, locating in Kendall County. Ill. as

pioneer residents. Mr. Burton improved a farm there upon which he and his wife resided many years and whence they went to Ottawa to live with a daughter, dying in that city when quite advanced in years.

HOMAS RICHARDSON, Sr. The subject of this biography stands prominent among the mercantile interests of Wellington and deals chiefly in dry-goods, having a fine large store, occupying No. 114 Washington Avenue, at Wellington. Engaging in business here in May, 1879, he is therefore one of the oldest established merchants of the place and carries a complete stock of everything in his line. He has built up a large patronage and his business ability and integrity are unquestioned.

Mr. Richardson was born near Frankfort, Ky., April 2, 1814, and lived there until a young man of twenty-one years. After completing his education he established himself in business at La Grange, Mo., and carried on general merchandising in that State for the long period of thirty-six years and about seven years at Lancaster, Schuyler County, Mo. He has been continuously behind the dry goods counter for fifty-five years, having begun August 20, 1835, and all this time has been in business for himself. With the exception of having been burned out at La Grange he has been uniformly successful. While a resident of Missouri he served in the various city offices and was President of the Board of Trustees of the La Grange Baptist College for fourteen years. In the early days he was an Old Clay Whig, but later identified himself with the Democratic party. For thirty-five years he has been a member in good standing of the Baptist Church and for probably twenty-five years has been connected with the Masonic fraternity.

In March, 1846, Mr. Richardson was united in marriage with Miss America C. Muldrow at Philadelphia, Mo., where Mrs. Richardson had been attending a Presbyterian institution of learning.

This union resulted in the birth of eight children, of whom only three are living, viz.: Lizzie, Thomas, a resident of Pueblo, Col., and John, who married Miss Belle Patton, of Wellington, and is engaged in merchandising in business with his father. Mr. Richardson is a man highly respected in his community and bears an unblemished reputation. His parents are Allen and Elizabeth (Payne) Richardson, who were residents of Kentucky and are now deceased.

CHARLES L. CROOKHAM, business manager of the *New Era* at South Haven, also holds the office of City Clerk, to which he was elected in May, 1888. He is still a young man, having been born September 13, 1863, but has already entered upon a promising career. His native place was Circleville, Ohio, from which his parents, Oliver and Mary J. (Walden) Crookham, came to Kansas in 1871. They located at Eureka, where the mother is still living. Oliver Crookham only survived his removal to the West three short years, being murdered in October, 1874, by one Alexander Herman, who is now serving a life sentence for the crime which was premeditated and unprovoked. Herman was the first criminal given a life sentence in Greenwood County. He had been hired by Mr. Crookham to break prairie, and when only half the job was completed, was requested by Mr. Crookham to discontinue his labors as his work was not satisfactory, which conclusion on the part of Mr. Crookham was upheld by arbitrators. Mr. Crookham paid the man his full price, and two years later, one day Herman went up to him and shot him without any words passing between them. Mr. Crookham was at the time husking corn on his farm.

Oliver Crookham was a man of excellent character, a Swedenborgian in his religious views, a consistent Christian, and an honest man. He was born, reared and married in Jackson County, Ohio, of which the mother of our subject was also a native, and they lived in Circleville sixteen years before coming to this State. After leaving Ohio they resided four years at Springfield, Mo. The paternal grandfather of our subject was George L. Crookham, a native of England, who emigrated to the United States when a young man, and located in Jackson County, Ohio. He was of studious habits, and through his own efforts obtained a good education, and spent much of his time as a naturalist. When employed he manufactured sugar from beets, and established some of the salt works in the Buckeye State. He was in the Government employ as a naturalist and a mathematician, and belonged to the National Mathematical Association. A man of broad and liberal ideas, he identified himself with the early abolitionists, and assisted fugitive slaves in making their escape to Canada. He was born in England, and spent his last days in Jackson County, Ohio, dying at the age of sixty-six years.

The maternal grandfather of our subject was Jonathan Walden, a native of Greenbriar County, in what is now West Virginia. He emigrated to Jackson County, Ohio, when a mere boy, was there married, reared a family, and died there about 1856. He traced his ancestry to the pilgrims who landed in the Mayflower, and who were of Scottish birth and antecedents. To Oliver and Mary Crookham there was born a family of six children, of whom Charles L., our subject, was the youngest. The days of his boyhood and youth were spent uneventfully on a farm, and in attendance at the district school. Later he entered the Kansas Normal College at Ft. Scott, from which he was graduated in June, 1886. In the fall of that year he made his first advent in South Haven, and established himself as a general merchant. Afterward he served as clerk in the bank six months. He is now engaged as a loan agent and in the insurance business. The *New Era* with which he is at present connected as business manager, was first established as a private enterprise, and purchased later by a stock company. It has a circulation of about four hundred, and is a newsy local paper, devoted chiefly to the interests of Sumner County.

Mr. Crookham, on the 27th of July, 1887, was joined in wedlock, at Eureka, Kan., with Miss Constance E., daughter of Robert and Elizabeth J.

F. M. Mills

(Bryson) Wiggins. The ancestors of Mrs. Crookham were of Irish origin, and first represented in the United States at a very early day. She was born August 27, 1865, in Canada. Of her union with our subject there is one child, a son, Arthur L. Mr. Crookham, politically, affiliates with the Republican party, and socially, belongs to South Haven Lodge, No. 114, I. O. O. F. In addition to his other interests, he is a member and Secretary of the South Haven Building and Loan Association, and Vice-President of the State Immigration Bureau of Sumner County.

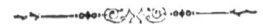

FRANCIS M. MILLS is one of the oldest settlers of Oxford Township, to which he came in 1871, sticking a stake on the claim which he still occupies, about the 23d of April, and beginning the labor of preparing a home at once. The land occupies the northeastern part of section 20, and was the outside claim from the village in that direction when Mr. Mills filed on it. Oxford then consisted of four buildings in process of construction, only the frames being up. Mr. Mills drew the lumber for his home from Newton, sixty miles distant, and was ten days in making the trip during which he experienced some very cold weather. He saw some antelopes and prairie wolves when he first set up housekeeping here, and was a witness to all the development in this section, assisting in the organization of the school district (No. 33) and in the building of the schoolhouse.

Mr. Mills is a son of John and Dorcas (Allison) Mills, both of whom were born in Augusta County Va., where their marriage also took place. They removed to Ohio, where the father cleared up a farm, upon which the family resided until his death, in 1839. The eldest son in the family—William Mills—was born in 1812, and he of whom we write, December 19, 1831. When our subject was fourteen years old the family removed to Sangamon County, Ill., where he grew to maturity, leaving the parental roof when of age, and going to Logan County, where he engaged in farm-

ing for some time. The mother also went to that county, where she died in 1864. During that year our subject went to Montana and engaged in mining, remaining in that Territory about five years, when he returned to his home in Logan County. The following spring he came to Montgomery County, in the eastern part of this State, and a year later to this county, and after having filed his claim and erected a dwelling, began his permanent residence here in May.

The lady who nobly shared in Mr. Mills' pioneer work here bore the maiden name of Harriet C. Shaw, and the rites of wedlock were celebrated between them in DeWitt County, Ill., January 21, 1863. The union has resulted in the birth of three children—Abbie L. died at the age of six years and twenty days; Fannie, at the age of nine months; the surviving daughter, Mary E., is now nine years of age and a bright and interesting young girl. Mrs. Mills was born in Orange County, N. Y., July 7, 1840, and is a daughter of Alexander W. Shaw, who was born in Westchester County, November 2, 1806, and after his marriage to Miss Adeline Welch, made his home in Orange County until his death, which took place in December, 1852. His entire life in that county had been spent on the same farm. After the death of her mother, in December, 1858, the daughter went to Illinois, where she resided until some time after her marriage.

Mr. Mills never fails to cast his vote with the Republican party, feeling a deep interest in the welfare of the country, though he has no personal political aspirations. He is a highly-respected citizen, and a man whose life has been usefully and quietly spent.

We invite the reader's attention to a lithographic portrait of Mr. Mills, presented in connection with his biographical sketch.

CHARLES RANDALL, a peaceable and law-abiding citizen of Avon Township, owns and occupies a snug homestead on section 12, of which he became the owner in 1871. He lives quietly and unostentatiously, making the record of an honest man and a good citizen, and reaping from his well-developed fields a comfortable income.

A native of Rensselaer County, N. Y., Mr. Randall was born October 17, 1818, but spent the most of his time until twenty one years old in Warren County, that State, being reared upon a farm. Later he visited Pennsylvania and Illinois, and in the spring of 1870, crossing the Father of Waters, established himself as a resident of Wilson County, this State.

After a sojourn of two years in the above-mentioned county, Mr. Randall, in the spring of 1871, arrived within the borders of Sumner County and pre-empted one hundred and sixty acres of land, which has since remained in his possession. He settled upon it in February, 1872, and commenced at first principles in the construction of a homestead. No small amount of labor was required in the cultivation of the primitive soil, the building of fences and the erection of his farm buildings, which, without making any pretentions to elegance, are reasonably convenient and comfortable. Mr. Randall prospered as a tiller of the soil, and invested his capital in additional land, until he is now the owner of two hundred acres, all of which has been brought to a good state of cultivation, and the taxes upon which assist in augmenting the contents of the county treasury to no small extent.

After coming to this county Mr. Randall was married at the home of the bride in Avon Township, April 20, 1875, to Miss Sarah A. Batt. This lady was born in Somersetshire, England, June 10, 1858, and is the daughter of William J. and Sarah A. (Brice) Batt, who were both likewise natives of that shire. The mother spent her last years in Sumner County, Kan., and the father is in New Zealand.

Nine children have been born to Mr. and Mrs. Randall, whom they named respectively: William C., who died at the age of six months; Davy, Henrietta I., Grace M., Francis R., Louis, Charles, Lena and Irving W. Mr. Randall, politically, is a sound Republican. He was elected Township Treasurer in the fall of 1887, and re-elected the two following years, serving now his third term. He is the friend of education and all the enterprises set on foot for the progress and welfare of the people, socially, morally and financially.

The father of our subject was Elisha Randall, who married Miss Melvina Prouty, and both were natives of New York State. Both died in Warren County, N. Y.

ALPHONSO B. RICE. One of the most attractive rural residences of Oxford Township is that owned and occupied by the above named gentleman, and which was erected in August, 1884, and was the first fine house built in the neighborhood. It is a two-story structure, the main part having a dimension of 16x28 feet, and with an addition 18x22 feet in the form of an L. The estate which surrounds it comprises one hundred and sixty acres on section 21, and is supplied with a fine orchard, grove, and other shrubbery, hedges, barn, wind-mill, and such farm buildings as are necessary to one engaged in general farming and stock-raising, all being well constructed, commodious and adequate. Mr. Rice raises excellent grades of stock, and his crops are among the best in quality and quantity.

Our subject is a native of Ohio, and a son of Alfred Rice, whose history may be found in the biography of Albert Rice, which occupies another place in this volume. His natal day was November 6, 1847, and when but a child he went with the other members of the family to Noble County, Ind., where he grew to maturity, completing his education at Kendallville. He then engaged in farming, leaving his mother's home at the age of twenty years to spend some time in the northern part of Michigan. In the fall of 1870, he came to Cowley County, Kan., and took up a quarter-section of land, and after proving up on it sold and purchased in the valley of the Arkansas, where he liked the country better. He is the second member of the family who settled in this county, and when he bought his farm it was nearly un-

broken, and his first dwelling was a little cottonwood house. His industry and energy have been
displayed in his management of the estate, and the
success he has met with in bringing it to its present state of perfection.

The marriage of our subject took place near
Moline, Allegan County, Mich., June 13, 1869,
the bride being Miss Sophronia M. Montague, an
intelligent and worthy lady, who has borne him
three children, two of whom—Laura Ellen and
Maud M.—still survive. Mrs. Rice was born in
Ohio, October 18, 1853, and was two years old
when her parents removed to Michigan, where she
grew to womanhood. Her father, Sandford Montague, is a native of Vermont, where he married
Miss Jerusha Washburn. He was thirty years old
when he removed to Ohio, whence he afterward
went to Allegan County, Mich., and there he and
his wife are still living, their present home being
near Bradley.

Mr. Rice is a believer in and supporter of the
principles of the Republican party. He is highly
respected as an honest, honorable and upright man,
and a citizen of reliability.

ILLIAM G. WHEALY. The industry
and enterprise exercised by this honored
pioneer of Sumner County has resulted in
the accumulation of four hundred broad acres of
land, finely located on sections 15 and 22, Avon
Township. To the cultivation and improvement
of this he has given his undivided time and attention since first settling upon it, bringing the soil to
a productive condition and erecting thereon substantial buildings. In addition to general agriculture he is considerably interested in stock-raising.
In his labors and struggles Mr. Whealy has been
aided and encouraged by the industry and counsel
of a sensible and excellent wife who has performed
her part in building up the home and providing
something to defend them from want in their declining years.

A native of the Dominion of Canada, Mr. Whealy

was born in Perth County, Province of Ontario,
March 21, 1843, and there attained to man's estate.
When twenty-three years old, he in the winter of
1866 repaired to the lumber regions of Michigan,
and the following spring returned Eastward as far
as Starke County, Ill. He sojourned there until
the fall of 1870, occupying himself in farming
pursuits. Next he crossed the Mississippi and
coming into Woodson County, this State, resided
there until the spring of 1871, then coming to this
county, pre-empted one hundred and sixty acres of
land on section 22, Avon Township.

Upon his arrival in this region Mr. Whealy put
up a small frame house, transporting the lumber
from Chanute, one hundred and thirty miles away.
This was the first dwelling erected between Wellington and Oxford. The country around was
thinly settled and for a number of years it was a
struggle with Mr. Whealy to carry on properly the
cultivation of his land and effect the needed improvements. Patience and perseverance, however,
finally gained the day and he found himself upon
a solid footing, financially. In the meantime, as
the country settled up and the necessity arose for
trusty men to take charge of public affairs, Mr.
Whealy was selected as a fitting man for the various
offices, officiating as Township Clerk and Trustee
and holding the latter office for seven consecutive
terms. The cause of education found in him a
stanch friend and the Republican party a faithful
supporter. He has been active in the ranks of the
latter and has exercised no small influence in party
politics in this region.

The marriage of William G. Whealy with Miss
Mary Magwood, was celebrated at the bride's home
in Kewanee, Ill., September 1, 1866. This lady
was born in County Monaghan, Ireland, January 17,
1845, and was the daughter of Thomas and Ann
(Gillis) Magwood, who were natives of County
Monaghan, Ireland. They are now deceased.
Eleven children came to bless the union of Mr.
and Mrs. Whealy, all of whom are living and form
a most intelligent and interesting family group.
They bear the names respectively of Thomas W.,
George K., Arthur C., Edward, Lizzie, Annie, Rebecca, Minnie, Julia, Cyrus H. and Benjamin H.
Mr. and Mrs. Whealy have for many years been

prominently connected with the Congregational Church. The parents of Mr. Whealy were Joseph and Elizabeth (Bradley) Whealy, natives of County Tyrone, Ireland, and who spent their last years in Ontario, Canada, and Dakota. Arthur C. was the second boy born in Sumner County and Miss Jennie Whealy, a sister of our subject, taught the first school in the county, at Oxford.

JOHN R. JOHNSTON. This volume would be incomplete were not mention made within its pages of the above named gentleman, who is a prominent business man at Oxford. He is a dealer in furniture and an undertaker, and has the exclusive trade at this point in both lines of his business. He is well-known throughout this section as an old resident of the county to which he came in the spring of 1876, and where for a time he was engaged in agricultural pursuits, opening up a fine farm. His natal day was December 1, 1830, and his birthplace Shelby County, Ky., where he lived till the Centennial year engaged in farming.

During the Civil War, Mr. Johnston was so fortunate as not even to lose a horse, though living in a country which was somewhat unsettled, and overrun in turns by the Union and the Confederate armies. He fed the soldiers of both troops, and so succeeded in avoiding their ill will.

On leaving the Blue Grass State, Mr. Johnston moved to Logan County, Ill., and after a short sojourn near Atlantic came on to this State and settled four miles west of the town in Oxford Township. He paid $800 for a tract of raw land, which he so improved that he was able to sell it a few years later for $6,500. He had broken the sod and thoroughly cultivated it, fenced the estate, erected an excellent house, barn, etc., set out numerous trees, and made of it, all in all, one of the best farms in the vicinity. After having lived on the estate six years, Mr. Johnston sold and moved to town, buying out an old establishment and engaging in his present business, which he has built up to a fine trade.

Mrs. Johnston bore the maiden name of Anna E. Young, and the ceremony which united her to our subject took place February 24, 1856, in Shelby County, Ky. She was born in the Blue Grass State, July 25, 1836, is a daughter of Catesby Young, and remained with her parents till her marriage. Mr. and Mrs. Johnston have reared a family of four children: Lucy Ellen is now the wife of A. M. Rees, of this city; Willie P., is the wife of C. F. Reed, of Edwards County; Shelby Thomas married Miss Maggie Bartlett, of this county; Farris Lee is the remaining member of the family circle.

While in Kentucky Mr. Johnston served as Constable, and since making his home in Oxford has been a member of the city council two terms. He has no desire for office, finding sufficient occupation in conduct of his business affairs, in the social circle and in his home. He votes the Democratic ticket. He is a member of the Christian Church, is regarded as of strict integrity in all business transactions, and is highly esteemed by his fellow citizens.

The parents of our subject were Permenus and Lucy (Reed) Johnston, the former of whom was a native of Virginia and the latter of Kentucky. Their marriage took place in the Blue Grass State where they lived until called from time to eternity. The occupation of the father was that of tilling the soil.

JOHN T. STEWART. The career of this gentleman affords an example of persevering industry, unflagging zeal, and a sturdy integrity which has met with its reward and secured to its exhibitor a very comfortable home and pleasant surroundings. It is seldom indeed that a Scotchman is found who does not display these traits of character and the subject of this biography is a worthy son of the race from which he sprang.

Mr. Stewart was a child of about three years

when his parents, John and Elizabeth (Bremner) Stewart, both of whom were natives of Scotland, emigrated to the New World and settled in Wellington County, Province of Ontario, Canada. They are still living upon the farm where they first located and which has been operated by the father, although in his own land he had followed the trade of a shoemaker. Both are members of the Presbyterian Church. Their family comprised ten children, named Eliza, Alexander, Jessie, John T., Ellen, Robert, Flora, David, Betsey J., and Collin.

The gentleman whose life we will briefly outline was born January 1, 1842, and leaving his native land in early childhood was reared on a farm in Canada, receiving a common-school education and acquiring the trade of a carriage-maker ere he grew to manhood. After having served an apprenticeship of three years, in 1861, he went to a place near Rochester, N. Y., and there worked at his trade a year. He then removed to Davenport, Iowa, and combined farming with work at his trade for several months, after which he again changed his location and did carriage work in Memphis, Tenn.

A few months later Mr. Stewart was to be found in Covington, Tenn., first working at his trade for an employer and conducting a business of his own for two years. His next removal was to Mountain Lake, Giles County, Va., where he remained until 1871, at which time he became a citizen of Kansas. His first location in this State was at Arkansas City, Cowley County, where he conducted a shop for a year and a half, after which he secured land in Sumner County, and turned his attention to farming and the stock business. He pre-empted one hundred and sixty acres of land and purchased an equal amount on section 21, Walton Township, which makes up a valuable tract of land and upon which Mr. Stewart has made all necessary improvements. His wife also owns one hundred and sixty acres on section 28, of the same township.

In 1870 Mr. Stewart became the husband of Jemima Q. Jackson, of Canada, who bore him one daughter, Maud M., who is now deceased. Mrs. Jemima Stewart departed this life in 1881, and after having remained a widower until 1886, Mr. Stewart contracted a second matrimonial alliance.

His bride on this occasion was Mrs. Margaret A. Mountjoy, of this county, widow of Henry C. Mountjoy, by whom she had three children: Henry L., Iona M., and Nettie I.

Mr. Stewart belongs to the Farmers' Alliance, and casts his vote and influence with the Republican party. He has been a member of the Presbyterian Church for twenty years and all who know the Scotch character will understand that he is a reliable and steadfast member, and that he deserves the hearty respect of his fellow men on account of his private character as well as for the ability displayed in his worldly affairs.

IRAM H. SHULL. There is probably not a finer home within the limits of Dixon Township than that which has been planned and built up by him with whose name we introduce this sketch. A man of more than ordinary intelligence and enterprise, he stands second to none in his township, and by his own efforts has acquired a competence, climbing up slowly from a modest position in life, and surrounding himself and his family with all of its comforts and many of its luxuries. Well informed, of correct habits and cultured tastes, he keeps himself posted upon the general topics of the day and is a lover of the fine arts, especially music, to which he has given much attention during his life, and is possessed of no mean talents as a singer and performer on musical instruments. In his youth he took a thorough course of voice culture and theory in the Miami Conservatory of Music at Xenia, Ohio, and for three successive years taught music in the High School at Fulton, that State. Later he was graduated from the Central Conservatory of Music at Columbus, Ind., and for six years was professor of Harmony and Musical Theory. Since that time he has kept up his interest and practice, and has now a number of private pupils.

The subject of this sketch was born May 5, 1844, in Stark County, Ohio, and is the son of David and Elizabeth (Herman) Shull, who were born, reared and married in Pennsylvania. They emigrated to Ohio in 1832, settling in Stark County during its pioneer days. The father took up land, became well-to-do, and was a prominent man in his community. He departed this life at the old homestead in 1870. The mother survived her husband ten years, dying February 10, 1880. Of the six children born to them, three only are living, the two besides Hiram H., being residents of Indiana.

Until a youth of eighteen years, Mr. Shull spent his time upon the old farm in Stark County, Ohio. He attended the schools of his native township, and became familiar with the arts of plowing, sowing and reaping. In 1862, during the progress of the Civil War, he enlisted as a Union soldier, in Company A, One Hundred and Fourth Ohio Infantry, and served three years. He participated in the battles of Covington and Danville, Ky., and while on picket duty at the latter place, was captured by the enemy. He was taken only a short distance, however, when he was paroled, and soon afterward, at Camp Chase, was exchanged. He then rejoined his regiment at Stanford, Ky., and under command of Gen. Burnside, was present at the siege of Knoxville, from the beginning until the close. He then went with his regiment after Longstreet to Strawberry Plain, and during the holiday season of 1863, suffered much hardship from cold and exposure, also from ague. He was subsequently with Gen. Sherman at Red Clay, Ga., and then, under the same General, went to Atlanta. He fought at Nashville and in the series of battles against the rebel Gen. Hood.

While at Pumpkin Vine River, Ga., Mr. Shull suffered a sunstroke which for a long time rendered him unfit for active duty. He, however, in due time, was on the field again, and fought at the battle of Columbia, near the Duck River, Tenn., where a shell was thrown by the enemy, killing a man on each side of Mr. Shull, and wounding one in front of him. The concussion so affected Mr. Shull that he fell unconscious and knew nothing until waking up in the hospital at Nashville, sixty miles from the spot where he fell.

Mr. Shull, however, soon returned to active duty again, in time to participate in the chase after Hood's army from Nashville. He was then transferred to Stoneman Barracks at Washington, D. C.,

and next his regiment was ordered to Ft. Fisher, N. C., being the first to enter the city of Wilmington. Here Mr. Shull was assigned to provost duty, and in due time rejoined Sherman's army in time to witness the surrender of the rebel Gen. Johnston, near Raleigh. The war now being ended, the regiment was sent to Cleveland, Ohio, where the boys received their honorable discharge.

When leaving the service, Mr. Shull sought his old haunts in his native county, and resumed his musical studies, remaining there until 1883. Then, resolving upon a change of location, he came to this State and purchased his present farm. He put up his residence that same year, an elegant dwelling not exceeded in point of finish and furnishing by anything in the township. Adjacent are the usual farm buildings, neat and convenient, and agriculture is here carried on after the most approved methods, and by the aid of modern machinery. The estate embraces four hundred and ten broad acres, all in one body, half of it being under cultivation, and one hundred and fifty acres, during the season of 1889, was planted to corn alone.

Mr. Shull assumed matrimonial ties December 9, 1869, being wedded at Dalton, to Miss Martha R. Dodd. Mrs. Shull was born November 24, 1844, in Stark County, Ohio, and is the daughter of John and Hannah (Gunn) Dodd, who were natives of England, and who settled in the Buckeye State over fifty years ago. The father carried on farming successfully, and died in Stark County in 1850. The mother survived her husband thirty-seven years, remaining a widow, spending the closing years of her life in Ohio, and passing away in 1887. The parental household included six children, three of whom are living.

Mrs. Shull acquired her education in the common school, and remained under the home roof until her marriage, receiving careful parental training and becoming familiar with all useful household duties. Only two of the three children born to Mr. and Mrs. Shull are living, viz: Clara E. and Sherman H. Mr. Shull, politically, takes a lively interest in the prosperity of the Republican party, and advocates the cause of temperance at every opportunity. He was at one time Clerk of the school board in his district, and at present officiates as Director. He also belongs to the Grand Army of the Republic, in which he has held some of the offices. For twenty-eight years he was chorister in the Presbyterian Church and is now an Elder. He has always taken an active interest in the Sunday School, and for over thirty-five years has rarely ever missed attendance, laboring actively in the instruction of the young. Mrs. Shull in religious matters, is in full sympathy with her husband, belonging to the same church. It will thus be seen that they occupy no secondary position among the social, moral and religious elements of their community.

GEORGE E. ROBINSON. Within the limits of this county no subject can be found better worthy of representation than the gentleman above named. His long life has been spent in useful labors, and while he has not occupied a prominent place in the public view he has exhibited, in his own quiet way, the traits of character most worthy of admiration, and such as have a wide influence over all by whom he is surrounded. He is now retired from active pursuits, and with his aged companion, enjoying the fruits of his former industry and the comforts which the competence they have secured ensures them.

The paternal ancestry of our subject were English, and in the maternal line he is descended from German stock. A number of his relatives were soldiers in the Revolutionary War, in which struggle his grandfather, Thomas Robinson, was a Colonel. Three of his uncles took part in the War of 1812. His father, Thomas Robinson, Jr., was a native of New Hampshire and, with his wife, Betsey McDonell, abode in Maine for years. In Somerset County, of the latter State, our subject was born June 20, 1819. The house in which that event took place was erected one year before, is still standing and is yet a substantial structure.

Mr. Robinson was reared to man's estate amid the scenes of his boyhood, became well acquainted with farming and lumbering, and after he was of age left the parental home and engaged in the latter occupation. The winters were spent in the woods and the summers in the mills during a period of some thirteen years. In 1852 he went to California, taking ship at New York City, crossing the Isthmus and continuing his journey by vessel on the Pacific, landing in San Francisco twenty-nine days after leaving New York. He followed gold mining in California about fifteen months, meeting with varied success, and then returning to New York City in the same manner as he had come.

Several years were spent by our subject in the Pine Tree State whence, in 1856, he journeyed West, and taking up his abode in Bureau County, Ill., resided there many years engaged in farming and stock-raising, among the beasts of his fields being Short-horn cattle. While there he served two terms as Supervisor of the township in which he lived. In 1881 he again turned his footsteps toward the setting sun, going to Nebraska and sojourning for a time in Beatrice, thence removing to Junction City, Kan., for a short period of time, thence to St. Joseph, Mo., making the latter place also his home for a short time only. In 1884 he came to Belle Plaine, where he has since made his permanent home. He owns one hundred and sixty acres of land in Harmon Township and his village residence with its plot of five acres.

The lady who for more than forty years has shared in the joys and sorrows of Mr. Robinson, was born November 28, 1823, and bore the maiden name of Nancy H. Malbon. Her parents were Nathaniel and Polly (Robinson) Malbon, her father a native of Maine and the son of a Frenchman who came to America when about eight years old. The rites of wedlock were celebrated between Mr. and Mrs. Robinson September 24, 1847, and they have been blessed by the birth of four children: George A., the first born, is deceased; Thomas R. lives in Kansas City, Mo.; Sade H. is the wife of F. C. Parker, Secretary of the School Board and Inspector of the school buildings at St. Joseph, Mo., and Burton S. is an express agent on the Denver, Memphis & Atlantic Railroad from Nevada, Mo., to Larned, Kan.

The gentleman of whom we write had not the early school advantages offered young men of this day and age, but being possessed of native intelligence and a desire to be well informed he has, by reading and observation, become conversant with general topics and the current events of the day, and his wife, whose early surroundings were similar to his own, is also well informed. In the accumulation of his property he has been ably assisted by his devoted companion, who has been his helpmate and counselor in all the chief events of his life from the time of their union. Both are members of the Presbyterian Church. Mr. Robinson is a member of the Masonic fraternity and of the Republican party.

IRA M. LEWIS is the owner and occupant of a half-section of land in Ryan Township, of which he took possession when there were but three houses in sight from his claim. Although he obtained a good insight into the trade of a carpenter when he was a young man, he has made farming his life work, and has shown ability and judgment in tilling the soil and in every department of labor connected with a successful farmer's career. His land is improved, intelligently cultivated, and makes an estate which any man might be well pleased to own.

The Buckeye State claims Mr. Lewis as one of her sons, his birth having taken place in Harrisville, November 7, 1837. He is the first-born in a family of twelve children, whose parents, Insley and Amy (Grissell) Lewis, were natives of Ohio. They were married in Columbiana County, and two years afterward removed to Jay County, Ind., where they made their permanent home. The father was a mechanic and the owner of a farm. The devoted husband and wife, and loving parents, "in death were not divided," both contracting typhoid fever, which occasioned their decease at the same time, in 1864.

The subject of this biography grew to manhood in Indiana, and began his life work by superintending his father's farm until he was twenty-three years of age. He had acquired a good common-

school education, to which his native intelligence and his keen observation have added much practical knowledge since he left the schoolroom. In 1863 he started for the pineries of Michigan and tarried at a place six miles from Battle Creek, that State. There he was drafted, but not being able to pass the required physical examination, he did not enter the service. In 1872 he removed with his family to Carroll County, Iowa, building the second house in the township in which he located. The Hawkeye State was the home of the family until 1877, at which time they were numbered among the inhabitants of Kansas, the first two years of their sojourn in this State being spent in Sedgwick County. At the expiration of that time a removal was made to the place which is now their home, and where Mr. Lewis is successfully giving his attention to the raising of crops and stock.

On August 11, 1861, Ira M. Lewis and Sarah J. Spayd were united in marriage at the home of the bride. She is a daughter of Reuben and Mary (Hart) Spayd, and was born in Darke County, Ohio, on Christmas Day, 1840. She acquired a good common-school education, and before her marriage was engaged in school teaching, a work for which her tact, excellent education and pleasant disposition admirably qualified her. Her father, a cabinetmaker by trade, was born in Dauphin County, Pa., October 24, 1811, and died in 1886. Her mother was born in Wayne County, Ohio, August 10, 1821, and her death took place July 12, 1882. Mr. and Mrs. Spayd were the parents of ten children, seven of whom now survive.

To our subject and his worthy wife five children have been born, two of whom are married and living in homes of their own. Estella J. is the wife of William A. Adams and the mother of three children; she occupies a pleasant dwelling two miles north of the parental home. Annie M., the fourth born, married John Miller, who lives on the northeast quarter of section 14, Ryan Township; they have one child; Linley L, Insley M. and John W. remain with their parents. All the children are well educated, and Estella has been a teacher.

Mr. Lewis belongs to the Farmer's Alliance, and is now a member of the Committee on Inquiry. He

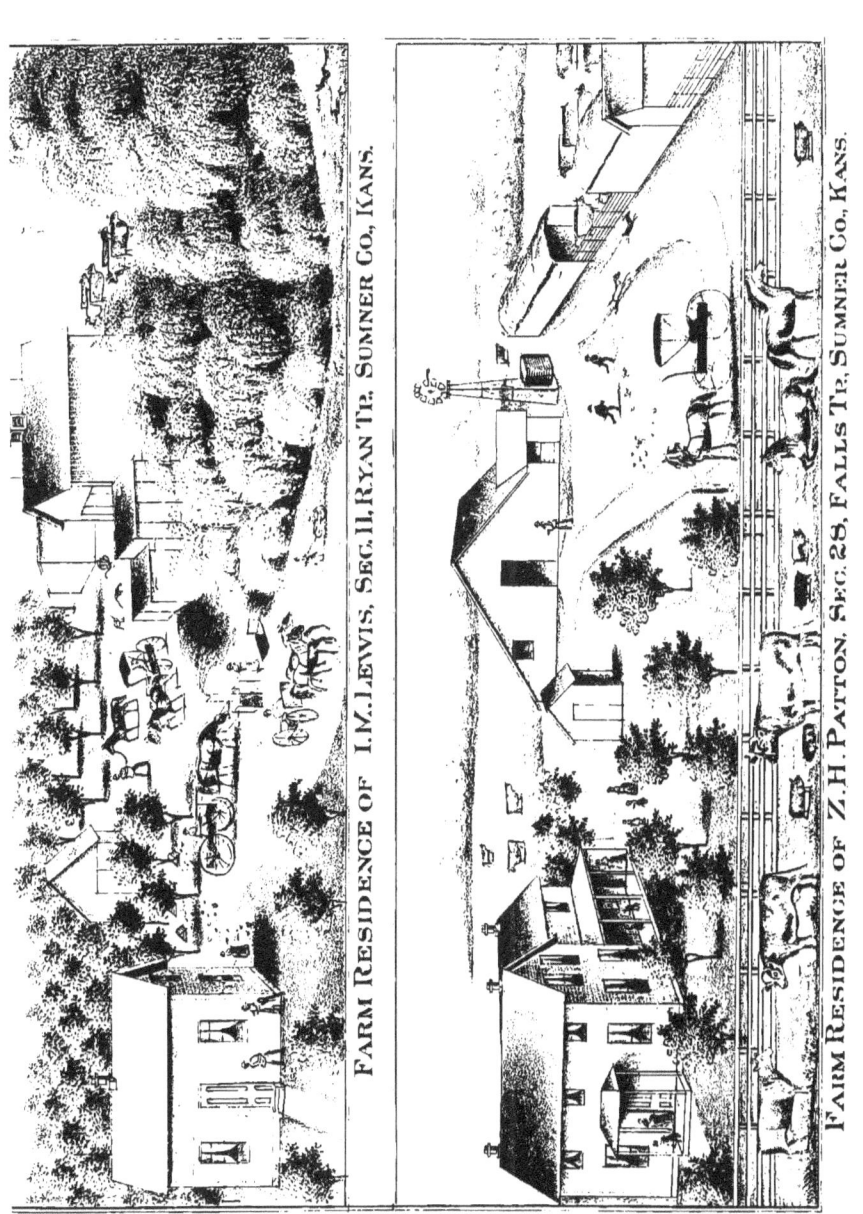

FARM RESIDENCE OF I.M. LEWIS, SEC.11, RYAN TP., SUMNER CO., KANS.

FARM RESIDENCE OF Z.H. PATTON, SEC. 28, FALLS TP., SUMNER CO., KANS.

is Treasurer of the School District, has been a member of the Board for several years, and takes a deep interest in the progress of the schools. He is also serving as Road Overseer. The Republican ticket is that which he always votes, and he is much interested in political movements. While in Indiana, prior to the Civil War, he lived in a settlement through which the underground railroad passed, and became somewhat acquainted with the workings of that road and quite interested in the abolition of slavery. Among his neighbors and fellow-citizens he is spoken of as a reliable citizen and an honorable man.

In this connection we present a lithographic view of the residence wherein Mr. and Mrs. Lewis are so pleasantly domiciled.

ZACHARIAH H. PATTON. The subject of this notice came to this county with a capital of forty-five cents, but is now numbered among its most thrifty and successful farmers. He is proprietor of one of the finest estates in Falls Township, embracing three hundred and sixty acres of as valuable land as is to be found on the Chikaskia River. A beautiful two-story residence embellishes the place and is represented by a lithographic view on another page; together with its surroundings it presents one of the most attractive pictures in the landscape of this region. The passing traveler invariably turns to take a second look at the homestead which has been built up only by the most unflagging industry and the exercise of good judgment and fine taste.

A native of what is now West Virginia, Mr. Patton was born in Gilmer County, November 28, 1843, and is the son of William and Mary (Smith) Patton, the former of whom was a native of Maryland and born in 1799. William Patton left his native State with his parents when a child, the family removing to Gilmer County, W. Va., where they all spent the remainder of their lives, William dying about 1868. He followed the vocation of a farmer and accumulated a good property. Both he and his estimable wife were for many years prominently connected with the Baptist Church. The paternal grandfather, likewise named William, was also a native of Maryland. The mother of our subject was born in the State of West Virginia, and died in Gilmer County that State, in 1885, after the death of her husband. Her father was John Smith, who traced his ancestry to Germany. To William and Mary Patton there was born a family of eight children, viz: John S., Zachariah H., Hannah E., Mary L., Phebe J., Susan K., Nathan L. and Anna C. Four of these are living.

The subject of this sketch was the second child of his parents and spent his boyhood and youth on the farm in his native county acquiring his education in the common school. After the outbreak of the Civil War, he, in 1862, joined the Confederate Army as a private in Company B, Twentieth West Virginia Cavalry and served until in November, 1863. Then, being wounded by a ball at Droop Mountain, he was rendered unfit for further service and receiving his honorable discharge returned home. He sojourned there until 1868, then started for the far West and locating in Kansas City, Mo., worked at anything he could find to do in order to make an honest living. In 1870 he came to Kansas and prosecuted farming in Neosha County until 1871. That year he came to this county and pre-empted sixty acres of land on section 28, Falls Township, of which he has since been a resident. He was prospered in his labors and later added two hundred acres to his real estate, this lying on sections 21 and 28. After a few years engaged in tilling the soil he gradually became interested in live stock, from which he has realized handsome returns. He knows all about the hardships and difficulties of beginning in a new country without capital, and has maintained a warm interest in the material welfare of his adopted home. He belongs to the Farmers' Alliance, and is a stanch supporter of the Democratic party.

Mr. Patton was married November 6, 1867, to Miss Phebe P. Spurgeon of Doddridge County, W. Va. This lady was born November 17, 1848, and is the daughter of John and Phebe (Smith) Spurgeon, who were natives of West Virginia and are now living in Kansas. The result of this union was a family of eleven children who were named respectively--William E., Charles, Laura D., Samantha J., Jessie, John, James L., Lenna, Nettie B., Luther and Joseph.

GEORGE W. ELLIS. In making note of the public-spirited citizens of Avon Township, the name of Mr. Ellis should occupy a leading position. He is a farmer in good circumstances, owning and operating a fine body of land, one hundred and sixty acres in extent, and located on section 29. He has erected good buildings, and provided himself with modern farm machinery, together with all the other appliances necessary for the successful prosecution of agriculture. He is one of the older settlers of this county, having pitched his tent here in 1870.

Mr. Ellis was born in Adams County, Ohio, November 7, 1835, and was there reared to manhood on his father's farm, learning the arts of plowing, sowing and reaping, and acquiring his education in the district school. His life passed in a comparatively uneventful manner until the outbreak of the Civil War, when he enlisted in the Union army, November 15, 1862, becoming a member of Company G, Seventieth Ohio Infantry. He served for three years, or until nearly the close of the war, experiencing all the vicissitudes of a soldier's life, but escaped comparatively unharmed, receiving his honorable discharge, and afterward returned to his native county, sojourning there until setting out for the West.

Upon coming to Kansas Mr. Ellis pre-empted one hundred and sixty acres of land on section 29, Avon Township, where he made his home until 1873. He then returned to his native State, and for twelve years thereafter engaged in farming in Adams County. Finally, in 1885, he returned to Kansas, taking up his residence once more in Avon Township, and again became owner of a quarter section of land, in the cultivation and improvement of which he has since been engaged.

Mr. Ellis was married, in Mason County, Ky., October 7, 1878, to Miss Josephine Burgle. Mrs. Ellis was born twenty miles from Paris, in France, and was brought to America by her parents, in 1852, when a child of three years. The family settled in Ohio, where she was reared to womanhood. Of her union with our subject there have been born two children—Landis and Andrew. Mr. Ellis, politically, is a decided Republican, while he and his estimable wife are prominently connected with the Methodist Episcopal Church, attending services at Wellington.

The regiment with which Mr. Ellis was connected was assigned to the Army of the Tennessee, and he participated in the battles of Shiloh, and the sieges of Corinth and Vicksburg; he was also engaged in the Mississippi campaign, and was with the troops of Gen. Hazen at the storming of Ft. McAllister, in 1864. He met the enemy at Mission Ridge, and marched with Sherman to the sea. He also participated all through the Atlanta campaign, and never once turned his back to the enemy, was never wounded or taken prisoner. He was mustered out at Savannah, Ga., receiving an honorable discharge in January, 1865.

GEORGE W. DURHAM. Second only to the influence of the home, is that exerted by the school, and the character and example of the teacher are even more potent than his precepts and mental instruction in molding the lives of the young, and preparing them for their future as citizens of this great republic. The position of a teacher is, therefore, one of great responsibility, and those who have charge of educational affairs should allow it to be filled only by persons possessed of upright characters and correct lives, as well as the tact which from a store of information can instill instruction into the receptive minds. It is a pleasure to all who are interested in the true growth and advancement of our country to find this principle carried out in the selection of instructors, and to feel assured that not only the mental but moral training of the youth is undertaken by competent teachers.

The subject of this biography is a young man of high mental attainments, cultured manners and fine moral character, and Sumner County is fortunate in having for several years enjoyed his services as an instructor. He was born in Warren County, Ky., July 5, 1861, and was reared and educated under favorable auspices, completing his studies at Smith Grove College, in his native county. He became a resident of this county in 1884, and has since been numbered among Kansas teachers, gaining a reputation and a popularity highly creditable.

At the home of the bride, on September 12, 1889, Mr. Durham was united in marriage with Miss Linnie K. Frable, a young lady who was well-fitted to become his companion, being cultured and refined, and like her husband, a worthy member of the Methodist Episcopal Church. Mrs. Durham was born in Pennsylvania, October 25, 1869, and is a daughter of Solomon and Mary (Schall) Frable, who were also natives of the Keystone State. The family moved to Sumner County in 1878, and Mr. Frable is now engaged in farming here. Mr. Durham is a Democrat in his political views, and never fails to support with his vote the principles in which he believes.

The Rev. Willis W. Durham, the father of our subject, was born in Barren County, Ky., fifty-four years ago. He is a Baptist minister, and is now employed by the Philadelphia Bible Association, as a traveling missionary in Southwestern Kansas, having taken up his residence in this county in 1884. He married Miss Susan J. Renfro, who was born in the same county in which he first saw the light, and who is now fifty-five years old. She is a daughter of Jesse J. and Pollie (Mitchell) Renfro, who were natives of the Old Dominion. At the age of twenty-one years Mr. Renfro went to Kentucky, and took charge of a plantation which he carried on for five years. He then purchased a farm, where, after having lived thereon sixty-eight years, he died at the advanced age of ninety-six. He had served as a soldier in the Mexican War. In politics he was a Democrat. Mrs. Renfro died when about seventy years of age. The parents of our subject reared six children, all still living, and named respectively: Alice E., George W., Dora W., Nathael T., Jesse J. and Amanda A.

UGH PAISLEY. The family of which this gentleman is a lineal descendant, is an old and honored one in Scotland, and to this fact the city of Paisley owes its name, and is a standing monument. His maternal ancestry were Irish, and the family of his mother is also a well-known one. Our subject is a man of honor, intelligence and geniality, and is accorded his just measure of respect by his fellowmen.

Mr. Paisley is the ninth of twelve children born to Robert and Mary (McCullough) Paisley, and his natal day was September 14, 1846. His parents were natives of Pennsylvania, were married in Ohio, and resided in the latter State until the death of the mother in 1863. Eight members of the parental family are now living. The father departed this life in 1882. He was a son of Hugh Paisley, who was an American soldier during the War of 1812.

During his youth our subject was afflicted with phthisic, but he was able to obtain an excellent common school education, and remaining with his father until twenty-five years of age, worked for twelve years in his grist and saw mill. In 1870, he came to Kansas, located in Sedgwick County, where he sojourned two years, after which he spent an equal length of time in Iowa. Returning to Sedgwick County, he was a resident therein for six years, and then, in 1880, came to Sumner County, and settled on a farm in Ryan Township, which he has since made his home. His farm comprises one hundred and sixty acres of land, all improved, and changed from the raw and primitive condition in which he took possession of it, to that of a well-cultivated and well-improved acreage. Mr. Paisley devotes his attention to general farming and stock-raising, and is winning a competence in his chosen field of labor.

The marriage of Mr. Hugh Paisley and Miss Matilda Neighburg, was celebrated in December, 1871, in Burlington, Iowa. Mrs. Paisley was born in Calmerlain, Sweden, April 13, 1817, to Adolf and Christina Neighburg, who were prominent people in their section of Scandinavia. The mother died in 1884, and the father in 1889. Their family comprised nine children, of whom three are now living. Mrs. Paisley is the second child, and came to America in 1872. She has borne her husband six children, of whom Adolphus A., Benjamin O., Merton H., Matilda, and Shaenie are now living. She has been a member of the Lutheran Church, and has many womanly and domestic virtues. Mr. Paisley belongs to the Farmers' Alliance. He has been Road Overseer, and is now Constable of Ryan Township.

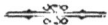

ILLIAM T. BOATRIGHT, a warm-hearted Southerner, with Northern proclivities, especially in politics, is one for whom nature has done much, and who has made the most of his opportunities, at times under adverse circumstances. He may be properly classed as among the most enterprising and public-spirited citizens of Creek Township, a man who keeps his eyes open to what is going on around him, and never intends to be left at the rear, where there is any worthy project in view, or any commendable enterprise to be encouraged. His native place was Graves County, Ky., and the date of his birth January 5, 1847. He was the tenth in a family of eleven children, the offspring of William V. and Sally W. (Gates) Boatright, who were natives of Virginia.

The father of our subject operated as a farmer and miller combined, and as early as 1821 left the Old Dominion, settling among the pioneers of Graves County, Ky., where he was married. In 1851, leaving Kentucky, he emigrated with his family, across the Mississippi into Platte County, Mo. They only lived there, however, about eighteen months, removing then to Gentry County, Mo. Mr. Boatright departed hence in 1867; his wife, Sally, survived him for a period of eighteen years,

remaining a widow, and died in Gentry County, Mo., in 1885. Eight of their children are still living.

William T. in the meantime, acquired such education as he could obtain in the common school, and worked with his father on the farm until after the outbreak of the Civil War. Then, a youth of seventeen years, he enlisted in Company D, Forty-third Missouri Infantry, which operated mostly in that State. During the Price raid, young Boatright was captured, October 15, 1864, at Glasgow, Mo., but was soon paroled and sent to Benton Barracks, near St. Louis. Later he returned to St. Joseph, and subsequently assisted in chasing bushwhackers, being in several skirmishes, and thus occupying his time until after the close of the war. He was mustered out June 30, 1865, and returning to the farm, remained with his father until his marriage.

The above-mentioned interesting event in the life of our subject occurred January 3, 1869, the bride being Miss Sarah E., daughter of Jackson and Mary (Compton) Burger, all natives of Kentucky. The Burger family emigrated to Missouri about 1855, settling in Platte County. In 1878 they came to Southern Kansas, and are still residents of this county. Their family consisted of eleven children. Mrs. Boatright was the eldest, and was born February 27, 1851, in Russell County, Ky. Of her union with our subject there have been born eight children, seven of whom are living, viz: Levi J., Laura A., James F., Orilla J., Jesse O., Charles W. and Viola M.

Mr. Boatright has always taken a warm interest in politics, and uniformly votes the straight Republican ticket. He is serving his second term as a director in school district No. 110, and for four years in Missouri served in a similar capacity. He is a member in good standing of the John Goldy Post, No. 90, G. A. R., of Milan, occupying the office of Junior Vice, and has also served as Sergeant Major. He began life for himself with a capital of $375, this comprising his portion of his father's estate. He came to Kansas in 1884, arriving in Creek Township, March 11, and that day he purchased his present farm, which was then but a tract of unimproved land. He now has ninety acres under the plow, with an orchard of sixty-five apple trees, and one hundred and fifty peach trees, besides pears and cherry trees. He has enclosed and divided his fields with substantial fencing, and in 1887, put up his present residence at a cost of over $600 besides his own labor. It is fair to suppose that in the course of a few years he will be able to retire upon a competence.

━━━◆━◆◆━━━

CHARLES G. EPPERSON, traveling correspondent of Kansas City *Daily Journal*, is a resident of Wellington, having an attractive home at No. 709, N. A. Street. He is the possessor of a bright intellect, being a forcible and vigorous writer, and has made himself an enviable reputation in the newspaper world. He was born in Lebanon, Boone County, Ind., February 17, 1810, and is the son of Charles and Martha (Woolery) Epperson, who are natives respectively of Virginia and Kentucky.

The Epperson family is of English extraction, and the first representatives here settled in Virginia prior to the Revolutionary War. Several members of it served in this great struggle, and the paternal great-grandfather of our subject, David Epperson, had a number of sons in the war; one, Thompson, was a Major. Charles Epperson, later, removed from Virginia to Kentucky, about 1810, sojourning there until probably 1839. We next find him in Montgomery County, Ind., where he lived until 1842. That year he pushed on further westward into Illinois, settling at Rio, in the northern part of it served in this County. He spent his last days in Oxford, Henry County, dying about 1849. His wife survived him only three months. They had lived together harmoniously for the long period of over fifty years. They reared a family of seven sons and four daughters, among them being Charles, the father of our subject, who was born in Virginia, August 11, 1802.

The father of our subject removed with his parents to Kentucky in his youth and there made the acquaintance of Miss Martha Woolery, to whom he

was married in Richmond, Madison County, and they lived in the Blue Grass State until about 1827. Thence they emigrated to Putnam County, Ind., and from there removed to Boone County, that State, about 1838. We next find them on the other side of the Mississippi, in Benton County, Iowa, taking up their abode at Marysville in October, 1847. This was during the early settlement of that region, and Charles Epperson improved a large farm from the wilderness. He became well-to-do, but in 1863 sold out and improved another farm in Harrison Township. He departed this life October 14, 1864. He was first a Whig and then a Republican, and a man warmly interested in the success of his party. For many years he was a member of the Christian Church. He was widely and favorably known, and stood high in his community, his word being considered as good as his bond. He left a valuable estate. The mother of Mr. Epperson is still living, making her home with her son, John, in Avon Township, this county, and has arrived at the advanced age of eighty-two years.

To the parents of our subject there was born a family of thirteen children, nine of whom are still living. John S., one of the Commissioners of this county, is a farmer by occupation, and makes his home in Avon Township; Hiram T. is farming near Vinton, Iowa; Mary, Mrs. Stefly resides in Boone, Iowa; Martha J. married J. P. Wood, and lives in Pulaski, Ind.; Minerva A. is the wife of E. G. Stowe, of McPherson County, this State; Charles G., our subject, was the next in order of birth; William W. is a commercial salesman, and makes his home in Cedar Rapids, Iowa; Kittie E. is the wife of P. D. Stout, of Jacksonville, Ill.; Albert G., a speculator, resides in Boone, Iowa.

The subject of this sketch was a lad of seven years when the family settled in Iowa, and he resided there until a man of twenty-five. He first attended school in Boone County, Ind., having for his teacher William Carey, he being then a little lad of five years. His teacher was little more than a boy. After an absence of forty-two years, Mr. Epperson visited his old home and found his former preceptor owner of the old Epperson homestead and worth $100,000. Pupil and teacher enjoyed a very pleasant visit. At Marysville young Epperson completed his education, and afterward assisted his father in carrying on the farm until his marriage.

In 1862 Mr. Epperson offered his services to the Government to aid in putting down the Rebellion, and was accepted and made a member of Company A, Twenty-eighth Iowa Infantry, and was assigned to the Army of the Mississippi. Soon after entering camp he was taken to the hospital sick, where he remained a short time, and was discharged.

In October, 1864, Mr. Epperson was wedded to Mrs. Mary C. (Van Cleef) Martin, whose husband had yielded up his life on the battlefield of Shiloh during the Civil War. Mrs. Epperson was a daughter of Richard N. and Susan Van Cleef, who were natives of Indiana. The father is now living in Guthrie, Iowa; the wife died in 1882. The young couple spent their first year upon the homestead, then removed to Cedar Rapids, and Mr. Epperson embarked in the lumber business as manager of the firm of J. S. Alexander & Co. On the 27th of March, 1867, he met with a severe affliction in the death of his wife, who passed away, leaving one son, Judson Elmore, who was born June 10, 1866, and who was a babe of nine months at the time of his mother's death. He is still living and makes his home with his father, being likewise a newspaper man.

After the death of his wife Mr. Epperson continued in business in Cedar Rapids until 1869, and then removed to St. Joseph, Mo. There he associated himself in partnership with J. B. Johnson, and egaged in the marble business. He began his newspaper career in February, 1873, as correspondent for the Daily Herald, of St. Joseph, and in May of that year accepted a position with the Wilcox & Gibbs Sewing Machine Company, which necessitated his removal to Louisville, Ky. In January, 1874, he was transferred to the office at St. Louis, Mo.

For a number of years Mr. Epperson had given his attention to the study of medicine, and while in St. Joseph took a course of lectures in the Eclectic Medical College, of St. Louis. In the fall of 1871 he repaired to Evansville, Ind., where he

commenced practice, and later, in order to receive further instruction in the profession, returned to St. Joseph, and while pursuing his studies in this direction, accepted a position on the Herald in order to earn money to meet his necessities. He found that the newspaper business was more congenial to his tastes than the medical profession, and, accordingly, abandoned the latter, giving to the former his entire attention.

Mr. Epperson continued his connection with the Herald until 1882, in the meantime traveling through New Mexico, accompanied by his wife and baby, Oscar, in 1880-81, and employing his facile pen in writing up something of the early history of the country as compared with its condition of to-day, and treating of its antiquities. He was accompanied on part of this trip by Capt. Jack Crawford, the scout—a man who had a large experience among the wild western regions. In 1882 Mr. Epperson resigned his position on the Herald, and coming to this county, began the improvement of a farm which he had previously purchased. In the meantime, in 1876, while on a visit to his brother in this county, he made the acquaintance of Mrs. Alice J. (Eggleston) Chamberlain, which resulted in a mutual attachment, and on the 28th of April, 1878, they were united in marriage at the home of the bride's parents, in Belle Plaine, Sumner County. Judge Elijah Evans officiating.

Mrs. Epperson was born in Springfield, Ill., November 25, 1856, and is the only child of Henry N. and Elizabeth (Artman) Eggleston, who are now residents of Wellington. The family came to this county in 1872, and Miss Alice officiated as one of the first teachers within its limits, a profession which she followed for seven years, beginning at the age of fifteen years. She was first married in August, 1874, to William R. Chamberlain, who died January 5, 1875. Mrs. Epperson attended the funeral services of President Lincoln at Springfield, Ill., and frequently saw the martyred President during his lifetime.

Residing on his farm from January 1, 1883, until January 1, 1884, Mr. Epperson then bought an interest in the Wellingtonian, a weekly paper, the official organ of this county, and then moved to Wellington. He associated himself in partnership with the Rev.

Samuel L. Hamilton, a Presbyterian clergyman of Wichita, and J. C. O. Morse, the Sheriff of this county, but in October following Mr. Epperson retired from the firm and again became the traveling correspondent of the St. Joseph *Herald*. In January, 1886, he again resigned this position to accept a similar one with the Kansas City *Daily Journal*, which he still holds.

Republican in politics, Mr. Epperson is a stanch supporter of the principles of his party through the columns of his paper, and is prominent in its councils. While a resident of Sumner County he was a member of the Central Committee representing Palestine Township, where he and his wife own two farms, the best in the State. Mr. and Mrs. Epperson are members of the Christian Church, and Mr. Epperson belongs to the Independent Order of Odd Fellows and the Ancient Order of United Workmen. Of the present marriage there have been born two children—Oscar Eggleston, July 7, 1880, and Charles Henry, October 17, 1883. In 1884 Mr. Epperson was a delegate from Sumner County to the State Republican Convention at Topeka, which was called to select delegates to the National Convention, which nominated James G. Blaine for President. In 1879 he accompanied the Hayes Presidential party on their trip through Kansas and to Springfield, Ill. The Eppersons have a very pleasant home in Wellington, and move in its highest social circles.

LBERT RICE is one of the early settlers of Oxford Township, and is the owner and occupant of a productive farm comprising two hundred and forty acres on section 22. This land was purchased by Mr. Rice in 1875 and was entirely raw and unbroken, and its present owner has made all the improvements upon it, which include a fine house, barn, wind-mill and such other buildings as are usually erected by a man of enterprise and industry, together with adequate fences and fruit and shade trees. The estate is devoted to the purposes of stock-raising and farming, in both of which the owner is proving very successful.

The paternal grandfather of our subject was Samuel Rice, who, being left an orphan, went on board a man-of-war, where he served until years of maturity. He then left the navy and married, and with his family soon removed to Ohio, from the eastern part of our country. His son Alfred was but a boy when the removal took place, and after reaching man's estate, he married Miss Elizabeth Furman, daughter of John Furman, of New York State, who, with his family, had removed to Ohio at an early day. Alfred Rice and his wife remained in Ohio until 1841, when they removed to Noble County, Ind., and there continued to reside until death. Mr. Rice cleared up a farm and made a home upon it, also working at the carpenter's trade in Kendallville. He reared a family of ten children, of whom our subject is one. The father died in 1848, and the mother lived to be eighty years of age, dying about the year 1886. Of the members of the parental family who lived to maturity, we note the following: Samuel married Miss Elizabeth Godwin, and now lives in Oklahoma; Amos is now deceased, leaving one child—Harriet; Elizabeth was the wife of Jerome Trowbridge, and died in Michigan; Isaac married Miss Edna Godwin and lives in Western Kansas; Alvin married Miss Maria Herrick and lives in ValVerde; Alphonso married Miss Sophronia Montague and lives in this township; William married Miss Emeline Miller, and they also live in this township.

The gentleman whose name initiates this notice was born February 6, 1844, in Noble County, Ind., and grew to maturity at Kendallville, first leaving his home to engage in the service of his country during the Civil War. Fired with the enthusiasm which swept like wild fire over the Hoosier State, when hostilities were declared, he enlisted in 1862, as a member of Company G, Forty-fourth Indiana Infantry, and was first sent to the Western army, but after a time was discharged on account of illness. When able to travel, he went to Iowa, and after regaining his health, again entered the service, his second enrollment being in Company I, Fourth Iowa Cavalry. He was sent to Tennessee, Mississippi and Georgia, the command being engaged in scouting and skirmishing mostly, and seeing much hard service. Mr. Rice was wounded in the left leg at Ripley, Miss., and after recruiting from this injury, continued his gallant work until the close of the war.

Receiving an honorable discharge, and returning once more to civil life, Mr. Rice made his home in his native State for several years, and then resided in Eaton County, Mich., three years, after which, in 1874, he came to this county, and the following year bought the farm upon which he is now living. Since that time he has been a continuous resident here, and has earned a high reputation among the citizens for intelligence, integrity and ability. He is a member of the Masonic order, and is now filling the office of Treasurer of School District No. 33. He has no desire for political preferment, but never fails to cast his vote in the interest of good government, his judgment leading him to take his place in the ranks of the Republican party.

The marriage of Mr. Rice took place in the Hoosier State, June 12, 1871, his bride being Miss Olive A. Thew, whose parental history will be found in a sketch of Joseph Thew, on another page in this work. This worthy and highly respected lady has borne her husband one son—Frank J., who is now seventeen years old, his birth having taken place May 13, 1872.

<hr/>

ILLIAM H. ALDRICH. This gentleman owns and occupies one of the finest homes in Sumner County. It embraces a highly-cultivated and valuable farm, embellished with an elegant residence and the outbuildings required for the shelter of stock and the storage of grain. The farm operations are conducted by the aid of improved, modern machinery, and in all its operations indicates the intelligence and enterprise of the proprietor. Mr. Aldrich is the owner of two hundred and sixty acres of land, and has dealt largely in real estate since coming to Kansas, buying and selling farm lands extensively. He came to this county in 1877, pre-empting first one hundred and sixty

acres on section 29, Falls Township, of which he has since been a resident. He started in life at the foot of the ladder and has made every dollar of his property by hard work and honest dealing. He has found live stock very profitable, and accordingly has given to this industry a large share of his attention.

Kalamazoo County, Mich., was the early tramping ground of our subject, and where his birth took place November 17, 1842. He is the offspring of an excellent family, being the son of Amos N. and Margaret (Heath) Aldrich, the former of whom was a native of Clyde, Wayne County, N. Y. Amos Aldrich when quite young removed with his parents to Jackson County, but later obtained work in Kalamazoo County, Mich., where he spent the remainder of his life. He learned the trade of a stone cutter in early manhood, but only followed it a comparatively short time, being more inclined to farming pursuits. He was a man looked up to and respected in his community, being for many years prior to his death a Class-Leader in the Methodist Episcopal Church, and was otherwise instrumental in furthering the interests of religion and morality. The paternal grandfather of our subject was Edward Aldrich, a native of New York State, and a farmer by occupation. He spent his last years in Kalamazoo County, Mich.

Mrs. Margaret (Heath) Aldrich, the mother of our subject, was born in Niagara County, N. Y., and removed with her parents in her youth to Kalamazoo County, Mich., where she made the acquaintance of her future husband. Their union was blest by the birth of nine children, all of whom are living, and who were named, respectively: William H., our subject; Nelson E., Joseph H., Margaret A., Arcena E., Martha D., Herbert S., Frank B. and John.

William H. remained a resident of his native county until a man of twenty-five years, acquiring such education as the district schools afforded, and becoming familiar with the various pursuits of farm life. He left Michigan in 1867, removing to Taylor County, Iowa, where he sojourned for a period of ten years. Then, in 1877, he cast his lot with the people of this county. While a resident of Iowa, he served as a Justice of the Peace, and since com-

ESIDENCE OF FRANK KUBIK, SEC.3. CALDWELL TP. SUMNER CO., KANS.

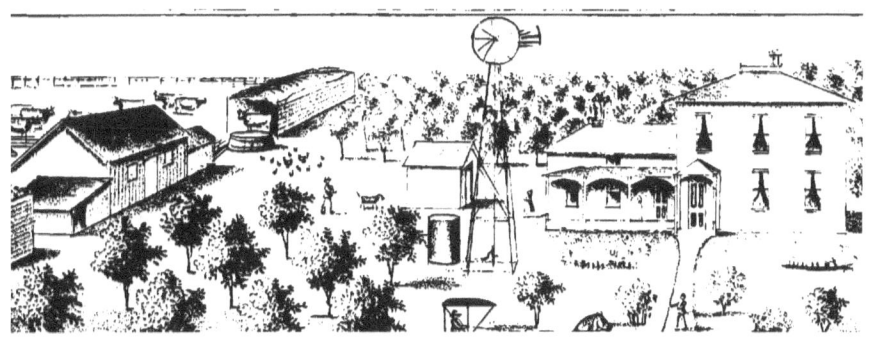

ing to Kansas has for one term been a Trustee of Falls Township. Both he and his estimable wife are active members of the Methodist Episcopal Church at Falls Center. Politically, Mr. Aldrich is independent, but favors prohibition.

While a resident of Taylor County, Iowa, Mr. Aldrich was married, September 17, 1868, to Miss Annie M. Warriner. This lady was born in Calhoun County, Mich., June 13, 1841, and is the daughter of Lemuel C. and Jane (Beedle) Warriner, who were natives of New York, and are now deceased. Four children have been born of this union, viz: Cassel, Lenna, Maggie and Nelson. Mrs. Aldrich owns a quarter-section of valuable land in Caldwell Township, from which she derives a good income.

Elsewhere in this volume will be found a lithographic view of the residence of our subject.

FRANK KUBIK. Kansas is the home of many foreign born citizens, whose industry, thrift and energy have been effective in developing the natural resources of the Sunflower State, and in advancing every good work within its borders. The department of farm labor has been fortunate in including so large a number of individuals who represent the best elements of their various nationalities, and who demonstrate by their lives that "man is the architect of his own fortune." The subject of this biography has proved himself to be a successful farmer and stock-raiser, and has built up a fine estate from a small capital. While doing so he has maintained a large family in comfort, and nobly assisted by his wife, has reared them to an honorable manhood and womanhood, which fact is the brightest star in his crown of rejoicing.

In the Kingdom of Bohemia, the gentleman of whom we write was born April 9, 1831. His parents, Joseph and Mary Kubik, had a family of six children, bearing the names of Joseph, John, Ann, Frank, Mary and Kate. With the exception of the latter, now the wife of Oscar Lender, of Racine,

Wis., our subject is the only survivor of the parental band. He was reared on a farm in his native country, and, at the age of twenty-three years, accompanied his parents across the Atlantic, and with them located in Racine, Wis., where the father and mother subsequently died. Joseph Kubik not only followed farming but was also proficient at the trade of a stone cutter.

The Badger State was the home of our subject until March, 1878, when he came to Sumner County, Kan., and bought one hundred and sixty acres of land on section 3, Caldwell Township. He subsequently pre-empted eighty acres on section 33, of the same township, and has since added by purchase to his acreage until he now owns four hundred and eighty acres of well-improved land on sections 34 and 3. He is a man of more than ordinary intelligence, and his citizenship and private character reflect credit upon his nationality and the home of his adoption. In 1864 he joined the Union army as a private in Company B, Twenty-second Wisconsin Infantry, and served until the close of the war.

In 1855, Mr. Kubik was united in marriage with Miss Mary Jenesta, a native of Bohemia, but at the time of their marriage, a resident of Wisconsin. The union was blessed by the birth of one daughter—Anna—born November 3, 1857. The loving wife and mother was stricken by death March 3, 1858. Mr. Kubik contracted a second matrimonial alliance August 22, 1859, being then united with Miss Anna Dauck, a lady of Bohemian nativity, whose eyes first opened to the light August 28, 1836. She is the daughter of Nicholas and Mary (Eclik) Dauck, who emigrated to America in 1853, settling in Wisconsin. The father died in that State and the mother in Minnesota.

Mrs. Anna Kubik has borne her husband twelve children, the date of their births being as follows: Frank, born July 18, 1860; Mary, September 18, 1861; Charley, May 27, 1863; Lydia, September 9, 1864; Lewis, April 13, 1866; George, August 17, 1867; Joseph, February 6, 1869; John, November 16, 1870; Jerry, February 11, 1872; Daniel, September 7, 1874; Pauline, April 8, 1876; Henry, November 17, 1877. All of this interesting group are still living, although four have left the parental roof for homes of their own. Frank, Jr., married Miss Mary Jeck, of Kansas, and after her death was united with Miss Catherine Renik, of Wisconsin, in which State they are now living; Mary married Anthony Ratt, a farmer of Sumner County; Lydia married Joseph Jenesta, a farmer in Racine County, Wis.; George became the husband of Miss Anna Bobek, of Sumner County, where he is engaged in farming.

Mr. and Mrs. Kubik are members of the Evangelical Church in Bohemia. A fine lithographic view of the residence of Mr. Kubik is shown elsewhere in this volume.

ENRY KNOWLES, of the firm of Knowles & Garland, is joint proprietor of one of the finest meat-markets in Southern Kansas. It was established in Wellington in 1882, by our subject and his son, F. E., and had not long been operated ere a fine trade had been acquired. On account of ill-health the son was obliged to abandon the business, and selling his interest to Mr. Garland, departed to California, Mr. Knowles does the buying for the establishment, having had quite an extended experience in the cattle trade, and being an excellent judge of flesh on foot.

The father of our subject was Daniel Knowles, son of Moses Knowles, and a native of New York State. He married Miss Sallie Spring, of Massachusetts, and his death occurred in February, 1823, a month prior to the birth of our subject, who therefore has but little knowledge of paternal history. The widow subsequently married a second time, her husband being Abner Goodrich, and after residing in New York State several years longer, went to Worcester, Mass., where she departed this life.

Henry Knowles was born in Livingston County, N. Y., March 18, 1823, and was reared there, attending school as opportunity offered during his early years. His step-father kept an hotel on Hemlock Lake, which was known as the "Half

Way House," and our subject made himself useful about the hotel, which was his home until twenty years of age, when he started in life for himself. He was industrious and willing, and found work at various kinds of employment during the following year. He was always inclined to make trades, and when twenty-one he went to Rochester, with a drove of cattle, which he sold, this being his first deal in that stock, and being accomplished in the interests of another man.

In 1847 Mr. Knowles went by lake to Chicago, and thence by team to McHenry County, Ill., where he bought a tract of land in what was known as the Burr Oak Openings, and on this wild acreage built a log house with a clay and stick chimney, and took up his pioneer work. Soon after he began dealing in stock, and as there were no railroads through that section cattle had to be driven to market. One of his first experiences in business was in driving a herd to Milwaukee, eighty miles distant, making the drive alone and on foot. The Cream City was then a small place, and it and Chicago were about of equal size. When the Chicago & Galena Union Railroad was completed to Marengo, Mr. Knowles shipped the first load of cattle ever sent from that place to Chicago. At that time cattle were unloaded at the freight depot and driven to the stock-yards at Madison Street, three-fourths of a mile west of the river.

After sojourning on his farm four years, Mr. Knowles moved into Marengo, and remained there engaged in the cattle and butcher business until 1878, when he came to this county and purchased one hundred and sixty acres of wild land seven miles north of town. He built a dwelling and at once began to improve land. He had been in ill-health for some time previous to his removal West, and was poor in purse, but his short-comings in that respect were balanced by a large fund of energy and thrift. After having operated his farm about two years he engaged in the cattle business in a small way, buying stock in the country and selling to the butcher in town. In 1881 he removed to this place and devoted his attention to buying and shipping cattle and hogs, and about a year later opened the market whose history has been before noted. He has been very prosperous and has accumulated a very nice property. He has erected a tasty and comfortable residence in town, and owns one hundred acres of land adjoining the city, and two outlying farms. He rents one of these estates, and supervises the work upon the other, where he feeds cattle for shipping.

The marriage of Mr. Knowles took place in 1815, his bride being Miss Sarah Waters, who was born near Johnsonsburg, Wyoming County, N. Y., on the 1st of March, 1826. She remained under the parental roof until her marriage, acquiring many household arts, those of spinning and knitting being included among them. Her father, Robert Waters, was born in New England, and was a soldier in the War of 1812, after which contest he settled in Wyoming County, N. Y. He was one of the pioneers of that section, and having purchased a tract of heavy timber land, cleared a large acreage and resided there until 1836, when he removed to the Territory of Michigan, and again took up pioneer labors as a citizen of Kalamazoo County. After spending five years on the frontier he returned to Wyoming County, N. Y., and purchased a farm, upon which he resided until his death. The mother of Mrs. Knowles was in her maidenhood Miss Amarila Knight, and was a native of the Empire State. She was a daughter of Simeon Knight, an early settler of Chautauqua County, whence he removed to Wyoming County, where he subsequently died. Miss Knight remained with her parents until her marriage to Mr. Waters, and became conversant with those household duties of carding, spinning and weaving, which are unknown to the present generation, and which she transmitted with good teaching of a more intellectual and moral nature, to her daughter. Her children were clothed in garments made from cloth which she had woven. Her decease took place in Wyoming County.

To Mr. Knowles and his worthy wife seven children have been born—Ellen and Alice are now deceased; Wesley and Frank E. are living in this county; Eva married Miner Youmans, and lives in Mayfield; Charles and Flora are deceased. Both the parents are members in good standing of the Methodist Episcopal Church, and Mr. Knowles has been a Class-Leader for many years. Both are thoroughly respected for their useful and upright lives, in a retrospect of which they find no cause for serious regret. Politically, he is a stanch Republican.

JAMES B. FOLKS. This gentleman is looked upon by his community as one of the best citizens of Chikaskia Township. In addition to developing a farm from a tract of wild land, he has reared a fine family of sons and daughters, who are now doing well in their various stations in life and reflecting credit upon their parental training. There is still spared to Mr. Folks his faithful life-partner, and the two are passing their declining years quietly together, enjoying the confidence and esteem of their neighbors, and justly feeling that they have not lived in vain. Mr. Folks is a man who does his own thinking, and still trains with the Republican party, although a radical prohibitionist. He, like many other sensible men, esteems it not wise yet to form a third party, believing that greater good can be accomplished by remaining in the solid ranks of Republicanism.

Born on the Atlantic coast, in the State of Maryland, September 19, 1826, Mr. Folks is thus a little past the sixty-fourth year of his age. He only remained a resident of his native State three years, going then with his parents to Ohio. His father, Jonathan Folks, was a native of Delaware, and a farmer by occupation. The mother, who bore the maiden name of Leah Folks, was not a relative of her husband, and was born in Maryland. To that State Jonathan Folks emigrated in early manhood, and there the young people were married. They removed to Ohio in 1829, and the father died there eleven years afterward, when his son, James B., was a lad of fourteen years. The mother is still living, making her home with her son, John H., in San Diego, Cal., and is eighty-four years old. The parental household included nine children, only two of whom are living—James B., and his brother, Capt. John H. Folks, a resident of San Diego, Cal.

Mr. Folks acquired a excellent education in Ohio, completing his studies at the South Salem Under College, in Ross County. He began teaching at the age of twenty-one, and followed this profession for twelve years thereafter, mostly during the winter season, while in the summer he made himself useful at whatever he could fine to do. After his children were sufficiently advanced in their studies he removed to Champaign, Ill., in order that the elder two might enjoy the advantages of the State Agricultural College. In the meantime Mr. Folks engaged in the pump and windmill business, at which he was occupied five years, leaving it then to his son, Willis. Subsequently he was engaged in the marble business for two years. In 1877 he came to Kansas, and for one season lived in the vicinity of Wellington. We next find him at Ft. Reno, where he was connected with the sutler's department for sixteen months. Then returning to his farm in this county, he engaged in the live-stock business, raising cattle and swine, in which he has since been largely engaged. He put up his present residence in 1882, and has himself effected all the other improvements upon the place.

One of the most interesting and important events in the life of Mr. Folks was his marriage, February 7, 1850, to Miss Eleanor M. Lindsey, at the bride's home in Ohio. Mrs. Folks was born December 30, 1830, in Ross County, Ohio, and is a daughter of Robert and Sarah (Robertson) Lindsey, who were natives of Pennsylvania and the parents of six children. They spent their last years in Ohio, the father dying in 1856, and the mother in 1858.

The household circle of Mr. and Mrs. Folks was completed by the birth of six children, all of whom are living—Florence J. is the wife of J. T. Shultz, of San Diego, Cal.; they have no children; Ida L. is the wife of J. D. Downey, of Indianola, Ill., and they have four children; Willis K. married Miss Emma Jessee, and is engaged in the coal and grain trade at Wellington, this State; they have one child; Clara E. is the wife of W. E. Thralls, of

Reno City, in Oklahoma, and they have one child; Louie M. is the wife of H. Llewellyn Jones, of Anthony, this State, and they have two children; husband and wife are engaged as abstractors; Ralph N. is engaged as a printer at Seattle, Wash.

Since early youth Mr. and Mrs. Folks have been identified with the Methodist Episcopal Church, in which Mr. Folks officiates as Steward. Both have been active workers in the Sunday-school, and Mrs. Folks has held the office of Superintendent. Politically, Mr. Folks affiliates with the Republican party, and is in sentiment a strong prohibitionist, taking an active part in local politics. He has been a member of the School Board for many years, and in Ohio was for a number of years Township Clerk. He is a Master Mason, and has held various offices in his lodge. The Folks homestead embraces two hundred and forty acres of land, while Mr. Folks has one hundred and sixty acres in California.

<hr/>

HARLES E. MURLIN, one of the leading business men of Jackson, is likewise regarded as one of the most valued members of his community, being enterprising, liberal and public-spirited, and the encourager of every commendable enterprise. His native place was Mendon, Mercer County, Ohio, and the date of his birth March 18, 1858. He comes of substantial stock, being the son of the Rev. Orlando Murlin, who was born in Kentucky, August 10, 1830.

The paternal grandfather of our subject was William Murlin, a native of Genesee County, N. Y., and born October 28, 1801. The latter was the son of John Murlin, who was born in Northumberland County, Pa., in 1770, and who was married in 1792, to Miss Sadie Danderer. They emigrated to Genesee County, N. Y., during its pioneer days, and resided there until 1817, then they removed to Kentucky, where they spent their last days. Their son William was reared in the Blue Grass State, and was married, December 25, 1821, to Miss Lydia Bigelow. The latter was born December 25, 1809.

and was thus made a bride at the age of sixteen years. In 1837 the pair with their little family removed to Ohio, settling among the pioneers of Mercer County, where Grandfather Murlin purchased a tract of heavily timbered land in Union Township. He first put up a log house, and cleared a farm from the wilderness, burning hundreds of large, fine logs, which, were they now in existence, would prove a fortune to any man. There he spent his last days, passing away June 10, 1886. When he took up his residence in the Buckeye State not a railroad had crossed its borders, and Pickaway, forty miles distant, was his nearest market until the completion of a canal. He lived to see the country settled up with an intelligent people.

The father of our subject was a lad of seven years when his parents removed to Ohio, where he was reared to man's estate. He was converted to religion in his youth, and at an early age officiated as an exhorter in the Methodist Episcopal Church, and finally became a circuit preacher. He is still living, making his home in Spencerville, Allen County, and is still laboring in the Master's vineyard.

Mrs. Esther (Hankins) Murlin, the mother of our subject, was the daughter of Timothy Hankins, who was born in Pennsylvania, and who settled in Mercer County, Ohio, about 1837. He likewise cleared a farm from the wilderness, being located on Eight Mile Creek, Union Township. There his death took place in 1887, after he had probably attained his fourscore years. To the parents of our subject there was born a family of nine children, viz.: Timothy W., Martin G., Matilda J., Charles E., Lydia, Lemuel H., Sarah E., Frank O. and Unity A. Charles E. attended the district school in his neighborhood, and by giving due attention to his books developed into a pedagogue at the age of twenty years, and was thereafter employed in this profession the greater part of the time for five years, in Allen and Mercer Counties. Afterward he employed himself as clerk in a dry-goods store in Cridersville, between three and four years. In 1884 he came to Kansas, landing in Wellington on the 15th of May. He secured a position as clerk in a store, but shortly afterward resigned, and going

to Rome assumed charge of the office of the Rock Island Lumber Company, entering upon the discharge of his duties January 1, 1885. This position he has since held with great credit to himself and satisfaction to those in whose interests he is operating. He also deals considerably in grain at times.

The 25th of December, 1879, was appropriately celebrated by Mr. Murlin by his marriage with Miss Arvilla Hall, which took place at the bride's home in West Cairo, Ohio. Mrs. Murlin was born in West Cairo, Allen County, Ohio, and is the daughter of Abram Hall, who was born in Huntington County, N. J., in 1826. Her paternal grandfather, William Hall, was a native of Sussex County, N. J., and born in 1799. He sojourned there until after his marriage. He then removed to Ohio, in May, 1835, settling in Carroll County, where he lived two years. Later he removed to Tuscarawas County, where he purchased land and prosecuted farming until 1853. Next he changed his residence to Allen County, purchasing also a farm there, in Bethel Grove District, where he died in 1876. His wife, Christina Smith, was born September 15, 1795, in Huntington County, N. J., and died in Allen County, Ohio. The father of Mrs. Murlin was nine years old when he removed with his parents to Ohio, where he was reared and married. He dealt in live stock, and finally took up his residence in West Cairo, where he now lives. He served in an Ohio regiment during the Civil War, from the beginning until its close, and has for some years been an invalid. The maiden name of his wife was Barbara Waltz. She was born in Ohio, and was the daughter of Samuel Waltz. Mr. L. Waltz, a resident of Wadsworth, Ohio, prepared and published some time since a history of the Waltz family in America. Much care was exercised in the preparation of the work, and it is highly valuable. There are several different branches of the family in America.

The first ancestor of Mrs. Murlin in this country was Frederick Reinhart Waltz, a native of Switzerland, who crossed the Atlantic in 1750, and settled in Pennsylvania. It is stated in the work above spoken of, that it is believed two of his brothers also came over. The line of descent from Frederick Reinhart Waltz is as follows: His son John, and next his son, S. P. Waltz; then Samuel Waltz, the grandfather of Mrs. Murlin. The mother of the latter died in West Cairo, February 4, 1877. To our subject and his estimable wife there have been born four children—Arthur D., Henry H., Grace and Esther A. The latter, who was next to the youngest, died when two years old.

WILLIAM P. McELHINNY. This gentleman is the owner and occupant of a pleasantly located, improved and valuable farm in Greene Township, comprising two hundred and forty acres on section 36, upon which he located January 19, 1876. He is engaged in farming, and the air of thrift and prosperity which marks his estate indicates that he is desirous of maintaining a front rank among the tillers of the soil, and to enjoy the comforts with which he has been blessed.

The parents of our subject were Robert McElhinny and Mary Creaghead, who after their marriage settled in Allegheny County, Pa., where the mother died when their son William was about eight years old. Some three years after her death, the father removed with his family to Meigs County, Ohio, where he died in November, 1886. He was a carpenter, and by his marriage with Miss Creaghead he became the father of three sons and three daughters.

The gentleman whose name initiates this notice was born in Allegheny County, Pa., April 5, 1843, and during his boyhood in that county, attended the common schools, acquiring a good foundation for the knowledge which he obtained in later years. He grew to manhood in Meigs County, Ohio, where for several years he was employed as a clerk in the business establishment of his brother in Middleport. Thence he went to Scioto County, where he acted as superintendent of a stone quarry belonging to H. D. Stewart during a period of four years, after which, for some two years, he was engaged in selling fruit trees. He then took up his residence in this county, where his industry and

prudence are reaping a merited reward, and he is favorably regarded by his fellow-citizens.

In Clay County, Ill., April 25, 1876, our subject was united in marriage with Lucy Chatlin, a lady of Christian character and many domestic virtues. Mrs. McElhinny was born in Scioto County, Ohio, April 19, 1837. The union has been blessed by the birth of two daughters—Lizzie M., and Sarah E.—whose minds are being developed and cultivated, and into whose hearts the principles of right living are being instilled, and who promise to attain to useful womanhood.

In the spring of 1863 Mr. McElhinny enlisted in the Union army and served about six months as a member of Company A, One Hundred and Fortieth Ohio Infantry. In politics he is a Republican, firmly believing that the principles of that party will best insure the future prosperity and welfare of the nation. As a citizen he is reliable and public spirited, as a neighbor and business man just and honorable, and in domestic life, kindly and considerate. Mrs. McElhinny is a member of the Methodist Church, of which her husband and children are attendants.

WILLIAM H. CARNES. This gentleman was elected County Clerk in November, 1889, and during his term of office will make his home in Wellington. He is already well-known as one of the most energetic young men in the county, where he has not only carried on a farm, but during the winter seasons has been engaged in school teaching for several years, and is held in good repute on account of his intelligence, geniality and uprightness. He is a native of the Buckeye State, was born in Union County, November 30, 1855, and is one of two children born to his parents, and the only survivor, his brother Joseph having died in infancy.

The parents of our subject, Cyrus N. and Eliza (Heminger) Carnes, were born in the Buckeye State, and the mother died when our subject was but a lad. The father is now living in Stark County, Ind., is a farmer and stock dealer, and is quite wealthy. In 1863 he enlisted in the Union army and served until the close of the war. Politically he is a Republican, and is a member of the Methodist Episcopal Church. He is of Scotch-Irish extraction.

The gentleman of whom we write was reared principally in Indiana, and educated in that State, in which, after completing his course of study, he engaged in teaching. In 1877 he came to Kansas, took up a claim in Creek Township, Sumner County, and after proving up on it returned to the Hoosier State, where he remained until 1882. He then came back to this county, and since that time has been engaged in farming and teaching as before noted. Like his father, he is a believer in the principles of the Republican party, which he supports with voice and vote.

The lady who presides with housewifely skill over the home of Mr. Carnes, was born in White County, Ind., December 2, 1858, and is the daughter of George W. and Agnes (Thompson) Cornell, who were also natives of the Hoosier State. She became the wife of Mr. Carnes June 18, 1881, and is the mother of two children: Alta, was born June 24, 1885, and Everett C., December 22, 1887. The parents of Mrs. Carnes became residents of Sumner County in 1877. Mr. Cornell is a farmer, and in his political affiliations joins with the Republican party.

JAMES C. O. MORSE, Sheriff of Sumner County, is one of the younger men who are taking front ranks in business enterprises and in public stations in the West, where energy and "push" are necessary, and win their meed of success. He was born in Cambridge, Henry County, Ill., January 15, 1855, and attended school quite steadily in his native State until fifteen years old, when his parents removed to Kansas, and he finished his studies in Wichita. After his father's death in the spring of 1875, he managed the farm on which he had previously assisted, and

remained in London Township, Sumner County, until the fall of 1879, when he came to this place. The following spring Mr. Morse went to Colorado, and after spending the summer there, went into New Mexico where he sojourned nearly a year, and then returning to this place he started a job printing establishment and a few weeks later purchased a half interest in the *Wellingtonian*, a weekly newspaper. He retained his interest in the journal and the printing establishment until October, 1881, when he sold out and became an assistant to Sheriff Henderson. It was not long before he was appointed Deputy Sheriff and he fulfilled the duties of that position until January, 1888, since which time he has served as Constable, and in the fall of 1889 was elected Sheriff of the county.

The Rev. John C. Morse, the father of our subject, was a native of Ashtabula County, Ohio, and a son of Elias Morse, who was born in Massachusetts, and who was a pioneer farmer in the Buckeye State. About the year 1850 the grandfather of our subject removed to Henry County, Ill., and purchased a farm one and one half miles from Cambridge, on which he spent his last years. His wife, whose maiden name was Sarah Dailey, also departed this life on the farm there.

The Rev. John Morse was reared in his native county, and removed to Illinois with his parents, their journey being made by the lakes to Chicago, and thence by team to their new home. During the first few years of their residence in the Prairie State there were no railroads in that section of the country, and Rock Island was the nearest market until the railroad was completed to Geneseo. When a lad of ten years of age young John was converted, and united with the Methodist Episcopal Church, and in his early manhood he began ministerial labors as a local preacher. He bought a farm west of Cambridge, on which his family resided until 1870, when he came to this State, making the removal with teams. Wichita was then but a small village and there was no railroad nearer than Emporia, one hundred miles distant. The Rev. Mr. Morse selected a location three miles north of Wichita, filed a claim on Government land and at once built a frame house, drawing the lumber from Emporia. The country around him was very sparsely settled, large herds of Texas cattle fed there, deer were abundant, and buffalo in large numbers were to be found a few miles west. As emigrants were frequently passing, there was a good home market for produce.

The Rev. Mr. Morse resided on the claim he had taken on first coming to the State, from November, 1870, until December, 1873, when he sold and purchased a tract of land in what is now London Township, this county. The farm was situated on both sides of the Ninnescah River, a number of acres had been broken, and there were a log house and stable on the north side of the river. Taking possession of this farm, its new owner superintended the work thereon and also continued his labors in spreading the Gospel until the time of his death, which occurred at Cambridge, Ill. (where he had been summoned on account of his father's sickness,) May 31, 1875. His widow is now a resident of this city. She was born in Coshocton County, Ohio, and bore the maiden name of Rebecca Jane Westlake. To her and her husband four children were born.

At the home of the bride, in London Township, in 1876, Mr. James Morse was united in marriage with Miss Rachel E. Chenoweth, who was born in Fayette County, Ohio. Her parents, Lewis F. and Martha (Morgan) Chenoweth, were natives of Madison and Franklin Counties, Ohio, and came to Kansas in 1871, first settling in Doniphan County and in 1873 removed to this county, the father buying a tract of land in London Township, which he improved and on which they still live. To Mr. Morse and his estimable wife two children have been born—Emma E. and Lucretia L. Mrs. Morse belongs to the Methodist Episcopal Church, and has many warm friends in the community, where her husband also is highly regarded.

GEORGE MORTON. This gentleman is one of the most prominent agriculturists of Oxford Township, and one of the largest land owners, and he also ranks among the early settlers.

as he came here in 1873. His home is situated on section 20, and bears marked improvements, including a fine orchard, neatly kept hedge, and a dwelling which is one of the finest farm houses in the vicinity. It is a two-story structure, 16x28 feet and 11x16 feet, and is well built and of a pleasing architectural design. The entire landed estate of Mr. Morton comprises seven hundred and twenty acres, and the most of his property has been accumulated by his own energy and able management since coming here.

The birth of Mr. Morton took place near Glasgow, Scotland, February 7, 1844, and he lived upon a farm in that country until 1866, obtaining a good education and a practical knowledge of agricultural pursuits. At the date mentioned he accompanied a Scottish colony to New Zealand, where he lived until about the close of the year 1871, when he came to the United States via California, and worked along for a place until he arrived in Wichita, Kan., where he sojourned two years. He then came to this county, bought out the claim to the quarter section upon which his home is, and proved upon it, receiving the only deed ever given to the place. He paid 36 per cent. for money to prove up with, made almost all the improvements, and as he was able, paid his indebtedness and purchased more land. The first addition to his acreage was purchased for the sum of $550 and $2,800 was paid for the next. Mr. Morton keeps both horses and cattle, has one quarter section mainly in pasture land, and carries on both grain and stock raising quite extensively.

At the home of the bride in this county, March 17, 1881, Mr. Morton was united in marriage with Miss Stella Russell. She was a daughter of John Russell, who now lives in Avon Township, and was born in Canada in 1855. She is well educated and possesses many housewifely and womanly virtues. The happy union has been blessed by the birth of four children, of whom three are now living—Minnie, George and Thomas. The parents were bereaved of their daughter Mary, on February 8, 1889.

Mr. Morton has been School Director for two years, and manifests an intelligent interest in the wellfare of the schools. He is a man of strict

E. L. Easter M.D.

honor and probity, and of a companionable nature, and is highly regarded by his fellow-citizens. He is a member in good standing of the Presbyterian Church. Mrs. Morton is a member of the Church of God.

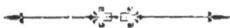

EDGAR D. EASTER. M. D., whose portrait is presented on the opposite page, is a practicing physician and dealer in drugs at Milan, and is rightly classed among the most prominent citizens of that flourishing town. He carries a full line of drugs, and has the exclusive trade in that branch of merchandise. He also has a line practice in his profession, which he has thoroughly studied, not only in America but also in Europe. His beautiful residence is built on the same lot with his drug-store, and is as attractive and cozy a home as anyone could desire. He also owns residence property and lots in Anthony, Harper County, Kan., and considers that city the best for its size in the State. The prosperity which has attended his efforts in life is a proof of his natural ability and his unbounded energy, for, with the exception of his early education, his extended knowledge and worldly possessions are due entirely to his own efforts.

The father of our subject was J. J. Easter, a native of Virginia, who was educated for the ministry, and who moved to Pennsylvania during his early years. When he had grown to manhood he bought a farm in Fayette County, and gave his attention principally to raising cattle and horses. He married Miss Mary E. Ebert, a native of the Keystone State, who bore him fourteen children. Of this large family ten are now living. During the Civil War the two oldest sons served their country as members of a Pennsylvania regiment. The father died in 1887, and the mother still survives at the age of sixty-eight years, and lives on the home farm.

Dr. Easter was the sixth child born to his parents, and opened his eyes to the light in Fayette County, Pa., June 7, 1851. Until his thirteenth year he attended the district schools, pursuing the elementary branches, and then became a pupil in the High School, after which he spent two years at work in a woolen factory. In 1869 he went to Iowa, and for a short time was employed in a woolen factory in Fairfield, next entering the office of Dr. P. N. Wood, now deceased, and spending a year in medical studies. Fully determined to acquire a thorough knowledge of his chosen profession, he engaged in the business of selling organs and sewing machines, as a temporary expedient by which to acquire means to prosecute his studies, and in this way saved enough to pay tuition for three and a half years.

We next find the young student in attendance at the Keokuk Medical College during nearly two courses of lectures, following which he bought out the office and good will of a physician in Van Buren County, contracting to pay $1,560, and going in debt for the entire amount. Four years and five months were spent in that county, whence, in 1878, Dr. Easter came to Kansas, and locating on a claim two miles south of Milan, built a sod-house and began life as a Kansas citizen, with a capital consisting of a team of horses and $35 in money. Eighteen months later he returned to Keokuk, accompanied by his wife, and both took a six months' course of lectures. Dr. Easter was graduated in 1881, while Mrs. Easter returned to the institution the following year, and won her diploma also.

Two years after the Doctor's graduation he crossed the Atlantic, accompanied by his wife, and in London, England, took a surgical course at St. Thomas College of Physicians and Surgeons, and a course in obstetrics at the women's hospital. After this addition to the theoretical and practical understanding of medical science, which he had previously possessed, the cultured couple returned to their home in June, 1884, and there, in December, 1886, the wife breathed her last.

Dr. Easter contracted a second matrimonial alliance, April 5, 1888, his chosen companion being Miss Allie M., daughter of Dr. G. M. Walker, of Rosemond, Ill. She is the older of two children born to her parents, and her natal day was March 12, 1865. She is a cultured and refined lady, was the recipient of a collegiate education at Lincoln,

Ill., and is a worthy companion for a man of her husband's intellect and acquirements. Her mother died in 1873, and her father is still practicing medicine in Rosemond.

Dr. Easter belongs to the Ancient Order of United Workmen, and is now one of the Examining Surgeons of that organization in Milan. He has also been a member of the Independent Order of Odd Fellows, in which he has held several offices. Interested, as all American citizens should be, in political affairs, he has decided in favor of the principles of the Democracy, and therefore casts his vote in their behalf. It is needless to state that he is not only respected by his fellow-citizens in Milan, but over a wide extent of country he is favorably known as a successful and learned physician and surgeon, and as a gentleman of integrity and honor.

ANIEL FEAGINS, a veteran of the late war, is well and favorably known to the people of Walton Township, where he owns a well-regulated farm of eighty acres on section 11. With the exception of the time spent in the army, he has been a life-long agriculturist and very successful. While in the service of his country he contracted a severe cold which resulted in the loss of his eyesight, and on account of which he draws a pension of $72 per month. He has learned to bear his affliction with equanimity and succeeds in a remarkable degree in making the best of circumstances. His course in life has been such as to establish him in the esteem and confidence of his fellow-citizens.

Fayette County, Ohio, was the early tramping ground of our subject, and where his birth took place February 10, 1817. He was the first born of Willis and Elizabeth (Jones) Feagins, the former of whom was a native of Kentucky and born May 1, 1795. Willis Feagins, when a young man, emigrated to Fayette County, Ohio, with his parents, where he sojourned until 1844. That year he sought the Far West, removing across the Mississippi to Davis County, Iowa, where he prosecuted

farming successfully and departed this life in 1873. For many years prior to his death he was a prominent member of the Methodist Episcopal Church, and politically, voted the Democratic ticket. Daniel and Violet (Combs) Feagins, the paternal grandparents of our subject, were probably natives of Virginia and both died in Fayette County, Ohio, Grandmother Feagins at the advanced age of one hundred and seven years. Grandfather Feagins served all through the Revolutionary War, with the rank of Major. The mother of our subject was a daughter of Thomas Jones, likewise a Revolutionary soldier, and a native of the Blue Grass State.

There were born to the parents of our subject eight children besides himself, and who were named respectively, Violet, Thomas, Catherine, Ellen, Susan, James, William, and Sarah J. Six of these are living. Daniel remained a resident of his native county until 1840, and then, a young man of twenty-three years, went to Iowa in advance of the family, settling on a farm in Davis County. He sojourned in the Hawkeye State until 1877, then came to Kansas, settling first in Cowley County, and thence removing in 1878 to this county.

While a resident of Iowa Mr. Feagins, in 1863, enlisted as a Union soldier in Company D, Third Iowa Cavalry, and was subsequently promoted to be Sergeant. He was in the service until July, 1865, and then, the war being over, received his honorable discharge at Edgefield, Tenn. He participated in many of the important battles of the war, including Big Blue and Nashville. The hardships and privations which he endured were borne with the fortitude and heroism which almost uniformly distinguished the conduct of the Union soldiers. They have been cited too often to need repetition here. The memory of those brave boys will be cherished as long as the United States stands as a nation. Mr. Feagins cast his first Presidential vote for Van Buren and has since remained a stanch adherent of the Democratic party. He belongs to the G. A. R. Post at Arkansas City.

While a resident of Iowa Mr. Feagins was married, June 13, 1846, to Mrs. Elizabeth Sanderson, who was a native of his own county in Ohio, and who was born July 28, 1824. Mrs. Feagins is the daughter of Jesse and Regina (Hinkle) Fisk, who were natives of Virginia and Pennsylvania. Her father spent his last years in Iowa; the mother is still living. She lived with her parents until her first marriage with Daniel Sanderson who died November 19, 1845. Mr. and Mrs. Feagins are the parents of eight children—James W., Daniel F., William T., Emily E., Elvira A., Mary E., Thomas J. and Jesse C.

WILLIAM C. GLAIZE, Cashier of the State National Bank at Wellington, came to Sumner County in April, 1884, and has held his present position since that time. This bank is located at the intersection of Lincoln and Washington Avenues and is one of the most reliable institutions of the kind in the county.

Mr. Glaize was born in Winchester, Frederick County, Va., September 21, 1852, and lived there until the spring of 1875. He attended the common school during his boyhood and youth and commenced his business career in the employ of his uncle, W. A. Rinker, with whom he remained three years. We next find him in Kirksville, Mo., as a member of the firm of Steer, Glaize & Co. Remaining in business there until the spring of 1881, he then sold out and located in Muscatine, Iowa, engaging in the same business. In the spring of 1882, he changed his field of operations to Washington, Iowa, associating himself with a Mr. Ball and continuing there until 1886. That year, coming to Wellington, he assisted in the organization of the State National Bank, which was organized on the 1st of August and opened its doors for business October 11, with A. H. Smith, President, William Myers, Vice President and Mr. Glaize, Cashier, the capital stock being $50,000. With the exception of the Vice President the officers still remain the same. Mr. Myers was succeeded by George Hunter. Mr. Glaize in addition to his connection with the bank as a stockholder, also has an interest in the Southern Kansas Farm, Loan & Trust Company, and is a heavy stockholder in the gas plant at Wellington. The bank building is a fine three-story

structure with a basement and occupying an area of 25x50 feet. It is thoroughly equipped and an ornament to the city.

Mr. Glaize was married at Kirksville, Mo., January 29, 1886, to Miss Nellie T. Bagg. Mrs. Glaize was born in New York, January 1, 1862, and is the daughter of John Bagg who came West at an early date and operated as a railroad bridge contractor both in Missouri and Kansas. Mr. and Mrs. Glaize are members in good standing of the Baptist Church, and Mr. Glaize, politically, is a staunch Democrat. During the progress of the Civil War he visited the South and was at Winchester at the time of the famous battle there and had a view of the conflict.

The father of our subject was George Glaize, likewise a native of Frederick County, Va. He was born October 4, 1822, and has spent his entire life within five miles of his birthplace. Although quite aged, he is still hale and hearty. The mother, born March 28, 1821, bore the maiden name of Harriet S. Rinker, and the parental family consisted of nine children. The maternal grandfather of our subject was Casper Rinker, a native of Virginia and who spent the greater part of his life in Frederick County.

REUBEN A. ANDERSON. This gentleman is recognized as one of the largest landowners of this county, holding the warrantee deed to one thousand and twelve acres, besides a large stock ranch in Barbour County. He gives considerable attention to the breeding of graded stock, while a part of his land is devoted to general agriculture. He is a man in the prime of life, having been born October 23, 1845, and his native place was Sullivan County, Ind. He came to Kansas in 1878, locating on section 31, London Township, of which he has since been a resident.

The subject of this notice was the eldest child of Absalom and Cynthia A. (Pierce) Anderson, the former of whom was born in Kentucky, in 1808. Six years later he was taken by his parents to Indiana, of which State he remained a resident thereafter until his death, at the age of fifty years. He followed farming successfully and was a man intelligent and well-informed, keeping himself posted upon political events and uniformly voting the Democratic ticket. His father, Robert Anderson, was a native of Scotland, whence he emigrated to America at an early day, settling in Kentucky and finally removing to Indiana where he spent his last days.

Mrs. Cynthia (Pierce) Anderson, was born in Ohio and is still living, being about sixty-eight years old and making her home in Kansas. She is the daughter of John and Sophia Pierce, who were likewise natives of the Buckeye State, whence they subsequently removed to Indiana, where they spent their last days. Grandfather Pierce was a farmer by occupation and both he and his good wife were members of the Baptist Church. To Absalom and Cynthia Anderson there was born a family of nine children, viz: Reuben A., Commodore P., Jonathan M., John P., Sophia, James A., Elizabeth, Robert C. and Charles. Only four of these are living, viz: Reuben, Jonathan, Robert and Charles. Reuben was reared and educated in his native county, living there until coming to this State. He is quite prominent in local affairs and served one term as County Treasurer. During the progress of the Civil War he enlisted October 9, 1861, at Terre Haute, in Company B, Thirtieth Indiana Infantry, and participated in the battles of Franklin and Nashville, Tenn., besides many minor engagements. He served until the close of the war, being mustered out October 18, 1865. On the 12th of July, 1866, he was united in marriage with Miss Eliza J. Nelson. This lady was a native of Indiana and by her union with our subject became the mother of nine children, viz: Ellazan, Arminna A., William A., Joseph, Lemuel L., James W., Reuben H. and two who died in infancy. Mrs. Eliza J. (Nelson) Anderson departed this life at her home on May 6, 1883.

Mr. Anderson contracted a second matrimonial alliance January 28, 1886, with Miss Lucinda Bowdre. This lady was born March 19, 1849, in Union County, Ohio, and is the daughter of Samuel and Nancy (Green) Bowdre, who were likewise born in the Buckeye State. The mother died in Ohio at the

age of sixty-six years. Mr. Bowdre is still living, making his home in Ohio and being now seventy years old. He has been a lifelong farmer and served as Justice of the Peace. Two children have been born to Mr. and Mrs. Anderson—Ruth A., July 1, 1887, and Maude H., April 21, 1889.

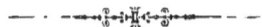

TRUMAN TUCKER. The lives perhaps of the majority of men pass on apparently like the smooth current of a river and those who only observe the surface know little of what lies beneath or how has been brought about the apparently smooth current. Those who have perhaps struggled under the greatest difficulties, have been the most quiet under all circumstances; but still have achieved frequently greater results than their more noisy brethren. The subject of this notice has builded well as far as character and disposition goes and is a man held in the highest respect in his community. Upon his well-cultivated farm of one hundred and thirty acres he has lived for a period of seventeen years, developing a good homestead and at the same time establishing himself upon a firm basis as a man and a citizen. He lives unpretentiously, yet comfortably, his home lying on section 13, Avon Township.

A native of Meade County, Ky., Mr. Tucker was born August 19, 1854, and when quite young was taken by his parents to Missouri where his father died when he was a lad of eight years. The family sojourned five years in that State and at a time when the climate was very unhealthy, and after the death of her husband the widowed mother returned with her children to the Blue Grass State where Truman was reared to manhood. They lived upon a farm and young Tucker acquired his education in the common schools. Leaving his native State he repaired to Henderson County, Ill., where he prosecuted farming eight years, and in 1869, crossing the Mississippi, established himself in Labette County, this State.

In Labette County Mr. Tucker was married May 1, 1870, to Miss Calsina George, a native of

Marion County, Iowa, and born March 26, 1850. The young people commenced their wedded life together on a farm in that county, sojourning there until 1872. Their next removal was to this county when they settled upon their present farm in Avon Township. In the meantime during the Civil War and while a resident of Henderson County, Ill., Mr. Tucker enlisted as a Union soldier, in Company I, Eighteenth Illinois Infantry, and served six months during the last part of the war. He cast his first Presidential vote for Lincoln, and is a stanch supporter of the principles of the Republican party. He and his estimable wife are active members of the Christian Church, endeavoring to carry out their professions in their daily lives.

They have made many friends during their long sojourn in this county and have welcomed under their hospitable roof its best citizens. Genial and companionable they are ever ready to extend a helping hand to those less fortunate than themselves and are possessed of that good breeding which is recognized at once in their intercourse not only with friends but with strangers. They are full worthy of representation among the better classes of people of this county. The mother of our subject died in Hancock County, Ill., in May, 1886.

EMELINE MUCKLEY, the subject of this sketch, is the widow of Michael Muckley, a pioneer of Sumner County, who was born in Stark County, Ohio, on the 7th of September, 1839. John Muckley, the father of Michael, was born near Baden, Germany, and came to America with his parents, who were among the first settlers of Stark County, and resided there during the rest of their lives. John M. was but a lad when he came to this country. He was reared in the home of his parents and received such an education as the county afforded at that time. Upon reaching his maturity he was united in marriage with a lady of the same county and they spent their life in Pike Township, Stark County, Ohio, on a farm.

Michael Muckley was reared on the farm of his parents and remained at home assisting his father to operate the place until the war broke out in 1861, when he tendered his services for the defense of his country and was assigned to duty with the Army of the Potomac. He enlisted in Company D, One Hundred and Seventh Ohio Infantry for a term of three years. He bore his part bravely in all the engagements that his regiment was called upon to take part in, and was one of the gallant supporters of the old flag in the glorious and decisive battle of Gettysburg, when the hitherto proud hosts of the Confederacy were shattered and driven back to their native place soon to dwindle away and surrender to the brave boys in blue. When the term of service expired for which Mr. Muckley had enlisted, he returned to his father's farm and operated a sawmill for some two years. He then entered a general store and engaged as a clerk for about one year, but his health proving unequal to the task he returned once more to the farm.

Shortly after leaving the store Mr. Muckley formed a partnership with an uncle and bought a tract of land upon which there was a sawmill and also a flouring-mill. Mr. Muckley superintended the work of the farm and also operated the two mills with good success. He resided there until 1878, when he sold out his interests and removed to Kansas. He settled in Sumner County at a time when Wichita, forty miles away, was the nearest railroad point and the nearest market. The county had but few settlers and was very little improved. Mr. Muckley bought a tract of land embracing the southwest quarter of section 22 in Jackson Township, and at once set to work to improve it and convert it into a fine farm. He resided there until his death, May 6, 1887. He had in the meantime erected a comfortable set of frame buildings and planted fruit and shade trees.

January 1, 1866, Michael Muckley and Emeline Howenstine were united in marriage. Mrs. Muckley is a native of Pike Township, Stark County, Ohio, where she was reared in the home of her parents. Her father, Jacob Howenstine, was born in Hagerstown, Md., and his father, also named Jacob Howenstine, was born of German parents in Germany. The grandfather of Mrs. Muckley removed from Maryland to Ohio, crossing the mountains in the usual style of the times with teams, and settled in Stark County when there were few other residents in the neighborhood. He took up Government land and made a comfortable home for his family. His last days upon earth were spent in the place where he had been a pioneer so many years before. The father of Mrs. Muckley was reared in Maryland and accompanied his father to Ohio when the latter emigrated to that State. The family located in Pike Township, and after some time Jacob H., Jr., started out for himself. He bought a tract of heavy timbered land in Pike Township and set to work cutting down trees to make room for the log cabin which was to be his home until such time as he could make a better. The cot then built was the birthplace of Mrs. Muckley, and similar lowly dwellings have been the homes of thousands of the best citizens of which America can boast.

The trials and hardships of the pioneers are a constant source of supply to the story-tellers of the present age. The open fireplace where the cooking had to be done, the rolling of the logs together only to burn them, because in the stage of development which they were then in, that was the only use that could be made of what would be almost of priceless value at the present time, and the many other things curious and pitiful that are related, were all, or nearly all, the lot of the parents of Mrs. Muckley during the early years of their life. Energy and industry overcame all the trials to which they were subjected, and they succeeded in making a fine farm and erecting good buildings. The father of Mrs. Muckley is still living on the place which he improved during the years of his youth and manhood, although his years number eighty-two. The mother of Mrs. Muckley was Margaret Miller, a native of Pennsylvania and daughter of John and Rebecca Miller. Mrs. Howenstine died in 1887, having reached a good old age.

Mrs. Muckley is one of a family of six children, whose names are as follows: Emeline, the subject of this notice; William and Jacob, who are residents of Huntington County, Ind.; Cyrus and Emery, who are living in Stark County, Ohio, and Almira who is married to David Evans. Since the death of her husband Mrs. Muckley has resided on the home farm, which she carries on with good success. She is a woman of much force of character and enjoys the esteem of her many friends; she is a devoted and worthy member of the Presbyterian Church, of which Mr. Muckley was also a consistent member during his life time.

ELI W. MORRIS. Although it has been but a few years since the above-named gentleman located in Harmon Township, he and his estimable wife have already established themselves among the most highly respected residents of the county, and have many warm friends therein who thoroughly appreciate their noble qualities of heart and mind. The father of Mr. Morris was christened Lorenzo D., and was born in West Virginia. His mother bore the maiden name of Mary Witt, and Tennessee was her native State. After the marriage of this couple they settled in Greene County, Ill., where four children were born to them, of whom our subject is the youngest. The death of the mother took place in March, 1842, and the father survived until June, 1887.

The natal day of our subject was March 15, 1841, and he grew to manhood in his native county, acquiring a good education in the common schools and a practical training from his worthy father. Upon reaching man's estate he engaged in farming in Macoupin County, and after tilling the soil there a year took his departure for the Pacific Coast, and in California carried on the dairy business three years. He then returned to the Mississippi Valley and again entered upon a farmer's life in Macoupin County, Ill., continuing so employed there until September, 1883, when he went to Arkansas and engaged in the cattle business. He prosecuted that business until May, 1887, and then settled in Harmon Township, where he now owns one hundred and sixty acres of land lying on section 28. The estate is thoroughly and intelligently cultivated and bears all needful buildings, which have been erected in a substantial manner and with due regard to their convenient location and attractive appearance. The whole estate has an appearance of order and thrift which plainly indicates to a passer-by that its owner is a thorough farmer and a man of good taste and good judgment. The internal arrangements of the dwelling, and the neatness and good cheer that abound within, as plainly mark the housewifely qualities and refinement of the lady who presides within its walls.

The wife of Mr. Morris is a native of Macoupin County, Ill., where their marriage took place February 13, 1879. The bride bore the maiden name of Arabella T. Bates and her natal day was February 3, 1853. She is the eldest of two children born to F. M. and Tabitha M. (Davis) Bates, the latter of whom died in Kentucky and the former during the war, in which he was an officer of the Confederate army. Seven bright children make up the jewels of Mr. and Mrs. Morris, and they bear the names respectively of Leon L., Nevada B., Paul F., Ethel B., Mary M., Jennie L. and Marvel E.

Mr. Morris belongs to the Farmers' Alliance, and both he and Mrs. Morris are members in good standing of the Baptist Church. Mr. Morris possesses the pleasant and affable manners which combined with his intelligence and good principles would naturally win friends, and it is not strange that even in his short residence in this county he is so well and favorably known.

ON. DANIEL F. JANEWAY, M. D. In the person of the subject of this notice we have that of a leading physician and surgeon of Argonia, a gentleman well-educated, intelligent, and thoroughly understanding the duties of his profession. In the fall of 1888 he was elected on the Republican ticket as a Representative to the Kansas Legislature from the Eighty-fifth District, holding until 1891. He is entirely in sympathy with the principles of his party, and a liberal and public spirited citizen, serving as Secretary of the school board, and otherwise identifying himself with the best interests of his community.

In Masonic circles he belongs to Chikaskia Lodge No. 285, in which he is Master, and he is also a member of Argonia Lodge, No. 272, I. O. O. F., in which he is Past Grand, and has been a Representative to the Grand Lodge. He is a member of the Southwestern Kansas Medical Association, and by virtue of his powers as Representative, served on the committee of Public Health in cities of third-class, and Manufactures.

The Doctor was born January 6, 1854, in Jefferson County, Tenn., and was the ninth in a family of twelve children, the offspring of Charles and Susannah (Hammer) Janeway, also natives of that State. Nine of their children are still living. The parents were married in Tennessee, December 21, 1836, and emigrated to Iowa in 1858, settling in Jasper County, where they now reside. The father is seventy-five years old, and the mother seventy-four. They celebrated their golden wedding in 1886.

The early education of Dr. Janeway was conducted in the district schools of Iowa, and later he attended Hazel Dell Academy at Newton, where he prepared for college. He entered the Freshman class at Penn College, Oskaloosa, from which he was graduated June, 1879, in the regular classical course, receiving the degree of A. B. For two years afterward he held the position of principal of public schools at Kellogg, and later was similarly occupied at Cottonwood Falls, this State. In the mean time he employed his leisure hours in the reading of medicine. In July, 1882, repairing to Kansas City, he entered the medical college there from which he was graduated March 1, 1884. He opened his first office in Argonia, Sumner County, where he has since resided and built up a fine practice.

Dr. Janeway contracted matrimonial ties July 28, 1881, with Miss Ada V. Moore. Mrs. Janeway is a native of Indiana, was the eldest child of her parents. Morris and Rebecca (Beals) Moore, and was born October 26, 1858. Her father was a native of North Carolina, and her mother of Tennessee. They came to this State at a very early day, settling in Chase County, where the father prosecuted farming successfully, and died in 1871. The mother was remarried to Z. W. Morgan, and is now living in Chase County. Of her first union there was born six children, five of whom are now living. Mrs. Janeway acquired an excellent education, completing her studies in the Normal School at Emporia. Subsequently she was employed as a teacher, some of the time in the schools of Argonia. With one exception, all her brothers and sisters are occupied in the same manner. Her sister, Belle, is a primary teacher in the First Ward at Wellington, Kan.

To the Doctor and his estimable lady there have been born three children: George M., May 25, 1882; Susan Lucille, October 24, 1885, and Rosa Lenore, June 27, 1888. Doctor and Mrs. Janeway are members of the Friends' Church. They occupy a neat home in the northern part of the city, and number their friends and acquaintances among its most cultured people.

ABEL L. TILTON, one of the earliest settlers of Oxford Township, entered a claim on section 1, in 1870, then returned to his home in Vermilion County, Ill., for his family, removing them hither the following year. The story of his trials and triumphs thereafter is similar to those which have been detailed so often in the compilation of this volume. Suffice it to say that he labored industriously, practicing economy, and in due time met with his reward.

A native of the Island of Montreal, Canada, A. L. Tilton was born February 18, 1832, and made his home there until about 1835, when he accompanied his parents upon their removal to Ohio, and subsequently removed to Vermilion County, Ill. Settling at Danville, Grandfather Tilton established a brick kiln and also operated as a contractor and builder. Among other work he constructed a dam across the Vermilion River for Amos Williams, who was one of the most prominent millers in that part of the State. Abel and his brother Fred assisted their father in his labors, and in 1838 they were engaged in hauling stone for the abutments of the Wabash Railroad, which was being built by the State. They also

carried the mail from Danville to Joliet, a distance of one hundred and ten miles with about seven others between. There was not a bridge between the two places, they having to ford the streams and the trip occupying two days. Many a time there was nothing in the mail bag, but they made it a point to fulfill their contract. Numbers of people in that region were then suffering from ague, and the mail-carrier, after his day's journey, frequently was obliged to cut the feed himself for his horse. The Tilton boys remained in the employ of Uncle Sam until the fall of 1840. Grandfather Tilton spent his last days in Illinois.

A very important event in the life of our subject was his marriage, February 21, 1860, with Miss Arminta Shepard, of Fairmont, Ill., after which event they settled on a farm in the vicinity of Rossville, Vermilion County, where he dwelt until coming to Sumner County, Kan. Upon his arrival here he selected a tract of land on the northeast part of section 1, Oxford Township, from which he constructed a comfortable homestead, putting up a frame house and other buildings and setting out quantities of fruit and shade trees. His children, later, after his decease, erected a modern dwelling, but covered in the old room which he had occupied, preserving it intact as he left it. He departed this life September 30, 1877. He was a staunch defender of Republican principles, and a regular supporter of the various churches which he attended, although not identifying himself in membership with them. Liberal and public-spirited, kind and charitable, he was a man bearing an irreproachable reputation, and was honored and respected by all who knew him.

Mrs. Arminta (Shepard) Tilton was born September 27, 1841, and was the daughter of Abraham Shepard, formerly of Ohio and now deceased. To her and her husband were born five children, all of whom are living with the exception of a son, Fred, who died three weeks prior to the decease of his father—Frank was born March 17, 1862, and is now a resident of Kansas City; John L. was born August 24, 1864, and is still living at the old homestead; he completed his studies in the schools at Oxford, and then assumed charge of the farm; Grace was born September 14, 1866, and Charles

RESIDENCE OF ABEL L. TILTON (DECEASED) SEC. I. OXFORD TP SUMNER CO. KAN

RESIDENCE OF CHARLES SHAFFER, SEC. 30. RYAN TP, SUMNER CO, KANS.

A., November 21, 1868. They are at home with their brother, John L. Frank belongs to the Ancient Order of United Workmen. After the decease of her husband Mrs. Tilton was married to J. J. Daniels, of Palestine Township, where they are now living.

A view of the homestead of the late Abel L. Tilton is shown elsewhere in this work.

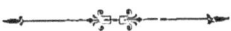

HARLES HENRY SHAFFER. The reliable German element of this county has played no unimportant part in its growth and prosperity. The sons of the fatherland have penetrated to every corner of Kansas, as well as other parts of the Great West, and are almost uniformly good citizens, well-to-do, self-supporting, and useful members of the community. Among the foremost farmers of Ryan Township may be mentioned Mr. Shaffer, who, like the most of his neighbors, commenced at the foot of the ladder, and now occupies a leading position in the agricultural districts.

A native of what was then the Kingdom of Westphalia, the subject of this notice was born December 13, 1849, and was the fifth in a family of six children, the offspring of George and Elizabeth (Lenze) Shaffer, who were also natives of Westphalia, where they lived after their marriage until 1849. That year the father emigrated to America, and settled on a farm in Reading County, Pa., whither his wife also came in 1850. There they spent the remainder of their lives, the father departing hence in 1862, and the mother in 1870. Five of their children are now living, one in South America and one in Germany, and the other three in the United States.

Mr. Shaffer was but a year old when brought to America, and his parents esteeming the school privileges of their native land superior to those of America, sent him back there when he was six years old, and he was thoroughly educated in the German tongue, remaining there six years. When leaving school he returned to this country, and at Philadelphia, being determined to go as a sailor, shipped on a merchant vessel as cabin boy for three years. At the expiration of this time he went as a regular sailor, and was on the lakes for two years. Then settling down on *terra firma* he engaged in the mercantile business in Ohio. In 1868 he set out for the West, and located in Black Hawk County, Iowa, of which he was a resident for three years, removing thence to Sioux County, where he lived six years.

In the meantime Mr. Shaffer spent two years in Montana, in the interests of the American Fur Company. In 1877 we find him at Joplin, Mo., where he worked in the lead mines nearly one year. He first struck the soil of Kansas in January, 1878, taking possession of the land which constitutes his present farm. It was then an uncultivated tract, upon which no improvements whatever had been attempted. By great perseverance and industry, while at the same time experiencing all the hardships and difficulties of life in a new country, Mr. Shaffer succeeded in opening up a good farm, and added to his landed possessions until he is now the owner of two hundred and forty acres, thoroughly improved and valuable. He put up, in 1883, as fine a residence as the traveler will find in all Ryan Township. In addition to raising the crops common to this region, he has been quite successful as a breeder of horses, cattle and swine. When coming to this place he was empty-handed, having by a series of misfortunes lost all that he had earned hitherto. Looking upon his surroundings to-day it must be admitted that he has labored to excellent advantage, and he forms a fine illustration of the results of unflagging industry and perseverance.

Mr. Shaffer was married, February 9, 1887, to Miss Carrie L. daughter of Leonard P. and Charlotte (Hines) Sayrs. The parents of Mrs. Shaffer were natives of New York State, whence they emigrated to Wisconsin in 1846, and from there came to Kansas thirty years later, settling first in Miami County. In 1883 they came to this county, and are now living in Argonia. There were born to them thirteen children, of whom Mrs. Shaffer was next to the youngest. Her birth occurred July 10, 1870, in Wisconsin. She applied herself to her books during her school days, and is an intelligent, pleasant lady, respected by all who know her. Mr. and Mrs. Shaffer are the parents of two children, a son and daughter—George Leonard and Catharina. Mr. Shaffer, during important elections, supports the Democratic party, but at home casts his vote for the man whom he considers will best serve local interests. He has been five years on the School Board of his district, and officiated as Trustee of Ryan Township for two terms. The Anti-Horse-Thief Association claims him as one of its most efficient members.

An additional feature of interest is a lithographic view, on another page of this volume, of Mr. Shaffer's pleasant home and surroundings.

ERBERT BARRETT. A prominent place among the business men of Oxford, Sumner County, is that held by the above named gentleman, who is the proprietor of a general dry-goods store in that flourishing town, and is also the principal organizer of the Bank of Commerce of Oxford, which was opened in April, 1889, by the firm of Barrett & Hardy. Mr. Barrett has been engaged in the dry-goods business in this place since March, 1879, when he bought out an old firm, and his aim has ever been to carry the best line of goods possible and retain his customers. He has built up one of the finest trades in the city, and his honorable dealing and manly character have won for him the hearty respect of his townspeople and those of the adjoining section of country.

Mr. Barrett was born in England, November 2, 1838, and is a son of M. and Ann (Evans) Barrett, who came to the United States when he was a lad of six years. They settled in Jo Daviess County, Ill., not far from Galena, where the mother subsequently died; the father is still living in that county. Our subject obtained a good High School education in his home town, Elizabeth, and finished his studies in Chicago, being graduated from Bryant & Stratton's Business College. He then engaged in clerking at his home, and after coming to

years of maturity began a general merchandise business there, which he continued until he came to this place. His was the fourth place of business in Oxford when he began dealing here, and he has not only succeeded in his mercantile pursuits, but has also accumulated other property, and filled positions of public importance.

For some time prior to the opening of his own banking institution, Mr. Barrett was Vice-President of the Oxford Bank. He has been Township Treasurer and Treasurer of the city schools, and served faithfully and ably. He owns some valuable farm lands near the city, and his finances are on a substantial basis enabling him to live in great comfort and bestow hospitality abundantly upon friends and acquaintances.

The marriage of our subject was celebrated in Elizabeth, Ill., October 29, 1869, his chosen companion being Miss Maria Weir, a young lady of intelligence and refinement who has ever been his most cherished friend. Mrs. Barrett was born in Pennsylvania, and is a daughter of Thompson Weir, one of the early settlers of Jo Daviess County, Ill. The union has resulted in the birth of two sons—G. M. and E. T.—both now in Winfield, Col.

ILKES E. BOZMAN. The mercantile interests of Argonia find a worthy representative in the person of the subject of this notice, who established himself in business at this place in 1886, and is enjoying a fair share of patronage. He has seen considerable of the great West, going when a young man of twenty years to California, by the way of the Isthmus of Panama, and was engaged at mining in the Golden State for a period of nine years, being fairly successful. He has been a keen observer, although quiet and self-contained, and possesses a good fund of general information, being a man with whom an hour may always be spent in a pleasant and profitable manner. He is held in high esteem in his community, both as a man and a citizen.

A native of Morgan County, Ohio, Mr. Bozman

was born August 8, 1831, and there grew to man's estate, acquiring such education as was to be obtained in the common school. After his sojourn on the Pacific Slope, he returned, in 1860, to his native State, and settling in Muskingum County, engaged in farming and stock-raising for about twenty-one years, coming then to Kansas. In the meantime, in 1864, he assumed domestic relations, being married in January, that year, to Miss Asenath, daughter of Thomas and Elizabeth Hiatt, the latter being natives of Virginia. Mrs. Hiatt departed this life at her home in Ohio many years ago. The father of Mrs. Bozman came to Kansas, and is now residing on a farm in Reno County. Of his first marriage there were born five children, only three of whom are living. Mrs. Bozman was born in Ohio, in January, 1833, to which State the family had removed about 1828-29.

Four children have been born to Mr. and Mrs. Bozman, the eldest of whom a daughter, Frances, is the wife of Dr. J. S. Baughman, of Argonia, and they have two children; Edward married Miss Bertha Hall, and they are living in Argonia; John Wilkes married Miss Nettie Hettrick; neither of these have children; William T. is unmarried, and makes his home with his parents, being a telegraph operator for the Santa Fe Railroad. Mrs. Bozman and her daughter are prominently connected with the Presbyterian Church.

While a resident of Ohio, Mr. Bozman served as a Justice of the Peace for the long period of eighteen years in succession. He was also a member of the School Board there for twenty-one years. A staunch Democrat and active in local politics, he was as at one time made the candidate of his party for the legislature, but was defeated with the balance of the ticket. His people were the old-line Whigs, with southern proclivities, and later identified themselves with the Democratic party.

The father of our subject was John Bozman, a native of Ohio, who, during the years of his active life, was engaged as a stock dealer and grazier. He was first married in his native State to Miss Eliza Brady, a native of Virginia, and they settled in Morgan County, where the mother of our subject died in 1845, when Wilkes E. was a lad of fourteen. The elder Bozman was subsequently married to Jane

Glass, and is now deceased, aged eighty-five years old. His wife is also deceased. Of the first marriage there were born four children, all of whom are living. The paternal grandfather was Wilkes Bozman, a native of Baltimore County, Md., and who removed to Ohio in 1808. He served during the War of 1812, and assisted at the bombardment of Ft. Henry. A prominent and successful man, he became an extensive farmer, leaving at his death two thousand acres of land in Morgan County, Ohio.

EDGAR BISSELL, who is the owner and occupant of a most excellent farm in Ryan Township, has passed through scenes which, if well described and furnished in detail would make up an account of the most interesting description. Amid the grand and rugged scenery of the Rocky Mountains he has spent much time, and that at a period when great bravery and courage were needed in those regions. His first visit to Kansas was made in 1855, and his permanent residence within the State dates from 1878. Although he can scarcely be classed among the pioneer settlers, there are few residents of the county who realize more fully the development of the section and the changes that have taken place since his first visit West.

The parents of our subject, Roderick and Fannie (Gaylord) Bissell, were born in Connecticut, were there married, and made that State their permanent home. The father was born in Litchfield County, was a manufacturer and lived until February 10, 1875. The mother, who has now reached the age of eighty-six years, is surrounded by all the comforts and luxuries of life in her elegant home in Winsted. The family of this worthy couple included six children, four of whom still survive.

The gentleman whose biography will be briefly sketched below, is the fourth in the parental family, and was born March 15, 1833, in Litchfield County, Conn. After having received a common school education, he attended the academy at Torringford, acquiring a more thorough and extended knowledge of the higher English branches, and prior to his majority he had also served an apprenticeship at the carpenter's trade. He began life for himself upon reaching man's estate, and not many months thereafter paid his first visit to the West, spending several months in roaming about the northern part of this State, visiting Ft. Riley, Lawrence and Topeka. He next paid a visit to Pennsylvania, and then settled down in Ft. Dodge for a period of two years.

In the winter of 1858–59, Mr. Bissell joined the throng whose cry was "on to Pike's Peak," and during the following two years he had the varying fortunes of a miner. The mines at that period were not supplied, as many are at present, with good machinery for drilling and blasting, with hoisting works, and the conveniences for separating ores, but the work entailed upon the miner was all of the pick and shovel, and pack-horse description. The prospect holes were deepened and widened by slow degrees, and if the upper stratum of rocks was supported at all, it was by the rudest arrangement of timbers. The rock was cleared away by the hand which had so gallantly wielded the pick, or if the dirt was searched, it was panned by the same hands, the process of gaining "pay dirt" in either case being irksome and prolonged. The man who was so fortunate as to discover nuggets of value, or even a lead which promised well, was in constant danger, as the camps were filled with men who, in their thirst for gold, would stop at no deed which would secure it. Not only was it necessary for one who would win success in the gold fields to be keen of observation in his search for metal, but he must be equally shrewd in his judgment of character, quick-witted and courageous, and with a large amount of physical endurance.

In the spring of 1861, Mr. Bissell determined to visit a region farther to the northwest, which is now comprised within the bounds of Montana, and which, at that date, was an unexplored and almost trackless region. The party which he joined crossed the Snake River, fifteen miles above old Ft. Hall, ferrying the river in their wagon-beds, being guided by old Tim Goodell. They stopped where Bannock City now stands, and there Mr. Bissell again began prospecting and mining. He was fortunate in his efforts, and the "output" of his two months' stay was very satisfactory. He was next to be found in Salt Lake City, Utah, where he saw and listened to the preaching of the notorious Brigham Young. Until 1866, Mr. Bissell remained among the mountains, mining and freighting. The latter occupation was one which required qualifications very similar to, one might say almost identical with those of a successful miner, together with a skill in managing horses, mules or oxen to which that of the ordinary four-in-hand driver bears but a slight resemblance.

The freighter's outfit comprises several yoke or span of animals, the number varying according to the route or the freight carried, the most frequent numbers being from five to thirteen span. These are attached to a wagon, behind which other wagons are trailed, the number of the "prairie schooners" also varying. The wagons, or at least a portion of them, are supplied with a strong brake, which the driver can operate by means of a rope when he is on foot. The long-handled skillet, the big coffee pot, the tin cups and a few other rude household utensils which the freighter uses at mealtime, generally form decorations to one of the wagons, which contains a supply of meal, coffee, bacon and blankets. In crossing the mountain passes and winding around the precipices, a skillful hand is needed to avoid accidents. Particularly is this the case upon meeting other outfits in the narrow gorges where there is scarcely room to pass; indeed, in many places, it is impossible to do so, and should some unlucky chance occasion a meeting here, one outfit must be backed out of the way, or lifted by bodily strength to one side. To avoid catastrophies, bells are used upon the animals which warn an approaching driver of danger.

After years spent amid such scenes and experiences, Mr. Bissell returned to his New England home for a visit with his family and friends, after which he again took up his residence in Iowa, remaining there about six years During that time, in 1869, he was united in marriage with Miss Leah E. Byerley, a daughter of George and Leah Byerley of North Carolina, both of whom are now deceased. Mrs. Bissell was born in Indiana. She is a member of the Lutheran Church, and possesses many

domestic virtues and acquirements. She has borne
her husband one son, Manney D., who has a good
common-school education. In 1878, Mr. Bissell
removed to Kansas, pre-empted one hundred and
sixty acres of land upon which he still lives, and
which he has placed in fine condition. The entire
acreage is improved, perhaps its most notable feature being a fine orchard of two hundred bearing
apple trees. It is the intention of Mr. Bissell to
erect a new dwelling this year, which, when completed, will be an added attraction of the estate.
He is engaged in farming, and also raises horses,
cattle and hogs.

Mr. Bissell is now Junior Warden of the Masonic
lodge in Milan. He has been Clerk of Ryan
Township, and a member of the School Board of
District No. 87. He takes an active interest in
political issues, is a strong believer in the principles
advocated by the Democratic party, in support of
which he always casts his vote. Not only has he
the respect of his fellow men, but he has the pleasure of knowing that other members of his family
have been honored by those among whom they
have lived. His brother, G. G. Bissell, who died
in Iowa, was Judge of the Miners' Court in Montana in 1861-62. Another brother, Dr. C. R. Bissell, now living in New York, was Judge of the
Miners' Court in Colorado in 1859.

HARPE P. G. LEWIS, President of the
First National Bank of Caldwell, and
prominently connected with the growth
and development of the city, was born in
Bucks County, Pa., June 24, 1849, and is a son of
Reading and Margaret (Shadinger) Lewis. The
paternal ancestry are of English origin, the first
settlements in this country having been made in
Connecticut. Thomas Lewis, the grandfather of
our subject, was a native of the same county in
which he of whom we write first saw the light, and
Reading Lewis was also born in that county. The
latter was born about 1821, and lived in Pennsylvania until 1873 when he removed to Newton,

Kan., whence ten years later he removed to Caldwell, in which city his death took place in January,
1888. He was a graduate of Jefferson Medical
College at Philadelphia and devoted most of his
life to the practice of the medical profession. He
was in easy financial circumstances. For many
years before his death he was a member of the
Friends' Church. His wife was born in Bucks
County, Pa., about 1827 and departed this life in
1862. She was of German ancestry, her forefathers
having been among the first settlers of the county
in which she was born.

Our subject is the eldest in a family of four
children, was reared in Bucks and Montgomery
Counties, Pa., and was the recipient of excellent
educational advantages, as well as the best of home
training. He acquired an academic education and
in quite early life taught school. In 1872 he went
to Macon County, Ill., and was engaged in teaching, and in carrying on the mercantile business and
buying grain at Argenta until 1878. He then followed his father to Newton, Kan., and the next
year took up his abode in Caldwell where he has
since resided. In Pennsylvania and at Newton he
read law, and in the latter place was admitted to
the bar and practiced his profession, and in connection therewith carried on a loaning business.
In 1881 he, with others, organized and put into
running order the Caldwell Savings Bank and was
made Vice-President of the institution, but in the
following year became President, continuing in
that capacity until 1887, when the bank was re-
organized as the First National Bank of Caldwell,
Kan. He has since served as President of the new
institution and he is also extensively engaged in
the real-estate and money-loaning business. He
started in life without a dollar, and has made all
he now possesses since he came to Kansas.

The marriage of Mr. Lewis was celebrated at
Argenta, Ill., in 1875, his bride being Miss Mary
A., daughter of Nathanial Griffin, and a native of
Champaign County, Ill. The estimable and intel-
ligent lady has borne her husband six children:
Anna, Edna, Ralph, Eugene, Francis, and Ernest.
Anna and Francis have been removed from their
parents by death. Mr. Lewis belongs to the social
orders of the Ancient Free and Accepted Masons,

and the Knights of Pythias. He is a staunch supporter of the Republican party. A man of more than ordinary intelligence and fine business qualifications, honorable in his dealing with mankind and exerting all his influence for the advancement of the material and moral interests of the city and vicinity, Mr. Lewis is regarded with respect by the citizens of Caldwell and wherever he is known.

MOSES GUM. Among the younger farmers of Morris Township, none are more deserving of special mention than he with whose name we initiate this sketch. He is well fixed, financially, being the owner of a fine body of land, thoroughly improved, with a neat modern residence, a good barn, substantial outbuildings and the other appliances of the model country estate. Socially and morally, as well as financially, Mr. Gum occupies an enviable position, being looked up to in his community as one of whom even better things may be expected in the future. His farming operations include the raising of the ordinary crops of Southern Kansas. He is also successful as a breeder of cattle, horses and swine. He takes an active interest in politics and is a Republican, "dyed in the wool" from his birth. His sentiments in regard to the temperance question are best illustrated in his own habits of total abstinence.

The fifth child in a family of seven born to Amos and Rebecca (Johnson) Gum, the subject of this sketch first opened his eyes to the light in Northampton County, Pa., September 2, 1854. Amos Gum, a native of Pennsylvania, was a miller by trade, but spent the latter years of his life in farming pursuits. His wife, Rebecca, was a native of his own State and after marriage they resided there until late in the year 1854 when they emigrated to Wisconsin. They were residents of the Badger State eleven years, removing thence, in 1865, to Iowa. In 1880 they went North to Dakota, settling in Hanson County, where they still remain. Amos Gum is now seventy-one years old and his wife,

Rebecca, seventy-three. There were born to them seven children, four of whom are living, the three besides our subject being residents of Nebraska and Kansas.

Mr. Gum received his schooling in Wisconsin and Iowa and when a young man of twenty years began farming on his own account. He came to Kansas from Iowa in 1878 and took up a claim on section 35, Morris Township, this county, where he has since made his headquarters. When ready to establish domestic ties he was married March 21, 1881 to Mrs. Mary H. (Pope) Manela. This lady is the daughter of T. J. Pope, of Kansas, and who was born May 7, 1850, in Indiana. Mr. and Mrs. Gum are the parents of two interesting children: Loyette, born July 24, 1882, and John Hoy, now three years old. Mrs. Gum is a member in good standing of the Missionary Baptist Church. Mr. Gum belongs to the Independent Order of Odd Fellows at Milan and is a warm defender of the principles of the order. He is also connected with the Farmers' Alliance. For three years past he has been a member of the school board of District No. 116, and for two terms has served as Treasurer of Morris Township. He was also Road Overseer for the same length of time.

The farm of Mr. Gum with its fine improvements is the result of his own energy and industry. The homestead embraces three hundred and twenty acres while he has sixty acres on section 12. The whole is improved and in a highly productive condition. His residence was erected in 1884 at a cost of $1,000. Mr. Gum has an orchard of two hundred and fifty apple trees and the same number of peach trees, together with the smaller fruits. It will thus be seen that he has aided largely in advancing the material interests of this township.

WILLIAM E. COX, Justice of the Peace at Wellington, is of Southern antecedents, possessing marked traits of character, transmitted to him from a very worthy ancestry. His native place was in Frankfort, Franklin County, Ky., and the date of his birth March 17, 1812. His father, Austin P. Cox, was born in Shelby County, that State. His paternal grandfather removed from Virginia to the Blue Grass regions at an early day and carried on farming successfully in Shelby County where he spent his last years.

Austin P. Cox when a young man commenced the study of law, going for this purpose to Frankfort about 1806–07. Upon the present site of that city there was then only a fort with a few settlers around it. The young barrister attained success and built up quite an extensive practice in the Court of Claims. He was President of the Board of Internal Improvements and otherwise a prominent man in his community. About 1859 he was appointed by the Governor as one of the commission to establish the State line between Kentucky and Tennessee. While in the pursuance of his duties he was subjected to much exposure and contracted a violent cold from the effects of which he died at his home July 20, 1861.

Mrs. Rebecca L. (Phillips) Cox, the mother of our subject was likewise a native of Kentucky and the daughter of William J. Phillips who was born in Maryland. Grandfather Phillips left his native State during the pioneer days of Kentucky and there spent his last years. There were born to the parents of our subject twelve children, viz: Elizabeth F., Sarah M., Charlotte L., Rebecca A., Laura S., Mary P., William E., Wallace H., Josephine C., Philip M., John C. and Willis T.

William E. Cox was reared and educated in his native county completing his studies in Sayers Academy. His business experience began as a clerk in the State Auditor's office and later he was employed in the office of the Adjutant General. He was thus occupied until in February, 1868, when he started for the West. Coming to Kansas he took up his abode in Montgomery County where he sojourned until the fall of 1869. He then started out to explore the western part of the State, visiting Sumner County in his travels, in company with two others. This county was not then organized and it was principally peopled by wild animals and Indians. Buffaloes were still plentiful and frequently roamed over the ground upon which stands

the present flourishing city of Wellington. Mr. Cox spent three or four months traveling through this section and then returned to Montgomery County, where he remained until the spring of 1871. He then came back to this county and located in Sumner City in time to witness the contest for the county seat. When the question was decided in favor of Wellington he came to this point and here has invested his labor and his capital. When first coming to Sumner County the Government survey had not been made and every foot of land was owned by Uncle Sam. Later it was sold at $1.25 per acre. Mr. Cox has viewed with warm interest the growth and development of his adopted State and as far as he could has assisted in advancing the prosperity of Sumner County.

The marriage of William E. Cox and Miss Mary D. Evans was celebrated at the bride's home in the city of Wellington in 1875. Mrs. Cox was born in Benton County, Iowa, June 10, 1849, and is the daughter of Judge Elijah and Amazetta H. (Forsythe) Evans. Her parents were natives of Indiana and spent their last years in Kansas. To Mr. and Mrs. Cox there have been born five children, viz: Helen, Nettie, Keith, Amazette and William E. Mr. and Mrs. Cox are members in good standing of the Methodist Episcopal Church and Mr. Cox votes the straight Republican ticket. He keeps himself posted upon the current events of the day —the political as well as the social questions—and is identified with Lodge No. 24, A. O. U. W. at Wellington.

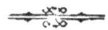

JOHN H. WENDELL, proprietor of the Star Livery barns at Caldwell, is numbered among the leading men of the city—a man enterprising and successful, and a general favorite, both in social and business circles. His native place was Adams County, Ill., and the date of his birth October 18, 1857. His parents were John H. and Annie C. (Kruse) Wendell, who were natives respectively of Missouri and Germany.

The Wendell family came to Kansas about 1867, John H., Sr., operated the most of his life as a merchant and hotel man and was successful in accumulating a comfortable property. In his religious belief he conformed to the doctrines of the Catholic Church. The seven children of the parental household included five sons and two daughters, of whom John H., Jr., was the fourth child. He was a lad of ten years when the family left Illinois and came to Kansas and lived with his parents at Neosha until 1868. That year he went into Butler County and in 1872 came to Caldwell, where he sojourned until 1880. He then went to Colorado, but in 1881, returned to Caldwell of which he has since been a continuous resident. He has been quite extensively engaged as a dealer in live stock, and as a trader is eminently a success. For several years he had the management of the stockyards in the interests of the Atchison, Topeka & Santa Fe Railroad at Caldwell. He established himself in the livery business in 1886, which he has since successfully conducted. He is a sound Republican, politically, and holds an honorable membership with the Independent Order of Odd Fellows.

Mr. Wendell was married October 18, 1883, in Caldwell, to Miss Lucy D., daughter of Jasper C. Mance. The mother of Mrs. Wendell bore the maiden name of Jessie E. Denton; her parents were natives of New York. The father is living in Falls Township and the mother is deceased. Two daughters, Bessie and Ethel, have been born of this union, the former April 10, 1884, and the latter October 8, 1885.

JOHN B. BROWNBACK. Among the many prosperous farmers of Falls Township, none occupy a higher position, socially and financially, than he with whose name we initiate this sketch. He commenced the battle of life at an early age on his own account, and without receiving any financial assistance, has, by a course of unflagging industry, and the practice of a wise economy, become independent. He is still in the prime of life, having been born April 8, 1842, and

is a native of Pickaway County, Ohio, of which his parents, Henry and Rebecca (Niece) Brownback, were early pioneers.

Henry Brownback was born in Pennsylvania, in 1810, and after emigrating to Ohio lived in Pickaway County until 1852. Then, pushing on further Westward to Illinois, he located in Shelby County, that State, where he still resides. He learned cabinet-making when a young man, but later abandoned it for the more congenial pursuits of farm life. He has been for many years an active member of the United Brethren Church, and is a citizen in good repute, greatly respected in his community. His father, Benjamin Brownback, was likewise a native of the Keystone State, and traced his ancestry to Germany. The mother of our subject was also a native of Pennsylvania, and born about 1814; she departed this life in Shelby County, Ill., in 1887.

To Henry and Rebecca Brownback there was born a family of eight children, whom they named respectively—Edward, Elizabeth, John B., William H., David, Jacob, Sophia and Joseph. Seven of these are living, making their homes in Illinois, excepting our subject, and Jacob, who lives in this State. John B., the third child, spent his early years on the farm in Shelby County, Ill., pursuing his studies in the district school. During the progress of the Civil War, he, early in 1862, enlisted as a Union soldier in Company C, Thirty-fifth Illinois Infantry, and served after the close of the war until September, 1865, receiving then his honorable discharge at Indianapolis, Ind. He experienced all the hardships and privations of life in the army, and participated in the following hard fought battles: Perryville, Stone River, Chickamauga, Missionary Ridge, Lookout Mountain, Resaca, Kenesaw Mountain, and was at the siege of Atlanta, and in all the battles of the Georgia campaign. Subsequently his command operated in Tennessee under the leadership of Gen. Thomas, taking part in the battles of Franklin and Nashville.

After leaving the army Mr. Brownback continued a resident of Illinois until 1874. That year, crossing the Father of Waters, he came to Sedgwick County, this State, and took up a claim in what is now Downs Township, upon which he lived three years. Then selling out he, in 1878, purchased

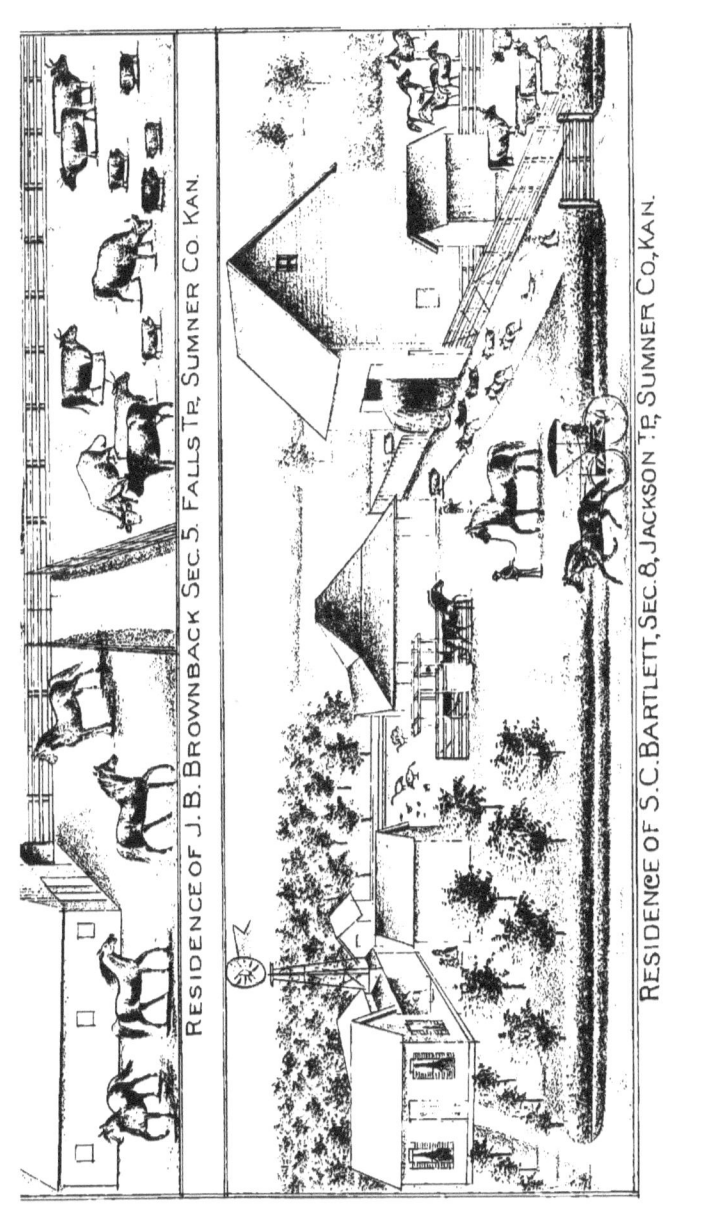

RESIDENCE OF J. B. BROWNBACK SEC. 5, FALLS TP, SUMNER CO. KAN.

RESIDENCE OF S. C. BARTLETT, SEC. 8, JACKSON TP, SUMNER CO., KAN.

land on sections 17 and 18, Falls Township, this county, and prosecuted farming there until 1883. That year he removed to Corbin, where he purchased land, and he also owns a farm on section 5, Falls Township. His landed possessions altogether embrace three hundred and ninety broad acres, thoroughly improved and equipped with suitable buildings. Stock-raising enters largely into his operations, and he is also engaged quite extensively in buying grain at Corbin.

Since the organization of the First National Bank at Caldwell, Mr. Brownback has been one of its Directors. He uniformly votes the Republican ticket, and has held some of the minor offices. He has little ambition for political preferment, finding more satisfaction in the peaceful pursuits of farm life. He is a member in good standing of the G. A. R. Post, No. 470, at Corbin.

One of the most important and interesting events in the life of our subject was his marriage with Miss Nancy E. Liston, which was celebrated at the bride's home, at Tower Hill, Ill., October 12, 1866. This lady was born in Clay County, Ind., September 13, 1845, and is the daughter of Perry and Mary A. (Riley) Liston, natives of Indiana. The eight children born of this union are named respectively—Perry, William, Flora, Effie E., Charles, Bertha, Jessie and Ettie. They are all living, and form a very bright and interesting family group, making their home with their parents.

A lithographic view of Mr. Brownback's residence is presented in connection with this sketch.

AMUEL C. BARTLETT. The solid element of the township of Jackson recognizes no more worthy citizen than Mr. Bartlett—a life-long farmer of more than ordinarily good judgment, and one who has been very successful. He comes of substantial New England stock and was born in Guilford, New Haven County, Conn., March 4, 1844.

The immediate progenitor of the subject of this sketch was John Bartlett, likewise a native of Guilford, Conn., and the son of Samuel Bartlett, who was born in the same town. The father of the latter was John Bartlett, who was a farmer by occupation, and as far as is known, spent his entire life in Guilford. Samuel Bartlett likewise followed in the footsteps of his father, spending his entire life in his native place. His son, John, the father of our subject, was reared in Guilford and was there married. He obtained a good education and taught school when a young man, but aside from this occupied himself as a farmer. His entire life was spent at the homestead of his birth.

Mrs. Lodoiska (Coan) Bartlett, the mother of our subject, was born in New Haven County, Conn., and was the daughter of Josiah Coan, a native of the same county, and a carpenter by trade, who also followed farming. Mrs. Bartlett died in 1851, when her son, Samuel C., was a lad of seven years. He was wholly orphaned by the death of his father, which took place in 1864. He remained a resident of his native county until the death of his father, then emigrated to Illinois and secured employment on a farm near Quincy. He sojourned there three years, then went into Pike County, Mo., where he secured land and prosecuted farming until 1875. Then selling out he started with a team for Texas, intending to settle there; he visiting Denison, Sherman, Dallas, and various other counties in the northern part of the State. Not being suited with the country he turned his horses' heads northward, riding up through the Indian Territory into Sumner County, this State.

Upon his arrival in Kansas Mr. Bartlett entered a tract of Government land—that which constitutes his present farm, and comprising the northwest corner of section 8, Jackson Township. At that time the small village of Wichita—forty miles distant—was the nearest railroad depot, and the nearest market for grain and stock. Only a few miles west deer and buffalo were plentiful, roaming undisturbed over the prairies and through the woodlands. Mr. Bartlett possessed the elements most needed to battle with the difficulties and dangers of frontier life, and proceeded with the improvement of his property, being greatly prospered. He brought the soil to a good state of cultivation, erected a fine set of frame buildings, and added to his landed possessions until he is now the owner of three hundred and sixty broad acres, all in one tract and well-improved. As a member of the community he stands second to none in Jackson Township. His estimable wife, to whom he was married in Pike County, Mo., October 8, 1865, was formerly Miss Mary C. Wheeler, a native of Cass County, Mo. The parents of Mrs. Bartlett were Edmund and Barbara A. (Robinson) Wheeler, natives of Kentucky, but now deceased. To Mr. and Mrs. Bartlett there have been born seven children, five now living, namely: Walter Edward, Lavina, Pearl, Samuel and Ernest. Charles Sumner, the third in order of birth, and an infant unnamed, are deceased.

In connection with this sketch of Mr. Bartlett may be found on another page of this work a lithographic view of his homestead.

SAMUEL BAIN. They who looked upon Kansas during the days of its early settlement witnessed scenes which in all probability will never be repeated here. It required more than ordinary courage and persistence for a man to maintain his position during the years when this part of the West was visited by various calamities, and when those men who then settled here were by no means in affluent circumstances. Mr. Bain, like his brother pioneers, came here poor in purse, but nature had endowed him with a large amount of resolution and perseverance, and he held to his first purpose of building up a homestead, in which he finally succeeded. He has brought his land to a good state of cultivation and realizes therefrom a comfortable income. He cares little for parade or show, and is content to dwell amid modest surroundings, his chief ambition being to live at peace among his neighbors, keep clear of debt and do good as he has opportunity.

The farm of Mr. Bain is pleasantly located on section 8, Avon Township, to which he came in 1872, and where he has since lived with the exception of two years spent in California. He was born in Jefferson County, Ind., August 20, 1823, and removed with his parents to Miami County, Ind., when a lad of twelve years. There he developed into manhood, obtaining a practical education in the district school and becoming familiar with the various pursuits of farm life. He also learned the trade of a carpenter. He remained a resident of Miami County until 1856, and then, a young man of thirty-three years, started out for himself, and going into Monroe County, Iowa, purchased a farm and engaged in its cultivation and improvement until 1872.

In the fall of the year above mentioned, Mr. Bain came with his family to this county, and with his children pre-empted a section of land including the north half of section 8, and the south half of section 5. He gave to the former his chief attention, making of it his homestead. He has not been wholly absorbed in his own personal interests, but has taken time to look after the school of his district, officiating as Trustee, and giving his support and encouragement to the various other enterprises calculated for the advancement of the people. He served as County Commissioner three terms, and has held the office of Justice of the Peace, under appointments by Govs. Osborne and Glick, and one term by election. The Republican party has received his uniform support since he became a voting citizen. He takes an active part in politics, and keeps himself well posted upon current events.

In October, 1887, Mr. Bain went to California, where he spent nearly two years. After the outbreak of the Civil War, he felt called upon to proffer his assistance in the preservation of the Union, and in February, 1862, enlisted in Company A. Thirty-sixth Iowa Infantry, serving two years. In the meantime, he officiated as Quartermaster Sergeant about ten months. He was married in Miami County, Ind., August 30, 1849, to Miss Experience Busick. Mrs. Bain was born in Pickaway County, Ohio, February 9, 1829, and is the daughter of Hezekiah and Matilda (Hazel) Busick, who were natives respectively of Ohio and Kentucky, and are now deceased. Of this union there were born four children: William E., who chose the occupation of a farmer, married Miss Mattie Hickenlooper and died in Avon Township. February 5, 1884; Maggie is the wife of William H. Pierce of California; Sarah L. married James Jordon and they live on a farm in Caldwell Township; Nancy J. is the wife of Andrew H. Swan, a farmer of Wellington Township. Mr. and Mrs. Bain have been consistent members of the Presbyterian Church for the long period of thirty-five years.

The father of our subject was William Bain, a native of North Carolina, who married Miss Margaret Jameson, of Garrett County, Ky. They emigrated to Miami County, Ind., during its pioneer days, and there spent the remainder of their lives. Their family consisted of nine children.

ILLIAM MYERS. This gentleman is a prominent resident of Wellington and the fortunate possessor of sufficient of this world's goods to enable him to spend his years in comfort retired from active business pursuits. He was at one time the possessor of considerable land near this place, and good judgment was displayed by him in selling at an opportune time, so realizing a decided advance on the first cost of his property. He possesses fine business ability and ranks among the honorable and reliable citizens of this community.

George Myers, the grandfather of our subject, was of German ancestry and himself a native of Pennsylvania. He owned a large tract of land in York County, where he carried on farming operations extensively and where he departed this life. He was the father of three sons, one of whom died young, while another went West in an early day. His third son, Henry, was born in York, York County, Pa., and having acquired the trade of a carpenter at the age of twenty-one became a contractor and builder in Carlisle. After an active life of forty years from that date he retired from business and spent the remainder of his life enjoying the fruits of his labors. At the age of eighty-five years he was gathered to his fathers, the date of his decease being December 2, 1883. He had married Miss Anna McFadden, who was likewise a native of York

County, and who also died in Carlisle, the date of the sad event being March 1, 1863.

The parental family comprised ten children, all of whom reached years of maturity: Emeline married William Skiles and after his death married Maj. A. A. Line, and now resides in Carlisle, Pa.; Susan married Joseph Gutshall, of Carlisle, and died in California, March 30, 1851; George W. went to California in 1849, and finally settled in Boise City, Idaho, where he died on the 19th of October, 1870; Henry was also a "'49er" and his death took place at Soda Springs, Idaho, October 21, 1871; John died in Carlisle, November 21, 1875; Henrietta became the wife of Samuel H. Gould and lives in Carlisle; in that place Luther M. also resides. So also does Anna, who married Joseph W. Ogleby; Lonesia married Samuel A. Brumbaugh, of Harrisburg, Pa., and they live in Beloit, Wis.

William Myers, of whom we write, is a native of Pennsylvania, having been born in Carlisle, Cumberland County, April 20, 1842. He was reared and educated in the place of his nativity, and while in his teens began to learn the trade of a carpenter and worked at the same with his father until of age. He then engaged in the service of the United States as a clerk in the Quartermaster's department at Nashville, Tenn., and remained there for three years under Charles H. Irvine. After the close of the war he returned to his home and in March, 1866, went to Bloomington, Ill., where he accepted a position as clerk in the station of the Chicago & Alton Railroad. After serving in a clerical capacity five years, he was appointed station agent and occupied that position eight years.

In 1879, on account of the ill health of his wife, Mr. Myers resigned his position in Bloomington and came here, arriving on the first train that ever brought passengers to this city. He had previously visited this section and had bought one hundred and sixty acres of land adjoining the town. Immediately following his removal here he built a comfortable dwelling and began improving his land, which he operated until 1886. In the spring of 1880, he accepted the agency of the Southern Kansas Railroad, and opened the station for this line on the 30th of March, of that year. He retained the position of station agent during the succeeding seven years and then resigned, having reached that degree of financial prosperity which enabled him to retire from active pursuits. The previous year he had sold one hundred and fifty acres of land for nearly $23,000, and now owns sixteen acres, upon which he resides and which forms a beautiful home.

The marriage of Mr. Myers took place July 3, 1867, his bride being Mrs. Martha B. Carpenter, a native of Rochester, N. Y. Her father, William Cook, was born in Plymouth, England, and was the son of another William, also a native of the Mother Country, who came to Canada with his family and settled in Kingston, where he died. William Cook, Jr., was reared and married in Halifax, Nova Scotia, and after his marriage resided in the Island of Cape Breton for some years. He then came to the United States and engaged in mercantile pursuits in Rochester, N. Y., for a time, whence he removed to Oberlin, Ohio, and there managed a college boarding house for a short period. His next removal was to Columbus, Ohio, in which place he was employed as a book-keeper by a hardware firm until his death, which occurred when he was forty-four years old, on the 30th of July, 1849. His widow continued to reside in that city until 1856, when she removed to Bloomington, Ill.

The maiden name of Mrs. Myers' mother was Mary M. Adams; she was born in Halifax, Nova Scotia, and was the only child of Thomas Adams, and a direct descendant of Henry Adams who emigrated from England about the year 1640 and was a pioneer of Braintree, Mass. Thomas Adams was a nephew of John Adams, the second President of the United States. He was a ship builder and followed his trade in Halifax and Cape Breton, and after her marriage made his home with, his daughter, departing this life at her residence in Columbus, Ohio. His wife was of German ancestry and bore the name of Amelia Sophia Cobright. William and Mary Cook, parents of Mrs. Myers, reared a family of eleven children, named, respectively, William P., Mary, Amelia, Thomas, Richard, Walter, Alexander, Ellen, Martha, Charles and Samuel.

Mrs. Myers was first married in Bloomington, Ill., in 1859, being united to Erastus S. Carpenter,

who was born in Rochester, N. Y., and followed the printer's trade. Mr. Carpenter departed this life in January, 1865, in the city in which his marriage had taken place, leaving one son, Edwin L., who now enjoys a lucrative position with the Rio Grande Western Coal Company. To Mr. and Mrs. Myers one son has been born, William H., who is now a student in Spaulding's Commercial College, Kansas City, Mo.

Mr. Myers is a member of Wade Bonney Post, No. 512, and the A.F. & A. M. of Bloomington. He was one of the organizers of the State National Bank and was its first Vice President.

MOSES R. JACKSON, who is engaged in cornice manufacturing in Wellington, was born in Harrison, Hamilton County, Ohio, August 8, 1883. His father, John Jackson, was born in Pennsylvania, and so also was his grandfather, Eben Jackson. The traditional history of the family lineage, is that they are descended from five brothers who came to America at an early period in the settlement of the colonies. The grandfather of our subject removed from Eastern to Western Pennsylvania, at the time of the first settlement in that part of the State, and located in the wilderness thirty miles from any white family, taking up Government land. He built a saw-mill and engaged in the lumber business, and rafted the first lumber ever floated down the Monongahela River to Pittsburg. In 1808 he removed to Ohio, making the trip on a raft down the Monongahela and Ohio Rivers. He settled on the present site of Cincinnati, in what was then a wilderness, and subsequently took a tract of timber land twenty miles distant, where he remained. A part of this land is now owned and occupied by his son, Ethan Jackson, and the town of Harrison occupies another portion of it. Ethan Jackson and his sons established a pottery which they conducted for some years, and in that place the old gentleman and his wife departed this life. Mrs. Jackson was a native of Pennsylvania, and bore the maiden name of Nancy McLean. Four children were reared to years of maturity—Neal, John, Daniel, and Ethan.

The father of our subject was a young lad when his father moved to Ohio. He learned the trade of a potter in Cincinnati, and was interested with his father and brothers in establishing the pottery, and prosecuted his trade nearly forty years. He resided in Harrison until 1868, when he removed to Livingston County, Ill., where he died late in the year 1872, his remains being taken back to Harrison for burial. His wife was born in Trenton, N. Y., and bore the maiden name of Ruth Ann Riggs. She died in Harrison in 1863, after having reared six children—our subject, Ethan, Isaac, Sarah J., John and Ruth Ann.

Moses Riggs, the father of Mrs. John Jackson, was a native of New Jersey, from which State he removed to Harrison, Ohio, and later to Pike County, Ill., where his death occurred. He was a millwright and miller. Besides his daughter Ruth, he had three other children. His only son, Cyrus, died in Franklin County, Ind.; Rhoda married John Durand, and is now living in Pittsfield, Pike County, Ill.; Emma married Alva Shaw, and they crossed the plains and settled in Oregon in 1846, being among the first whites to settle there; Mr. Shaw took the first sheep to the Territory.

The subject of this sketch was reared and educated in Harrison, and while a youth, in the intervals of study, assisted in the pottery. His father had a tin shop in connection with that establishment, and in 1849, young Jackson entered the shop and learned the tinner's trade, which he subsequently followed until July, 1862. He then took up arms in defense of the Union, becoming a member of Company B, Ninety-sixth Ohio Infantry, in which he served three years, when he was discharged on account of the expiration of his service. He next engaged in farming on the estate of his father-in-law, and continued thus employed until 1866, when he located in Fairbury, Ill., and there followed his trade for twelve months. At the expiration of that time he opened a shop in Chatsworth, in partnership with his brother Ethan, the connection continuing until 1873, when he sold, and a short time after located in Wichita, Kan., which was then a city of about two thousand inhabitants, and

the western terminus of the railroad. In that city he continued his trade as foreman of a shop until 1881, when he came to this place, where he filled a similar position for four and a half years, after which he established himself in the business which he is now conducting. He has a thorough knowledge of his trade, and turns out excellent work, and in every relation of life displays an honorable character.

In Miss Phœbe, daughter of Moses and Phœbe Marsh, Mr. Jackson discovered the qualities which he desired in a life companion, and with her he was united in marriage in 1857. The bride was born in Butler County, Ohio, and like her husband, is a worthy member of the Brethren Church. Their happy union has resulted in the birth of three children—E. Edwin, George J., and John.

JEROME W. KENDRICK, an early pioneer of Sumner County, pre-empted in 1876, the northwest quarter of section 22, in what is now Jackson Township, and taking up his abode thereon, has continued to live there. He settled upon a tract of wild prairie at a time when the country around him presented a desolate appearance, inhabited principally by wild animals. There was not a railroad station nearer than Wichita, and the present flourishing city of Wellington was a hamlet containing only a few hundred people. The transformation which has taken place during the intervening years has been watched by Mr. Kendrick with the warmest interest, while he has contributed by his own labors to bring about the great change which, within a period of twenty-five years has passed over the face of the Sunflower State.

A native of Butler Grove Township, Montgomery County, Ill., the subject of this notice was born February 11, 1844, and is the son of the Rev. John C. and Rebecca (Ware) Kendrick, both natives of New Hampshire. The parents were reared and married in the old Granite State, and about 1830 emigrated to Illinois, locating in the wilds of Montgomery County. The removal was made overland with teams before the days of stages or hotels, and the travelers carried with them their beds and provisions, camping and cooking, and sleeping by the wayside. The Kendrick family first settled in what is now Butler Township, but only remained there a short time, the father later entering a tract of Government land in what is now Fillmore Township. This land was all prairie, and no railroad was built through that region for many years thereafter. The nearest market was at St. Louis, sixty-five miles distant, and from three to five days were employed in making the round trip.

The elder Kendrick improved forty acres of land upon which he lived a number of years, then selling out, returned to Butler Grove Township, and purchased one hundred and twenty acres where he made his home until his death, which occurred about 1868. His wife, Rebecca, was the daughter of Benjamin Ware, who spent his last years in New Hampshire; she passed away in 1856, twelve years prior to the decease of her husband. Their family consisted of nine children. John C. Kendrick united with the Methodist Episcopal Church in his youth, and began preaching, becoming a member of the Conference. After his removal to Illinois he traveled the circuit as a local preacher, receiving little or no remuneration for his services.

The subject of this sketch attended the pioneer schools of Montgomery County. Ill., which were mostly conducted during the winter season, and as soon as old enough he was required to make himself useful about the farm. On account of the ill health of his father, he at the age of fifteen, assumed many of the cares and responsibilities of the head of the household. He remained with his parents until his marriage, and then purchasing a farm adjoining, lived there until 1876. Then selling out he started for the farther West, driving overland with a team to Booneville, Mo., and at that point chartered a car which conveyed him and his goods to Osage Mission, whence he came with a team to this county. The story of his later toils and struggles, is the common one of those who settled upon the frontier, and his prosperity has only been achieved by the most unflagging industry, and the exercise of a close economy. He was successful as a tiller of the soil, and in addition to the cultiva-

tion of his land, has erected a good set of frame buildings, and gathered around himself and his family the conveniences and comforts of modern life.

Miss Rebecca Livengood, a native of Hancock County, Ohio, became the wife of Mr. Kendrick on the 28th of November, 1866, the wedding taking place at Hillsboro. Ill. The household now numbers nine children, viz: Carrie C. J., George A., Ida May, Nellie G., Ella R., John J., Jennie F., Minnie E., and Pearl Ethel.

Mrs. Kendrick is the daughter of the Rev. John J. Livengood, a native of Pennsylvania, who removed to Ohio in his youth, and was there married to Miss Amanda Byers, a native of that State. They removed to Illinois about 1851, settling in Montgomery County. Mr. Livengood was reared in the doctrines of the Lutheran Church, and prior to this time had become a preacher. After the removal to Illinois, he was assigned to a charge in Hillsboro, having four appointments in that vicinity. He lived there until 1864, then removed to Butler Grove Township, and purchased the farm upon which he still resides. He labored faithfully in the Master's vineyard until 1871, then retired and spent his remaining years in quietness at Hillsboro, passing away March, 1886. His wife had died at the home farm in Butler Grove Township in February, 1879. Mr. Livengood was a Republican, politically, and Mr. Kendrick is a Democrat.

ILLIAM CORZINE, Vice-President of the First National Bank at Caldwell, is also engaged extensively in the live-stock business, being one of the largest land-owners of Sumner County. Of Southern antecedents, he was born in Tobias County, N. C., January 5, 1835, and is the son of John R. and Elizabeth (Madden) Corzine, the former of whom was a well-to-do planter during his residence in the South.

John R. Corzine, in 1838, emigrated to Jersey County, Ill., where he sojourned for a period of fourteen years, then changed his residence to

Montgomery County, that State. In the latter he spent his last days engaged in farming. He was a strict member of the Baptist Church from early manhood and possessed of the unquestioned integrity which gained him the confidence and esteem of all with whom he had dealings. His wife, Elizabeth, was born in Roan County, N. C., and was the descendant of an old and honored family of high respectability. She also like her husband died in Montgomery County, Ill. There were born to them six children, viz: William, Sarah J., Noah, Jefferson, Francis M. and Elizabeth A.

The subject of this sketch was the first-born of his parents and was reared on a farm in Jersey County, Ill. He attended the common school and in 1852 removed with his parents to Montgomery County, where he commenced farming for himself and was thus occupied there until 1873. In the meantime he was prospered, but decided to invest his capital in Kansas lands, and coming to this county purchased nine hundred and sixty acres on sections 16 and 24, Falls Township. He still maintains possession of this land, which is now valuable. He gave his attention strictly to farming until 1882, then removed with his family to Caldwell, of which he has since been a resident. He still has the general management of his farming interests and as a leading stockman of this county, holds membership in the Cherokee Strip Live Stock Association. He started out for himself unaided and his possessions are solely the result of his own industry and good management. For three years he served as County Commissioner, and is recognized everywhere as a liberal and public-spirited citizen, willing to aid in any project which will result in the advancement and welfare of the people around him. He is an uncompromising Democrat, politically, and has taken the third degree of the Ancient Free & Accepted Masons. The Caldwell First National Bank has become one of the leading institutions of its kind in this county, owing its prosperity largely to the standing of its Vice-President, who is also a leading director.

Mr. Corzine was first married in 1858 near Litchfield, to Miss Sarah Forehand, of Montgomery County, Ill. This lady was a native of Tennessee, and departed this life at her home in Falls Township in 1875. There were born to her and her husband six children, viz: James A., Emma J., Thomas J., Ida E., Mary and Albert. Mr. Corzine in 1877 contracted a second marriage with Miss Margaret S. Blackwelder, of this county, and who is still living. Of this union there are no children.

ENRY J. BEILET. This gentleman is not only one of the substantial citizens of the county, financially speaking, but is one of its educated citizens and a man of enterprise, morality and good citizenship. His natal day was March 9, 1843, and Texas claims him as one of her sons. His father, Joseph Beilet, was born in Germany and came to America when a young man, making his first settlement in Philadelphia, Pa. He became one of the early settlers of Texas, and being a man of more than ordinary intelligence became a prominent citizen, and was the incumbent of several minor official positions. He served as a private in the Mexican War. In politics he was a Democrat, and in religion was a member of the Lutheran Church. He was not only influential among his fellowmen, but displayed excellent business ability and at the time of his death was in good financial circumstances.

The gentleman whose name initiates this sketch was the fifth in a family of ten children, and was reared and educated in his native State, finishing his schooling as a student in St. Mary's College. In 1869, he went to Louisville, Ky., and learned the trade of a painter, which he followed but a few years ere he was compelled to abandon it, as he found it was injuring his health. Returning to Texas in 1872, he entered upon the business of stock-raising and has since kept up his interest in stock, his principal business at present consisting of buying and selling good grades. In 1880 he came to this county and purchased one hundred and sixty acres in Sumner Township, where he now lives; he also owns considerable real estate in Nebraska and altogether is in a condition of prosperity commendable to his prudence and industry and highly satisfactory to any man whose ideas of comfort are not exorbitant.

The family of Mr. Beilet is made up of his wife and three charming daughters—Mary E., Annie L., and Birdie. Mrs. Beilet bore the maiden name of Laura J. Wright and was born in Iowa, April 19, 1858, to Henry and May (Heart) Wright, who were natives of Ohio. The Wrights came to Kansas in 1871, and settled in this county, where the father is still carrying on his occupation of a farmer. The rites of wedlock were celebrated between the daughter and our subject May 27, 1880.

 H. D. CLEVELAND. This gentleman is the proprietor of the Capital Livery, Feed & Sale Stable, in Wellington, and has one of the finest establishments of the kind in Sumner County. His stables are located on Lincoln Avenue, and there he usually keeps for work sixteen to twenty horses, and he also has a fine line of trade in boarding. He has been carrying on the establishment here since 1878, and is one of the oldest livery men now in the city. He has also been quite extensively engaged in buying and selling stock. He is quite an old settler of this State, having landed in Wichita in 1872, when that prosperous city was but a small village, and there engaged in the grocery business, in which he continued some three years. He then changed his employment to that in which he is now engaged, and a few years later removed his stock to this city, of which he is now a prominent business man.

Mr. Cleveland is a son of Joseph and Sallie (Barrett) Cleveland, natives of Niagara County, N. Y., where they were married and where for many years the father was engaged in farming. In 1856, they removed to Stephenson County, Ill., about eight miles from Beloit, Wis., thence removing to Sheboygan County, Wis., where Mr. Cleveland continued his former occupation until elected Sheriff, which office he held four years. He also served as Supervisor six years. In 1869 he removed to Iowa, and in 1774 came to this State, and is now

living in Pawnee County. His wife died in Wisconsin in 1868.

The subject of this brief biography was born in Niagara County, N. Y., February 24, 1848, and remained in his native county until eight years old when he accompanied his parents farther West. Young as he was at the breaking out of the Rebellion, Mr. Cleveland was anxious to devote his youthful energy to the cause of the Union, and therefore placed his name on the muster-roll of Company F, Second Wisconsin, the date of his enlistment being March 22, 1864. He was first sent to Washington and then went to the front, being present at the first battle of Bull Run. After the expiration of his first term of enlistment he entered the Thirty-sixth Wisconsin, as Captain of Company F, which he had raised. This command was also sent to Washington and thence to the seat of conflict, and Mr. Cleveland participated in all their engagements, from the battle of the Wilderness through to Richmond. His services included participation in the battles of Spottsylvania Court-house, Cold Harbor and Welton Railroad, and many smaller engagements, with the usual amount of hard marching and camp duties. At Spottsylvania Court-house, he received a flesh wound in the leg, and was an inmate of the field hospital for a time. He attended the Grand Review at Washington and was mustered out at Chicago, June 18, 1865.

At the cessation of his soldier's life, Mr. Cleveland returned to Wisconsin and there engaged in buying horses for the Western markets until the fall of 1869, when he removed to Iowa and engaged in the livery business in Cedar Falls, also owning a farm in Grundy County. From Iowa he removed to Austin, Minn., where for three years he was engaged in the sale of agricultural implements, after which he became a resident of this State and employed as before noted.

The lady in whom Mr. Cleveland found the companion he desired was Miss Anna Porter, who was born in Cumberland County, Ky., June 23, 1856, and there made her home until about six years of age, when her father, R. Porter, was killed, after which her home was in Bowling Green. In that city the rites of wedlock were celebrated be-

Calvin L. Read

tween herself and Mr. Cleveland June 5, 1883. Their happy union has been blessed by the birth of three children—Alida P., Grover and Chester.

Mr. Cleveland belongs to the Grand Army of the Republic and to the Ancient Order of United Workmen. He is a reliable citizen, an honest man, kindly in his domestic relations, and receives his due measure of respect from his associates.

ALVIN L. READ. No more popular man can be found in a "day's journey," nor one more worthy of the regard in which he is held, than he whose name stands at the head of this biography, and whose portrait appears on the opposite page. He settled on his present location in Dixon Township, in 1879, and during the decade of his residence here has been actively and officially interested in various social organizations, in political and educational matters, and has always manifested an intelligent interest in every movement which has for its object the welfare of the community. His farm is now rented to a tenant, and comprises one hundred and sixty acres, eighty of which are under the plow.

Truman Read, the father of our subject, was a native of Windsor, Mass., and the son of Joshua Read. He was a carpenter by trade as well as a farmer, and during the War of 1812, served in the American army. In the Empire State he married Miss Sallie Brown, who was also a native of Windsor, Mass., and they made their permanent abode in Yates County, N. Y., where Mrs. Read died in 1842. The father of our subject subsequently married Rebecca Hennebergh, who is still living on the old homestead, her husband having departed this life in 1877. The first marriage of Truman Read was blessed by the birth of eight children, four of whom are now living.

The subject of this sketch is the seventh in the parental family, and was born February 3, 1834. He received a good common-school education, and remained at home, helping his father until he was twenty-one years of age. He has always been en-

gaged in farm pursuits, except during the Civil War, and began life for himself by renting a farm which he carried on until his patriotism was roused to a pitch of enthusiasm by the efforts made to destroy the Union, and he abandoned his peaceful calling to take his place in the ranks of his country's defenders. In 1862 he became a member of Company A, One Hundred and Twenty-sixth New York Infantry, and until June, 1865, was far from home and friends, undergoing the hazards of army life.

About the 1st of September, 1862, Mr. Read was sent with his comrades to Harper's Ferry, Va., and on the 15th of the same month, they were taken prisoners by Stonewall Jackson's army. After having been kept on parole at Chicago for two months, they were exchanged and sent to Washington, and placed upon picket duty at Bull Run until 1863. They were then attached to the Second Army Corps at Gum Spring, Va., and took part in the trying scenes of Gettysburg. Returning to Virginia, they crossed the Shenandoah and Potomac Rivers to the banks of the Rappahannock, remained there for a time, and then moved over to Culpeper on the Rapidan River, where they remained until Lee undertook to flank the army, when they again returned to Bull Run. The command started South again, went into the Mine Run expedition, and then into winter quarters. In May, 1864, they broke camp and entered upon the Petersburg Campaign, and in April, 1865, they followed Gen. Lee's army to the surrender at Appomattox Court House. During these years Mr. Read had taken part in the battles at Harper's Ferry, Gettysburg, Auburn Run, Va., and Bristol Station.

Although this outline of the movements of the command to which Mr. Read belonged, does not include many of the most terrible and noted battle fields, those who are acquainted with a soldier's life know that it was not the less arduous or hazardous. Indeed what are commonly called minor engagements, and the minor duties of campaigning, require perhaps more true courage than that called for during a great battle, as in the latter there is an excitement, and even an exhilaration of spirit "when the fight is on," that leads men generally to forget their personal danger, and the very number engaged lessens the individual chances of injury. It is therefore true that the greatest bravery is frequently displayed during the scenes which history does not record, or passes over with but a slight comment. Mr. Read was one of a special detail of one hundred men to act as Gen. Hancock's Provost Guard, and was serving in that capacity at the close of the war. He was on duty at Washington during the Grand Review in 1865.

When mustered out of the service, Mr. Read returned to his home in New York, and soon after settled in Oceana County, Mich., on a farm which he operated for twelve years. He then removed to Arkansas, and after sojourning in that State about eighteen months, came to Kansas in 1879, and took up his residence on the farm where he still lives. In 1856 he became the husband of Maria Gerould of New York. They have one child, Anson Revell Read, now living in New York, where he owns and operates a vineyard.

Mr. Read takes an active interest in politics, and always votes the Republican ticket. He is a member of the school board in District No. 160, and has been Road Overseer. He has been Tyler in Argonia Lodge, A. F. & A. M., of which he is a member; is now Master of the Grange; is Commander of Argonia Post, No. 312, G. A. R., in which he has formerly held other offices; and is President of the Farmers' Alliance.

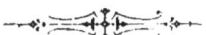

JOHN F. RUGGLES. This gentleman is one of those prosperous farmers of the county, who settled within its limits at an early period in its history, and who have witnessed the development of its agricultural and business interests, and the change from wild land which was the haunt of buffalo, bear, deer, and other wild animals, to well-kept and productive farm lands dotted with peaceful herds.

Mr. Ruggles was born in Lewis County, Ky., on New Year's Day, 1850, and is a son of Moses and Eliza (Roberts) Ruggles, the former of whom was of New England ancestry, and born in the same county in which his son, our subject, first saw the light. The mother was born in Fleming County, Ky., and was a daughter of one Samuel Roberts. The paternal grandparents of our subject were Thomas and Louisa (Bourse) Ruggles, both of whom were born in New England, the grandfather being of English ancestry. They were among the early settlers of Lewis County, Ky., where Thomas Ruggles took up a tract of timber land, upon which he cleared a considerable acreage, changing the wilderness to a fertile farm. There the father of our subject was born in April, 1816, and grew to maturity, his early life being passed before railroads were built in the Blue Grass State, and when Richmond, Va., was the market for hogs and cattle, to which the people drove them from farms far distant. Being reared to agricultural pursuits, Moses Ruggles, upon attaining to manhood, bought some improved land a mile distant from his father's homestead, and there took up his employment, and is still residing on the same place. He has lived to see that section develop into a well-settled and wealthy country, and now finds a much nearer market than Richmond for all that he desires to buy or sell. His wife, the mother of our subject, departed this life about the year 1854, when he of whom we write was scarcely more than a babe.

John F. Ruggles passed his boyhood and youth in his native county, leaving the parental roof at the age of eighteen years, and going to DeWitt County, Ill., where he began life for himself by working on a farm. He then rented land and carried on agricultural pursuits there until 1875. The previous year he had visited this section of country and purchased land in Wellington Township, to which, at the date mentioned, he came as a settler. Wichita was the nearest railroad station, whence he traveled to this county by stage. The only improvement upon the place which he had purchased was a small dwelling, and all the conveniences which now mark the place have been accomplished by him. He is the fortunate possessor of a half section of land which is all enclosed, and which is improved for general farming or used as pasture land. The industry and practical ability of Mr. Ruggles are plainly indicated by the appearance of everything about the estate, and as one who has assisted in the development of the county, and been for a number of years one of its reliable citizens, he is entitled to and receives the respect of his fellow-men.

The marriage of Mr. Ruggles was celebrated in 1871, the bride being Miss Armenia, daughter of Samuel and Harriet (Grovsy) Wilson, who was born in Lewis County, Ky., and who has been a faithful and loving wife and mother since the date of their union. Seven children have come to brighten their fireside. They are named, respectively: Hattie L., Dollie J., Annie L., Eliza J., Katie L., and Samuel W. and Vadie L., twins.

OHN J. STANDS, an extensive farmer residing in Jackson Township, Sumner County, was born in Pike Township, Stark County, Ohio, February 24, 1850. His father, Henry Stands, was a native of Pennsylvania, where he was reared and married. When a young man, he learned the trade of a weaver, and worked at that branch of industry in his native State for a number of years. In those days hand-looms were in use, machinery not having as yet made its appearance to benefit both the workman and his employer. Sometime after marriage he removed to Ohio, where he rented land and engaged in farming. He met with gratifying success, and after a time was enabled to purchase a partly improved farm in Pike Township, upon which he moved, and where he resided until his death in 1885. He had lived to see Stark County, Ohio, develop from a wilderness to a wealthy and populous country. The maiden name of the mother of our subject was Lydia Holm. She was born in Ohio, and now resides on the family estate in Pike Township, Stark County, where she enjoys the confidence and esteem of a large circle of friends. Henry and Lydia Stands were the parents of fourteen children, of whom ten were reared to maturity.

The subject of this sketch was reared on his father's farm, and commenced to assist him in his labors as soon as he was old enough to be of any use. He continued to reside with his parents until his marriage, when he struck out for himself. He rented land in the neighborhood of his old home, and operated it as a farm until the year 1878, when he removed to Kansas. Although his native State was endeared to him by many ties of kindred and the hallowed associations of his youth and manhood, yet as it offered him no prospect of obtaining a new home for himself in the future, he concluded to sever the chain binding him to his native soil, and seek a home in the great and glorious West, where he could call the land his own. Hearing good reports of Sumner County, he decided to locate in it, and has never had occasion to regret his choice, as it has fully met his expectations in every respect.

The removal of Mr. Stands and his family was made from his native State to his new home, via railroad to Wichita, then the terminus of the line in that direction, and from that point to their final location by teams. Upon his arrival in the county he bought one hundred and sixty acres of slightly improved land, including the southwest quarter of section 20, Jackson Township. Energy, industry, and good management have secured for our subject a large measure of success, and he has been enabled to add by purchase to his original tract of land, until he now has a fine farm of four hundred acres, all good land and enclosed by a thrifty and beautiful hedge. He has erected good buildings and planted fruit and shade trees, which will in the near future amply reward him for his labor in their behalf. He manages his business of a general farmer and stock-raiser with intelligence and skill, and can show as good land and improvements as can be found in the county.

In 1874 our subject and Miss Christina Kahler were united in the bonds of matrimony. Mrs. Stands was born in Tuscarawas County, Ohio, and is a lady well-fitted by nature and education to be the wife of a good man. She is an earnest Christian worker, and exemplifies the precepts of religion in her daily life, and as a consequence enjoys the respect and esteem of all with whom she comes in contact. She is a member of the United Brethren Church, and is a regular and devoted attendant upon all its services. Mr. Stands is a Republican in politics, and exerts his influence for the success of his party. Mr. and Mrs. Stands have been charged with the rearing of six children, named respectively: Bertha E., Ollie M., Irving S., Della N., John H., and Myrtle L.

THOMAS A. DAVIS has been a resident of this county since 1876, and is the owner of a pleasant and well-improved farm on section 30, Sumner Township, and engaged in general farming and stock-raising. In addition to his agricultural employments, he finds time for labors in behalf of the cause of Christianity, and is the local Baptist preacher at Mayfield. He was Justice of the Peace for a number of years, and has high repute among his fellow-citizens as a just Judge, a kindly neighbor, and a worthy citizen.

The ancestral line of our subject is traced through a number of generations of North Carolinians to English ancestors. His grandfather was Daniel Davis, and his father William Davis, who was born in 1819, and is now living in Jackson County, Mo., whence he removed in 1845. He is engaged in tilling the soil, and has an honorable record as a private during the late war. The mother of our subject was born in 1818, to Thomas and Mary Winfrey, and was christened Nancy. Her father was a farmer, and like her husband's family, she and hers were natives of North Carolina. She also is still living. The parental family comprised Thomas, Elvira, Caleb J., John S., and Mary J.; all are still living except Caleb J., who died at the age of seventeen.

Mr. Davis was born September 6, 1839, in North Carolina, and being but a lad when his parents removed to Missouri, his rearing and education were completed in the latter State. He finished his course of study in 1858, and taught school until 1861, when he determined to devote his strength, and his life if need be, to the cause of the Union. He therefore enlisted in Company I, Second Missouri Cavalry, and served his country faithfully until June, 1865, when he was honorably discharged

and mustered out of the service. The principal battles in which he participated, were Lexington, Lone Jack, Prairie Grove, and Helena, and in many minor engagements, brilliant cavalry dashes and scouting exploits, he bore a gallant part.

At the conclusion of the war Mr. Davis adopted the occupation of farming, and until the year 1870 was thus engaged in Missouri, and he then entered upon a mercantile career, pursuing it until the fall of 1876, when he pre-empted the land upon which he yet resides, and again turned his attention to the pursuit of agriculture.

On January 14, 1860, Mr. Davis was united in marriage with Miss Emily S. House, a native of Jackson County, Mo., whose natal day was October 17, 1843. She was a daughter of Samuel and Julia House, who were natives of Kentucky and North Carolina, respectively. Mrs. Davis breathed her last July 30, 1884, leaving six children to mourn the loss of a loving mother, and to whom she left as a heritage, the knowledge of her kindness and consistent Christian character. She was a member of the Baptist Church. Her children are named respectively: Caleb S., Julia A., John H., William, Henry J., and Isaac W. By a second marriage, Mr. Davis has one child, DeForest, who is now living in Missouri.

FREDERICK S. PHILLIPS is making a specialty of fruit-growing and has, at his pleasant homestead on section 10, a growing orchard comprising one hundred apple trees, besides pear trees, an abundance of raspberries, blackberries, grapes, strawberries and other small fruits. For eight years after coming to his present location he followed the trade of a blacksmith, and had a shop on his farm. Gradually he gave up this business to engage in other departments of labor in connection with his farm, which consists of forty acres of well-improved land.

Of sturdy English ancestry, our subject was born March 30, 1827, in Hunterdon County, N. J. His parents were Jonathan and Sarah Phillips, likewise natives of New Jersey, of which State their forefathers were among the very earliest settlers. It is said that to these early representatives of the Phillips family were issued during Queen Anne's reign, deeds to large tracts of land in New Jersey. Jonathan Phillips was twice married, our subject being the eldest child by the second marriage. He was reared to manhood in his native State, and until the age of sixteen was mainly occupied in the details of farm life. At that time, however, he commenced to learn the blacksmith's trade, serving a four years' apprenticeship, and afterward following it in New Jersey for a period of thirty years. His early education was received in subscription schools, and was limited to the mere rudiments of knowledge.

Mr. Phillips is numbered among those valiant patriots who offered their lives in their country's defense. In 1862 he enlisted in Company G. Thirtieth New Jersey Infantry, which was incorporated with the Army of the Potomac. He participated in the battles of Chancellorville, Fredericksburg, Gettysburg, and other minor engagements. He enlisted as Second Lieutenant, serving in this capacity during his active campaign of nine months. He endured with hardihood the severe marches accompanying army life, for, being of a sturdy frame and compact build, he suffered less from hardships and exposure than most of the soldiers.

On the 20th of January, 1849, our subject was united in marriage with Miss Caroline Johnson, who, like himself, was a native of Hunterdon County, N. J., and was born October 26, 1827. She was a daughter of Asher and Mary A. Johnson, of the same State, and of an old family probably of English origin. Eight children were born to Mr. and Mrs. Phillips, of whom five survive, namely: Emma A., wife of John Watson, of Trenton, N. J.; William, a resident of Stockton, N. J.; Eva, wife of George Bruner, and a resident of Colorado; Sallie, who married Charles Gartner, of Mulvane, Kan.; Lewis, who lives in Colorado. The deceased are—Mary H., Asher J., and one who died in infancy.

Leaving his Eastern home in January, 1877, Mr. Phillips cast his lot among the people of Sumner

County, Kan., where his family followed him the ensuing March. By dint of toil and good business management, he has made for himself and family a comfortable home, and there is passing the close of a well-spent life. He has gained the respect of the community by his upright, consistent character, and is associated with the Grand Army of the Republic, at Mulvane. Politically, he affiliates with the Republican party, and is an earnest worker in the interests of anything calculated to benefit the county where he makes his home.

EDWARD C. JEFFRIES. Nineteen years ago there might have been seen the team and wagon of an emigrant slowly making its way across the country to Palestine Township in the month of July, and which upon arriving on the northeast quarter of section 6, halted and the travelers alighting, proceeded to look around them in contemplation of that which they expected would be their future home. The outlook was not remarkably encouraging, being a broad stretch of open country over which wild animals roamed at will and which had been scarcely disturbed by the foot of a white man. Upon the land selected there stood a little 12x14 frame house which had been put up by some discouraged "squatter" but into which Edward C. Jeffries and his family soon removed and proceeded to make the best of circumstances.

The Jeffries family, as may be supposed, were not over-stocked with this world's goods, although Mr. Jeffries had paid for his claim the snug sum of $500. He was of a hospitable disposition, which quality was shared by his excellent wife, and that little house during that first fall sheltered from time to time four other families who sojourned there temporarily. Neighbors were few and far between and in the fall of 1872 Mr. Jeffries went only about twelve miles west of the present site of Belle Plaine to kill buffalo for his winter meat, laying low as many as five or six in an hour. Large herds of these animals then roamed over that section of country. Upon one of these expeditions while out hunting Mr. Jeffries' attention was attracted by a movement in the grass and he discovered the head of an Indian who was stealthily watching his movements. The savage upon being discovered mounted his pony and rode at a rapid rate over the hill, pointing an arrow in his bow at the white man. Mr. Jeffries leveled his repeating rifle on his threatening foe and they each came to a halt, thus regarding each other and each waiting for further demonstrations. Finally the Indian wheeled and left, much to the relief of the peaceable white man.

In due time there was constructed from this primitive tract of land one of the best farms in Palestine Township, presenting now the picture of a pleasant country home where peace and plenty abound. The first dwelling has been supplanted by a commodious frame residence, near which have been built a substantial barn, corn cribs, granaries and other necessary structures, while Mr. Jeffries has planted over a thousand fruit trees, including apple, peach, pear and cherry, besides blackberry and grape vines. The farm is mostly enclosed and divided with hedge fencing. No more fitting monument could be erected to him whose perseverance and energy have met with such ample reward.

The subject of this notice was born in Wood County, Ohio, May 12, 1836, and was reared there on a farm, acquiring a practical education in the district school. His parents, George and Rebecca (Buse) Jeffries, were natives of Pennsylvania and born near the town of Little York. At an early date they removed to Harrison County, Ohio, with their respective parents and endured all the hardships incident to pioneer life. Later the mother became a resident of Wood County, that State where her death took place in 1864. Prior to the removal there they had sojourned for a short time in Cincinnati, where the father died in 1848. The mother was a consistent member of the United Brethren Church. The paternal grandfather, Samuel Jeffries, was of Scotch ancestry and it is believed was born in the Land of the Thistle.

Edward C. Jeffries remained a resident of the Buckeye State until after the outbreak of the Civil War and at an early period in the conflict enlisted as a Union soldier in Company K, Sixty-seventh

Ohio Infantry, being mustered in as a private November 7, 1861. He served three years, then veteranized, and on March 18, 1865, was given a First Lieutenant's commission with which rank he served until the close of the war. Prior to this he had acted as Commissary Sergeant. He participated in many important battles, including the fight at Winchester, met the enemy in the Shenandoah Valley near New Market, and in front of Richmond and was at the battle of Black Water, Morris Island, Chapin Farm, Bermuda Hundred, Petersburg, and had the satisfaction of witnessing Lee's surrender at Appomattox. His company was held afterward about twenty miles north of Richmond until December 7, 1865, when they repaired to City Point where Mr. Jeffries received his honorable discharge, and the company later was disbanded at Columbus, Ohio.

Mr. Jeffries returned home without a scratch, able to enter at once upon the duties of a civilian. Esteeming one of the first of these duties to be the establishment of a home, he had prior to this taken unto himself a wife and helpmate, Miss Ellen North, to whom he was wedded April 24, 1865. This lady was a native of his own county and the daughter of William and Matilda (Skinner) North, the father a native of Philadelphia, Pa., and the mother of Perry County, Ohio. Mr. and Mrs. North became residents of Wood County with their respective parents early in life and during the pioneer days of that region. Grandfather Joseph North and his wife, Catherine, it is believed were both natives of Pennsylvania. Upon emigrating to Ohio, they settled in the heavy timber among Indians, bear, wolves, wild hogs and other animals, and they laboriously constructed a homestead from the wilderness. There they spent their last days. On the maternal side, Grandfather John and Elizabeth (Oakley) Skinner, likewise natives of the Keystone State, were early pioneers of Perry County, Ohio, whence later they removed to Wood County and underwent an experience similar to that of the North family. Those courageous spirits have long since passed away and it becomes the duty of their descendants to hold their names in remembrance.

In the spring of 1867 Mr. Jeffries removed with

his little family to Benton County, Iowa, where they sojourned until coming to Kansas. There has been born to them one child only, a son, George L., who, with his parents, is a member of the Methodist Episcopal Church, in which Mr. Jeffries is one of the pillars and officiates as Trustee. Mrs. Jeffries' family, as far back as she has the records, were all identified with this religious denomination. Her parents accompanied her to Kansas, remaining with her until their decease, the father dying November 29, 1880, and the mother February 19, 1881. Although usually fortunate Mr. Jeffries has met with reverses like most other men. In 1871 his crops were destroyed by the grasshoppers which put the family upon very short rations for the following winter and spring. Money likewise was scarce, and during the fall of that year Mr. Jeffries hauled corn from Ft. Reno, thus making money enough to meet his expenses.

Politically, Mr. Jeffries affiliates with the Republican party. He has served as Treasurer of Palestine Township since 1887, and as Trustee from 1884 to 1886. He belongs to Belle Plaine Post, No. 337, G. A. R., and his son to the Sons of Veterans. Mrs. Jeffries is an efficient worker in the Relief Corps.

~~~~~~~~~~~~~~~~~~~~~~~~~~~~~~~~~~~~~

ANIEL GILCHRIST, a farmer and stockraiser of Belle Plaine Township and the owner of two hundred and sixty acres of land therein, is a native of Caithness Shire, Scotland, where his eyes first opened to the light April 10, 1838. He is the son of William and Margaret (Dunbar) Gilchrist and is the oldest living member of the parental family. An older brother, William, is deceased; John lives also in Belle Plaine Township; Alexander is deceased; and Margaret is the wife of J. W. Dand, of Belle Plaine. The mother now lives in that town, but the father departed this life in 1883.

The early years of our subject were spent in the usual occupations and recreations of boyhood, and

at the age of sixteen years he began an apprenticeship at the carpenter's and joiner's trade, serving four years. He subsequently pursued that occupation as a journeyman and followed it for a period of about thirty years. On May-day, 1860, he was united in marriage with Miss Mary Brims, a daughter of Donald and Catherine Brims, who was born in Scotland in 1828. A son William, born July 1, 1861, came to bless this union. The wife and mother participated in her husband's fortunes until November 25, 1889, when she breathed her last, leaving behind her a wealth of love and affection, and greatly missed both by her family and the people who knew her so well. She was a consistent member of the Presbyterian Church.

Mr. Gilchrist emigrated to America in 1861, passage being taken at Glasgow, on the steamer "Caledonia," of the Anchor Line, which after an ocean voyage of sixteen days made a landing at Quebec, Canada. Thence Mr. Gilchrist went to Montreal, where he followed his trade for four years, after which he removed to Boston, Mass., residing near that city two years, working in a sash, door and blind factory. In 1865, he became a citizen of Chicago, Ill., and during the following years was employed as a journeyman carpenter in that city. His next removal was to Sumner County, Kan., and his first settlement was on Cow Skin Creek, on section 19. That location was his home for four years, after which he settled on section 25, Belle Plaine Township, which has since been his home.

The home farm of Mr. Gilchrist comprises one hundred and sixty acres, which at the time of his settlement upon it was in a primitive condition with the exception of having had the sod turned on about twenty-five acres. There was no house whatever on the land and the condition in which the estate is now seen has resulted from the energy and hard labor of the owner, and his son, who from his boyhood proved an efficient helper. They endured the hardships subject to pioneer life, the devoted wife and mother being a helpmate and counselor, and encouraging the father and son in every effort.

Mr. Gilchrist has served for three terms as Treasurer of School District No. 76. In politics he is a

Democrat while his son is an equally stanch Republican. The sturdy elements of the Scotch character have been well manifested in the career of Mr. Gilchrist, and it is a pleasure to his many friends to know that he is prospering in his worldly affairs, and to feel that he is interested in all movements which pertain to the public good in the section of which he has been so long a worthy resident.

THOMAS N. CORNWELL. A mixed population has been blended together very harmoniously in the settlement of this county, men having come from nearly all parts of the United States. The subject of this notice, one of the well-to-do farmers of Palestine Township and comfortably located on section 5, is a native of Old Virginia and was born in Fauquier County, August 31, 1832. About six years later his parents, Benjamin and Nancy (Grant) Cornwell, removed to Madison County, Ohio, locating on a farm in the heavy timber, or upon land which the father, by the exercise of great industry and perseverance transformed into a farm. He felled the heavy timber, grubbed out and burned the stumps, plowed, harrowed and sowed, and this process repeated season after season in due time placed the family in comfortable circumstances.

Amid these scenes young Cornwell was reared to man's estate. He assisted his father in the development of the farm, remaining under the home roof until 1854, being then a youth of twenty-two years. In the meantime, in 1853, the mother had passed away. In 1856, Benjamin Cornwell emigrated to DeWitt County, Ill., and died the following year. Prior to this, in 1854, Thomas N. had gone to Illinois, of which State he remained a resident until 1880. He there met his fate in the person of Miss Margaret James, to whom he was married in 1858. This lady was born July 26, 1837, in Fayette County, Ohio, and was the daughter of William and Susan (Belford) James, who removed from Ohio to DeWitt County, Ill., during the early settlement of the Prairie State. They

there spent the remainder of their lives. The grandfather, William James, emigrated from Maryland to Ohio at an early date and died there. On the maternal side Grandfather William Belford, removed from Virginia to Illinois, likewise in pioneer times, and there he died.

Mr. Cornwell prosecuted farming in Illinois until the fall of 1880, then disposing of his interests in that region came to Kansas and invested his capital in his present farm of two hundred and forty acres. With the exception of an old box house, which had been erected by some pioneer who had become discouraged and abandoned it, there were no improvements upon the place. Mr. Cornwell's first business was to provide a shelter for his family, and he then began at first principles in the construction of a farm. He has been greatly prospered in his labors, bringing the soil to a good state of cultivation, planting fruit and shade trees, erecting buildings and bringing about the other improvements naturally suggested to the enterprising individual. He and his family are now domiciled in a fine, large frame dwelling, a view of which appears in connection with this sketch. Adjacent to the residence is a substantial barn and other good buildings, an orchard of about five acres, and there are also twenty acres of timber which has chiefly grown up since he came here.

The household circle of Mr. and Mrs. Cornwell was completed by the birth of nine children, seven of whom are living, viz: Albert, Stephen, Alvin, Elmer, James, Anna and Ida. The two deceased died in infancy. The wife and mother departed this life February 4, 1884, at the homestead in Palestine Township; she was forty-six years of age, and her death cast a gloom over the neighborhood. Mr. Cornwell formed a second matrimonial alliance March 17, 1886, the lady being Mrs. Ruth E. (Hatfield) Shay, who was born September 9, 1840, in La Porte County, Ind., her parents being Moses and Nancy (Christy) Hatfield, natives of Virginia and Ohio respectively. They removed to Indiana at an early day, but after the late war removed to Missouri, where the mother died, aged about sixty-six years. The father is still living in Harrison County, Mo., and has now reached the advanced age of eighty-six years. Mrs. Cornwell was first

FARM RESIDENCE OF T. N. CORNWELL, SEC.5. PALESTINE TP, SUMNER CO. KAN.

FARM RESIDENCE OF Wᴹ A. DARBY, SEC. 2. BELLE BLAINE TP, SUMNER CO. KAN.

FARM RESIDENCE OF ISAAC VANCUREN, SEC.8, PALESTINE TP, SUMNER CO. KANS.

married, January 7, 1858, to Isaiah Shay, the ceremony being performed in Tazewell County, Ill. Their five children were named, respectively; Kittie, Ira, Mary, Rachael and Iva. Kittie died near Belle Plaine in 1887. All are married and have families, with the exception of Ira who makes his home in Palestine Township.

Mr. and Mrs. Cornwell belong to the Christian Church, attending services in Belle Plaine, and in which our subject serves as a Deacon. In Illinois he was an Elder. He has always been interested in educational matters, believing in giving to the young all the advantages, fitting them to become useful and intelligent members of society. He has served as Treasurer most of the time since coming to Palestine Township. In DeWitt County, Ill., he represented Texas Township in the County Board of Supervisors a number of years. He also in Illinois identified himself with the Independent Order of Odd Fellows, and he is a charter member of Belle Plaine Lodge, No. 498, and the Encampment at Belle Plaine. The paternal grandfather of our subject was Payton Cornwell, a native of Virginia, in which State his father located upon coming to America from England. On the maternal side his grandfather, Isaac Grant, was of Scotch ancestry and died in Virginia.

ISAAC VANCUREN. The subject of this notice holds a prominent position in the agricultural community of Palestine Township, and is successfully cultivating two hundred and forty acres of good land, pleasantly located on section 8. As a farmer, he is thorough and skillful, and as a member of the community, is held in high respect. By birth, he is an Ohio man, a native of Belmont County, and was born October 29, 1839. When a mere boy, his parents, Cornelius and Catherine (Hagen) Vancuren, changed their residence from Belmont to Hocking County, where they spent the remainder of their lives. The mother first passed away, being then sixty years old. Cornelius Vancuren lived to the advanced age of eighty

years. Both were church members, worthy and conscientious people who lived at peace with their neighbors and enjoyed the respect of all who knew them. The father, politically, was a Democrat, and had served as a soldier in the war of 1812.

Mr. Vancuren was reared to man's estate in Hocking County, Ohio, and when ready to establish domestic ties, was wedded, in March, 1849, to Miss Eliza A., daughter of Solomon and Mary A. (Flenner) Yantes. This lady was born in Pickaway County, Ohio, but her parents later removed to Hocking County, where they spent the closing years of their lives, dying in the faith of the Lutheran Church. The paternal grandfather, Henry Yantes, was born, it is supposed, in Germany. Both he and his wife, Catherine, died in Pickaway County, Ohio. On the mother's side, Grandfather George Flenner, with his wife, Elizabeth, died in Sandusky County, Ohio.

Mr. and Mrs. Vancuren lived on a farm in Hocking County, Ohio, until the spring of 1865, then removed to Shelby County, Ill., locating there also upon a farm, and remaining three years, when they removed to Macon County, where they remained until February, 1877. Their next removal was to this county. Mr. Vancuren at once purchased one hundred and sixty acres of land, which is now included in his present farm. Later he added to his landed possessions, until he has now two hundred and forty acres, all in productive condition and devoted to general agriculture. The family first occupied a small house, and beyond a few acres of ground having been plowed, this was the only improvement upon the place. The nearest market was at Wichita, to which place the farmers of this region conveyed their produce overland with teams. Mr. Vancuren labored industriously in the construction of his homestead, and its present condition indicates to what good purpose he employed his time. Besides the cultivation of the soil and the erection of buildings, he planted a grove of forest trees and numbers of apple trees, besides the smaller fruits. The family enjoy all the comforts and many of the luxuries of life.

Seven children came to bless the union of Mr. and Mrs. Vancuren, all of whom are still spared to them. The eldest born, a daughter, Catherine, is the wife of Anthony Hahn, and they live in this county; Mary J. is the wife of James L. Vaughan, of Winfield; Elizabeth, Mrs. Benjamin Aurbert, lives in Dalton, Ill.; Rebecca J. is the wife of Henry Graban of Washington; John and William remain at home with their parents; Harriet A. is the wife of William Daily, and they live in Winfield. Mr. and Mrs. Vancuren are connected with the Christian Church at Belle Plaine, and occupy a good position in their community.

The paternal grandfather of Mr. Vancuren was a Tory during Revolutionary times, and after the war was over, settled in New York State, where it is supposed he spent his last days. On his mother's side, Grandfather David Hagen, it is supposed, was born in Ireland. He lived in Pennsylvania many years, and died there. On another page of this volume may be found a view of Mr. Vancuren's residence.

---·--+·❈❈·+-·---

ILLIAM ALFRED DARBY. Here and there we find a man of advanced thought, ahead of his time, keeping himself well posted upon the march of events, and taking a warm interest in the various enterprises calculated to benefit the world in general. Mr. Darby is one of the most public spirited men of Belle Plaine Township, and is a farmer by occupation, operating one hundred and sixty acres of well-developed land on section 2. He came to this county in the spring of 1871, from Independence, this State, and during his eighteen years residence among the people of this community, has fully established himself in their confidence and esteem.

Mr. Darby was born in West Virginia, March 18, 1812, and when a child, was taken by his parents to Richland County, Ohio. His boyhood and youth were spent amid the quiet pursuits of farm life, and he acquired his education in the common school. The family left the Buckeye State about 1860, removing to Logan County, Ill., and later crossing the Mississippi, took up their abode in Independence, this State. William A. remained there one winter, then coming to this county, pre-

empted one hundred and sixty acres of land—that which constitutes his present farm—and where he has since resided. This was then a tract of wild land, without any improvements, and it has taken no small amount of labor and capital to bring it to its present condition. The results of perseverance and industry have been illustrated in a marked degree in the labors of Mr. Darby, who is now in possession of one of the most desirable homes in this part of the county.

Mr. Darby came to this section an unmarried man, but in due time formed the acquaintance of Miss Angeline Lawless, to whom he was wedded in Belle Plaine Township, April 25, 1875. Mrs. Darby was born in Russell County, Ky., April 5th, 1855, and is the daughter of James and Nancy (Cook) Lawless, who are now living in Harmon Township. The young people began the journey of life together at their own home, and toiled mutually in gathering around themselves the conveniences and comforts of modern life. Mr. Darby is a reader, and keeps himself posted upon political events, giving his cordial support to the Republican party.

The father of our subject was John O. Darby, who married Miss Sarah Neal; they were natives of Virginia and Pennsylvania respectively. They became the parents of eleven children, and spent their last days in Richland County, Ohio.

Among other lithographic views of well-developed farms in Sumner County, we present that of Mr. Darby, with some of its improvements and principal buildings.

❧─·0·─·─·❈❈❈·─·─·0·─❧

ESLEY S. NORTH. This gentleman ranks among the leading farmers of Palestine Township, being the owner of eighty acres of choice land on section 32. This land has been thoroughly improved and embellished with good buildings, including a neat modern dwelling, with stables, corncribs, etc.; adjacent to them is an orchard of five acres, with an abundance of the smaller fruits. Mr. North makes a specialty of stock-rais-ing, principally Poland-China swine. He is amply worthy of a representation in this work as a thor-ough and skillful agriculturist and a useful mem-ber of the community.

A native of Wood County, Ohio, Mr. North was born February 5, 1838, and spent his early years learning the arts of agriculture. His parents, Will-iam and Matilda (Skinner) North, were natives re-spectively of Germantown, Pa., and Perry County, Ohio. Each emigrated with their parents at an early date to Wood County, Ohio. The paternal grandparents of our subject were Joseph and Cath-erine (North) North, and on his mother's side his grandparents were John and Catherine (Oakley) Skinner. They all took up their abode in the Buckeye State about 1836, among Indians and wild animals, the latter including bears, wild cats, wolves and other dangerous creatures. Each fam-ily put up a little log cabin and began the con-struction of a farm from the heavy timber at a time when the nearest settlement was forty miles away.

To the above-mentioned settlement these pion-eers had also to repair in order to get their milling done, traveling laboriously through the heavy tim-ber where scarcely a trail sometimes was discernable. There was a little trading post at Perrysburg, about twelve miles distant, where dry goods could be procured. They took up a portion of canal land, paying to the Government $1.25 per acre, and im-proved their farms with the aid of rude imple-ments. There their children were born and reared, and there all the grandparents died. The land which they thus reclaimed from the wilderness is now valued at over $100 per acre.

The subject of this sketch upon reaching man's estate was married in his native county, July 1, 1860, to Miss Amelia M., daughter of Michael and Fanny (Payne) Moore. Six years later leaving the Buckeye State they came this side of the Missis-sippi, locating in Benton County, Iowa, Mr. North purchased land upon which he operated until the fall of 1871. His next removal was to this county and he pre-empted one hundred and sixty acres of land, a tract of wild prairie, which is now included in his present farm. In those days about a day's

drive west there was found an abundance of buf-falo, and other wild animals infested the country. Occasionally a buffalo would be seen in Palestine Township. Mr. North, with a company of his neighbors, frequently went hunting in the fall, kill-ing buffalo for their winter's meat, upon which the early settlers lived almost entirely. Deer and an-telopes were still numerous in this part of the coun-try.

Mr. North and his family, when first coming to this county, lived for a time in a small, frame house, 12x14 feet in dimensions. The nearest market was first at Newton and then at Wichita, where the set-tlers transported their grain and stock, following a trail across the open prairie. Religious services were held in private houses, until the Methodist built a church at Belle Plaine. Schools were con-ducted in vacant-claim shanties on the subscription plan.

Four children were born to Mr. and Mrs. North, the eldest of whom, a daughter, Emma, is now the wife of C. B. McAllister, of Belle Plaine Town-ship; Ossie died in 1879, when an interesting maiden of sixteen years; Alta and Daisy remain under the parental roof. Mr. and Mrs. North and their daughter, Emma, are members of the Pres-byterian Church. The family holds a good posi-tion in the community, and have an attractive home replete with all the comforts and conve-niences of modern life.

<hr>

MAJ. GEORGE W. DOUGHTY, Sr., Post-master of Dalton, was appointed to his present office in 1885, and is the only man who has been its incumbent since its estab-lishment. The following year, in February, 1886, he was appointed a Notary Public, and thus has sufficient business to keep him employed. He came to this point in 1884, and purchased twenty-five acres of land, upon which he proceeded to lay out a town, putting up first his own residence and a store building. The former was destroyed by fire on the morning of the 20th of November, entailing a loss of over $5,000. In due time, Mr. Doughty rebuilt, and now has a comfortable and well-appointed home. Among his fellow citizens he is regarded as a man of strict honesty, and he has been no unimportant factor in the development of Avon Township.

A native of Roane County, Tenn., the Major was born May 28, 1838, and was reared to man's estate under the home roof in that county. His father, Sampson Doughty, was a carpenter by trade, which he followed for thirty years at Lenoirs, Tenn. George spent his boyhood days in his native county, remaining there until a youth of nineteen years. Then going to Georgia, in company with his brothers, he settled near Resaca, where he engaged in the manufacture of agricultural implements until 1861.

The Rebellion now having broken out, and being surrounded as he was by the most ultra secessionists from the very commencement of the strife, and being one of the few men in the South who dared to express their Union sentiments, he at once became a target for all the fire-eating Southerners for miles around. For many months his life was a continual round of hair-breadth escapes and persecutions that would seem almost incredible if related at this day to those who did not witness, or have personal knowledge of, similar experiences during that terrible time when traitors sought to destroy the unity of the Nation. Going back to Tennessee, he joined the Union Army, being the only man from Gordon County, Ga., to enlist in the Federal forces. This was done in the month of March, 1863, young Doughty becoming a member of the Thirteenth Tennessee Cavalry, and being commissioned Major upon the organization of the regiment. He served as such until the 10th of March, 1865, when he resigned and returned to his native town to engage in the manufacture of leather. He sojourned there this time for seven years, then struck out for the Southwest, crossing the Mississippi, and going into Dennison, Tex. There he engaged in the lightning rod business for a period of twelve years and until coming to Kansas.

Maj. Doughty was married in Clinton, Tenn., January 21, 1868, to Miss Sallie Owen. This lady was a native of that place, and accompanied her husband to Texas, dying in Denison, November 13, 1881. She was a lady of many estimable qualities, and a member of the Baptist Church.

Maj. Doughty identified himself with the Masonic fraternity, in which he has risen to the Royal Arch degree, and he is a member in good standing of the Nathaniel Lyon Post, No. 5, G. A. R., at Dennison, Tex. In politics, he was formerly an Old Line Whig, but upon the abandonment of that party, cordially endorsed Republican principles. The Major, on the 19th of February, 1886, in alighting from a passenger train at Argentine, this State, on the Southern Kansas Railroad, was thrown down by the train, striking the steps and breaking his arm, which subsequently was amputated. He also sustained other serious injuries. He is a man genial and companionable in disposition, and makes friends wherever he goes. His name will be held in remembrance by the people in Avon Township long after he has been gathered to his fathers.

OHN L. PEGRAM. In his migrations it is seldom the lot of the biographer to meet as fine a couple as Mr. Pegram and his amiable and excellent wife. They occupy a high position, socially, in Dixon Township and have a pleasant and comfortable home in the shape of a well-developed farm on section 8. A career of prudent industry has made them financially well-to-do, and the sterling qualities of their characters, have drawn around them hosts of friends. They are among the pillars of the Methodist Episcopal Church at Argonia in which Mrs. Pegram is an especially faithful laborer, having charge of two classes in the Sunday-schools and doing good in other channels as opportunity presents.

A native of Guilford County, N. C., Mr. Pegram was born April 28, 1814, being the fifth child of Daniel and Jane (McMichael) Pegram, who were also natives of that State. They were reared and married in their native county where the father prosecuted farming, hiring colored people to do his work, as, although a Southern man, he was decidedly opposed to slavery, and would take no part in the ownership of human flesh. Politically, he was an old line Whig, and nearly all his life was a Class Leader in the Methodist Episcopal Church. He died in North Carolina in 1854, following the wife who had passed away the year previously. Five of the eight children comprising the original household are still living, the four besides John L., making their homes in Texas and North Carolina.

The subject of this sketch, having become orphaned by the death of his parents when a boy of eleven years, was obliged to look after himself and commenced working on a farm at $8 per month. He was thus employed until a youth of eighteen years and then, in 1862, during the second year of the war, was conscripted into Millett's Battalion of Infantry, State troops of the Confederate Army, and ineligible to go out of the State. He was thus held until June, 1864, much against his will, doing duty at Camp Instruction in Raleigh. Then, being allowed thirty days furlough, he was assigned to the Twenty-ninth North Carolina Infantry and under Gen. Joseph E. Johnston repaired to Kenesaw Mountain and for six days was under the hot fire between the Union troops and the Confederates. The latter then fell back to Atlanta, followed by Gen. Sherman. Young Pegram watched his opportunity and escaping from the ranks hid in the brush until both armies had passed him, leaving him inside the Union lines upon which he soon reported to Gen. Thomas. Shortly afterward he took the oath of allegiance at Chattanooga and remained with the Union troops until his release.

After the war was over Mr. Pegram emigrated to Bartholomew County, Ind., and in the vicinity of Hope, began working for a stockman. Shortly afterward, however, he removed to Tipton County, where he worked one season. We next find him at Kokomo, at which place he remained a resident for a period of twenty-one years, being engaged as clerk in an hotel part of the time and for eleven years was in the employ of the Panhandle Railroad. In 1881 he made a visit to his old home in North Carolina. Upon his return he located in Grant County, Ind., where he commenced farming, remaining there until 1887. In July of that year he came to Kansas and settled on the land from which

he has since constructed his present fine farm. In addition to general agriculture he is considerably interested in the breeding of horses and swine.

While a resident of Indiana, Mr. Pegram formed the acquaintance of Miss Eliza J. Reeder, to whom he was married October 1, 1877. This lady was born September 18, 1849, in Howard County, Ind., and is a daughter of James M. and Jane (Burbridge) Reeder, who were natives of Ohio. They emigrated to Indiana quite early and are still living being residents of Kokomo. They are quite aged, Mr. Reeder having been born in 1805, and his wife, Jane, in 1819. There was born to them a family of nine children, three of whom are living.

To Mr. and Mrs. Pegram there has been born one child only, a son, Rephelius, August 1, 1878, at Kokomo, Ind. Parents and son are connected with the Methodist Episcopal Church, in which Mr. Pegram is Steward and Trustee. He is also Chaplain of the Farmers' Alliance. He takes an active interest in politics, and while a resident of Indiana was frequently sent as a delegate to the various Republican conventions, uniformly giving his support to this party. Mr. Pegram serves as Director in his school district. He was upon one occasion nominated Justice of the Peace, but declined the proposed honor. Mrs. Pegram comes from a good family, her maternal grandfather having been Judge William Burbridge, of Crawfordsville, Ind.

~~~·····ᐁᕒ~·ᐁᕒ~~~

ENRY F. HARBAUGH. Among the agriculturists of Greene Township, none are more worthy of representation in a volume of this kind than the above named gentleman, whose enterprising character, intelligent mind, and useful labors in the teacher's profession, as well as in the business which he is now following, places him in the front rank of the citizens of the county. He was born in Trenton, Tuscarawas County, Ohio, on the 1st of August, 1849, and was but three years old when his parents removed to Washington County, Iowa, where he grew to manhood. There he acquired a fundamental education in the common schools, supplementing it by an attendance at the High School, and becoming thoroughly versed in the common English branches.

The father of our subject, Eli Harbaugh, was a cabinet maker, and also carried on a farm, in the work of which our subject assisted as his strength would permit during his youth, and on which he labored several years after attaining his majority. The mother, whose maiden name was Catherine Engel, departed this life April 2, 1872, after having reared a family of eleven children, of whom our subject is the eldest. The father still survives, and is now a resident of Barber County, Kan.

At the age of twenty-five, he of whom we write, went to California with the intention of making that country his home, but not being as well satisfied with his surroundings there as he had anticipated he remained but two years and eight months, when he returned to Washington County, Iowa, and there remained until he became a citizen of Kansas. In that county he taught school during the winter seasons for several years, and also engaged in pedagogical labors during some of the summer terms. Since coming to this county he has taught two terms, and here, as in his former fields of labor, he has been successful in the work of instruction, and has been popular with pupils and parents.

In April, 1878, Mr. Harbaugh came to this county and purchased one hundred and sixty acres of land on section 20, Green Township, upon which he made his home, and where he now has one of the best improved farms in this section of the country. Since taking up his abode here he has added one hundred and sixty acres to his original purchase, and has made excellent improvements on the entire estate, his residence, barn and other buildings being especially good, adequate in size and numbers, and thoroughly first class in every respect. Mr. Harbaugh is engaged in general farming, and is quite an extensive dealer in stock, exhibiting a marked degree of enterprise in carrying on both branches of his employment.

The lady who ably presides in the home of Mr. Harbaugh, and who in her domestic affairs and elsewhere exhibits good judgment, a kindly spirit, and a marked intelligence, bore the maiden name of Lizzie Blattner, and was born in Washington County, Iowa, May 24, 1857. In her native county, March 10, 1880, she became the wife of Mr. Harbaugh, to whom she has borne four children: Nellie M., George E., William G. and John P. William G. died when a little more than twelve months old, and the others form a bright group by the family fireside.

In the fall of 1889, Mr. Harbaugh was elected Trustee of Greene Township, in which he has formerly held the office of Township Clerk. He has also been a member of the School Board, and evinces an earnest interest in the cause of education, as in other elevating and developing movements. He has taken quite an active part in political affairs, and is an ardent Prohibitionist. He is a Director and Treasurer of the Sumner County Farmers' Mutual Insurance Company, and is a member of the Farmers' Alliance. Mrs. Harbaugh was appointed Postmistress of Concord by ex-Postmaster Gen. Gresham, and has held the office since that time.

GEORGE PFEIFER, the subject of this notice, was born in Harrison Township, one and one-half miles west of Dayton, Montgomery County, Ohio, March 30, 1849. His father, Adam Pfeifer, was born and reared in Germany, and was the first member of his family to emigrate to America. He came to this country about the year 1840 and located in Montgomery County, Ohio. As he had been reared to agricultural pursuits he sought that kind of work and labored for farmers for some time receiving his pay monthly. Being economical in his habits he saved enough from his wages to begin for himself at the time of his marriage. He rented land for a few years but was soon enabled by good management and industry to buy a farm of his own. He purchased unimproved land in Madison Township and built a house into which he moved and then proceeded to make all the improvements customary at that time on the best farms.

As Mr. Pfeifer was able he bought small tracts adjoining his original purchase and after some years traded the whole place for an improved farm in Clay Township, the same county. He operated his new place some years then again traded, giving his farm in exchange for fourteen miles of turnpike extending from Dayton to Brookville, and known as the "Dayton and Wolf Creek turnpike." He retained possession of that property until his death. He also owned a house and lot in Trotwood, a village on the "pike," and that was the family residence at the time of his death in 1865. The maiden name of the mother of our subject was Mary Grim. She was born in Germany and came to America when a young lady. She lived in Montgomery County, Ohio, until her marriage which took place in that State. The parental family consisted of nine children, six of whom were daughters. They are all living and enjoying a fair degree of prosperity.

George Pfeifer was reared and educated in his native county and as soon as able to do so was put to work assisting his father on the farm. After the death of the latter our subject worked on farms for some time then bought an interest in a threshing machine and threshed for farmers in the neighborhood for four seasons. When not engaged at that he followed farming. In 1876 he rented a farm and operated it until 1879, when he removed to Kansas and rented land in Harvey County for one year then located in Sumner County. He purchased the place where he now resides, the northwest quarter of section 25, Jackson Township. There were some slight improvements made when it came into his possession and to that he has added until now he has an excellent farm of one hundred and sixty acres all fenced, well cultivated and good buildings erected. He has five acres in orchard trees and in all respects is prosperous and delighted with the country.

In 1876 Mr. Pfeifer was married to Miss Minnie Wogaman, a native of Madison Township, Montgomery County, Ohio. She is the daughter of Martin and Eliza (Bradenburg) Wogaman, and is an excellent woman in every respect. Mr. and Mrs.

Pfeifer are the parents of three children, named respectively—Clarence, Lena and Harry. They are worthy members of the Presbyterian Church. Mr. Pfeifer upholds the principles of the great Democratic party and takes quite an interest in its success.

Martin Wogaman, the father of Mrs. Pfeifer, was born in Montgomery County, Ohio, and his father, John Wogaman, was a native of Pennsylvania, and removed from there with his parents to Ohio during the early years of the settlement of Montgomery County, and was reared in the county in which his parents located and there married Miss Mary Burkett. Mrs. John Wogaman was a native of North Carolina and accompanied her parents to Ohio when quite young. The great-grandfather of Mrs. Pfeifer bought a tract of Government land nine miles west of the present site of Dayton. It was heavily timbered and difficult to clear but he succeeded in making a good farm out of it and resided on it until his death. For many years Cincinnati was their nearest market and depot of supplies. Deer, bears, wolves, wildcats and other game were plentiful and rather undesirable acquaintances except when laid low by the huntsman's unerring aim.

John Wogaman inherited land from his father-in-law and added to it by purchase until he had quite an extensive estate. He resided on his farm until his death, which occurred in 1883, when he was nearly eighty years of age. The father of Mrs. Pfeifer was reared on his parents' farm and when grown to maturity took a wife in the same county and made his home on a farm in Jackson Township, Montgomery County, where he resides at present. He owns a good farm of one hundred and forty acres, all under superior cultivation and well improved in every respect. The mother of Mrs. Pfeifer was born in Dayton, Ohio.

The grandfather of Mrs. Pfeifer, John Bradenburg, removed from Maryland to Dayton where he settled and worked at his trade, for he was a mechanic, and made his home there during the remainder of his life. The maiden name of his wife was Mary Suman. She was a model wife and mother and her last days were passed in the peaceful enjoyment of her children's love and care. The

mother of Mrs. Pfeifer has survived the storms of
life to the present time and bids fair to live to be a
blessing to her descendants for many years to come.
Mr. Pfeifer is a stanch Democrat and highly esteemed in the community in which he lives. He is
a member of the Farmer's Alliance, an organization
that has been of much service to the tillers of the
soil, especially in the West where means of transportation are limited.

JEREMIAH D. GREENMAN. The beautiful farm which is owned and occupied by
the above-named gentleman, comprises three
hundred and twenty acres of the finest land
in Caldwell Township. Everything about the place
denotes the present prosperity and the past industry
of the owner, and still further betokens that it is
the home of an intelligent and refined family.
Among the many improvements upon the estate
a fine orchard is noticeable, and is a profitable as
well as an attractive feature.

The paternal ancestry of Mr. Greenman were of
Welsh stock and Rhode Island was the birthplace
of more than one generation. The grandparents,
Jeremiah and Mary (Eddy) Greenman were natives
of Providence, whence about the year 1808 they
moved to Washington County, Ohio. The grandfather had been a seafaring man, served in the
Colonial army during the Revolutionary war, and
drew a pension for injuries received in the service.
The next in the direct line of descent was another
Jeremiah Greenman, who was also born in Providence, R. I., his natal day being August 8, 1794.
Being but a lad when his parents moved to Ohio,
he grew to manhood there and, November 26, 1818,
married Miss Letitia McCoy, who was born in
Washington County, June 26, 1799. On June 1,
1836, this couple started for the West, and, embarking
in a family boat, floated down the Ohio River to its
mouth, thence going by steamboat to Pekin, Ill., and
continuing their journey by teams to what is now
Waynesville, Ill. They shortly afterward entered two
hundred acres of land in what is now Padua Town-

ship, McLean County, where Mr. Greenman died
October 17, 1843, his wife surviving until September 5, 1878. The father was interred in Dawson's
Cemetery, at Old Town, McLean County, Ill., while
the mother lies buried in the cemetery on our subject's farm. They were not members of any
church but were remarkable for the integrity and
correct principles which governed their lives.
Their family comprised nine children, as follows:
Thomas M., Sarah E., Emeline, Henry C., George
W., Elizabeth J., Jeremiah D., Mary L. and a son
who died in infancy.

The birth of the subject of this biography occurred in McLean County, Ill., November 20, 1839,
and he was reared on his father's farm there, receiving a common school education and a practical
training in the duties of farm life. When the war
cloud arose in 1861, no State was more prompt
than Illinois to respond to the call for troops, and
young Greenman with hundreds of his compeers
eagerly laid aside the arts of peace and took up
arms in his country's cause. Joining the Union
army as a private in Company K, Eighth Illinois
Infantry, in 1861, he participated in the battles of
Ft. Henry, Ft. Donelson, Shiloh, and in the other
work of his regiment during a period of fourteen
months, when, owing to disability, he was discharged. As soon as his health was restored, he
began to look eagerly toward the front with a desire to again participate in the work which was
going on, and in 1865 he enlisted as a member of
Company B, One Hundred and Fiftieth Illinois Infantry, in which he served until February, 1866,
when he was discharged at Atlanta, Ga.

There being no further need of his services on
the field of battle, Mr. Greenman returned to his
native county in Illinois, and remained there until
1876, when he removed to Kansas. He pre-empted
one hundred and sixty acres of land and subsequently added an equal amount by purchase, making up the acreage before mentioned, which he has
so conducted as to merit his reputation as one of
the leading farmers of the township. He began
his battle in life with no capital except what nature
had bestowed upon him, and his prosperity has
been gained without financial assistance, being due
entirely to his own efforts and the co-operation of

RESIDENCE OF DR. W. F. WILLHOITE, CORBIN, SUMNER CO. KAN.

CALDWELL.

FARM RESIDENCE OF J. D. GREENMAN, SEC. 32. CALDWELL TP., SUMNER CO. KAN.

his worthy wife, who in her own department has shown herself a capable manager.

Mrs. Greenman was born in McLean County, Ill., May 1, 1843, and bore the maiden name of Sarah E. Vanscyoe. She is a daughter of Perry O. and Mary (Newcomb) Vanscyoe and her union with our subject was celebrated on Christmas Day, 1863. Eight children have come to gladden the house of Mr. and Mrs. Greenman with their affection and growing intelligence. They have been christened Perry D., Alvin H., John L., Millie E., Mary C., Jeremiah M., Mary L., and William L.

Mr. Greenman belongs to the Independent Order of Odd Fellows, the Grand Army of the Republic, and to the Republican party. An honorable man, upright in his dealings with all with whom he comes in contact, and kindly in every social and domestic relation, he well deserves the high reputation which he has among his fellow citizens.

An additional feature of interest to the readers of this volume is the lithographic view of the residence owned and occupied by Mr. Greenman.

ILLIS F. WILLHOITE, M.D., in addition to a successful practice as a physician and surgeon, is also conducting a thriving trade in drugs and medicines. He is a regular graduate of the Physio-Medical College of Indianapolis, Ind., from which he emerged in 1883 with the proper credentials, and began the practice of his profession at Colfax, Ill. A year later, in July, 1884, he came to Kansas, locating in Corbin, of which he has since been a resident. He has a full understanding of the duties of his profession, and is building up a successful business.

The subject of this notice was born in McLean County, Ill., January 5, 1859, and is the son of Lewis J. and Mary A. (Willhoite) Willhoite, who were natives of Owen County, Ky. The father was born April 24, 1829, and lived in the Blue Grass State until a man of twenty-five years. In 1851, he changed his residence to McLean County, Ill., where he still remains. His life occupation has

been that of a farmer, by which he has accumulated considerable property. For the last twenty-five years he has been a member in good standing of the Christian Church. Politically, he is an uncompromising Democrat. The paternal grandfather, Lewis Willhoite, Sr., was likewise a native of Kentucky, and the son of John Willhoite, who was born in Virginia. The latter served as a soldier in the Revolutionary War. The family traces its ancestry to Germany, and was first represented in this country during the early Colonial days.

Mrs. Mary A. Willhoite was born April 27, 1829, and was the daughter of Willis C. Willhoite, being distantly related to her husband. There were born to them five children, viz: Maria I., Henry L., Willis F., Mary E. and Ellis L. Willis F., the third child, was reared on the farm in McLean County, Ill., obtaining such education as was afforded by the common schools. When twenty-one years old, he began reading medicine with Dr. N. Loar, of Bloomington, and in due time entered college, as before stated. Under the influence of his honored father, he imbibed Democratic sentiments, and remains a firm adherent of that party. Socially, he belongs to the Independent Order of Odd Fellows, and in his religious views is, also like his father, a devout member of the Christian Church.

Dr. Willhoite was wedded February 23, 1886, to Miss Allie J. Stagner, of McLean County, Ill. Mrs. Willhoite was born in that county, and is the daughter of John S. and Julia (Goblen) Stagner. There have been born of this union two bright little daughters—Grace M. and Nona J. The family occupy a neat residence situated in the south part of the town, and represented by a lithographic view, to be found on another page.

ESSE BARNES. There are always in every community a few men evidently born to be leaders. Those who attain the greatest influence are the men who usually pursue the even tenor of their way quietly and without ostentation, but still carry with them the moral suasion which causes them to be looked up to and tacitly recognized as possessing the sound judgment which may be relied upon and the substantial traits of character which make them worthy of being assigned to positions of importance and responsibility.

The gentleman with whose name we introduce this biographical outline, is not only a thriving farmer and business man of Avon Township, but has been no unimportant factor in promoting its social and moral interests. He is prominently connected with the Methodist Episcopal Church and a faithful worker in the church and Sunday-school. All the enterprises which tend to the moral advancement of the people have uniformly received his cordial support. In politics he is a staunch Republican, although he has never sought office, but he keeps himself posted upon the march of events and stands ready to do his duty whenever occasion requires it.

A native of St. Clair County, Ill., Mr. Barnes was born June 29, 1829, and was reared there on his father's farm until reaching man's estate. He acquired a practical education in the common school and was content to engage in the peaceful pursuits of agriculture. He was first married in his native township in 1850 to Miss Louisa Davis and there were born to them seven children, viz: William J., Laura, Marcus, Etta, Franklin, Mary N., and Corrington. Mrs. Louisa (Davis) Barnes departed this life in Mercer County, Ill., January 18, 1866.

Mr. Barnes contracted a second marriage at the home of the bride in St. Clair County, Ill., with Miss Sarah Myer. Of this union there has been born a daughter, Jessie. From St. Clair County Mr. Barnes removed to Mercer County, Ill., and engaged in farming, sojourning there for a period of twelve years. Then, in November, 1876 he came to this county and settled in Avon Township of which he has since been a resident. His farm comprises one hundred and sixty acres of well-developed land upon which he has erected convenient and substantial buildings and gathered around himself and his family all the comforts of modern life. There is not a man in Avon Township who stands higher in the estimation of his fellow-citizens.

Joseph Barnes, the father of our subject, was a native of Kentucky and received a good education. He followed the profession of a teacher for many years and also prosecuted farming successfully. He was a man highly respected in his community and departed this life at his home in Illinois in 1872. The maiden name of the mother was Elizabeth Barry.

＊＊＊＊＊

CLARK R. PERSONS, Cashier of the Bank of Belle Plaine, is a lineal descendant of an old New England family and the son of a worthy couple who were born in New York. He is one of the best educated and most intelligent citizens of the county, has acquired a wide fund of information through his observation and investigation in different parts of the United States, and has accumulated a large amount of property, his real estate and stocks being estimated at about $20,000.

Mr. Persons was born in Wyoming County, N. Y., March 13, 1847, and is the oldest son in the family of Solomon H. and Mary R. Persons. His father having been a farmer, he was reared amid the surroundings of rural life, receiving an elementary education in a district school and later attending the Academy at East Aurora, N. Y. He engaged for a short time in teaching school, but spent the greater part of his time in the intervals of study in the work of the farm. When twenty-two years old he went to Nebraska and crossed the plains with a surveying party, spending perhaps two years in the Western Wilds.

Drifting back as far as Ohio, Mr. Persons remained in that State until 1876, being in the employ of the Lake Shore Railroad Company as a clerk at Genoa, about three years. During the Centennial year he secured the position of chief clerk for the agent on the Sante Fe Railroad at Wichita, Kan., and officiated in that capacity until the fall of 1879, at which time he was appointed station agent at Wellington. He was the first agent the Sante Fe Railroad had at that point and he remained in charge of affairs there until the summer of 1881, subsequently to which he engaged in the drug business with F. B. Snyder. The business was conducted under the firm name of F. B. Snyder & Co.. the connection continuing over a year, when Mr. Persons sold out his interest and in the fall of 1886 came to Belle Plaine.

The firm of Fultz Millard & Co.. opened a banking business here, which was conducted under that head for about three years, and then merged temporarily into the firm of C. R. Persons & Co. After having been conducted until October 15, 1889, by the above named firm, it was re-organized into the bank of Belle Plaine. E. T. Williamson becoming its President and the gentleman of whom we write its Cashier. The concern is duly incorporated under the laws of Kansas with a capital stock of $15,000, an ample reserve fund, and does a banking business consistent with the size of the town and the contributory territory. Mr. Persons is a heavy stockholder in the bank and he also owns property in Wellington and a farm in Osborn Township. He served a term as Mayor of Wellington and since coming to Belle Plaine has become known as a public-spirited citizen. In politics he is a Democrat.

On May 27, 1871, the rites of wedlock were celebrated between Mr. Persons and Miss Clara S. Dean, a native of Ohio, and a daughter of B. and Nancy Dean. Mrs. Persons is an intelligent and well-bred lady, is a member in good standing of the Methodist Episcopal Church, and both she and her husband take an active interest in social matters. They are popular in the circle in which they move and are regarded with respect by all who know them.

JOHN GOLIGHTLEY. Kansas has provided a home for representatives of the best nationalities on the face of the earth, including old England, from which Mr. Golightley came in 1871. He landed first at Quebec, whence he proceeded to Wisconsin, but he only sojourned a few months in the Badger State, coming then to Brown County, Kan. Of that county he was a resident about five years and then removed to Harper County. After a sojourn there of one year he came to this county and worked by the

month for several years. He was prudent and saved his earnings and in due time purchased one hundred and sixty acres on section 36, Harmon Township, of which he has since been a resident.

Mr. Golightley was born in the County of Durham, England, October 21, 1846. His parents were Robert and Jane Golightley who came from pure English stock; they were born in England and spent their last years there. The parental household included nine children, eight of whom are living.

The subject of this sketch attended the common schools during his boyhood and at an early age was trained to habits of industry and economy. In his native England he was employed mostly at farming, living there until a young man of twenty-five years. After coming to Kansas he was married in Belle Plaine, September 13, 1883, to Miss Elizabeth Johnson. This lady, a native of the Dominion of Canada, was born in the Province of Ontario in 1852 and came with R. Robertson to Kansas about 1882. Their union has resulted in the birth of two sons—Robert and George—aged six and four years respectively. Mr. Golightley, politically, is a Republican. He gives his chief attention to his farm and his family, caring very little for the honors of office. He lives in a modest manner in an unpretentious residence, but surrounded by the comforts of life.

GEORGE R. STEELE was born in Virginia, January 25, 1849, and is a son of Eli and Virginia (McGuire) Steele. His father was also a native of the Old Dominion, was a son of Ralph Steele, of Fairfax County, and was killed during the late war when thirty-six years of age. He was a member of the Twenty-Second Cavalry Regiment of Virginia. Mrs. Eli Steele was a daughter of James and Betsey (Brown) McGuire, her parents also being Virginians, and she was the mother of three children—George R., Ralph and Mary E.

The subject of this biography was reared on a farm in his native State, and received a good common-school education. In 1872 he went to Cedar County, Mo., and a little later changed his location to Wyandotte County, Kan., remaining in the latter County until 1876, following the occupation of a farmer. He then went to Bent County, Col., remaining there until 1885, when he returned to Kansas, and located in Sumner County, where he has since been actively engaged in farming, stock-raising and grain buying. He now resides at Mayfield, and is filling the office of Trustee of Osborn Township.

At the bride's home, January 20, 1876, the rites of wedlock were celebrated between Mr. Steele and Miss Rachael Bousman, whose many womanly virtues and graces had won his high esteem. The bride was born in Miami County, Ind., April 17, 1857, and is a daughter of Samuel and Elizabeth (Hall) Bousman. The happy union of Mr. and Mrs. Steele has been blessed by the birth of six children—Nellie M., Maggie R., Edith C., Georgie C., and Hazel and Hiley (twins), who form a bright and charming group around the family fireside. The mother of our subject died in 1855, in Virginia, leaving three children, whose names we give above. His father married again, in 1858, in Virginia, to Miss Louisa Lockhart, daughter of John M. Lockhart. She became the mother of three children, named Charles W., James M. and Hammilton W. They are all living.

REBECCA R. WALLACE, one of the oldest pioneers of Belle Plaine Township, came to this county in the summer of 1874, and purchased land, on which she still lives. It is located on section 14, comprises three hundred and twenty acres, now in a fine state of cultivation and well improved, forming an estate remunerative and attractive. There were but twenty acres of broken ground upon it when her settlement was made, and she and her boys have brought it to its present condition. She has witnessed the gradual development of the country from a sparsely settled and uncultivated region, into a productive and prosperous one, and during the years of its growth she and hers experienced some of the hardships incidental to their surroundings.

Mrs. Wallace is still quite hale and hearty for a lady of her age, being somewhat advanced in years, as she was born March 19, 1821. She is a native of Bourbon County, Ky., and a daughter of Hughes and Elizabeth (Payne) Bowles. Her parents were natives of Virginia, and the lineage on both sides is of French stock. Her father was twice married, and had a large family, of whom the following survive: Anderson resides in Illinois; Mrs. Elizabeth Hall in the same State; Mrs. Wallace; Julia, wife of P. J. Hawes, of Butler County, Kan.; David in Illinois; Jesse P., in Mulvane, Kan.; and William F., in Illinois.

When she was about twelve years old the lady of whom we write accompanied her parents to DeWitt County, Ill., where they were among the early settlers, and where they died. She received but meager educational advantages, but with a desire to become well informed, she has taken advantage of the opportunities afforded her throughout her long life, and is very well versed on the general topics of the day. She grew to maturity in Illinois, and there, March 3, 1840, became the wife of Charles C. Wallace. Like herself he was a native of Bourbon County, Ky., born January 13, 1819, to Andrew and Hester (Campbell) Wallace, who, during his youth, removed to DeWitt County, Ill. Amid the pioneer scenes of that State he grew to manhood, and remained a resident there until his death, which took place in 1852. He was the father of four sons and daughters, three of whom are now living. Of these Elizabeth is the wife of C. A. Steward; William R., whose sketch occupies another page in this volume; and James D. resides in this county. The deceased child bore the name of Charles C.

James D. Wallace, the youngest surviving member of the above family, was born in DeWitt County, Ill., May 8, 1850, and was reared on a farm in his youth, and entered the regular army in his nineteenth year. His enlistment dated from February, 1869, and he was a member of Company F, Sixth United States Cavalry. During the period of reconstruction he did service in Texas; in the Indian Territory assisted in keeping the red men in their place on the Reservation, and did guard duty in Wichita in 1870, when there were but a few hundred people in that town. In 1870-71-72 he was stationed with his regiment at Ft. Riley, and was on duty in Sumner County, preventing the Indians from leaving their Reservation. The five years which is the Regular Army period of enlistment having expired, he was discharged, February 15, 1871, at which time he held the rank of Sergeant-Major of the United States Cavalry at Ft. Hays. He had been a Sergeant with the escort party that accompanied the Russian Grand Duke Alexis, over the plains during his buffalo hunt.

Upon leaving the service young Wallace returned to his native State, and the following year became a resident of this county and State. On the 1st of September, 1878, he was united in marriage with Miss Alma Epperson. For eight years he traveled as a salesman for the grocery house of Ridenour, Baker & Co., of Kansas City. In politics he is a strong Republican.

ALBERT MORRILL. He with whose name we introduce this biographical record, bore an important part in the early settlement of Oxford Township, arriving here as early as December, 1870. He filed a claim occupying a part of section 13, west of the Arkansas River and one-half mile south of Oxford Post-office. There was then not even a house to mark the site of the town. Wild game of all kinds was plentiful and a year or two after settling here Mr. Morrill purchased one hundred and eighty-five buffalo hides at $1.50 per hide, tanned. His only neighbors were John and William Burnett with John's wife and her mother who had preceded Mr. Morrill to this region that same year, settling one mile north. La Fayette, John and Perry Binkley, and John Horton traded with the Indians.

Mr. Morrill made his way to this region from Webster County, Iowa, driving overland with a team and reaching his present location just at nightfall. He occupied himself that winter trading with the Indians and getting out timber for his first house. The nearest trading point was Emporia and the nearest mail station, Winfield, and Wichita. The following winter Messrs. Morrill, Buckley, Corbin and Doyle, the latter a surveyor, laid out six blocks of Oxford, calling it Neptuwa, after an Indian Chief. In March following they sold their interest to a town company who changed the name and proceeded with its improvement. In the spring of 1871 a goodly number of emigrants came, crossing the Arkansas River in an ash "dug-out" belonging to Mr. Morrill & Co. The first prairie boat was built in the summer of 1871.

After completing his first dwelling Mr. Morrill sent his son-in-law after his family. Mr. Morrill in the meantime having charge of the store which he had bought out. He then took up a tract of land which he supposed to be two hundred acres in extent, but at the survey there were found to be only one hundred and thirty-six acres. It lay in its primitive condition and Mr. Morrill broke the soil and first planted fifteen acres of corn of as good quality as he has ever raised since. He planted fruit and forest trees and effected the usual improvements suggested to the enterprising and progressive farmer. Later he embarked in stock-raising, bringing into this county the first Magee swine and with one exception being the first man to introduce this breed of swine into the State of Kansas. He continues to make a specialty of these and has at the present time a herd of very fine animals. He handles thoroughbreds entirely. He has invested his capital in additional land, having now a well-developed farm—two hundred and sixteen acres in extent—and has erected a more modern dwelling near the first one.

Mr. Morrill assisted in organizing school district No. 1, and was mainly instrumental in putting up their schoolhouse. He also instituted the first Sunday-school, conducting the services in one place after another as the houses were built up. He was the only man making a profession of religion at that time in this region and conducted the first prayer meeting, which was held in a "dug-out." He officiated as Sunday-school Superintendent and had for his assistant later, Capt. John Folks, who was editor of the Oxford *Press*, the first paper published in this place. Mr. Morrill was then, as he is now, a Methodist in religious belief and he assisted in organizing the first society of this denomination in Oxford Township. The first man to preach for them was Rev. Mr. Perkins, a Presbyterian. Meetings for some time were held in schoolhouses. Mr. Morrill officiated as Class-Leader and Steward for a period of forty years. In his pious labors he received the assistance of his devoted wife and later their four children also became members of the Methodist Episcopal Church. Mr. Morrill first voted with the old Whig party, but upon its abandonment identified himself with the Republicans. He belongs to the Farmers' Alliance in which he officiates as Chaplain at Oxford.

The native place of Mr. Morrill was at Napoli, Cattaraugus County, N. Y., where his birth took place May 4, 1827. His father, Masten Morrill, was born at Danville near St. Johnsburg, Vt., January 15, 1788. The latter was reared to manhood in his native place and was there married to Miss Sally Osborn, January 19, 1816, who was born near the early home of her husband, October 1, 1795. The parents of Mr. Morrill lived together for the long period of nearly sixty years. Masten Morrill was one of the early settlers of Olean, N. Y., but the family of ten children, nine of whom lived to mature years, was reared in Cattaraugus County. In 1861 they removed to Illinois, settling at Leon, Whiteside County, where the parents spent their last days. Their remains were laid to rest in the little burying ground which Mr. Morrill instituted on his own farm for the settlers from New York State. Most of the family were buried there. The wife and mother departed this life December 2, 1877. Mr. Morrill passed away September 22, 1882. He had been a professor of religion for many years.

Arriving to man's estate in his native county, the subject of this notice was married March 22, 1848, to Miss Hannah Boardman. This union resulted in the birth of eight children, only four of whom are living: Cynthia L. became the wife of Perry Binkley, of Oxford; Charles M. is a practicing physician of Prophetstown, Whiteside County,

Ill.; Marion is occupied at farming in Sumner County, Kan.; Willard C. is a resident of Oxford Township. Mrs. Hannah Morrill, who was born August 27, 1828, at Napoli, Cattaraugus County, N. Y., departed this life at the homestead in Webster County, Iowa, February 11, 1866.

The present wife of our subject to whom he was married in 1866 was in her girlhood Miss Jemima Jadwin. This lady was born in Tuscarawas County, Ohio, December 1, 1811, and is the daughter of Andrew and Mary Ann (Packer) Jadwin, who, when she was a child of six years left the Buckeye State, removing to Indiana. Locating in DeKalb County, Ind., they there spent the remainder of their days. Their daughter, Jemima, subsequently went to Iowa where she lived until her marriage. Ten children, one deceased, have been born of this union. Those who are living are named respectively: Ernest, John Delbert, Frederick, Minnie, Grace, Albert, Lettie, Alma and Flossie.

GEORGE C. CARPENTER. Without making any great pretensions to elegance, the home of Mr. Carpenter, in point of solid comfort, is probably not excelled by any in his community. It lies in the shape of a well-developed farm on section 4, Chikaskia Township, comprising one hundred and sixty acres of choice land, improved with good buildings and supplied with the necessary farm machinery. Besides stock-raising and general agriculture, Mr. Carpenter makes a specialty of fruit-growing, having an orchard of seven hundred trees, including apple, peach, plum, cherry, apricot and nectarine. He takes a lively interest in politics, voting the straight Republican ticket and is a man of decided views, keeping himself thoroughly posted upon all the leading topics of the day. Of the seven children born to him and his estimable wife, five are living. Robert V. married Miss Frances V. Ward, is the father of two children and lives in Ryan Township; George B. married Miss Nancy DeMoss, and is also a resident of Ryan Township; he is the father of one child; Clara B. is the wife of Joseph L. Kearns, of Chikaskia Township, and they have two children; Ira W. and Mary E. remain with their parents.

The youngest in a family of eight children, Mr. Carpenter was born December 1, 1833, in Warren County, Ohio, where he acquired the rudiments of a common-school education. He commenced the battle of life for himself when a lad of fifteen years, in the State of Indiana, to which his parents removed when he was less than two years old, continuing in the agricultural districts of the Hoosier State, until 1857. That year he removed to Appanoose County, Iowa, of which he was a resident for a period of nineteen years. In 1876 he changed his residence to Monroe County, Mo., where he sojourned four years. His next removal, made in 1880, was to this county and to his present farm.

Mr. Carpenter, in the meantime, while a resident of Indiana, was married September 1, 1856, in Ripley County, to Miss Nancy, daughter of Benjamin and Nancy (Funkhauser) Kaster. Mrs. Carpenter was the seventh child of her parents and was born in Ripley County, Ind., February 9, 1837, being one of fourteen children. Her parents were natives of Pennsylvania and resided there until 1828, going thence to Indiana. The father died at the old homestead in Ripley County, in 1854. The mother subsequently remarried and spent her last days in Lucas County, Iowa, passing away in February, 1885.

During the progress of the Civil War, Mr. Carpenter in July, 1862, enlisted as a Union soldier in Company F. Thirty-sixth Iowa Infantry, and was first sent with his regiment to Camp Lincoln, Iowa, and then to Benton Barracks, Mo. Thence they were ordered to Memphis, Tenn., becoming a part of the Sixteenth Army Corps under Gen. Hurlbut. Later they were assigned to the Seventh Corps, commanded by Gen. F. Steele. Mr. Carpenter participated in the bombardment of Ft. Pemberton and was in the battle of Helena, Ark., at the capture of Little Rock and Prairie De Ann, in the fight at Elkin's Ford, Mark's Mill and numerous other engagements, skirmishes and raids. At the battle of Mark's Mill he received a gunshot wound in the left jaw, the ball entering the left corner of his mouth and passing through his neck came out behind the jugular vein, breaking his jawbone in three places and taking off a piece of his tongue. After this he was considered fully entitled to an honorable discharge, which was given him October 24, 1864. With good care and skillful treatment he recovered from this painful injury and in the course of a few months was enabled to resume his farming operations. The improvements upon his farm have all been effected by his own enterprise and industry. Ninety acres of his farm are under the plow and each year sees something added to its beauty and value. The present residence was erected in 1881.

The father of our subject was George Carpenter, Sr., a native of Virginia, who, in 1800, removed to what was then the Territory of Ohio, settling near the present site of Cincinnati, which was then designated as Ft. Washington, at Waynesville, Warren County. He commenced farming in the wilderness, sojourning in what subsequently was named the Buckeye State until 1835. That year he removed to Indiana where he prosecuted agriculture until his death in 1850.

The mother of our subject bore the maiden name of Susan Cozad. She was a native of Maryland and was taken by her parents to Ohio when quite young where she met her future husband. There were born to them eight children, six of whom are living. The mother departed this life in Indiana, in 1874. Mr. Carpenter, of this sketch identified himself with the Independent Order of Odd Fellows, in Iowa, with which he still holds membership. He also belongs to the Grange and Corbin Post No. 426, G. A. R. at Corbin, in which he has held the offices of Surgeon and Junior Vice-Commander.

ANIEL W. BENTON. The subject of this biography was born in Pickaway County, Ohio, August 10, 1832. He is a son of Elias Benton, who was born in Litchfield, Conn., August 9, 1795. Daniel Benton, the grandfather of our subject, was born in Connecticut. September 12, 1761. His wife was Margery Frisbee, and their marriage was celebrated in 1789. His father, the great-grandfather of our subject, was Nathaniel Benton, a native of Connecticut, where he was born August 25, 1726, and was united in marriage to Miss Abigail Gillett. He settled in Litchfield, Conn., during Colonial times, where he followed the occupation of a farmer. He died in that town in 1800, and was followed to the silent land by his wife some ten or twelve years later. Daniel Benton was reared in his native place, and resided there till 1821, when he started with his family for the far West, as Ohio was then called, and journeyed with a team to that State, and located at Somerset, Ohio. They crossed the Ohio River at Wilksburg, Va., on the 1st of August of that year. As soon as the family was fairly well established in their new home, Mr. Benton returned in the same year to Connecticut to finish some important business that it had been found impossible to transact before leaving that State. On his way back to Ohio to the waiting family he was stricken by a mortal disease, and died in the town of Harmony, N. J., where his remains were interred. His wife survived till the year 1835, when she too, paid the debt of nature and lies quietly sleeping in the Salem churchyard in Pickaway Township.

Elias Benton was reared in his native town and received a liberal education in the common schools of the place. He took the Freeman's oath while a resident of Connecticut, and in 1821, accompanied his parents to Ohio. After the death of the father, he took up a tract of timbered land in Pickaway County, upon which he put up a log cabin, which was afterwards the birthplace of the subject of this sketch. The cabin, according to the fashion of the time, was built with a large fire-place, and as Mrs. Benton had no stove, she performed all cooking operations by the open fire. Rail-roads were an unthought of possibility in that section at that time, and for many years the farmers hauled their produce to the river towns, where they exchanged them for cash, or, most likely, for goods of some description. Upon one occasion, Mr. Elias Benton had his wheat made into flour, and in company with a neighbor, built a flat-boat on the Scioto River, and by that means, transported the flour to New Orleans, where, after waiting six months, they received their payment of 35 cents per bushel.

In a few years the log cabin in which Mr. E. Benton began housekeeping, gave place to a small frame dwelling, where the family lived a few more years, then it in turn gave way to the present substantial structure of brick. The residence of Mr. Benton was the first brick dwelling to be erected in Pickaway Township. He lived there many years, and reared his family in habits of industry and economy. He spent his last days in Hardin County, Ohio. His death occurred on the 18th of May, 1886. He had lived to see Ohio develop from a wilderness to a well-settled and wealthy country. It was his good fortune to be present at the ceremonies attendant upon the commencement of the Ohio canal, when the first spadeful of earth was lifted at Licking Summit, July 4, 1825, in the presence of the Governor, De Witt Clinton, and many others of note in the State. It was a gala day for Ohio, and a time long to be remembered by those present on the occasion.

Elias Benton was thrice married: his first wife was Rosanna Cherry, to whom he was united June 20, 1820. After her death he again married, his second wife being Elizabeth Johnson Caldwell, who was born June 12, 1797, and died May 7, 1865. Their marriage was celebrated January 20, 1823, and the union resulted in the birth of six children, as follows: Orlando was born July 7, 1826, and died October 17, 1852; William Johnson, March 6, 1828, died December 25, 1833; Maria Jane, born April 19, 1830, married Joseph Wright, November 9, 1852, and died November 18, 1860; Daniel W., the subject of this sketch; Almira, born February 11, 1834, died March 25, 1853; Sarah Ellen, born May 22, 1838, married John Saylor, November 13, 1856. On the 12th of February, 1867, Mr. Benton was married the third time, the lady being Mrs. Catherine Cherry.

As stated before, Mr. Benton received a good education and was a man of literary tastes. He frequently employed his pen on articles for the newspapers, also in writing a history of the Benton family, which latter work was published in book form in 1878, when the author was eighty-three years old, and blind. The book is an interesting one, and we are indebted to it for the principal portion of the facts herein recorded. One of the stories related in the book just mentioned, reveals one of the curious laws passed by the State of Connecticut in the early days of its history. The Legislature enacted a law to the effect that every taxable person not identified with any church, should be assessed a certain amount for the support of the Congregational church, to which most of the legislators belonged. The law had the effect of making many non-church members hasten to one or other of the various religious bodies, where they signed themselves as members, by which means they escaped paying the tax. The Methodists and Episcopals received many additions to their numbers in that way. One day Daniel Benton, upon his arrival home, announced the fact that he had that day signed himself as a member of the Protestant Episcopal church, and stated that they would thereafter attend the services of that denomination. In that manner it transpired that the father of our subject was reared a Protestant Episcopal. Mr. Benton also states in his book that the public school teachers were obliged to teach the catechism in the daily sessions of school, but were permitted to teach the one that was desired by the parents of the pupils. Politically, Mr. Benton was a Whig, and always took an active interest in the affairs of the country. He served many years as Justice of the Peace, and enjoyed the esteem of his neighbors and friends. He was an extensive and judicious reader, delighting principally in historical works, and his retentive memory enabled him to lay up a large fund of valuable and interesting knowledge. His mental faculties were preserved unimpaired to the day of his demise.

The subject of this sketch was reared in his native State, and resided with his parents until after his marriage. In 1856, he removed to Hardin County, where he bought a farm and made his home till 1887, when he emigrated to Kansas. He located at Ft. Scott, where he bought city property, and also purchased farm land in the neighborhood. He made his home in that city until 1889, when he disposed of a portion of his interests in that place, and removed to Wellington and purchased the farm which is his home at present. He has two hundred

and forty acres of fine land adjoining the city of Wellington, upon which are a superior set of frame buildings adapted to all the wants of a farm carried on in accordance with the best methods employed in modern agriculture. In addition to the farm just mentioned, Mr. Benton owns three hundred and twenty acres in Harmon Township.

The marriage of our subject took place September 18, 1855, the lady of his choice being Miss Harriet Maria Wharton. Mrs. Benton was born in Frankfort, Ross County, Ohio, February 9, 1836. Her father, Rev. Henry Wharton, was a native of Clermont County, Ohio, and his father, John Wharton, was a native of Virginia, of English ancestry. John Wharton was a pioneer of Clermont County, where he improved a large farm, and passed the remainder of his days in the State of his adoption. His wife was Eleanor (Salts) Wharton, a native of Virginia, of English ancestry. The father of Mrs. Benton was reared in his native county, and when quite young professed conversion and united with the Methodist Episcopal church of that place. In 1834 he was admitted to the Ohio Conference as a preacher, and from that time forward was an active and efficient worker in the ranks of the ministry of that denomination. His field of service extended to many different points within the bounds of the Conference, but at all places he was highly esteemed for his eminent piety and superior pulpit ability. His death occurred in 1864, when he was sixty years of age. His wife was Sarah (Winters) Wharton, a native of the same county as her husband. The father of Mrs. Wharton, William Winters, was of Welsh ancestry. He was a farmer by occupation, and followed that calling throughout his life. His wife was Nancy (Carr) Wharton, an estimable woman who performed all the duties of life in a manner pleasing to her family, and in accordance with the dictates of her conscience.

Mr. and Mrs. Daniel W. Benton have had six children born unto them, as follows: Henry W., an attorney at Minneapolis, Minn.; Guy Potter, Principal of the Ft. Scott Public Schools; Clarence and Eva are students at Winfield College, southwestern Kansas; Mary and Marguerite are at home. The entire family, except Henry and his wife, are members in good repute in the Methodist Episcopal Church, South. Henry and wife are members of the Presbyterian church. Mr. Benton is an ardent Republican in politics, and a strict temperance man in practice and principle.

JAMES L. M. STRANGE. The subject of this notice first struck Kansas soil in the fall of 1881, locating first on a rented farm in Cowley County. Two years later he came to this county and purchased the land which he now owns and operates, this embracing one hundred and sixty acres on section 11. It was originally an open prairie with no improvements, but by the exercise of industry Mr. Strange is now in the possession of a good homestead, with his land all fenced, provided with substantial buildings and indicating at all points the intelligence and progress of the proprietor. The most of the land is devoted to the raising of wheat, with the exception of ten acres in pasture.

The subject of this notice was born in Adair County, Ky., October 23, 1839, and is the son of William Strange, likewise a native of the Blue Grass State within which he spent his entire life. He was cut down in his prime, however, dying in 1846, at the early age of about thirty-five years. The paternal grandfather was Archelus Strange, a native of Virginia, and who was married there to Miss Elizabeth Coffee. Soon afterward they removed to North Carolina and from there to Adair County, Ky., where they spent their last days. There were born to them twelve children, viz.: Clayborne, Louis, Abram, William, the father of our subject, Archelus, Levi, Larkin, Elizabeth, Betsey, Polly, Wenston and Ellen. Elizabeth, Clayborne and Wenston are the only survivors, they being residents of Arkansas and Kentucky.

The mother of our subject bore the maiden name of Damarius Davis; she was born in Adair County, Ky., and with her family of five children, after her husband's death, removed to Warren County, Ky., where James L. M. was reared on a farm. Our subject obtained such education as the

common schools afforded and when reaching man's estate was wedded to Miss Sarah J., daughter of Ransom and Lettie (Bevil) Conklin. Mrs. Strange was likewise a native of the Blue Grass State. Of her union with our subject there were born eight children, the eldest of whom, a daughter Lillie, is the wife of W. A. Hiser of South Haven Township; Elmeta V. married M. H. Elliott and lives in South Haven, Kan.; William R., Molly B., Tandy W., Nannie D., James L. W., and Sally, remain at home with their parents. Mr. and Mrs. Strange are consistent members of the Christian Church at South Haven, and Mr. Strange belongs to Lodge No. 336, A. F. & A. M. at Smith's Grove, Ky.

The father of Mrs. Strange was born in Tennessee and her mother in Virginia. They came to Kansas in the fall of 1881, locating, like Mr. Strange, in Cowley County where they still live. Grandfather Howell Bevil a native of Virginia, removed to Kentucky at an early day and there spent the remainder of his life.

JOHN C. THRAILKILL, of Wellington, is successfully engaged in the grocery trade, having a thriving business located on North Washington Street. He is one of the old settlers, having come to this region in March, 1872, when the present flourishing city was a village of probably five hundred souls. He has grown with its growth and contributed materially to its welfare and advancement.

The subject of this sketch was born in Trenton, Grundy County, Mo., May 18, 1844, and when a child two years of age, was taken by his parents to Andrew County, that State, where he grew to maturity. He was given a fair education in the common schools, and when starting out for himself engaged in the mercantile business at East Nebraska City, Iowa, where he sojourned from 1867 to 1872. Then, selling out, he came to Kansas, and has since been a resident of Wellington. Prior to his settlement in East Nebraska, however, he had been to this locality and entered a claim in the vicinity of

Belle Plaine, which he proved up, obtaining his clear title. He established himself in the grocery business at Wellington in 1877, prosecuting this until 1883. Then selling out, he embarked in the live stock business, and was thus occupied until 1889, buying and feeding. He is now in the enjoyment of a lucrative trade, and occupies a well-equipped store, keeping a full line of all the goods pertaining to his business. Although meddling very little with politics, he usually votes the Democratic ticket, and he belongs to the Masonic fraternity.

Mr. Thrailkill was married in Nebraska City, Neb., April 13th, 1876, to Miss Jonnie Cockrill, a native of Kentucky, and who removed with her parents to Western Iowa when a child. Her father, J. B. Cockrill, engaged in the mercantile business, and died June 5, 1887, in Wellington, Kan. The mother is still living, making her home in Wellington. Our subject and his estimable wife are the parents of three children, namely, Clyde, Lee and Ray.

The subject of this sketch was the son of John Thrailkill, a native of Tennessee, and who married Miss Emily Moore. They first removed to Missouri, where the father engaged in mining, and then in merchandising. He died in Missouri in August, 1854. The mother died October 14, 1888, at St. Joseph, Mo.

ROBERT J. SMITH, dealer in agricultural implements and also engaged in the real-estate and loan business at Wellington, came to the city in 1883 and has made for himself the reputation of an honest man and a good citizen. His native place was Brown County, Ohio, and the date of his birth February 18, 1839. His boyhood and youth were spent in a comparatively uneventful manner in attendance at the district school, and he afterward served an apprenticeship as a tanner, harness-maker and in the saddlery business. Upon the outbreak of the Civil War he enlisted as a Union soldier in August, 1861, in Company A, Seventieth Ohio Infantry. His regiment was assigned to the Army of the Tennessee under the command of Gen. Sherman. Mr. Smith participated with his comrades in the battles of Shiloh, Corinth, Vicksburg, Jackson and Mission Ridge, besides other minor engagements. At the expiration of his term of enlistment he repaired to Knoxville, Tenn., but immediately returned and re-enlisted, in January, 1864, in the same company and regiment.

Soon afterward followed the siege of Atlanta and the Fifteenth Army Corps, of which Mr. Smith was a member, started for Savannah, Ga., and joined in the famous march to the sea. During this trying journey Mr. Smith did not ride one hour. He participated in the charge of Ft. McAllister under Gen. Hazen, and thereafter fought at Columbia, and Rolla. His division was then sent to Little Rock, Ark., and at the close of the war he was mustered out at Camp Denison, Ohio. He was never too ill to report for duty, never in the guard house and never captured or wounded, although experiencing some hair-breadth escapes. He likewise never missed a battle or skirmish in which his regiment was engaged.

Upon returning to the pursuits of civil life Mr. Smith engaged in harness-making at his father's old stand in Decatur, Ohio, where he lived until coming to Kansas. On January 14, 1869, he was married, in Adams County, Ohio, to Miss Lina McClung. This lady was born in that county in August, 1841, and is the daughter of James McClung, an Adams County farmer, who is now deceased. The four children born of this union are still living and at home with their parents, bearing the names, respectively, of Frederick M., Herschel B., Robert Charles and Nora. They are being carefully trained and will be given good educational advantages. Mr. Smith, politically, is a Republican, and in his religious views sides with the doctrines of the Presbyterian Church, being connected with this church at Wellington. He also belongs to the Grand Army of the Republic.

The father of our subject was John S. Smith, who was born in Washington County, Pa., in 1813. He removed to Ohio at an early day was there married to Miss Ruth Simpson. He engaged in harness-making and saddlery at Decatur, that State, and with his estimable wife is still living. The latter is now seventy three years old and a member of the United Presbyterian Church.

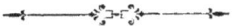

JOHN W. CHAPMAN. This gentleman is well worthy of representation in this volume, not simply on account of his financial prosperity and as the owner of a beautiful farm in ValVerde Township, but as a loyal, intelligent and upright citizen, useful in his day and generation, and a living example of worth of character.

Mr. Chapman is of Southern parentage and ancestry, and is a worthy descendant of an honored line in America, the early members of the family having settled in Virginia on their emigration from England. The paternal grandfather was one Daniel Chapman, of North Carolina, and in that State Thomas Chapman, the father of our subject, was born in 1803. Daniel Chapman removed with his family to Robertson County, Tenn., when his son Thomas was but a lad, and there the boy grew to maturity, making that his home until 1840. He married Miss Rachael Garrison, who was born in Tennessee about the year 1802, and who died in Marion County, Ill., in 1846, about six years after she and her husband took up their residence there. Thomas Chapman spent his life in the pursuit of agriculture, and was in easy circumstances. He served in the Black Hawk War and also in the Florida War of 1836. He was a member of the Methodist Episcopal Church for many years before his death, which took place in 1874. The old gentleman, father of our subject, enlisted during the War of the Rebellion, notwithstanding his advanced age, and was discharged on account of his inability to endure the hardships. The parental family comprised nine sons and daughters, namely: Jane E., Susan E., Richard M., Mary, Nancy, Sarah, John W., Daniel W. and Louisa. Susan E. is now deceased.

The gentleman of whom we write was born in Robertson County, Tenn., October 23, 1837, and was reared on his father's farm in Marion County, Ill.,

acquiring an excellent common-school education. He had been taught to love his country as a sisterhood which should be unbroken, and upon the breaking out of the Civil War he took his place in the ranks of the Union army, entering the service in 1861, as principal musician of the Fortieth Illinois Infantry, in which capacity he served the term of his enlistment, three years. He not only was present during many minor engagements and cheered his comrades on weary marches, and in the waiting hours in camp, but participated in the noted battles of Shiloh, Corinth, Vicksburg, Jackson, Chickamauga, Lookout Mountain, Missionary Ridge, Siege of Knoxville and all of the hard-fought conflicts of the Georgia campaign.

At Atlanta, Ga., in August, 1864, Mr. Chapman was honorably discharged and he then returned to Marion County, Ill., making that his home until 1882, when he removed to Sumner County, Kan. He purchased land and entered upon the life of a Kansas farmer, adding to his acreage and improving the estate until it reached its present state of high cultivation and development. He now owns three hundred and twenty acres, lying on sections 5 and 9, ValVerde Township, on which is an excellent residence, good barns, a fine orchard of several acres, and other minor improvements which every enterprising and progressive farmer makes. Mr. Chapman is giving his entire attention to the stock business and to tilling the soil, and is proving successful in his enterprise.

On March 11, 1857, the marriage ceremony was performed which united Mr. Chapman and Miss Margaret Rogers, of Marion County, Ill. The young and charming bride was born in Mississippi, January 18, 1840, and lived to make a happy home until April 18, 1870, when she breathed her last. The union resulted in the birth of five children: Wilber C., Fannie G., Ruth G., Laura L., and an infant that died unnamed.

Mr. Chapman was again married September 11, 1870, the lady with whom he was united being Mrs. Abigail Massey, who was born in Clay County, Ill., in 1837, and died May 4, 1878. Mrs. Abigail Chapman bore her husband five children—Aaron C., Fred M., Bertha A., Merida W. and Flora M. Mr. Chapman contracted a third matrimonial alliance December 5, 1878, his companion being Miss Lida A. Songer, of Clay County, Ill., who was born there August 13, 1851. This union has been blessed by the birth of six children: Pearl, John R. Forest A., Bessie J., Daisy F. and Dwight L.; the last two are twins.

Mr. Chapman belongs to the Farmers' Alliance, and to the Masonic fraternity. He gives his political support to the Republican party. He is a member in good standing of the United Brethren Church.

LANCELOT JOHNSON. The pioneer history of Sumner County and the men who were instrumental in its early growth and development forms a most interesting story which will not part with any of its importance as time rolls on. Among those who came to this region nearly a score of years ago and who battled with dangers and difficulties was Mr. Johnson, who is now looked upon as one of its most honored residents. He established himself on section 6, Oxford Township, on the 28th of May, 1871, taking up from the Government the quarter section which he now owns. He put his stakes in front of his present residence at a time when the now flourishing town of Oxford had just been laid out and contained one small store conducted by Mr. P. Binley. The latter purchased furs from the Indians and made a precarious living as best he could. There were no improvements, whatever, on the uplands and but one shanty between Oxford and Mr. Johnson's claim.

Soon after Mr. Johnson selected his location he was joined by two neighbors; in fact, fourteen claims were taken in one day by a delegation from Iowa. In those days there was a community of feeling among the pioneers which led them to take an interest in each other's welfare and very soon all were not only acquaintances but friends. Mr. Johnson proceeded with the improvements of his property, breaking the sod and putting in a full crop that same year. He filed his claim at Augusta and obtained his outfit for farm-

ing at Independence, and for building purposes made his lumber from cottonwood. At first he was obliged to haul water from Oxford. The neighbors joined together in obtaining water, one going at one time and another the next. The only ladies in the colony was Miss Cordie, the daughter of Mr. Johnson, and Mrs. Frank Evans. The ladies were sheltered in a tent while the men lived in their wagons, the camp being on the present farm of Mr. Carpenter.

The first shanty of the colony, a structure twelve feet square, was put up by Mr. Johnson and within it Mr. Johnson and family lived for two summers. In the winter Mr. Johnson and his daughter repaired to Independence.

On the 1st of January, 1872, Mr. Johnson removed his wife and family to this place and then proceeded with the improvement of his property until 1879. He then embarked in sheep-raising, transferring the scene of his operations to Meagher County, Mont. In that region he took another claim, remaining on it until proving up, then sold it and returned to Kansas and sojourned upon his his farm until 1884. Upon the latter Mr. Johnson had planted a good grove and set out quantities of hedge for fencing. After prosecuting general agriculture he became interested in stock-raising and in this, as with the other, was uniformly successful.

Liberal and public-spirited, he was ever a friend of education and progress, assisting in organizing the school district and officiating as Director.

Mr. Johnson, about 1884, put up a more modern dwelling at this place assisted by his son. The latter then went to No Man's Land, where he is now engaged in stock-raising. Mr. Johnson, although making no pretentions to being a politician, votes the straight Republican ticket and keeps himself posted on matters of general interest. He is a member in good standing of the Christian Church. Such has been his course in life, his honesty and fair dealing with his fellow-men, that he has gained the unqualified respect of all those with whom he has come in contact.

A native of Shelby County, Ky., Mr. Johnson was born September 23, 1827, and when a child of two years was taken by his parents to Orange County, Ind. Later they removed to Putnam County, that State, thence to Boone County, and finally to Benton County, Iowa, where young Johnson developed into manhood. He left the parental roof when about nineteen years old and commenced learning the carpenter's trade, then going to St. Paul, Minn., he sojourned there one year. Returning then to Iowa he prosecuted his trade in Benton County and finally purchased land five miles from Vinton, the county seat of Benton County, where he made his home for a period of twenty-five years. In the meantime he was married, March 5, 1850, to Miss. M. J. Forsythe.

After the outbreak of the Civil War Mr. Johnson enlisted in October, 1862, in Company K., Sixth Iowa Cavalry, and leaving home November 3, following, was sent to the Northwest to fight the Indians. His duties led him all over Dakota Territory, and he returned home November 3, 1865, after a service of three years and nine hours. He had now a family of five children. He continued a resident of of Benton County, Iowa, until 1870, although in the meantime he had sold his farm. That year they came to Kansas and purchased a town lot in Independence, where they lived until their removal to Oxford Township, this county.

Mrs. Johnson was born in Decatur County Ind., February 5, 1830, and is the daughter of J. S. and Jane (McCoy) Forsythe, the former a native of Kentucky and the latter of Indiana. Mr. Forsythe lived for a time in the vicinity of Lebanon, Boone County, Ind., where he was among the first settlers. He engaged in merchandising and for some years was Sheriff of Boone County. In 1841 he crossed the Mississippi into Linn County, Iowa, settling at Marion, but two years later changed his residence to Benton County. He was married in the latter county where the wife and mother died in 1849. In Iowa, as he had been in Indiana, Mr. Forsythe was prominent in local affairs, serving as County Judge and Township Supervisor and holding other public positions until quite aged. Finally, leaving the Hawkeye State in 1873 he came to Kansas and spent his last years in Avon Township, dying in 1876 at the age of seventy-nine years.

Five children were born to Mr. and Mrs. Johnson, of whom only three are living. John A. mar-

ried Miss Lundy King, and is the father of five children; he has already been spoken of as a resident of No Man's Land. Eva is the wife of E. Platte, and they live on a farm near Greensburg, adjoining the county seat. Cordie remains at home; Ida married James Johnson, who died in 1884 and she died in 1888, both being the victims of consumption. Their son, Allen W., died when three years old.

Alexander Johnson, the father of our subject, was born in Ohio and married Miss Sarah Allen, of Kentucky. They made their home in Shelby County, that State, until coming West, as already stated, and reared a family of ten children to mature years. Mr. Johnson died in Iowa April 13, 1855, at the age of sixty-six years. The mother died about 1875-76, in Iowa. She was a member in good standing of the Christian Church. Mr. Johnson had served as a soldier in the War of 1812.

DEACON JAMES T. CHURCH. The subject of this sketch is particularly well known in the religious circles of Wellington, being one of the pillars of the Baptist Church, in which he has officiated as Deacon for many years. He was born in Lancaster, Fairfield County, Ohio, November 19, 1828, and is the son of Isaac Church, a native of Cape May, N. J. The latter was reared in his native State, and became an architect and builder. He was converted in his youth, joining the Baptist Church, and for many years officiated as a minister of that denomination. Upon leaving New Jersey he established himself in the city of Philadelphia, where he continued preaching. About 1820 he emigrated to Ohio, and located among the pioneers of Fairfield County.

After his removal to Ohio, the father of our subject being located in the town of Lancaster, engaged as a carpenter and builder, while he also continued his labors in the Master's vineyard. With the exception of a short time spent afterward in New Jersey, he remained a resident of Lancaster until his death, which occurred about 1853-54. He was married in early manhood to Mrs. Susan Dunlap. She was the mother of our subject and his twin sister, and passed away about 1832, twenty years prior to the decease of her husband. The Rev. Isaac Church was four times married.

The subject of this sketch attended the primitive schools of Lancaster, Ohio, and after reaching manhood completed a business course in the Commercial School at Ottawa, Ill. He was only four years old at the time of his mother's death, and when a boy of eight years went to live with an uncle in the same county, where he was reared on a farm and remained until reaching his majority. He was then given $100, with a horse and saddle, and started out to seek his fortune. Locating in Fairfield County he engaged with a firm of contractors six months, then secured a position as clerk and book-keeper in the employ of Mahlon Ashbrook, in Pickaway County. This gentleman also conducted a sawmill, distillery, etc. Young Church remained with him one year, then returned to his old home in Fairfield County and engaged in sheep raising, and also dealt in sheep in company with his uncle, John M. Ashbrook. He was thus occupied two years, then engaged in farming. He purchased land in Fairfield County, and continued there until 1857. Then selling out he went to Ottawa, Ill., and engaged in the grocery trade and the manufacture of vinegar. In 1866 he sold out once more, and engaged in the lumber and grocery trade until 1877. He now met with reverses, losing all of his property, and we next find him in Chicago, Ill., as a dealer in groceries. Later he embarked in the lumber business, on the Lumber Exchange, until 1880.

In the above mentioned year Mr. Church came to Kansas, locating first at Humboldt, and engaging in the lumber trade one year. In 1882 he sold out and removed to Lincoln, Neb., where he prosecuted the lumber business a few months, and then, in 1883, came to Wellington. Here he opened a lumber yard and instituted a branch yard at Caldwell, conducting these until January, 1889. His next move was to form a partnership with J. L. Wood, and they opened an office for the practice of law, also attending to collections and insurance.

Mr. Church was married, October 9 1853, in Fairfield County, Ohio, to Miss Laura C. Kagy. This lady was born in Fairfield County, Ohio, March 19, 1832, and is the daughter of Lewis B. and Francina P. (Ashbrook) Kagy, who were natives of Virginia, and pioneers of Ohio. To Mr. and Mrs. Church there were born two children—Francina and Mary. The first mentioned was married to Ricardo Miner, and they live in Phoenix, Arizona; they have one child, George E. Mary is the wife of C. A. Foss, of San Diego, Cal., and they have three children –C. Stanford, James C. and Laura C. Politically, Mr. Church is a stanch Republican.

~~·→=✦=←·~~

JOHN P. NICE is one of the most practical and prosperous farmers in ValVerde Township and an exponent of the excellent traits which are to be met with among the Teutonic races. His residence and barn are the finest in the township, and taken all in all, his farm, although not so large as many, is one of the most attractive in the entire county. Hard work, a wise economy, and a determination to succeed, have been the levers by which he has won success since he came to Kansas a poor man.

The birth of our subject took place in Prussia, April 15, 1846, and he is the youngest of three children born to Mathew and Gertrude Nice. The mother died in Germany, and in 1853 the father emigrated to America, settling in Grant County, Wis., where he lived until 1887, when he too, departed this life. Three years after his own passage across the Atlantic, his children—Gertrude, Nicholas and John P.—followed him to America, and our subject grew to manhood on his father's farm in Wisconsin. He remained in that State until 1871, and then became a citizen of this county, making Oxford his first abiding place. There he carried on a mercantile business for a time, but in 1883, moved to his present home on section 16, ValVerde Township, where he owns one hundred and sixty acres of land. The estate is not only furnished with the fine residence and barn before

mentioned, but with all other buildings necessary
for the carrying on of the work of the farm, and
with such fences, trees, and shrubs as make it beautiful and add largely to its value.

The lady to whose housewifely skill and amiable
character, Mr. Nice owes the comforts and pleasure
of his home life, was born in Austria, in 1855, and
bore the maiden name of Mollie Potacek. At the
time of their marriage in 1875, she was a resident
of this county. Their happy union has resulted in
the birth of four children, William, Avice, Lena,
and an infant who died unnamed. Mr. Nice has
held some minor offices, exercises the elective franchise in behalf of the Democratic party, and is a
member of the Farmers' Alliance. He does not
belong to any religious organization but is a Catholic in belief.

OSCAR J. HACKNEY. In 1871 this gentleman left Logan County, Ill., for the Kansas
frontier, coming by rail to Newton, which
was then the western terminus of the road, and
thence by stage to Wichita, then an unpretentious
village, where he was met by a brother and driven
to this county, his arrival being in the month of
September. Wellington had just been platted and
contained but few houses, and in the western part
of the county deer and buffaloes abounded, while
the surrounding country was still in the possession
of the United States Government. Mr. Hackney
took up the southeast quarter of section 25, in
what is now Wellington Township, and at once
erected a house and began a successful career as a
Kansas pioneer farmer. He has added to his
landed estate, and now owns five hundred and
twenty acres of fine land, one hundred and sixty
acres being in Avon and the rest in Wellington
Township.

Mr. Hackney was born in Jefferson County,
Iowa, April 26, 1847, and was a child of about five
years when his parents removed to Logan County,
Ill., where he was reared and educated until about
sixteen years old. In the meantime the Civil

War had broken out, and all over the Northern
States the tidal wave of patriotic enthusiasm had
rolled, carrying with it to the front many a lad
who, though young in years, was old in devotion
to his country; while many a lad was compelled to
remain at home on account of his youth or insuffi-
cient strength, whose heart was with the forces and
who waited longingly for the day to come when he
could enter the army.

In 1863 young Hackney enlisted in Company
H, Seventh Illinois Infantry, and soon after his
enrollment was taking his part in campaign life in
Alabama. From that State the following year he
went to Georgia, joining Sherman's forces at the
famous field of Resaca, and subsequently participating in the battles, skirmishes and weary marches
from that point to Atlanta, being present during
the siege and at the capture of that city, and in
the battle of Altona Pass. During the latter engagement he was seriously wounded, and was laid
up for two months, after which he rejoined his
comrades and marched with the victorious army to
Washington, via Petersburg and Richmond, where
after participating in the Grand Review he was honorably discharged and mustered out of the service.
Returning to his home he rented land, and devoted
himself to the peaceful occupation of farming,
quitting Logan County only to become a citizen
of Kansas.

The wife of Mr. Hackney is a native of Logan
County, Ill., and bore the maiden name of Lena
Clark. She is a daughter of John and Eliza Clark,
and with the educational advantages afforded in
her childhood and the careful training of her worthy parents, was well fitted to discharge all her
duties in life upon reaching womanhood. Her
union with Mr. Hackney was celebrated January
28, 1868, and six children have come to bless their
fireside—Edward, John, Frank, William, Mamie
and Kate.

Mr. Hackney belongs to James Shields Post, No,
57, G. A. R. Until the year 1872 he was a Republican, but since that time his suffrage has been
given to the Democratic party. During Gen.
Grant's presidential term he received the appointment of Postmaster at Wellington and served two
years in that capacity. He is enterprising and

G. A. Sommerville

prudent in his agricultural work, keeps himself well informed regarding current events and general topics of information, and is regarded as a good citizen and honorable man.

The father of our subject is now living at Winfield, Kan., to which place he removed in 1880. He was born in Ohio, and is the son of a farmer who removed from the Buckeye State to Illinois, thence to Iowa, returning subsequently to the Prairie State and spending his last years in Logan County. Jacob T. Hackney accompanied his father to Illinois, and thence to the Territory of Iowa, and was a pioneer settler in Jefferson County. In 1852 he purchased a farm three miles from Mount Pulaski, in Logan County, Ill., upon which he made his home until his removal to this State. His wife, the mother of our subject, bore the maiden name of Lucy Chapman, and was a native of Lexington, Ky. She departed this life at her home in Logan County, Ill., some years since.

EORGE A. SOMMERVILLE. The name of this hardy pioneer, whose portrait is presented on the opposite page, has been familiar to the people of Oxford Township since 1873, when he took up his abode in a then thinly settled region, selecting land on section 36, to the extent of three hundred acres. He comes of sturdy ancestry and was born in Harrison County, W. Va., January 24, 1812. His father, Alexander Sommerville, was born in Scotland and emigrated to the United States a single man. He married Miss Grace Miller and they made their home in the Old Dominion thereafter until the death of the father.

The father of our subject engaged in various pursuits and was looked upon as a man of more than ordinary ability. He was elected Sheriff of Harrison County when his son, George A., was a mere boy, and retained the office for many years. In the meantime the home of the family was in Clarksburg, the county seat, where George A. developed into manhood. The elder Sommerville,

also followed the profession of a teacher for a number of years. The parental household included eleven children, all of whom grew to mature years and of whom George A. was the seventh in order of birth. Alexander Sommerville departed this life at the old homestead in Virginia in 1839. The mother survived her husband for a period of twenty years and in the meantime removed to Indiana where her death took place in 1859.

Upon leaving his native State Mr. Sommerville repaired to Elkhart County, Ind., where he sojourned three years and then took up his abode in Kosciusko County. In the meantime he was occupied in agricultural pursuits and on the 6th of December, 1840, was married in Kosciusko County, to Miss Delilah Firestone. Mrs. Sommerville was born in Logan County, Ohio, in 1822 and was the daughter of Samuel Firestone. When she was a young lady the parents removed to Indiana where they lived until called home to a better land. Six children were born to Mr. and Mrs. Sommerville of whom two only lived to mature years, both sons— Marion, a resident of Harper, Kan., and Jasper, who lives one and one-half miles north in Oxford Township.

The land which Mr. Sommerville first took up had undergone but very slight improvement, although there was a frame building on the place. He thus practically commenced at first principles in the construction of a home, breaking the land, making fences and setting out fruit and shade trees. He was prospered in his labors and in due time found himself in the enjoyment of a competence. He retired from active labor in 1881, renting the farm, but still makes his home there. Mr. Sommerville has given to each of his sons eighty acres of land and has sufficient left to yield him a comfortable income. The first schoolhouse in his district was put up the first summer he located there. He has been Treasurer four years and School Director for two years. He gives his unqualified support to the Republican party. He has been for some time a member of the Missionary Baptist Church and is looked upon as a representative man whose career has been such as to gain him the esteem and confidence of his fellow-citizens. Mrs. Delilah Sommerville departed this life at her home in Oxford Township, August 14, 1884. She was a member of the same church as her husband and an active Christian.

WARREN WOLLAM, one of the enterprising and progressive farmers of Greene Township, was born in Columbiana County, Ohio, November 9, 1851, and is a son of Alfred Wollam, a tiller of the soil in the Buckeye State. In 1863, Alfred Wollam, with his family, which consisted of a wife, seven sons and two daughters, removed to Mercer County, where he and his wife still reside, and where our subject grew to manhood.

Mr. Wollam, of whom we write, acquired an excellent education, and early in life adopted the profession of a teacher, spending the winters in professional work, and during the summers working upon his father's farm until he was twenty-two years old. He taught sixteen terms of school in Mercer County, seven of them being successive in his home district, and since coming to Kansas has spent one term in similar employment.

At the home of the bride in Mercer County, Ohio, August 16, 1873, Mr. Wollam was united in marriage with Miss Elscina, daughter of Wesley Copeland. The bride was torn in Auglaize County, Ohio, June 15, 1854, and has been an able assistant and loving companion since their marriage. After that event the young couple continued to reside in Mercer County until the spring of 1883, when they removed to Kansas, locating on section 29, Greene Township, where they have ever since resided. There Mr. Wollam now owns one hundred and sixty acres of fertile and productive land on which excellent buildings have been erected and other good improvements made. Since coming to this State he has devoted considerable time to carpentering and has built several houses in Greene Township. He is a good workman at the trade, as well as a successful farmer. The family of Mr. and Mrs. Wollam comprises four living children:

Nellie, Alfred, Oma, and Carl, and two infant daughters. Eva and Gertie, were removed from them by the reaper—Death.

Mr. Wollam is an active worker in the Farmers' Alliance, and has been business agent since the organization of the society here. He has held the office of Trustee of Greene Township for three successive terms. He takes an active part in political matters, laboring earnestly for the advancement of the Republican party. In July, 1888, he was sent as a Delegate to the State Republican Convention. In the fall of 1889 he was the Republican candidate for County Clerk, but was defeated by William H. Carnes. Few men of his years within the bounds of Kansas possess a wider fund of information, a more agreeable manner, or a more energetic nature than does he, and his reputation among his associates is that of an upright man and reliable citizen.

ALEXANDER BARNES, a homesteader of 1876, established himself that year in London Township, taking up one hundred and sixty acres of land on section 32. The country around him was then mostly in a wild condition, where few people had settled, presenting thus not a very cheerful outlook. Mr. Barnes, however, had abundant faith in the future of his adopted State, and held his ground, while others, to a certain extent, were coming and going. He carried on the cultivation of his land as rapidly as possible, erected the necessary buildings, planted fruit and shade trees, and in due time found himself the possessor of a snug homestead. He prosecutes general agriculture, and makes a specialty of attending strictly to his own concerns, meddling very little with public affairs, otherwise than to maintain his allegiance to the Democratic party.

A native of what is now West Virginia, Mr. Barnes was born in Brook County, November 4, 1835, and lived there until a young man of twenty years. He then emigrated to Illinois, accompanied by his brother, and subsequently moved to Iowa, of which he was a resident until coming to this county. After leaving his native State, he was married February 1, 1858, to Miss Harriet Barker. This lady was born in Fulton County, Ill., on the 9th of August, 1841, and is a daughter of John and Rachel (Harris) Barker, who were natives of Ohio. Mr. Barker followed farming as his chosen vocation, and is now deceased. Ten children have been born to Mr. and Mrs. Barnes, whom they named respectively: John W., Warren A., Elmer, Carrie, Mattie, Melvin, Walter, Clyde, Dollie, and Cora. They are all living, making an exceedingly bright and interesting group. Carrie married David E. Rogers, and lives in this township.

The father of our subject was Alexander Barnes, Sr., a native of Maryland, who emigrated to the western part of the Old Dominion when a young man. Later we find him in Washington County, Ohio, where he followed his trade of carpenter, and spent his last days. The parental household consisted of ten children. The mother is long since deceased, having died in Ohio at the advanced age of eighty years.

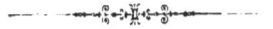

JAMES H. WILLIAMS. The subject of this notice lives quietly and unostentatiously at a snug homestead in Harmon Township, where he has three hundred and twenty acres of choice land, occupying a part of section 19. He came to this county in the fall of 1884 from Sangamon County, Ill., where he was born August 8, 1842. He spent the first twenty years of his life on his father's farm, little occurring to disturb the even tenor of his way until the outbreak of the Civil War. He celebrated his twentieth birthday by enlisting as a soldier in the Union Army in Company E, One Hundred and Fourteenth Illinois Infantry, and rendered a faithful service of three years or until the close of the war. The regiment was assigned to the Army of the Tennessee and he endured the various hardships inseparable from life in the army, but preserved his health and strength

in a remarkable degree, escaping capture and wounds from the enemy. He was present at the battles of Jackson, Vicksburg, Brandon, Nashville, Mobile, Ft. Blakely and numerous other engagements.

After receiving his honorable discharge from the service of Uncle Sam, Mr. Williams returned to the place of his birth and sojourned there until 1868. In the meantime he was married March 12, 1868, to Miss Caroline F. Hedrick. The newly wedded pair settled in Christian County, Ill., where Mr. Williams engaged in farming and where they lived until the spring of 1881. Then returning to Sangamon County they resided there until the fall of that year and then set their faces toward the country west of the Mississippi. Mrs. Williams, like her husband, is a native of Sangamon County, Ill., and was born August 11, 1851. Her parents were Alfred and Nancy Hedrick, natives of Tennessee and Ohio. The father resides in Taylorville, Ill., the mother is deceased.

To our subject and his estimable wife there have been born five children, viz.: Herbert L., Frederick, Emma, Hattie and Rosa. Hattie died when an interesting child of twelve years; the other children are at home with their parents. It is hardly necessary to state that Mr. Williams thoroughly believes in the principles of the Republican party to which he has given his support since becoming a voting citizen. He was elected Township Trustee in the fall of 1885, serving two terms and was re-elected in the fall of 1889. He has been a member of the school board of his district and occupied other positions of trust and responsibility. He and his wife, with their son Frederick and daughter Emma, are members in good standing of the Christian Church.

The home surroundings of Mr. Williams and his family present a picture of plenty and content which is delightful to contemplate. The dwelling is a comfortable structure and adjacent is a goodly assortment of fruit and shade trees, together with the various other appurtenances usually belonging to a rural home. Mr. Williams keeps a fair assortment of live stock and realizes each year from his well-cultivated fields a sufficient income to supply his wants and enable him to lay by something for a rainy day. Isaiah B., and Phebe Williams, the parents of our subject, were natives of Vermont and Kentucky and came to Illinois when small, where they have since resided. They live in Custer, Ill.

~~~~~~~~~~~~~~~~~~~~~~~~~~~~~~~

ANDREW S. OMO. Among the honored veterans of Jackson Township none are held in greater respect than Mr. Omo and his estimable wife. They commenced the journey of life together over fifty years ago, a journey in which their interests have been mutual, and which has been singularly blest by affection and contentment. Both are remarkably well preserved, and from choice still continue the performance of their daily duties, finding in them a solace far more comfortable than idleness. Mr. Omo has passed his seventy-seventh birthday, having been born in 1813, and his native place was at Little York, York County, Pa.

In reverting to the antecedents of the subject of this notice, we find that he is the son of Simon Omo, who was born in Paris, France, and entered the army when a lad of fifteen years, serving under Napoleon. He thus spent seven years of his life, and at the expiration of this time was detailed to cross the Atlantic with three vessels for provisions. The vessels laid at the port of Philadelphia nearly three months, and in the meantime Simon Omo and three of his comrades deserted. They had but fifty cents between them, and were unable to speak the English language. They struck out for the country, and luckily found a well-to-do Frenchman on a farm, who gave them a square meal besides provisions to take with them and $2 in cash.

Thus equipped, the father of our subject and his comrades proceeded to Lancaster, Pa., and young Omo engaged with a blacksmith to learn the trade. He served an apprenticeship of four years, and continued with his employer a number of years longer. Then, being married, he located at Little York, where he continued to sojourn until

1820. That year he removed to Union County, and was a resident of Lewisburg one year. Subsequently he rented a tract of land four miles south of New Berlin, where he lived two years. Next he removed into the town, where he resumed work at his trade and resided many years.

Finally, selling out, Simon Omo left the Keystone State, emigrating to Allen County, Ind., where he spent his last days with his children. His death took place in 1871, after he had reached the advanced age of ninety-three years. His wife, the mother of our subject, bore the maiden name of Mary Mosher. She was born in Lancaster, Pa., and descended from German and Swiss ancestry. She departed this life in New Berlin, Pa., about 1859. There were born to her and her husband eight children.

Mr. Omo, of this notice, remained a resident of Union County, Pa., until 1852. In addition to blacksmithing, his father also engaged in the manufacture of brick, and Andrew learned the trade, which he followed in Union County until the date above mentioned. Then, removing to Lycoming County, he officiated as Superintendent of a brickyard there three years. In the fall of 1855 he set out for Iowa, making his way by railroad to Rock Island, Ill., which was then the western terminus of the Great Western Railroad. Thence he took a stage to Tipton, Iowa, crossing the Mississippi on a steamboat at Rock Island. He purchased land in Cedar County to the extent of a half-section ten miles northeast of the town and one and one-half miles east of the present site of Clarence. He put up a frame house and then returned to Pennsylvania for his family. The nearest markets to his land were at Davenport and Muscatine, forty miles away. Mr. Omo settled upon his land, which he brought to a good state of cultivation, and whereon he erected comfortable buildings.

Sojourning in the Hawkeye State until 1876, Mr. Omo then sold out and came to Kansas, locating in Pawnee County and taking up a timber claim as a homestead. In common with his neighbors, he suffered from drouth, grasshoppers and other ills, but lived there until 1883. Then, selling out at a sacrifice, he came to Sumner County and purchased one hundred and sixty acres of land on section 25, in what is now Jackson Township. His house is now but a few rods from Rome station—a roomy and convenient structure, where Mr. Omo and his excellent wife entertain travelers in that home-like manner more like a private family than an hotel. At the time Mr. Omo took possession of his land only sixty acres had been broken, and the only improvement was a small "box" house. It is hardly necessary to say that the premises presented a widely different appearance from that of to-day. Mr. Omo in due time put up a more modern residence and planted about fourteen hundred fruit trees, which are now in a good bearing condition, including a large and choice variety. As time passed on, he gathered around himself and his family the other comforts and conveniences of modern life. His course has been signalized by industry and perseverance, while as a man and a citizen Mr. Omo has conducted himself in such a manner as to gain the confidence and esteem of all who know him.

The marriage of Andrew S. Omo and Miss Sarah Rudy was celebrated at the bride's home, in New Berlin, Pa., August 10, 1839. Mrs. Omo was born in Union County, Pa., May 6, 1821, and is the daughter of Philip and Sarah (Overmoyer) Rudy, who were natives of Pennsylvania, and spent their last days in that State. To Mr. and Mrs. Omo there was born a family of sixteen children, of whom the following were reared to mature years. Agnes, the eldest living, is the wife of Harvey Lowrey and the mother of four children; her husband is deceased, and the widow resides in Wellington, Kan. A. Percival during the Civil War served as a Union soldier in an Iowa regiment; he is married and the father of eight children, making his home in Pratt County, Kan. Simon A. is married, and has two children; Sarah J. is the wife of Robert Laporte and the mother of two children; Laura married Edwin Olive, and also has two children; Henrietta, Mrs. Donald Cory, is the mother of eight children; George Ira is married, and has four children; Alice, Mrs. James Hagerty, is the mother of four children; Cyrus died when thirty years old; Jerome is married, and lives in Montana; Frederick is married, and has two children; Lizzie remains at home with her parents; Maggie is the

wife of William Newton. Mr. and Mrs. Omo pride themselves on the possession of thirty-two grandchildren and six great-grandchildren. They form a large and pleasant family, and are recognized as among the most respectable elements of Sumner County. Mrs. Omo, a kind, motherly woman, is a member in good standing of the Presbyterian Church.

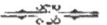

JONATHAN D. BILLITER is a typical Southern gentleman, brave and high spirited, enthusiastic in his support of any measure to which he gives adherence, the soul of hospitality, and generous and whole-souled to those in need. The paternal ancestry were Scotch, and North Carolina was the home of both the parental lines for more than one generation.

The parents of our subject, Mathew and Sarah J. (Yates) Billiter were born, reared and married in the State above mentioned, and there the father carried on his occupations of a mechanic and a farmer until his death in 1847. The widow subsequently married Richard Ransom of the same State, who has since died, and she still lives there at the age of seventy-two years.

The gentleman of whom we write was the youngest of three children born to his parents, and is the only one who now survives. His natal day was September 17, 1846, and the place of his birth, Forsythe County, N. C. He received a common-school education and an excellent home training, and began life for himself at the age of twenty years without financial assistance and in possession of only the clothes he wore. He adopted the occupation of a farmer, has made it his life work and successfully prosecuted it for nearly a quarter of a century.

Mr. Billiter was in his teens when the Civil War broke out but, young as he was, was deeply interested in the internecine strife and at the age of eighteen years he took up arms in behalf of the Confederacy. He enlisted in Company B, Third North Carolina Infantry, and took part in the bat-

tles at Petersburg, Ft. Fisher, Kingston, Goldsboro
and Smithfield, bearing himself gallantly in every
conflict, and enduring cheerfully the toils incidental
to a soldier's life which proved so monotonous when
unmixed with the excitement of battle. He was
attached to the army of Gen. Joseph E. Johnston
and was present at the surrender of Goldsboro, N.C.
Whatever may be our opinion regarding the rights
and wrongs of the Civil War, honor belongs to all
who abandoned home and friends for the field of battle and who displayed in the thick of the fight their
bravery and devotion to the principles in which they
believed, and it is a pleasure to the biographer, while
deeply regretting the losses of the great struggle, to
note the worthy conduct of American citizens from
the North and the South during those sad years.
Both the brothers of our subject served in the
Twenty-first North Carolina Regiment—John, the
second son, dying in the service, and Phillip L.,
going through the war and surviving until 1871.

In 1866, Mr. Billiter went to Missouri and settled
in Jackson County, where he remained twelve
years. While there, November 17, 1869, he was
united in marriage with Miss Margaret E. Benton,
a most estimable lady, who has shared his fortunes
since that day, adding to his joys and endeavoring
to assist and encourage him in every good work.
Mrs. Billiter is the fourth of twelve children born
to her parents, is a native of Tennessee, and her
natal day was August 11, 1844. She received a
common-school education, and by reading and observation has added to the knowledge thus obtained
an excellent fund of information.

The parents of Mrs. Billiter are C. L. and Mary
(Gentry) Benton, natives of North Carolina and
Kentucky, respectively. They were wedded in Indiana, lived in that State two years, thence removed
to Tennessee and nine years later returned to the
Hoosier State where they sojourned four years. In
1856 they removed to Missouri, settling in Harrison
County, where they resided four years, removing
thence to Decatur County, Iowa. After a sojourn
of four years in the Hawkeye State they went
again to Missouri, spent a year in Clay County,
and then took up their abode in Jackson County.
There Mrs. Benton died in 1869. After living in
Jackson County five years Mr. Benton removed to

Cass County, where he now resides with his second
wife, his age being sixty-nine years. He served in
the Union army during the Civil War as a member
of Company A, Thirty-fourth Missouri Infantry.
Of the children borne by the mother of Mrs. Billiter
eight are now living.

In 1878 Mr. and Mrs. Billiter removed from
Jackson County, Mo., to Kansas, locating upon
a farm in Ryan Township, Sumner County, where
they have since resided. When they began their
occupancy of the farm it was all raw land, but it is
now in an excellent condition of cultivation and
improvement, with one hundred and thirty-five
acres of the quarter section which comprises it under plow. Cattle, horses and hogs are raised in the
numbers usually to be found on a quarter-section
of Kansas land.

The family of Mr. and Mrs. Billiter comprised
four sons and daughters—John C., Edgar F., Sarah
Lutitia and James Dawson. John C. died in 1879.
Mr. Billiter is a member of the Farmers' Alliance,
is actively interested in politics and votes the Democratic ticket. He served two terms as Township
Treasurer and one term as Township Trustee. He
is Elder in the Christian Church and Superintendent of the Sunday-school, and his wife also is a
member of the same religious organization. Both
are prominent in the community in which they live,
are well known and held in high repute by their
fellow-citizens.

LESLIE COOMBS. The subject of this notice
is numbered among the prominent and well-
to-do farmers of Downs Township, being
the owner of three hundred and sixty broad acres
of land and having his residence on section 15. A
part of his land lies on this section and the balance
on sections 11 and 16. He came to this county in
1881 and has proved a valuable acquisition to its
agricultural interests, having had a life-long experience as a farmer and dealer in live stock and
prosecuting his labors in that thorough and syste-

matic manner which forms an excellent example for others to imitate. He was born in LaRue County, Ky., February 21, 1852, and is the son of Walter W. and Sarah E. (Churchill) Coombs, who were likewise natives of the Blue Grass State.

Walter W. Coombs was born July 8, 1829, and spent his entire life in his native State, being, however, cut down in his prime when only thirty-three years of age. His father, Samuel Coombs, likewise a native of Kentucky, was born in 1799 and died in that State. The mother of our subject is still living in Kentucky, being about sixty years old, having been born February 4, 1830. Her parents were Armstead and Mary (Brown) Churchill, natives of Virginia and members of well-known Virginia families. To Walter W. Coombs and his estimable wife were born a family of five children, viz. Churchill, Leslie, Susan, John A. and Ida. Three are living, two residing in Kentucky with their mother and our subject.

The subject of this sketch spent the days of his boyhood and youth amid the peaceful pursuits of farm life in his native county and at an early age gained a good insight into the arts of plowing, sowing and reaping. After coming to this county he was married April 2, 1885, to Miss Fanny Rasdall. Mrs. Coombs is likewise a native of Kentucky and was born in Warren County, March 21, 1866, thus being twenty years old at the time of her marriage. Her parents were Clay and Belle (Clayton) Rasdall natives of Kentucky who came to this county in 1880 and are still residing here in Downs Township.

RUBEN NEAL. This model farmer and stockraiser of Falls Township, is considered one of the most liberal and public-spirited men in his community, and by his genial an I companionable disposition and courteous treatment of all around him, finds friends wherever he goes. He has been no unimportant factor in advancing the agricultural interests of this section, his own example of thrift and industry furnishing

an incentive to those around him to do likewise as far as in them lay. He has one of the most attractive homesteads in the township, comprising three hundred and twenty acres of highly-improved land, embellished with tasteful and convenient modern buildings. He has found stock-raising extremely profitable, and to this industry gives the most of his attention.

The native place of Mr. Neal was on the other side of the Atlantic in Lincolnshire, England, where his birth took place February 19, 1851. He comes of stanch English ancestry, being the son of Rev. William H. and Phebe (Dudley) Neal, who were both descended from good families and who emigrated to America during the same year in which their son Ruben was born. They settled in the city of Buffalo, N. Y., where the father for many years officiated as a minister of the Methodist Episcopal Church, serving with distinction, being possessed of marked ability and a good education. He remained connected with this denomination until 1878, then went over to the Society of Friends, and later, coming West, is now installed as pastor of a Quaker Church in Emporia, this State. He is now aged about sixty-six years, having been born in 1824, while his estimable wife is two years younger. They are the parents of three sons—Ruben, William H. and John T. The two younger are residents of Buffalo, N. Y., and Bay City, Mich.

Mr. Neal was reared in the city of Buffalo, N. Y., where he attended the city schools and upon becoming his own man, chose farming for his vocation. He followed this in Erie County, N. Y., until 1876, then determined to seek his fortunes in the far West. Coming to this county he pre-empted one hundred and sixty acres of land on section 30, Falls Township, where he settled and has since resided. Subsequently he purchased another quarter section, these lying on sections 19 and 30, so that he now has in all three hundred and twenty well-tilled acres, comprising as fine a farm as is to be found within the limits of this county. When coming to this region he was entirely without means, having even to borrow the money to pay for entering his land.

The first dwelling of Mr. Neal in Kansas was a sod house, which he constructed at a cost of $6, and which he occupied with his family for two years. He is now domiciled in a fine two story frame residence, finished and furnished in modern style, and has an equally fine barn and conveniently arranged outbuildings. Providence smiled upon his efforts from the beginning, and he is in the enjoyment of this fine property, free from incumbrance, and with the prospect of a sufficiency for his old age. He operates almost altogether in high-grade stock of all kinds and has contributed in no small degree to the live stock interests of this county, assisting in raising the standard and laboring with his brother farmers in eliminating the poorer grades, so that each year there is noticeable an improvement throughout Sumner County in this respect.

Politically, Mr. Neal is a sound Republican. He and his excellent wife are active members of the Methodist Episcopal Church at Caldwell, contributing a liberal support thereto and being among its chief pillars. Mrs. Neal was in her girlhood Miss Clara Broughton, daughter of William and Adelaide (Palmer) Broughton, and was married to our subject at Buffalo, N. Y., January 1, 1875. Her native place was Covington, Wyoming County, N. Y., and the date of her birth September 6, 1856. Eight children came to bless this union, four of whom are living, viz: John F., George H., William R., and Howard. Jessie, Phœbe and two infants unnamed are deceased.

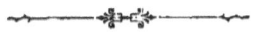

NORMAN GRIST, an early settler of Sumner County, Kan., resides on section 1, Belle Plaine Township. He was ushered into this world May 27, 1842, in Bradford County, Pa. His parents, Lyman and Caroline (Ellis) Grist were also born in that State, and their ancestors are supposed to be natives of New England of English stock. Lyman and Caroline Grist were the parents of nine children, named, respectively: Savannah, who is the wife of Morris Wilcox and lives in Bradford County, Pa.; Mary, the wife of George Burgess, resides in Barber County, Kan.;

Thomas H. makes his home in Wisconsin; Salina is the wife of Andrew Melville, of Bradford County, Pa.; Norman, the subject of this sketch; Ann, John and Sarah are at home, and one is deceased.

The subject of this notice was reared on a farm in his native State, where he secured a fine physical development and a fair elementary education in the common English branches taught in the country schools of that State. Although the means of obtaining a good education were far more limited in those days than in the present time, yet our subject was undismayed at the prospect and kept "pegging away," learning a little here and a little there until he has managed to obtain a large fund of useful and interesting knowledge embracing all the essentials of a liberal education.

When the dark cloud of Civil War burst upon the devoted head of the nation, our subject was only a boy of eighteen years but, in response to the call for troops to defend the old flag from misguided zealots who would have trailed the starry banner in the dust, he enlisted April 24, 1861, in Company I, Sixth Pennsylvania Reserves and was assigned to duty in the Army of the Potomac. He remained with that portion of the Federal troops during the entire war, a period of over four years. He made an honorable record as a gallant soldier and was faithful to his duty during all the vicissitudes through which that famous army passed. He fought in the battle of Manassas and during the Peninsular campaign his regiment was engaged in guarding railroads leading from Whitehouse Landing on the Pamunky River to the main body of the army. He was also in the second battle of Bull Run when the boys in blue were a second time put to flight by the lads in gray, and in the battles of South Mountain and Antietam where the "blues' cleverly turned the tables on their exultant foes and drove them across the Potomac.

Mr. Grist was in the fiercely fought battle of Fredricksburg where he was wounded in the left shoulder. This necessitated his removal to the hospital where he was detained some three months, and during that time the battle of Chancellorsville was fought. As soon as his wound was healed our subject rejoined his command and participated in the conflict at Gettysburg when the tide of victory turned in favor of the Northern arms. He was afterward in the three days' fight in the Wilderness; at the siege of Petersburg where, while assisting to capture the Eidon Railroad, he was wounded in the right side, which sent him to the hospital once again, but he recovered in time to be present at the surrender of Lee at Appomattox. When the latter event took place our subject was a member of the Fifth Corps under Sheridan. He was finally discharged, July 1, 1865, and returned to his home in Pennsylvania. While in Washington he participated in the grand review of the troops which took place in the presence of the President and all the high officials in addition to the principal generals. It was a grand sight and one not easily forgotten.

Upon returning to Pennsylvania our subject took up his life again at the old home, but soon wearied of the place and resolved to try the West to make a fortune. He went to Fayette County, Iowa, where he resided several years. February 24, 1869, he was married to Miss Libbie Davis, a daughter of John and Ann (Fox) Davis, who were both natives of Wales. Eight children have come to their home to share their love and claim their care, named, respectively: Harry B., Carrie A., Maggie M., Earl J; Hattie, who is deceased; Kate, Lura and Fay.

In the spring of 1871 our subject emigrated to Sumner County, Kan., and pre-empted one hundred and sixty acres of land, upon which he now resides. It was all new, unimproved land and our subject turned the first furrow on the section. By energy and persevering industry he has brought it up to its present state of high cultivation and productiveness. The usual hardships of a pioneer life have fallen to his lot but cheerful courage has enabled him and his excellent wife to surmount them all, and they are now rewarded for their faith in the possibilities of the country which they found in such an undeveloped state, by its present fine condition as regards education, morals and refinement.

For some years Mr. Grist has not enjoyed good health, rheumatism and other ailments have contributed to undermine his physical well-being, but he is a patient sufferer and keeps up good heart not wishing to dampen the pleasure of his family by useless repining. He is a member of the Old Set-

tlers Society and finds himself regarded as a representative farmer and veteran soldier. No one is more deserving of the respect and esteem which he receives than the subject of this biography. He has seen the growth of the county from nothing, as it were, to its present thriving condition and rejoices in the progress which has been made. He is a Republican in politics and favors whatever will help to build up the community in material or intellectual prosperity. Mr. Grist is now Clerk of the School Board and has served one term as Director, in which position he gave good satisfaction.

REV. ROLLIN H. SEYMOUR, proprietor of the Waldon House at South Haven, is well-known to the people of this vicinity, and is doing the entire hotel business of the city. He located at this point in 1886, putting up the present structure, which has become an almost indispensable institution to the traveling public. It is conducted upon first-class principles, and "mine host" is not only a favorite with his guests, but among the people of the entire community.

Of Eastern antecedents, the subject of this notice was born in New Haven County, Conn., August 24, 1834. He lived there on a farm until a lad of fourteen years. His father, Stephen Seymour, was a member of the firm of Ives, Kendrick & Co., brass manufacturers at Waterville, where he lived until about sixty-eight years old. Then, retiring from active labor, he removed to Waterbury, Conn., where he spent his last days, dying at the age of about seventy-one years. He was a member of the Episcopal Church, to which the various other members of the family belonged.

The mother of our subject bore the maiden name of Flora Harrison. She was the daughter of Aaron Harrison, and was born in Wolcott, Conn., of which her parents were residents many years. Grandfather Harrison was a musician of considerable talent, and officiated as Drum-Major in the War of 1812. He died in Camp at Branford,

Conn. The parents of our subject both died at
the old homestead. Grandfather Seymour was a
native of Wales, whence he crossed the Atlantic
with three brothers and their families and located
on the Connecticut River, where they all spent
the remainder of their lives. They were prominent members of the old Welsh colony which made
for itself a name during the early settlement of
Connecticut, and were members of the Episcopal
Church. The Harrisons traced their ancestry to
England.

After reaching his fourteenth year young Seymour began to assist his father in the office at the
factory, and two years later he entered a good
school in the city of New Haven, where he took
a four years' course, in the meantime assisting his
father during vacations. After completing his
studies he worked in the factory for a time, and
later entered the Middleton Theological Methodist
Episcopal College, having identified himself with
this religious denomination at the age of twenty-
one years. He soon exhibited uncommon talent
as a pulpit orator, was ordained, and preached until
about 1881.

The elder Seymour at one time entered upon the
hazardous undertaking of going to England for
the purpose of bringing two English mechanics to
the United States, these being Samuel Forest and
Israel Holmes, the plan being to convey them from
the Old Country in a water cask, as there was a
severe penalty for importing such service to this
country. The enterprise, however, proved successful, they being placed in the cask and fed
through the bung-hole until they were out of
English waters. They worked in the factory many
years, and died in Waterbury, Conn. at a ripe old
age.

To the parents of our subject there was born a
family of eight sons, all of whom lived to mature
years—the eldest, Mason S. S., has for thirty years
been practicing medicine successfully on Long
Island; Charles H. was graduated from Trinity
College at Hartford, and is now a prominent
clergyman of the Episcopal Church; Rollin H.,
our subject, was the third in order of birth; William G., who won considerable distinction as an
artist, died at the age of twenty-eight years, in

Haverhill, Mass.; Harry A. is living on a farm
near Watertown, Conn., and is a large grower of
fine-wool sheep; John O. died at the age of eighteen years; Ralph died when two years old; Benjamin F. was graduated from Trinity College, and
from Francova Eva, at Montreal, Canada, after
studying in the latter seven years, and was an
Episcopal clergyman, also professor of French and
German in a college at Puget Sound. Prior to his
removal to the West he held a Professor's Chair in
a school in Pennsylvania.

The subject of this sketch was married in September, 1857, at Norfolk, Conn., to Miss Ellen L.
Brown, of that city. About that time he associated himself in partnership with one Samuel
Ives, in New Haven, engaging in the mercantile
business. In the spring of 1863 he disposed of his
interest in the concern to his partner, and his
home was broken up by the death of his wife,
which occurred that same year. In 1865 he contracted a second marriage with Mrs. Agnes S.
(Murphy)Bauce, of Salsbury. He continued to
reside in New Haven until October, 1868, then
coming to Kansas, located at Junction City, and
became a contractor for the erection of brick buildings. In the spring of 1870 he removed to Ottawa
County, where he engaged in the live-stock business, and also kept supplies for stockmen.

Five years later Mr. Seymour removed to Norton
County, and now turned his attention more closely
to religious matters, entering the ministry of the
Methodist Episcopal Church, in which he had
officiated on Sundays for many years. As time
passed on he organized a number of churches in
the Northwestern District of Kansas, but was
finally compelled to resign his labors on account
of ill health. We next find him a resident of
South Haven, in which he put up the first hotel.
At Norton he also erected the first hotel, the first
store and the first residence, having taken up land
as a homestead claim. He was for some time
President of the Town Site Company there. He
was a third time married at Alma, Neb., in 1886,
to Mrs. Mary A. (Ramsey) Simpson, and they have
one child living, a daughter, Bessie M.

Soon after the outbreak of the Civil War Mr.
Seymour, in June, 1861, enlisted as a Union sol-

dier in Company B, Forty-third New York Infantry, as a private. On the 21st of September following he was commissioned Second-Lieutenant of his regiment, in Hancock's Brigade, and served in that capacity until wounded by a gunshot, May 5, 1862, at the battle of Williamsburg. He was struck three times, once in the knee, once on the foot and once in his side. He carried the latter ball until January, 1877, when it was removed. As may naturally be supposed he has been a great sufferer from this, and for two years his side was wholly paralyzed, and is only now partially restored to its natural condition. He was honorably discharged on account of wounds received while in line of duty.

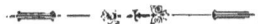

ALEXANDER K. CULBERTSON, the founder of Drury, which he laid out in 1877, on his farm, has his residence in South Haven Township, on section 6, where he has erected a fine dwelling and gives his attention to agricultural pursuits. He is the owner of five hundred and ten acres of land, being thus well-to-do, financially, and is a self-made man, the architect of his own fortune, indebted simply to his own energy and industry for his possessions. A native of Ohio, he was born near Zanesville, Muskingum County, March 18, 1844, and is thus in the prime of life, and the midst of his usefulness. His career since coming to the Sunflower State has furnished an admirable example of persevering industry, and should be a source of encouragement to the young man beginning at the foot of the ladder in life, and having only his own resources to depend upon.

Mr. Culbertson is descended from substantial Pennsylvania stock on his father's side, being the son of William B. and Louisa B. (Moody) Culbertson, the former of whom was born in Chambersburg, Pa., about 1808. William B. Culbertson, when an infant, was taken by his parents to Muskingum County, Ohio, where he was reared to man's estate,

and chose farming for his life vocation. At this he was very successful, becoming the possessor of a fine property. He did not live to be aged, departing this life in March, 1861, when about fifty-three years old. His father was Samuel Culbertson, likewise a native of the Keystone State, and of Irish extraction.

The mother of Mr. Culbertson was born in the city of Portland, Me., November 12, 1809, and departed this life January 22, 1890, at Muncie, Ind. The ten children of the parental family are recorded as follows: William M. is engaged as a coal and lumber dealer at Lawrence, this State; Granville M. died in infancy; Harriet A. is the widow of A. E. Fillmore, of Zanesville, Ohio; Sidney E. is the wife of Jefferson Van Horne, a banker of Zanesville; Louisa and Stillman are deceased; Ida L. is the wife of A. E. Lyman, a boot and shoe dealer of Muncie, Ind.; George V. died when a promising young man, about twenty-four years old; Samuel W. died when about twenty-seven years old; and the subject of this sketch. Samuel W. was the eldest.

The subject of this sketch was the sixth child of his parents, with whom he spent the years of his boyhood and youth, residing on the home farm near Zanesville, Ohio, and acquiring a practical education in the district schools, also attending school in Zanesville. He lived in the Buckeye State until a man of twenty-seven years, then in March, 1871, turned his steps toward the farther West, coming to this county and pre-empting one hundred and sixty acres of land on the Chikaskia River. This embraced the northeast quarter of section 1, Falls Township, where he put up a log cabin and lived six years. At the expiration of this time he changed his residence to his present homestead, and is now the owner of five hundred and ten broad acres. He deals largely in sheep and cattle, and has been no unimportant factor in developing the agricultural interests of Sumner County. He is a sound Republican, politically, and belongs to the Farmers' Alliance, and has held some of the minor offices.

On the 8th of March, 1877, Mr. Culbertson was wedded at the bride's home in South Haven Township, to Miss Drury Davis. This lady was born in

Nodaway County, Mo., June 12, 1855, and is the daughter of Hiram and Mary J. (Broyles) Davis. Her parents were natives of Virginia, and are now residing in Oklahoma. There have been born of this congenial union three children, all sons; William B., Sidney B. and Berryman K. In addition to being a thorough and skillful farmer, Mr. Culbertson is considered one of the most liberal and public-spirited men in his community, encouraging the projects calculated to advance the interests of the people, socially, morally and financially.

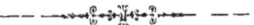

NELSON H. SNOWDEN has for several years been Superintendent of the Sumner County Poor Farm, and so successful and satisfactory has been his management that he is re-engaged for the years 1890-91. He is a native of the Hoosier State to which his grandfather, James Snowden, moved from Ohio, settling among the early inhabitants of Union County and entering a tract of Government land, located partly in Harmony and partly in Liberty Townships, building a log house in the latter. At that time and in that section timber was valueless, and in clearing the land large logs were rolled together and burned. The grandfather cleared and cultivated his farm and lived upon it until his death. His son Jacob, the father of our subject, was born in Ohio, but was a mere child when his parents moved to the Hoosier State where he spent the remainder of his life. Having grown to manhood, he married Miss Eliza A. Langston, and purchased a tract of land in Harmony Township, upon which he built the log house in which our subject was born. There were no railroads in that section for many years, and the nearest market was Cincinnati, forty-five miles distant. Like his father before him, Jacob Snowden cleared his farm, and there ten children were born to him, nine of whom lived to mature years. His death took place December 15, 1869, and his wife survived until August, 1878, both passing away on the home farm.

The natal day of our subject was January 1,

1852. In his youth he attended school as regularly as was possible, and as his strength would admit assisted in the work upon the farm, of which he took charge at the death of his father and upon which he continued to reside until 1875. He then entered the employ of the Pittsburg, Cincinnati & St. Louis Railroad, and after four years spent in railroading, again took up his labors on the home farm which he rented until 1884, at which date he became a resident of this county.

At the home of the bride's parents, G. W. and Ellen Mills, in Houston County, Minn., July 11, 1877, Mr. Snowden was united in marriage with Miss Emma Mills, a native of Henry County, Ind., and a young lady whose character and acquirements promised well for the future happiness of the home. Mr. and Mrs. Snowden are the parents of two children—Cora and Louis. In politics Mr. Snowden is a sound Republican. He belongs to the Christian Church and endeavors in his daily life to carry out the Golden Rule and fulfill all the duties which devolve upon him as man and citizen, in a worthy manner.

JOHN C. LAMBDIN. This gentleman has a large circle of acquaintances throughout the State of which he is a pioneer, and is held in high esteem by all who know his life and character. He was the first Probate Judge of Butler County, which he assisted in organizing in 1858, and the title which was then bestowed upon him, is the one by which he is familiarly known to this day. In 1859, he was elected a member of the Territorial Council, and served in the sessions of 1859-60. Although capable of serving a constituency in any department of public life, he declines to be a candidate for office, preferring to serve his fellow-men in a private capacity.

Judge Lambdin was born in Pittsburg, Pa., October 15, 1819, and is the only survivor of a family of six children. His boyhood was passed in Cincinnati, Ohio, and he received only a common-school education. When about seventeen years of age, he went on to his father's farm in Clermont County and remained there until 1837, when he re moved to Johnson County, Ind., and engaged in a manufacturing business. He moved the business to Paris, Ill., in 1851, and to Point Commerce, Ind., about two years later, remaining in the latter place until May, 1857, when he started for Kansas. A few months later we find Mr. Lambdin located in Butler County, at Chelsea, and soon after filling the positions of public responsibility before noted, and in the intervals of public life, devoting his time to farming and stock-raising.

When the Civil War broke out, Kansas was not behind her older sisters in her desire to uphold the Union and it was not long until almost every able bodied man living in the section with Judge Lamb din had joined the army, even his two sons having left their home for a life on the tented field. He de termined to send the remainder of his family back to Illinois, and he too joined the Union forces as stock Quartermaster of Lane's brigade. He subse quently left that command, assisted in the organi zation of the Indian brigade of five regiments and re-entered the service as Quartermaster of the Fifth regiment of Indian troops, serving in that capacity until the fall of 1863, when he was called to Leav enworth and put on Provost Marshal duty in the Southwest. In that capacity he served until the close of the war, when he returned to Butler County, and resumed the arts of peace.

Judge Lambdin again took up his former occu pations of farming and the stock business, and he also conducted a mercantile business at Eldorado for more than fifteen years. In 1881 he moved to Caldwell, but has been engaged in no regular busi ness since except that of looking after his real estate business. He was Superintendent of the Water Works, the first year the system was put in, and al though he declines office is one of the most liberal and public-spirited citizens of the town, manifest ing a deep interest in every scheme which is pro mulgated for the public good and contributing generously to all in which his judgment concurs. Being possessed of mental abilities of no mean or der, and desirous of adding to the knowledge ob tained in his early years, he has taken advantage of every opportunity which reading and observation

would afford and has become well informed on cur rent topics and in various lines of thought. He be longs to the Masonic fraternity and to the Knights of Pythias.

Judge Lambdin has been twice married. His first matrimonial alliance was contracted in 1839 and he became the husband of Miss Caroline Beachbard of Madison, Ind., who was spared to him and her fam ily until 1853. She was the mother of three sons, William R., Joshua T, and John W. The first two served during the late war; John W. is now de ceased. After having remained a widower until 1855, Judge Lambdin became the husband of Mary V. Vaught, of Paris, Ill., who has borne him one son —Robert M.

In the paternal line, Judge Lambdin is of Welsh descent, his grandfather, Robert Lambdin, having emigrated from Wales to America prior to the Rev olutionary War and settled in Maryland. John Lambdin, the father of our subject, was born in that State about the year 1776, grew to maturity there and married Miss Mary Roberts, a lady of Irish extraction. They removed to Pittsburg, Pa., whence, in 1821, they departed to Cincinnati, Ohio, where Mrs. Lambdin died in 1857. A portion of their time was spent on a farm in Clermont County. Mr. Lambdin was a carpenter and one of the most skilled workmen of his day; his financial circum stances were easy. He was a member of the Metho dist Church, and his death, which occurred in 1852, found him prepared for the scenes of futurity.

HOMAS DUNBAR, a successful general farmer of South Haven, may usually be found at his headquarters on section 16, where he has one hundred and sixty acres of land in a high state of cultivation and makes a specialty of stock-raising, mostly good grades of cattle and horses. He came to this county in 1876 when the greater part of the land in this region was the prop erty of the Government and when wild animals were plentiful, including deer, antelope, turkeys and wolves. The nearest market was at Wichita to which the produce of the few farmers who had settled in this region was hauled laboriously overland with teams, across the prairie, in many places unmarked save by an Indian trail.

Upon first coming to this region Mr. Dunbar took up his abode in a little frame house, 14x20 feet in dimensions, which he occupied for three years and in the meantime proceeded with the improvement of this property. He sold this farm in 1879, purchasing that which he now owns. His career has been marked by close application to his calling and straightforward dealings with his fellow-citizens by which he has established himself in their confidence and esteem.

A native of New York State, Mr. Dunbar was born in the romantic regions around Lake Champlain, February 1, 1844. Two years later his parents, John and Mary (Linton) Dunbar, removed to Canada, locating at Ormston, where the father occupied himself as a carpenter. About 1853 they changed their residence to Lashute, on the North River, and there the father died in 1867, aged sixty-five years. He was a native of Northern Scotland, where he was reared in the doctrines of the Presbyterian Church and where he was married to his first wife, who died there. His second wife, Mary Linton, the mother of our subject, likewise a native of Scotland, was born in the city of Edinburg and when a mere child was brought by her parents to Canada; they settled in Montreal where the parents died in the faith of the Presbyterian Church.

Mrs. Dunbar after the death of her husband, removed with her family of eight sons to Livingston County, Ill., and later came to this State of which she is still a resident, making her home with three of her sons in Gunnison County. Thomas, our subject, on the 25th of February, 1888, was wedded at the bride's home in South Haven Township, this county, to Miss Jenny E., daughter of Henry and Melissa (Jourdan) Clayton, a native of Byron County, Ky. Mrs. Dunbar came to Kansas with her mother in 1883, her father having died in Kentucky. Mrs. Clayton was subsequently married to Stephen Riggs and is now a resident of South Haven Township. Mr. and Mrs. Dunbar have had one child, a son, Bruce, who died when five months

old. Mrs. Dunbar is a member in good standing of the Christian Church. Mr. Dunbar was reared in Presbyterian doctrines but is not at present identified with any religious organization. Politically, he votes independently.

THOMAS J. MYERS has been a resident of Wellington for nearly a decade, and has been engaged in buying and shipping livestock. He is the third son of Abram and Margaret Myers, and the parental history will be found in the biography of L. K. Myers, in this book. Our subject was born in Knox Township, Jefferson County, Ohio, on the 4th of December, 1830, and during his boyhood attended the pioneer schools of the county, which were taught in the log house where the benches were made of hewn logs, with wooden pins for legs. He was a lad of ten years when his parents moved to Carroll County, where he attended school during the winter months, and and the rest of the year assisted his father in clearing land and tilling the soil. There were no railroads in that section for a number of years, and all their transportation was done on the Sandy and Beaver Rivers, and the Ohio Canal.

In 1853 Mr. Myers, with a brother and three sisters, made the journey to Indiana with teams, and spent the winter in Whitley County, whence the family went to Iowa. Soon after their arrival in the Hoosier State our subject and his brother took a contract to build a mile of railroad, a short distance west of Columbia City. Work on that part of the road ceased in the spring of 1854, and Mr. Myers secured a situation as fireman on another part of the road, which he resigned after a short time to follow the rest of the family to the Hawkeye State. He traveled by stage to Goshen, Ind., thence by rail to Rock Island, Ill., where he again boarded a stage which landed him in Washington, Washington County, Iowa. He there secured a ride in a carriage to Winterset, nearly one hundred and fifty miles distant, and then continued his journey on foot. He walked hard all day, and made a distance of fifteen miles.

Coming upon a log cabin after dark Mr. Myers asked the privilege of remaining during the night. The house consisted of one room, and the two bedsteads in it were made by boring holes in the wall and inserting poles, the other ends of which were supported by posts. There was not a chair in the house, and neither lamp nor candle. Corn bread and fat meat constituted the supper, which Mr. Myers ate from the top of a chest while sitting on a small trunk. The inmates of the cabin consisted of a man and wife and seven children, but notwithstanding the meager accommodations, a kindly welcome was accorded to the stranger. Being very tired he passed a very comfortable night, but arose in the morning not feeling well, with twelve miles yet to walk. He had heard of the town of Pisgah, and expected to see something of a place, but on reaching its site found it consisted of one log cabin, occupied by a Mr. Locke, who was one of the first settlers of Union County. Mr. Myers was quite exhausted when he reached this place, but succeeded in hiring a horse from Mr. Locke, and made the rest of the journey more speedily and with a little more comfort.

The father of our subject had entered a tract of Government land, upon which the family lived, and during the winter our subject and his brother L. K., entered and sold several tracts of land in Union County, and in the spring of 1855, began to improve the land the father had taken, continuing together there until 1859. Our subject then removed to Afton, and engaged in mercantile business. The nearest railroad station was at Ottumwa, one hundred miles distant, and the greater part of his goods were teamed from there. In connection with his mercantile employ Mr. Myers had bought and shipped live stock, and some three years after becoming a resident of Afton he abandoned the former business and devoted his attention entirely to the latter, remaining in that city until 1880, when he came to this place, bought a home, and entered upon the same pursuits, shipping his stock to Kansas City and Wichita.

The wife of Mr. Myers bore the maiden name of Elizabeth Roberts, and the rites of wedlock were

celebrated between them in 1861. She is a daughter of Dr. J. F. and Tamar (Smith) Roberts, the latter of whom died when she was an infant. The father was born in Culpeper County, Va., and it is probable that his father, Benjamin Roberts, was also born in that State. In 1822 the grandfather moved to Ohio, and having purchased land in Athens County, tilled the soil there for a number of years. His wife, Mary Delaney, died in Perry County after having lived to a good old age. Mr. Roberts departed this life also ripe in years, in Athens County. His son, J. F., received a liberal education, and took up the study of medicine in his early manhood, being graduated from the Medical College at Columbus, Ohio, and successfully practicing his profession for many years. His skill was displayed in Meigs and Vinton Counties, Ohio, until 1859, and he then removed to Afton, Iowa, where he continued his professional labors for two years. He next opened an office in Brookfield, Mo., and some time later went to Centralia, Ill., where his death took place in April, 1889, at the age of sixty-five years. His daughter, now Mrs. Myers, received an excellent education, and is a worthy and efficient companion. She has borne her husband two children—Frank L. and Harry W.

In politics Mr. Myers advocates the principles of the Democratic party. His wife and two sons are members in good standing of the Presbyterian Church, and both have many friends in the community, where their uprightness, intelligence and friendly natures are well known.

AARON KING, late of Oxford Township and who owned one of the most valuable quarter sections of land in Sumner County, departed this life March 31, 1889, leaving behind him the record of an honest man and a good citizen. He pitched his tent at his late homestead on section 6, June 1, 1871, and maintained his position through the scourges of grasshoppers, drouth and chinch bugs, and was one of the three men who.

with their families, spent the winter following in one small dwelling. Upon coming to this region Mr. King drove overland from Vinton, Iowa, looking out for a location as he traveled and being one of the first men to cross the Arkansas River. He dug a cellar and while on a trip to Thayer, one hundred and twenty miles away, Mrs. King arrived August 25, 1871, and put up with the family of a Mr. Carpenter, remaining there until Mr. King had completed a roof to shelter his family.

The Carpenter domicile comprised one room only 16x21 feet in dimensions and into it three families moved and lived there until Mr. King had his own home ready. This domicile sheltered thirteen persons, including two children, but they had all come to this region with a mutual purpose in view and assisted each other. They bought their supplies from peddlers in the eastern part of the State and paid $2.50 per bushel for seed corn of a very poor quality. Wichita at that time was a hamlet of a few houses and one saloon. Mr. King proceeded with the improvement of his land, setting out fruit trees, hedge and forest trees, from the latter of which they still obtain all the fuel needed.

Mr. King was elected the first Director in his school district and Mrs. King was Chairman of the first meeting and administered the oath of office to him. They voted upon the question of building a schoolhouse and by the aid of the women present, carried it in the affirmative. Mr. King served as Director a number of terms and Mrs. King was the one who invited the minister to preach first in that vicinity, the services being held at Mr. Carpenter's house, and there a Methodist Episcopal church was organized. After the schoolhouse was erected the services and Sunday-school were conducted in it and Mrs. King was Superintendent of the latter for several years. She has been connected with this church for the long period of fifty years.

The subject of this sketch was born in Cuyahoga County, Ohio, July 30, 1842, and was the son of William King who spent his last days in Ohio. He grew to mature years in his native State and then removed to Indiana where he was married to Miss Lydia Hoover. Of this union there were born seven children, all of whom are living.

Mrs. King was born near Batavia, Ohio, March 11, 1822, and is the daughter of Richard and Margaret Allison, the former of whom was born in Cayuga County, N. Y. His wife was formerly a Miss Patton. Mr. Allison died in Ohio. The mother subsequently removed to Indiana and made her home with her daughter until her death. Miss Allison was first married to David Craig, October 12, 1842, and they settled in Rush County, Ind. There were born to them four children, only two of whom are living: Demetrius, in the Choctaw Nation, and Huldah M., the wife of Enoch Platt. Mr. Craig died in Vinton, Iowa, (to which place he had removed with his family) January 6, 1857.

OLOMON MILLER. This peaceable and law-abiding citizen of Falls Township, came to Sumner County in 1877, and preempted eighty acres of land on section 2, to which he subsequently added another eighty acres, and is now in the possession of a well-improved farm provided with convenient and suitable buildings. Upon his arrival here he was without capital, and has not only evolved from the soil of the Sunflower State a comfortable living, but managed to lay by something for a rainy day.

A native of Tuscarawas County, Ohio, Mr. Miller was born May 29, 1847, and lived there with his parents until 1810. The family then emigrated to Grant County, Ind., where they spent their last days. The parents were John and Susan (Penrod) Miller, natives of Pennsylvania. John Miller was an enterprising and industrious farmer, becoming well-to-do, and was a leading member of the Presbyterian Church. Possessing decided views, he was not easily turned from his convictions, and from the time of becoming a voting citizen, gave his unqualified allegiance to the Democratic party. The parental household included nine children, viz: Polly, Daniel, Lizzie, Henry, Mary A., Solomon, Rachel, John and Susan. Three of these are living.

Mr. Miller was the sixth child of his parents and

ES. OF SOLOMON MILLER, SEC. 2. SOUTH HALF FALLS TP. SUMNER COUNTY, KANS.

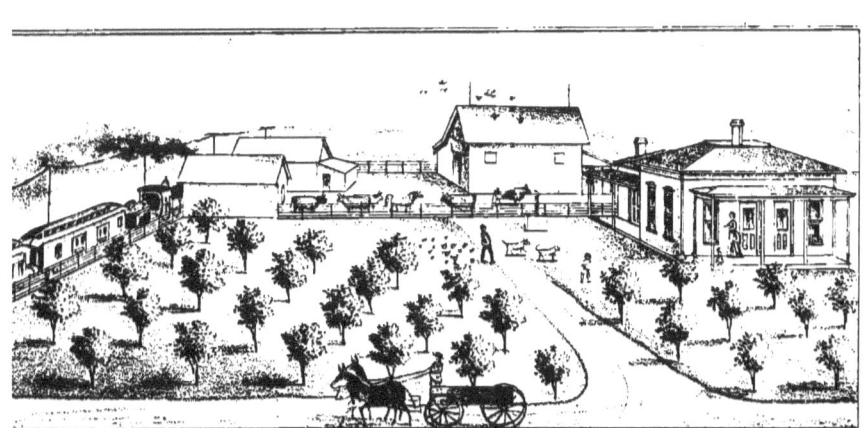

RESIDENCE OF ANDREW CZAPLINSKI, SEC. 32, CALDWELL TP. SUMNER CO. KANS.

was reared on a farm in Grant County, Ind., acquiring his education mostly in the district school. He worked with his father until after the outbreak of the Civil War, then, in 1862, joined the Union army as a private in Company K, One Hundred and Eighteenth Indiana Infantry. He repaired with his regiment to Cumberland Gap, and shortly afterward was injured in a railroad accident, which so disabled him that, being unfit for further military duties, he was obliged to accept his honorable discharge. Returning then to the farm in his native county, he remained there until coming to this State, in 1877. Mr. Miller finds his religious home in the Methodist Episcopal Church, and is a member in good standing of the Grand Army of the Republic. He keeps himself posted upon current events, and is identified with the Farmers' Alliance.

Miss Mary E. Kirkendall of St. Joseph County, Ind., became the wife of Solomon Miller, in February, 1861. The young people commenced the journey of life together in Grant County, Ind., where Mr. Miller prosecuted farming on his own account until removing west of the Mississippi. To him and his excellent wife there were born three children, viz.: Rachel A., Sarah C. and Mary J. Mrs. Mary E. Miller departed this life at the homestead in Falls Township, October 15, 1873. In 1875 Mr. Miller contracted a second marriage with Miss Margaret Clevinger, of Howard County, Ind. There have been born of this union two sons—Henry and William—bright and intelligent lads, who remain at home with their parents.

A lithographic engraving of the residence wherein Mr. and Mrs. Miller are so comfortably domiciled is presented in connection with this sketch.

NDREW CZAPLINSKI. A well-improved farm of two hundred and forty acres indicates the perseverance and industry of this well to-do resident of Caldwell Township, who came to this region poor in purse, and who has by his own exertions and perseverance, sur-

rounded himself with all the comforts of life. He was born in the Province of Posen, Prussia, November 30, 1835, and comes of substantial German ancestry. His parents, Toney and Josephine Czaplinski, were natives of the same Province as their son, and there spent their entire lives. The father was a distiller of liquors. There was born to them one child only—Andrew, of whom we now write.

The subject of this notice was reared in his native Province, and received a common-school education. He was trained to habits of industry, and at an early age went to work at the manufacture of fur goods. When reaching his majority, he determined to seek his fortune in America, and accordingly crossed the Atlantic, settling first at Toledo, Ohio. He worked there at his trade until the outbreak of the Civil War and soon after the call for troops, enlisted as a private in Company B, Thirty-seventh Ohio Infantry, which was assigned to the Army of the Cumberland, and to the Fifteenth Army Corps, under the command of Grant and Sherman. Mr. Czaplinski participated in many of the important battles of the war, being at Vicksburg, Missionary Ridge, and upon other hard-fought fields. At Vicksburg, on the 22d of May, 1863, he was wounded by a gunshot; from this, however, he recovered in due time, rejoining his regiment, and on the 25th of November, following, at the battle of Missionary Ridge, received a second wound which disabled him for further service. He received his honorable discharge at the city of Washington, September 9, 1864.

Returning now to his native haunts in Toledo, Ohio, Mr. Czaplinski established himself in the mercantile business, at which he continued until 1871. The following year, resolving upon a change of location and occupation, he pre-empted one hundred and sixty acres of land on sections 32 and 33, Caldwell Township, this county. He proceeded in true pioneer style to cultivate and improve his land and here he has since made his home. He added to his first possessions by the purchase of eighty acres on section 28, and has brought the whole to a productive condition, erecting thereon suitable buildings, and gathering about himself and family the comforts and conveniences of modern life.

The subject of this sketch was married in Toledo, November 7, 1865, to Miss Elvina Demki. This lady is a native of the same Province as her husband, and was born January 12, 1845. She came to America with her parents in 1864, settling in Archibald, Ohio. Eight children have been born of this union, viz.: Hugo, Laura, Oscar, Charles, Hammond, Ada, Annie and Lydia. Laura and Oscar died at the ages of ten and seven years, respectively.

Mr. Czaplinski has gathered around himself and his family the comforts and conveniences of life, and a lithographic view of his pleasant homestead, with its principal buildings, is a valuable addition to the ALBUM.

DE WITT S. BLACKMON. A well-regulated farm of one hundred and sixty acres indicates the industry and perseverance which have signalized the operations of Mr. Blackmon since the year 1877, during which he settled on section 14, Walton Township. Aside from dealing somewhat in farm lands, he has given his attention strictly to agricultural pursuits, making a specialty of stock-raising. A native of Lewis County, N. Y., he was born November 24, 1829, and is a son of Sylvester and Clarissa (Peck) Blackmon, who were natives, respectively, of Connecticut and Vermont.

Sylvester Blackmon emigrated at an early date to Lewis County, N. Y., whence he removed, about 1839, to Defiance County, Ohio. He followed farming successfully in the Buckeye State and died at the homestead where he first settled, in 1864, at the age of about eighty-two years. He became well-to-do, leaving an estate worth about $10,000. He was one of the early members of the Masonic fraternity in that State and, politically, was first a Whig and then a Republican. The wife and mother died at the homestead in Defiance County, Ohio, during the boyhood of her son, DeWitt S. The parental family included six children, viz.: Per-

melia, Delia, Maria, Mary, DeWitt S. and Fanny. Our subject and his sister Permelia are the only survivors, and the latter is a resident of West Virginia.

A boy of ten years when going with his parents from his native State to Ohio, Mr. Blackmon was reared in Defiance County on the home farm, living there, with the exception of the time spent in army, until 1877. That year, coming to Kansas, he purchased one hundred and sixty acres of land on section 11, Walton Township, of which he has since been a resident. While a resident of Ohio, he, in 1862, during the progress of the Civil War, enlisted as a private in Company B, Forty-Seventh Ohio Infantry, and served until June, 1865, when, the conflict being ended, he repaired to Washington, D. C. and received his honorable discharge. His duties as a soldier were performed in that faithful and uncomplaining manner which gained him the respect of his comrades and the approval of his superior officers. He served in the Army of the Tennessee under Gen. Logan and was in all of the principal engagements of his regiment from the taking of Atlanta to the surrender of Lee.

The paternal grandfather of Mr. Blackmon served in the War of 1812, while his paternal great-grandfather shouldered his musket and fought with the Colonists during their struggle for independence. He attained to the ripe old age of ninety-nine years and nine months, spending his last years in New York. Mr. Blackmon is a member in good standing of the Masonic fraternity and also belongs to the Farmers' Alliance. In politics he is independent.

Nearly thirty-eight years ago, on the 14th of July, 1852, Mr. Blackmon was married to Miss Elizabeth Butler. The bride was born in Coshocton County, Ohio, December 31, 1831, to John and Sarah (Devall) Butler, who were natives of Ohio, and spent their last years there. This union resulted in the birth of ten children, viz: Clara, Vinal, John, DeWitt S., Jr., Elizabeth, Mary, Allen, Albert, Mattie and Maude. John, Allen and Albert are deceased. The Blackmon homestead invariably attracts the eye of the passing traveller as presenting a picture of one of the most elegant homes in Sumner County. The fine residence in all its appointments is indicative of cultivated tastes and ample means, and its surroundings reflect great credit upon the intelligence and enterprise of the proprietor. The family occupies no secondary position among the best residents of the township.

NEWELL S. COZAD. There is probably not within the limits of Falls Township a more prosperous or enterprising citizen than he with whose name we introduce this sketch. He is descended from an ancestry possessing marked peculiarities and who were noted almost uniformly for their wealth and influence in the communities where they resided. The landed possessions of Mr. Cozad embrace one thousand broad acres in Sumner and Kingman Counties, this State, including one of the finest farms on section 15, Falls Township, where he settled in the spring of 1880. He also owns three hundred and forty town lots in Caldwell and valuable real estate in Cleveland, Ohio, where he spends the greater part of his time. In addition to the prosecution of farming extensively, he is also largely interested in live stock, of which he possesses a thorough knowledge and which yields him large returns.

The subject of this sketch was born in Cleveland, Ohio, July 23, 1831, and is the son of Samuel and Mary (Condit) Cozad, the former of whom was a native of New Jersey. The parents of Samuel Cozad upon leaving that State settled in Washington County, Pa., when their son was a child of two years. Ten years later they removed to Cleveland, Ohio, where the father departed this life in 1870. He was a successful farmer and a man of large means leaving an estate valued at $300,000. His farm occupied ground now included in Wade Park, which is one of the most popular resorts of the people of the Forest City. Samuel Cozad in early life was a Presbyterian in his religious views, but afterward, in company with fifteen others, organized the Euclid Avenue Congregational Church in Cleveland, and was largely instrumental in the

erection of the church edifice. He contributed liberally to the support of the society until his death. In early manhood he had served as a soldier in the War of 1812. His father, likewise named Samuel, was a native of New Jersey and of French descent.

The mother of Mr. Cozad was likewise a native of New Jersey, where she was reared to womanhood. When she was nineteen years old her parents removed to Ohio, they likewise settling in the city of Cleveland where Miss Mary met her future husband and where they were married. She died in Cleveland, Ohio, September 5, 1871. Grandfather Abner Condit was likewise a native of New Jersey. To Samuel, Jr., and Mary Cozad there was born a family of six children, viz: Silas H., Hettie A., Mary C., William, Newell S. and Martha J. Hettie and Newell are the only surviving members of the family; the former is the wife of J. D. Bennett and is living in Kingston, N. Y.

Mr. Cozad was reared at the old homestead in the vicinity of Cleveland and attended the city schools until sufficiently advanced to enter an academy. Later he was in college two years. He then took up the study of law and was admitted to the bar in Cleveland about 1855. He practiced two years only but, being inclined to a more active life, then abandoned the profession and turned his attention to farming and gardening near the city, which vocation he prosecuted successfully until 1876. That year, coming to Kansas, he purchased land and began dealing in cattle with such success that he has since prosecuted the business and become independent financially. In the meantime his son Charles, under the able tuition of his father, has also developed fine business qualifications, and the two together are members of the Cherokee Strip Live Stock Association, having large pastures in the Territory and operating under the firm name of Cozad & Son. Mr. Cozad is a devout member of the Presbyterian Church, to which he gives a liberal support, and in politics he is a sound Republican, strongly advocating prohibition doctrines.

Soon after the outbreak of the Civil War Mr. Cozad, in 1861, joined the army with the "Squirrel Hunters" from Cleveland, a body of men organized to protect the southern border of Ohio. In 1864 he joined the regular army, enlisting in Company D, One-hundred and Fiftieth Ohio Infantry, serving one hundred days. His services being then no longer required, he received his honorable discharge and returned to the pursuits of civil life.

The marriage of Newell S. Cozad and Miss Sarah J. Coe, of Cortland, Ohio, was celebrated at the bride's home June 16, 1858. Mrs. Cozad was born in Cortland, May 7, 1835, and is a daughter of John and Mary (Meek) Coe, who were natives, respectively, of Ireland and Pennsylvania. The latter spent their last years at Cortland, Ohio. To Mr. and Mrs. Cozad there have been born a son and daughter, the latter named Mary A. and now the wife of George W. Bradford, of Caldwell. Charles N. is unmarried and remains at home with his parents. The home farm has been brought to a high state of cultivation and embellished with modern buildings. Everything which cultivated tastes and ample means can afford has been brought together in the improvement of the premises, and it is not only a matter of pride to the people of the neighborhood, but is the means of enriching the county treasury each year by a handsome sum in the way of taxes. Mr. Cozad occupies no secondary position among the prominent men of this county and has contributed his full quota toward advancing its material interests.

JOHN STIGER was born in Dale Township, McLean County, Ill., on the 9th of November, 1845. His father, William Stiger, is a native of Bedford County, Pa., and his grandfather was also a native of the same State. Abram Stiger, the grandfather of our subject, was reared in his native State, and continued to reside there for some years after his marriage. His wife was a native of the old Keystone State, and their marriage was celebrated at her home in the usual style of those times. Hearing the marvelous tales that were related of the unsurpassed richness of the soil of Illinois, Abram Stiger packed his household goods and family in wagons, and in that manner they were drawn to their new home in McLean County, Ill. They were among the early settlers of that county, and as there were no railroads built, or even thought of, they were obliged to travel slowly across the country, in order that the cattle and teams should not be too much fatigued with the long journey.

The father of our subject was but a boy when his parents located in Illinois. He grew to manhood on his father's farm, receiving such education as the schools of the time afforded, and has a vivid recollection of the times, when, for want of a nearer market and better facilities for transportation, they were obliged to haul their produce to Chicago in wagons drawn by horses or oxen. He has lived to see the wonderful transformation wrought by the advent of railroads in the State of his adoption. He is still a resident of the place where his childhood and youth were passed, and has no desire to remove until he receives the summons to go up higher. The mother of our subject was Miss Mary Beeler. She was a native of Dale Township, McLean County, Ill., and a daughter of William and Betsy Beeler, who were natives of Ohio, and pioneers of Dale Township.

John Stiger was reared in Dale Township, where he attended school during the early years of his life, but as soon as he was able to work, was obliged to do what he could to help his father carry on the farm. He remained with his parents until his twentieth year, when he started out for himself. For a time he worked by the month for his grandfather Beeler, and resided in his house, then rented a farm and operated it by himself. Being industrious and economical, he prospered in his undertaking, and was able to lay up a fair share of wealth besides furnishing himself and family with the comforts and conveniences of modern rural life.

Mr. Stiger was a resident of Dale Township, McLean County, until the year 1883. In the fall of that year he removed to Sumner County, Kan., and located on section 34, southwest quarter of Jackson Township, where he bought one hundred and sixty acres of land. He now has an excellent farm, well improved, having fruit and shade trees, and good buildings, and neither himself nor family have ever regretted leaving their old home in Illinois.

September 5, 1865, Mr. Stiger and Miss Mary Banner were united in the bonds of matrimony, and the union has been blessed by the birth of eight children, namely: William, Edward, Amy, Julia, Alice, Ora, Burtie, and Effie. Mrs. Stiger is an estimable lady, and commands the respect and esteem of all who know her. She is a native of Forsythe County, N. C., and daughter of Joshua Banner, a native of the same State. The grandfather of Mrs. Stiger, Joshua Banner, as far as known, spent his entire life in North Carolina. The father of Mr. Stiger grew to manhood, and was married in his native State, and resided there until the year 1865, when he removed to Illinois, and settled in Dale Township, McLean County. The entire journey was made in wagons drawn by horses, and consumed a great deal of time. They camped by the way, and during the trip Mr. Banner caught a cold which terminated fatally, about two weeks after their arrival in Illinois. Mrs. Banner was thus left a widow with seven children to support. She was a woman of energy and spirit, and succeeded in keeping her family together until they were grown and able to do for themselves. Her maiden name was Amy Ogburn, and she is a native of North Carolina. She is now living with a daughter in Colorado. The family of Mr. Stiger attend the Methodist Episcopal Church, of which Mrs. Stiger is a worthy member, she having united with that denomination in Illinois.

ILLIAM ALLEN McDONALD. There is probably not a more talented lawyer in Sumner County, or one understanding the intricacies of his profession more thoroughly than Mr. McDonald, who established himself in the city of Wellington, in January 1, 1875. He was born in Circleville, Pickaway County, Ohio, December

1, 1846, and is the son of Patrick McDonald, a native of County Donegal, Ireland, and of Scotch ancestry.

He emigrated to America early in life and located in Circleville, Ohio, where his death took place in 1849, when his son, William A. was a child of three years. He had been married in Circleville to Miss Rebecca Loofborrow, a native of Fairfield County, Ohio, and the daughter of Maj. Wade Loofborrow, who was a soldier in the War of 1812, whom it is believed was a native of Pennsylvania, and of German ancestry. The latter settled in Fairfield County, Ohio, during its pioneer days, and followed farming there the remainder of his life. To Patrick McDonald and his wife there was born two children. The brother of our subject, John Wade McDonald, now practicing law at San Diego, Cal., was one of the pioneers of Sumner County, and held the offices of Probate Judge and County Attorney, respectively, during his residence in the county. The mother died in 1849; the same date of the death of her husband, both dying with the cholera.

Young McDonald was thus left an orphan early in life, and was taken into the home of his maternal uncle, B. F. Loofborrow of Delaware County, Ohio, where he attended the common school, obtaining a very good education. In 1861, when a youth of not quite fifteen years, the Civil War having broken out, he enlisted as a Union soldier, November 26, 1861, in Company I, Eighty-second Ohio Infantry, and participated in many hard-fought battles, among them the second battle of Manassas or Bull Run, besides minor engagements. At Bull Run he was severely wounded and sent to a hospital, but before being fully recovered, rejoined his regiment. Later he participated in the battles of Chancellorsville and Gettysburg, and was slightly wounded at both places. He fought at Chattanooga and Mission Ridge, and went with his corps to the relief of Burnsides at Knoxville. He returned to Chattanooga, and on the 1st day of January, 1864, his term of enlistment having expired, he veteranized, and was granted a furlough of thirty days. At the expiration of this time he rejoined his regiment at Columbus, Ohio, and soon afterward they were ordered to Bridgeport, Ala.,

Two weeks later Mr. McDonald was placed on detached duty, and returned to Columbus to assist in collecting, drilling and forwarding recruits, drafted men, and substitutes to the front. He was thus occupied until the close of the war, and received his honorable discharge July 12, 1865.

Upon retiring from the army, Mr. McDonald, desirous of increasing his store of book knowledge, attended school until March, 1866, at the Ohio Wesleyan University at Delaware. He entered upon his business career as a dealer in live-stock, especially horses, making his headquarters at Huntsville, Ala. He had all these years improved his opportunities for reading and observation, and in due time became an important factor in politics in Alabama. On the 29th of April, 1869, he was appointed Register of the Land Office at Huntsville, which office he held for a period of five years. In the meantime he improved his leisure hours by studying law. In December, 1871, he started Westward, and in January, 1875, arrived in Wellington, this State, where he entered in earnest upon his law studies, devoting to them his whole time. He was admitted to the bar in Wellington, in 1876, Judge W. P. Campbell presiding, and at once opened an office, and since that time has engaged in a continuous and successful practice. He is considered one of the leading members of the profession in this part of Kansas.

Mr. McDonald was married July 1, 1876, at the bride's home in Wellington, to Miss Sarah M. Bates. This lady was born in Yates County, N. Y., in April, 1847, and is the daughter of Charles and Mary (Payne) Bates. Her father died December 3, 1872. The mother is still living, and resides in San Diego, Cal. Mrs. Bates was the first woman to reside in Wellington. The only child born of this union, a daughter, Mary Della, died when three months old. Mr. McDonald cast his first Presidential vote for Gen. Grant, but from 1876 to 1888, affiliated with the Democratic party. During the Presidential election of the latter year, he gave his support to Gen. Harrison. He has served two terms as City Attorney, and as an ex-soldier, belongs to James Shields Post, No. 57, G. A. R., of which he is Past Post Commander, and also Post Judge Advocate of the Department of

Kansas. Socially, he belongs to Wellington Lodge, No. 24, A. O. U. W., and is also a member of the Masonic Lodge at Wellington.

He was also a member of the Twentieth and Twenty-second National Encampment at San Francisco, Cal., and Columbus, Ohio, 1886 and 1888, respectively. Mrs. McDonald is a member of the Methodist Church.

GEORGE H. WINSOR. One of the finest farms in Oxford Township is that owned and occupied by the above-named gentleman, who came to this section before either county or township were organized, and who assisted in forming school district No. 1, which extended to the Territory, and in other pioneer work of this vicinity, besides making for himself a beautiful home. His estate comprises a quarter of section 31, and was staked out by him in the early part of April, 1871, before the section survey had been made. He was looking for a location with living water, and finding a spring and branch, and a dry building spot above the spring, he put up a log house and a Kansas barn—i. e., a board frame covered with straw or willow withes twisted in closely. Mr. Winston used the former. He now has a fine grove of five acres on the branch, which will furnish wood enough to keep his fires going for years, and an excellent orchard, together with all the usual improvements of a progressive farmer. The residence is of a pleasing design and first-class construction, and two stories in height, and both main portion and L are 26x24 feet. It was erected in 1883.

The birth of Mr. Winsor took place at Dartmouth, Devonshire, England, October, 3, 1822, and the parental home was at the mouth of the Dart River till our subject had reached the age of twelve years, when a removal was made to Upper Canada. The mother, Mary (Couch) Winsor, departed this life in the fall of 1860. The father, George Winsor, Sr., having moved to Marion, Iowa, died there in October, 1873, at the age of seventy-eight years.

The gentleman of whom we write grew to maturity in Canada, and on October 21, 1845, near Simcoe, was united in marriage with Miss Mary Wiltse. The bride was a native of Vienna, Chautauqua County, N. Y., and a daughter of Mr. and Mrs. Nathaniel Wiltse, natives of Dutchess County, N. Y. During her early childhood her parents removed to Canada, where she was educated and married.

Mr. Winsor learned the boot and shoe business at Simcoe, and engaged in the same in that place, and later in St. Charles, Kane County, Ill., whence he removed to Marion, Iowa, after a sojourn of a year. Some time after taking up his abode in the latter place, he changed his line of business, and engaged in the sale of agricultural implements, which he continued until 1866, when he located in Miami County, and bought an Indian Head Right, which he sold four years later to become a resident of Kansas.

Seven children are now living of the ten born to Mr. and Mrs. Winsor. Edward W. is prosecuting the ice business in Chicago; Frank is on a farm in Avon Township; Jennie, wife of James Holliday, lives in this county; George G. is now living in Avon Township; Harry and A. D. are graduates of the Kansas Normal School, and are engaged in teaching; Lizzie is also a teacher. All have been given excellent educational advantages, Mr. Winsor having resided in Oxford for two years before there was a school here, in order that they might not lack school privileges.

After his return to his farm and the organization of a new school district, Mr. Winsor was made Director and filled that office during a period of ten years. He has voted the Republican ticket until within the last four or five years, since which time his allegiance has been given to the Union Labor party. While ever interested in good government, he has never aspired to political honors, but has endeavored to serve his country in a more quiet way, as one of the cool-headed and reliable citizens. He is of a social and benevolent nature, and belongs to the Masonic order, the Independent Order of Odd Fellows and the Farmers' Alliance. He

possesses excellent judgment, not only in business matters but in affairs which relate to the welfare of the community, and is highly respected by his fellow-citizens as one of the most upright and reliable of their associates.

WILLIAM C. F. CUMMINGS, one of the early pioneers of this county, made his first appearance in South Haven Township, in 1873, and pre-empted one hundred and sixty acres of land on section 26. He put up a plank house 16x28 feet in dimensions, and occupied this several years while he proceeded with the improvement of his property. His nearest market for some time was at Wichita, to which his grain and produce was transported laboriously overland with teams. The country was in its wild and uncultivated state, with not even a wagon road, and nothing to mark a path to any point except an Indian trail. The red man still prowled around, while buffalo and other wild animals were plentiful, deer, antelopes, and a great many wolves. The present site of South Haven was marked by a solitary store.

Notwithstanding the disadvantages under which he was obliged to labor, Mr. Cummings was prospered, and in due time added eighty acres to his original purchase. He placed one hundred and eighty acres under the plow, reserving the balance for pasture and meadow. He planted an orchard of apple trees, and set out two hundred peach trees, besides trees of the smaller fruits. The necessary buildings were also erected, the plank house giving place to a modern and comfortable residence. Mr. Cummings resided there until the fall of 1884, when he removed to South Haven, where he has a pleasant home, including a neat frame dwelling with the other necessary structures, and five lots. He still retains possession of his farm property, and has the management of its operations.

The subject of this sketch was born in Erie County, Pa., June 7, 1823, and was reared as a farmer's boy. The father, John Cummings, was a native of Strasburg, Pa., where he lived until reaching manhood, and then went to Erie County, that State. There in due time he was married to Miss Sarah, daughter of Michael McKelvy. Grandfather McKelvy was a native of Virginia, whence he removed with his family to Erie County, Pa., during its pioneer days. John Cummings, died in that county in 1829. The paternal grandfather, John Cummings, Sr., was a native of Germany, and emigrated to America when a young man, settling near Strasburg, Pa., where he spent the remainder of his life.

When a youth of sixteen years, William Cummings imigrated to Buffalo, N, Y., where he learned blacksmithing with his brother John, and where he lived five years. Then starting out again, he commenced traveling over different parts of the United States and Canada, working at his trade as opportunity afforded. He likewise spent three years on the lakes as fireman on steamers running from Buffalo to Chicago. Finally he located in Kendall County, Ill., where he took unto himself a wife and helpmate, being married in 1856, to Miss Anna E., daughter of James and Margaret (Wilson) Mack. Mrs. Cummings was born in Glasgow, Scotland, and came to America with her parents in 1846, when a child of six years. They lived for a time in New York City, then removed to Illinois, and from there to Wright County, Iowa. In the latter county the parents spent their last days. The father was a native of Paisley, and the mother of Glasgow, Scotland. They were married in the latter city, where for a number of years Mr. Mack occupied himself as a weaver. In their own country they were members in good standing of the Baptist Church.

After their marriage Mr. and Mrs. Cummings removed to Wright County, Iowa, where Mr. Cummings worked at his trade, and also prosecuted farming about nine years. We next find him in Davis County, Mo., where he sojourned about seven years, after which he returned to Iowa. From there, in 1873, he came to this county.

There have been born to Mr. and Mrs. Cummings, eleven children, six of whom are living, viz: Addie, Mrs. James Clark, of South Haven; Anna, Mrs. William Noble, of Sumner County;

Wilson; Mattie, the wife of Albert Moss, of South Haven; Charles, and Daisy. The five deceased are Marion, who died at the age of six years; Rosanna, who died when four years old; William who died aged sixteen months; Andrew, and Allen, twins, who closed their infant eyes at the ages of two and three months. Mrs. Cummings is a member in good standing of the Christian Church. Mr. Cummings, politically, votes the Democratic ticket, but otherwise than serving as Justice of the Peace for one term, has had very little to do with public affairs.

John Cummings, the father of our subject, went to Canada during the War of 1812, and being a citizen of the United States, was arrested as a spy, convicted and sentenced to be shot. He, however, succeeded in effecting his escape before the day appointed for execution, receiving, it is believed, assistance from the Masonic lodge, of which he was a member.

CHARLES W. SMITH, the leading agricultural dealer of Wellington, was born near Fulton, Oswego County, N. Y., September 29, 1859. His father, James Smith, was born in Ireland, and the paternal grandfather of our subject was also, as far as known, a native of the Emerald Isle, in which he spent his last years. He was a member of the Methodist Church and reared his family in that faith. James Smith remained a resident of his native land until sixteen years of age, when he accompanied his brothers, George and Samuel, to America and all settled in Oswego County. The father of our subject had been reared to agricultural pursuits, and after living in Oswego County a few years he bought a tract of timber land three miles from Fulton and cleared a farm from the wilderness, residing there until 1865. He then sold out and removed to Fulton, where he engaged in the butchering business and where he is still living. The maiden name of his wife was Elizabeth Jane Mason and she is also a native of Ireland.

Her father, James Mason, came to America with his family and spent his last years near Fulton, where he had purchased a farm. James and Elizabeth Smith reared four children—George L., Emma J., R. J., and our subject.

The gentleman of whom we write attended school quite steadily until fifteen years of age and then commenced working in a grocery store, continuing in the employ of one man for four years, when with a friend he started out to seek his fortune in the West. Young Smith was the fortunate possessor of $30 in cash as a capital with which to begin his life. The two boys visited different places in New York and Ohio, and finally reached Bryan, in the latter State, out of funds. They started on foot from there and walked one hundred and twenty miles to Lenawee County, Mich., where they found employment in a sawmill at Ottawa Lake. After working a few weeks and so replenishing their pocket books, they went to Adrian and there made a contract with the city council to number the houses, stores, etc., in that city. After completing that job they went to Hudson and, their money being soon spent, they sought work on a farm.

The lads spent but a few days in agricultural labor when they started out in the interest of a Detroit firm to sell Harper's Circulating Library, and traveled in Southern Michigan from April until July when they went to the City of the Straits. There our subject met a merchant from Augusta, Kalamazoo County, and returned with him to his home, where he clerked in a general store about six months. He was then offered a better position with a farm-implement house and accepted the offer, becoming very successful in that line of mercantile work and making large sales. After a few months a Kalamazoo firm made him a very flattering offer, but his employers, rather than lose his services, took him into partnership. This connection continued about two years when it was terminated by the death of one of the partners and Mr. Smith went to Kalamazoo, where he entered the service of C. A. Crosby & Co., a firm which was afterward incorporated into the Kalamazoo Wagon Company, and traveled in their interest until 1883.

Mr. Smith then resigned his position and came to this place, where he engaged as salesman for C. G. Larned & Co., implement and hardware dealers, with whom he remained two years. He then engaged in business for himself and is now carrying a full line of farm implements of the best quality, barbed wire, wagons, carriages, etc. His building, which is known as the Wigwam Implement House, is a commodious and substantial structure 50x120 feet, and the business which is carried on within it is conducted according to the highest principles of business integrity and honorable dealing.

In 1883 the rites of wedlock were celebrated between Mr. Smith and Miss Kate S., daughter of John G. and Martha M. Schmucker. The bride was born in Pennsylvania and is one of those intelligent and noble-hearted women who are well fitted to make a happy home. The happy union of Mr. and Mrs. Smith has been blessed by the birth of two children—Ruby L. and Mildred M.

Mr. Smith is a member of Anchor Lodge No. 9, K. of P., and of Wellington Lodge No. 133, I. O. O. F. In politics he is a stanch Republican, and his first vote for President was cast for James A. Garfield. Few young men can look back over a more successful career than has been that of our subject and he may justly be pleased with the reputation bestowed upon him by his fellow-citizens. Both he and his wife belong to the Presbyterian Church.

ELIJAH M. ADAMS. Few of the prominent residents of Bluff Township are unfamiliar with the personality of the gentleman who bears this name, and who, although only coming here in 1882, has made for himself a record eminently creditable, pursuing the even tenor of his way at a well-regulated farm of one hundred and sixty acres on section 33. Besides this property he has twenty acres on section 4. He is a self-made man in the strictest sense of the term, having commenced life at the foot of the ladder, and has by his own efforts climbed up to a good position, socially and financially. He is prominently connected with the Methodist Episcopal Church, has officiated as Township Clerk, and uniformly votes the Republican ticket.

A native of Johnson County, Mo., Mr. Adams was born May 3, 1848, and was the sixth in a family of twelve children, the offspring of Daniel and Susan (McCrary) Adams. He spent his boyhood days at the homestead in his native county, attending first the common schools and later the academy. He completed his education in the Missouri State Normal School, at Warrensburg, and remained a resident of his native county until 1883, coming then to Kansas, and settling upon a claim which he had taken in 1876. On the 21st of March, the first-mentioned year, he was married to Miss Louie A. Smith, of Johnson County, Mo. This lady was born in Wisconsin, February 25, 1866, and is the daughter of LaFayette and Sarah (Custard) Smith, natives of Pennsylvania. Mr. and Mrs. Adams became the parents of four children, viz.: Ida, Alfred, Eva and Lotta. In the sketch of W. P. Adams, which will be found on another page of this work, there is furnished a more extended notice of the Adams family. Elijah M. has given considerable attention to fruit culture, having a large orchard of apple trees, and numerous varieties of the smaller fruits. He is a thorough and skillful farmer, and has done his share in furthering the agricultural interests of this county.

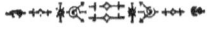

MOS CANN. A pleasant and valuable farm in Wellington Township is owned and occupied by the above named gentleman, whose citizenship in this county dates from the fall of 1873, when he purchased one hundred and sixty acres of prairie land, twenty acres of which had been broken, and upon which there was a small house. Innumerable droves of buffaloes crossed the plains a few miles west, deer and antelopes were plentiful throughout the region, and farm products had to be hauled to Wichita, thirty miles distant, that being the nearest market. Mr. Cann has seen the country change from that primitive and thinly settled condition into a populous district, spanned by railroads, where the wild game of those early years is replaced by herds of domestic animals, and the far-reaching landscape is covered with fertile farms.

Before entering upon a brief sketch of the life of our subject, a few words in regard to his progenitors will not be amiss. His paternal grandfather, William Cann, was born near Washington D. C., was reared to manhood there, and served as as a Justice of the Peace in the Capital City. His grandchildren have now in their possession a bond which was given for a deed, and which bears the signature of George Washington. From Washington William Cann moved to Pennsylvania, in which State the father of our subject was born. About the year 1820 he became a pioneer settler of Butler County, Ohio, the removal from the Keystone State being made by boat down the Ohio River to Cincinnati, and thence by sleds to the location which he had selected, where he took up a tract of timber land and cleared a farm, and where he resided until his death.

Amos Cann, Sr., father of our subject, grew to manhood in his native State, where he married Miss Elizabeth Biddinger, whose father, Frederick Biddinger, was a farmer and also a native of the Keystone State, and who, like the Canns, became a pioneer settler of Butler County, Ohio, where his death occurred. Mr. Cann accompanied his parents to Ohio, and clearing a tract of timber land there, built a substantial log house, in which our subject was born some years later. Cincinnati was but a small village at the time of his removal to Southern Ohio, and for many years after, though still a small place, was the only available market.

The people in those days spent their time almost entirely at their own homes, the facilities for friendly intercourse and travel being limited, and many household duties were then necessary, which have been done away with by the introduction of modern machinery and railroads. The mother of our subject carded, spun and wove all the cloth used by her family. On one occasion her husband, while in Cincinnati, was offered three lots on Main Street, between Fifth and Sixth Streets, for a linen vest he wore, the cloth for which she had made.

The senior Amos Cann had but meager educational advantages in his youth, but being very ambitious to acquire a good education, he spent all his leisure moments in reading and studying by the light of pine knots, and thus acquired a thorough fund of information, turning it to account as a teacher in his native State and later in Ohio, where he was one of the early pedagogues. This worthy representative of the old regime was gathered to his fathers in April, 1881. His widow is now residing on the homestead, in Butler County, Ohio, and enjoys a full measure of regard as one of the pioneer mothers of the county.

The gentleman whose name initiates this sketch is one of the eleven children born to his parents, and first opened his eyes to the light January 19, 1840, in the log house twelve miles southwest of Hamilton, Ohio. He was reared and educated in the home county, and as soon as his strength would admit began to assist in farm work, taking more and more active part in the labors of the estate as he grew toward manhood. He was an inmate of the paternal household until his marriage, and then rented land in the vicinity, carrying on agricultural labors there until the period of his becoming a resident of this county. He had previously visited this State, though not this part of it, and determined to set up his household gods within its borders. His removal here was made by rail to Wichita, thence by wagon to this county, where he now has a finely improved and thoroughly cultivated farm, which bears an excellent set of buildings, including a tasty and comfortable dwelling.

The lady who for a quarter of a century has been the valued companion of Mr. Cann, and to whose careful management and amiable disposition the comforts of his home are largely due, is a native of the same county and State in which he was born, and in which they were united in marriage January 12, 1865. She was christened Phœbe, and is a daughter of Pierson and Margaret Appleton. She has borne her husband five children: Henry, Sylvester, Maggie, Charley and Amos.

Mr. Cann is now a member of the Democratic party, although for many years he advocated the principles of Republicanism. He is a reliable citizen, an intelligent, enterprising and honest man, and has an excellent standing among his fellow-citizens.

JOHN A. BLAIR. Only about twenty-five families had made settlement in this county when Mr. Blair crossed its borders with the intention of making it his future home. The face of the country then presented a vastly different appearance from that of to-day, wild animals being plentiful, and the primitive dwellings of the pioneers, few and far between. It needed men of more than ordinary courage, facing such an outlook, to finally resolve upon permanent settlement, but Mr. Blair was equal to the emergency, and establishing himself as a resident, has since maintained his position.

Commencing with modest means and dependent upon his own resources, Mr. Blair, by a course of great industry and prudence, advanced step by step until he has now become one of the most prominent residents of the county, and is one of its most extensive live-stock dealers. His operations along the Cherokee Strip have probably not been exceeded by those of any man in the vicinity. He is a Westerner by birth, his native place being Plainfield, Hendricks County, Ind., where he first opened his eyes to the light September 20, 1851. His immediate progenitors were Enos and Margaret (Morgan) Blair. The father was a native of North Carolina, whence he emigrated with his parents to Hendricks County, Ind., in boyhood, residing there until a young man of twenty years.

Enos Blair, in 1871, came to Kansas and settled in Caldwell, when it was little more than a hamlet. He made his continuous residence there until 1887, then removed to Alamosa, Colo., where he now resides. During his sojourn in the Hoosier State he carried on farming successfully, dealt in live-stock, and was also interested in pork-packing at Indianapolis for several years. He became wealthy, but subsequently met with financial reverses which nearly ruined him. After coming to Kansas he continued his live-stock operations. He also became interested in newspaper work, and for a number of years was editor and publisher of the Caldwell *Post*. He had been reared in the Quaker faith, to which he adhered until business cares absorbed his mind to the exclusion mostly of religious matters. He was identified with the Ancient, Free and Accepted Masons and the Independent Order of Odd Fellows, and votes the Republican ticket. He is now retired from active business.

Mrs. Margaret (Morgan) Blair was born in Knoxville, Tenn., and coming to Kansas with her family, died in Caldwell, in 1871. The household circle was completed by the birth of five children, viz.: Julia, Will P., John A., Hattie and Francis M. The two daughters are deceased. John A. spent the early years of his life in his native township, attending first the common school, and later entered Earlham College, at Richmond, Ind.; he also studied in a private school at Indianapolis. After coming to Kansas he occupied himself as a clerk until 1871, and during that year he was appointed Postmaster of Caldwell, holding the position until 1881. In the meantime he also engaged in the mercantile business. During the year last mentioned he disposed of his store and stock and turned his attention to live stock, becoming a member of the Cherokee Strip Live Stock Association, of which he has been Secretary since the time of its organization. He is a Knight of Pythias, Uniformed Rank, and is also a member of the Masonic fraternity. He cast his first Presidential vote for Grant, and has since maintained his adherence to the Republican party.

When approaching the twenty-third year of his age Mr. Blair was married, March 17, 1874, to Miss Katie Wendell. Mrs. Blair was born in Adams County, Ill., June 5, 1859, and is a daughter of the late John H., Sr., and Anna Catherine (Kouse) Wendell, both of whom are deceased. There have been born of this marriage two daughters—Mabel and Marguerite. Mr. Blair has always signalized himself as a liberal and public-spirited citizen, and the uniform encourager of the enterprises calculated to build up the interests of his adopted town. He is amply worthy of representation in a work designed to perpetuate the names of the leading men of Sumner County.

JOHN H. PORTER, a farmer residing on section 20, Wellington Township, was born five miles east of Madisonville, the county seat of Monroe County, Tenn., February 28, 1862. His father, William W. Porter, was born in Washington County, of that State, and his grandfather, Boyd Porter, is supposed to have been a native of Virginia. The latter moved to Washington County during its early settlement, and there improved the farm upon which he spent his last years.

The father of our subject was reared in his native county, and learned the trade of a tanner. He purchased a farm near Riceville, and established a tannery here, managing his farm and operating his tannery until 1862, when he sold out and removed to Monroe County, purchasing property and establishing himself in similar occupations there. In 1876 he visited this county and bought two hundred and forty acres of land on sections 20 and 29, of Wellington Township. Sumner County was sparsely settled at that time, and there were no railroads within its limits, so Mr. Porter deferred moving here, but continued to operate his farm and tannery in Tennessee for several years. He had sold his property there, and almost completed his arrangements for removal to this State, when he was stricken by disease, and May 21, 1885, breathed his last. The maiden name of his wife was Elizabeth Swan, and she was born in Knox County, Tenn. Her father, James Swan, was a native of the same county, was a blacksmith by trade, and spent his last years at his home near Campbell's Station. She passed from time to eternity in July 21, 1881.

The parents of our subject, and all of the family are members of the Presbyterian Church, in which the father was an Elder for many years. The first and third born of the children, James and Francina are missionaries in Japan; Belle is now the wife of S. D. Jewell, of New York. The other members of the family circle in their order are: our subject, Ella E., Jennie A., Lillie, Mamie G., and Dora.

In accordance with the wishes of the father, all the children, with the exception of James and Francina, came to Kansas and located upon the land the father had purchased. Our subject being the only son here, has superintended the improving of the land, has erected an excellent and adequate set of farm buildings, and has the estate under thorough and intelligent cultivation. It is located three miles from Wellington, and its situation adds to its value from a monetary point of view, as well as to its desirableness as a residence.

Mr. Porter received the advantages of the best schools of his native county, and supplemented his earlier education by a course of study in Knoxville Business College, and is one of the best informed young men in the county. He is displaying excellent judgment and practical ability in his agricultural work, and has already built up an excellent reputation for his manly character, and gives promise of becoming one of the most prominent and influential citizens of the county when a few more years shall have been added to his life.

THOMAS J. HOLLINGSWORTH, M. D. Although only establishing himself at South Haven, in December, 1888, Dr. Hollingsworth has already succeeded in building up a good practice, this being done by a strict attention to the duties of his profession, and his attitude as the encourager of those movements and enterprises calculated for the good of the community. He was born in Clay County, Mo., September 1, 1854, and obtained his preliminary education in Wyandotte County, this State. Later he attended the State University of Missouri, from the medical depart-

ment of which he was graduated in 1877. He began the practice of his profession in Wyandotte County, and later followed it in Kansas City, Mo., and in the city of the same name in this State. From the latter he removed to South Haven.

Of Southern antecedents, Dr. Hollingsworth is the son of Jeptha H. and Sarah F. (Jessup) Hollingsworth, who were natives of Todd County, Ky. They removed to Missouri in the spring of 1853, and located in Clay County. The elder Hollingsworth organized the first Battalion of Confederate soldiers in Bates County, of which county he was at that time resident. A short time afterward he removed his family to Collin County, Tex., while he remained in the service until the close of the war, acting under a Captain's commission. Then returning to Platte County, Mo., he engaged in stock-raising two years. Next he sold out, and coming to Kansas, located in Wyandotte County, where he was interested in live stock until his death May 27, 1888, at the age of fifty-nine years. The wife and mother died at the same farm March 4, 1881. The elder Hollingsworth was a well-educated man, having been graduated from the Louisville Law University, and he for a number of years was engaged in the practice of law in Kentucky and Missouri.

The mother of our subject was a niece of Gen. Thomas S. Jessup, who was at one time a member of the Kentucky Legislature, and later represented his district in Congress at Washington, in which city he died many years ago. She was carefully educated, completing her studies at a Female Seminary in Greenwood, Ky. She united with the Cumberland Presbyterian Church at the age of sixteen years, to the faith of which she consistently adhered until her death. The father of our subject was a member of the Missionary Baptist Church, with which he identified himself at the age of twenty years, and in which he was an earnest worker from that time on.

The paternal grandfather of our subject, Jeptha Hollingsworth, Sr., was a native of South Carolina, and traced his ancestry to Scotland. He was left an orphan when a mere child. When reaching man's estate he settled in Kentucky, and was married to Miss Mary Gordon, who was born there.

They lived in the Blue Grass regions many years, but finally removed to Missouri, where they spent their last days. Grandmother Hollingsworth was a member of the Baptist Church. On the maternal side Grandfather William Jessup was a native of Ireland, and closely related to the O'Connells of that country. He emigrated to America when quite young, and was married in Kentucky, where he reared a family and died.

Dr. Hollingsworth of this sketch was married in Chicago, Ill., November 29, 1881, to Miss Lois Kenyon Fellows, daughter of Mrs. Mary K. Fellows. Mrs. Hollingsworth was born September 27, 1861, in Syracuse, N. Y., of parents who were natives of New York. To the Doctor and his good wife there have been born three children, the eldest of whom, Jeptha B., died young. The survivors are Albert B., and Lola M. F. The Doctor affiliates with the Democratic party, and is a member of Pomeroy Lodge, No. 88, I. O. O. F. at Pomeroy, this State.

ANDERSON GILBERT FORNEY. This gentleman and his brother, J. W., occupy leading positions among the farmers and stock-raisers of Palestine Township, having about one thousand acres of land, and dealing largely in good grades of cattle, of which they usually feed about five hundred head annually, besides draft and road horses. The term "self-made" may properly be applied to them, as when coming to this section, they had but little means, but by great industry and a wise investment of that which they managed to save, they are now comparatively independent. Besides this land they have two other good farms and property in Wichita, Wellington, and Belle Plaine. Anderson G. may usually be found at his headquarters on section 7, Palestine Township, where he has a comfortable home, and apparently everything around him to make life desirable.

A native of Guernsey County, Ohio, Mr. Forney was born December 3, 1847, and spent his early years in the agricultural districts. His primary studies were conducted in the common school, and later he entered Cambridge College, Ohio. When leaving school, he occupied himself at teaching, and in 1867 was married in his native county, to Miss Samantha, daughter of David and Eliza J. (Hamilton) Dull. Mrs. Forney was also born in that county. Her father was a native of Pennsylvania, and her mother of Ohio. Her maternal grandfather, James Hamilton, was of Scotch birth and parentage. He emigrated to America at an early period in his life, and settled in Pennsylvania, where it is believed he spent his last days.

In 1869 Mr. Forney took a trip to Iowa, having in view the location of a permanent home, but finding nothing desirable, returned to Ohio, where he remained until the spring of 1871. His next venture was to this county, and he pre-empted one hundred and sixty acres of land, which is now included in his present farm. He put up a frame shanty which he occupied with his little family for several months, and commenced at first, principles in the construction of a farm from the primitive soil. He hauled his provisions from Emporia by team, the journey occupying about two weeks, and paid $2 for corn, $9.50 per barrel for salt, and twenty-five cents per pound for bacon. Wild animals were still plentiful, including deer, antelope, buffalo, and turkeys. Mr. Forney upon one occasion assisted in catching a buffalo with a lasso. His companions in the sport were John Gilchrist and L. Martin St. Clair. They loaded the animal into a wagon, and hauled it into the town of Belle Plaine, where it soon died, surrounded by an admiring crowd. Indians were often seen strolling over the country, but they did not offer to molest the settlers.

There were born to Mr. and Mrs. Forney eleven children, two of whom, Emma and Sylvester, died in infancy. The survivors are Amanda B., Frank W., Jennie H., Cora, Rosa Nell, Charles D., Mary D., Josie, and Benjamin Harrison. Mr. Forney gives his political support to the Republican party. He has served as Township Clerk, and been Clerk of the School Board since taking up his residence here. A man of liberal and progressive ideas, he keeps himself thoroughly posted in regard to current events, and is an earnest worker with the Farmers' Alliance of Home Valley.

The subject of this notice is the son of John and Eliza (Wilson) Forney, who were also natives of Guernsey County, Ohio, where the mother died in 1863, in the faith of the Methodist Protestant Church. The father is still living there. The paternal grandfather, Abraham Forney, was born in Maryland, where he lived until reaching man's estate, and was then married to a Miss Curtis. They emigrated to Ohio in 1802, the year in which it was admitted into the Union as a State. Grandfather Forney opened up a farm in the wilderness, and there, with his estimable wife, reared his family, and spent his last days. The father of our subject occupies that same homestead. Grandfather Forney shouldered his musket during the War of 1812, assisting in driving the British finally from American soil. Mr. Forney belongs to the A. O. U. W. Lodge No. 83, of Belle Plaine.

JAMES W. BELLER, now a resident of Perth, was born in Berkeley County, Va., August 29, 1838. Abisha Beller, his father, likewise a native of that county, was born in 1779. He served in the War of 1812, and was by occupation a planter. Legacia Beller, James W. Beller's grandfather, was born in France. He came to the United States when a child, located in Virginia and died in Berkeley County at an advanced age. He served in the Revolutionary War, and was a farmer, cultivating a large plantation.

Margaret (Morgan) Beller, the mother of the subject of this notice, was born in Berkeley County, Va., in 1797, and died at the age of sixty-three years. To her and her husband, Abisha, there was born a family of thirteen children, of whom James W. is the only surviving member. He was given a good education, being graduated from Prof. Frarey's High School in Jefferson County, Va. Soon after the outbreak of the Civil War he enlisted, September 6, 1861, in Company H, First

Maryland Dragoons, and was mustered out at the hospital in Williamsport, Md., December 16, 1862. He re-enlisted, January 14, 1863, in Battery D, Second Pennsylvania Heavy Artillery, as a private, and was promoted by special order No. 161, Current Series 64, Adjutant General's office, Washington, D. C., dated April 28, 1864, by order of Abraham Lincoln and countersigned by Edwin M. Stanton, Secretary of War, as Second Lieutenant, and assigned with brevet rank of Captain to the command of Battery E, Prov'l, Second Pennsylvania Heavy Artillery, and was taken prisoner by the Confederate Army, July 30, 1864, in the crater, caused from blowing up of the rebel fort, in front of Petersburg.

Mr. Beller for a period of seven months was held a prisoner of war in the "officer's prison" at Columbia, S. C., being at the expiration of this time paroled and passed through the lines at Wilmington, N. C. He arrived at Camp Parole, Annapolis, Md., on Sunday, March 3, 1865. He was in all the principal battles of the Army of the Potomac, except those of the Peninsular campaign and the fight at Gettysburg; during the latter his battery was stationed at Ft. Ethan Allen, in the defense of Washington, D. C.

After he was mustered out of service Mr. Beller returned to Martinsburg, which had now become West Virginia, and where he resided for several years. He there engaged in the sale of engines and sawmills for the firm of Griffith & Wedge, at Zanesville, Ohio. In 1879 he went to Porter County, Ind., where he was a contractor and builder, and where he also engaged in the mercantile business. He was married there in 1879, to Miss Matilda Miller, who died April 15, 1885. In 1880 he came to Kansas, and for some years was a resident of Labette County. On the 1st of March, 1887, he came to this county, settling in Perth, where he is now engaged in the real-estate business and insurance, and is also a Notary Public. Politically, he is an active, working Republican.

On the 19th of January, 1887, Mr. Beller contracted a second marriage in Martinsburg, W. Va., with Miss Lizzie L., daughter of Dr. John and Mary (Eldertice) Carpenter. This lady was born near Gettysburg, Pa., and was of illustrious ancestry,

Her maternal great-grandmother was a member of the Royal family of the Stuarts of Scotland, whence she went with her family to Ireland when a young girl, and was there married to a Mr. Alderdice, which name was afterward written Elderdice. They left Ireland and came to the United States about the year 1797, during the reign of persecution by Catholics, they being Scotch-Irish Presbyterians. They landed at Baltimore, Md., when that city was a small town, and letters written by Mrs. Beller's great-grandmother, and now in her possession, show that there were no postal facilities beyond the Alleghany Mountains.

Mrs. Beller is a very superior lady, possessing marked literary talent, and for some years has been a contributor to various newspapers and magazines. For some years also she was associate editress of the Martinsburg (W. Va.) *Herald*, and wrote up a history of the county and of the prominent men of Martinsburg for the special edition of that paper. She was for a time court stenographer, serving under the Hon. Judge Charles J. Faulkner, now the United States Senator from West Virginia.

Dr. John Carpenter, the father of Mrs. Beller, came to Kansas in 1889, arriving on the 15th of November. He was born in Adams County, Pa., January 20, 1805, and in 1826 removed with his father's family to Rochester, N. Y. He studied medicine at Rochester, and at Cincinnati, Ohio, being graduated at the latter place. He practiced near Gettysburg, Pa., for a period of thirty years, residing there at the time of the famous battle, and acted as surgeon for the wounded during and after the conflict. He removed to Martinsburg, W. Va., in 1868, and practiced medicine in that city for twenty-one years. His wife, Mary (Elderdice) Carpenter, died there in 1881, at the age of sixty-seven years. Dr. Carpenter's maternal ancestors, the Zimmermans, came from Switzerland to this country before the advent of William Penn. When Penn arrived he undertook to naturalize the people, and to change all the German and Swiss names into English. A part of the people agreed to this, while others refused to accept the change. Among the latter was one of the Zimmerman's, and that branch of the family are spread out

through New York, Pennsylvania, Maryland and the West, as Zimmermans, while Mrs. Beller's branch of the house use the English version of Carpenter. Dr. Carpenter has in his possession title deeds to lands in Adams County, Pa., a part of which was then called the "Manor of Maske," that date back to Penn's residence and were given under his hand and seal. Dr. Carpenter's grandmother, who in her maidenhood was Miss Lamon, was captured by the Indians in what is now Adams County, Pa., about the year 1765, when she was a child. Subsequently, after she had grown to be a young lady, she was recaptured by the Provincial Army and returned to her family. The Doctor is probably the only person living who saw the famous Sam Patch make his fatal leap over the Genesee Falls, at Rochester, N. Y., in the year 1828–29, he being not quite positive as to which year it occurred. He has lived a useful and long life, been eminently successful as a physician, and respected and esteemed by all who have known him.

~~----·∞∞{¦¦}·∞∞----~~

THOMAS TRACEWELL. In noting the pioneer settlers of Avon Township, the name of Mr. Tracewell should occupy a prominent position as he came to the frontier in the winter of 1877 and located upon the quarter section of land which he had purchased in September preceding. He has maintained his position through the scourges of drouth, grasshoppers and chinch bugs, and still preserves his faith in the future of the Sunflower State. He lives comfortably and unostentatiously, occupying a substantial residence and has convenient outbuildings for the shelter of stock and the storage of grain. This property is pleasantly located on section 23, and is represented on another page of this work by a lithographic engraving. Mr. Tracewell has not only acquitted himself as a thorough and skillful agriculturist, but by his integrity of character has attained to a good position among his fellow citizens.

The subject of this sketch was born in St. Clair

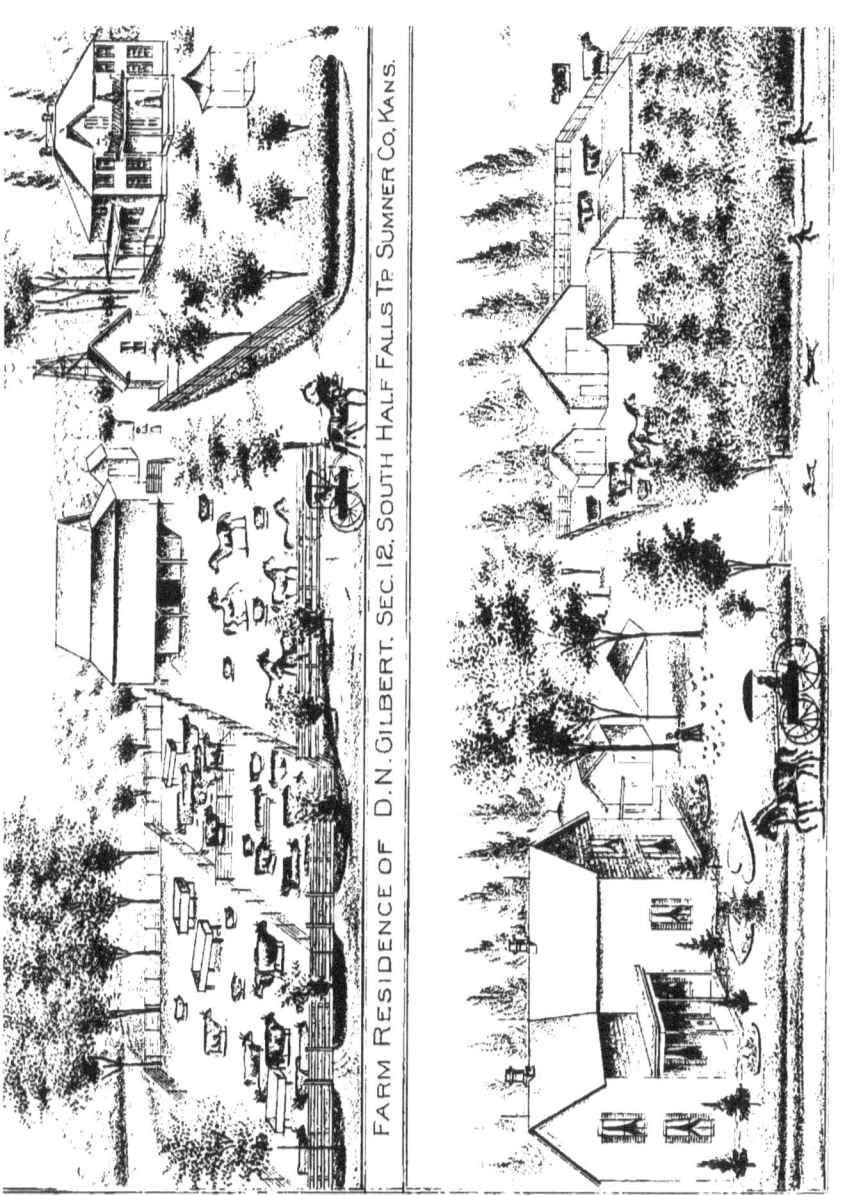

FARM RESIDENCE OF D. N. GILBERT, SEC. 12, SOUTH HALF FALLS TP. SUMNER CO., KANS.

County, Ill., December 29, 1840, and there spent the first thirty-seven years of his life. His boyhood and youth were passed in the manner common to farmers' sons, he attending the district school mostly during the winter season and growing up familiar with the arts of plowing, sowing and reaping. He remained a member of the parental household until ready to establish a fireside of his own, and was then united in marriage with Miss Sarah J. Hill, April 15, 1874.

Mr. and Tracewell commenced their wedded life together on a farm in their native county of St. Clair, Ill., where they sojourned until coming to Kansas. Mrs. Tracewell was born May 20, 1851, and is the daughter of Samuel A. and Nancy C. (Sargent) Hill, who were both likewise natives of St. Clair County, Ill., where they were reared and married; thence in 1880 they came to this county and settled on a farm in Dixon Township. To Mr. and Mrs. Tracewell there have been born three children, only two of whom are living—Edward A. and Jesse H. Eugene died when about four months old.

The father of our subject was Edward Tracewell, a native of Virginia, who married Miss Margaret Glover, a native of Tennessee. They first settled in St. Clair County, Ill., where they spent the remainder of their days, the father occupied in the peaceful pursuits of farming. Thomas Tracewell is a stanch supporter of the Democratic party, but aside from serving as Constable and as a member of the school board he has avoided the responsibilities of office. He forms one of the solid elements of his community, a man who casts his influence on the side of morality and good order and who lives at peace among his neighbors.

EMANUEL M. RIFFEL. In noting the prominent citizens of Downs Township, Mr. Riffel cannot be passed by without due mention. He is a gentleman approaching the sixty-seventh year of his age, having been born May 21,

1823, and his native place is York County, Pa. His father, Henry Riffel, was likewise a native of the Keystone State and born in Adams County. He died at the old home at the age of eighty-three years. He was a brickmaker by trade, but his last years were spent on a farm. An industrious and law-abiding citizen, he became well-to-do and uniformly voted the Democratic ticket.

The paternal grandfather of Mr. Riffel was Melcher, a native of New Jersey, who moved to Pennsylvania and spent his last days in Adams County. He was a farmer by occupation and during the Revolutionary War carried a musket in behalf of the Colonists. The mother of our subject bore the maiden name of Lydia Wolford. She was born in York County, Pa., and was the daughter of George and Eliza Wolford, who were among the earliest settlers of that State. Grandfather Wolford followed farming and was a conscientious member of the Lutheran Church. Mrs. Lydia (Wolford) Riffel departed this life about 1881 in York County, Pa., at the age of seventy-nine years.

The subject of this notice was the eldest of the seven children born to his parents. He was reared on the farm in his native county and educated in the common school. When quite young he began an apprenticeship at carriage-making, which he completed in Maryland, to which he had repaired in 1840. In 1849, he emigrated to Cincinnati, Ohio, where he sojourned three years, working at his trade, then went into Butler County, that State, and sojourned there until 1885. That year found him first west of the Mississippi and upon Kansas soil. Locating in Perth, this county, he established himself in business as a carriage-manufacturer, which he has since successfully followed. He differs in his political views from those entertained by his honored father, being a sound Republican.

While a resident of Cincinnati Mr. Riffel was married June 30, 1850, to Miss Hannah Mitchell. This lady was born in Pennsylvania October 21, 1833, and is the daughter of John and Mary (Baughman) Mitchell, who, upon removing from Maryland settled in Cincinnati, Ohio, where they both died at an advanced age. They were natives respectively of Pennsylvania and Maryland. Of this union there were born seven children, namely: John, Charles, Mary, William, Thomas N., Ernest and Harry. John died when a babe of three and one-half months; William was called hence when a promising youth of eighteen years; Harry died when fourteen months old. The survivors are living in different States.

WILLIAM P. ADAMS. The farmers and stockmen of Caldwell Township have a worthy representative in this gentleman, and his career affords a fine example of what can be accomplished by persevering industry, integrity and wise economy. He began life with no capital except his native abilities, his physical energy, and his determination and he is now the owner of a well-improved farm, comprising one hundred and forty-six acres on section 7, and is regarded as a very successful agriculturist and fruit-grower.

The parents of our subject are Daniel and Susan (McCrary) Adams, now residents of Johnson County, Mo. The father was born in North Carolina but at an early date emigrated to his present place of abode, where he has been County Judge and Justice of the Peace. He has followed farming throughout his life and has accumulated considerable means. His father, John Adams, was a native of North Carolina and became a resident of Johnson County, Mo., in 1833. John Adams served under Gen. Jackson in the War of 1812, and his father was a Revolutionary soldier and a participant in the battle of King's Mountain. The mother of our subject was born in Tennessee and has borne her husband twelve children, namely: John A., Elizabeth, William P., Jane, Christina, Elijah M., Ellen, Robert, Thomas, Emma, James and Frances.

The gentleman of whom we write was born in Johnson County, Mo., May 29, 1841, was reared on the farm and received a common-school education. When about nineteen years of age he entered the Federal army as a private in Company G,

Seventh Missouri Cavalry, serving his country to the best of his ability from the date of his enlistment in 1863 until the close of the war. His regiment belonged to the First Brigade and he participated with his comrades on many a hard fought field.

Mr. Adams moved from his native county to Humboldt County, Iowa, in 1875, but sojourned there only a few months ere becoming a resident of Kansas. He took up a claim which has since been his home and which energetic and systematic management has brought to a high state of perfection and which now forms one of the most attractive places in the vicinity. Among its excellent improvements are a fine residence and orchard, in the former in which he secures needed rest from the toils of life and pleasing recreation in the bosom of his family, while in the care of the latter he gains both pleasure and profit.

The marriage of Mr. Adams and Miss Josephine McCurdy took place September 8, 1870, and has been blessed by the birth of four children: Lena, Ruby, Ralph and Irwin. Mrs. Adams is a daughter of William J. and Margaret (Smith) McCurdy, and was born near Dalton, Ga., and is a lady of estimable character and agreeable manners. Mr. Adams is a member of the Grand Army of the Republic and he and his wife belong to the Cumberland Presbyterian Church.

HUMPHREY B. OSBURN came to Sumner County in the fall of 1880 and settled on section 21, Greene Township, where he has since been a resident and where he is carrying on the occupations of farming and stock-raising in which all of his years of maturity have been spent. He owns a large and valuable estate, comprising six hundred and forty acres on sections 24 and 25, and is one of the most highly respected residents of the township as well as one of its large land owners.

The birth of Mr. Osburn occurred in Davis

County, Mo., and his natal day was March 15, 1835. His father, Martin Osburn, was a farmer, and our subject not only obtained the best education possible under the surroundings of his early life, but also acquired a practical and thorough knowledge of agriculture, which has stood him in good stead since he began life for himself. He was about twelve years of age when the family moved to Andrew County, Mo., where he grew to manhood and remained until his thirtieth year. He then moved to Nemaha County, Neb., where he resided three years, after which he settled in Worth County, Mo., and continued to abide there until his removal to this county, where he has accumulated property and been a useful citizen.

The marriage of Mr. Osborn took place in Andrew County, Mo., his chosen companion being Miss Emma Bohart, who grew to womanhood there, but is a native of Buchanan County. Six living children brighten the lives of Mr. and Mrs. Osburn, a cluster of maidens who bear the names of Anna C., Sarah E., Elsie, Martha, Alice and Fannie. Three sons, James, Martin and Humphrey F., have been taken from them by death.

Mr. Osburn has held the office of School Treasurer ever since coming to Kansas. Politically he is a Democrat and never fails to cast his vote in the interest of his party. Both he and his wife have high standing in the Christian Church, of which they have been members for many years.

ROBERT W. LEMOND. The mercantile interests of Hunnewell are prominently represented by the subject of this notice, who is President of the City Council, Clerk of the School Board and who is seldom without some office of trust and responsibility. He is a gentleman in the prime of life, having been born March 27, 1847, and his native place in Gonzales County, Tex. He was reared to manhood in the Lone Star State on a stock farm, and acquired his education by walking four miles to a district school, which he attended five months, this comprising his book-learning. He, however, has improved his leisure time and keeps himself posted upon current events and by his habits of thought and observation, has formed an intelligent character which no one would suspect of having been deprived of the ordinary school advantages of a civilized community.

Young Lemond remained with his parents, John and Nancy (Brown) Lemond on the farm in Texas until May, 1863. The Civil War being then in progress, he, although being but sixteen years old, enlisted in Company E, Ford's Regiment of the Confederate Army and served as a non-commissioned officer until November following. He was then promoted to be First Sergeant with a regular commission and served in that capacity until the the close of the war. In the meantime he had also had command of the company.

Returning now to the old farm in Texas young Lemond sojourned there until 1882, being associated with his father as a live-stock dealer, they keeping from one thousand to five thousand head of horses and cattle on their ranche. These they disposed of largely in the Kansas markets, to which they drove large herds periodically.

John Lemond departed this life at Gonzales, Tex., in 1878, aged sixty-three years. He was a native of North Carolina, whence he removed to Texas at an early day. His wife, Nancy, survived him until 1884, dying at Gonzales when about fifty-five years old. The parental household consisted of eight children of whom Robert W. was next to the eldest and of whom besides himself, there is only one survivor. One brother, Alexander, was killed while in the Confederate service during the late war. Upon leaving Texas Robert W. located on a ranche in the Indian Territory, where he sojourned until 1885, coming then to this county. He was married at Hunnewell, July 17, 1883, to Miss Lena, daughter of G. A. and Lucinda (Vernon) Hale. Of this (his second) marriage, there have been born two children—Walter and an infant unnamed. The first wife of Mr. Lemond, to whom he was married in Texas, was Mrs. Mattie (Price) Apath. That union resulted in the birth of three children, viz: Cornelia A., Kate H. and Robert W. Mrs. Mattie Lemond died in 1879 at

Coleman, Tex. She taught school some years in Texas and for one term Mr. Lemond was her pupil.

Mr. Lemond in March, 1887, after locating in Hunnewell associated himself in partnership with George K. Van Hook, under the firm name of Van Hook & Lemond. They have a full line of general merchandise, including groceries, hardware, flour, wood and queensware, and carry a stock of from $2,000 to $4,500. Their sales aggregate probably $12,000 per year. Mr. and Mrs. Lemond are prominently connected with the Presbyterian Church in which Mr. Lemond officiates as Superintendent of the Sabbath-school. He mixes very little in political affairs aside from giving his hearty support to the Democratic party.

D AVID M. HARDMAN. Among those who arrived in Oxford Township in time to assist in its early growth and development was Mr. Hardman, who pitched his tent on section 1, in the fall of 1876. He had come to this vicinity the year previous and still remains upon the land which he purchased as a claim, and upon which he has effected nearly all of the improvements which to-day attract the attention of the passing traveler. His farm embraces two hundred and forty acres of fertile land, which is finely adapted to general farming and stock-raising.

The subject of this sketch was born in Wayne County, Ind., June 9, 1835, and lived there until reaching mature years. His father, Israel Hardman, was a native of Kentucky, and born October 12, 1801. The latter removed with his parents to Dayton, Ohio. Grandfather David Hardman was one of the hardy pioneers of Kentucky, and was with the famous Daniel Boone at the siege of Blue Lick and Boonesboro. He married a Miss Leatherman, of Virginia, and removed to Ohio during the time of the pioneer days of the Buckeye State, settling near Dayton. There his son Israel, the father of our subject, grew to mature years and was married

to Miss Elizabeth Wagoner. Later Israel Hardman emigrated to Indiana and settled in Wayne County, where he followed farming until 1855. That year he removed to Appanoose County, Iowa, where he sojourned until his death, in 1878. He was a member of the German Baptist Church. The mother had passed away in 1860.

David M. Hardman, during his younger years, learned carpentering. He remained under the home roof until after his mother's death. In the meantime he was married, September 7, 1859, to Miss Elizabeth Ullrick, the wedding taking place at the bride's home. A year or two later Mr. Hardman set out overland to California, where he built a mill on Center Creek in Amador County. He superintended the operations of this until the fall of 1866, in the heart of the mining regions. He then returned to his old haunts in Iowa, via the Isthmus and New York City, arriving at his destination in December, that year, after an absence of five years.

Again resuming operations as a carpenter, Mr. Hardman also engaged in millwrighting, remaining there until his removal to this county. He came here with the expectation of putting in the machinery of the Oxford Water Mill, the first structure of any importance in the county. Upon his arrival here he assumed a half interest in the enterprise in company with Joseph Hewett, completed the mill and then sold out. This mill was driven by water-power from the Arkansas River, having a fall of ten feet in a mile race. Mr. Hardman was obliged to build a dam across the river above the island in the form of a V, running from the island up stream, instead of straight across. After withdrawing from the mill Mr. Hardman purchased the land which he now owns. The bottoms were flooded in 1876, where the year previous, there had been raised seventy-five bushels of corn to the acre. This flood swept down millions of cottonwood trees, thousands of which were taken to different counties and planted. These trees have now grown to be sixteen and eighteen inches in diameter, forming fine wind-breaks and a grateful shade in summer. Mr. Hardman while carrying on the improvements of his property has, nevertheless, maintained an interest in the welfare of his adopted township, serving as a School Director in his district, and giving his support and encouragement to the various enterprises tending to the good of the people. He votes the straight Republican ticket, and is identified with the Ancient Order of United Workman.

Mrs. Hardman was born in Wayne County, Ind., December 23, 1839, and is the daughter of John and Margaret (Gatz) Ullrick, who removed to Iowa in 1855. Mr. Ullrick was a native of Hesse, Germany, and for nine years served in the German army, being in the wars against Napoleon. There were born to him and his estimable wife three children, all natives of the Fatherland. Upon emigrating to America they settled in the city of Baltimore, where they sojourned from 1830 until 1835, and then removed to Hagerstown, Pa. In 1855 they turned their steps Westward, locating in Iowa, where the mother died in 1878, at the age of seventy-four years. Mr. Ullrick only survived his wife one year, dying in October, 1879, at the advanced age of eighty-four years.

Of the four children born to Mr. and Mrs. Hardman only two are living—Laura F. and Charles Warren—who remain at home with their parents. Katie and Ralph are deceased. Mr. and Mrs. Hardman have made many friends during their long sojourn in this county, where their upright lives and hospitality have secured them the universal respect of all who know them.

GEORGE W. FRIEND. Illinois is acknowledged to be one of the most prosperous States of the Union, but Mr. Friend, in October, 1877, concluded he could remove to something better west of the Mississippi, and accordingly gathering together his family and household goods, set his face toward the State of Kansas. Coming to this county he selected one hundred and sixty acres of land, on section 29, Harmon Township, and proceeded to build up a homestead. He was prospered in his labors, bringing the soil to a

good state of cultivation, erecting substantial buildings, and effecting the other improvements naturally brought about by the enterprising and progressive farmer.

Mr. Friend has been materially assisted in his labors by his estimable and capable wife—a lady who has proven a most efficient helpmate to her husband, encouraging him in his worthy endeavors, and by the wise and prudent management of her household affairs has been no unimportant factor in the accumulation of their property. Mrs. Friend has illustrated in no small degree the manner in which a woman may influence the well-being and prosperity of a husband and a family. Mr. Friend gives his attention to general farming and stock-raising, making a specialty of minding his own concerns, and has been prospered in proportion. The family occupies no secondary position among the best social elements of their community.

The subject of this sketch was born in Chambersburg, Pa., February 3, 1838, and lived in his native city until a boy of seven or eight years. He then removed with his parents to Baltimore, Md., of which they were residents four years. From there they went to Havre de Grace, that State, and not very long afterward to Philadelphia, Pa. In 1857 they struck out for the West, and took up their abode in Springfield, Ill.

After the outbreak of the Civil War Mr. Friend, in August, 1862, entered the ranks of the Union Army, as a member of Company E, One Hundred and Fourteenth Illinois Infantry. Soon afterward he went with his regiment to the front, and participated in the siege of Vicksburg, and the battles of Jackson, Henderson Hill, Ft. Drusey, Pleasant Hill, Yellow Bayou, Lake Chicot, Tupelo, Nashville and Mobile. He was for about one and one-half years on detached service, in the pioneer corps. He escaped wounds and capture, and at the close of the war was mustered out of the service at Camp Butler, Springfield, Ill., receiving an honorable discharge.

After leaving the army Mr. Friend established himself in Springfield, Ill., as a clerk in a clothing store, remaining there one year. Later he engaged in the mercantile business for nearly ten years, and until the fall of 1877. He then entered upon a new departure, coming to Kansas and engaging in agricultural pursuits. These he has found congenial to his tastes and health, and has been fairly prosperous in his undertakings. He votes the straight Republican ticket, and has held the office of Township Trustee for the past year. Both Mr. and Mrs. Friend are members in good standing of the Methodist Episcopal Church, attending services at the Plain View school-house.

The marriage of George W. Friend and Miss Adeline Taylor was celebrated at the bride's home, in the city of Springfield, Ill., October 9, 1859. Mrs. Friend was born in Sangamon County, Ill., January 23, 1841, and is the daughter of Jefferson Taylor, a native of Kentucky. The mother is deceased, and the father lives in Sangamon County, Ill. Her father's family consisted of seven children, six of whom are living. Of her union with our subject there have been born three sons and one daughter, viz.: Elmer; Norah, who died at the age of five years; George and William H. Mr. Friend as a Union soldier belongs to Belle Plaine Post, G. A. R., at Belle Plaine.

ILL. T. WALKER. The subject of this notice is one of the influential men of the city of Wellington, and this part of Kansas, possessing more than ordinary ability and highly spoken of by all who know him. He follows the practice of law and makes a specialty of the pension business. He has been a resident of Wellington since April, 1885, and makes his headquarters at a well-equipped office on Washington Avenue.

Mr. Walker was born in Hancock County, Ind., October 17, 1849, and there grew to mature years, pursuing the common branches of study in the schools of that locality. He completed his literary education in Spiceland Academy in Henry County, Ind., after which he for a time was engaged in various pursuits and then commenced the reading of

law. He was admitted to practice at the age of twenty-seven years, in November, 1876, commencing his maiden efforts at Scottsburg, Scott County, Ind. He continued there until April, 1885. In the meantime he officiated as Master Commissioner of the Circuit Court of that county from the time the office was created until it was abolished in 1883.

Mr. Walker, in 1882, was a candidate on the Republican ticket for Congress in the Third Indiana district. The district being largely Democratic he was defeated. In 1884 he was a member of the Republican National Convention which nominated James G. Blaine for President. The same year he represented his district on the Indiana Republican State Central Committee, serving with efficiency. In 1873-'75 he was an officer of the State Senate of Indiana, and in 1881, at the regular and special session of the House of Representatives of Indiana, was an officer of that body.

Upon locating in Wellington Mr. Walker engaged for a time in general law business, gradually working into the pension practice to which he seems peculiarly adapted, having the bulk of this business for all of Southern Kansas. In April, 1886, he was elected Police Judge of the city of Wellington and re-elected in 1887 without a dissenting vote. During the session of 1887 he was assistant chief clerk of the Kansas House of Representatives. He has always been a Republican in politics and is a member in good standing of the Presbyterian Church. He has for many years been a Knight of Pythias and at the present time is Grand Prelate of the Grand Lodge of Kansas.

At Greenfield, Ind., December 3, 1871, Mr. Walker was wedded to Miss Kate Pierson. Mrs. Kate Walker survived her marriage less than a year, dying October 17, 1875. Mr. Walker contracted a second marriage July 1, 1881, with Miss Kate McKinney, of Loogootee, Ind. This lady was born in Washington County, Ind., November 30, 1852, and removed with her parents to Martin County, where she remained until her marriage. Her parents were Griffin and Mary A. (Williams) McKinney, who were natives of Indiana and Kentucky, respectively, the father deceased. Griffin McKinney who died in August, 1886, aged seventy-one years, was born in Mon ezuma, Ind. in 1815, and was a soldier in the Mexican war. He had traveled when a young man over Spanish North America and the northern portions of South America. The mother is still living. Mr. and Mrs. Walker are the parents of one child, a daughter, Mary Pearl.

The father of our subject was Robert Walker, a native of Clinton County, Ohio, and born March 10, 1821. When six years old he was taken by his parents to Rush County, Ind. They remained there a few years and then removed to Hancock County, Ind., and lived there until 1871. He married Miss Martha A. Tibbets and they reared a family of eight children, seven of whom are still living. The Walker family in 1874 removed to Scott County, Ind., where the parents still reside. Robert Walker has long been a member of the Masonic fraternity and is also a Knight of Pythias.

DAVID W. DORSETT. It is nearly a score of years since this gentleman took up his residence in this county and began at once to take rank as an upright citizen, an industrious man, and a kind neighbor. His home is pleasantly located on section 22, Harmon Township, and comprises eighty acres of fertile and thoroughly cultivated land, bearing an excellent set of farm buildings and such other improvements as are to be expected of a man of his ability.

Mr. Dorsett is the fourth child in a family comprising nine sons and daughters. His parents, Samuel and Elizabeth (Walker) Dorsett, are natives of North Carolina, in which State they lived until 1841, when they settled in Adams County, Ill., where they sojourned forty years. They then moved to this county and are now honored residents of Harmon Township.

Our subject is a native of North Carolina, where his eyes first opened to the light April 1, 1842, and he was therefore but two years old when the family removed to Illinois. There he grew to manhood, was educated, and entered upon the pursuit of agriculture. Though a native of the South and of Southern parentage, he was not in sympathy with the States that desired to leave the Union, and with all the ardor of his young soul he desired to assist in the preservation of the Government which he had been taught to revere. On July 30, 1862, though not yet of age, he was enrolled in Company B, Fiftieth Illinois Infantry, and until the close of the war faithfully served his country in the ranks, being mustered out of service at Washington, D. C. and honorably discharged "when the cruel war was over."

Returning to his former home, Mr. Dorsett continued to live in Illinois until the fall of 1871, when he came to this county and pre-empted one hundred and sixty acres of land where he is now sojourning, being therefore one of the oldest settlers in this county. He has served both as Trustee of Belle Plaine Township and Treasurer of Harmon Township, and also as Justice of the Peace, and in every position of public responsibility has shown himself worthy of the trust reposed in him. He is a member of Belle Plaine Post, Grand Army of the Republic, at Belle Plaine.

In Miss Harriet Baxter, a native of Carroll County, Ohio, born April 1, 1850, Mr. Dorsett found united the qualities which he desired in a companion, and after a successful wooing he was united with her in marriage, the ceremony taking place in Schuyler County, Ill. Mrs. Dorsett is a daughter of John and Ellen (Moore) Baxter, now residents of Brown County, Kan., and is the fifth of the ten children born to them. Her happy union with our subject has been blessed by the birth of seven children: Samuel B., Elizabeth E., Orie L., Ellie B., Loren E., Willie F. and Della F.

FRED JAY. The subject of this notice is a favorite in the amusement circles of South Haven, conducting a billiard hall, and at all times deporting himself as a gentleman. He is a little over thirty-one years old, having been born

August 6, 1858, and his native place was Portage City, Wis. While he was still a mere child his parents, John C. and Lucy C. (Waters) Jay, removed to Southern Iowa where they sojourned for a time, then changed their residence to Northern Missouri.

The next removal of the Jay family was to Winneshiek County, Iowa, and we next find them in Hancock County, that State, located on a farm and where the boyhood days of their son Fred were chiefly spent. He attended the district school and assisted in the lighter labors of the farm, remaining there until 1882. Then a young man of twenty-four years, he went up into Dakota and purchased a claim where he engaged in farming about two years; he also operated as an insurance agent, and at the same time sold agricultural implements. In the meantime his mother kept house for him until his marriage, which occurred July 21, 1885. The lady of his choice was Miss Frances E. Mosier, who was born in Morgan County, Mo., in 1856.

Remaining in Dakota until the fall of 1885, Mr. Jay then, with his wife, parents and sister, and the husband of the latter, set out overland by team for this State, and after an enjoyable trip of two months landed in South Haven. Soon afterward Mr. Jay purchased his present residence. The first season he occupied himself in buying and selling corn. In January, 1887, he purchased an interest in the billiard hall and later became sole proprietor, and is now in the enjoyment of a profitable business. He owns considerable city property and is generally well-to-do. To Mr. and Mrs. Jay there has been born one child, a daughter, Cora.

JAMES H COX. He, with whose name we introduce this biographical outline, is accredited with being one of the most extensive and prosperous farmers of Falls Township. Intelligent and enterprising, he has been the architect of his own fortune and is the owner of eight hundred acres of valuable land, all in one body. His possessions have all been accumulated since coming to this State. He came to this county in 1876 and pre-empted one hundred and sixty acres of land on section 12, Chikaskia Township, where he lived until 1882. Then, selling out, he purchased the whole of section 3, Falls Township, where he established his homestead, and he also owns one hundred and sixty acres on section 10 of this township. He gives his entire attention to farming and stock-raising, of which he makes an art and a science and from which he realizes handsome returns.

A native of Carroll County, Ohio, Mr. Cox was born March 4, 1841, to Zebediah and Elizabeth (Ryan) Cox. Zebediah Cox was born in Maryland in 1801 and emigrated to Ohio when a young man. He spent the remainder of his life in the Buckeye State, dying in Harrison County, in 1865. He learned carpentering during his early manhood, but subsequently engaged in farming as a more congenial pursuit. The paternal grandfather of our subject was Sheridan Cox, a native of Maryland, who spent his last years in Ohio. Mrs. Elizabeth (Ryan) Cox, likewise a native of Maryland, was born in 1809, and died in Wyandot County, Ohio, in 1858.

To the parents of our subject there was born a family of nine children, viz: Sheridan, Joshua, Samuel, Mary, Hiram, James H., Rachel, William and Martha. They are all living with the exception of Hiram, who died when about twenty-one years old. James H., the sixth child, was reared in Carroll and Wyandot Counties, Ohio, attending the common school and becoming familiar with the various pursuits of farm life. When a young man of twenty years, leaving the parental roof, he journeyed to McLean County, Ill., where he sojourned for a time, then removed to Livingston County, of which he was a resident until coming to Kansas. His career presents a remarkable illustration of the results of energy and perseverance he having started out in life dependent upon his own resources without means or influence, and he is now numbered among the leading men of the county. He is a staunch supporter of the Democratic party, but cares very little for political preferment, simply serving in some of the minor offices. Socially, he belongs to the Independent Order of Odd Fellows, and the Farmers' Alliance.

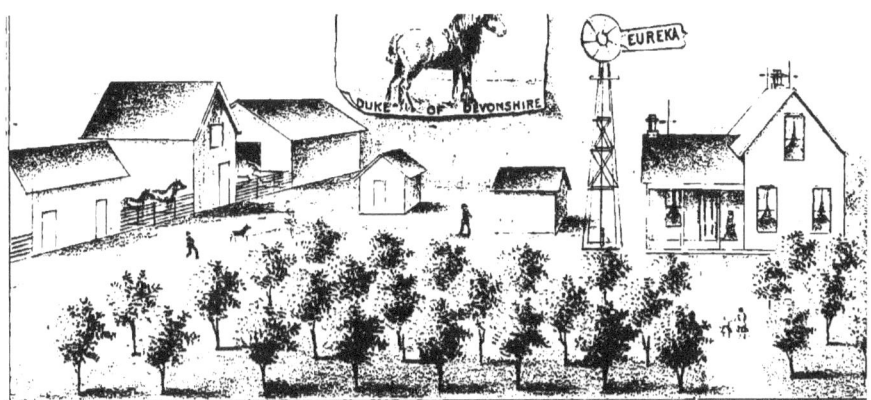

FARM RESIDENCE OF J.H.COX SEC 3. FALLS TP SUMNER CO KAN.

RES. OF A.A.ENDERS SEC.17, SOUTH HALF FALLS TP. SUMNER CO, KAN.

At Pontiac on the 12th of May, 1872, occurred the marriage of James H. Cox with Miss Nancy Hallock. Mrs. Cox was born in McLean County, Ill., September 17, 1856, and is the daughter of Washington and Catherine (Skaenes) Hallock, who were natives of Ohio. Mrs. Hallock still lives in Illinois; Mr. Hallock is deceased. To Mr. Cox and his estimable wife there have been born five children, viz: George, Emma, Samuel, Nelson and Edna, all of whom are living.

We invite the reader's attention to a lithographic engraving of Mr. Cox's residence on another page.

OHN W. NYCE. There is not a more popular man in the city of Caldwell than he with whose name we introduce this sketch. Indeed he is widely and favorably known throughout Sumner County, as one who has been identified with its best interests and who has contributed materially to its growth and development. He is at present the Mayor of Caldwell and Cashier of the Stock Exchange Bank, and has occupied various other positions of trust and responsibility since becoming a resident of this place.

The subject of this sketch was born in Delanco, Burlington County, N. J., July 15, 1855, and is the son of John and Martha (Allyn) Nyce, who were natives respectively of New York and New Jersey. John Nyce was a lawyer of fine abilities and attained to a high position in his profession, which he followed for many years in Milford, Pa. At the outbreak of the Civil War he joined the Thirty-third Pennsylvania Infantry, as Second Lieutenant of a company, and subsequently rose to the position of Major, serving in that capacity until the battle of Antietam. Then, being wounded, he was for a time unfit for service. After his recovery he was promoted to be Colonel of the One Hundred and Seventy-fourth Pennsylvania Infantry, a position which he filled with great credit to himself until

the expiration of his term of service. He was a man quiet and unobtrusive in his manner, never seeking notoriety of any kind, but he held some of the minor offices of his town.

Although successful as a money getter, the father of our subject never succeeded in accumulating much means, on account of his liberality. He was a devoted Christian, and for many years prior to his decease, a member in good standing of the Methodist Episcopal Church. He also officiated most of his time as Sunday-school Superintendent. He came of a long line of honorable ancestry, of German extraction, and was gathered to his fathers on the 11th of April, 1880, caused from a wound received through the lung at the battle of Antietam, at the early age of forty-nine years. The wife and mother, who bore the maiden name of Martha A. Allyn, is still living, making her home in Caldwell; she is a lady possessing many estimable qualities and greatly beloved in the community. She is now fifty-four years of age and traces her ancestry to Scotland. The parental household included six children, viz.: John W., Bertha, Belle C., Clara E., Mattie B. and George M.

He of whom we write was the eldest child of his parents, and spent his early years at Stroudsburg and Milford, Pa. He completed his studies in the academy, and later read law under the instruction of his father, to such good purpose that in 1877, he was admitted to the bar. He followed the profession in Milford until May, 1881, in the meantime serving one term as District Attorney. He determined to seek the West, believing that it could furnish a better field for his ambition, and accordingly in the month above mentioned, he came to Kansas, and taking up his residence in Caldwell began dealing in live stock. In 1882, however, he abandoned this and entered the Stock Exchange Bank of Caldwell as book-keeper, and was shortly afterward promoted to Assistant Cashier. He proved himself to be competent and trustworthy, and in 1884 was made its regular Cashier, which position he still holds. In 1886 he was elected Clerk of the District Court of Sumner County, and served one term. In addition to his other responsible duties, he officiates as Treasurer of the Cherokee Strip Live Stock Association, a position requiring bonds of $200,000. Mr. Nyce is a Mason in high standing, and a Knight Templar, and a member of Isis Temple, Mystic Shrine of Kansas, and he also belongs to the Encampment of the Independent Order of Odd Fellows; he is a Knight of Pythias, Uniformed Rank; is identified with the Ancient Order of United Workman, and is Captain of the Sons of Veterans, Col. John Nyce Camp, No. 5, at Caldwell. Politically he is a sound Republican.

The marriage of John W. Nyce and Miss Maggie A. Quick was celebrated at the bride's home in Milford, Pa., May 9, 1881. Mrs. Nyce was born March 19, 1862, in Milford, Pa., and is the daughter of Peter A. L. and 'Catherine (Angel) Quick, natives of Pennsylvania. Mr. and Mrs. Nyce are the parents of two sons: John W., Jr., and Peter Q. The family residence is pleasantly located in the south part of town, and forms one of its most attractive homes.

------- ⟶≥≷⟨⟨⟶ -------

ILLIAM H. LASSELL. The tasteful and attractive home of this gentleman is located on section 29, Bluff Township, and its appearance and surroundings are conclusive evidences to the passerby that the owner is in a condition of financial prosperity, and that the family is possessed of refined tastes. These indications would not be belied by closer investigation, as the estate is one of the best farms in the township, the dwelling, barns and other improvements being excellent and adequate, and the entire place pervaded by an air of neatness and order highly creditable to its owner and operator. The interior of the residence presents equal signs of good management, and the family are found to be cultured, cordial and agreeable.

Mr. Lassell was born in Clinton County, N. Y., May 25, 1840, to Harris and Lydia (Fisk) Lassell, and is the sixth in a family of seven children. The eyes of his father first opened to the light in Swanton, Vt., March 8, 1803, and when a young man he

took up his abode in Otsego County, N. Y. There he married a young lady of that county, and engaging in the mill and lumber business, continued to reside in the Empire State until 1853, at which time he moved to Green County, Wis. In the latter State he followed farming until his death, which occurred in January, 1885. He accumulated considerable means, and left an estate worth $12,000. He was a member of the Masonic fraternity, and of the Republican party. Mrs. Harris Lassell was born April 12, 1802, and died in Green County, Wis., February 14, 1873. She was the mother of seven children. Ellen and Lewis, the first and fourth born being now deceased. The survivors are: Eliza, the wife of R. W. Button, of Colton, Cal.; Luther J., a lumberman and miner in Arizona; Lorenzo H., a lumberman in Washington; and Emily A., the wife of Charles Smiley, a farmer in Albany, Wis.

The gentleman who is the subject of this biography was reared to the age of twelve years in his native county of the Empire State, and spent the remainder of his years to early manhood in Green County, Wis. In 1859, when nineteen years of age, he crossed the plains to California, and remained on the Pacific Slope until 1868, when he returned to Green County, Wis., and engaged in farming there during the succeeding eight years. He then moved to Bremer County, Iowa, and in 1878 came to Sumner County, Kan., and pre-empted one hundred and sixty acres on sections 28, 29, 32 and 33, of Bluff Township. He has since made his home here. has acquired an excellent reputation among his fellowmen, and proved himself a useful citizen. He has served as Justice of the Peace, is a member of the Masonic fraternity and of the Republican party.

The marriage of Mr. Lassell was celebrated March 11, 1874, his bride being Miss Celia Taylor, of Avon, Rock County, Wis. Her parents, James H. and Caroline (Conger) Taylor, are natives of Fairfield, Vt., and emigrated to Wisconsin about the year 1845, still surviving at their home there. Mrs. Lassell was born in Delevan, Wis., July 7, 1848, and possesses some rare accomplishments. She was graduated from the White Water (Wis.) Normal School in 1872, and had taught school several years before her marriage. Five bright boys and girls cluster about the fireside of Mr. and Mrs. Lassell, and gladden their parents' hearts by their growing intelligence and youthful courtesy. They bear the names of Caroline L., Harris J., Ada M., Wallace A. and Louisa A.

MELANCTHON L. BRIGGLE, a prosperous farmer residing in Jackson Township, was born in Pike Township, Stark County, Ohio, October 16, 1847. His father, Joseph Briggle, was a native of Wurtemburg, Germany. The father of Joseph, also a native of Germany, emigrated with his family to the United States and settled in Pennsylvania. After a few years residence in that State he moved on further West and located in Ohio. As there were no railroads or canals built, their only mode of performing the journey was by means of teams, which was the usual method of travel adopted by the emigrants of those days. He was a farmer by occupation, and resided on his farm in Ohio during the remainder of his life.

The father of our subject was only six years of age when his parents came to America, and remembers but little of the voyage, which was not then made as quickly and easily as at the present time. He was reared in Pennsylvania, where he learned the trade of a stonemason. He accompanied his parents to Ohio, but found upon his arrival that there was small demand for his services as a mason. Instead of idly bemoaning his fate he manfully set out to secure the work in other places that was denied him at his home. In the spring following his entrance into Ohio he slung his kit of tools on his back and trudged on foot, there being no railroads, back to the State of Pennsylvania, where he readily procured work at his trade. He did this for five successive years, going to Pennsylvania in the spring and returning to his Ohio home in the fall when the work for the season was over. He worked at his trade on the Pennsylvania

Canal when that great waterway was in process of construction. He also found employment upon the public works that were being built in Pittsburg. In this manner he secured sufficient means to purchase a farm of one hundred and sixty acres in Pike Township, Stark County, Ohio, upon which he settled. Although starting in life in such an humble manner, his persevering industry secured him a fine estate of one hundred and eighty acres of excellently improved land, well stocked and provided with good buildings. His last years were spent in the enjoyment of well-earned repose amid the scenes of his manhood's struggles and triumphs. The mother of our subject was Catherine Beard, a native of Pennsylvania, who removed with her parents to Stark County, Ohio, during the early days of that county. The parental family consisted of twelve children, nine of whom are living.

The subject of this notice attended the school of his district during the early years of his life, but as soon as he was able to be of use on the farm was put to work, and from that time forward did not have many idle days to spend either in mischief or in the pursuit of knowledge. He continued to reside under the parental roof until he had reached the age of twenty-five, when he removed to a town near by and engaged in the carpenter's trade for two years. He then returned to the farm, and in connection with his brother George, bought the homestead and operated it with good success until 1883. In that year he removed to Kansas and located in Sumner County on his present place, which he purchased shortly after entering the State.

The farm of Mr. Briggle is situated on section 15, and embraces the northwest quarter. It is enclosed by a thriving hedge, and subdivided into forty-acre tracts, all neatly fenced and finely cultivated. His family residence and all other buildings, of which he has all that are necessary, are substantially and tastefully built frame structures, and contribute their share toward making the place a cosy and prosperous home.

Our subject was married in 1875 to Miss Agnes Muckley, a native of Stark County, Ohio, and a daughter of John and Mary Muckley. The father was of German descent, and was highly esteemed in his neighborhood. Mr. and Mrs. Briggle are the parents of two children, whose names are—Virgil M. and John C. They are held in high regard in the community in which they live, and are fully deserving of all the kind words which they receive from neighbors and friends. They are consistent Christians, and find a religious home in the Presbyterian Church. Mr. Briggle is a staunch and devoted adherent of the principles of the Republican party.

ON. WILLIAM L. CHAMBERS. During his residence in Wellington, Mr. Chambers has become widely and favorably known to the citizens of this part of the county. In former years he was engaged in the practice of law, and in the fall of 1888 was elected Justice of the Peace, which position he still holds. He was born in St. Clair County, Ill., September 8, 1831, and is the son of William Chambers, a native of Hagerstown, Md. William Chambers was reared in his native State, and after serving in the War of 1812, went to Kentucky, and was married near Scottsville, to Miss Sarah M. McReynolds, a native of that place. Mr. Chambers, who from his youth up had been piously inclined, now entered the ministry of the Methodist Episcopal Church, and labored in the Master's vineyard until about 1830. We next find him in St. Clair County, Ill., where he purchased land and engaged in farming a few years, then removed to Greene County. His next removal was to Waverly, Morgan County, where he resumed preaching. He also purchased land, and operated as farmer and preacher until after the death of his wife, when he severed his connection with the conference, and for some years was a local preacher.

The father of our subject, in 1851, removed to DeWitt County, Ill., and purchased a tract of wild prairie land, also property in the town of Clinton. He took up his abode in the latter, and while preaching proceeded with the improvement of his property which he had purchased near the town, and resided there until 1858. Then, selling out, he removed to Christian County, and purchased land six miles from Taylorville, where he made his home until his death, which occurred in the fall of 1859.

To the parents of our subject there was born a family of six children, and of the second marriage of William Chambers there were born three children. William L. pursued his early studies in the old log schoolhouse near his childhood home, a structure finished and furnished in the fashion of those times, with puncheon floor and slab seats and desks. His surroundings, however, did not lessen his love of learning, and he made such good headway, that in 1857 he entered McKendree College, at Lebanon, Ill., of which he remained a student until 1859. He then commenced the study of law, in the office of Lawrence Welden, at Clinton, Ill., with whom he remained until 1862.

The Civil War now being in progress young Chambers laid aside his personal plans and interests in order to assist in the preservation of the Union. In August, that year, he enlisted in Company B, One Hundred and Seventh Illinois Infantry, being mustered in as a private. Not long afterward he was promoted to be Quartermaster-Sergeant and then First Lieutenant and Regimental Quartermaster. He served in this joint capacity three or four months, and was then ordered to the headquarters of Gen. Cooper, Commander of the Second Brigade, and Second Division, Twenty-Third Army Corps, and served as Quartermaster of the brigade. Later he was ordered by the commanding general, Crouch, of the Twenty-Third Army Corps, to serve as Quartermaster of that division, and in addition was Quartermaster of the post at Salisbury, N. C., and of transportation. This occupied his time until the close of the war, when he received his honorable discharge at Salisbury, June 21, 1865. His duties in the army led him over the States of Kentucky, Tennessee and Georgia, and after the fall of Atlanta he repaired to Washington with his comrades and was present at the Grand Review.

After leaving the army Mr. Chambers returned

to Clinton. Ill., where he resumed the study of law, and in 1866 was admitted to the bar before the Supreme Court at Springfield. He opened his first office in Clinton, and in due time became Assistant Assessor for Internal Revenue of DeWitt County. In 1868 he was elected Register of Deeds, and resigning the office of Assessor served four years. He then returned to his law practice, but in the meantime had been of such good service to the Republican party, that in 1876 he was elected to represent DeWitt and Macon Counties in the State Legislature. He afterward had the satisfaction of casting his vote for John A. Logan for United States Senator. He remained a resident of Clinton, practicing law until 1879. That year he came to Kansas, settling in Wellington, of which he has since been a resident.

The subject of this sketch was married, November 26, 1866, at the bride's home in Waverly. Ill., to Miss Ellen E. Woods. Mrs. Chambers was born in Morgan County, Ill., and is the daughter of Mason F. and Sarah I. (Chesnut) Woods, who were natives of Kentucky, and pioneers of the above-mentioned County. Her father is deceased, and her mother lives in Waverly. Three children have been born to Mr. and Mrs. Chambers, bearing the names of Edwin C., Kate S. and William M. The latter, who was the eldest, died in Wellington in 1885, when a promising youth approaching the sixteenth year of his age. Mr. Chambers belongs to the Grand Army of the Republic, in Deming. N. M., where he opened an office in 1884, and practiced two years. He is a Mason, and has attained the Royal Arch degree. Politically, he is a staunch Republican.

WILLIAM G. MOORE. The spring of 1871 first found Mr. Moore interviewing the frontier with the idea of a permanent settlement. The outlook in this region was anything but encouraging, much of the land being the property of the Government and over which roamed Indians and wild animals, including buffalo, deer, antelopes, wolves and wild turkey. After erecting a domicile Mr. Moore could stand in his doorway and look over a long stretch of country without a dwelling where now may be seen schoolhouses, farm residences, fertile fields and all the other evidences of civilization. He, himself rejoices in, the possession of a snug farm, one hundred and sixty acres in extent, one hundred and twenty of which are under the plow and yielding abundantly the best crops of the Sunflower State. In addition there are comfortable buildings, an orchard of apple trees in good bearing condition, besides pear, cherry, crab and peach trees, all planted by the hand of the present proprietor.

A native of North Carolina, Mr. Moore was born in Guilford County, February 2. 1834. About 1840 his parents, John L. and Mary F. (Bishop) Moore, leaving the South emigrated to Hamilton County, Ind., with their little family, where the father purchased a farm in the green woods, erected a log cabin in primitive style and commenced the improvement of his land. The family sojourned there until 1852, then crossing the Mississippi, established themselves on a farm in Appanoose County, Iowa. Thence they removed to Taylor County, that State, and there the father died in the fall of 1862, aged fifty-one years; the mother is still living, making her home with her son, our subject, and is now about seventy-eight years old. Mrs. Moore, notwithstanding her years, is in remarkably good health, very active, and frequently walks to town and to church, one and one-half miles away.

To John L. and Mary F. Moore there was born a family of eleven children, of whom William G. was the eldest and of whom only five survive. The second son, Hubbard, enlisted in the Union army during the late war and died in the service at Little Rock, Ark. A younger son, Enoch T., was also in the service and came home without a wound. The paternal grandfather, John Moore, was a native of North Carolina where he reared his family and died in the faith of the Baptist Church. On the maternal side of the house, Grandfather Aaron Bishop was a native of Maryland and when a young man went to North

Carolina where he was married to Miss Louisa Caffe, a native of that State. They lived on a farm and reared a family at a time when table knives and forks were manufactured from wood. Later, pewter cutlery and dishes came into vogue and were considered very fine. The Bishop family religiously as far as is known, was mostly identified with the Society of Friends. One of the early progenitors, Robert Bishop by name, likewise a resident, first of Maryland and then of North Carolina, finally removed to Delaware County, Ohio, settling among its earliest pioneers and there spent the remainder of his life. He also was a Quaker in religious belief.

The subject of this sketch was married in Hamilton County, Ind., in 1852 to Miss Angeline, daughter of Hardy and Martha (Thompson) Ward. Mrs. Moore was born in North Carolina and while an infant of a few months was taken by her parents to Indiana. In the fall of 1852 they removed across the Mississippi to Missouri, settling in Howard County. Later they came to Kansas and were residents of Coffee County about four years, then returned to Missouri where the father died in the fall of 1867. The mother is still living, making her home with her son. The paternal grandparents of Mrs. Moore were James and Martha (McDonald) Thompson, natives of North Carolina. He died in North Carolina as did also his wife.

The maternal grandparents of Mrs. Moore were Samuel and Sally (Womell) Thompson, likewise of North Carolina; the mother of the latter lived to the advanced age of one hundred and one years. William G. Moore in the fall of 1852 removed to Iowa and a year later to Missouri. In 1856 he returned to Iowa and in 1857 came to this State, locating in Coffee County, near Burlington, the latter then consisting of one house in which was kept a store of dry-goods and groceries. The building was about twelve feet square formed by posts driven into the ground, sided up and covered with clapboards. Mr. Moore pre-empted land and prosecuted farming, marketing his produce at Kansas City. He sojourned there until the fall of 1866, then returned to Iowa, coming from there to Kansas.

There have been born to Mr. Moore and his ex-

cellent lady thirteen children, the eldest of whom, a daughter, Isabel, died in infancy. Sarah E. and James O. remain with their parents; Mahala is the wife of Reuben Dodson, of Sumner County; William H. died when about seven months old; Lilly Q. is the wife of Amos Chambers of Sumner; Rosa B. married Myron Lusk and lives in Sumner County; Ichabod K. died when two years old; Katie E. is one of the most popular and successful teachers in the South Haven schools; Thomas A., Elmer L., Ella E. and Clara P. are deceased. Mr. Moore, politically, is a sound Republican and has served as Township Treasurer one term, School Treasurer six years and School Director three years. He is a member in good standing of Lodge No. 111, I. O. O. F., while he and his wife are prominently connected with the Methodist Episcopal Church in which Mr. Moore officiates as Trustee. He has also served thirteen years as Treasurer of his Odd Fellows lodge.

JESSE T. STURM. In compiling the main facts connected with the history of Mr. Sturm, one of the most highly respected citizens of Wellington, we find that he was a native of Virginia, and was born in Marion County, February 11, 1841. His father, Jesse Sturm, Sr., was likewise a native of that county and the son of Jacob Sturm, who was born and reared in Germany. The latter at an early day emigrated to America, being accompanied by two brothers; he was then a young man, and settled in the Old Dominion during the Colonial times. He served in the Revolutionary War on the side of the Colonists, and after the close of the great struggle purchased a large tract of land in Marion County, Va., and cleared a farm from the wilderness. He also erected a gristmill, which he operated, and there spent the remainder of his days. His wife was a native of his own county.

Jesse Sturm, Sr., was reared to manhood in his native county, where he learned farming and milling. When reaching manhood, he purchased a tract of timber land there, of which he cleared quite an area, then selling a part, laid out the town of Worthington, erecting a mill and several other good buildings. The mill was operated by him, and he also conducted an hotel. In 1849, selling out the above-mentioned interests, he purchased a farm and mill site along the line of Marion and Harrison Counties. There he put up another mill, which he operated until 1873. He then sold out all his interests again and purchased another tract of land on the same stream, building another mill and operating this by steam. He purchased a home in the village of Wyatt, where he spent his last days, passing away October 10, 1883, at the age of seventy-six years.

The mother of our subject bore the maiden name of Matilda Davis. She likewise was a native of Marion County, Va., and the daughter of Caleb Davis, who was born near Moorfield, that State. The latter was a farmer by occupation, and spent his declining days in Marion County. Mrs. Matilda (Davis) Sturm died in Wyatt, Va., November 11, 1886. The parental family consisted of ten children, eight of whom lived to mature years. Jesse T. was reared and educated in Marion County, also in Harrison County, Va., and assisted his father in the labors of the farm and mill. During the second year of the war he enlisted, August 20, 1862, in Company H, Fourteenth West Virginia Infantry, and served until July 3, 1865, in the Army of West Virginia. He participated in the battles of Bulltown, Lynchburg, Carter's Farm, Winchester, Fisher's Hill and Cedar Creek. At the latter place his regiment was surprised and routed when Sherman made his famous ride at Winchester. Mr. Sturm saw the hero as he reached the line. Although Mr. Sturm was struck by a bullet and knocked down, he soon recovered and assisted in finishing the fight at Fisher's Hill, being the first man over the ramparts at Winchester, and he fired the first shot at Bulltown. In the first-mentioned place Mr. Sturm and his brother-inlaw, Lieut. Hess, with about twelve others, went in advance of the line of battle, running into an ambuscade of the enemy, and Mr. Sturm was the only one left standing when the regiment came up. Lieut.

Hess was shot, and fell dead at his feet. The clothing and equipments of Mr. Sturm were perforated by forty-two bullets. He was then promoted to be Color-Sergeant, which position he retained until his discharge.

Upon leaving the army, Mr. Sturm engaged in farming and lumbering at Mannington, W. Va. In 1870 he commenced teaching vocal music, which he followed until the spring of 1872, when he started for the country west of the Mississippi. Leaving West Virginia in March, 1872, he traveled by rail to Florence, Marion County, and then purchasing a team and wagon, drove through to this county. Soon thereafter he filed a claim to a tract of land in what is now Falls Township. The country was thinly settled, peopled principally by wild animals, including deer and buffalo. Newton, eighty miles distant, was the nearest railroad station. Mr. Sturm repaired thither, and purchasing lumber, hauled it to his claim, where he put up a house and commenced the improvement of his property. That first year he harvested a fine crop of corn from the soil. He has operated upon the maxim that "a rolling stone gathers no moss," and to-day retains possession of the land, which under his careful management has been transformed from a wild, uncultivated waste to a valuable homestead. He gradually added to his possessions, and is now the owner of three hundred and twenty broad acres. He erected good buildings and supplied himself with all the necessary machinery for successful farming. He lived there until the 23d of September, 1888, then wisely retiring from active labor, took up his abode in Wellington.

On the 11th of February, 1866, occurred the marriage of Jesse F. Sturm to Miss Lavinia J. Hess. This lady is likewise a native of Marion County, Va., and was born January 28, 1847. Her parents were Peter and Orpha (Sandy) Hess, who spent their last years in Worthington, W. Va. To Mr. and Mrs. Sturm there have been born six children, viz: Leonidas W., Leodas B., Lola M., Leiten L., Leonora L. and Lucius M. Mr. and Mrs. Sturm are members in good standing of the Christian Church. Mr. Sturm belongs to Upton Post, No. 27, G. A. R., of which he is a charter member, and to Wellington Lodge, No. 133, I. O. O. F. He votes the straight Republican ticket, and has served as Trustee of Falls Township, School Director, Justice of the Peace, Road Commissioner, and in 1887 was elected County Treasurer.

The ability displayed in the management of the finances of the great county of Sumner, and the uniform kindness and courtesy shown to all parties with whom he came in contact, raised our subject in the esteem of the people of his county, and in 1889 he was re-elected to that important and lucrative office by a largely increased majority, and is now about entering upon its duties for a second term.

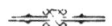

MANLEY D. COVELL. As an exponent of progress and enterprise Mr. Covell stands foremost among the leading men of Avon Township. At present he is giving his chief attention to the breeding of Percheron horses, and is one of the best judges of horse flesh in this section of the country. For many years he was an importer, and has for the last fifteen years made a specialty of breeding the pure registered Percherons, of which he has thirty head on his homestead in Sumner County. More than ordinarily intelligent and well-informed, he is naturally looked up to in his community, where he has been no unimportant factor in advancing its material interests. His well-regulated homestead is situated on section 30, comprising three hundred and twenty acres of land, whereon have been erected good buildings, and which is complete in all respects as a rural residence.

Mr. Covell came from his native place—Delaware, Ohio—to this county in March, 1883. He was born in March, 1822, and is the son of Calvin Covell, a native of Vermont, and a carriage-maker by occupation. The father came to Delaware, Ohio, about the year 1816, and was married to Pamelia Dopson, October 19, 1820. They had a family of eight children, who lived to maturity, and who were named as follows: Manley D., our subject; Clarissa Electa, who married William

Likes, and at her death left one son, now living: Mary E., who became the wife of G. W. Emerson, and they are now living in Delaware, Ohio; Lyman Sanford, who was united in marriage with Miss Laura Abbott, of Tiffin, Ohio; they live in Delaware, Ohio, and have one daughter living, Anna B.; Louisa Ann (Mrs. Isaac W. Hickle), who lives in Cumberland County, Ill.; of their five living children three are boys and two girls; Pamelia J. (Mrs. M. C. Cochran) lives in Delaware, Ohio; Calvin Edgar was twice married, his first wife being Miss Sarah Mills, and the second Miss Margaret Emerson; Adeline Josephine became the wife of Milton Scott, and lives at Clarence, Cedar County, Iowa; they had four children, one of whom, Fannie, is deceased.

Our subject, after completing his education, learned the trade of a carriage-maker under the instruction of his father, and was engaged in this at Delaware for several years. Later, in Ohio, he became interested in farming, and there began the importation and breeding of Percheron horses. He finally resolved upon seeking the Far West, and came to Kansas in 1882, selecting the land in Avon Township, upon which he removed the following year. This embraces three hundred and twenty acres, and is finely adapted to the business to which it is devoted. Mr. Covell usually keeps about thirty head of pure-blooded Percheron horses of all ages, and his transactions extend not only throughout the State of Kansas, but the two States adjoining.

Mr. Covell was first married in his native place to Miss Louisa Lee, who became the mother of seven children, three now living—Charles, Anise and Addie. Mrs. Louisa Covell died in Delaware, Ohio, in 1872. Our subject contracted a second marriage in Franklin County, Ohio, with Mrs. Anise Lee, widow of Theron Lee, and likewise a native of the Buckeye State. This lady is the daughter of Alvin and Betsy Fuller, and was born January 30, 1828. Her parents are deceased.

For nearly fifty years Mr. Covell has been a faithful member of the Presbyterian Church, identifying himself with it in Delaware, Ohio, in the winter of 1840, and has been an Elder therein since 1861. Politically, he is a sound Republican. He meddles very little with public affairs, but has been a reader all his life, and keeps himself thoroughly informed upon the leading questions of the day. Mrs. Covell is a lady of more than ordinary intelligence, and in all respects a true helpmate to her husband, proving of assistance, financially, in the prudent and economical management of her household affairs, and assisting him also in sustaining his reputation among his fellow-citizens. They have a pleasant and attractive home, and occupy a leading position in the community.

ANNIBAL A. TAYLOR, one of the pioneers of Sumner County, was born in Ohio County, Ky., November 25, 1843. His father, Levi Taylor, was a native of the same county, and his father, the grandfather of our subject, was a pioneer of Ohio County, Ky., in which place he spent his last days. The father of our subject was left an orphan at a very early age but continued to reside in his native county, where he was reared to agricultural pursuits. When grown to manhood he bought a tract of heavily timbered land on the bank of Green River and there built a log house in which the subject of this sketch was born. He cleared a farm and resided there until his death in 1885. The maiden name of his wife, the mother of our subject, was Kittie Catherine Taylor. She was a native of Virginia, of which State her parents, Septimus and Priscilla Taylor, were also natives. They removed to Kentucky and were among the earliest settlers of Ohio County where they spent their last days. The mother of H. A. Taylor died in 1879. The parental family embraced eight children, all of whom were reared to maturity. They were named respectively, Septimus C., Mary, Lewis, Victor, Silas, H. A., Volney and Quintus S.

The subject of this sketch was reared in his native county and assisted his father in tilling the soil during his youth and early manhood. When quite well grown he engaged in occasional trips of

flat-boating on the Green River, going as far as Evansville. He made two trips down the Mississippi River to New Orleans with a flatboat loaded with hoops, poles and staves for the market. These various expeditions were keenly enjoyed by Mr. Taylor and were also profitable in a pecuniary point of view. He continued to make his home in Kentucky until 1868, in which year he went to Champaign County, Ill., where he rented land and lived on it until 1871.

In 1871 Mr. Taylor concluded to emigrate to Kansas where he could secure Government land and make a better home for himself than he could in the more populous State of Illinois. Accordingly he started with a pair of horses and a wagon and drove the entire distance to Sumner County, which was then opened up for settlement. Only a year before his arrival buffalo had roamed over the plains which were then unsurveyed and untenanted by anything superior to the wild animals which were shortly to be displaced by the settlers and their domestic creatures. Mr. Taylor made a claim to a tract of Government land, including the northwest quarter of section 11, in what is now Jackson Township, and filed on the same at the land office at Wichita. He then returned to Kentucky where he resided until 1876, in which year he again turned his foot-steps Westward and located on his land in Sumner County. During his absence the railroad had been extended from Emporia to Wichita, which materially increased the value of his land besides facilitating the operations of travel and transportation. He continued to reside on his farm until 1881 when he rented it to a good tenant and went to Colorado where he spent the summer near Gunnison. In the fall of that year he returned to his farm and has resided on it from that time to the present.

The subject of this sketch was twice married. In 1877 he took Miss Martha J. Fulkerson to wife but his married happiness was of brief duration, as she was claimed by the pale messenger from the unseen land in the fall of 1879, and borne swiftly away from the sorrowing friends who would fain have detained her yet awhile longer. She was the daughter of Enis and Sissera Fulkerson and a native of Muhlenberg County, Ky. The second union of Mr.

Taylor took place in January, 1882, when he espoused Miss Phœbe Frame, a native of Montgomery County, Ill. There is one child living—Howard. Mr. and Mrs. Taylor are excellent people and consistent Christians. They find a congenial religious home in the bosom of the Methodist Episcopal Church, of which they are earnest and efficient members.

NOAH E. HEIZER, an old resident of this county, was born in Fayette County, Ind., January 4, 1826, and spent his early life there on a farm. His father, Joshua Heizer was a native of Virginia, whence he emigrated to Indiana in 1818 and acquired his education in the primitive schools at a time when Indians and wild animals roamed through the heavy timber. The father built a log cabin and cleared up a farm from the wilderness.

The mother of our subject, who in her girlhood was Jemima Cory, was a native of Warren County, Ohio, and going to Indiana to visit her brother, there met her future husband to whom she was soon married. They became the parents of seven children, of whom Noah E. was the fourth in order of birth. The parents spent their last days at the old farm, the father dying at the age of fifty-six. The mother lived to the advanced age of eighty-five. Both were members of the Presbyterian Church. The maternal grandfather, Noah Cory, it is believed was a native of Pennsylvania, from which he emigrated at an early day to Ohio and there died.

The subject of this notice was married in Fayette County, Ind., to Miss Margaret, daughter of Nehemiah S. and Nancy (Wherrett) Raszell. The parents of Mrs. Heizer were natives of Kentucky whence they removed at an early day to Indiana, settling at Greensburg, upon the site of which Mr. Raszell erected the first brick house. Both he and his wife died in that State. The paternal grandfather, Charles Raszell, settled in the woods near Greensburg at an early day and died in that city

when over one hundred years old. He was married in Virginia to Nancy Holden; she died in Kentucky and Grandfather Raszell later was married to Miss Jennie Doles who died in Indiana.

Mr. Heizer lived in Indiana until February, 1877, then came to Kansas, settling first in Cowley County. He lived there until March, 1884, then purchased eighty acres of land from which he constructed his present farm. Five of the six children born to him and his excellent wife are still living. Mr. and Mrs. Heizer are prominently connected with the Methodist Episcopal Church, attending services at South Haven. Mr. Heizer belongs to the Farmers' Alliance. While a resident of Cowley County he served as Township Trustee.

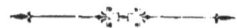

M. B. HOLMES is the senior member of the firm of Holmes & Co., grocers, in Wellington, where he has been engaged in business since 1874, with the exception of two years. He is in charge of one of the largest and most prominent groceries in the place, and is highly respected by all who know him for his integrity and business ability.

The parents of our subject were Samuel and Jane (Streator) Holmes, for many years residents of Quincy, Ill., in which place our subject was born July 19, 1839. His father was a native of Thompson, Conn., having been born in 1812, and took up his residence in Quincy at an early date. The senior Mr. Holmes was engaged in pork-packing and later in railroad work, having been the builder of the east end of the Hannibal & St. Joseph, and of the Quincy & Palmyra Railroad, and President of the latter. He was an incorporator of the Quincy Bridge and an extensive business man, and during the latter part of the '50s was Speaker of the Illinois House of Representatives. He departed this life in 1868 at the age of fifty-six years. His widow survived until 1872, when she too passed away, her age being sixty-one years.

The subject of this biography grew to maturity

in his native town, acquiring an excellent education in that town, where subsequently he engaged in the grocery business and also in grain dealing, finding his principal occupation in that employment until he came to Kansas. He is a member of the Ancient Order of United Workmen and the Modern Woodmen of America. He gives his suffrage to the Democratic party, but has no political aspirations of a personal nature.

On May 20, 1885, Mr. Holmes was united in marriage with Mrs. Mary W. Peck, of St. Louis. Her maiden name was Mary Whitmore and she was born in St. Louis in 1849, growing to maturity in that city, and there marrying Rudolph, son of Charles H. Peck. By him she had two daughters—Mary and Lyda—who are now living with our subject.

MONS DAVIDSON. No resident of Wellington is more highly respected than the above-named gentleman, whose citizenship of Kansas dates from the fall of 1870, and who is well known as a man of ability and integrity of character. His life shows in a marked manner through what discouragements and trials some men arrive at prosperity and win a high reputation, and should be an encouraging lesson to other youths. Mr. Davidson was born in Norway, January 3, 1837, and is a son of Arne and Britavia Davidson. He grew to the age of thirteen years in his native country, and then accompanied his parents, two brothers and a sister to America, landing in New York, July 5, 1850. It was the intention of Mr. Davidson, Sr., to locate in Wisconsin, and the family went as far as Chicago, where they waited for an uncle of our subject to come from Wisconsin with a team, as there was no railroad to that section. When the uncle arrived, he found the father nearly dead of the cholera, and a few hours later he breathed his last. The uncle was taken sick at the burial, and he also died in a few days, and in a short time the mother and one

brother of our subject, his aunt, two cousins, and two uncles were also dead, leaving two orphans thirteen and eight years of age, without friends or relatives near them, in a strange land, with whose language even they were unfamiliar. J. R. Kinzie, a kind-hearted man, for whom Kinzie Street, was named, took the orphans in charge and found a home for the younger with a Mr. Hubbard, himself retaining charge of our subject. The following fall our subject's uncle by marriage sent his sons with an ox-team and took the boys to his home in Wisconsin, where our subject remained one and one-half years.

Young Davidson then hired himself out to a Mr. Jewell until he was twenty-one years of age, this being a period of six years. He then went to Warren, Ill., and apprenticed himself to D. H. Dean, a blacksmith, with whom he remained three years, after which he went to Hillsdale, Mich., having determined to devote his savings to acquiring a better education. He attended the college from 1861 till the fall of 1863, when he gave up his intention of graduating to engage in the service of his adopted country in the war that was then going on.

Mr. Davidson enlisted in Company I, Eleventh Michigan Cavalry, which was attached to the Fourteenth Army Corps, his first service being in following the famous Gen. Morgan and assisting in the routing of his band. His regiment then took part in the attack at the King Salt Works, Va., and the next winter again attacked that place and captured it. They also fought with Breckenridge between Withville and Salt Works, and in many skirmishes and raids. Near the close of the war they were engaged at Salisbury, N. C., where they captured many prisoners, and after which they joined in the pursuit of Jefferson Davis. Mr. Davidson was discharged at Knoxville, Tenn., and mustered out of service at Jackson, Mich., after having faithfully fulfilled the duties which devolved upon him in every department of a soldier's life.

Before going into the army, Mr. Davidson was united in marriage with Miss Ora A. Francisco, of Grass Lake, Mich., who was attending Hillsdale College, and continued her studies there for some time after he had joined his regiment. Upon leaving the army, Mr. Davidson first took up the arts of peace at Warren, Ill., where he built up a home and improved some land that he owned. Moving thence to Wyota, Wis., he engaged in business with his brother for four years, and then returned to Warren, where he remained until 1876, when he came to Wichita, intending to work at his trade there. Finding no job, however, he went to the western part of Sedgwick County, and took up one hundred and sixty acres of land, on which he proved up and made good improvements, living on it four years, when he was burned out by prairie fire. He then came to this place, and for a year worked by the day, after which he rented a shop and began business for himself. He afterward purchased the lots with nothing but a little shanty on them. They are finely located on Lincoln Avenue, a half block from Washington Street, and there Mr. Davidson has erected a fine two-story brick building, 50x75 feet, in which he finds abundant occupation.

To Mr. Davidson and his estimable wife four children have been born. Three of these are still living. Charles H. is a book-keeper in this place; Nellie V. is a teacher; William M. is still attending school. All are intelligent and well-informed, filling their spheres in life in an honorable manner. Mr. Davidson has served his fellow-citizens as Alderman, and is regarded as one of the representative old settlers. He belongs to the Baptist Church, and is a useful and honored member of that body.

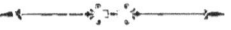

ON. S. HARVEY HORNER, who is the present representative from Sumner County to the Kansas Legislature on the Republican ticket, has been for many years identified with the interests of Caldwell and vicinity, and is evidently one of its most popular men. The possessor of more than ordinary capabilities, he has made a good record as a business man and a citizen, and has attained to his present high position solely through his own efforts, having started in life entirely dependent upon his own resources. He was born in Darke County, Ohio, June 8, 1851, and is consequently in the prime of life and the midst of his usefulness.

Mr. Horner was the sixth in a family of nine children, the offspring of John C. and Mary (Burns) Horner, the former of whom was a native of Adams County, Pa., and born in 1819. John Horner left his native State in 1835, when a youth of sixteen years, locating in Gettysburg, Ohio, and was thereafter a resident of the Buckeye State until his death, which occurred at Versailles in 1882. He accumulated a comfortable property, following the pursuits of farm life, and was an active member of the Cumberland Presbyterian Church. He was married in early manhood to Miss Mary Burns, who was born in Ohio about 1824 and died in Versailles, that State, in 1876. The paternal grandfather was John C. Horner, a native of Pennsylvania, whose father owned the farm upon which later was fought the famous battle of Gettysburg, Pa. The family is of Irish extraction and was first represented in this country during the Colonial days.

The subject of this sketch was reared on a farm in his native county, receiving such educational advantages as were afforded by the common schools. He was more than ordinarily bright and intelligent, and at the age of sixteen years began reading medicine. His attention, however, was turned in another direction and thereafter, until 1876, he was occupied as clerk in a drug-store at Versailles, Ohio. That year he sought the Great West, coming to Wichita, this State, and was employed as clerk in a drug-store there until 1879. That year he took up his abode in Caldwell, of which he has since been a resident. He soon established a drugstore on his own account, which he has since conducted very successfully, incorporating with it a jewelry business, from which he also realizes handsome returns. He is now well-to-do financially, and occupies no secondary position among the leading men of his community. Liberal and public-spirited, he is one of the first to lend a helping hand to every worthy enterprise, being in favor of education and every measure tending to elevate society and benefit the people. He has served as a member of the City Council, also as City Treasurer and City Clerk. He is likewise a Director of the

Stock Exchange Bank, and is a large stockholder in the Caldwell water works. As a member in high standing of the Masonic fraternity he has taken all the degrees, and belongs to the Encampment degree. I. O. O. F., Uniformed Rank of K. of P., and the Modern Woodmen of America.

Mr. Horner was married, October 25, 1878, to Miss Julia York, then a resident of Wichita, this State. Mrs. Horner was born in Winchester, Ill., January 11, 1862, and was the daughter of John and Mary (Blackburn) York, the former of Illinois and the latter a native of England. The result of this union is a bright little daughter—Marie, born November 17, 1887.

JUDGE JOHN E. HALSELL, now residing in Wellington, and engaged in legal practice there, is a native of the Blue Grass State, having been born in Warren County, September 11, 1826. His parents, William and Mary (Garland) Halsell, were early settlers in that county, where the father was engaged in farming. William Halsell was born in Butler County, Ky., and when gathered to his fathers was eighty-two years of age. To him and his wife eight children were born, who lived to maturity.

The gentleman of whom we write acquired a fundamental education at the common schools near his home, finishing his literary course at Cumberland University, Lebanon, Tenn., and taking up the study of legal lore in the same institution. He was graduated from the Department of Law in 1849, and located for practice at Bowling Green, Ky., where he continued his legal labors for thirty years. During the early period of his practice there he was elected County Attorney, which office he held for four years, and was also elected Circuit Judge of the Fourth Judicial District of Kentucky. He held different local offices, Mayor, etc., and was elected to Congress from the Third Congressional District of Kentucky, serving in the Forty-eighth Congress and also in the Forty-ninth. While a

member of the Legislative Assembly he was Chairman of the Committee on Private Land Claims, and a member of the Committee on Patents, and served his constituents satisfactorily and with credit to himself. Until his election to Congress he practiced regularly in Warren and adjoining counties.

In April, 1887, Judge Halsell located at Wellington, entering into partnership with Judge Ray, and in the short space of time since he came here has acquired a reputation as one of most able attorneys in this part of the State. The firm to which he belongs is now Halsell & Mumford. Judge Halsell has had no political aspirations, but being a firm believer in the principles of Democracy, and in the duty of exercising the right of franchise, he is ever ready to cast his vote with his favored party. Of a social and benevolent nature, he is naturally interested in the societies, and belongs to the Independent Order of Odd Fellows and the Masonic fraternity.

Judge Halsell was united in marriage, in April, 1876, with Mrs. Carrie Spencer nee Porter, of Todd County, Ky. The union has been blessed by the birth of one son, John T. Halsell. The accomplished wife of Judge Halsell is a daughter of the Rev. Thomas Porter, of the Cumberland Presbyterian Church, and was born in Todd County, where she lived until after her marriage with our subject.

JOHN C. JAY, at present a resident of South Haven, where he settled in 1885, is a native of New York State. His early years were spent in an uneventful manner on a farm and when reaching man's estate he was married to Miss Lucy C. Waters, who was born and reared not far from the childhood home of her husband. They lived in their native State until 1849, then removed to Columbia County, Wis., and later to Portage County, that State. In 1859 they changed their residence to Ralls County, Mo., and afterward, in 1861, removed to Macon County. That same fall, going into Iowa, they lived for a short time in Van Buren County. Then in the fall of 1862 they returned to Portage County, Wis.

In 1863 Mr. Jay removed with his family to Ft. Atkinson, Iowa. In 1865 we find them in Castalia, that same county, and from there they removed to Hancock County. Next they journeyed to Dakota and from there came overland with a team to South Haven. Mr. Jay's family consists of a daughter, Emma D., and a son, Frederick, who is represented elsewhere in this work. Socially, he belongs to the Masonic fraternity. His parents were Jesse and Margaret (Clark) Jay, both natives of New York State where they reared their family and died.

The paternal grandfather of our subject was Joshua J., a native of New York State, where he was reared among strangers, his parents having died when he was quite young. After reaching manhood he married Miss Rachel Bailey and later they removed to Ohio, where they spent the remainder of their days. On the maternal side Grandfather Elias Clark, also a native of New York State, was of Irish ancestry. He married Miss Hiley Cole, who was a native of New York and who traced her forefathers to Holland, some of whom came to America with the Plymouth Rock Colony. Mr. Jay recollects seeing in his young years an old family Bible marked by a blood stain of one of his ancestors who was murdered by the Indians; and there were also holes in several of the leaves, bearing a spear mark of the Indian who killed the person who was reading the Bible at the time of the massacre; that old book is supposed to be still in possession of some member of the family not at present known by Mr. Jay.

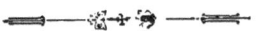

A BRANAMAN, who is the Cashier of the Sumner National Bank in Wellington, was born in Milledgeville, Carroll County, Ill., February 21, 1854, and was a child of about five years when taken by his parents to Tama

County, Iowa, where he grew to maturity. He finished his education at Tama City High School, and was preparing for college when his eyes failed, and he was obliged to abandon his purpose. He afterward entered a law office, and in 1875 was admitted to the bar, and practiced in Tama City for five years. Although a very young man he was given the offices of City and School Treasurer, and was actively engaged in political work although he did not seek official honors. In the summer of 1880 Mr. Branaman moved to Grundy Center, Iowa, and engaged in the banking business, continuing so interested there until he moved to this city, about the middle of April, 1886. At that time the old John G. Woods Bank became the Sumner County Bank, with J. G. Woods as its President; Paul Weitzel, Vice President; and our subject Cashier. Two years later it was re-organized as a National Bank, Mr. Branaman retaining his former position, Mr. Weitzel continuing Vice President, and Dr. S. W. Spitler becoming President of the new institution. The bank has a firm standing in the community, and has a capital stock of $75,000.

The parents of our subject are Henry and Nancy J. (Fowler) Branaman, who are now living in Tama County, Iowa, where the father is engaged in the grain business. He was born in Louisville, Ky., June 9, 1831, and was but a small boy when taken to Indiana, where he grew to manhood and married. In 1854 he moved to Carroll County, Ill., and for some years was engaged in farming there, leaving that county for the place of which he is now a resident.

During his residence at Tama City, Mr. Branaman, of whom we write, was united in marriage with Miss Rosa V. Morris, the ceremony taking place June 15, 1873. The charming bride was born in Pennsylvania, December 1, 1854, and is a daughter of C. E. and Elizabeth Morris, who moved to Illinois when she was five years old, and thence to Tama City in 1866. Her happy union with our subject has been blessed by the birth of two children—Minnie E. and Charles H., both of whom will be given the best educational advantages which their parents' love and prosperous circumstances can compass.

The subject of this notice has been Treasurer of

the School Board in Wellington. In 1887 he was Secretary of the County Republican Central Committee, and in 1888-89 was Chairman of the same. He is highly spoken of as one of the leading citizens, and a man of business ability and of strict integrity in all transactions.

JOHN C. PECKHAM, a well-known citizen of South Haven, well-to-do and living retired from active labor, has just passed his sixty-ninth birthday, having been born January 7, 1821. He is a native of Holmes County, Ohio, born and reared on a farm, of parents who located in that region during the period of its earliest settlement. They hewed out a homestead from the heavy timber, and there spent their last days. The mother, however, was cut down in the prime of life, dying when her son, John C., was a mere child. She was a lady of many estimable qualities, and a consistent member of the Christian Church. Eleven children were left motherless at her death, of whom John C. was among the younger. The mother bore the maiden name of Cynthia Cook. William Peckham, the father of our subject, after the decease of his first wife, was subsequently married to Mrs. Rebecca (Ralston) McLaughlin, and there were born to them six children who were all reared upon the same farm, and there the father and stepmother died. The latter was a member of the Presbyterian Church. Mr. Peckham belonged to the Christian Church. He and his first wife were natives of Rhode Island, where the paternal grandparents of our subject lived for many years. After the death of Grandfather Peckham the son brought his mother to Ohio, and she died in Holmes County at the advanced age of one hundred and one years.

The subject of this sketch was married in his native county in 1848, to Miss Isabel, daughter of James and Sarah (Leadon) Hackenberry, a native of the same county, where her father located when a boy. The parents of the latter were among its

earliest pioneers, and James, the son, was there reared to man's estate. He died in Missouri about 1872. In 1849 John C. Peckham removed to Marshall County, Ind., where he sojourned ten years. We next find him in Maries County, Mo., and from there, in 1863, he removed to DeKalb County, that State, where he prosecuted farming until 1878. That year he became a resident of this county, purchasing a farm about two miles northwest of the present site of South Haven. He occupied himself in agricultural pursuits until February, 1889, when he wisely decided to retire from active labor, and is now enjoying the fruits of his industry.

During the progress of the late Civil War Mr. Peckham enlisted as a Union soldier in Company A, Thirty-second Missouri Infantry, and served one year, at the expiration of which, on account of illness he was obliged to accept his honorable discharge. Politically, he is a Republican, but has very little to do with public affairs otherwise than casting his vote at the general elections. He belongs to South Haven Post, G. A. R., at South Haven, and with his estimable wife is prominently connected with the Christian Church. There have been born to them six children, all of whom are living, and named respectively: Sarah J., Alice, James W., Eliza, Emma and Ella. The family residence is nicely located in the east part of the city, and is the frequent resort of its best people.

FRANKLIN P. LOGAN is one of the many young men who are acquiring competencies by the pursuit of agriculture, and gaining a foremost rank among the practical and prosperous farmers. He is the owner of a tract of fertile land on section 5, Caldwell Township, marked with such improvements as are expected of an enterprising tiller of the soil, and gives his attention to farming and the stock business thereon. He is now filling the position of Trustee of the township, and has held many minor offices, serving his fellow-men in a satisfactory manner. He belongs to the Farmers' Alliance, and his voice and vote uphold the principles of the Democracy.

Our subject is the son of James and Margaret (Clendenning) Logan, who were natives of Ohio. James Logan was born in LaFayette County, in 1819, to Thomas and Ann Logan, the former of whom was born in Ireland and the latter in North Carolina to Irish parents. When but a boy the father of our subject accompanied his parents to Cass County, Ind., where he spent the remainder of his life, engaging in farm pursuits when he had reached a suitable age, and leaving an estate of $10,000 at his death. His demise took place in 1874. He had always avoided publicity, and pursued the even tenor of his way occupied with his own personal affairs and private life. His wife was born March 30, 1823, being a daughter of Thomas and Nancy (Brown) Clendenning, natives of the Emerald Isle, and her death took place in Cass County, Ind., February 6, 1877. The family of which our subject is the fourth member comprises Nancy A., now the wife of George W. Campbell, a lumber dealer of Cass County, Ind.; Mary E., the wife of Artemus Smith, a farmer and stockman in the same county; John T. also lives in Cass County, Ind.; our subject; Charles L., a farmer of Cass County, Ind.; and Martha L., deceased, who was the wife of E. C. McDonald, of Sumner County, Kan.

Franklin P. Logan, the subject of this sketch, was born August 11, 1853, in Cass County, Ind., reared on his father's farm, and was the recipient of such educational advantages as were to be obtained in the common schools. In 1877 he became a citizen of Kansas, pre-empting one hundred and sixty acres of land, which he still occupies, where he has since resided, devoting his attention to farming and the stock business.

The wife of Mr. Logan bore the maiden name of Mary E. Jones, and their marriage was celebrated February 5, 1879. The bride was born in Howard County, Ind., and is the third of twelve children born to James M. and Elizabeth (Freed) Jones. Her parents rank among the first settlers of Sumner County, to which they removed in 1871, and in which

they still make their home. Mr. and Mrs. Logan are the parents of three children—Clara I., Vida I. and Ethel I. Under the careful oversight of their estimable mother they give promise of becoming young ladies who will be a credit to any society, and in whom their parents can rejoice more and more as years go by.

AARON P. HARTMAN, proprietor of the "Two Orphans" livery barn at Caldwell, is looked upon as one of the reliable and well-to-do citizens of the place, who is contributing his full quota to its material interests. He comes of substantial stock, being the son of John and Margaret (Crisinger) Hartman, and was born in Somerset County, Pa., March 16, 1841. The family is of German descent and both the parents of Aaron P. were natives of Somerset County, Pa., where they spent their entire lives, the father engaged in farming. The home circle included four children, of whom Aaron P. was the eldest born. He was reared in his native town of Berlin and early in life learned blacksmithing, but not being particularly inclined to this employment, soon abandoned it. After the outbreak of the Civil War, he, in 1862 entered the Union Army as a private in Company C. One hundred and Forty-second Pennsylvania Infantry, serving until the close of the struggle. He participated in many hard-fought battles, and endured with his comrades all the vicissitudes of a soldier's life. He served until the close of the war, receiving his honorable discharge and returning to his native county sojourned there, variously employed, until 1871.

We next find Mr. Hartman in Lee County, Ill., where he lived a few years, then set out for the farther West, and established himself as a resident of the Sunflower State. In 1885 he came to Caldwell, but was not engaged in any regular business until July, 1889, when he became interested in his present enterprise. He started in life without other means than his habits of industry and resolute will and it cannot be denied that he has made for himself a good record. He is a Mason in good standing, a supporter of the principles of the Republican party. He was married to Miss Mary Miller, the wedding taking place at the bride's home at Great Bend, this State. By a former marriage Mr. Hartman became the father of one child, a son, Albert, who is now living in Illinois.

LEANDER A. PARKS of South Haven Township, made his advent in this region in March 1878, purchasing the land which he now owns and occupies, and from which he has constructed a good farm. Only fifteen acres of the soil had been broken and there were no improvements except a rude log cabin. The farm now presents the picture of smiling and productive fields, with a good residence, a substantial barn and other outbuildings, a flourishing apple orchard and trees of the smaller fruits. In addition to this property Mr. Parks has a like amount, one hundred and sixty acres, about six miles west, which he has also improved, and which is now valuable.

Of Southern antecedents, Mr. Parks, a native of Logan County, Ky., was born March 8, 1819 and spent his early years in the agricultural districts. His parents, David and Mary (Sawyers) Parks, were natives of North Carolina, where they were reared and married. Thence in 1815, they removed to Logan County, Ky., and there spent the remainder of their lives. The mother passed away when about fifty years old. David Parks survived his wife many years living to the age of eighty. Both were members of the Presbyterian Church in which the father officiated as an Elder. Five of their children lived to mature years, two having died in infancy. Leander A. was the third in order of birth. The paternal grandparents removed at an early day from Pennsylvania to North Carolina. Grandfather Parks was probably a native of Pennsylvania, while his wife was born in Ireland.

The subject of this notice attained to manhood in his native State and was married in Logan County in 1842, to Miss Hannah H. Sawyer. Miss Sawyer was a native of the same county as her husband and the daughter of James and Hannah (Henderson) Sawyer who were born in North Carolina and who died in Kentucky. Of this union there were born three children—Sarah, Robert and David. Sarah is deceased; David is in Kentucky; Robert lives in Sumner County. Mrs. Hannah Parks died in Kentucky in February, 1848, aged thirty-one years.

Mr. Parks contracted a second marriage October 6, 1848, with Miss Louisa E. Henderson, a native of Kentucky. Her father, Andrew Henderson was born in North Carolina and married Mary Maben, a native of Ireland, who came to America with her parents and located in South Carolina. There she was reared from infancy to womanhood. She died at quite an advanced age in Logan County, Ky., to which she had removed with her husband soon after marriage. Grandfather Michael Henderson married Hannah Barnett and both were natives of Pennsylvania. They removed first to North Carolina and then to Logan County, Ky., where both died when about ninety years old.

Mr. Parks when a young man identified himself with the Presbyterian Church of which he has been a member for the long period of more than thirty years and in which he officiates as an Elder. Mrs. Parks also belongs to that church. Of this marriage there have been born four children, viz: John W., Mary M., Cyrus O. and Leander N., the latter of whom died in infancy.

HON. WILLIAM J. LINGENFELTER, at one time a member of the State Senate and likewise a Representative, is now numbered among the most able men of this county—one who has been largely instrumental in promoting its best interests. Aside from his services as a public official, he has been quite extensively engaged in farming and makes his headquarters at a fine homestead, embracing three hundred and twenty acres of choice land in South Haven Township. He also has the same amount of land in Stafford County adjacent to the village of Hudson and an interest in another body of land adjoining St. John, the county seat of Stafford County. He is a man popular in his community, one in whom the people have confidence and whose ability as an official and whose worth as a citizen is universally recognized.

Mr. Lingenfelter was born in Jefferson County, Pa., August 17, 1840, and was there reared to manhood on a farm. His parents were John N. and Catherine (Mank) Lingenfelter, natives of Bedford County, Pa., and born near Claysburg, in what is now Blair County, where they were married. In 1839 they removed to Jefferson County with their three children and there were subsequently added to the household circle eight more children, William J. being the eldest born in that county. The children and the father are all living, the latter continuing to reside at the old homestead in Jefferson County; the mother died there May 23, 1863, at the age of forty-seven years. She was a member of the Evangelical Church. The father of our subject was seventy-four years old January 2, 1890. He has been for many years a member of the Methodist Episcopal Church, one of its chief pillars and holding the various offices. Although a man of decided views and an ardent supporter of his party, he would never accept the responsibilities of office.

The paternal grandfather of our subject was a native of Virginia whence he removed to Pennsylvania at an early day and was married to Miss Margaret Zeth, who was born near Hagarstown, Md. They reared their family in Bedford County, Pa., then removed to Jefferson County, in 1840, and there died at the ages of about seventy-six years each. Both were members of the German Baptist Church. An earlier progenitor of the family, George Lingenfelter, was a native of Virginia and a soldier in the Revolutionary War. He was married in his native State to a Miss Dively who was born in Virginia and after rearing their family they removed to Bedford County, Pa., where they spent their last days. The father of George Lingenfelter was born in the Grand Duchy of Baden, Germany, whence

he emigrated to America at a very early day and located in Virginia.

Jacob Zeth, the maternal grandfather of our subject, was born in Hesse Cassell, Germany, and when seventeen years old joined the Hessian soldiery and thus made his way to America. While the boats were in waiting in New York harbor he swam ashore thus making his escape from the troops and joined Washington's army, fighting on the side of the Colonists until the war was over. He was present at the battle of Yorktown and after the close of the war engaged in the mercantile business near Hagarstown, Md., where he accumulated quite a fortune. He was there married to Miss Burgoo, a native of France, and born near the city of Paris. They reared a family of children and died in Maryland.

The education of William J. Lingenfelter was conducted in a log schoolhouse heated from a huge fireplace, with slabs for seats and desks and a floor of puncheon. When eighteen years old he began attending Strattonville Academy in Clarion County, Pa., where he pursued his studies one year. Afterward he was a student at Whitehall Academy near Harrisburg one year. He afterward went to the oil regions of Pennsylvania where he commenced drilling wells and remained for about eighteen months. Returning then to his native county he engaged as clerk in a general store and was thus occupied until 1863.

The Civil War now being in progress Mr. Lingenfelter enlisted as a Union soldier in Company C, Two Hundred and Sixth Pennsylvania Infantry in which he served about six months as a private. When leaving the army he again went into a store and was thus occupied until January, 1865. Then going to Tennessee he rented a large plantation and raised a crop of cotton and corn. His employers of the store had solicited him to go there, they furnishing all the money necessary and giving him one-third of the profits. Each partner thus realized about $800.

Mr. Lingenfelter returned to Pennsylvania in December, 1865 and in March following emigrated to Missouri and purchased a farm in Gentry County. He also engaged in general merchandising at Riding City, remaining there one and one-half years,

In the meantime he was elected Surveyor of De Kalb County, as his farm was on the county line and his buildings in De Kalb County. He resigned that office on account of ill health and later commenced teaching, which profession he followed until 1872. That year he came to Kansas and pre-empted one hundred and sixty acres of land on section 3 and later purchased eighty acres adjoining. With the exception of an occasional dugout, there were no settlers in this region at that time aside from a few who had located upon the present site of South Haven and Wellington. The buffaloes had been driven back, but three strays were killed in this vicinity in 1872. The nearest market was at Wichita and for a number of years the meat used by the settlers was chiefly buffalo, antelope and deer. Black and grey wolves (coyotes) were still plentiful and frequently made night hideous with their howling.

Mr. Lingerfelter purchased three hundred and twenty acres of land about four miles east of Wellington where he lived until 1876, carrying on its improvement and cultivation. In 1876 he returned to Pennsylvania to visit his father and attended the Centennial Exposition. During his absence he was nominated for County Superintendent of Schools, but he declined the proffered honor. However, he was declared the candidate and being absent was defeated, although running ahead of his ticket. Upon returning from Pennsylvania he resumed farming.

In May, 1877, Mr. Lingenfelter was married to Miss Mary C., daughter of Joseph and Elizabeth (Montgomery) Gregson. This lady was born in Fulton County, Ind. That same spring the newly-wedded pair settled upon the farm which has since been the family homestead. In the fall of 1882 Mr. Lingenfelter was elected to represent this county in the Kansas Legislature and served one term. In 1884 he was elected to the Senate, serving also one term of four years. He was earnestly solicited to accept the nomination for a second term, but declined. His party in this district in 1884 was in the minority more than seventeen hundred and the fact that Mr. Lingenfelter was elected against this, indicates in a marked manner his popularity with the people.

To Mr. and Mrs. Lingenfelter there have been born three daughters, viz: Rosa J., Mary C. and Susan E. One son born July 20,1883,died October 6, 1886.He was a very bright and promising child and his death was a severe blow to the afflicted parents, to whom were extended the sympathies of the entire community. Mr. Lingenfelter is a liberal minded and public-spirited man—one who has uniformly given his encouragement to the projects tending to promote the best interests of Sumner County, socially, morally and financially.

TEPHEN DOWIS is a Southern gentleman by birth, education and lineage. His grandparents were natives of the Carolinas, and Kentucky was the native State of his father and himself. In the paternal line he is of Irish extraction. Jesse Dowis, his grandfather, was born in South Carolina, and died in Knox County, Ky., when upwards of eighty years of age. In the latter county, William Dowis, the father of our subject, opened his eyes to the light in 1812, and breathed his last in 1862. His occupation was that of a farmer, and politically he was a Democrat. The mother of our subject is still living in that county, and is now sixty-five years of age. She bore the maiden name of Alla Hart, was born in North Carolina, and is a daughter of Stephen and Alla Hart, who, after living many years in the State in which she was born, took up their abode in Knox County, Ky., and there breathed their last. The parental family comprised ten children—Lucinda, Nancy J., Jesse, Stephen, Mary A., John P., Robert P., Susan, Nancy and Rachael. Of these Mary A., Stephen, Susan, Nancy and Rachael now survive.

The subject of this biography was born in December, 1842, in Knox County, Ky., reared on a farm, and educated in his native county, receiving an excellent home training from his worthy parents. Although he was not yet of age when the Civil War broke out, he entered the Union Army, August 28, 1861, as a member of Company I, Seventh Kentucky Infantry, and devoted the opening years of his manhood to the service of his country. He participated in the battles of Richmond (Ky.), Vicksburg, Arkansas Post, Jackson (Miss.), and in many minor engagements, remaining in the service until October 5, 1864, when he was honorably discharged and returned to his home.

A few months after resuming civil life Mr. Dowis took to himself a companion in the person of Miss Elizabeth Elliott, the rites of wedlock being celebrated between them February 8, 1865. The bride was born in Kentucky, April 17, 1844, is a daughter of Hiram and Adeline (Steele) Elliott, and a lady whose estimable character endears her to many friends.

In January, 1884, Mr. Dowis came to Kansas, and selecting a location in Downs Township, this county, bought a farm, upon which he lived until 1886, when he rented it and engaged in the mercantile business at Perth. The business is conducted under the firm name of Dowis & Son, and is steadily increasing, owing to the tact displayed in its management, and the honorable manner in which its patrons are treated. The junior member of the firm, Greene E. Dowis, was born July 17, 1868, and is the only child of our subject and his estimable wife. The young man gives promise of becoming a thorough and successful business man, as he already exhibits a mercantile capacity creditable in one so young.

⊹⊶⊷✦⧉✛⧖✦⧉⊷⊶⊷

GEORGE W. FAUCHIER is an old settler of this county, his settlement in Harmon Township having been made in 1873, at which time he began to develop the northwest quarter of section 27, where he now owns and operates eighty-five improved and thoroughly cultivated acres. He is actively pursuing his farm life, and with his chosen companion enjoying the fruits of his industry and the esteem of their many friends.

Mr. Fauchier was born in Montgomery County,

Ind., June 4, 1830, and was twelve years old when his parents moved to Parke County, thence going to Howard County, where he grew to manhood. He received as good an education as could be obtained in the counties in which his home was, and on arriving at a suitable age learned the carpenter's trade, which he followed in his native State until October, 1866, when he changed both his residence and his occupation. At that date he determined to make for himself a home farther west, and selecting Franklin County, this State, settled there and engaged in farming, leaving that county to take up his abode here at the date before mentioned.

The grandfather of our subject was John Fauchier, a French Revolutionist, who, being exiled from his native land, sailed to Boston, Mass., and made for himself and family a home on American soil. His son, John B., father of our subject, was born in Boston, and adopted the occupation of a farmer. He was married in Kentucky, to Miss Sarah Broyles, a native of Virginia. The result of their union was the birth of fifteen children, of whom our subject was the fourth. John Fauchier died in Howard County, Ind., and his widow died in the same county, February 7, 1890, aged eighty-five years.

The marriage of our subject took place in Howard County, Ind., February 3, 1853, and his bride was Miss Martha A. Scott, a native of Putnam County, where her birth occurred December 11, 1834. Her father, Thomas M. Scott, was born in North Carolina, and her mother, whose maiden name was Leta Anderson, was a native of Tennessee. The parents settled in the county where Mrs. Fauchier first saw the light, subsequently removing to the county wherein she was married, and in the latter they departed this life. Their family consisted of eight children, and Mrs. Fauchier is the second in order of birth. To our subject and his estimable wife four children have been born: James J. married Miss Alice I. Collins; Sarah J. is the wife of F. P. Willey; Rachel C. is the wife of J. S. Farris; and Enos F. married Miss Hattie Dorsett.

Mr. Fauchier has held some of the school offices,

and has proved an efficient servant of the people in the cause of education. For seven years he was Justice of the Peace. Since the organization of the Republican party he has been a sound believer in the principles embodied in its platform, and has been an active worker in the political field. Mrs. Fancher is a member of the Christian Church. Both are honored by their fellow-citizens for their intelligence, uprightness, kind hearts, and earnest endeavor to fulfill all their duties in life.

EDSON WIGGINS. A pleasantly located farm of two hundred and forty acres on section 26, Sumner Township, is the home of this gentleman, who is engaged in the occupations of farming and stock-raising, and who has been a resident of the county for twenty years. His home is one of comfort and good cheer, and while not occupying any prominent public position, Mr. Wiggins in his own quiet and straightforward manner performs the duties of citizenship and of the individual in a manner entitling him to the respect of his fellow-men.

The parents of our subject were natives of Vermont, and in that State he of whom we write was born August 2, 1837. His father, Peter Wiggins, was a farmer by occupation, and died in his native State at the age of sixty-eight years. The mother, who bore the maiden name of Elmira Stephens, is still living, and is now seventy-two years old. The parental family comprised seven children, namely: Elizabeth, Albert, Charlotte, Edson, Elias S., Frank and Calista; of these, Edson and Calista are the only survivors.

Edson Wiggins was reared on a farm, early acquiring a practical knowledge of the occupation which he has since followed, and being the recipient of a good common-school education, grew to manhood in possession of the thrifty and sturdy characteristics which seem to belong to natives of the Green Mountain State. In 1865 he became a resident of Kansas, spending the first five years of

his citizenship in Jackson County, whence, in 1870, he moved to Sumner County. He pre-empted one hundred and sixty acres of Government land, adding to the acreage as prosperity attended his labors, and making upon his estate such improvements as are expected of an enterprising agriculturist.

The marriage of Mr. Wiggins was celebrated in June, 1876, the lady with whom he was united being Miss Amanda Cross, who was born in Ohio, March 13, 1845. Her father, Albert Cross, was one of the early settlers of Kansas, and was engaged in farming. His death took place when he had reached the ripe age of seventy-two years. He had held several minor offices, and for many years was a Justice of the Peace. To Mr. and Mrs. Wiggins five children have been born, named respectively: Lizzie, Albert, Elsie, Laura and Frank. The latter died when one year old; the survivors are being carefully trained by their estimable mother, and receiving such educational advantages as befits their years.

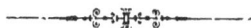

WILLIAM W. LEMMON, M. D. Few physicians in this county have attained to a more enviable position, considering the time they have been in practice, than Dr. Lemmon, who is popular and prominent among the people of South Haven, where he established himself in 1884. For two years after locating here he was engaged in the drug business, but has since abandoned this, his time being all occupied in his professional duties. He is a Western man by birth, his native place being Dubois County, Ind., where he first opened his eyes to the light September 15, 1845. He spent the first eighteen years of his life upon a farm, where he grew up healthy in mind and body, and was trained to those principles of right and honesty which have characterized his dealings with his fellow men.

Soon after the outbreak of the Civil War young Lemmon enlisted as a Union soldier in Company E, Twenty-fourth Indiana Infantry, and served as a private three years. He saw much of active service, participating in the battle of Ft. Gibson, the siege of Vicksburg, the fight at Jackson, Miss., and was at Ft. Blakeley and other important points held by the enemy during the war. Although often in the thickest of the fight, he escaped without injury and received an honorable discharge. Returning then to Indiana, he supplemented his education by an attendance of two years at Asbury (now DePauw) University, in Greencastle, and then spent two years on the old farm.

At the expiration of this time, Mr. Lemmon decided to take up the study of medicine, and entering the Medical College at Indianapolis, he was graduated from that institution in 1873, after taking a full course. Later, he attended lectures three terms at Detroit and Indianapolis. Locating in Washington, Ind., he there began the regular practice of his profession, and later removed to Hunnewell, Kan., from which place he came to South Haven in 1884.

Dr. Lemmon was married in Greencastle, Ind., March 10, 1874, to Miss Matilda, daughter of Edward H. and Desire (Waterhouse) Crow. Mrs. Lemmon was born May 29, 1850, in Greencastle, and by her union with our subject has become the mother of four children—William G., Helen, Jacob and Eddie; the latter two are deceased. The little family occupies a snug home in the southern part of the town, and number among their friends and acquaintances its most cultured people. The Doctor meddles very little with political affairs, but keeps himself posted upon current events and votes the Republican ticket. He is a charter member of Post No. 407, G. A. R., at South Haven, which was organized in 1887, and has now a membership of about forty. He held the post of Commander for two years. He also belongs to Lodge No. 407, A. F. & A. M., at Greencastle, Ind., and the Commandery.

The father of our subject was Jacob Lemmon, likewise a native of Dubois County, Ind., where he was reared to man's estate. There also he was married to Miss Elizabeth Corn, a native of Kentucky, and they became the parents of nine children. The mother departed this life at Greencastle, Ind., in 1869. She was a lady of many

estimable qualities, and a member in good standing of the Cumberland Presbyterian Church. Jacob Lemmon survived his wife six years, dying on the old home farm in Dubois County, Ind., in 1875. The paternal grandfather of our subject, also named Jacob, removed from Virginia to Kentucky at an early date, and finally to Indiana, where he and his wife spent their last days.

The parents of Mrs. Lemmon were natives respectively of Kentucky and Maine, and the various members of the family belonged to the Methodist Episcopal Church. Mr. and Mrs. E. H. Crow are still living in Indiana, and are the parents of eleven children.

SAMUEL NUTT. The main points in the history of this prominent citizen and well-to-do resident of South Haven may be gained in the following comparatively brief outline. A native of Vermont, he was born May 29, 1840, and lived there until a youth of fifteen years. His father, Isaac B. Nutt, was a native of Massachusetts, whence he removed to Vermont in early manhood. He was there married to Miss Sarah Monroe, a native of that State, and within its limits they spent the remainder of their lives. Mr. Nutt dying December 1, 1853. He served as a minute man in the War of 1812. The mother subsequently removed to Massachusetts, and Samuel being the youngest at home, virtually became the head of the family. They were left in limited circumstances, and at an early age Samuel began learning the trade of a shoemaker, at which he worked in Massachusetts until the outbreak of the Civil War. The mother in the meantime had died, in 1857, in the faith of the Baptist Church.

On the 15th of April, 1861, the subject of this notice enlisted as a Union soldier in Company H, Thirteenth Massachusetts Infantry, and in August following was promoted to be Corporal. He remained in the army until the fall of 1862, when he was obliged to accept his honorable discharge on account of continued illness. It was believed by all that he simply went home to die. He had participated in the battle of Winchester and other minor engagements, and experienced the various hardships and privations of a soldier's life. After the close of the war, leaving New England, he went to New York City, where he engaged in the boot and shoe business as foreman of a factory and where he continued variously occupied in different branches of his business until 1875.

January 1, 1867, at Worcester, Mass., the subject of this notice was united in marriage with Miss Mary E. S., daughter of Samuel and Sarah (Foster) French. Mrs. Nutt was born in Grafton, Mass., February 14, 1841. Her parents were also natives of the Bay State. Her paternal great-great-grandfather was one of the earliest settlers of Massachusetts, locating probably not far from the time at which the Bay Colony sought that region for its home. He was of Irish birth and parentage, and spent his last days in Massachusetts. The next in line of descent was Joshua French, who was one of fourteen sons born when the United States was composed of fourteen colonies, in one of which each one settled. Joshua chose Massachusetts for his abiding-place, within which he spent most of his life, dying in New York State.

On the maternal side the grandfather of Mrs. Nutt was Abner Foster, a native of Worcester County, Mass., and of English ancestry from the second generation settling on American soil. His wife, Judith Weatherbee, likewise traced her ancestry to England, and she also was of the second generation, many of whom fought valiantly in the Revolutionary War. Grandfather Benjamin Nutt, a native of Massachusetts, was a Captain in the Vermont Rangers during the struggle for independence, and received an honorable wound in the service. He spent the greater part of his life in Vermont, where he reared his family and died.

In 1875 Mr. Nutt, leaving New York City, emigrated to Linn County, Iowa, and located at Central City, where he engaged in the boot and shoe business. He remained there until 1878, coming thence to Rooks County, this State. He changed his residence to South Haven in April, 1881, when the present site of the town was unmarked save by a blacksmith-shop, an hotel, a general store and a drug-store. That same season he put up his present residence and shops, and established himself in the boot and shoe business, which he has since conducted successfully. In the meantime he had become prominent in local affairs, being elected the first Mayor of the city soon after its organization, in the fall of 1887. Politically, he affiliates with the Union Labor party, and while a resident of Rooks County served as Justice of the Peace, and has been the candidate of his party for State Treasurer and Sheriff of the county.

To Mr. and Mrs. Nutt there have been born two sons—Vincent S. and Vivian J. Mr. Nutt while a resident of New York City identified himself with Lodge, No. 632, A. F. & A. M., and he also belongs to Palestine Chapter, No. 255, in which he has taken seven degrees. He is also a Knight of Labor at South Haven, being a member of Lodge No. 8,685, with which he became identified at its organization, and in which he is a Master Workman. He also belongs to the Anti-Monopolists of Springfield, Mo., and is National Vice-Foreman. He is a liberal-minded and public-spirited citizen, one who keeps himself thoroughly posted upon events of general interest, and who is always to be found on the side of the enterprises calculated to benefit the people at large.

REV. AVAN LA VANCE, M. D. This veteran in the medical profession is a man whose personal history possesses very many points of interest, he having had a large experience of life and being possessed of that quality of observation in regard to what has been going on around him in the world, which has proved of great value in a moral and intellectual point of view. He is a gentleman of fine tastes and has one of the most attractive homes in South Haven. The interior has been decorated largely by the handiwork of its inmates, the Doctor and his amiable wife and their daughter, Viola, all of whom possess rare skill with the pencil and brush. It is at once recognized as the home of culture and refinement and is no less indicative of ample means.

Dr. La Vance was born in the city of Paris, France, June 22, 1818, but when a mere child removed from there with his parents, Joseph and Anna (Napoleon) La Vance, they settling on the Rhine where their son was reared and educated. In 1831 they emigrated to America, locating in Bangor, Me. In that city the parents spent the remainder of their lives, both dying at about the age of sixty-eight years. They likewise were natives of France and of pure French ancestry. When a young man the subject of this sketch began the study of medicine in the Eclectic College of New York City and the Old School of Boston, Mass., from both of which he was graduated. He began the practice of his profession at Dorcester, Mass., when about twenty-two years old. Later he was a resident of Boston seven years and he also resided in Plymouth a number of years. From there he went to New York City and thence, in 1819, to California. The wild life of the West, however, not being congenial to his tastes he returned the following year and two years later took up his abode in Henderson, Ky.

After a three year's residence in the above-mentioned place, Dr. La Vance turned his eyes once more westward and we next find him in Carlinville, Ill. He remained there until 1867, then came to this State, locating in Marion during the pioneer days of that region. He now entered upon a widely different field of labor from that to which he had been accustomed, riding on horseback across the open prairie, frequently forty miles, when there were no roads or bridges and he had nothing to guide him but his compass. Indians still infested the country and the intrepid physician never ventured out without a brace of revolvers to protect himself from them and other natural enemies. The few white settlers were located principally along the creeks and the red man was troublesome and dangerous. The settlers put up a substantial schoolhouse at Marion which they enclosed with a stone wall and this served as a fort to which they retreated in times of danger. Dr. La Vance in addition to the practice of his profession interested himself in the settlement of the country, locating many farms

for the emigrants. He practiced in that region until 1881, in the meantime watching the growth and development of the country with warm interest and assisting to this end whenever possible. He finally decided to cast his lot with the people of South Haven and settled here when the present flourishing town was a village of a very few houses. His intention was to gradually retire from practice, but at South Haven he found quite a number of old Illinois friends who still call upon him, unwilling to be put aside.

The first marriage of Dr. La Vance took place in the city of New Orleans with Miss Sarah, daughter of Abraham and Sarah (Jackson) Moore. This lady was born in Louisiana and died at New Orleans in 1840, where the Doctor had located temporarily. There were born to them two children, both of whom died young. The present wife of our subject, to whom he was married January 6, 1857, at Montgomery, Ill., was formerly Miss Parthenia, daughter of Daniel and Eveline (Hamilton) Bagby. She was born in Macoupin County, Ill., March 20, 1839. This union resulted in the birth of five children one of whom, Napoleon, died when two years old; Rizpah is the wife of Ira P. Smith of Montgomery County, Ill.; John resides in South Haven, and Eldora the youngest is at home with her parents. Viola is the wife of C. B. Wolfe of Wabaunsee County, Kan.

Mrs. La Vance and her daughters are members in good standing of the Christian Church, in which the Doctor has labored as an Evangelist for more than thirty years. He organized the church at Palmyra, Ill., and while living there officiated as Elder, and he has also organized a number of societies since coming to Kansas. He is still devoted to his ministerial labors, confining his attention mostly to this State, although sometimes called out of it. The Sunday-school has ever received his earnest and faithful attention. He was born and reared a Catholic, in the faith of which church his father lived and died. The son was converted to the Protestant religion when a young man and at once began preaching and working in the Sunday-school. The mother, who had been born and reared a Catholic, changed her religious views at the same time that her son embraced Protestantism and died a member of the Protestant Methodist Church. Dr. La Vance has exercised a wide influence and has been the means of causing many adherents of the Catholic faith to come under the pale of the Christian Church. He is a man of broad and liberal views and fine intelligence—one of those who will be remembered long after he has been gathered to his fathers.

JAMES F. ROBERTSON, M. D. In every qualification which pertains to good citizenship, this young gentleman has a prominent place, and in the professional ranks of Caldwell he is an able, well-informed and busy man. He has built up an excellent practice in the medical profession during the few years in which he has been a resident here, occupies a leading position among the practitioners of the place, and has a reputation second to none. He may well be called a self-made man, as his education was the result of his own exertions, and the knowledge which he acquired from books and observation, has been made of practical use by his discrimination and wise application of theories.

From worthy parents Dr. Robertson derives the characteristics which belong to the "canny Scot." His father, Amelious Robertson, was born in Scotland, in October, 1819, and was brought to America by his parents when a child. The family settled in Black Hawk County, N. Y., and in 1836 removed to Wood County, Ohio, where the remainder of his life was passed, and where he breathed his last, July 5, 1888. His occupation was that of a farmer. His wife, Margery Frazier, was born in Scotland, May 5, 1821, and still survives. She came to America with her parents when about fifteen years old, the family settling in Wood County, Ohio. Amelious and Margery Robertson were the parents of eight children, of whom our subject is the second in order of birth.

Dr. Robertson was born in Haskins County, Ohio, May 2, 1855, and was reared on the farm in Wood County,acquiring a common-school education there.

In 1874, he began reading medicine with Drs. Peck and Powers, of Prairiesburg, Ohio, and after attending the Detroit (Mich.,) Medical College three sessions, was graduated with high honors in the spring of 1877. He at once located in Haskins County, Ohio, began the practice of his profession, and remained in that place until 1882, at which time he removed to Caldwell, Kan. He has since been constantly engaged in professional work, and together with his professional reputation, has acquired a worthy one as a private individual.

Dr. Robertson has been a member of the Caldwell City Council for six years, and is still serving on that board. He belongs to the Free and Accepted Masons, the Encampment of the Independent Order of Odd Fellows, the Knights of Pythias, and the Ancient Order of United Workmen. At the home of the bride in Haskin, Ohio, June 17, 1879, he was united in marriage with Miss Cornelia J. Meagley. The bride was a native of the town in which she was married, was born in 1831, and is a lady of intelligence, refinement, and those sterling traits of character which endear her to her acquaintances. She and her husband are the happy parents of one son, Wright.

AARON T. BALL, Cashier of the Bank of Geuda Springs, although still a young man, has displayed decided business qualifications, and exhibits a high morality and courteous bearing in private as well as in public life, winning respect and friendly regard on all sides. He is a son of the Hoosier State, and the youngest of six children born to John and Mary J. (Bryant) Ball. His father was born near Louisville, Ky., about the year 1818, and having moved to Fulton County, Ind., when a young man, spent the remainder of his life there, breathing his last in 1854. He was a farmer, possessed of considerable means, held some minor offices, and was for many years connected with the Methodist Episcopal Church. The mother of our subject was born in Fulton

County, Ind., and in that county breathed her last.
The brothers of Aaron Ball were christened An-
sel B., Daniel U., George W., John H., and William.

The subject of this sketch first opened his eyes
to the light October 8, 1850, in Fulton County Ind.,
and was reared on the parental estate, acquiring an
excellent education at Ft. Wayne. He was Deputy
Auditor of the county seven years. In 1869, he
went to Red Cloud, Neb., and after sojourning
there a year, returned to his native State, going
again to Red Cloud in 1879, and remaining there
in the employ of the Chicago, Burlington & Quincy
Railroad until 1882. He next removed to Geuda
Springs, Kan., engaged in the general mercantile
business for a period of two years, when he sold
out, and until August, 1888, had no regular occupation. The Bank of Gueda Springs was then organized, and he has since been its cashier; he is
also a stock-holder in the institution.

At the home of the bride in Warsaw, Ind., October 7, 1875, Aaron Ball and Miss Mary McGrew
were united in marriage. Mrs. Ball was born near
Goshen, Ind., March 10, 1855, possesses an estimable character and many womanly virtues, and her
chief object has ever been to make her home happy,
and attractive to her husband and the son who was
born to them, October 30, 1876. The bright lad
who is the only offspring of Mr. and Mrs. Ball,
bears the name of Chester B. Mr. Ball belongs to
the Independent Order of Odd Fellows, in the Encampment Degree. He is a believer in, and supporter of the principles of the Republican party.

WILLIAM H. BROWN. Among the first
settlers of South Haven may be mentioned
Mr. Brown, who pitched his tent in the
embryo village in June, 1885, and established himself in the livery business. There were then but
comparatively few people who could act as patrons
to such an enterprise, but by the exercise of patience, with a seasonable amount of waiting, satis-

factory results began to develop. Mr. Brown has
now a large barn stocked with a fine assortment of
horses and vehicles, and is doing a paying business.
He runs a hack line to and from the railroad depot,
and by his courteous treatment of those with whom
he has dealings, has fully established himself as a
successful business man.

A native of Steuben County, N. Y., the subject
of this notice was born September 17, 1836, to
Samuel and Mary (Burr) Brown. The following
year Samuel Brown resolved to seek the farther
West, and taking with him his little family, emigrated to Tazewell County, Ill. He settled upon a
farm, and there William H. grew to be a lad of fifteen years. The family then changed their residence to Jefferson County, and later the parents
removed to Fulton County, where they spent their
last years, dying at an advanced age. They were
most excellent and worthy people, and members in
good standing of the Baptist Church. There had
been born to them twelve children, of whom William H. was the sixth in order of birth.

The paternal grandparents of our subject were
Thomas and Mary Brown, who lived in New York
State a number of years, and then accompanied
their son to Illinois. Thomas Brown was a noted
preacher of the Baptist Church for many years, an
active worker, preaching until past his threescore
years and ten, and organizing many societies of
that denomination both in New York and Illinois.
No fancy salaries were paid in the pioneer days,
and Grandfather Brown's labors were mostly gratu-
itous. His duties were performed mainly on the
Sabbath day, while during the week he attended
to the cultivation of his farm. He passed away
firm in the faith which he had professed for so
many years, justly feeling that he had earned the
reward of a good and faithful servant.

The early education of William H. Brown was
obtained in the district schools of Tazewell County,
Ill. When the family removed to Jefferson County
the latter contained a large area of land still belonging to the Government. He assisted his father
in transforming a portion of this into a comfortable homestead, much of the soil being turned by
the old fashioned wooden mold-board plow. In
Jefferson County he developed fully into manhood,

and when ready to establish a fireside of his own was joined in wedlock with Miss Mary Estes.

Soon after their marriage Mr. and Mrs. Brown removed to Fulton County, Ill., settling on a farm where they lived about two years. There their eldest child, Columbus, was born. Illinois, however, was not quite far enough West to suit Mr. Brown, and so, in 1857, gathering together his little family and his household effects, he pushed across the Father of Waters into Douglas County, this State. Settling on a homestead claim, he operated in true pioneer style until 1872. That year he came to this county, and locating near Caldwell engaged as a dealer in live-stock about two years. Then, removing to Hunnewell, he established himself in the livery business, and was thus occupied until coming to South Haven.

Mr. Brown was wedded, October 23, 1873, at Wichita, to Mrs. Lydia (Moliere) Edwards. This lady was born in Indiana, December 31, 1841, and is the daughter of William and Mary (Anghee) Moliere, who were natives of Pennsylvania, and are now deceased. Mrs. Brown was first married, in Indiana, January 12, 1860, to Samuel Edwards, who served in the Union army during the late Civil War, and subsequently located in Sumner County, this State, of which he was one of the earliest pioneers, and where he died in 1872. There was born to Mr. and Mrs. Edwards one child, a son, Myron, who is now a resident of South Haven.

Mr. Brown while a resident of Hunnewell served as a member of the City Council two terms, and has held the same position the same length of time in South Haven. During the progress of the Civil War Mr. Brown, in August, 1862, enlisted in the First Kansas Battery, under the command of Norman Allen, of Lawrence. Mr. Allen died in July, 1863, and was succeeded in the command by M. D. Tinney. Mr. Brown served until the close of the war, in the meantime being promoted to Corporal. He participated in a number of important engagements, being at Newtonia, Mo., Ft. Wayne, Kane Hill, Van Buren and others. In the spring of 1863 he returned to Lawrence, and from there was ordered to Ft. Leavenworth, where the battery obtained fresh horses, and thence proceeded to Rolla, Mo. Next they went to St. Louis, and from there

to Indianapolis, Ind., after which they drove the raider Morgan from the soil of Ohio. Returning then to St. Louis they went from there to Cairo, and next to Columbus, Ky. After sojourning there one month they returned to Cairo, where they remained five months.

Afterward Mr. Brown was at Chattanooga, and in August, 1865, returning to Ft. Leavenworth, received his honorable discharge. Although not being wounded or captured, his health was undermined by the exposures and hardships which he endured, and which induced rheumatism, from which he has since suffered. He belongs to South Haven Post, G. A. R., and South Haven Lodge, No. 111, I. O. O. F., being a charter member of both lodges. Mrs. Brown belongs to Rebecca Lodge, No. 97, I. O. O. F.

JAMES P. ELSEA is a large land owner, one of the most extensive cattle men in this section of the country, and who, although doing some general farming, devotes his attention almost wholly to the handling of stock, buying, feeding and shipping, in large numbers. He owns five hundred and sixty acres of land in this county, and an extensive range in Barber County, having a controlling interest in about nineteen hundred acres there. At this writing he has about one hundred and seventy-five head of cattle, and his herds number far more at some seasons.

Mr. Elsea was born in Elkhart County, Ind., December 4, 1847, and there grew to manhood, acquiring a fair education under the fine system of the Hoosier State, and residing in his native county until the spring of 1873. Having chosen Kansas as his future home, he came to this county in April of that year, and pre-empted one hundred and sixty acres of land on section 32, Greene Township, where he still makes his home. During some six or seven years he spent much of his time in the Indian Territory, looking after the cattle which he fed upon the ranges there, and he also spent two or three years in Barber County, although this has been his home since he first took up his claim here. He spent two years upon the Pacific Coast in California.

Mr. Elsea is a Democrat, and is deeply interested in the welfare of the party, although he has no political aspirations. He belongs to the Masonic fraternity. He is one of the most energetic of men, jolly and companionable, and with the exception that he still pursues a life of single blessedness, his citizenship has in it no cause of complaint. As may well be supposed, he has many friends, and is warmly welcomed in social circles.

VOLNEY S. WIGGINS, one of the pioneers of Sumner County, was born near Circleville, Pickaway County, Ohio, August 14, 1855. His father, H. H. Wiggins, was born in the Province of Ontario, Canada, and was a son of Samuel Wiggins, a pioneer of that province, where he cleared a farm and engaged in agricultural pursuits, continuing to reside there until his death.

The father of our subject received his early training in the province, and when a young man went to Ohio and purchased a tract of land near Circleville. Thinking he could better his condition by going West, in 1858 he left his family and made his way to Louisa County, Iowa, where he purchased a tract of prairie land on the Iowa River. There were a few acres broken, and that, with a log house of which he immediately took possession, constituted the improvements. A few nights after his arrival there he was awakened by a strange sound, and jumping out of bed found himself nearly waist deep in water. There had been a sudden rise in the river, and the banks had been overflowed, an occurrence which did not often happen.

The father was soon joined by his family, and continued to improve the farm, upon which they lived until after the Civil War. He then sold and

bought a tract of wild land near by, which was the family residence until 1869, when he again sold out and journeyed farther Westward. This time he located in Crawford County, Kan., buying a claim to a tract of land one and a half miles east of Girard, which he at once began to improve. He had resided upon this place five years, when he found that it was railroad land, to which he could secure a title only by paying a large sum to the railroad company. He therefore abandoned it, and again started Westward, on this occasion coming to this county, where he was one of the pioneers. Deer and antelope still roamed over the prairie, and a few miles west buffalo abounded. He made claim to the southeast quarter of section 1, in what is now Osborn Township, and prosecuted the labors incidental to the improvement of the primitive soil. For some years there was no railroad nearer than Wichita, and that city was the nearest market for farm products. Prior to his death, which occurred March 18, 1889, he had seen the county develop to one of the most populous, and which contained more miles of railroad than any other in the State.

The wife of H. H. Wiggins and mother of our subject, bore the maiden name of Lucinda Jones. She was a native of New York, and a daughter of Nathaniel Jones, who was, as far as known, a native of the same State, and who was a carpenter by trade. Mr. Jones removed from New York to Ohio, and lived in Pickaway County a number of years, after which he went to Iowa, and thence came to this State, where for some years he lived with his daughter, Mrs. Wiggins. He subsequently went to the home of a son in Michigan, and there departed this life. Three children were born to the parents of our subject—Hiram, Volney and Charles.

The gentleman whose name initiates this sketch was three years of age when his parents moved to Iowa, in which State he attended the pioneer schools. When his parents came to Kansas he accompanied them, and as soon as he was large enough he began to assist his father in the work of the farm, and adopting his father's employment has always been engaged in agricultural pursuits. In 1882 he located upon the farm which he now owns and occupies, and which comprises the south half of the southwest quarter of section 6, Wellington

Township. He stands well among his fellow citizens as a young man of industrious habits, intelligence, and good principles, and one who merits their respect.

The home of Mr. Wiggins is brightened by the childish forms of three children—Samuel, Lucinda J. and Josephine—who have blessed his union with the lady who exercises such pleasant and orderly control of the household affairs. This lady, formerly Miss Lucy Rumble, native of Tower Creek Township, LaSalle County, Ill., and daughter of Charles and Elizabeth Rumble, whose sketch will be found elsewhere in this volume, was united in marriage to Mr. Wiggins on December 3, 1882.

GEORGE J. MILLER is the owner and occupant of a pleasantly located, well-improved farm of one hundred and sixty acres on section 34 Wellington Township. This land was purchased by him in 1879, and was then in the primitive condition of unbroken prairie. Taking possession of it in 1880, he has erected a set of farm buildings, which, though built of wood, are substantial and well designed. He has fenced and otherwise improved the estate, among the notable features of its adornment being many fruit, shade and ornamental trees.

The subject of this sketch was born in Bennington, Wyoming County, N. Y., July 27, 1853, and is the oldest member of the parental family. His father, George Miller, was born in Germany, and came to America when a young man. He learned the trade of a miller in his native land, and followed this for some time, later purchasing a farm in Bennington Township, where for many years he prosecuted agriculture. He is now living in Warsaw, the same county. The maiden name of his wife, the mother of our subject, was Kate Clar. Her father, Adam Clar, was a native of France, and spent his last years in Wyoming County. Beside our subject the members of the parental family were Margaret, John, Charles, Sarah and Lizzie

The subject of this sketch received his early education in the public schools of his native town, and prosecuted the study of higher branches at the Union School at Batavia. When not engaged in the schoolroom he assisted his father on the farm, early acquiring a practical understanding of a farmer's life and labors. At the age of twenty years he left the parental roof-tree and started out in life for himself, visiting different parts of the State of Michigan during the next few months. He then went to Ohio, and after spending the winter in another section, visited Toledo, where he accepted a position with the Water Company for a year, following which he entered the employ of the Summit Street Railway Company, remaining with them until he became a citizen of Kansas.

Though young in years Mr. Miller exhibits a judgment and discrimination equal to that shown by many older men, and manages his estate prudently and discreetly. He possesses an upright and manly character, and is highly respected among those with whom his lot is cast.

WILLIAM B. COLDWELL. This gentleman is a Justice of the Peace in Oxford, and is well known as a stock-raiser, his specialty being Jersey cattle, of which he has the best herd in the county, made up of the A. J. C. C. registered Jerseys. Mr. Coldwell is not only widely known as a Jersey cattle dealer, but has for a number of years filled a prominent position in Oxford as a business man and a public servant, and he still holds positions of public responsibility for which a long experience in mercantile and clerical capacities has well fitted him. His home estate comprises seventy acres adjoining the town, and he also owns one hundred and sixty acres in another part of the township.

Mr. Coldwell is a son of T. M. Coldwell and a grandson of Abiram Coldwell. The latter was a native of Virginia and the son of a man who came from Scotland. He grew to maturity in the Old

Dominion and there married a Miss Montgomery, after which he moved to the eastern part of Tennessee and engaged in farming, subsequently going to Dickson County, Tenn., where he died. He reared a family of fifteen children. Of these, Thomas M. was born in December, 1808, in Dickson County, and there grew to maturity on his father's farm. After his marriage to Miss Elizabeth Bell, he removed to Shelbyville, where he engaged in the sale of groceries and produce, and where he remained until his death, which took place in 1871. He was an able financier and a successful business man, but lost heavily in the war, saving but $250 out of the wreck made of his fortunes at that time. He was an Elder in the Presbyterian Church for more than a quarter of a century. He was kind and affectionate in his home relations and a prominent and respected citizen of his county. He was the father of nine children, of whom all but one are still living.

The subject of this sketch is the first-born in the parental family. The second son and child, Emmett, is now engaged in the foundry business at Birmingham, Ala.; Alice is the wife of William E. Mathews, of Shelbyville, Tenn.; Mary, who died in November, 1872, was the wife of B. F. Peacock, of this township. John is now agent for the Adams Express Company in St. Louis, Mo.; he came to Oxford in 1871, and resided here twelve years. The above-named children were born to the first wife of T. M. Coldwell, and after her death he married Miss Jane Cannon, of Rutherford County, Tenn., who became the mother of four children. Joseph C. is pastor of the Presbyterian Church at Elizabethtown, Ky.; Emma is still at home; Abbie is the wife of Mr. Black, of Louisburg, Tenn.; Maggie is with her mother.

The subject of this sketch was born in Shelbyville, Tenn., January 18, 1839, and grew to man's estate in his native place, finishing his education at Shelbyville Academy. At the breaking out of the Civil War, in 1861, he went to Nashville, Tenn., and entered the Commissary Department of Gen. Thomas' command, having charge of Taylor depot, with two or three million dollars' worth of stores, shipping to the front all the time. He next entered the large retail dry-goods house of Col. W.

W. Berry & Co., on College Street, Nashville, and subsequently handled the penitentiary productions—wagons, stoves, etc.—in the same city, with Messrs. McCampbell and Michael. He next held the position of Inspector of Customs in New York City during the years 1869–70, and then returned to his youthful home to assist in settling his father's estate.

In October, 1872, Mr. Coldwell came to this place, where there were but few people, and where deer were so plentiful that he could shoot all he wanted within the distance of half a mile, and herds of antelope were to be seen on Slate Creek. There were several Indian scares after he came here, but it was found that they were gotten up by desperate characters who had gathered here from various points, and the object was to steal horses. In the fall of 1873 Mr. Coldwell went into Harper County on a hunt and found but one white man in that county. His first claim here was the northeast quarter of section 22, upon which he made improvements, and in 1874 moved to the land which he now occupies, where he has also erected good buildings and placed the land under excellent cultivation, erected a windmill, and set out fruit and shade trees. At the same time he engaged in the dry-goods business, opening one of the first establishments of the kind in Oxford and after a time beginning a trade in agricultural implements, which he continued for ten or twelve years. He then engaged in the breeding of thoroughbred Jersey stock and good grades of horses, and, as before stated, has become well known in this business.

Mr. Coldwell was Secretary of the Committee which was appointed to secure a wagon bridge across the Arkansas River, his coadjutors being H. Barrett, Jasper Summerville, G. J. Hess and Dr. I. J. Maggard. They raised a private subscription and the county gave assistance, and the highway was secured. Our subject is manager of the co-operative store at Wellington, which is controlled by the Farmers' Alliance, and has been elected Secretary of the Oxford Farmers' Elevator and Mill Company, composed of members of the same body, which is soon to erect the buildings indicated in the title of their association. Mr. Coldwell has never desired office, but has been willing to serve his fellow citizens when called upon to fill any position which does not require his absence from home. He has therefore served as Township Clerk, and in 1888 was elected as Justice of the Peace. He has also been Chairman of the Democratic Township Committee. Of more than ordinary intelligence, undoubted ability and excellent character, Mr. Coldwell is highly respected by all who know him.

The wife of Mr. Coldwell bore the maiden name of Nellie Malaby, and their marriage was celebrated at her home, in Palestine Township on the last day of 1878. The bride was born in Pennsylvania April 27, 1854, and moved to Illinois with her parents, and in 1871 came with them to this county, where her mother is still living. Her father, the late George A. Malaby, was one of the early settlers of this county. He married Miss Esther Johnson, and their family comprised five sons and six daughters. Mr. and Mrs. Coldwell are the happy parents of five interesting children, who are named respectively: Irma, Irene, Irving, Ivan and Ion.

AMES W. HOUSEWORTH. The work of the biographer is particularly pleasant when to a record of financial prosperity and success one can add that of a useful career on the field of battle and in various departments of local affairs, and a character above reproach. Such a life and character may well be recorded for the benefit of future generations, who will eagerly glance backward to learn what worthy examples have been given by their progenitors. The gentleman who is the subject of this sketch can look back over years well spent since his early manhood, and turning his thoughts to the future, may confidently hope for still more extended usefulness through his personal efforts and the family whom he has reared.

Mr. Houseworth is the third in a family of fifteen children, twelve of whom grew to maturity. Their parents were Abram H. Houseworth, who

was born near Orange Court House, Va., and Lucy A. Blackwell, who was also a native of the Old Dominion. This worthy couple were married in Kentucky, and resided there until 1812, when they removed to Clark County, Ind., locating on a farm. They sojourned in the rural districts but a short time ere removing to the county seat, where Mr. Houseworth again occupied himself at his trade of a mechanic. Four years later they returned to their farm, upon which they remained until 1878, when they settled in Carroll County, Mo. The mother departed this life in 1885, and the father in 1888.

The gentleman of whom we write was born at Simpsonville, Shelby County, Ky., June 29, 1841, and was still an infant when the family removed to the Hoosier State, in the district schools of which he received a good common-school education. He began life for himself when he still lacked a year of his majority, by enlisting at the breaking out of the Civil War in Company B, Eighty-first Indiana Infantry. The command was sent to Nashville, Tenn., and forming a part of Gen. Rosencrans' army, took part in the battle of Stone River, and thence went to Chattanooga, later participating in the battle of Chickamauga, and fighting almost continually until the siege of Atlanta.

Under the command of Gen. Thomas they next participated in the engagement at Jonesboro, whence they returned to Nashville, fighting in the battle of Franklin on their way thither, engaging in another hard contest at their objective point and driving away Gen. Hood's army. Their next movement was to Huntsville, Ala., following which they entered East Tennessee, and then went to North Carolina on a scouting expedition. At the conclusion of this expedition they returned again to Nashville, where they remained until mustered out of service, at Camp Harper, in June, 1865. During the battle of Stone River, Mr. Houseworth was struck on the left elbow by a minie ball, but remained with his company notwithstanding the wound. He entered the ranks as a private, and was promoted to the position of Corporal.

After being honorably discharged, Mr. Houseworth returned to his father's farm, happy in the consciousness that there was no cause for regret in a retrospective view of his conduct during the war, and that the years which he had devoted to the service of his country had been well and nobly spent. During the winter after his return home he attended school, and the following spring rented a farm, which he operated about a year. He then purchased thirty-two acres, which he lived upon until 1868, when he removed to Missouri and settled in Carroll County, where he purchased a farm of forty acres, which was his home until 1877, when he came to Kansas and settled on the farm which he now occupies. This comprises two hundred acres in Ryan Township, and when he took possession of it every acre was in the raw condition of the Sumner County prairie. One hundred and sixty acres are now devoted to crops, and the owner divides his attention equally between the raising of crops and stock. The estate bears the usual improvements, the dwelling, which was erected in the year 1879, having been added to in 1887, forming a pleasant and commodious residence. In 1887 Mr. Houseworth went to Garfield County and took up one hundred and sixty acres of land as a soldier's homestead, and on that tract he has broken forty-five acres of ground and dug a good well.

The marriage of Mr. Houseworth was celebrated in Indiana, March 26, 1866, his bride being Miss Elizabeth Mitchell, who was born in Clark County, of that State, January 30, 1840. She was the recipient of a good common-school education, has many womanly virtues, and possesses a character which endears her to many hearts. Her parents, John and Rachel (St. Clair) Mitchell, were natives of Pennsylvania, but lived for a time in Ohio and later in Indiana. Mr. Mitchell was a farmer. He died in 1879, and his wife in 1858.

Mr. and Mrs. Houseworth are the parents of six children: Theodore E., Rachael Estella, John Leno and Abram Leman (twins), Frances Olga and Lucy Gertrude. The oldest son is now teaching in School District No. 137; Rachael Estella teaches five miles north of Milan; Abram Leman is teaching four and one half miles northwest of Argonia.

Mr. Houseworth is a member of the Farmers' Alliance, and of John Goldy Post, No. 90, G. A. R., of Milan, being Chaplain in the latter organiza-

tion. He is Director of School District No. 123, and has been elected Justice of the Peace; he is also serving his second term as Trustee of Ryan Township. While a resident of Missouri, he was twice elected Township Collector, and was also Registering Officer. He takes an active interest in politics, and votes the Republican ticket. Mrs. Houseworth is a member of the Methodist Episcopal Church and Mr. Houseworth of the Christian Church, and he has taught in the Sunday-school.

EBERLE D. WHITESIDE. In noting the business men of Caldwell, the name of Mr. Whiteside deserves more than a passing mention. In reverting to the incidents of his early life, we find that he was born in Casey County, Ky., January 13, 1863, and is the son of Christopher and Elizabeth (Wilson) Whiteside, who were natives of Kentucky. The latter lived in the Blue Grass State until about 1865, then emigrated to Illinois, and four years later to Cherokee County, Kan. The elder Whiteside spent his early years mostly in farming pursuits, but is now engaged as an hotel-keeper at Neosha. He bears the reputation of an honest man and a good citizen, is a worthy member of the Christian Church, a Democrat in politics, and belongs to the Masonic fraternity. The mother is also still living. The parental family included nine children, who were named respectively: William A., James T., Mattie, John, Eberle D., Eliza, Kittie, Lizzie, and Charles C.

The subject of this sketch was the fifth child of his parents, and was reared on the farm in Cherokee County, this State, acquiring a practical education in the common school. He made good use of his time and opportunities for the acquisition of useful knowledge, and for a time followed teaching. Later he entered the printing office of the Columbus *Times*, where he learned the "art preservative" and was engaged at this until 1883. That year he became the employe of the Long Bell Lumber Company, with which he has since continued, having charge of this business at Caldwell since 1885. He possesses fine business qualifications, and is evidently bound to make of life a reasonable success. He votes the Democratic ticket, and belongs to the Ancient Order of United Workmen.

On the 29th of December, 1886, Mr. Whiteside was wedded to Miss Mamie Hammett, of Columbus, Kan. Mrs. Whiteside was born in Martha's Vineyard, Mass., May, 1865, and is a daughter of John M. and Cordelia (Tilton) Hammett, likewise natives of the Bay State, and now of Columbus, Kan. There has been born to Mr. and Mrs. Whiteside, one child, Gladys E., July 29, 1888.

ILLIAM D. MOORE, proprietor of the Wellington Foundry, Stove and Machine Works, is numbered among the stirring business men of the city, and established himself in his present business in January, 1886, being located at the intersection of Harvey Avenue and C Street. He gives employment to several men, and is contributing his full quota to the industrial interests of Sumner County.

Essentially a Western man, Mr. Moore was born in Sangamon County, Ill., July 6, 1856, and was reared to manhood on his father's farm twelve miles south of Springfield. He completed a thorough education in the university at Champaign, being graduated in the Class of '83, from the mechanical and civil engineering departments. Soon afterward he assumed the position of Assistant Superintendent of River Survey on the Mississippi River in the employ of the Government. He was thus occupied one year, and then went into the Champaign machine shops, where he worked also one year, and acquired a practical knowledge of the business. At the expiration of this time, coming to Wellington he purchased a small foundry, and was ready for business on the 1st of January, 1886.

From the start Mr. Moore has been prosperous,

being obliged to increase his facilities, and now has one of the best-equipped shops in the city, giving employment to ten men during the busy season. He devotes his entire attention to his business, having neither time nor inclination for politics, simply casting his vote in support of the Democratic party.

The subject of this sketch was married at Auburn, Ill., February 17, 1887, to Miss Mattie Hill, Mrs. Moore, like her husband, was born in Sangamon County, Ill., and is the daughter of William R. and Jane (Mason) Hill, the former of whom was a a native of Kentucky, and the latter of Illinois. Mrs. Moore received excellent parental training, and remained under the home roof until her marriage.

The father of our subject was Morrison M. Moore, who was a native of Virginia, and born about 1810. He removed to Kentucky when a boy where he grew to man's estate, and then emigrated to Sangamon County, Ill. There he was married to Miss Sarah Crow, and they became the parents of eight children, all of whom are living. Mrs. Moore was born in Kentucky, and removed with her parents to Illinois when a young girl, about 1830. She and her husband are still living at the old farm in Sangamon County, and the elder Moore votes the Democratic ticket. Our subject and his family occupy a neat home in the northern part of the city, and enjoy the acquaintance and friendship of its best people. Mr. Moore has recently determined to engage in the manufacturing of stoves.

W. SHEARMAN. Among those who have borne no unimportant part in building up the town of Wellington, and whose interests have centered here for these many years, the subject of this notice deserves special mention. Notwithstanding that he has witnessed changes that seemed more like a dream than a reality, and was in Wellington during its earliest settlement, he is still a man in the prime of life, having been born September 23, 1836. His native place was Yates County, N. Y., where he was reared on a farm and attended the common school. The death of his mother, when he was a boy of thirteen years, resulted in his going out in the world to earn his own living, and he worked on the farm in the summer, and in the winter season in the timber. When a youth of nineteen years, he went into Chemung County, N. Y., and for some time thereafter was engaged as a traveling salesman for a boot and shoe house. He then returned to his native county, and engaged in the grocery business at Penn Yann, remaining there until 1851. Afterward he changed his residence to Niagara County, and became Superintendent of Gen. Whitney's farm, holding the position seven years. In 1858, he repaired to Louisiana and became overseer of a plantation, sixty nine miles above the city of New Orleans.

We next find Mr. Shearman again in the North, in consequence of the outbreak of the Rebellion, located near Geneva, N. Y. In 1862 he enlisted as a Union soldier in Company F, One Hundred and Twenty-sixth New York Infantry. The regiment soon afterward was ordered to Harper's Ferry. In September, that year, Mr. Shearman was captured with 13,000 others. The next day they were paroled, sent to Chicago, Ill., and Mr. Shearman was discharged on account of disability. In February, following, he returned to New York State, and lived one year in Ontario County. He then clerked one year in Penn Yann, and going from there to Elmira, engaged again as a salesman for a boot and shoe house three years. He next established himself in the grocery business at Penn Yann, sojourning there until 1871, although for two years, he was not engaged in any active business.

In the year last mentioned, Mr. Shearman turned his face towards the Great West with the intention of settling in some new town. Coming to Kansas, he visited a brother in Leavenworth, and there learned that a new town named Meridian had just been started in Sumner County. He accordingly set out for that point, going by rail to Emporia, then the Western terminus of the Santa Fe Road, and from there by stage to Wichita. There being no stage from this point as he expected, and deter-

mined not to abandon his enterprise, he started out on foot with another man, and about two and one-half miles southeast of the present site of Wellington, he found the village of Meridien. This consisted of a few tents near the timber. The proprietors of the land offered Mr. Shearman two lots if he would put up a store building and embark in merchandising. He stopped over night with them, and the following day two gentlemen named Wood and Godfrey invited him to their camp, one mile distant. Upon arriving there, they unfolded to him their plans. They were about to lay out a village where Wellington now stands, and offered him two business lots and two residence blocks for himself and his brother.

Mr. Shearman had already made arrangements with a friend at Emporia to send him lumber, and who at once dispatched teams for this place, and on the 4th of April, in company with others, commenced laying out the town. As soon as his lumber arrived, he put up the first building erected in Wellington, and as it approached completion, placed within it a stock of general merchandise, including most everything in general use. This, with the exception of Mr. Godfrey's drug store, was the only store in the town for many years. Mr. Shearman gave his sole attention to his mercantile business about eight years, and then served two years as under sheriff. When the Wells-Fargo Express Company established an office here, he accepted the agency and discharged the duties of this position until the office was consolidated with that of the Adams Express Company. He then embarked in the grocery business, which he is still conducting.

When Mr. Shearman came to this county, deer, antelope and buffalo were numerous, and the land was owned by the Government. It was sold for $1.25 per acre to homesteaders, who are now in possession of valuable and productive farms. Mr. Shearman has lived to see the surrounding country settled up with an intelligent and prosperous people, and a city, numbering probably 6,000 souls, grow up from the prairie. Since attaining his majority, Mr. Shearman has voted the Democratic ticket. He was the first Trustee of Wellington Township, and was a member of the Board of County Commissioners during the erection of the court house in 1881. He has been a member of the City Council, and served as Mayor three years. As one of the old landmarks he is known to a large portion of the people of Sumner County, and will be gratefully remembered long after he has departed hence.

The first marriage of Mr. Shearman occurred December 11, 1866, the bride being Miss Ophelia Bennett. This lady was likewise a native of New York State, and died in Penn Yann in 1868. In 1879, Mr. Shearman contracted a second marriage with Miss Alwilda DeArmand, who was born in Butler County, Ohio. Of the first marriage there was born one child, a daughter, Helen, who is now the wife of P. J. Ivers. The second union resulted in the birth of three children—Grace, Shirley and John.

The father of our subject was John Shearman, a native of Dublin, Ireland, and the son of George Shearman, who probably was born in the same country, and spent his entire life there. George Shearman was an attorney, and successfully engaged in the practice of his profession. The maiden name of his wife was Rebecca Brown. She was born in England, and died in the city of Dublin at the advanced age of one hundred and five years. Both were Episcopalians in religious belief. Four of their children emigrated to America—James, John, Frank and George—settling in Yates County, N. Y. Frank and James never married. George reared a family. John acquired an academic education in his native city and sailed for America when a a youth of nineteen years. Later he engaged in farming in Yates County, N. Y., and two years after marriage removed to Wilkesbarre, Pa., and embarked in the distillery business. After a twenty years' residence there he returned to Yates County, and purchased a flouring mill, which he operated some years. He died in that county in 1867, at the age of ninety-seven years.

The mother of our subject bore the maiden name of Anna Woodruff. She was born in Connecticut, and was the daughter of Elisha Woodruff, who probably was also a native of that State, and who emigrated to Yates County, N. Y., during its pioneer days, purchasing a tract of timber land in the wilderness. This was long before the days of canals

and railroads, and for a time the nearest mill to Grandfather Woodruff was at Elmira, seventy-five miles distant, to which he carried his grist on horseback. He cleared a farm, and resided there until his death. Mrs. Shearman spent her last days with her son in Tompkins County, N. Y. To her and her husband there have been born nine children, four sons and five daughters, viz.: Frank, Charlotte, Bradley, Rhoda, Anna, John, Mary, A. W., and one who died in infancy.

ENRY L. BENEDICT, Postmaster at Milan, is one of those deserving citizens whose history the biographer takes great pleasure in writing. For more than a decade he has resided in Ryan Township, and during those years he has filled positions of responsibility among his fellow-men, and has ever been found faithful in the discharge of his duties, both in those public capacities and in those of private life. His loyalty and devotion to his country were manifested during the Civil War, and proved him a worthy son of a father who had served in the War of 1812, under the leadership of William Henry Harrison.

The paternal grandfather of our subject was Obadiah Benedict, a native of Scotland, and a Quaker in his religious belief; his wife was of Welsh ancestry. Among the progeny of this worthy couple was Asahel Benedict, who was born in the State of New York, and adopted the occupation of farming. During the second contest for American relief from British tyranny, he became a teamster, driving oxen and carrying stores and ammunition, and using a musket on various occasions. He participated in the battle of Tippecanoe, and during the war became very strongly attached to Gen. Harrison, with whom he at one time swapped horses.

Asahel Benedict married Miss Evelina Moore, a native of Connecticut, and a daughter of Chandler Moore, of England, who served in the Colonial Army during the Revolution, and was wounded by a sabre cut at the battle of Brandywine. This couple was united in marriage in Ohio, and permanently resided in that State, having been among the earliest settlers of Franklin County. They were the parents of nine children, two of whom are now living. Four sons grew to manhood, and all served in the Union Army during the Rebellion—Anson was a member of the Fourteenth Ohio Infantry, and died from disease at Kingston, Ga.; Flavel T. belonged to the Ninety-fifth Ohio Infantry, and served under Gen. Thomas at the battle of Nashville, during which he received a death wound; Charles W. belonged to the Third Ohio Infantry, and was captured by the Confederates in the early years of the war, but was exchanged, and continued to serve his country until the close of the contest. The mother of this family died in 1839, and the father survived until 1881, when he passed away at the age of eighty-nine years.

The gentleman whose name initiates this sketch was the second member of the parental family, was born in Franklin County, Ohio, April 1, 1827, and was reared to the age of sixteen at the place of his birth. He received a common school education in the district schools, and at the age of thirteen years began life for himself as a farm hand, working by the month. Three years later he went to Louisiana, and was engaged in checking timber and in sawmill work near New Orleans for about four years, after which he spent a year getting out timber in the swamps. He became of age while there, and cast his first vote for Gen. Zachary Taylor for President.

After the lumbering and milling experiences in the South, Mr. Benedict turned his face Northward and settled in Washington County, Ind., on a farm, continuing to reside in the Hoosier State and occupy himself with agricultural labors until 1871, with the exception of the time which he devoted to his country's service on the field of battle. At the date last mentioned he removed to Kansas, settled on a farm in Cowley County, and six years later removed to the farm which he now occupies. His estate comprises one hundred and sixty acres of land, all improved, and supplied with a full assortment of buildings in good condition, and everything about the place indicates

that its owner is thoroughly acquainted with the details of his chosen occupation, and a capable judge of the needs of the country, and consequently discriminating in regard to stock and crops. Mr. Benedict was appointed Postmaster at Milan, June 24, 1889, and beside conducting the office, which is a fourth-class and money order one, he handles a stock of groceries.

"The shot heard round the world" had scarcely ceased to re-echo throughout the land ere Mr. Benedict had determined to do what lay in his power to prevent the dissolution of the Union. He enlisted July 13, 1861, as a private in Company K, Twenty-third Indiana Infantry, and six months later was promoted to the rank of Corporal. The command was sent to St. Louis, and thence to Paducah, Ky., and served under Gen. U. S. Grant until after the fall of Vicksburg, following which they were under the leadership of Gen. Logan, Gen. McPherson and of Gen. F. P. Blair. Still later Mr. Benedict was a member of the force under command of Gen Gresham, and still later fought under Gen. Sherman. He participated in the trying contests of Fts. Henry and Donelson, on the bloody field of Shiloh, throughout the siege of Vicksburg, at Raymond, Jackson (Miss.). Champion Hill and Black River. He took part in a running fight with Bragg's army, in the Sherman raid to Meridian, Miss., in the affray at Big Shanty, and in the notable engagement at Kenesaw Mountain; he celebrated the Fourth of July, 1864, by taking part in the rattle of musketry and the clash of arms on the Chattahoochie River, and during the following day also spent the hours in renewed attempt to preserve the life of the Nation that had been born eighty-eight years before. A few days after this engagement, the three-years term of service for which the regiment had been enlisted having expired, they were sent to Rothwell, Ga., discharged, and going to Chattanooga, Tenn., were there mustered out of the service. Although Mr. Benedict did not attain to a high rank, and his name was not blazoned before the world as a great general or the leader of some dashing exploit, he is nevertheless as brave, gallant and worthy a soldier as could be found in all the ranks. Praise and honor are justly due to the great leaders whose capacity to plan and to execute campaigns led victory to perch upon the banners of the Union forces. But to the noble men, who, like our subject, left home and loved ones and endured all the privations, dangers, and arduous toils of "life on the tented field," no less is a meed of honor due; no less is the heart of a lover of his country thrilled by recollection of all they suffered and all which we owe to them. And what shall be said of the noble women who, after bidding their loved ones a fond good-bye, took up the great burden of anxiety and suspense regarding their safety, adding it to the other burden of family support, which so often devolved upon them. The wife of Mr. Benedict was left with four small children when he took up arms, and during the weary months of his absence she filled a father's place to them, exercised a wise oversight over their worldly affairs, and proved that she too could sacrifice and endure in her country's cause.

This lady, who for many years has stood by Mr. Benedict's side, sharing in his trials and his joys, and with him endeavoring to worthily fill their sphere in life, bore the maiden name of Sarah E. Andrew. She is a daughter of Thomas Andrew, a native of North Carolina and a mechanic, who departed this life in 1878, and of Lucy Dollans, a native of Virginia, whose death took place in 1874. Mr. and Mrs. Andrew were the parents of eight children. Mrs. Benedict was the third in order of birth, first opened her eyes to the light May 24, 1831, and was united in marriage with our subject September 13, 1849. Two of her brothers, William and John, entered the Union Army, and the latter died in the service in 1865. To Mr. and Mrs. Benedict eight children have been born, and six are now living. These are named respectively: John A., Caroline, Robert A., Charles H., May and Crowder.

Mr. Benedict belongs to John Goldy Post, No. 90, G. A. R., and was Vice Commander in 1888. He is much interested in educational matters, and has been a member of the School Board for several years. He was Treasurer of Ryan Township in 1887, and he is one of the gentlemen who named it. In politics he is always actively interested, and is a never failing supporter of the Republican ticket.

Both he and his wife are members of the Methodist Episcopal Church, in which he is a Trustee and the Chairman of the Board, and the entire family take an active part in the work of the Sunday school. Mrs. Benedict has been a member of the church since 1842, having identified herself with that religious body at the age of eleven years.

JAMES C. DAVIS is the owner and occupant of the southeast quarter of section 25, Jackson Township, where he has resided for several years, and where he has erected a good set of farm buildings, planted a fine orchard, and made other improvements such as are usually accomplished by a thorough farmer. His grandfather, Samuel Davis, was born in Wales, in which country the ancestors had been living for generations. He came to America and in Vermont continued his labors as a farmer, and in that State departed this life.

Samuel Davis, Jr., son of the above, and father of our subject, was born in Rutland County, Vt., and reared to agricultural pursuits. He first removed to New York, and about 1820 went to Ohio, becoming a pioneer resident of Miami County. He took up a tract of heavily timbered land in Stanton Township, erected a log cabin, and resided there until 1834, when he sold and purchased other timber land in Union Township, Mercer County, building a log cabin in that wilderness also, and again undergoing the hardships and trials of a frontiersman. Deer, bears, wolves, coons, wild cats and gray foxes were numerous, there were no railroads or canals for several years, and the nearest town of any note was Pickaway, forty miles distant. He cleared a farm, and as there was no sale for timber, many fine logs which he cut were rolled together and burned to get rid of them. On that place he resided until a short time before his death, when he took up his abode with his children. His wife, who was born in New York, bore the maiden name of Laura Spicer, and was a daughter of Samuel and

Sarah (Rudd) Spicer. She died at the home of her children in March, 1865. She had reared seven children: Samuel, Laura, Justus, James, Mary, Sarah and Eliza. Justus and James took part as soldiers in the late war.

James C. Davis was born in Miami County, Ohio, September 8, 1827, and being a lad of seven years when his parents removed to Mercer County, he was practically reared in the latter. There were no free schools at that period, and institutions of learning were kept up by subscription, and were held in log houses, with benches made by splitting logs, inserting pins for legs and hewing the upper side smooth. As soon he was large enough, young Davis began assisting his father on the farm, and continued so employed until 1849, when he bought a tract of timber land near the parental homestead, built a log cabin, and commenced housekeeping. He cleared the land and worked it, residing there until 1864, when he entered the one hundred days' service as member of Company K, One Hundred and Fifty-sixth Ohio Infantry. At the expiration of his term of service he resumed farming, and remained upon his original homestead until 1882, when he came to Kansas, locating in this county. A year later he sold his Ohio farm and bought that upon which he is now residing.

At the home of the bride in Mercer County, Ohio, July 12, 1849, Mr. Davis was united in marriage with Miss Mary H. Gordon, a native of Hardin County, Ky. Her grandfather, John Gordon, was born either in Scotland or Ireland, and came with his father, Hugh Gordon, to America, locating in Virginia. In 1801 they went to Kentucky, settling in Washington County, where he cleared a tract of land, and where both the grandfather and great-grandfather remained until their death, the latter being one hundred and three years at the time of his decease. The wife of John Gordon bore the maiden name of Mary Latham, and after the death of her husband she went to Illinois, and spent her last years with her children there.

Henry Gordon, the father of Mrs. Davis, was born in Fauquier County, Va., and was reared and married in Kentucky, in his manhood settling in Hardin County, where he lived until 1840, when he removed to Mercer County, Ohio, buying a tract of timber land, which he cleared and made his his home until his death. His wife, Miss Catherine Drury, was born in Bennington County, Vt., and was the daughter of Samuel Drury, a saddler, who after working in New York City, went to the Green Mountain State, where he married Miss Hannah Branson, later removing to Lake Geneva, N. Y., thence to Hardin County, Ky., where both subsequently died. The mother learned the trade of a mantau-maker in Albany, N. Y., and also learned to spin and weave, as was the custom in that day. Her daughter, Mrs. Davis, also learned to spin and weave, and now has in her possession coverlets of her own manufacturing. She also learned the trade of a tailoress.

ORRANCE R. DONLEY. This sturdy veteran bears the distinction of being one of the oldest living settlers of Sumner County and the oldest settler in the village of Oxford. He came to this region when the present site of Oxford was marked simply by a sawmill, and here he has since maintained his residence, watching the growth and development of the country and proving himself a worthy and useful citizen.

When Mr. Donley came to this region, in the winter of 1871, he staked out a claim just west of the town of Oxford and also made a home at the mill which he had removed from Winfield. This latter was operated by steam, and the first structure of the kind in the county. Three years later Mr. Donley traded the mill for land. Later he and Mr. Chandler embarked in the furniture trade, and put up a substantial new building in the central part of town, bringing into the latter the first full stock of furniture, they operating under the firm name of Chandler & Donley. A year later, however, Mr. Donley disposed of his interest in the business, and in due course of time commenced dealing in live stock, being thus occupied for a number of years. He was also at one time engaged in a store of general merchandise and groceries, in company with Mr. A. Gridley, who had the post-office in the store and who was the second post-master there.

His real estate comprises a farm of one hundred and sixty acres, which is conducted under his supervision. Mr. Donley settled in Oxford Township prior to its organization or that of the school districts. He has served as Township Trustee, and was a member of the town council two terms. He has supported the principles of the Republican party since becoming a voter.

A native of Cattaraugus County, N. Y., Mr. Donley was born April 2. 1845, and lived there until a youth of eighteen years. In the meantime he pursued his studies at the schools of Little Valley and Perryville. During the progress of the Civil War he, in 1863, joined a construction corps and assisted in building bridges, houses, platforms, store-rooms, etc., in the meantime assisting to build the bridge at Bull Run and Bridgetown. Later he went to Richmond. Va., expecting to assist in building the bridge across the James River, but the war ended before it was completed.

We next find Mr. Donley in Salamanca, N. Y., where he purchased property and conducted a grocery store for eighteen months. Then coming to Junction City, Kan., during the time of the building of the Union Pacific Railroad, he again commenced working with a construction corps. The following spring he repaired to Omaha, Neb., sojourning there until 1864. That year he went to Texas, via Ft. Smith and Memphis, purchasing horses and cattle, and driving the latter to Abilene, Kan. Wichita was then a hamlet of a few log houses. Subsequently Mr. Donley was in Labette County, this State, and afterward made an overland trip to Ft. Smith in order to recover the baggage he had left there. That same winter Mr. Donley purchased a sawmill at Chetopa, Kan., which he removed first to Winfield and then to Oxford. During these years, although making several changes, he prospered financially, and is now independent.

On the 25th of November, 1878, Mr. Donley was united in marriage with Miss Virginia B. Cheuvront at the bride's home in Oxford Township. Mrs. Donley was born in West Virginia. June. 13, 1856, and was the daughter of Morris Cheuvront, who, upon leaving the old Dominion, settled near Fairmount, Ill., where his daughter, Virginia, grew to womanhood. Later the family came to Kansas. Of this union there have been born four children—Torrance E., Morris, June and a babe, Hernon.

The father of our subject was Torrance R. Donley, Sr., who married Miss Margaret Cain. They spent the greater part of their lives in Cattaraugus County, N. Y., where their remains are laid to rest.

JOHN BOTKIN is one of the first settlers of Sumner County, and is the owner of several farms within its limits, which he rents while himself living in Wellington, practically retired from active pursuits. He has had an extended observation of life on the Plains and in the Rocky Mountain regions, and can tell many an interesting tale of experience in the Western wilds. He was born in Morgan County, Ohio, May 8, 1812, and is of remote Scotch ancestry, although the family for a time resided in Ireland, and probably one generation at least was born in the Emerald Isle.

The first of the family to settle in America was Robert Botkin, who was born in Ireland, and on coming to this country located in Lancaster County, Pa., where he operated a farm, and also ran a ferry-boat across the Susquehanna River at a point known as Crab's Ferry. He had a son who bore his own name, and who was but a boy when they came to America. Robert Botkin, Jr., was reared and married in Lancaster County, whence he went to Fayette County, and later to Greene County. In the latter he rented land and farmed for many years, spending his latter days in Morgan County, Ohio, with his children. His wife was Miss Sarah Horner, a native of Lancaster County, and a daughter of Robert and Sarah (Cook) Horner. Her death took place in Greene County, Pa., where her son,

Amos H., the father of our subject, was born, October 15, 1815.

Amos H. Botkin was reared in the Keystone State, and when about of age went to Ohio, making his home in Belmont County for a time, and then removing to Morgan County, where he was engaged in farming and where he continued to reside until 1850. He then removed to Indiana, and locating in Clark County, fifteen miles from Charleston, lived in the Hoosier State two years. He next started for Iowa with a team, and after spending a few months in Christian County, Ill., continued on to the Hawkeye State and became an early settler of Van Buren County. He bought a tract of land there, and another in Davis County, and resided upon the former until 1878, when he came to this place, where he has since made his home. The maiden name of his wife was Sarah Ann Bony, and she was born in Washington County, Pa. Her parents were Jacob and Sarah (Ault) Bony, who were natives of York County, Pa., whence they removed to Ohio in 1830, making their first settlement in the Buckeye State in Guernsey County, and later changing their residence to Morgan County. They subsequently removed to Iowa, where Mr. Bony spent his last years. He was a shoemaker, and followed his trade all his life.

John Botkin, whose name initiates this sketch, was but four years old when his parents removed to Clarke County, Ind., and was in his seventh year when they settled in Iowa. There he attended the pioneer schools, and in the intervals assisted his father in improving the farm. He was still residing with his parents when he determined to devote his energy to the Union cause, and in April, 1863, though not yet of age, he enlisted in Company G, Seventh Iowa Cavalry. He served until after the close of the war, his duties carrying him into Missouri, Arkansas, Kansas, Wyoming, Colorado, Dakota, Idaho, Utah and New Mexico, and including much hard riding, as all the marches from State to State and from Territory to Territory were made on horseback. The various phases of cavalry campaigns became familiar to him, and he also acquired a considerable knowledge of the untrodden wilderness, and unsettled plains and valleys of that little known region on the eastern slope of the Rockies.

After being discharged from the army in June, 1866, Mr. Botkin returned to Davenport, Iowa, and thence to the paternal home, where he remained eleven months, after which he crossed the plains to the Rocky Mountains. At that time innumerable numbers of buffaloes traversed the plains, and deer, antelope, elk and mountain sheep were plentiful. Mr. Botkin spent nearly three years in Wyoming Territory engaged in getting out timber to be used in the construction of the Union Pacific Railroad, and also in getting wood and hay for the Government. Returning again to his home, he remained in Van Buren County a few months, and then started to cross the plains again, but at Columbus, Neb., he met his brother Simon, and concluded to come to Southern Kansas to locate.

The brothers therefore bought teams and drove across the country nearly four hundred miles, arriving in Wichita in June. That flourishing city was then a small village, and Indian tepees lined the banks of the Little Arkansas River. Our subject took a claim on a school section, but remained in that vicinity but a few weeks, when he again pursued his investigations, and in September settled in the southwestern quarter of section 27, in what is now Wellington Township, this county, and is included in the present city limits of Wellington. At that time there was not a house where the city now stands, and the land was owned by the Government. The general survey was not yet completed. There was no railroad nearer than Emporia, and Wichita was the nearest post-office. Mr. Botkin built a log house covered with sod in lieu of shingles, and began to break the soil and improve the land. The following spring the village was platted a half-mile distant. Mr. Botkin continued farming and stock-raising until 1887, when he took advantage of the boom here and sold his farm to a syndicate and built where he now resides. After selling his original farm he bought other tracts of land in different parts of the county, and is deriving a comfortable income from their rental.

On January 11, 1877, the rites of wedlock were

celebrated between Mr. Botkin and Miss Anna, daughter of Daniel and Anna E. Ellington. The bride was born in Clark County, Ill., and possesses many womanly virtues. Their family comprises four living children—Everett, Grace, Laura and Bessie. Harry, the fifth child, died at the age of twenty-nine days; John Q. died when nine months old.

Mr. Botkin is interested in the social orders, and holds membership in the James Shields Post, No. 57, G. A. R., and in Wellington Lodge, No. 150, A. F. & A. M. He is an intelligent and reliable citizen, a man of good character, and has many friends in the community.

AVID STEPHENS. In noting the leading pioneers of Sumner County, due mention should be made of Mr. Stephens, who established himself as a resident of South Haven Township, at a time when the nearest market was at Wichita, to which point he and his neighbors hauled all their produce overland with teams. For several seasons there were to be seen only a few rude dwellings in the open country where wolves and antelopes were plentiful. He has since been a continuous resident of the township, and has evinced that warm interest in its growth and development which is only felt by intelligent members of the community. He is a Virginian by birth, and first opened his eyes to the light in Rockingham County, March 11, 1825.

The early years of Mr. Stephens were spent on a farm in his native State, and about 1831 his parents, Louis and Elizabeth (Alder) Stephens emigrated to Madison County, Ohio. The father took up a tract of new land and prosecuted farming in the Buckeye State until 1849. That year he pushed on further westward into Knox County, Ill., where he purchased a piece of raw prairie, from which he built up a valuable homestead, and there spent his last days, passing away in August, 1887, at the advanced age of eighty-four years. The mother survived her husband one year, dying in August, 1888, at the age of eighty-three. They were the parents of ten children, seven of whom survive, and of whom David was the third in order of birth.

The paternal grandfather of our subject, was Mark Stephens, a native of Germany, who emigrated to America when a young man, paying his passage by working at seven cents per day. When landing he located in Virginia, and in due time was there married to Miss Mary Wolf, a native of Germany. They settled on a farm in the Old Dominion, and became well-to-do, rearing a fine family of children, and there closed their eyes to earthly scenes.

On the maternal side Grandfather Michael Alder, was likewise a native of Germany, also crossed the Atlantic early in life, settled in Virginia, and married Miss Barbara Moyers. Grandmother Alder was likewise a native of the Fatherland. To them was born a family of sons and daughters, and they spent their last days on the soil of the Old Dominion. They passed through many thrilling scenes, having located in a wild country where Indians were numerous. About that time Jonathan Alder, an uncle of Michael, was captured by the Indians when a boy of eight years, and lived with them until a man of thirty years. He died in Ohio.

Mr. Stephens when a young man went from Illinois to Virginia, and was there married to Miss Arminda, daughter of Evan and Margaret (Burnsides) Hinton. Mrs. Stephens was born in Virginia. Her parents were also natives of the Old Dominion, and her paternal grandfather, a staunch tory, who located there at an early day, also died there, together with her parents. Soon after their marriage, Mr. and Mrs. Stephens took up their abode on a farm in Knox County, Ill., where they sojourned until 1874, coming then to this county. Mr. Stephens purchased one hundred and sixty acres of land about two and one-half miles north of the present site of the city, and establ'shed himself with his little family in a small box house, which constituted their domicile for several years. From this land the father improved a good homestead, and secured eighty acres adjoining. He placed one hundred and eighty acres under a good state of cultivation, planted an orchard of apple

trees, also other fruit trees, and effected good im
provements. He sold this farm in 1880, and lived
thereafter near South Haven until 1886, when he
removed to South Haven.

Eight children were born to Mr. and Mrs. Ste-
phens, one of whom, Evan, died when quite young.
The seven survivors are named respectively: Ezra,
Evan, Ruhama, Charles, Wilson, Albert, and Les-
ter; Mrs. Stephens departed this life in Knox
County, Ill., in 1870, in the faith of the Methodist
Episcopal Church, of which she had been a consist-
ent member several years.

In 1886 Mr. Stephens contracted a second mar-
riage at South Haven, with Mrs. Rachel (Polk)
Swiney. This lady was born in Hamilton County,
Ohio, and when quite young removed with her parents to Madison County, Ind., where she was first
married to Thomas Swiney. They settled in Knox
County, Ill., where Mr. Swiney died in 1884. Mrs.
Stephens is a member of the Methodist Episcopal
Church. Mr. Stephens, politically, affiliates with
the Democratic party, and is a member of Pacific
Lodge, No. 400, A. F. & A. M., at Knoxville, also
of the Independent Order of Odd Fellows, at the
same place.

AMES H. OWENS. The agricultural interests of Sumner County, are worthily represented by Mr. Owens, who was one of the
pioneer farmers of Oxford Township, where,
besides his home farm of two hundred and forty acres
on section 10, he also owns two quarter-sections a
little further West. He came to this region in 1875
and selected a fine location west of Oxford Center,
where he now has one of the most attractive homes
in the township. He commenced at first principles
in the construction of his farm, which had been
subjected to very little improvement when he assumed ownership. He put up a fine residence in
1877, which still stands flanked by a substantial
barn and all other necessary outbuildings, besides
forest and fruit trees and shrubbery. He avails
himself of first-class machinery in the prosecution

of his calling, including a costly windmill, and he
has operated with such thoroughness and skill, that
he has secured the reputation of being one of the
most successful farmers in the county. His landed
possessions altogether embrace six hundred and
twenty-four acres, forming as fine a body of land
as can be found in the Sunflower State. He rents
all but the home farm.

For the past seven years Mr. Owens has been
quite extensively engaged in the breeding of thoroughbred Short-horn cattle. Of these he has a
very fine herd from which he sold in the fall of
1889, forty-nine head at a good round sum. He is
also a successful breeder of blooded horses. In
bringing his farm to its present fine condition, he
has expended much time, labor and money, but
they have proved a wise investment. Mr. Owens
is a liberal and public-spirited citizen, a stanch supporter of the Democratic party, and a member in
good standing of the Christian Church. He is a
man of standing in his community, exercising no
small influence among his fellow-citizens, by whom
he is universally respected.

Born in Posey County, Ind., December 4, 1836,
Mr. Owens lived there until a youth of fifteen years.
His parents were James H. and Sarah (Cox) Owens,
natives of North Carolina, the former of whom removed to Indiana when a child of five years. The
mother died at the birth of her son, James H. The
father and son removed to DeWitt County, Ill., in
1851, where the former carried on farming, and the
latter acquired his education in the common school.
When eighteen years old he began farming for
himself, prosecuting this successfully until his marriage on the 4th of March, 1862, with Miss Jane
Marquis. The young people began the journey of
life together on a farm in Macon County, Ill.,
where they sojourned until coming to Kansas. The
elder Owens in the meantime died in 1864. While
in Illinois, James H. held the office of Township
Commissioner until resigning, and since that time
has carefully refrained from accepting the responsibilities of office, although he is acknowledged as
a leading man of this township.

Mrs. Jane Owens was born in Posey County, Ind.,
September 22, 1836, and is the daughter of Pleasant Marquis, who spent his last years in Posey

County. Ind. Of her union with our subject there have been born five children, four of whom are living: Minnie is the wife of A. A. Richards, of Wellington; Robert remains with his father; Fanny died when two years old. The two younger are Effie and Alfred. Effie is attending school at Wichita. Mr. Owens believes in education, and has carried out his theory in regard to his own children.

WILLIAM H. NOTTINGHAM was reared to farm pursuits, and among the young agriculturists of the county has a high rank as one who is thoroughly acquainted with the details of farm work, and wise in his adoption of methods for adding to the resources of the soil. He gives his entire attention to farming and the stock business, and the one hundred and sixty acres of improved land on section 3, Caldwell Township, which is his place of abode, presents an orderly and attractive appearance to the passer-by.

Mr. Nottingham is a native of Vinton, Benton County, Iowa, was born July 29, 1856, and received an excellent common-school education in the schools of his native town. When fourteen years of age his parents became residents of Sumner County, Kan., and after assisting his father upon the home place until he had arrived at a suitable age to do so, he pre-empted some Government land, and began his individual life as a farmer.

The parents of our subject are Morgan J. and Caroline (Underwood) Nottingham, early settlers of Sumner County, to which they came in 1871. Morgan Nottingham was born in Virginia, fifty-four years ago, and was five years of age when his parents removed to Ohio. In the year 1850 he took up his residence in Benton County, Iowa, whence he came to this State and county, pre-empting one hundred and sixty acres of land in Oxford Township. Although he learned the trade of a carpenter in his early life, he has followed farming the most of the time, and is still so occu-

pied. He is numbered in the ranks of the Republican party, and in the social order of the Ancient, Free and Accepted Masons. He is Justice of the Peace and a worthy member of the Christian Church. His wife was born in Franklin County, Ind., in 1873, at the age of thirty-three years. She had borne seven children—William H., L. G., Ella M., Susie, Anna D., James W. and John.

At the home of the bride, January 9, 1883, the the subject of this biography was united in marriage with Miss Lula King, an attractive and intelligent young lady, whose birth occurred in Kosciusko County, Ind., January 14, 1863. She is a daughter of Aaron and Lydia (Hoover) King, natives of Ohio. Both parents are now deceased. The union of Mr. and Mrs. Nottingham has been blessed by the birth of three children—Bernerd F., Murl and Ray—and they have suffered the loss of the second born. Mr. Nottingham follows his father's example in being a staunch member of the Republican party and a consistent member of the Christian Church. He belongs to the Farmers' Alliance.

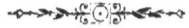

WILLIAM N. BLAMPIED is one of the pioneers of Sumner County, Kan., and resides on section 3, Belle Plaine Township, where he came in the summer of 1871, although for two previous years he had sojourned in the Sunflower State. He is a prominent citizen, both socially and politically, being a supporter of the principles of the Republican party, and identified with any movement tending to improve the county.

Having been born August 6, 1850, Mr. Blampied is now in the prime of a useful life. Guernsey County, Ohio, was his native place, and his paternal ancestry is supposed to have been of French extraction. His father, Thomas Blampied, enlisted in the Union army in 1862; he was taken prisoner in Monocacy, Va., and died in the Lynchburg prison from hardship and exposures. The mother,

Hannah (Helm) Blampied is now living in Belle Plaine, Kan. She was a native of the Old Dominion, and removed to Ohio at an early day in the history of our country, where she married Thomas Blampied, a native of the Buckeye State. Their family comprised four children, of whom three survive: Rachel, wife of Harry Halpin; Milton, William N.; our subject; Mary is deceased.

Our subject remained in Ohio until he reached the nineteenth year of his age, and in his youth worked at harness-making for about two years. He also served two years in the Ohio State Militia and did duty at Camp Chase, being subject to State call. He enlisted as a private in Company G, Forty-seventh Regiment, Ohio National Guards. After serving with them he returned to Guernsey County, and once more engaged in farming. He left the Buckeye State about 1868, and went to Polk County, Mo., where he worked as a farm laborer for a few years. He sojourned in Davis (now Geary) County, Kan., and in other counties of the same State about two years, coming in the summer of 1871 to Sumner County.

Not a furrow had ever been turned on the one hundred and sixty-acre farm, which Mr. Blampied then commenced to improve, transforming it from a wild tract of raw land to a well-regulated estate. Some of this property has been sold, the farm now consisting of one hundred and twenty acres. Mr. Blampied was married in Ohio May 22, 1873, to Miss Sarah J. Rose, who was born in Harrison County, Mo., August 16, 1855. Her father, Timothy Rose, was a native of Ohio, and her mother, (Catherine (Castor) Rose, a native of Pennsylvania. Mrs. Blampied accompanied her mother to Ohio when eleven years of age, her father having been killed during the Civil War in Missouri by Quantrell's gang, and it is said that Quantrell himself committed the murder. In company with eleven men he was returning home on a furlough, when all except one, fell victims to the enemy's unerring fire. Mrs. Blampied has two brothers, Benjamin and Timothy, both residents of Ohio. After the death of her husband, Mrs. Rose was again married to William Vansickel, by whom she had five children, namely: Ida B., wife of Willard Little, of Ohio; William M., of Ohio; Eddie, who is de-

ceased; Joseph and Harry, who live in Ohio. Mrs. Vansickel died in Ohio in December, 1886.

When Mrs. Blampied was a girl, she removed with her mother and other members of the family to Guernsey County, Ohio, where she remained until her marriage. To her and her husband have been born eight children, namely: Ida A., Elmer C., Lillian, Charles, Jesse, Willis H., (deceased) and Ora V., (deceased), and an infant daughter unnamed. The children are receiving good educations in the district schools, and are being carefully trained for future positions of responsibility. Mrs. Blampied is a member of the United Brethren Church and with her husband occupies a prominent position in society. They have endured hardships of frontier life, and have been interested witnesses of the development of the country from a wild state to a land of plenty, where well-cultivated farms are the rule and not the exception.

HENRY H. JACOBS. The subject of this notice, the present Postmaster of Perth, first struck the soil of Kansas March 20, 1886, coming directly to this county and locating on the northeast quarter of section 14, Downs Township, where he has since successfully prosecuted farming pursuits. He was born March 9, 1837, and is a native of York County, Pa. His father, George Jacobs, was also born in that county, in 1804, and died there in his prime, aged forty-five years, five months and seventeen days. He was a farmer by occupation, and a member in good standing of the Lutheran Church. The Jacobs family was of German extraction and noted principally for their substantial and reliable traits of character and the industry which has made of them well-to-do citizens, who have always been useful members of their community.

Mrs. Elizabeth (Cromer) Jacobs, the mother of our subject, was born in Pennsylvania in 1807, and is still living, making her home with her daughter in Perth. The parental household included seven children, viz.: Susannah, Mary, Henry H., George W., Amelia S., Elizabeth A., and John Q. Elizabeth died at the age of four years, four months and twelve days; John died when a little lad of five years; Henry H., the third child of the family, spent his boyhood and youth after the manner of most farmers' sons, attending the district school and assisting his father on the farm. He remained a resident of his native county until coming to this State. His homestead lies adjacent to the town limits of Perth, and he was appointed to the office of Postmaster in 1889. He is also connected with the Farmers' Mutual Insurance Company of Sumner County. In politics, he is decidedly Republican.

In November, 1862, during the progress of the Civil War, Mr. Jacobs enlisted as a Union soldier in Company F, One Hundred and Sixty-fifth Pennsylvania Infantry, serving until July of the following year. He is a prominent man in church matters, and assisted in the organization of the Lutheran Church at Perth. He was married in his native county, February 2, 1860, to Miss Elmira F. Heagey. Mrs. Jacobs was born in Adams County, Pa., March 8, 1841, and is the daughter of Henry and Rachel (Schriver) Heagey, who were likewise natives of that State, and spent their last days in Pennsylvania. Six children have been born to Mr. and Mrs. Jacobs, whom they named respectively: Luther H., Elmer E., Annie E., Emery G., Allen G, and Melvin H. Luther died at the age of nine months and twelve days, and Elmer was taken from the home circle, aged one year and thirteen days. The other children are with their parents.

 B. FREEMAN is a prominent and rising young physician of Wellington, where he has been engaged in the practice of his profession for about four years. He has built up an excellent and growing practice among the better class of citizens, and is highly spoken of by those who know him as a man of ability in his chosen field of labor and of strict integrity in all transactions.

Dr. Freeman was born in Metcalf County, Ky., in 1859, and is a son of Albert L. Freeman, who was born in the same county about thirty years prior to his son's birth. The father was married in that county to Miss Juliette S. Morrison and carried on his occupation of tilling the soil there until 1885 when he removed to this county. Here the parents and their three children now live, two sons, E. P. and W. L., being engaged in farming. The entire family are members of the Cumberland Presbyterian Church in Wellington.

The gentleman whose name initiates this notice received an excellent education, acquiring the fundamental branches in his native State and completing the literary course in Cumberland University at Lebanon, Tenn. He then read medicine under Dr. J. W. Good, of Hiseville, Ky., taking his lectures in the Medical Department of the Louisville University and being graduated therefrom in the class of 1885. Thinking the West afforded a better field for a young physician than localities in the East where there were so many old established practitioners, he came to Kansas and opened an office in Rome, this county, where he sojourned but nine months ere coming to this place, with the result already noted.

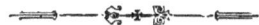

JOHN W. PARKS, a successful general farmer of Sumner County, came to this region from the Blue Grass State within which he was born, on the 27th of October, 1851, in Logan County. He was reared there on his father's farm, the father being Leander A. Parks who is represented elsewhere in this work. When a young man of twenty-three years John W. came to Kansas and took up a claim of one hundred and sixty acres on section 32. Two months later, however, he returned to Kentucky, but came back to Kansas the following spring and purchased one hundred and sixty acres of land, which is now the property of his brother R. N. After fencing his fields and effecting other improvements, Mr. Parks traded this property to his brother for that which he now owns and operates.

Having now established himself on a firm basis and secured the wherewithal to keep a family, Mr. Parks was married, April 5, 1888, to Miss Sarah Rinehart. This lady is the daughter of George Rinehart, a native of Carroll County, Ohio, and who is now a resident of this county. When Mr. Parks first came to this section his nearest grain market was at Wichita. Wild animals were plentiful and buffalo could be found within a day's drive west. In the fall of 1873 Mr. Parks set out with a party of four men on a buffalo hunt, and during their absence of two weeks killed twenty-two of the monarchs of the plain.

Mr. Parks, in addition to being a good farmer, has become a popular citizen. He was elected Township Treasurer in the fall of 1889, an office of which he is still an incumbent. He belongs to the Farmers' Alliance, and with his estimable wife is a member in good standing of the Presbyterian Church.

CHARLES WICHERN, the oldest settler of this county, who is now a resident of Wellington, was born near Hamburg, Germany, October 28, 1839. His grandfather John Henry Wichern, was a native of Hamburg, and spent his entire life in his native land. He was a well educated man and an accomplished linguist and acted as translator in the courts. His son, John H. Wichern, D. D., was also born in Hamburg and attended the schools very steadily in his youth, afterward studying theology and then engaging in home missionary work independently of any church or society. He held various official positions under the Prussian Government. He was for a time an officer of the Department of the Interior,

the whole prison department being under his supervision. He was a member of the Evangelical Church and was the founder of several benevolent and educational institutions. Like his father he spent his entire life in his native land, where his death took place in 1881. He was the father of nine children—Caroline, Elizabeth, Charles, Sophia, Henry, Amanda, John, Mary, and Louis. All were reared to maturity except Mary, who died young.

The subject of this sketch was the eldest son, and the only member of the family who ever came to America. He attended the Hamburg schools very steadily until he was sixteen years of age, and then went to Prussia and advanced his education by attendance at an academy and university. At the age of twenty-one he entered the Prussian army and after being in active service a year, was promoted to a Lieutenancy and served in the Reserve Corps until 1869. During this time he acquired the reputation of an energetic and active young man, a credit to himself and his worthy parentage. He then came to America, and after sojourning for a time in Virginia, in 1870 started to go to California but stopped at Salina, Kan., and concluded to investigate the territory of Southern Kansas. There being no railroads, he purchased a pony and started for the head waters of the Little Arkansas River, and on arrival there found Indians and buffalo in abundance and no white settlers.

Having heard of the new town of Wichita, which had just been laid out, he concluded to make his way there and on his arrival found a few buildings in process of erection. The surrounding country was owned by the Government and was very sparsely settled. He stopped with a man named Weikert and from his home started out to find a suitable place to establish a ranch for cattle-raising. He wished to find a tract including both prairie and timber land close to water, and finally selected the northwestern part of section 3, township 30 south, range 1 west, now known as Sumner County. The land had not yet been surveyed but he built a house of cottonwood logs and went to Emporia, one hundred and twenty-five miles distant, which was the nearest railroad station, and there procured lumber with which to finish his cabin. When the Government survey was made he was obliged to move his house a short distance.

Immediately after locating, Mr. Wichern engaged in the stock business but in the winter of 1871-72 his herds all died and he then undertook general farming, in which he has been highly prospered. He has added to his landed estate, and at the present time owns three hundred and twenty acres, three hundred of which is under cultivation. He continued to reside upon his farm until 1884, when he rented the estate and came to Wellington, where he has since lived and where he is deservedly popular and respected. In politics Mr. Wichern is independent, voting for the candidate whom he thinks best fitted for office. He is a member of the Methodist Episcopal Church. He not only possesses an excellent education, but keeps himself well posted regarding general topics and current events, and manifests an intelligent interest in public enterprises, doing his share in bringing up the status of the county in good citizenship, morality and intelligence.

ALONZO M. REECE, is one of the prominent farmers in this county, owning a finely improved farm of eighty acres, on which he built for himself one of the finest dwellings in this part of the country, and where he has the largest orchard in the vicinity coming into fruitage. He is engaged in general farming and stock-raising and keeps good grades of stock.

William J. Reece, the father of our subject, was born in Clark County, Ohio, July 5, 1831, and about seven years later made his advent into Logan County, Ill., with his father, Samson Reece, who was a member of the first colony that came to that county. There he grew to maturity and on the 23d of December, 1853, was united in marriage with Miss Hannah Hull, was born in Madison County, Ohio, in 1836. Marrying young and starting in life with but one horse and $100, the father of our subject accumulated a fine property,

and became one of the most respected men in this county, in which he held various township and county offices. He was a member of the Cumberland Presbyterian Church, in the faith of which he died in 1882. His widow is still living on the old farm. The parental family comprised four children—our subject, Oswald T., Maria C. (now deceased), and William J.

The subject of this sketch was born on the paternal acres in Logan County, Ill., October 10, 1854, and received a good education in his county, in which he lived until 1876. At that date he came to this State and county and first rented a farm at Oxford upon which he lived two years. He then went to Harper County and took up a claim near Harper City upon which he proved up, and he then spent a year "on the range" and in March, 1883, returning to this county, bought the farm upon which he is now living and made the improvements upon it. Mr. Reece is one of the representative men of the township and is highly respected by all who know him. He has been Trustee of the township two terms and proves an efficient and satisfactory public officer.

In Logan County, Ill., December 24, 1874, the rites of wedlock were celebrated between Mr. Reece and Miss Lucy E., daughter of J. R. Johnson, whose history is found elsewhere in this work. Mrs. Reece was born in Pleasureville, Henry County, Ky., March 7, 1855, and is an educated and cultured lady. To herself and husband five children have been born. Carrie died at the age of two years. The survivors are Floyd, Gertie, Cora and Bessie.

WILLIAM H. FITZ HUGH, M. D. The gentleman with whose name we introduce this biographical record, and whose homestead is familiarly known as "The Hive," has the honor of being the largest land-owner and stock-raiser in township Seventy-Six. He possesses the warrentee deed to eight hundred acres, having his home on section 27, where he has erected substantial buildings and sits under his own vine and fig tree, comparatively independent. He developed the greater part of this farm from land lying in its primitive condition and has been more than ordinarily successful in his labors as a tiller of the soil and his investment of capital.

In noting the career, especially of a successful man, it is natural to revert to his antecedents. The father of our subject was William H. Fitz Hugh, a native of Washington County, Md., and born October 17, 1794. He was of English descent and followed the peaceful pursuits of agriculture. In early manhood he was married to Miss Maria A. Hughes, a maiden of his own county and who was born April 1, 1801. After marriage they settled in Hagerstown, where they reared a family of nine children and spent their entire lives. Of the sons and daughters born to them four are living.

Dr. Fitz Hugh was born in Hagerstown, Md., January 30, 1826. He was reared to manhood on his father's farm and attended the common school there until a lad of eleven years. Afterward he received instruction from private tutors at home. When sufficiently advanced in his studies, he became a student of the Pennsylvania College at Gettysburg, where he attended three years. Then he pursued his studies further in the academy at Hagerstown until a youth of eighteen years.

The study of medicine was entered upon by young Fitz Hugh at Hagerstown, Md., under the tutorship of Drs. Dorsey & Son, in whose office he remained about three years. Later he attended lectures at the University of Maryland. In the meantime, however, he enlisted as a soldier in the United States army and served in the Mexican War about eighteen months. He participated in the battles of Contreras, Churubusco and Molina Del Rey, and was present at the storming of Chapultepec. In the last engagement he was wounded in the head but soon recovered. Upon leaving the army he returned to Maryland and attended another course of lectures at the University, receiving his diploma.

Entering upon the practice of his profession at Martinsburg, Va., Dr. Fitz Hugh resided there nine months when on account of the death of his father he returned home and resumed charge of the farm. Upon withdrawing from this he dropped his professional duties for a time and engaged as a clerk in the store of his uncle in Pennsylvania for one year. The next four years were spent on the old farm, which he operated as a renter. On the 27th of November, 1856, he was united in marriage with Miss Amelia J. Alves at the bride's home near Henderson, Ky. The newly wedded pair took up their abode in Hagerstown where they lived until April, 1857, then removed to Logan County, Ill., where Dr. Fitz Hugh again turned his attention to farming and where, with the exception of two years spent in Pennsylvania in the employ of his uncle, he sojourned until April, 1877.

In April of the year above mentioned Dr. Fitz Hugh came to Kansas and secured eight hundred acres of land on section 27, in Seventy-Six Township, of which he has since been a resident. He named this estate the "hive" after the old farm in Maryland. He commenced his live-stock operations upon a large scale, and he deals in cattle, sheep and swine. He has all the facilities for the successful prosecution of this industry, while his good judgment and ample store of information upon all subjects connected with agriculture can scarcely do otherwise than insure success.

To the Doctor and his estimable lady there have been born two children only, William H., Jr., who married Miss Emmie Alves, and Alves, who is a resident of Wellington. The Doctor has always taken a warm interest in politics and gives his support to the Democratic party. While a resident of Illinois he officiated as Collector of the township for several years. The Doctor and his wife are regular attendants and liberal supporters of the Episcopal Church. The paternal grandfather of Dr. Fitz Hugh, also named William, served as a soldier in the Revolutionary War, and for a time was Aid-de-camp to Gen. Washington. His great-grandfather won distinction as an officer in the British army. William H. Fitz Hugh, Sr., father of our subject, suffered the affliction of blindness several years prior to his death.

Mrs. Fitz Hugh was born near Henderson, Ky., October 7, 1833, and is the daughter of Dr. William J. and Augusta (Hughes) Alves. Her father was the owner of a plantation known as "Hurricane-

nia." Dr. Fitz Hugh enlisted as a private in the Mexican War and on account of excellent service rendered was promoted, first to be Sergeant and then Second Lieutenant, with which rank he was mustered out.

OHN R. SPARR, one of the most highly-respected young farmers of Illinois Township, operates one hundred and sixty acres of land on section 12, and by his straightforward methods in his business affairs, gives promise of occupying in the near future a leading position in his community. He was born in Blair County, Pa., June 14, 1865, and is the son of John Sparr, a native of Center County, that State. The latter when two weeks old was taken by his father to the vicinity of Williamsburg, Pa., where he was reared by his grandparents, Christian and Mary Sparr, his mother, Mrs. Sarah (Fontz) Sparr having died in April, 1820, two weeks after the birth of her son. John Sparr, Sr., upon reaching man's estate, was married in Huntingdon County, Pa., to Miss Susan J. Shultz, who was a native of that county. They settled upon the old Sparr homestead and John Sparr, Jr., departed this life May 13, 1865. His remains were laid to rest in the old family cemetery. The paternal great-parents of our subject was early settlers of the Keystone State and are supposed to have been of German birth, or at least of German ancestry, and the family were almost without exception members of the Lutheran Church, in the faith of which John Sparr, Sr., likewise passed away.

On the maternal side the grandparents of our subject were John and Mary (Beaver) Shultz, natives of Huntingdon County, Pa., wherein they spent their entire lives, dying on the old farm where they reared their family. They also were members of the Lutheran Church. An early progenitor was Henry Shultz, also a native of Huntingdon County, and who married Miss Sarah Solma, of that county. They belonged to the Ger-

man Baptist Church. Anthony Beaver, the paternal great-grandfather of our subject, married Miss Susan Clapper, both of whom it is supposed were natives of Pennsylvania and of German ancestry.

In the fall of 1873 the mother of our subject came to this county with her five children and pre-empted one hundred and sixty acres of land in London Township. They commenced farming in a primitive style, marketing their produce at Wichita and Wellington. Their first dwelling was a structure 10x12 feet in dimensions, built of cottonwood boards. But few houses were in sight, the country being open and the land mostly the property of the Government. Mrs. Sparr kept the post-office in her own house one year. In January, 1875 the sons put up a more substantial dwelling which the family occupied until 1878. Buffalos roamed the country a short distance west, while antelopes and wolves were numerous. There were no churches and religious services were held in schoolhouses and private dwellings. Both John Sparr and his wife were members of the Lutheran Church in the faith of which the father died about 1865.

John Sparr, father of our subject, was married twice; his first wife was Sarah Hall, and a native of Pennsylvania. She died in that State leaving two children, named—Lucy J., now deceased, and William M., living now in Iowa.

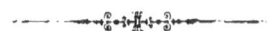

APT. JOSEPH A. CORBETT. Who is there in Chikaskia Township unacquainted with or, at least, unfamiliar with the name of Capt. Corbett, who is one of its most stirring citizens and the hero of a history of more than ordinary interest. He has been for many years successfully engaged in farming and is the owner of four hundred acres of choice land, well improved and finely situated on section 9. There are few enterprises of any importance and none affecting the progress and advancement of the people to which he has not given his hearty assent. An active member of the Republican party, he takes a lively interest in politics, remaining loyal to the old flag since the time when, in the State of Kentucky, his rebel neighbors twice put the rope around his neck, threatening to hang him on account of his adherence to the Union. He has served as Justice of the Peace in Chikaskia Township, has officiated as a member of the school board in his district, is President of Dobbs Farmers' Alliance, and at Milan belongs to the A. H. T. A., is Secretary of the Masonic Lodge and Post Commander of John Goldy Lodge, No. 90, G. A. R. In his farming operations he raises the crops common to this region and is somewhat interested in live stock.

The fourth in a family of five children, the subject of this notice was born October 20, 1838, in Gallatin, Sumner County, Tenn., and is the son of Joseph and Agnes L. (Bigus) Corbett, who were natives, respectively, of Pennsylvania and Virginia. The father emigrated to Tennessee when a young man, where he was married and employed himself as a carpenter. He left Tennessee with his family in 1854, removing to Kentucky, and thence, in 1857, crossing the Mississippi into St. Charles County, Mo. The mother died there that year, the father lived until 1865, spending the closing years of his life in Kentucky. There are living of the parental family only two children, the one besides Joseph A. being D. W., a resident of Kentucky. One son, William D., was a very prominent physician and died in Hickman, Ky., in 1878, from the effects of yellow fever. On account of the services which he had rendered during that terrible epidemic, Gov. Blackburn recommended the appropriation of funds by the Legislature for the erection of a monument over the grave of him who had so faithfully performed his duties amid disease and death.

Leaving home when a youth of sixteen years, young Corbett commenced the battle of life wholly dependent upon his own resources, having no capital and few friends or advisers. He was a courageous and adventurous lad and soon, in 1857, he joined an expedition to chastise the Mormons, the enterprise being under the command of Gen. Albert

Sidney Johnston. This occupied seven months. Afterward Mr. Corbett lived in Missouri one year, then returning to Kentucky located in Butler County and engaged in farming two years and until after the outbreak of the Civil War. On January 1, 1862, he enlisted as a Union soldier in Company B, Twenty-sixth Kentucky Infantry, which was attached to the Army of the Cumberland in Gen. Buell's division. Prior to this, however, he had been in the smoke and heat of battle, eight miles west of Russellville, Ky., where there were about three thousand rebel cavalry as the outposts of Gen. Buckner's army at Bowling Green, Capt. Netter of Company B, Twenty-sixth Kentucky Infantry, took sixteen men, including Mr. Corbett, who had volunteered to accompany him, and procuring turpentine carried it in canteens to a bridge across the Whip-poor-will River, which was guarded by sixteen rebels, with whom they had a desperate fight but carried the day, firing the bridge and thus cutting off communication. They left their wounded in care of a Union man who lived in the vicinity and escaped from a whole battalion of rebels who pursued them for forty miles.

After entering the regular service our hero took part in some of the principal battles of the war, viz: Shiloh, Perryville, Kingston, Ft. Fisher and Wilmington. After the fight at Perryville, the regiment was transferred to the Eastern Army under the command of Gen. Scofield. In the meantime Mr. Corbett had been promoted to be Sergeant and in 1864, at the end of his term of enlistment, he veteranized. He frequently executed important commissions, and at one time with a squad of four men under his command was left to guard an immense quantity of stores left on the bank of the Cumberland River at Harpeth Shoals. He succeeded in saving the stores in the face of the army of Gen. Wheeler, five thousand strong, being assisted by Capt. Allen of the gunboat "St. Clair" and his marines.

In December, 1864, Sergt. Corbett was commissioned as First Lieutenant by President Lincoln, being attached to the One-hundred Twenty-fifth United States Infantry as Regimental Quartermaster. He remained in the service after the close of the war, and in August, 1866, was presented with a captain's commission and made the acting assistant Quarter-master at Ft. Cummings, New Mexico, where he sojourned three and one-half years. Then on account of failing health he was obliged to send in his resignation.

Returning now to Kentucky, Capt. Corbett followed the peaceful pursuits of agriculture until 1883. That year he left the Blue Grass regions, and coming to Kansas took up his abode in Wellington, and was there engaged as a dealer in real estate two years. His next removal was to his present farm. He took unto himself a wife and helpmate in the person of Mrs. Mary J. Johnson, the wedding being celebrated at the bride's home in Kentucky, May 20, 1882. Mrs. Corbett was born June 25, 1854, in Smith County, Tenn., and is the daughter of John and Amanda (Walker) Kittle, who were natives of that State, and there spent their entire lives, the father dying in 1857 and the mother in 1876. Their family consisted of five children, of whom Mrs. Corbett was the third, and only one living. The Captain and his excellent lady are the parents of one child only, a daughter, Sierra Florieta, who was born February 11, 1883. Mrs. Corbett is connected with the Missionary Baptist Church at Milan. In his younger years the Captain also belonged to the Baptist Church.

AMES Q. BROWN, who has been a resident of this county since 1875, is well worthy of representation in a volume of this nature, his good citizenship, his fine moral character, and his intelligence and practical ability in agriculture, alike entitling him to respect. His paternal ancestry is of Scotch and English blood, and the long line of honored lineage have transmitted from generation to generation, sturdy qualities of manhood, and a record for industry and honor which are the best inheritance a man can have.

Going back to the fifth generation prior to our subject, we find James Brown, who was born in 1686, and died in 1770. The next in the line is another James, born in Dorchester County, Md., in 1710, who married Priscilla, daughter of Judge Thomas White, and who died in 1791. Following him comes his son, White Brown, who was born in the same county as himself, the date of his birth being March 23, 1749. After reaching years of maturity, White Brown engaged in tilling the soil in Delaware, and was a resident of that same State until 1801, when he emigrated to the Northwest Territory, and settled in what is now Ross County, Ohio. He was one of the first settlers in that almost untrodden wilderness, where bear, deer, wild cats, coons, beavers, and wild turkeys were numerous for many years, and where many privations and hardships and frequent dangers beset the pathway of the frontiersman. He settled on military land, buying a large tract for twelve and a half cents per acre, which is still owned by his descendants. His land was heavily timbered, with an excellent water-power on it, and after damming the stream, he put up one of the first mills ever built in that section. He cleared his farm and operated it and the mill, continuing to reside there until he had reached the advanced age of ninety-three years, when he departed this life. His wife bore the maiden name of Anna Withgott, and she, like her husband, earned the respect of their contemporaries for her cheerful and arduous labors in the development of a new country, and in the proper rearing of her family.

The father of our subject was christened Nelson, and was born in Newcastle County, Del., he being twelve years old when his parents went to the Northwest Territory. He learned the trade of cloth manufacturing, and built a woolen factory on Deer Creek, the same stream his father's mill was on, and after operating the factory some years, abandoned it and devoted his attention entirely to farming. He was a large land owner, holding thirteen hundred acres in Ross and Pickaway Counties, and on his farm he resided until his death in 1862. He was an old-line Whig, and upon the disintegration of that party, became a Republican. His wife was Miss Anna Maria, daughter of John and Sarah Hughes, who was born in Maryland, and who departed this life in Chillcothe, Ohio. She was a worthy member of the Methodist Episcopal Church.

The parental family comprised twelve children, and nine reached maturity. These are: Ellen, Sarah, White, James, Eliza, Rebecca, Elizabeth, Allen F., and Alice.

James Q. Brown, the subject of this sketch, was born in Ross County, Ohio, November 13, 1828, and was reared and educated there, beginning to assist his father in the woolen factory as soon as he was large enough, and later bearing his share in the farm labor. He remained with his parents until twenty years old, and then farmed in connection with his father for a time, and in 1849 went to Illinois on horseback. He located in Pike County, and with his brother bought an improved farm, upon which he lived seven years. He then changed his location to Macon County, and bought a four hundred-acre farm seven miles from Decatur, making that his home until 1864, when he sold it and moved into the town.

While a resident of Decatur, Mr. Brown dealt in land and lumber, continuing to abide there until 1873, after which he spent two years in Cameron, Mo., whence he came to this county. He purchased one hundred and sixty acres in Wellington Township, where he still lives, and where he has erected buildings suited to the various needs of agricultural life, has fenced and otherwise improved the place, which, when he took possession, had no improvements but twenty acres of broken sod, and made of it a highly productive and attractive estate. In addition to this Mr. Brown has one hundred and sixty acres in Sumner Township. At the date of his arrival here, Wellington was a village of about two hundred and fifty inhabitants, and a few miles west deer and buffalo were still plentiful, while Wichita, thirty miles distant, was the nearest railroad station.

The marriage of Mr. Brown took place in Pike County, Ill., in 1856, his bride being a native of that county. She bore the name of Sarah F. Chenoweth, and a daughter of Samuel and Rachael Chenoweth, whose sketch occupies another place in this volume. The happy union has been blessed by the birth of two children: Seymour N. married Sarah G. Gatliff, and lives in Wellington; Cleo resides in Kingman.

Mr. and Mrs. Brown have been members of the

Methodist Church for many years. He is a Republican, and never fails to cast his vote in the interest of good government, manifesting an intelligent interest in everything which pertains to the good of the community. Possessing well-informed minds and pleasant manners, Mr. and Mrs. Brown are deservedly popular among their neighbors and associates. The wife of Seymour N., died January 21, 1889, in Wellington, leaving one child, named Charley C., aged nine years, who makes his home with his grandparents, our subject and wife.

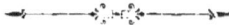

ENRY BOWERS, a retired farmer now living in Wellington, is of German ancestry, and two generations of his progenitors were natives of the Keystone State, where the line was planted in Colonial times. There Daniel Bowers first opened his eyes to the light, and so also did his son, John, who was born in 1803. About six years after the birth of the latter, the family removed to Ohio, and among the pioneers of Stark County, Daniel Bowers carried on his employments of farming and butchering. The later years of his life were passed in Allen County, and he died at a ripe age.

John Bowers grew to manhood in Stark County, and there married Miss Elizabeth Bysel, who was born near Harrisburg, Pa., and while quite young, was brought by her father to Ohio. Mr. Bowers took up a tract of timber land, and cleared and resided upon it until 1835, when he undertook the labors of a frontiersman in Hancock County, by opening up a tract of timber land about six miles from the present site of Findlay. At that time a few log houses constituted that village, and he built a dwelling of the same kind on his farm. Timber was so abundant in the region, that it was practically valueless, and large black walnut logs were rolled together and burned, to get rid of them. Deer, bears, wild turkeys, coons and wolves were numerous, and the nearest market was Sandusky, sixty miles distant, while for many years railroads were unknown in that region. The settlers were practically home livers, and Mrs. Bowers cooked by a fire-place, carded, spun and wove flax and wool, and clothed her family in cloth made by her own hands. After some years a railroad was extended to Findlay, wooden rails with a strip of iron nailed on the top, forming the track.

Mr. John Bowers cleared a small tract of the land which he had obtained, and after sojourning upon it about three years, sold the property and bought another piece of timber land twelve miles west of Findlay. There he cleared a good farm, upon which he resided until his death, which took place July 6, 1887. His wife passed away on the home farm in 1876. Their family comprised seven sons and three daughters, and the subject of this biography was the first born: Jonathan is now living in Hancock County, Ohio; Andrew J. lives in this city; Philip B., in Seattle, Wash.; Daniel on the homestead in Hancock County, Ohio; Wesley at Geuda Springs, this county; John served in an Ohio Regiment, and was killed at the battle of Chickamauga; Lydia married John Haddox; Elizabeth married D. F. Brooks; and Sarah A. married Moses Fermin. All the sisters are living in the Buckeye State.

The maternal grandfather of our subject was Philip Rysel, who moved from Pennsylvania, to Stark County, Ohio, about the year 1823. He leased a tract of land for a time, and then bought a flour mill on the line between Stark and Wayne Counties, and operated it until his death. During his last years he made his home with a son in Wayne County.

Henry Bowers was born near Canton, Stark County, Ohio, March 11, 1826, and was a lad of nine years when his parents moved to Hancock County. The removal was made with teams through the wilderness, and the father's circumstances being very limited, his children were obliged to assist him as much as possible in clearing the farm, and securing their inheritance. Our subject attended the pioneer schools, and in the intervals labored on the homestead. The schoolhouse was built of logs with the chimney on the outside, constructed of earth and sticks, the floor of puncheon, and roof and door of boards; the windows were of greased paper, and the seats were made by splitting logs, leaving one side smooth, and inserting pins in the other for legs.

Mr. Bowers resided under the parental roof until his marriage, when he bought a tract of Government land in Putnam County, built a log house, himself splitting the puncheon for the floor and clap-boards for the roof, and in this primitive abode the young couple began house keeping, the wife doing her cooking and other household work by the fire-place, as was the custom at that time on farms, and in the frontier settlements. The land upon which they located was timbered, and Mr. Bowers cleared a considerable tract, upon which they lived for six years.

In 1857, Mr. Bowers purchased some prairie land near Gridley, in McLean County, Ill., thirty acres of it being under cultivation, and a log house standing upon it. On this farm the family resided until 1875, good buildings being in the meantime erected, and the acreage thoroughly cultivated and improved. At the date above mentioned, they removed to this county, which Mr. Bowers had visited the year before, and where he had purchased one hundred and sixty acres of land near this city. Twenty acres of the estate were broken, and there was a small frame house upon it. The nearest railroad ran through Wichita, and Wellington was a village of two hundred inhabitants. As soon as the family settled in their new home, Mr. Bowers set to work to farther improve the estate, and when the boom came he took advantage of the high price of land, and sold the greater part of his quarter-section. He still owns twenty acres adjoining the city, and is now also the fortunate possessor of two farms which are rented.

Mr. Bowers has been twice married. The first ceremony took place in 1848, the bride being Miss Lydia A. Fisher, who was born in Stark County, Ohio. She departed this life in 1880, after having borne nine children—Martha J., Levi B., Jasper P., Clinton, Annie, John, Eddie, Minnie, and Abbie D. The second marriage of Mr. Bowers took place in 1881, and the lady with whom he was then united was Miss Mary J. Layman. Her parents, John H. and Catherine (Royer) Layman, were the children of German parents, and were born in Pennsylvania, the father in Cumberland County, and the mother in Lancaster County. Their family comprised five children—Lucinda, Mary J., Sarah A., Daniel, and H. W. Mr. Layman moved to Ohio about the year 1836, and settled in Portage County, where he bought timber land and cleared an excellent farm, upon which his death took place in 1887. In that county Mrs. Bowers first opened her eyes to the light.

Mr. Bowers is a member of the Methodist Episcopal Church, with which he united in 1853, since which time he has served as Treasurer and Steward, and also as Class-Leader for many years. His first wife was a worthy member of the same denomination, and the present Mrs. Bowers is a member in good standing of the Christian Church. In his early life Mr. Bowers was a Democrat, but differing with the party on the question of slavery, at the formation of the Republican party, he identified himself with it, and has ever since given it his suffrage. The upright character, industrious habits, and friendly nature of Mr. Bowers are recognized and appreciated by all with whom he comes in contact, and they accord him a corresponding measure of respect and good will.

ON. ALEXANDER HANNIBAL SMITH. There are few people sojourning any length of time in Sumner County, who are unacquainted with at least the name of Mr. Smith, who is recognized as one of its most popular and prosperous citizens. Nature has endowed him with fine abilities, intellectually, and with great kindliness of disposition, besides the qualities which have made him successful financially. He is of Southern birth and antecedents, his birthplace having been in the vicinity of Bucksville, Cumberland County, Ky., where he first opened his eyes to the light March 30, 1836.

John C. Smith, father of the subject of this notice, was born in Fauquier County, Va., and was the son of Mathew Smith, a native of the city of

Edinburg, Scotland. The latter left home when a boy, and came to America during the colonial times. He located in Virginia, but later entered the Continental Army, in which he arose to the command of a company, being given a captain's commission under Gen. Nathaniel Green, his brother-in-law. He was shot through both limbs and crippled for life. Later he became the owner of land in Virginia, where he spent his last days.

Mathew Smith married Miss Pamelia, a sister of Gen. Nathaniel Green, who, after the death of her husband, removed, in 1811 to Kentucky. The journey was made overland with ox-teams, and the widowed mother was accompanied by her nine children, taking with her her household goods and farm implements. She was a woman of great courage and resolution, and entered a tract of Government land in the timber of Cumberland County, where, with the assistance of her children, she improved a farm, building up a good homestead.

Late in life she removed to Warren County, where she spent her last years. Her son, John C., the father of our subject, was a lad of nine years when the family removed to Kentucky, where he was reared to man's estate. After his marriage he purchased a tract of timber land in Warren County, in what was known as Smith's Grove Valley. He put up a log cabin in the most primitive style, with puncheon floor, and the chimney built outside of earth and sticks. In this pioneer structure the subject of this sketch was born. The mother was a very industrious woman, devoted to her family. She span and wove wool and flax, manufacturing thus all the cloth used in the family, and making up the garments with her own hands. The father cleared a considerable extent of his land, and was prospered in his labors, being finally enabled to erect a good brick house. For some time after the Smith family settled in that region, wild game of all kinds was abundant, including deer and turkeys.

Mrs. Sally D. (Gearhart) Smith, the mother of our subject, was born in Cumberland County, Ky., and was the daughter of Peter Gearhart, a native of Germany. Grandfather Gearhart was reared to farming pursuits, and emigrated to America when a young man, locating in Virginia. He was there married and removed to Kentucky at an early day, settling among the timber of Cumberland County. He cleared a farm and died there. The parents of our subject resided on that farm until their decease, the mother passing away in 1855, and the father in 1857. Six of the ten children born to them lived to mature years, namely: Alexander H., Herschel P., Mereenia, Carroll J., Dobney W., and Julius O.

The subject of this notice was reared to man's estate in his native county, and acquired his early education in the subscription schools, conducted in a log schoolhouse. The temple of learning was erected and furnished in the most primitive manner, the seats being of split logs, upheld by wooden pins, and the chimney built outside of earth and sticks. Light was admitted through an aperture made by removing a log from one side of the building, and closed by a wooden shutter. The school was conducted mostly during the winter season, while in summer young Smith assisted his father on the farm. He remained with his parents as long as they lived, and then being the eldest child, the care of the family devolved upon him. He managed the farm, and reared the children, taking the place of both father and mother, the youngest child being then two and one-half years old, and his oldest sister, a little girl of seven. The father had made a will, giving to Alexander the homestead with the provision that he was to look after the children until they should be able to take care of themselves. He fulfilled the duties assigned him in an admirable manner and continued to reside on the old farm until 1880. He was a Union man during the Civil War, but took no part therein, and although that section of country was overrun by both armies, he did not in any wise suffer from personal outrage or loss of property.

Disposing of his interests in the Blue Grass State in the year above mentioned, Mr. Smith came to Kansas and purchased city property in Wellington, also farm lands in Sumner County. He has one hundred and sixty acres adjoining the city limits besides other lands in different parts of the county, and has been identified with many of the enterprises which have assisted in the growth and prosperity of Wellington. He was instrumental in the organization of the State Bank, of which he was elected President, and still holds this office. During his early manhood he was a Whig, politically, but later developed into a Jeffersonian Democrat. He was prominent in the politics of his native State and represented Warren County in the Kentucky Legislature, casting his vote for James B. Beck for Senator. Since coming to Kansas, among other positions of trust and responsibility, he served one term as Mayor of Wellington. As a financier he stands pre-eminent, and is now in the enjoyment of not only a large share of this world's goods, but the confidence and esteem of his fellowmen. Of late years he has operated extensively as a money loaner.

Mr. Smith was married in his native county, in 1857, to Miss Rebecca Shobe. Mrs. Smith, like her husband, was born in Warren County, Ky., and there reared to womanhood, receiving a common-school education, and becoming versed in all useful household duties. The twelve children born of this union were named respectively: Herschel P., Jesse G., Moses S., Carrie C. L., Anna, Golsen N., Girden B., Walter, Hannibal, P. F., Talmadge and Dudley.

R. S. EWING SMITH. The gentleman with whose name we introduce this biographical record is recognized as the leading dentist of Wellington and a member of the profession who thoroughly understands his calling in all its details. He was born in the town of Princeton, Gibson County, Ind., and is the son of Jesse Smith, a native of Glasgow, Scotland and who was born in 1794. The latter when quite young emigrated with his mother and sisters to America, locating with them in Raleigh, N. C. There Jesse was reared and educated and remained until 1830. That year he emigrated to Indiana and located among the early settlers of Princeton. This was before the days of railroads and canals and the removal was made overland with teams.

Jesse Smith during his younger years had learned the trade of a carpenter, which he followed after removing to Indiana until 1845. That year he pushed on further westward into Jefferson County, Ill., and purchasing a farm near Spring Garden, sojourned there until 1876. That year he came to this State and settled in Wabaunsee County, near Alma. His death took place at the home of his son, Alonzo, in 1877.

The mother of our subject bore the maiden name of Rhoda P. Dimmick. She was born in Vermont and was the daughter of Adam Dimmick, a native of New York State, who removed to Vermont and then to Indiana, being one of the earliest settlers of Gibson County. He cleared a farm from the timber and there spent his last years. To the parents of our subject there was born a family of twelve children, of whom the record is as follows: William died at the age of ten years in Indiana; John B., during the Civil War served in the Thirty-sixth Illinois Infantry and died in the army; Octavia became the wife of James Prigmore of Spring Garden, Ill.; Augustus practiced dentistry in Sedalia, Mo., and is now deceased; B. Frank is a resident of Weir, Kan.; S. Ewing, our subject, was the next in order of birth; James died in Lutesville, Mo.; Delia died in Kansas; Halla and Matilda, are twins; the first mentioned became the wife of Jonathan Casebolt, the inventor of the curve to the cable car system and lives in San Francisco, Cal.; Matilda married George Thomas of Linnville, Ind.; Thomas is a resident of Union, Ind.; Alonzo resides in Wabaunsee, this State.

After the removal of the family to Illinois Dr. Smith made his home for a time with a sister, Mrs. Prigmore. Her husband was a wheelwright with which trade Dr. Smith became quite familiar and at the same time completed his studies in the common school. In 1859 he went to Philadelphia and studied dentistry, remaining there two years. At the expiration of this time the outbreak of the Civil War turned his attention in another direction and in 1861, returning to Illinois he enlisted, in February, 1862, in Company I, Sixtieth Illinois Infantry, and served until the close. The greater part of this time he was under the command of Gen. Thomas. At the battle of Lookout Mountain he was wounded and sent to the hospital at Madison, Ind. As soon as able to be of assistance in any way, he was de-

tailed to the hospital service and remained in the army until the expiration of his term of enlistment.

We next find Dr. Smith in Philadelphia where he practiced dentistry two years, then removed to New York City, where he sojourned until 1876, having his office at No. 710 Broadway. In the year above mentioned he set his face toward the Great West and coming to Kansas located in Council Grove, Morris County. In 1882 he repaired to Kerr City, Fla., and in the fall of 1883 he purchased one thousand acres of land at Lake Kerr where he planted an orange grove. In 1885 he traded three hundred acres of this land for the Commercial House, the leading hotel in Manhattan, Kan., which he still owns. In 1885 he removed hither to look after his property, remaining until 1888. That year he came to Wellington and opened an office and during a year's time has built up a large practice. He still owns seven hundred acres of his Florida land upon which he has expended large sums of money in improvements.

Dr. Smith was wedded January 25, 1865, at the bride's home in Indiana to Miss Anna Lund. This lady was born in Madison, Ind., and died in Oregon in 1868, leaving one child, F. Ewing, eleven months of age and who was legally adopted by S. D. Ewing, of Ohio. The Doctor contracted a second marriage in 1872 with Miss Helen Love.

Mrs. Helen (Love) Smith was born near Auburn, N. Y., and is the daughter of Volney Love, a native of Niles, that State. Her paternal grandfather was Capt. Samuel Love, a native of Scotland who upon coming to America settled in New York State. He served in the War of 1812 as commander of a company and died in the service. He had married Miss Sarah Bassett, who, after his death became the wife of the father of President Fillmore and spent her last years in Aurora, N. Y. Volney Love was reared on a farm and later conducted a hotel at Skaneateles, N. Y., and at Niles. In 1860 he came to Kansas, settling among the pioneers of Wabaunsee County. He purchased a tract of land and engaged in farming some years prior to the building of a railroad in this region. Later he removed to Alma, Kan., where he was in the United States mail service and where his death took place in the fall of 1876.

The maiden name of the mother of Mrs. Smith was Lydia Coon. She was born in Scipio, Onondaga County, N. Y., and was the daughter of Eli and Margaret (Van Auken) Coon and was married in her native State. She is still living, making her home in Florida. Her two children living are Mrs. Smith and Ida May, the wife of Luther Bovece of St. Augustine, Fla.

Mrs. Smith understands the profession of dentistry nearly as well as her husband and is his efficient assistant in his business. The Doctor belongs to the Congregational Church and is a member of the Masonic fraternity, the Ancient Order of United Workmen, the Knights of Honor and the Grand Army of the Republic.

UDGE JAMES A. RAY, Judge of the District Court of Sumner County, established himself as a resident of Wellington on the 22d of March, 1883, and with the exception of one year, which he spent as Internal Revenue Agent in the employ of the Government, has been continuously engaged in the practice of law. He was born near Bowling Green, Ky., August 22, 1818, and there spent his boyhood and youth, completing a practical education in the common schools. He commenced the reading of law at home and later entered the law office of Halsell & Mitchell and was admitted to practice in 1874. He commenced the duties of his profession in his native town, remaining there three years thereafter. He then removed to Cumberland County, Ky., and accepted the position of Deputy Collector of Internal Revenue, still continuing, however, his law practice. During that time he had many adventures with the Moonshiners whose operations had become quite extensive in that region.

In 1885 Mr. Ray was appointed Judge of the District Court, the district then comprising four counties, he filling a vacancy and serving one year.

He has always been an active supporter of the Republican party, and was at one time the City Attorney at Wellington. While a resident of Kentucky he was active in politics, but since coming to Kansas has been too busy with the duties of his profession to give much attention to public affairs. His religious views coincide with those of the Presbyterian Church, and with which he is connected in Wellington. He bears the reputation among his fellow citizens of an honest man and a useful member of the community.

Judge Ray was married in Berksville, Ky., August 22, 1879, to Mrs. Nana (Dodd) Eckles who was born in Adair County in 1851. Mrs. Ray when quite young went with her parents, Henry and Sarah J. Eckles, to Cumberland County, where she sojourned until her marriage. Of this union there have been born five children, viz: Lawrence W., Roscoe C., Anna, Frederick A. and Clifford. To Mr. and Mrs. Dodd there was born one son, Charles B. who remains with his mother.

The father of our subject was Benjamin Ray, a native of Warren County, Ky., and who married Mrs. Louisa E. Chapman. He farmed in Kentucky until about 1878, and then retired from active labor. Besides our subject, there are living three other sons and one daughter. W. D. is the Republican Postmaster of Russellville, Ky., Charles L. is farming in Texas; Joseph W. lives in Bowie, that State; Katie, Mrs. Hobbs, is a resident of the same place.

AVID N. GILBERT. Among the farmers and stock dealers of Falls Township, the above named gentleman deserves mention, both on account of his excellent character and the share he has in the interests of the county. He has been a resident here since 1875, his home being on one of the best improved farms of the township, the estate comprising two hundred and forty acres on section 12. For several years after his arrival here he dealt largely in sheep, but now gives his attention to farming and cattle dealing. His financial success proves his ability, as he was poor when he began his career, and he has made all that he possesses and is now quite well-to-do.

From a long line of honorable ancestors whose home was in Virginia, and one of whom settled in that State in Colonial days, Mr. Gilbert derives his origin. Prior to the emigration to the Colonies the family had lived in England. The parents of our subject were Samuel and Melvina (Crutcher) Gilbert. The father was born in Lincoln County, Ky., about the year 1801, but spent the most of his life in Taylorsville, Spencer County, where he died in 1877. He was a miller and mechanic, and at one time was quite wealthy but was bankrupted through paying security debts. From early manhood until his death he was a member of the Methodist Episcopal Church. Mrs. Melvina Gilbert was born in Spencer County, Ky., dying there when our subject was but seven years of age.

Our subject was the only child of his parents, and was born December 28, 1829, at Taylorsville, Spencer County, Ky. He was reared in his native town, receiving a common-school education, and in early life doing wool-carding with his father. In 1850 he went to California, but a year later returned to the States and located in Buchanan County, Mo., where he lived until 1856. He then located in Leavenworth County, Kan., where he was successfully engaged in farming and stock-raising until 1873, when he moved to the city of Leavenworth, where he lived until 1875, when he sold out his interests there and became a resident of Sumner County. Here he has since resided, continuing to meet with success in his chosen vocation, and adding to his worldly possessions.

During the war Mr. Gilbert belonged to the Kansas State Militia, and has commissions as First Lieutenant and Captain. He has held various minor township offices, among them that of Justice of the Peace. Politically he has been a Greenbacker since the institution of that party. He is a member of the Farmers' Alliance.

The first marriage of Mr. Gilbert took place in Buchanan County, Mo., October 22, 1852, the bride being Miss Mary Martin, of that county. She was born in Washington County, Ky., in 1828,

and lived until May 1882. She became the mother of four children—Martha A., Samuel J., William W. and Zula V.—all yet living. On October 6, 1881, Mr. Gilbert contracted a second matrimonial alliance, being on this occasion united with Mrs. Elizabeth J. Alexander, of DeLand, Fla. She was born in Taylorsville, Ky., January 15, 1830, and was the widow of William Alexander, by whom she had six children—John L., Katie, William, Anna, Susie and Joseph. Her present marriage has been childless.

A view of Mr. Gilbert's residence will be found on another page.

AARON A. ENDERS. Few men in Falls Township have so valuable a farm or so pleasant a home as he whose name introduces this sketch. His estate consists of one hundred and sixty acres of finely improved land on section 17, of which he took possession in 1885. The dwelling is one of the noticeable ones of the vicinity, and all the buildings upon the estate are well built, affording adequate shelter for crops and stock. The entire attention of Mr. Enders is turned to farming and the stock business, and his capability is being abundantly displayed. His excellent financial standing is due to his own efforts, every dollar that he possesses having been made by himself.

The birth of Mr. Enders occurred in Dauphin County, Pa., August 15, 1842, and on the farm where he first saw the light he was reared to man's estate. He received a good common-school education, and an insight into the business he is now following, his father being a life-long farmer. At the age of twenty-one years he began railroading, but afterward followed mining in his native State three years. He then learned the trade of a stonemason, working at it until 1876, when he turned his attention to farming. In 1881 he came to this county, purchased the land which he now occupies, and in a short time moved upon it..

The parents of our subject are Samuel and Leah (Etter) Enders, who are natives of Dauphin and York Counties, Pa., respectively; they were reared, married, and still live in that State. The father is a member of the German Reformed Church, while his wife is a member of the United Brethren Church. Socially Mr. Enders belongs to the Knights of Pythias. His family consists of the following children —Isabella, Aaron A., Rebecca, Louisa, Charles and Ann J. The Enders family is of German stock, the great-grandfather of our subject having been born in the Fatherland.

Aaron Enders and Miss Susan A. Miller celebrated their marriage rites January 6, 1870. The bride was born in the same county as her husband, her natal day being February 5, 1845. Her parents, Christian B. and Mary (Wartle) Miller, now live in this county. She is an estimable woman, looking well to the ways of her household and winning respect from all about her. She has borne her husband three children—Otto, Leedora and Claude. Mr. Enders is a member of the Republican party and of the Farmers' Alliance. He is a man of intelligence and good character, whose life, though unmarked by any remarkable event, is well worthy of record in a volume of this nature. On another page will be found a fine view of the home and surroundings of Mr. Enders.

R OBERT F. INGRAM. Although not yet thirty years of age, the subject of this sketch may be called an old settler of Kansas, and in her borders few, if any, men can be found who have exhibited more energy and capability than he. He was born in West Virginia, April 1, 1863, and was about four years old when his parents came to Kansas, settling in Johnson County, near Olathe. After remaining there some eight years a removal was made to this county, and

section 31, Osborn Township, became the home of the family.

When fourteen years old young Ingram began life for himself, and for some years prior to the death of his father, which took place in 1882, he had sole charge of his father's affairs. When he became of age, he purchased and removed to the farm which he now occupies in Ryan Township. It comprises eighty acres of section 25, is thoroughly and intelligently cultivated, and about sixty head of stock are carried upon it. The present residence was erected in 1886, at a cost of $1,600, and is as fine a dwelling as can be found in the township. Mr. Ingram also owns eighty acres in Missouri. Besides carrying on his home place he runs two steam threshers, and such is the confidence of his fellow-citizens in his judgment that they have made him Road Overseer, feeling satisfied that the interests of the agriculturists will be safe in his hands.

On January 27, 1886, the interesting ceremony took place which transformed Miss Edith P. Waters into Mrs. R.F. Ingram. The bride was born on the 10th of November, 1865, to Gardner and Sarah Waters, and is the fourth of their five children. Mr. and Mrs. Waters were natives of Missouri. The father, who was a farmer, died in 1870, and his widow subsequently married F. B. Crigmore, and now lives in this county. Mr. and Mrs. Ingram were the parents of two children, both of whom died in infancy.

Mr. Ingram takes a deep interest in politics, and exercises the elective franchise in behalf of the candidates on the Democratic ticket, his judgment concurring in the principles which they are expected to uphold. He and his wife belong to the Christian Church, are regular attendants at the Sunday-school, and their intelligent minds, cordial natures and upright lives, endear them to a host of friends.

The parents of our subject, William and Elizabeth Ingram, were natives of West Virginia, and were married in that State. The father served in the Fiftieth Pennsylvania Infantry during the Civil War, and his death was occasioned by disease contracted in the army. The mother died in 1868, and the father subsequently married Miss

Margaret Fletcher, who is now living in Osborn Township, this county. The first marriage of William Ingram was blessed by the birth of seven children, six of whom are now living, our subject being the fourth in order of birth; the second marriage resulted in the birth of six children.

VAN R. JONES, one of the early settlers of Oxford Township, came to this region in March, 1871, and secured a quarter section of land on Slate Creek. Subsequently he traded for that which his widow now occupies. He put up a good frame house that same year, and was joined by his wife in February, 1872, the latter driving from Humboldt. Together they lived and labored until the death of Mr. Jones, which occurred February 9, 1885.

The subject of this sketch was born in Merionethshire, North Wales, November 8, 1821, and lived there until a man of twenty-nine years. He then emigrated to the United States, settling in 1850 in Madison County, N. Y. From there he removed to Dayton, Ohio, and in the vicinity of that now flourishing city, engaged in farming. There also he married Miss Clara Davis, March 15, 1856. They removed to East Virginia in May following, purchasing a farm in Loudoun County, and sojourned there until the outbreak of the Rebellion. After the second battle of Bull Run they removed to Washington, Mr. Jones having been taken prisoner and held for four months, notwithstanding the fact that he was neither a citizen of the United States or a soldier in the Union Army. After being released he lived with his family in Washington until 1871, and then they all came to Kansas. Mr. Jones was reared in the doctrines of the Church of England, to which he afterward loyally adhered.

Mrs. Clara (Davis) Jones was born at Pompey Hollow, Onondaga County, N. Y., March 13, 1833, and is the daughter of Allen Davis, a native of Cooperstown, N. Y., whence he removed to the above-mentioned place. He was there married to

Miss Chloe Benson, and they lived in Pompey Hollow until the death of the mother, which occurred September 23, 1847. Next they removed to Madison County, N. Y., where Miss Davis remained with the family until her marriage. Allen Davis met his death by drowning in Oneida Lake in June, 1872, at the age of seventy-two. To Mr. and Mrs. Jones there were born six children, of whom but two are living: Edward R., the main stay of his mother, was born in Washington, in 1866, and has charge of the homestead; Nellie A., also lives with her mother; John died at the age of five years; Molly died when sixteen months old; Robert and Catherine died at the ages of three months and six years, respectively. Mrs. Jones is a lady highly respected in her community, and a consistent member of the Episcopal Church.

At the organization of the school district in which they lived, Mr. and Mrs. Jones were present, and the latter was the only one casting her vote for a schoolhouse who is still living here. Mr. Jones, although by no means a politician, kept himself well informed upon public events, and officiated as a Justice of the Peace. He was a Greenbacker, with Democratic proclivities.

ARREN J. WOLLAM is an enterprising and progressive farmer of Green Township, who was born in Columbiana County, Ohio, November 9, 1851, and is a son of Alfred Wollam, a tiller of the soil in the Buckeye State. In 1863 Alfred Wollam with his family, which consisted of a wife, seven sons and two daughters, removed to Mercer County, where he and his wife still reside, and where our subject grew to manhood.

Mr. Wollam, of whom we write, acquired an excellent education, and early in life, adopted the profession of a teacher, spending the winters in professional work, and during the summers working upon his father's farm until he was twenty-two years old. He taught sixteen terms of school in

Mercer County, seven of them being successive in his home district, and since coming to Kansas has spent one term in similar employment.

At the home of the bride in Mercer County, Ohio, August 16, 1873, Mr. Wollam was united in marriage with Miss Elscina, daughter of Wesley Copeland. The bride was born in Anglaize County, Ohio, June 15, 1851, and has been an able assistant and loving companion since their marriage. After that event the young couple continued to reside in Mercer County until the spring of 1883, when they removed to Kansas, locating on section 29, Green Township, where they have ever since resided. There Mr. Wollam now owns one hundred and sixty acres of fertile and productive land, on which excellent buildings have been erected and other good improvements made. Since coming to this State he has devoted considerable time to carpentering, and has built several houses in Green Township. He is a good workman at the trade, as well as a successful farmer. The family of Mr. and Mrs. Wollam comprises four living children—Nellie, Alfred, Oma and Carl; and two infant daughters, Eva and Gertie, were removed from them by the reaper—Death.

Mr. Wollam is an active worker in the Farmers' Alliance, and has been business agent since the organization of the body here. He has held the office of Trustee of Green Township for three successive terms. He takes an active part in political matters, laboring earnestly for the advancement of the Republican party. In July, 1888, he was sent as a delegate to the State Republican Convention. In the fall of 1889 he was the Republican candidate for County Clerk, but was defeated by William H. Carnes. Few men of his years within the bounds of Kansas possess a wider fund of information, a more agreeable manner or a more energetic nature than does he, and his reputation among his associates is that of an upright man and reliable citizen.

————◆◇◆————

WILLIAM H. LASSELL. The tasteful and attractive home of this gentleman is located on section 29, Bluff Township, and its appearance and surroundings are conclusive evidences to the passerby that the owner is in a condition of financial prosperity, and that the family are possessed of refined tastes. These indications would not be belied by closer investigation, as the estate is one of the best farms in the township, the dwelling, barns and other improvements being excellent and adequate, and the entire place pervaded by an air of neatness and order highly creditable to its owner and operator. The interior of the residence presents equal signs of good management, and the family are found to be cultured, cordial and agreeable.

Mr. Lassell was born in Clinton County, N. Y., May 25, 1840, to Harris and Lydia (Fisk) Lassell, and is the sixth in a family of seven children. The eyes of his father first opened to the light in Swanton, Vt., March 8, 1803, and when a young man he took up his abode in Otsego County, N. Y. There he married a young lady of that county, and engaging in the mill and lumber business, continued to reside in the Empire State until 1853, at which time he moved to Green County, Wis. In the latter State he followed farming until his death, which occurred in January, 1885. He accumulated considerable means and left an estate worth $12,000. He was a member of the Masonic fraternity, and of Republican politics. Mrs. Harris Lassell was born April 12, 1802, and died in Green County, Wis., February 14, 1873. She was the mother of seven children: Ellen and Lewis, the first and fourth born, being now dead. Of the survivors Eliza is the wife of R. W. Button, of Colton, Cal.; Luther J., a lumberman and miner in Arizona; Lorenzo H., a lumberman in Washington; and Emily A., the wife of Charles Smiley, a farmer in Albany, Wis.

The gentleman who is the subject of this biography was reared to the age of twelve years in his native county in the Empire State, and spent the remainder of his years to early manhood, in Green County, Wis. In 1859, when nineteen years of age, he crossed the plains to California and remained on the Pacific Slope until 1868, when he returned to Green County, Wis., and engaged in farming there during the succeeding eight years. He then removed to Bremer County, Iowa, and in 1878 came to Sumner County, Kan., and pre-empted one hundred and sixty acres on sections 28, 29, 32 and 33 of Bluff Township. He has since made his home here, has acquired an excellent reputation among his fellow men and proved himself a useful citizen. He has served as Justice of the Peace, is a member of the Masonic fraternity and of the Republican party.

The marriage of Mr. Lassell was celebrated March 11, 1871, his bride being Miss Celia Taylor, of Avon, Rock County, Wis. Her parents, James H. and Caroline (Conger) Taylor, are natives of Fairfield, Vt., who emigrated to Wisconsin about the year 1845, and are still residing there. Mrs. Lassell was born in Delevan,Wis., on the 7th of July, 1848, and possesses some rare accomplishments. She was graduated from the White Water (Wis.) Normal School in 1872, and taught school several years before her marriage. Five bright boys and girls cluster about the fireside of Mr. and Mrs. Lassell, and gladden their parents' hearts by their growing intelligence and youthful courtesy. They bear the names of Caroline L., Harris J., Ada M., Wallace A. and Louisa A.

— ·✦✧✦ ·—

JOHN C. WEBBER, M. D. The legal profession of Perth and vicinity finds a worthy representative in Dr. Webber, who established himself at this place in 1886. Being equipped with a thorough knowledge of the duties of his profession, he soon established himself in the esteem and confidence of the people, and is now in the enjoyment of a good practice. He is essentially a Western man, and was born in Davis County, Iowa, March 17, 1857.

The subject of this notice is the son of David Webber, who was born near Vincennes, Ind., in 1836, and who died at the early age of thirty-seven years in Sibley County, Minn. In early life he emigrated to Missouri and thence to Davis County, Iowa. He went to Minnesota in 1870, and lived but three years thereafter, dying after a short illness, in 1873, from the effects of a suddenly-contracted cold while out in a snow storm. He was a chair-maker by trade, an industrious and law-abiding citizen, and a staunch supporter of the Republican party.

The paternal grandfather was Nathaniel B. Webber, who was born in the State of Maine in 1801, and who died in Texas at the advanced age of eighty-three years.

The mother of our subject, who bore the maiden name of Frances S. Kein, was born in South Carolina, and is now living in Davis County, Iowa. There were born to her and her husband six children, viz: John, Sarah, Mary, Ambrose, Isaac and David, all of whom are living, and those besides John C., making their homes mostly in Iowa.

Dr. Webber spent his early years in a comparatively uneventful manner under the home roof, attending the common school, and being variously employed until making up his mind to adopt the medical profession, he spent two years at the Southern Iowa Normal school at Bloomfield. After the proper time spent in reading medicine, he entered the College of Physicians and Surgeons at Keokuk, Iowa, from which he was duly graduated, and commenced the regular practice of his profession in Savannah, Iowa, where he met with good success for the following five years. He was married May 10, 1884, in Iowa, to Miss Florence Brunk. He then came to Perth where he has since remained. This lady was born in Grayson County Ky., August 6, 1863, and is the daughter of Samuel and Ann (Gray) Brunk, who were likewise natives of the Blue Grass State. Upon leaving that region, in 1870, they removed to Davis County, Iowa, where they now live and where the father is engaged in farming. The Doctor and his amiable lady are the parents of three children, namely: Gaillard, Glen and an infant unnamed. The family residence is pleasantly situated in the southeast part of the city, forming an attractive home, and the Doctor and Mrs. Webber enjoy the friendship and acquaintance of the best people of their community.

——◇——

JUDGE JOHN T. SANDERS. The city of Wellington recognizes in Judge Sanders one of its most important and useful citizens. He has been connected with many of its important enterprises and has uniformly given his

support and encouragement to whatever would assist in its advancement and welfare. He was at one time Mayor of the city, and served nine years as a member of the Board of Education, being President of the same for five years. He holds the office of Probate Judge, having been first elected in 1886, and after serving two years, was re-elected in 1888. The varied duties associated with the position he has discharged with eminent ability and to the general satisfaction. Politically, since becoming a voting citizen, he has been identified with the Republican party. He was a charter member and the first Commander of James Shields Post, No. 57, G. A. R., and also belongs to Wellington Lodge, No. 150, A. F. & A. M., Wellington Lodge, No. 133, I. O. O. F., and Sumner Chapter, No. 37, R. A. M.

A gentleman still in the prime of life, Mr. Sanders was born June 20, 1842, his native place being Spring Mills, Richland County, Ohio. His father, James Steel Sanders, was a native of Virginia, born in Frederick County, February 13, 1809, while the paternal grandfather, Isaac Sanders, was a native of London, England, and was born about 1765. Isaac Sanders came to America when eighteen years of age and located in Frederick County, Va., where he died in 1822. He was by occupation a weaver, and was twice married. His first wife bore him two children, Joshua A. and William. The latter died in Virginia when young, and the former passed away in Mississippi about 1833.

Isaac Sanders contracted a second marriage with Elizabeth Steel, who was born in 1776, in Frederick County, Va., and died in Richland County, Ohio, September 7, 1859. Her father, Thomas Steel, was born in Ireland, and her mother in Wales. At an early day they emigrated to America, and located in Virginia. Elizabeth Steel Sanders had four brothers and two sisters, all natives of the same county in the Old Dominion. She bore Mr. Sanders seven children, as follows: Mary Ann, Elizabeth, Rebecca, Thomas, James S., William C. and Sarah. All are dead with the exception of James S. and Sarah.

After spending his boyhood in Virginia, James S. Sanders emigrated to Westmoreland County, Pa., in 1825, and four years later was married at Greens-

burg, that county. In 1835 he removed to Ohio, settling in Richland County, which was the home of the family for a number of years. His means were limited and the opportunities for a poor man not so good as those offered further West.

Accordingly, in 1846, the elder Sanders started with his family for Indiana with an ox-team and a covered wagon. They carried their household effects, cooking and camping by the way-side. Locating in Lake County the father took up a tract of Government land in the timber, four miles from any settlers. The family lived in the wagon while a log cabin was being erected, this being chinked with chips and clay. The chimney was built outside of earth and sticks. The mother had no stove and did all her cooking by the fireplace. They kept sheep and raised flax, the mother breaking the latter, and spinning and weaving both flax and wool. She thus made all the clothing for the family, and everything required for the household.

There then roamed in the wilds of Indiana, deer, bear, wolves and other wild animals, and whatever the larder lacked in other provisions, there was always plenty of meat. The Sanders family were prospered in their labors at felling the trees and tilling the soil, and the father accumulated land until he had about two hundred acres, all of which they cleared. After several years, selling out, they purchased three hundred and twenty acres of timber, four miles distant. The greater part of this was also cleared, and an orchard was set out and good buildings erected. The country grew up around them, peopled by a happy and prosperous community, and the Sanders family became well-to-do.

James Sanders, however, not yet satisfied with his surroundings, sold out again, but now wisely retiring from active labor, left the farm and removed to the village of Westville, where he and his estimable wife are still living. The maiden name of the mother of our subject was Mary Haines. She was born April 1, 1808, in Westmoreland County, Pa., and was the daughter of Frederick Haines, of German descent, who was born in Northampton County, Pa., where he married Joanna Jarret, of English ancestry. Soon after their marriage they emigrated to Westmoreland County, Pa., where were born to them nine children, four boys and five girls. The mother died about 1841, and the father about 1857. Three of the children survive.

To James and Mary Sanders there was born a family of eight children: William P., the eldest living, is a resident of Bremer County, Iowa; Catherine E. married John Shaw, and is a resident of Westville, Ind.; Reuben H. lives in Door Village, Ind., and is a minister of the Methodist Episcopal Church; James F., a resident of McCallsburg, Iowa; Johanna M. married Lemiah Shaw, and she is deceased; Benjamin F. is a resident of Chicago, Ill.; John T. was the next in order of birth; Rachel J. is the wife of Sanford Culbertson, and lives in Westville, Ind.

The subject of this sketch was a boy of six years when his parents removed to Indiana. He distinctly remembers many of the incidents of the overland journey, and of pioneer life there. His early studies were conducted in the old log schoolhouse, the benches of which were made by splitting small trees, hewing off one side and inserting wooden legs. He usually attended school three months during the winter season. The balance of the year he assisted in clearing land and tilling the soil. He remained under the parental roof until 1860, and then commenced working out by the month, being thus occupied until after the outbreak of the Civil War.

Resolving now to have a hand in the preservation of the Union, young Sanders, a youth of nineteen years, enlisted, June 25, 1861, in Company B, Twentieth Indiana Infantry, for three years, or during the war. This regiment participated in the most important battles of the war, namely: the Chickahominy, Hampton Roads, Norfolk, Oak Grove, Peach Orchard, White Oak Swamp, Malvern Hills, Kelly's Ford, the second battle of Bull Run, Fredericksburg, Chancellorsville, Gettysburg, the Wilderness, Spottsylvania, Cold Harbor and Petersburg, and a number of minor engagements. In the fall of 1862 Mr. Sanders was seized with inflammatory rheumatism, and conveyed to the hospital in Philadelphia, from which, there seeming little hope of his immediate recovery, he was honorably discharged Dec. 23, 1862. He returned home, but seven days later, being much encouraged by the

improvement in his physical condition, he re-enlisted in Company G, Twelfth Indiana Cavalry, in which he served until January 7, 1865. He then participated in the battles of Franklin, Nashville and Hurricane Creek, near Huntsville, Ala. In the latter battle he was wounded in the side, and a bullet passed through both arms, completely disabling him forever from doing manual labor. He was taken to the hospital at Huntsville, and from there to Nashville, later to Indianapolis, and in due time was discharged on account of disability and returned home. He had been mustered in as Sergeant, in which capacity he served until retiring.

Being unable to perform manual labor Mr. Sanders now commenced learning telegraphy, and was soon given a position as night operator at LaFayette, Ind., by the Louisville, New Albany & Chicago Railroad Company. Six months later he was made Station Agent at Wanatah, La Porte County, and continued thereafter as agent and operator for a period of thirteen years. He resigned his position as station agent to accept one as a traveling salesman with the firm of Walter A. Wood & Co., with whom he associated nearly two years.

We next find Mr. Sanders occupied as Station Agent on the St. Louis & South Eastern Railroad, at Mt. Vernon, Ill. Two years later he resigned this position also and accepted one with the Missouri Pacific Railroad Company, first as telegraph operator at Chamois, Mo., and shortly afterward as Station Agent at Herman, that State. Later he was with the Adams Express Company, temporarily assigned to the office in Dodge City. On the 27 of September, 1879, he arrived in Wellington and opened the first express office in the place in the interest of the Adams Express Company. That same day the first express matter was brought to this place by train. When the Wells, Fargo Company extended their route to this point their office was consolidated with that of the Adams, for a time Mr. Sanders had charge of both. He continued his labors as agent for the Wells, Fargo Company until 1886. Then having been elected Probate Judge, he resigned to accept the latter office.

The marriage of John T. Sanders with Miss Hessie E. Crawley, was celebrated at the bride's home, in La Porte, Ind., in April, 1868. Mrs. Sanders was born in Greencastle, Ind., and is the daughter of John and Nellie Crawley, who are now deceased. Of this union there have been born two children, a son and daughter: Claude is a stenographer and clerk in the general office of the Atchison, Topeka & Santa Fe, at Topeka; Maude A. will graduate from the High School in Wellington, at the close of the spring term of 1890.

GEORGE W. GELBACH, junior member of the firm of Dowis & Gelbach, general merchants of Perth, pursues the even tenor of his way as a man giving due attention to the details of his business, and is held in general respect in his community. Like many of the substantial citizens of Sumner County, he is a native of Pennsylvania and was born in Adams County, March 11, 1864. His father, Joseph Gelbach, likewise a native of that county, is still living there on a farm and is now about fifty-five years old. Honest, industrious and steady-going, he is respected by his neighbors and uniformly votes the Democratic ticket.

The ancestors of our subject originated in Germany, where his paternal grandfather, John Gelbach, was born in 1771. He emigrated to America at an early day, settling in Pennsylvania, where he followed blacksmithing and died at the advanced age of ninety-four years. The mother of our subject was in her girlhood Miss Eliza Raffensburger. She was born in Gettysburg, Pa., in 1843, and died at the early age of thirty-seven years. Her parents were Jacob and Eliza (Miller) Raffensburger, natives of Pennsylvania and of English extraction.

To the parents of our subject was born a family of eight children, all of whom are living. They bear the names respectively of John, Mary, Jennie, Laura, Allie, Charles, George W. and Grace. It will thus be seen that George W., of this notice was next to the youngest born. He was reared in his native township and completed his education at

the Millersville State Normal School. After emerging from this institution he commenced teaching, which profession he followed in Pennsylvania until 1884. That year he came to this county and occupied himself as before, until 1887, in the meantime also serving as Postmaster at Perth. That year he associated himself with his present partner, and has since given his attention to mercantile business.

Mr. Gelbach was maried October 13, 1889, at Perth, to Miss Josie Rosdall. This lady was born in Kentucky, September 11, 1869. Mr. Rosdall came to this county in 1877, and is engaged in farming in Downs Township. He is a man of decided views and votes the straight Democratic ticket.

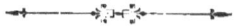

JACOB LEIGHTY. Among the business men of Conway Springs none stand higher in the estimation of their fellow-citizens than Mr. Leighty, whose thorough workmanship, honorable business methods and upright character, alike entitle him to their respect. He has been engaged in the harness business in this place since February, 1888, prior to which time he had been a resident of Wellington for two years, and in that place also, as in other towns in which he has lived, he was ranked among the best citizens.

The birth of Mr. Leighty took place in Connelsville, Fayette County, Pa., January 25, 1846, and in the same county, his father, Daniel S. Leighty, was also born. The latter was a son of Jacob Leighty, who lived in the section of Pennsylvania where his son and grandson were born, and where he breathed his last. Daniel Leighty was a carpenter by trade, and in 1856 removed his family to Warren County, Ill., which was his home until his death. In 1861, he joined the Union army as a private in the First Illinois Cavalry, was captured by the Confederates at Lexington, Mo., but was afterwards paroled and re-enlisted. In the Eleventh Illinois Cavalry he served until January, 1864, when at Vicksburg he was stricken down with chronic diarrhœa which caused his death. For many years he was a member of the United Presbyterian Church; his political adherence was given to the Republican party. His wife, in her maidenhood Miss Rebecca Gilchrist, was also a native of Fayette County, Pa., and belonged to a notable family of Scotch-Irish, who emigrated to America before the Revolution, making their settlement in the Keystone State. Her death occurred in Warren County, Ill., March 12, 1874. To her and her husband seven children were born, named respectively, Joseph W., Mathew, Jacob, Elizabeth B., Edward, Anna and Walter.

The gentleman whose name initiates this sketch was reared to his tenth year in his native county in the Keystone State, and then accompanied the other members of the family to Illinois, where he continued his studies in the common schools, acquiring a good understanding of the branches taught therein. His early life was spent on a farm, which he left at the age of eighteen to begin work at the harness-maker's trade at Galva, Ill. He enlisted in May, 1864, in the One Hundred and Thirty-eighth Illinois, was discharged the 14th of October of the same year. In 1867 he returned to his home and remained there two years after which he engaged in the harness business in Osage City, Kan. Some three years later he returned to Warren County, Ill., established himself in business at Monmouth, and carried on the establishment there until August, 1882, when he returned to Osage City and there remained two years. From that time until February, 1886, he had no permanent location, but at that date he established himself in Wellington, Kan., whence he subsequently removed to Conway Springs, as before noted.

Mr. Leighty was united in marriage with Miss Ida B., daughter of Thaddeus and Octavia (Shaw) Clarke, of Monmouth, Ill. They were married January 20, 1880. The parents of Mrs. Leighty are natives of Illinois and Ohio respectively, and to them were born seven children: E. Joe, Ida B., Elva J., Cora M., Nellie M., David E. and Bessie E. Her father was an enterprising and prominent journalist. His death occurred at Monmouth, Ill., in 1873. Mr. Leighty belongs to the Ancient Order of United Workmen and is a staunch member of the Republican party.

BIOGRAPHICAL.

INDEX.

Views.

PORTRAITS

www.ingramcontent.com/pod-product-compliance
Lightning Source LLC
Chambersburg PA
CBHW022013110726
47901CB00006B/1512